BEYOND THE SKY

THE SKYWARD SAGA BOOKS 1-3

A.R. KNIGHT

STARSHOT

THE SKYWARD SAGA - BOOK ONE

A.R. KNIGHT
STARSHOT
THE SKYWARD SAGA

I watch her from behind the thick tree as she moves among the ferns and vines, yellowed now from lack of rain. A mosquito buzzes in front of me, but doesn't land thanks to the sticky sap covering my skin, keeping me free to concentrate.

Because she's been getting better.

My mosswrap slides with me as I move around the trunk, its rings of woven, soft green keeping me cool and quiet as I pad out behind her. She, on the other hand, is wearing a stained, ragged shirt, things she calls trousers extend down to her ankles where they meet thick brown— and now hopelessly scratched—boots. They break twigs, snap plants as she moves, making her easy to follow. She wears a shining gray tube tied to her waist, and I've never seen her use, but the shining gray tube is compelling all the same. Today, I'm going to get it.

There's a wild hoot from somewhere ahead—a startled bird, and she whips her eyes towards it, her arms tense, and I make my move. A one-two step over the branch, directly into the clear middle of a pile of fresh-fallen leaves, tapping the silent ground, and then, with a press of my right calf, I jump. I'm too far away for a tackle, but just right for the back of her legs. She manages to catch the moving air and half-turns as I fly into her, which only makes things worse for her balance, as now I'm pushing her sideways rather than forward.

She crumples to the ground with a grunt and I'm on top of her, scrambling for the tube. I get my hand on the hilt when I feel something sharp against my throat.

"Wrong target, Kaishi," Viera whispers. "The knife is deadlier up close than the pistol."

I flick my eyes down to the simple leather hilt and shining metal blade—forged, so Viera says, back in her homeland beneath the mountains. If I ever get my own knife, it'll be black-glass, and it'll shimmer as it sucks in Ignos' light.

"You've never shown me how it works," I say back, but I let my hands off her pistol.

Only then does she take the knife away.

"Not going to, either, unless things take a turn." Viera waits for me to get off of her, and then she follows me to her feet, sighing at the new dirt stains on her clothes.

"What kind of turn?"

"A bad one." Viera slots the knife back into the slit near the top of her boot.

Before I can get more details, a mournful call rings through the woods. It's haunting, and it winds through the jungle trees like the spirits of my ancestors. A hollowed caller. One of three we have, and they're all prizes. Blow it from the top of the Tier and you're going to catch its sound even in other villages.

Father says it makes other tribes jealous. Mother says it

sings a beautiful song. I don't see why the hollowed caller can't do both.

I'm not waiting for the second blast. I flash a quick thanks at Viera for playing the game and check the vine-tie holding my hair together—there's nothing worse than loose strands catching on branches while sprinting through the forest—and I'm running.

Feet, bare and scuffed, pound dead leaves into dirt as I pad along the pathway back to the main square. Ferns tickle my legs. Trees make half-hearted swipes towards my head.

My route isn't the only way back home, and soon enough I'm seeing motion in the woods around me. Hunters, farmers, people moving because sitting in the village all day is a recipe for losing your mind.

They're all coming back now, and they're not quiet about it. Whoops and calls ring out, greetings mingle with questions and answers about quarry, the weather, and what's cooking. I join in, and nobody cares that the priest's daughter isn't at the ceremony yet.

Because, mostly, I'm the priest's daughter. Not the priest. Never will be.

When I walk into my village, I see eight stone houses. Built flat, as if someone started out with cubes and then gave up when they realized our stone doesn't play nice with right angles. We don't have etchers, here in the jungle. Our stone comes by our hands. The mortar that binds it together is mixed with the power of our arms, and spread with rocks.

But I'm not looking at the houses. I'm focused on the one thing that keeps our village going. The Tier, and ours is a big one. The largest that I've ever seen, and I've been to some other tribes on tours with my father, seen their Tiers. Rocks dug up from the ground support logs and moss, which we've piled on top of each other to create a living mound. Wherever a slate presents itself, our people have carved their version of Ignos and his burning halo.

Dusk makes for perfect viewing time: Ignos is kissing the far horizon, and plants his last lights right on the Tier's top. On the altar there, a smooth stone slab pinned between twinned pillars bearing Ignos' circle wreathed in shards. Anything put on that altar is centered between Ignos, making for an easy transition from this life to the next.

Ignos isn't alone up there now. My father stands in front of the altar with a trio around him. One is holding the hollowed caller—a yellowed stick of bamboo with spaced holes—and I recognize a boy not much older than myself.

Normally he's out hunting with the rest, but apparently he's done something right—you don't get to blow the caller unless you've earned it. The other two are what I call my father's followers. They trail him around town and help him get whatever he needs.

Right now, that's a black-glass knife and a person, pinned with his back on the altar.

"Kaishi!" Mother's voice brings me away from the scene and over towards her. She's standing outside our house with a look that promises a thousand punishments if I don't veer her way this second, so I do.

"I'm not late," I say the words to kill the fight before it starts. I fail, and I know this by the measure of my mother's right eyebrow and how high it rises.

"Don't presume to know what I'm about to say," Mother scolds. "It's rude, and childish."

"Aren't children supposed to be childish?" I say,

because I've so far escaped the rite of adulthood: getting a husband or a wife.

Don't get me wrong—I'm a fan of this. Plenty of nice, unattached hunters in our village, but there's a resistance I have to destiny. Or rather, what others think is my destiny. But I keep quiet about that because I'm not suicidal.

"Clearly," Mother replies. I think Father loves her, in part, because she has this razor sarcasm and she's not afraid to cut with it. "It's not what you have done, but what you haven't."

Now she points me back towards the Tier and I can trace that finger with the sense of a child being told just where their mistake lies. It's the black glass knife, the one now held by Father. He's raising it high to catch the Ignos' light, so that it practically glows up there.

And I know.

"I forgot," I say, which is the truth.

Honest.

"Yes. Your father cleaned it himself."

"We don't usually have sacrifices every day."

"This isn't a usual time," but before Mother can continue the lecture, the hollowed caller blows again.

This time it's a staccato blast. If you're not here now, it's saying, you're going to miss something good, so Mother closes her mouth into a tight frown, grabs my arm like I've seen six summers instead of sixteen, and we're off.

My tribe isn't small, but we compress well into tight rows for the ceremony. There's an aisle in the middle, where, in a few minutes, the body currently on the altar will be carried. My mother pulls me right between the gathered people. We're all wearing our moss-wraps; emerald and brown mosses that we grow and weave together. Some tribes have fur, others use cotton, but we're too deep beneath the trees for that.

Any parts the moss doesn't cover, and plenty that it does, we coat with various salves; stuff that helps keep the bugs away or helps heal cuts and bites. The smells mingle with burning incense, another village feature and the core of one of my favorite things: taking a sprint along the outskirts of the town and enjoying the scents. Right now it's a spicy smoke, and at the edges I inhale the first hints of dinner: Pork, buried earlier in the day with hot coals.

I'm not the only one thinking about food; we pass by a young boy, half my age or less, who, because he's surrounded by his towering parents and other adults, can't see what's going on and is taking the loss of opportunity to stare back towards the cook fires. I seize a moment and tap him on the shoulder.

Come with me, I mouth. The time for talking is past—Father has already started the prayers—but the boy gets it. Takes my offered hand and heads with us to the front of the crowd. The perks of being the priest's daughter? A front row spot for every sacrifice.

Blood spatters come free.

You might think the offer on the altar would struggle. He's likely a hunter, though I don't recognize the tattoos on this one. He's probably been taught to fight, to kill and take what he can to survive. Only here he's being held by an older man covered in feathered bracelets, whose arm is bony and, while strong, is no more capable of keeping a man like our sacrifice down than I would be.

Only the captive lies still.

Honor.

That's what Father tells me the first time I witness one

of these. The sacrifice honors Ignos and brings some glory to our tribe, but it's also redemption for our captive. A chance for him to reclaim some of what he's lost by getting captured in the first place.

Go to Ignos in peace and accept your place in his home, and be glad of it.

The argument doesn't work with every sacrifice, though. Some fight to the end. Struggle and plead. Those are always the messy ones. I try to look away when those happen, but Mother forces me to watch. To witness the disgrace.

Fighting when there's no chance makes it all hurt more.

Father goes through another set of prayers. He's asking Ignos for water, for food, and for a healthy tribe. It's the standard trio, and I don't fault him for lacking originality. Neither does the rest of the village, and we all say our parts when we should.

The next part is rough, but the captive makes it easy. Several quick cuts with the black glass blade and we're looking at his heart. Father's holding it up to Ignos' last light as it touches the head of the carved altar.

Then it's done. No lightning, thunder, or earthquakes. If Ignos heard, he's not making it obvious.

When the crowd goes, the boy squirms away with them, leaving me alone with Mother. She doesn't want to get started again with everyone here, and I'm thinking it's partly because nobody has an appetite for fighting after watching someone get ripped apart, literally, right in front of them. So we stand and wait, because my one job is coming down the steps towards me.

Father, softening the gesture with a broad smile, hands me the blood-soaked black glass knife with both hands. I accept it in the same way, and the warm liquid slips between my fingers. I try not to think that the red was, moments ago, inside someone and only succeed when Father starts talking to me.

"You'll have it cleaned this time, Kaishi?" he says the words without malice, with the hint of a joke, because Father knows I've already heard it from Mother. "We have been lucky. There's another one ready for tomorrow."

"Do you think he heard it?" I ask. "Ignos?"

"It's not whether he heard our prayers," Father replies. "But whether we deserve an answer."

He is described in superlatives. A living weapon. Death incarnate. The last thing you see before your eyes go dark. All of these and more, on a hundred worlds, have been used to whisper about his coming.

More generally, and to himself, he goes by the name he has earned:

Sax.

A single syllable, because he is as of yet a three-letter Oratus. No ship under his command, no army at his beck and call. Not that he needs or wants those; each would take him away from the blood. From the visceral feel of his claws doing the work they're made for.

He's looking at them now. Checking them in front of a broad mirror. All twenty of them. Five on each hand, and he has four of those. They're attached to arms: two on each side, sprouting from a long torso that, due to his gray scales, shimmers like rippling water on a cloudy day. Twin legs, a tail and his head, thick and dominated by his large oval eyes and wrap-around mouth, round out the limbs. Nearly four meters tall, Sax doesn't come in a small package.

As he checks his body's weapons, Sax keeps an eye on the Oratus next to him. Same body, same height, only Bas is closer to rose gold in color. Sax looks at her with a mix of confidence and love, the sort of bond shared by a Pair.

Bas doesn't notice, because she's already started putting on her mask. She presses her left foreclaw—the upper set of arms—into the mirror. At first, it seems like the claw might push through and shatter the thing. Send glass everywhere. Instead, the surface of the glass warps; sucks in her claw and then oozes out over it. Liquid metal.

The mask flows forward over Bas's claw, her arm and the rest of her. Once Bas is completely covered, eyes and all, the mask appears to sink into her skin. Becomes translucent, as though her pinkish scales were covered by a slight fog.

Sax follows her lead. They all need masks; required for missions with a high risk of attack or exposure to vacuum, and this one has both. Behind him, he hears, or rather, through cavities in his skull full of tiny, vibration-sensing antennae, detects the other half of their set laughing. The usual for those two. Go back to the beginning of their fifty mission stretch and you'd find Sax seething at their hissing.

Now, he ignores it.

When the time comes, Gar and Lan won't be laughing. They'll pull the triggers on their miners, same as Sax. Gar would probably shoot first.

The mask is cool, but quickly warms to Sax's skin. It actually burns a little. Increases Sax's body temperature to ideal levels for performance. While the mask is getting to equilibrium, Sax and Bas step back from the mirror to see the next part of the show.

Oratus claws are like diamonds—they can cut through just about anything—but they're not much help against an enemy at range. The mask helps against weapons fire, but pop enough holes in it, and the mask will fall apart too. Better to eliminate the problem.

The mirror helps them with that. With a wave of Sax's claw, the mirror flows up towards the ceiling and reveals blue metal shelves holding an array of deadly tools. Sax moves first, with the confidence of knowing exactly what he wants and how to get it. The target is a pair of black sticks about my height.

Sax calls them batons. He picks them up with his fore-claws and sets them across his back. They stick to the mask, like a magnet.

Next comes a belt for his waist, followed by a variety of fun and games. Things to be thrown, fired, or tasted, depending on the situation. Next to him, Bas makes her own choices, and when they're both done, they take a second to stare at each other. Check the list, make sure nobody's forgotten something.

Neither of them has.

"Evva says this might be the last one," Bas breaks the silence, and while her mouth moves, the sound actually comes through the mask.

The four of them are already connected.

"There are always more," Sax replies, his voice like grinding sand.

"But what if it is?"

"Then we'll have to find something else to kill," Gar joins the conversation, and their group, in the center of the room. There's not much to say to that, because everyone agrees with Gar's assessment. Oratus are like miners—they serve a purpose, and Sax has a hard time thinking of what that might be if not to tear the galaxy's enemies apart. Lan saves him the trouble by joining in, completing their set.

They're ready to go.

I'm holding the torch in both hands and watching the flames dance to the nighttime breeze. It's not heavy—the stick of wood isn't much longer than my forearm, and the burning rag doesn't send the fire high—but Father says that holding with two hands signals devotion to the task.

As I'm going to offer a prayer to Ignos, the god that determines whether my family and tribe lives or dies, devotion seems appropriate.

It's dark in the jungle after Ignos goes down. If I'm standing in the village, where most of the trees have been cut to make room, I could see the stars. Underneath the canopy, though, I'd be wading in a sea of black without the torch. As it is, my eyes can't make out much more than my own feet and the overgrown path beneath them.

My ears, though, find a world of their own.

While bird calls drop away as Nomis—the silver sister of Ignos—rises, other animals take their place. Buzzing insects swarm around the light, some of them as large as my hand. The sap I've spread over my skin keeps most off of me, and years of practice mean I don't flinch when a moth lands on my wrist and flares its owl-eyed wings.

My steps startle a spider monkey somewhere above, and it hoots as it swings away, alerting its family to my coming.

Fear doesn't strike me here, even though I'm alone. Our hunters, and those of other tribes, cross these areas enough that any large predators have either learned to stay away or found themselves in our fires. Those same tribes don't have an interest in taking me, even if they were out at night. Sacrifices are about honoring Ignos, and a sixteen year-old girl doesn't have much honor to provide.

Not yet, anyway.

When I reach the clearing, there's a small stone totem standing at the far end. About as tall as I am, and bearing another carving of Ignos. This one, though, is white-spotted and washed out. Father says it's been here since before the village, and that it's partly the reason why our tribe has survived so long; others make pilgrimages here for their own people, and their gifts pay their peaceful passage. Food and tools that help our village grow.

I'm the only one here now, though, which is good. Solitude helps me get closer to Ignos, or at least that's what I think as I kneel before the totem and begin the rites. With my eyes closed, I set the torch to the side, though I have to twist it into the hard dirt. A sign we could use some rain—normally this clearing is a muddy mess. Everyone knows when you've been here because you come back with coated knees.

It's a ritual prayer. Asking for guidance, strength, and the usual array of graces. Only at the end do I break into originality. Start a one-sided conversation with a god that is so great and mystifying that I have no idea if he can understand me, or if he cares.

"I don't know if you're listening," I say, and I put my hands on the totem. We're not supposed to touch it, but nobody's watching, and maybe it'll get Ignos' attention. "I'm asking you for something tonight. Again."

I pause. This is the hard part, because when I don't say it then it doesn't feel so real. I can distract away the feeling with my chores, or conversation, or just by running through the jungle. But I didn't come here to be distracted, so I say it anyway.

"I need a destiny. Father says I can't be a priest, and Mother tells me I'll be getting a husband soon. I don't want that, Ignos. I don't want what they want for me. Show me something else, please!"

It's a plea, and I'm a little ashamed as I say it. Blushing, even, there in the dark, because I know most of the village would say the same thing if they had the chance, but they don't. They make do with the struggles, and embrace the happy moments: a successful harvest, a dance around the fires, a hunt that brings back enough to feed the family.

Who am I to ask for more?

I'm opening my mouth to take it all back, beg forgiveness, when a breeze kicks up and I feel my torch go out. My eyes open to the purest dark I've seen in a while, though I'm able to pick up the torch by the heat of it. Not the first time this has happened, and every Solare knows how to pick their way through the ferns and trees at night.

The dark, though, is why, when the whole sky burns a minute later, I go blind.

Only for a second, and it's not really blindness but shock at the white burst overwhelming everything. I blink rapidly as the glow recedes to a single, huge ball hurtling above the trees. The leafy canopy means I catch the fire in spots as it barrels close and then over my head.

It's hard to see anything in that angry orange and black, but I track the burning ball anyway. At least until it vanishes beneath the tree tops. First comes the snapping and cracking of trees, and then a rippling bang. Like a thunderstorm letting loose over a lake. The ground shifts and I fall to all fours, my fingers digging into the dirt like it's a cliff I'm trying to climb.

Then it's done.

Stillness takes over and for a moment everything is stunned quiet. I take a breath. The first insects test their buzzing. Gradually, the jungle restarts its symphony.

When I stand, holding the burned-out torch, I don't turn back towards my village. I saw where the bright flash landed. It didn't look far. I'm thinking of my prayer, too. And destiny.

Ignos might have heard me, and given me an answer. All my parent's stories about heroes started with one thing: when given the chance, the hero acted. So I move past the totem, take a walk into the uncut brush.

It's slow going without a light and wandering into unfamiliar territory. Bugs bite—ants and other critters undeterred by my sap coating—and animals running away from the crash find me and turn around.

Unseen branches scratch my face and a thorn leaves its mark on my hand. I don't turn back, though, because I know what lies behind me.

Eventually I break through into what wasn't a clearing moments before. Now it's a fiery disaster. Trees hold bits of flame like I might hold a cup of water. Dirt and rocks are piled up everywhere, as though someone went digging with abandon. I notice too that most of the debris are black, and hot.

I step onto the dirt.

It sears the soles of my feet, so I dance until I find a but of slightly cooler rock, then take a look.

There's a pit in the middle, almost as large as one of our houses. Deeper than I am tall, and in the center is something that, to me, appears like an oval boulder. In the flickering orange, it's obviously pitted too. Bits and pieces taken out of its sides, though the unmarked parts shine. I've never seen anything like it, but that meshes with what I'm thinking. Ignos' sent along something completely new.

Something just for me.

I take the next steps slow and careful. Test the dirt to make sure each step isn't too hot. Even so, burns get added to my growing list of injuries.

Never let it be said that Ignos doesn't make you work for your dreams.

I clamber to the edge of the hole. Now that I'm closer, I can tell the oval isn't too much larger than Father. Four or five of him, squashed into the same shape, would make for the entire thing.

As though the oval knows I'm looking at it, it begins to steam. White streams emerge from what grows to be a line around the middle of the oval, floating up into the sky. Then, before I can decide what to do, the oval pops in half. The top part rises up and falls away from me and I notice it's attached with a small silver hinge to the oval's far side.

What's more interesting, though, is what's inside Ignos' gift. It looks like a black sea, though when I concentrate, I can pick out traces of purple. The ink—because I don't know what else to call it—appears still, and I take that as a sign to come closer.

I'm not completely convinced; I take the descent into the pit slow and make sure to identify the easiest way to scramble out if the oval turns out to be unfriendly.

I reach out with one hand to touch the oval's outer shell. The lip of the opening. It's warm, though not as hot as parts of the dirt. If my mind wasn't in total shock, I might wonder why, but instead I note that it's safe to touch and keep going closer.

Both of my hands are on the lip, which rises just about to my chin, and I'm peering into that purple-black ink. There's something in there. I can make out a shadow, shifting in the firelight.

I reach for it, trained by years of grabbing at fish, slip on that narrow lip, and fall inside.

Sax raises a single claw and the ship takes note. The mirrors slide back into place and hide the remaining arms. Behind Sax, a door, till that moment unified with the pearly sheen of the ship's walls, shunts open with the hiss of compressed air. Careful not to let his tail get in the way, Sax leads the group from the room and down the ship's outer corridor.

And stops immediately. He's forgotten what Evva said. They're late to the fight, and as the ship's outer hull turns translucent—a neat effect of well-placed screens—the four of them bear witness to chaos.

What look like whole flocks of birds dip and dart through black space. A black palette marred by the orange gas giant staring at them, its churning atmosphere dotted with specks as ships criss-cross in front of it. Constant light shows erupt as pilots try their hands with energy weapons, though Sax knows there are plenty more projectiles flying through that vacuum; invisible and just as deadly.

Sax is drawn to the biggest blot of the bunch. Makes sense—that's what he's here for. It's a disc, sort of, and it hangs there in space, dwarfing everything around it. You'd think it would be the center of the fight, seeing as it's the most important ship here, but it looks like the battle has drawn away from it.

"They've set us up," Sax says. "Should be a smooth ride."

"How many do you think, on a seed ship that size?" Gar asks the question, and Sax can almost hear him salivating.

"Enough for all of us, and more besides," Sax replies. "Evva says you'll have to share, Gar."

The commander said nothing of the kind, but that's the implication Sax had when Evva told him they were going with a full assault crew. At least four shuttles, stocked to the brim with soldiers. Sax had made sure they were the only Oratus though. Nobody to take his credit. Still this is a big commitment for the Chorus military, the Vincere.

"So long as they understand they're getting the scraps and no more," Gar hisses.

At the end of the hall, a circular door spins open. Evva's on the other side. Not directly, but standing in a Sphere. From their eyes, it looks like she's stuck her head into a giant, bluish ball. On the inside, Evva is seeing everything the sensors can give her about the fight and letting her float around in it like some sort of god. Sax has tried it before. It twisted his stomach around and cost him a good meal.

Beyond Evva is the rest of the bridge. Aside from the seemingly huge windshield—screens again, overlaid on heavy armor—the bridge is consumed by pods. Flaum, furry creatures with big eyes and long snouts, sit at some, chattering to each other or to ships outside. Sax resists the urge, though Lan's low growl says she doesn't.

Normally, these things are prey. Normally, they're snacks to tear apart on course to the real meat.

Evva leaves the Sphere before Sax gets through his hypothetical destruction of the Flaum, and she's everything Sax would expect a fourth letter Oratus to be. Her lime green scales are scatter-shot with luminous medals, as though someone had blasted Evva with a cannon full of honors. Each one glows in the light, playing rainbow tricks on Sax's eyes.

"We are ready to begin, commander," Sax says, though a flash behind Evva—some ship meeting a fiery end—draws his eyes away from her.

"Your shuttle is ready," Evva replies. Her voice, not through the masks, sounds filtered until Sax looks back at her. Then the mask reshuffles priorities and brings Evva's next sentence in clear and clean. "Your orders are to proceed directly to the core. Find the Seed Sevora and eliminate it. No need for prisoners."

"Of course," Sax replies.

"You should all know," Evva says, and Sax perks up because her voice has changed here. It's not the commander talking, it's Evva. "The Chorus declared a tenth cycle. The Great Peace, they're calling it. It's up to us to deliver that here, make it so the last nine cycles of war aren't wasted."

"The Great Peace? We're still fighting," Bas says.

"Not for much longer," Evva motions a claw out towards space.

"We think this is their last one. The final seed ship. Destroy it, and we've finally won."

Evva's injecting emotion there, and Sax knows why. She's alone on this bridge for a reason. Brilliance, sure, but also because her pair vanished in a seed ship raid gone wrong. Oratus keep their grudges deep, and Evva's gives the four of them a boost.

"We honor your lives," Evva continues, back in formal form.

"We are honored to serve," Sax replies, and hears the others say the same.

It's going to be a good hunt.

When I wake up I know I'm suffocating. I can feel, pressing against my eyes, the cool liquid that must be the ink inside the oval. I also feel my nerves tell me someone's staring my way.

I'm not alone.

As I move my arms—the ink is sludge-like, heavier than I expected—something twitches in my brain. Like a headache blinking on and off, only sharper. I push past it because what I need right now is air.

My feet hit the oval's hard bottom and press, raising my head clear. The ink doesn't drip away clean. It sticks, like fruit juice. I start brushing it away from my mouth, gulp in the first gasp of air, and that's when noises erupt in my head. A mix of animal cries, grinding rock, and sounds that I can't identify at all. They cluster together, writhe and burst, and dimly, beyond, I can still make out the crackle of dying flames and nothing else around the oval.

That, more than anything, confirms that I'm only hearing this in my own head. That, more than anything, drives a stake of fear into my heart.

Fear.

The word appears. Like a dream, or a sudden inspiration. Along with it comes a crystal clear tone, as if the word were spoken by, say, a blown hollowed caller. Not the right sound at all.

Fear.

The word comes again, along with the tone, but this time there's adjustments, like speech, as it climbs through the letters. Like a child learning to sound out a word. Like I did when I was young.

I look down at the ink I'm swimming in, and I find that it's lower than I thought. No, it's evaporating. Vanishing into the night. The pool shrinks until it's barely up to my waist.

I.

Yes, I think, that's me.

Me.

I shake my head. Try knocking it from side to side to see if something might pop out. Or if I've broken part of my brain and it's causing these strange bursts. The motion only makes my ears ring.

New words take time.

It's a sentence and not something I just said. I freeze. Maybe, I think, if I stop doing anything else I'll be able to tell what's going on. Really, I'm reaching for anything. Running through what my tribe teaches when a predator's encountered.

Or an enemy.

Not an enemy.

It's responding to me. The tones are saying the words as they flash into my mind, though I'm not hearing them in my ears, exactly. More like when I imagine someone speaking to me and I can hear their voice despite them not actually talking. It's a feeling.

I'm not your imagination.

That much is obvious. Even though I'm a dreamer, I'm not this good at fooling myself. So I launch to the next question: if this isn't my imagination, and it isn't outside of me, then what is it?

You are Kaishi?

How does it know my name?

I know much more than that, Kaishi. I know where you were born. I know your father is the priest of your village. And I know you hate cutting your hair.

My name and Father's position, I could excuse. Common enough knowledge for people that live around here. Even neighboring tribes know who my father is, and I've been to a few of them on trading trips, so I could be recognized, though the lack of light in this pit would make it difficult.

But my hair? I've never told a soul.

I never complain, even when Mother takes the knife to my tangled knots. It's a chance to be brave, after all.

Getting through that logic brings me back to my question.

Namely, what is this?

The voice doesn't respond. Then my left arm goes numb. I look at it, start to move my right to touch it, when that goes numb too. My legs twinge, and suddenly I can't feel anything.

Interesting. There seems to be a problem with you, Kaishi.

I agree with that. To add to things, there are sounds coming from the jungle now. Whistles and shouts. I recognize the voices and calls. My own tribe, probably coming to see what happened over here.

Meanwhile, I'm stuck in the oval, unable to feel my toes.

Yes, that is a side effect. The issue appears to be with total control. That I cannot achieve it.

Total control of what?

You.

There is one thing I know of that can control a person if it wishes to. One thing with the power to make a Solare act different than normal, and that is Ignos.

The idea connects the fragments for me. Pulls together the prayer at the totem, the strange flash in the sky and now the voice in my mind. This voice, this thing talking to me, must be Ignos, or at least a part of him.

I wait for the voice to confirm, but it's silent. I'm, however, happy to keep running down this thought. If Ignos is talking to me, why? Couldn't he do as he wished without messing with my head?

Even a god needs to see the world through his subject's eyes.

The sounds are getting louder and I'm guessing Father's warriors will be breaking into the clearing any second. I'd love to get out of the oval, but I still can't move my arms and legs.

First, look down.

I follow Ignos' instructions and glance at the bottom of the oval. The ink is almost all gone, and in the last bit there is a strange green cube. It's a brighter green than any I've seen before—the closest being a newly sprouted leaf on a spring morning. It's crawling with spidery blue veins.

Take it.

As Ignos says the words, my arms are free to move again. Legs too. I'm tempted to run, but angering the god inside my head seems like a poor choice, so I reach and put the palm of my hand on the cube. It jitters slightly, like a scared animal. Then the veins snap off the green cube and reach back towards my hand. I try to jerk away, but the veins have me.

Stay still. It will hurt less.

Now Ignos tells me, after the veins have their tiny hooks in my skin. They're wrapping themselves around my hand, and crawling up to my wrist. I manage to quell my nerves, partly because I'm so covered with cuts and bites already that a few more barely register.

The cube melts and I watch as what was once solid breaks apart and flows up along the blue veins. Over my hand—it's like sap, only not sticky—and around my wrist. The green streams coil around me and, suddenly, harden. Like a torch going out, the green fades to a grim brown.

I call it the Cache. We'll need it.

Ignos' voice sounds pleasant as he says this. Like he's describing a flower, or breakfast. I don't have time to ask why, though, as I see the ferns around the pit split open to reveal the mighty warriors of Father's tribe. They're carrying spears, slings, bows, and they're all staring at me in confusion.

Which, I would be too if I were them.

There's not a story, a lesson from Mother, or an ancient saying that describes what to do if a god takes up residence in your head. So my wide eyes match the tribe's and I answer their silent questions with the only thing I can think of, "I found something."

This doesn't help anyone, but it does spur Father to break through the line of warriors and scramble down into the pit. He rushes over the dirt and, reaching into the oval, pulls me out. I'm not a baby, though, so I have to help him.

Use my own legs to climb over the lip. I'm overjoyed that they both work, that the numbness is gone, and in that instant happiness I start to talk because now I'm not staring at a crowd, I'm looking at my father's concerned face.

"It's a gift, Father," I say. "Ignos answered my prayer. He's with me now."

Father takes this the same way I would have if one of the villagers had told me the master of all creation had taken up residence in their mind. He tilts his head, closes his eyes briefly, and then looks past me to the oval. Notices that it's empty.

"A gift," Father speaks slowly, like he did when I was little and he wanted me to stop crying.

I'm annoyed that he doesn't immediately understand, so I repeat the words, "He came from the sky, Father. Ignos is talking to me right now."

That last bit is a stretch. Ignos isn't talking now, and I don't know why. Later, I'll understand that his frequent silences are when he's processing new information. Taking in all the things he doesn't know and understand, and then comparing them to the Cache, the bracelet on my wrist, to see if there's something similar inside its stores.

"Ignos speaks to you?" Father says. He doesn't drop the skeptical tone. "What is he saying?"

Say what I tell you. As if I were speaking it.

Ignos' command comes charging through my mind, and strings of words follow it. Fantastical descriptions of stars and worlds far beyond our own. It doesn't make sense, but I've been raised to trust what a god tells me, so I repeat it anyway. As I talk, Father's expression does work, twisting between confusion, disbelief, and fear.

"All of these things, unknown to you and your tribes, are part of my kingdom," I say as Ignos directs. "It is now time to prepare for you to join that kingdom, which is why I am here now. Call your neighboring tribes and bring them to heed my words so that we can begin."

Ignos goes on, through me, about miracles to come. The words are grand and sweeping. The sort of speech Father might make, but that I have never done. This, I think, convinces Father more than anything. Wondrous stories I can make up. Sermons like this take more effort. Require knowing the emotional cadence of the crowd.

Ignos does. I do not.

At the end of Ignos' speech, Father steps back from me. I see a new look in his eyes, one that brings with it a twist of knotted pain. I'm not his daughter in that look. I'm something else. Both feared and revered. I turn away from that hurting stare and see the warriors have been listening, and it's even worse with them: Some are on their knees, bowing towards me. Others are openly weeping or looking up at the sky in search of the miracles I promised.

Father interrupts with a call to go back to the village. A pair of warriors stay behind to look over the oval and search for anything I might have missed. The rest escort us back.

The village is wide awake waiting for us, and our crew breaks apart into a dozen re-tellings of my words. Father takes no time for any of them, instead pulling me to our family's house. As Father leads me inside, he looks at Mother and says, "Our daughter claims she has been touched by Ignos."

Then he turns to me, and with as grave an expression as I've ever seen, says, "She will need to sleep, as tomorrow will bring her first ceremony. If Kaishi speaks the rites well, then our village will have a new priestess. If she does not, then Ignos will not brook her mockery, and we will have another sacrifice."

They're already hanging as the rest of the grunts enter the shuttle. Flaum, their furry bodies coated in standard-issue hardplate uniforms and Whelks, who wear nothing and carry their rifles in their ocher, stubbly gel arms. Both species birthed in prolific numbers, which is why they fill the vast majority of the sub-roles necessary to keep the Vincere up and running.

Gar, if Sax asks him, would rate the Flaum higher than the slug-like Whelks, but only because Gar prefers the taste of fur.

Sax has his four arms and two legs wrapped around the bars on the roof inside of their assault shuttle. Bas is next to him, and Gar and Lan have similar poses on other bars behind. It's a ridiculous look to the soldiers below, but they know not to point and laugh because the ones who do tend to meet swift, terrible ends.

Besides, there's a point to the exercise. One that Sax knows is coming now that the shuttle has lurched into motion. They're leaving the command ship and starting the cruise through battle-filled space.

If Evva's done her job, then the rest of the Vincere fleet will be running cover for them. Their fighters and frigates ought to be filling every possible attack route with more firepower than even the Sevora care to brave.

The front of the shuttle—on these, the pilots stay at the back—shifts translucent. Ahead of them, growing steadily larger, sits the orange gas giant and the seed ship. A perfect view of their target.

"How many fall in the first minute?" Bas asks the four of them, through the masks. "Half?"

She's talking about their soldiers, below. Sax doesn't need to hear the creatures to know they're nervous, as fodder ought to be before it runs into death.

"A third," Lan replies. "It's a seed ship, not a war vessel. They won't be ready."

"We've given them enough notice," Sax says and the other three hiss in agreement. Leaping late to a fight is bad enough, but it's taken them too long to get the shuttles loaded and ready to launch. Which means Vincere command didn't think a seed ship would be here, this far outside of populated space.

As they get closer, Sax picks out the quadrant divides that slice up the seed ship. Four sections with a circle in the middle. That's where the Seed Sevora would be. The one running the whole operation. Get to that creature and Sax could set the ship on a death spiral into the gas giant. Let the planet's gravity do the rest.

The seed ship's outer hull appears a faded green, which confirms Lan's assessment. The emerald color means the Sevora want this one to start new worlds. Get new species. A red seed ship would be militarized and ready to deliver thousands of battle-ready troops to a target.

Vincere logs say there used to be plenty of other colors

too, but Sax hasn't seen those. He briefly wonders why the Sevora would color-code their ships and asks the group, but they don't have an answer and he lets the question drop.

Besides, it's prep time.

"Stim up," Sax says, and everyone, except Bas, who claims she doesn't like the stuff, dips one of their foreclaws into a small vial of bluish liquid held on their belts.

The Stim sticks to his claw as he brings it out of the vial, which has a membrane that seals itself after he's dipped, and Sax raises the coated claw to his mouth. Opens slightly and sticks the claw inside. Licks, with his forked tongue, the Stim off.

Tastes like sugar.

Stim hits him hard. It always does. But it's the sort of slam that's fun. Sax's dual hearts spool up to hyper speed, his pupils blow wide, and there's a slowing that happens. Like someone's told the universe to take a breath. Sax has time to contemplate the shuttle, to check his miners, his mask, and confirm the others in the set are doing the same.

Time too to look up.

To see their shuttle ram into the seed ship's hard metal hull.

A trio of hunters move a boar, freshly dressed and cleaned, into a pit full of hot coals warmed in one of the many cooking fires. They waste no time shoveling more coals and dirt over the top. It'll cook over the course of the ceremony and be ready to serve as the celebratory dinner.

I'm watching all this as I hack at a coconut under the tilting light of Ignos. The sweet milk inside is going to be cool even on a hot, sweaty afternoon like this one. It's been almost a full day with a god in my head, and Ignos, it turns out, likes to talk. Though I'm guessing the coconut fascinates him, because he stays quiet until I chop a small hole. When I lift the coconut up and taste the first bit of cool, sugary milk, though, Ignos breaks through into my head so fast that I almost spit up everywhere.

Fascinating! I would say that the terries on Vimelia are quite a bit more succulent, however, and not quite as sweet.

He's been using words like those too. Things I don't understand. At first I asked questions, but when those led to equally strange answers, I gave up. I figure Ignos has a lot going on that humans aren't meant to understand anyway.

Also, I have a ceremony to worry about.

Fear not, Kaishi. Everything I'm telling you will make sense eventually.

I'm not worried about Ignos' nonsense. I'm concerned about how I'm supposed to preach to hundreds of my own tribe. Father's words last night weren't idle ones either; it's not unheard of among the tribes to have someone claim they're hearing from Ignos directly. It usually follows that they're proved wrong when one of their "miracles" goes awry. The punishment for that sort of thing is a swift trip to the top of the Tier.

They don't come back down. Not in one piece, anyway.

So now I'm planning my phrases. Running them through as I sip from the coconut.

Do you not trust me, Kaishi? I will give you the words, as I did last night.

Words like those would get me killed. Ignos surprised everyone, sure, but those were ramblings in the middle of midnight to a group of tired warriors seeing something they'd never seen before. None of what Ignos said came from our sacred rites, and promises of far away stars wouldn't do anything for families hoping for rain right here in the jungle.

Father always says that being a priest is about delivering hope and softening despair, so I'm trying to figure out how to do that.

I've seen many speeches delivered, Kaishi. In places far beyond your imagining. In words beyond your comprehension. Trust that I can find the right thing to say.

I look up at the trees framing our village, at the Tier standing tall. On many of those trees, small ants scurry back and forth in search of food. Owls and spider monkeys hang on branches, engaging in their own daily rituals. Bird calls ring through the air; mates exchanging news. If Ignos could understand all of them, then perhaps he could give me the words I needed.

Look at your wrist, Kaishi. That's where we'll find what we want.

The bracelet is still there, tight. I tried to take it off last night, but it wouldn't budge, so I gave up. Too tired then to care much. As I look at it, the dull brown seems to flash green for a moment, as if it knows, somehow.

Every recorded speech we have lives in the Cache. I'll find the right one, and your people will hold you up as the greatest priestess in Solare history.

Did I mention that Ignos has a penchant for hyperbole? He might be a god, but the rate he speaks about me becoming a legend of this and a queen of that is a little much, even for my ambition-starved soul. Part of me is even insulted—does Ignos really think we're this easy to fool?

I'm not trying to trick you, Kaishi. Once we have their hearts, we can use the Cache to find the miracles to capture their minds. Then, you'll have everything you could ever dream of.

I shake my head, which causes my father, who's walking my way, to quirk a smile at me. It's a different version of his usual grin. One that's sad in the corners.

"Deep in conversation with Ignos?" Father says as he takes a seat next to me.

"You could say that," I reply. "Have you ever spoken with him?"

Father shakes his head. "I pray to him, and his replies come in wordless forms. From what I see with you, however, I think I prefer it that way."

I laugh, and it threatens to veer into a sob. Ignos' descent towards the horizon is bringing what's about to happen into focus and the idea that this may be the last time Father and I are going to sit here talking shrivels me up inside. Father, in that way parents do, senses this and puts a hand on my shoulder. The pressure helps. It's a base for me to stand on.

"You know the rites," Father says. "You've heard me speak them often enough. Say the simple ones and you'll be accepted."

Yes, I know them. Prayers for rain, for food, for health. They're not difficult.

They won't make you a legend either.

"You really think those will be good enough?" I ask. "How many are coming?"

"I don't know. We sent runners, but it seems our neighbors are nervous. Last night's event hasn't helped. Nor have they."

I see where he's nodding, and I know what he's talking about because how could I not? Viera's been staying in the guest house for nearly two months now, after her friends left. She's pale-skinned, and she's a Lunare, so she's either here to kill us or trade with us.

I don't tell him about the games we play, what Viera's been teaching me. Some things Father doesn't need to know.

"She's the only one left," I offer.

"For now," Father replies. "Viera makes no secret that her friends are coming back."

"I thought they were good for us. They traded with all the tribes?"

"With one eye on everything we would not give them, like your mother's necklace and my headdress." Father is really talking about the turquoise. Those bright blue gems belong with the priest and his wife, whomever that is.

I don't have anything to say to that and Father sighs a moment later, stands up and holds out his hand for me to take. I do and he pulls me up. Places his palms on my shoulders and draws me in for a hug.

"Kaishi, convince them you hear what the Ignos' says," Father whispers. "Our village needs a priestess, and your parents need you."

Then he's gone towards the Tier. I notice too that he's carrying the black-glass knife in a loop around his waist. It's clean, though I didn't do it.

Ignos shatters the moment, as he often does, with an angry tone.

You're too primitive to answer my questions. To help me remove the block.

I ask Ignos what 'the block' might be, but get no answer.

As the sky turns purple and orange, I make my way towards the Tier. Some of the crowd is already there, assembled for what promises to be the most interesting sacrifice in some time. Which is when it hits me. I'm performing the ritual, which means I'll have to do the sacrifice. Cut into the man and take out his heart.

I start to sweat. I've never done that before. Even with Father up there, guiding me, the thought of cutting through the living skin of another person is terrifying.

You saw the entire sky light on fire. Picked your way through a dark and dangerous jungle to find something you've never imagined before. Went up to it and met me, and you're scared of something you've seen so many times?

Ignos, of course, is right. This shouldn't be so hard.

That's what I tell myself as I walk between the gathering people to the foot of the Tier. I've climbed up and down these stones before.

Dawn is the best time, when the rocks are cool and at the top you can see the blanket of mist covering the entire jungle. Trees poking their green leaves through. Now the stones are warm and I lift each leg, place each hand slow, taking care to plant my feet correctly. One step at a time. Nobody will trust a priestess that falls.

I glance up and see Father's already up at the top, along with the man blowing the hollowed caller. A sound I don't really hear as I'm so focused on climbing. The sacrifice is there too, along with the usual pair of assisting elders. This one is a scrawny hunter, and unlike yesterday's, his face is full of fear.

You and me both, I want to say, but that would be cruel. He's going to die regardless. I'm only dead if I fail.

Which isn't going to happen.

Ignos is suddenly full of encouragement. As if the god realizes his chosen body might go under the knife if he can't come up with something good. If I misremember a crucial phrase, or botch the cutting.

But I manage the first stage well enough. Make it to the top, next to the altar. Ignos' light is still hot up here, even at dusk. Like he's staring right at me across the horizon, and now I know why Father seems to spend the whole ceremony looking down at us or with his eyes closed. Doing anything else means blindness.

When I angle down to my village, though, I don't see the rows of people I'm looking for. Instead, the crowd is pushing into itself. Cowering against one another, because there's an army—no, that's too big of a word, a patrol—surrounding them. Maybe three dozen. Only these aren't wearing the capes and cloths of our hunters. Many of these sport patchwork brown skins of bears on their heads, and all of them hold weapons.

Kukri. I can catch the black-glass glint from up here. The shards are jammed into the tops of wooden sticks, the glass cut like an eagle's talons. Like the knife Father still holds, they're capable of tearing a person apart. I know because our village has only one, taken from a long-ago prisoner. It sits, unused, in someone's house. Our bows and arrows make for more effective hunting. Nobody would bother with kukri in the jungle.

Which, it hits me, is what these warriors are. They're not Solare. They're from outside, the plains to the West. We call them Charre, and in some distant past they left the jungle behind for clear skies and the brutality that comes when there's no place to hide.

As I'm processing this, one of the Charre, the only one I can see wearing the faded tan furs of a lion around his neck and shoulders, comes forward towards the Tier. Our villagers don't stop him, but shrink back, with mothers putting arms around sons, and fathers moving to shield them both. It's time for the ritual, so nobody is armed. Other tribes wouldn't think of a raid now—showing such disrespect for Ignos would be unthinkable.

Which is why I'm not so surprised when the lion warrior waves at me to carry on. Now that he's closer, I can see that he's not much older than I am, though his chest bears a few scars and his dark arms appear covered in tattoos. He notices my stare and gives me a smile in return, as though I'm supposed to treat their interruption as nothing.

They're here for you.

Ignos says it the same moment I'm piecing it together.

Our village isn't the largest, our tribe isn't the wealthiest. The only reason these Charre might come to our little town is because they heard a woman talking about how she communes with their god.

"Begin the ceremony, Kaishi," Father says. "There is no other option, now."

I take a deep breath. Feel the humid jungle air fill my lungs, and when Ignos begins to feed me lines, I say them. One after another. I lose myself in the recitation, so much so that I don't even know what I'm saying. It could have been complete nonsense, except I see the crowd falling into words. Even the Charre turn towards me, let their kukri hang loose in their hands. At the base of the Tier, the lion warrior drops to his knees.

I speak the last line and my voice falls silent. Father moves forward with the knife, and I know right now that I cannot kill this man. I'm not ready, and I don't know how.

"I can't," I whisper, turning and taking the black-glass knife from Father anyway, to hide our voices.

"You must," he replies, though I can tell he's sorry to say so.

I stand over the sacrifice, who now has both elders' hands pinning his back to the altar. His white eyes roll towards me. His lips are drawn back, and I can tell he wants to scream but can't quite bring himself to it. Can't shed that last end of his dignity.

I hesitate.

Give the sacrifice to the Charre. There is no dishonor there, right?

If Ignos himself tells me there is no dishonor, then there cannot be. My relief at the escape pushes me to point the black-glass knife down the steps towards the lion warrior, who starts in surprise.

"We give this honor to you, visitors, so that you may leave our village in peace," I say, using the same words Father has said before, though that was trading trinkets, not whole persons.

The lion warrior covers any shock, sliding on a straight face. He stands, "I came to see a priestess, and I believe I have." The warrior shifts to look at the crowd and I see that his back, too, is tattooed in a black-inked version of Ignos, a dark halo and colored rays shining up to the warrior's shoulders. "Your priestess has bought your survival with the offer of this sacrifice. She can buy your freedom as well, with her own."

Ignos' shock runs through my mind, mingling with mine. Quick enough, though, Father is next to me, whispering in my ear.

"You must go, Kaishi," he's saying. "Do not fight. Do not resist, or they will kill us all and take you anyway."

I had expected Father to deny this warrior's demands. To call my village to fight in my defense, but even as his words churn my stomach I see their point.

I asked Ignos for a destiny and he's delivered.

To save my family, my village, I move down those steps. Go past the lion warrior, and feel him walk behind me. Hear his call to gather the sacrifice and prepare to leave.

He lets me say goodbye to Mother, Father, and I know I'll never see them again.

The thing about gravity is that, this far from the gas giant, there's not much of it. Only enough to boost the Oratus' momentum. Which works in their favor, because when the shuttle's pointed tip pierces the seed ship's hull, allowing the nose to crash through, Sax and the others let go of the hanging bars and shoot forward towards that translucent shuttle bow.

Where they'll splat into a gooey pile if things don't work as they should.

But the shuttle is a Vincere craft, and the Flaum that maintain it do so with the constant penalty of death for any failure whatsoever. Vigilance isn't just expected, it's enforced. So the shuttle's nose bursts like a blossoming star; pointed triangles flaring out and leaving a wide open window into the seed ship for Sax and the other three to fly through.

For the barest second as he launches from the shuttle, Sax feels the tug of vacuum pulling him back towards space. Then, again, the shuttle does its job: those flared ends fold back against the seed ship's inside hull, and from each one slides out metal slats. They mesh with each other and create a seal against outer space, and now the fun's beginning.

The four Oratus soar into what looks like the seed ship's growth quadrant. Dark blue lights shine from the top of a smooth ceiling down onto open clusters of terminals and liquid-filled tanks that quickly give way to a forest of glass tubes, most full of greenish ooze and the floating bodies of all sorts of species. They're tall, going from floor to ceiling, which in the seed ship means a towering height. Ten times Sax's own. The Oratus have to watch themselves or they'll splatter against those tubes too.

Not that they have much control after being flung out of the shuttle. Sax, with the Stim giving him plenty of time to look as the four of them fly over the Sevora's thin defense, has a second to torque himself around before he hits the first tube.

He tenses his muscles.

And bounces.

His claws slide across the glass, pulling him around the tube and then Sax kicks off, launching himself further towards the back of the section. Bas, Gar, and Lan do the same, jumping from one tube to the next, leaving behind the growing laser-light show as their soldiers engage the Sevora.

Who, it looks like, are using Flaum too. Only these aren't the same as the Vincere soldiers. Mostly because the Vincere conscripts are actually Flaum, all the way through. On the Sevora side, though, they're just bodies. Flaum hands holding the rifles, fingers pulling the trigger, with a Sevora in their heads calling every shot.

Which is why Sax, with every tube he hits, digs his claws in just enough to crack the glass. To splinter it inside the tube and start the fluid spilling. The leak will kill the half-grown specimen inside. Prevent one more Sevora from getting the body it wants. If the mission succeeds, all of these test tube species will die anyway, but Sax prefers confirmed kills to hypothetical ones.

The seed ship's own homespun gravity, coupled with the gas giant's, starts to pull the set down before they've reached the end of the tube forest. Sax calls, through the mask, for his team to drop now so they don't get too scattered, and the next tube he hits serves as his ride to the ground.

At the base, it's a hard metal landing. Terminals whiz and beep as Sax crashes into a deserted cluster of tubes. Monitors show waving lines and green numbers. Sax ignores it all and orients himself towards the back of the section. They have to get further into the seed ship, and they don't have long to do it.

A chittering noise slips in through Sax's mask. Followed by more. Looks like some of the Sevora saw them flying overhead. Weren't fooled by the assault troops spilling from the shuttle. Sax reaches for his own miner and draws it from his belt. The miner is made for an Oratus, with circles that close neatly where each claw ought to go. Precise, deadly control.

Only the chitters aren't coming closer. Maybe Sax is wrong. Maybe they didn't notice.

But now Sax has noticed them.

He creeps around the tubes, careful to place his claws lightly on the metal floor. The soft gravity here means such steps aren't hard. Sax just has to be careful so an accidental twitch doesn't send him floating.

What Sax sees when he pokes his head around the side of a tube cluster and into a wide hallway, is a trio of Sevora Flaum setting up a gouter on a tripod. A large cylinder attached to a pair of wheeled containers as large as Sax, the gouter will, in another moment, start spraying hot chemical doom through the air towards the Vincere troops.

The gouter's liquid would melt a mask in no time, and would melt a hull too, which is why, when it cools, the stuff hardens into a stiff seal. The Sevora don't see Sax, so he takes a moment to put his miner back. No sense wasting energy.

Or fun.

Sax bursts around the corner, claws digging hard into the floor, then he leaps at the Flaum settling in to the gouter's targeting chair. The Flaum's friends turn at the shriek of tearing metal, but all they have time to do is scream before Sax hits. His claws do the work on the gunner, while Sax uses his tail to wrap around the left one's neck.

Constricts enough to feel the jolt that says the job's done, and then he's turning to the last one. Sometimes Sevora know their end is coming, and they face it bravely. Stand there silent as Sax claims them for his kill count. This one, though, cowers. Backs away from the Oratus as Sax climbs out from the gouter's chair. Behind him, Sax uses his tail to bash apart the chemical feeds, ruining the weapon for any future parties.

"Tell me, Sevora," Sax hisses as he towers over the tiny Flaum. "What are you hoping will happen? That I'll spare you because you look so pathetic?"

The Sevora stares back at Sax through the Flaum's big black eyes. There's still a small weapon hanging from the Sevora's holster. If drawn and shot perfectly, it might pierce the mask. Give Sax a scar. Sax wants the Sevora to reach for it, to see if Sax is faster. He doesn't get the chance.

Bas dashes by in front of him, and without breaking stride, her claws leave a fatal rend that has the Sevora collapsing to the ground.

"Stop playing with your food," Bas says through the mask as she hurtles on towards the edge of the section.

Sax can't argue with her logic, and he bounds after her. They're almost to the gate leading further into the seed ship. Which is good, because, by Sax's counting, their time is almost up.

The Charre have grown like a nightmare. I first heard of them years ago, through stories told by passing traders. If we had a penchant for sacrifice, the Charre have an obsession. They feed on conquest. On taking land and people and abusing both. Father would curse them and, in equal breath, our own ancestors for letting Solare fall into such squabbling decline.

When the Lunare appeared, however, everything seemed to change. Caught between two greater powers, Father and the elders held long nights debating about which side to join. Staying independent meant death, of that they were certain. Still, they had pushed back a formal decision, waiting to see which of the two would prove more dangerous.

Now here I am, being pushed through the jungle by kukri-wielding warriors, a victim of that indecision. My anger, though, funnels to the only possible target: the lion-sporting chief who walks next to me while his band spreads out around us.

As we move away from the village, his stance changes.

Out of the eyes of the crowd, he relaxes, even presumes to offer me a friendly smile. He's not much older than me, and his frame, as I look at him, says he's a powerful hunter, though every glance is undercut by the fact that he could order me killed should the mood strike.

The shape of his eyes and his smooth skin—he has white-lance scars on his chest and legs, mingling with the tattoos, but his face has been spared—boosts the appeal. He radiates a charm, an ease with the power he holds, but it's nothing against my wall of rage. I'm almost surprised at how angry I am, but the shock of being taken transmutes itself to fire easily.

"My name is Malo," he says, and I nearly spit at his face.

"I don't care," I reply.

You should. His smile looks genuine, and he might be the only friend you have now.

Ignos is right, of course, but I'm human and can't accept the current state of things without flaring up. Malo sees this and swallows, looks around as if hoping one of his warriors will offer an excuse to end the conversation. But he doesn't break stride and stays by my side.

A brave move.

I thought you asked for a destiny? Is this not what you wanted?

Again I cede the point. Why ask for a change if you're going to be devastated when it happens? My counter argument goes like this:

Damn destiny, I want my family back.

"I'm sorry," Malo tries conversation again. "I know it's hard."

"I don't know how you expect this to go," I reply, cooling my heat long enough to form a real sentence. "You took me from my home. You've surrounded me with killers. I'm not going to be your friend."

"I don't need you to be my friend," Malo replies. "I do, however, need you to listen."

That I can do. Listening lets me simmer in my self-pity, and I revel in it while Malo talks about the rules of traveling with a Charre army. When food is served, how sleeping works, and the marching schedule. All of it's aggressive. Dawn to dusk and with expedience. Even the hunters in our tribe don't approach the Charre's hours on the move.

Malo's words lay lightly on my mind as I race through memories of my parents, childhood, and routines that I'm now realizing may be forever gone. Eventually Malo becomes aware that I'm not asking questions or even looking at him—my eyes have drifted to some vague point in front of us—and he stops. Waits for me to ask him to keep going.

I don't, because I'm recalling the pig planted beneath the earth and how, right now, Father is probably taking a bite of it. Part of me hopes he can't eat it after losing his daughter, and another part is ashamed at the same.

"Can you tell me your name?" Malo's question interrupts.

"Kaishi," I say.

"Look around at my warriors and tell me what you see." Malo sweeps his own gaze around the band.

They're not all visible in the night as some are scouting through the brush, but there are at least a dozen around us. I don't expect the question, and that prompts me to follow his suggestion and peer around.

All of the warriors carry weapons and have tattoos. Most wear the giant, toothy maws of bears in the same way Malo sports the lion skin. I see something else, too: many of the warriors are blinking, stepping on roots here and there.

Those carrying spears in addition to their kukri have them hanging low rather than at proper marching height.

"They're exhausted," I say, and the breach in the Charre's invincible myth is a comfort.

"We ran all morning and afternoon to reach you," Malo says. "We didn't want to lose time."

"Lose time?"

"Ignos sent a sign, Kaishi. Surely you saw it? A great fire in the sky?"

I nod.

"We were camped north of here, waiting to meet another of our bands, but when we saw where the fire touched the earth, we left to head this way. We ran into one of your village's messengers as we traveled, he was quick to tell us what had happened."

"I went there. To where the fire touched." There doesn't seem to be much point in hiding it. "That's where I found Ignos. He talks to me, and then I say his words."

"Then you are precisely what we need," Malo says. "Whispers float through our cities that hordes from the mountains are coming, and that they have constructs so massive only Ignos himself could have built them. That they hold weapons which can spit fire."

"What does that have to do with me?"

"You are divine, Kaishi." Malo's hands twitch towards me as he says this, as though he wants to grab my shoulders. "At least, if you are telling the truth. What the Emperor needs now is someone to show that Ignos is still with us. To prove that the Lunare are not the chosen people."

As Malo speaks these words, his face transforms and his eyes pick up the same fervor that I saw when he bowed to me at the base of the Tier. He wants to believe me. He wants me to be the miracle his people need.

You can be, Kaishi. They are looking for hope. You can be more than that—you can be real. Keep this one close to you. We can use him.

Use him? The word is oily, somehow, and I recoil from it.

You're naive. Everyone can be used, and to carry out my mission, you will need to use many.

Ignos' mission. Preparing us for a new future. That is more important than any discomfort I might feel over simple terms. So when I realize Malo's staring at me with worry, I do what I can to dispel it.

"Ignos asks me questions sometimes," I say.

"A god asks you questions?"

Malo's point is a good one, but I've come up with my own answer to it already, one that Ignos confirmed when I suggested it hours ago. "He's testing my faith."

Ignos says I should keep Malo close, so I climb the mountain of my rage and seek cool understanding on the summit. "You've seen my home, Malo, tell me about yours?"

This sparks another, different expression from the soldier who I'm starting to think has a thousand faces. His lips turn up at the corners, he looks to some point west, and his mouth opens slightly before he talks, as if measuring the words for their worth. "Have you heard of Damantum?"

The name is familiar, like a minor character in a story often told. I shake my head.

"Then you have missed the greatest city in all the world." Malo's hands start to sweep as he talks. "Damantum covers an island with gold that glitters in the light of Ignos. Lush gardens float on its gentle waters. Markets throng in every street, offering wonders of which you and I can barely imagine."

I'm sure Malo would keep going, but I interrupt him,

because there's only so much adoration I can stand, "You sound like the Lunare. She talks of her mountain cities in the same way."

After I say this, I realize Malo likely has no idea who I'm talking about, but, to my surprise, Malo glances behind us. I follow and there, her hands bound but feet moving free, flanked by two warriors, marches Viera.

"Unlike the Lunare, what I speak of is true," Malo says. "When we reach Damantum, you will understand."

"Why did you bring her?"

"To see if, underneath her boasts and lies, we may learn something of her brethren," Malo says. "And once we do, her sacrifice will be a glorious one." He looks at me, the fervor returning to his face. "I hope you will wield the knife."

The far end of the first section is marked by a gateway; a broad arch bordered by soft green globes spaced every couple of meters. Every seed ship is made up of twelve sections split by these gateways, and getting through them before the Sevora lock the gates is imperative.

Bas reaches the gateway first after scaling the twenty shallow, flat steps leading up to the door. As she does so, with Sax coming hot behind her, those soft green globes flip to a bright red. They'd taken too long, and now every second spent on this side of the gateway would give the Sevora time to organize a defense on the other side.

To the right, next to a red globe at Sax's chest level, there's a black protrusion. Like a bulb, only opaque.

"Mind scanners," Lan says as she and Gar join them on the landing. Sax notes that Gar's mid-claws, like his own, are red and wet.

"Unless one of you has managed to get infected, we're not getting this gateway open."

"I tried," Sax offers. "But they died too quickly."

"Good," Gar replies. "Because I would try to tear you apart if they hadn't."

"I would like to see you try." Sax opens his mouth slightly, shows row after row of razor teeth.

"Cutters," Bas interrupts, and she completes the interruption by stepping between Gar and Sax. "We burn our way through."

That's all she needs to say. The four of them pull small canisters with smaller tubes attached at right angles around them. They each stick their claws into the tops of those tubes and push down, mixing the volatile gasses, while the claw holding the weapon clicks the release.

Lightning-blue beams spit out from the ends and slam into the gateway. Their fire concentrates on a small section, tracing out a square for them to fit through. The miners are so bright that Sax can't stare right at them, but instead at the curling, blackened bits of metal falling to the floor beneath.

In the distance, behind them, there's the sound of equipment exploding. Bangs and pops signaling the destruction of seed ship gear. The Vincere forces have won the first battle, and too quickly. Victory means whatever Sevora forces remain will be retreating right towards the four of them.

"Bas, trade you," Sax says, handing his cutter to his pair, who gives him her miner. The motion causes a brief blip in the burning, but the delay is worth it.

None of them wants to catch a laser bolt to the back.

Malo doesn't halt the march until the jungle canopies disappear and stars shine. I've seen stars from our clearings, of course, but it's my first time this far west and having an entire horizon splashed in Nomis' glow stops me.

We're at the head of a valley that, after days and days of hiking, should lead us to the volcano that marks the true base of Charre territory. Malo's laid out the course for me, and while I'm excited at seeing someplace new, every step takes me away from familiarity.

Which is why, lying down on my cotton mat, placed over the rock-sand ground, I'm not able to fall asleep. The desert has its own sounds, but they're not the ones I know. Monkeys and owls aren't calling, the whistle of wind through the trees is missing, and even the insects buzz differently.

Though, I notice, they still bite.

The Charre replace the noises I know with clanking, chopping ones. Cook fires spring up, though I tell Malo I'm not hungry. Truth is, I don't know if I am or not—

everything is too much right now. So I stay there on the thin mat, feel the rocks dig into my back, and talk to Ignos.

You tell me these Charre are greatly feared?

As much as any one group can be, I suppose. Fear, I think, might be the wrong word. It doesn't do us much good to be afraid in the jungle because there are so many ways things can go bad. Rather, I would say the Charre, of all people, are the ones most likely to destroy what we have. If that is fear, then yes, we fear them.

And yet, they seem to value you.

It's not me they care about. It's him. Ignos is who they're looking for.

But they believe you. Malo does, at least. He's your path to power.

Power for what?

Anything. Once you have the resources, that bracelet on your wrist will give you everything you could ever need.

I look at the Cache, but it's not much now. A simple thing sitting on my arm. It doesn't flash, or whisper secrets in my mind. I try to will it to do something. Tell it to light up.

"Work," I say to it.

"Who are you talking to?" Malo asks, sitting down beside me.

Before I respond, he hands me a bundle of maize in a thin tortilla.

"I said I wasn't hungry." I take it anyway and Malo smiles.

"Everyone's hungry after a hike like that. I can't have you tired tomorrow. It's going to be a long walk."

The food is bland, but my stomach likes it fine and I devour the whole thing in three bites. Malo even has a skin of water for me, and I squeeze some out into my mouth. It's warm, stale, and delicious.

After I'm done, Malo takes the skin back and notices I'm looking at his hands. Trying to see if he brought more. He laughs. I can't help but crack a small smile too. Then Malo's up and away, back a second later with another tortilla. This one, along with the maize, has bits of meat in it. I recognize the iguana, though the strange green circles scattered throughout are new to me.

"Take it in small bites," Malo says. I don't really listen and take a third of the tortilla in a single chomp.

The warmth comes slow, but it builds into incredible heat. The insides of my mouth burn, and as my eyes go wide, Malo hands me a small bowl full of a light orange juice. I drain the whole thing, the mango sweetness staving off the feeling that I'm about to die right there.

What are you doing? Did he poison you? Why are you burning?

I suck in mouthfuls of air, and then I notice Malo is laughing again.

"A little bit at a time, priestess."

I note the title and wonder if that's going to be me from now on.

The priestess.

Focusing on that does more than the mango juice to quiet the burn, and, as my mouth calms down, I find myself reaching for the tortilla again. Malo holds it away.

"You'll take it slow this time?" Malo says and I nod.

I'm true to my word, and, with little bites of fire, I finish the tortilla. When I'm done, Malo's expression is more serious than I'd expected.

"What's wrong?" I say.

"You'll have to learn to like the peppers," Malo says, and

I can tell this isn't a casual conversation any more. "In Damantum, you'll eat with priests. Maybe even the Emperor. They will look for signs Ignos isn't with you. That you're lying. No priestess of the Charre will refuse our own food."

"Everyone likes these in Damantum? I'll be doubted because of a pepper?"

"By those who fear your power, yes. I've seen many of my own warriors placed on the altar because the priests found some way they had displeased Ignos." Malo's annoyed, and this is the first time I really see why he's the leader here. "There are those in Damantum who would trample over anyone in their path. We have days ahead of us, priestess. If you would like, I want to use our evenings to teach you how to survive in my city."

I don't need Ignos' advice to say yes to that one, and shortly after Malo vanishes into the night, saying we should both get what sleep we can. Except now I'm thinking about the den of snakes I'm walking into and its enough to keep my mind churning.

I hear laughter not far off. I roll over on the mat and look and there's the Lunare, Viera, talking with a pair of Charre around their fire. They've unbound her arms, which means they must think she's not a threat. Viera's in the middle of some story, and her hands are waving around, her ragged clothes looking ridiculous, and I can see why the Charre don't think she'll cause any harm.

But you don't agree. Why?

Because the Lunare have a history. Because they trade, yes, but they also take. The Solare, what tribes we have left, have been squeezed between the Charre to the West and the Lunare in their mountains to the East. Oceans cover the other two directions, trapping us. Father believes Ignos will save those of us who are left, and I believe him. I do. But we're running out of time.

You didn't answer my question, Kaishi.

Why is Viera dangerous? Because I know what the Lunare leave behind when they raid a tribe. The burned-out corpses with dark holes in their bodies. Houses torn apart and looted. Anyone not dead is, we think, taken away. To what end, we don't know.

I don't think Viera's like the others—I'd even call her my friend but Father's warned me enough times that she's going to bring trouble that I can't dismiss it entirely.

Then why do your tribes not band together and strike? Defend and attack as one?

It's not like the Solare haven't tried. It's not like my father and the other elders haven't met with other tribes and talked of an alliance. Every time he returns with a shaking head and grumbles of power, and how hard it is to give up a little, even in the face of losing it all forever. So we trade what we can with the Lunare and hope they'll leave us alone.

Then why don't you try something different?

I look over at the fire and Viera, still chattering. It doesn't take much thought to see where Ignos is going with this, and I'm not tired yet anyway, so I sit up from my mat and, after pulling my mosswrap around me to cut the chill night breeze, head over towards their fire.

The Charre warriors glance at me as I approach and the simultaneous moving of those big, brown bear heads and their gleaming teeth swinging in my direction makes me pause. They won't hurt me, I tell myself, because if they'd wanted to have me dead, it would have happened before dinner. No sense wasting food on a body.

"Hearing my stories?" Viera speaks to me. "How do they match up? Figure a priestess has to have some good ones of her own."

The flames give her face a luminous glow, and the shadows play between her large eyes and the wisps of snow-white hair playing down her forehead. Interrupted, Viera's hunching over the fire, as though she's trying to hug the flames. Before I ask how she can stand the heat, Viera straightens, turns, and leans her back over the burning brush.

"Are you cold?" I ask, ignoring her question.

I have stories. Plenty. We've swapped some during our jungle runs.

"You see the snow on top of the mountains?" Viera replies, and I note that she's talking in Solare tongue. "You probably think it's cold for us. That we should be used to it?"

The warriors return to watching Viera with quirked smiles, and I realize that they don't understand a word of what the Lunare is saying. They're laughing because holding one's self over a fire looks ludicrous. I'm so used to both languages that swapping between Charre and Solare tongues comes as naturally as breathing.

"But we go deep," Viera continues. "Our pathways hollow so far that we catch the heat of the world. It's like this fire here, but everywhere and all the time. So yes, I'm cold."

I take my own seat near the fire. The sand is warm on my legs, soft and smooth. Straight back the way we came, beyond the camp, the jungle trees dance back and forth in the breeze. The Lunare live deep in the mountains. I can't imagine what it would be like to not see the sky, and turn away from the thought.

"They can't understand you," I say, and it takes a second for Viera to realize that I'm talking about the warriors.

"You can't understand me?" Viera says the words in Solare and the warriors greet the phrase with blank stares. "Interesting. I guess that means I can spend all day insulting them and nobody will know."

"I will," I say.

"Yes, you will," Viera says the reply slowly and sits back from the fire, looking at me. "Why'd you come over here, Kaishi? Lonely?"

"Because you were talking so loudly I couldn't get to sleep," I reply.

"It's a habit of mine." Viera shrugs. "Is this a warning? Is Ignos going to strike me down if I don't let his priestess rest?"

The casual blasphemy bites my ears, and I'm about to scold her for it when Ignos rushes through my mind.

Look past the flaws to what she can bring us, Kaishi. I will forgive anything said against me so long as you achieve my goal.

Ignos makes sense, so I give Viera a toothy smile, "He might, if I ask him to."

Viera laughs at this, and it's a bouncing, joyful thing. How she can make such a sound in a situation like this is beyond me. When Viera looks my way again, her green-yellow eyes are shining with mirth.

"I thought I would be stuck with dead-eyed warriors," Viera says. "I'm happy they took you along, Kaishi."

"Happy? How can you be happy surrounded by enemies?" I blurt out the question, because there's nothing in the Lunare's tone that speaks of sarcasm.

Viera is, as far as I can tell, genuinely enjoying herself.

"Do you know why I stayed behind when my people returned to the mountains?" Viera asks and I shake my head. "Because of these." The Lunare points to the sky and the starry tapestry. "They're beautiful. So much more so than the rock ceilings that have kept my nights company for so long."

"The stars won't walk for you," I say. "And I don't think these warriors will mind leaving you behind."

"Then I think we'll have to work together, Kaishi," Viera says. "This isn't just another jungle run. It's an adventure, one I think you've been waiting for. I know I have."

"I just want to go home."

"You won't, Kaishi," Viera's smile falls away.

"Why?"

"I love the stars, Kaishi, and so do most of the Lunare. We like your jungle, and we like these sandy plains." Viera takes a long breath, savoring the air. "Visiting is nice. Trading is better. But why stop there?"

"What do you mean?"

"We're coming, Kaishi, and we're going to take everything you and your people have."

Sax sets himself up atop the landing and waits for targets. There's no cover up here, but Sax has options. Moments later, the first scrambling Sevora —Flaum and Whelks, because both Sevora and the Vincere value prodigious breeders—come into view. Some of them pause at the sight of Sax, two are brave enough to reach for weapons.

Sax leaps. Presses his legs against the landing and launches himself straight up. Gravity is light enough that he doesn't simply fall back down, but floats. This, with the Stim, gives him plenty of time to aim. To roast, with red and yellow blasts of energy from his miner, the two initial threats and, quickly enough, more. They burst into burning confetti, superheated by Sax's miners, and soon enough the Sevora rethink their withdrawal.

They scatter back into the tube forest as Sax returns to the ground. He doesn't think there's another way out of this section, so they'll be back, but the soft bang behind him means Sax won't be here to greet them.

Which makes them the lucky ones.

Sax feels a touch on his tail. Familiar. Bas's way of saying 'let's go'. Sax keeps his eyes backward, looking towards their shuttle and any further Sevora attacks while Bas, keeping her tail on his, guides the Oratus through the hole they've cut in the gateway. Only when he's ducked through does Sax turn and look at the section they've entered.

If the last one held the tubes growing the species, this one holds their next stop. It's composed of wide purple-black pools. Each one as large or more than the shuttle Sax and the others came in on. The pools aren't quiet either; they burble and churn with movement beneath the surface.

Gar doesn't wait. He lifts his cutter, aims it towards the nearest pool, and fires. The pool itself heats up, begins to boil with the amount of energy pouring into it. There's a big reason this is a bad idea: the cutters are their best way through the gateways, and there's at least two more before the seed ship's center. Wasting energy on immature Sevora that'll die anyway if the mission succeeds is stupid.

But Sax waits a few moments before ordering Gar to stop. He knows how satisfying this is. He wants to do it himself, but Bas still has his cutter.

"When the ship falls, you'll get them all," Sax says as the cutter's light dies out.

"This is more fun," Gar replies, and they all hiss in knowing agreement.

The pools are criss-crossed by catwalks. Railed bridges spotted with feeding stations and consoles showing temperature and concentrations of minerals Sax neither knows nor cares about. They walk on by, occasionally swiping with claw or tail to break things to pieces.

Pointless, nourishing destruction.

I twist and turn the rest of the night after Viera's warning. The Lunare are coming? With the Charre pressing from the other side, my tribe wouldn't last long. Neither would any of the Solare.

Unless you find an ally.

Ignos makes a good point. If we pressed ourselves into the service of one side or the other, we might survive. It would mean giving up our independence, but I'm not so naive that I believe we're keeping that anyway.

Why are you here, Kaishi?

The question comes with a hint of more. Ignos does this from time to time; makes asks designed to lead me to other conclusions. I don't mind it much, but here in the early morning, tired, with my god beginning to brighten the Eastern sky, I'm not that patient and go with the obvious answer:

I'm here because the Charre came and stole me away from my family and my home.

No, you're here because you have an opportunity.

If Ignos had been my mother, or another village elder, I

would have laughed. Pushed the suggestion away. But there's only so much defiance one can have in the face of their god. So I stay quiet and wait for Ignos to continue.

At least some of these warriors believe in you. Malo, the leader, certainly does. Together, we can turn them, Kaishi. Together, we can make them all believe in you.

And then what? I tell them to leave my people alone? How long till they decide I'm not much use as a priestess and tear me apart?

If they believe you are a goddess, they will not touch you.

There's a new word. One that at once makes clear Ignos's plans for me and spawns a thousand questions about why, why bother with a random Solare girl when there are already people—the Charre's Emperor, say—who hold the positions of power Ignos is clearly looking for.

Because you found me, Kaishi.

There are easy rebuttals to this, but I don't have time to make them because Malo and his warriors are calling for the march to start. I scramble and put on my mosswrap. I'm about to start rolling the mat up when a warrior appears, gently pushes me away, and proceeds to take care of my gear.

I insist that I'm capable of handling my own stuff and the warrior just laughs. Puts the mat inside a pack harness looped over his shoulders, and walks off. I follow, because nobody's telling me what to do and I don't want to get left behind.

The Charre move quick in the early morning, despite sore muscles from the day before. At least, I'm guessing everyone feels the same knots and spasms as I do. Malo says we have to cover as much ground as possible before Ignos gets high and the heat makes travel difficult. I say that it's plenty difficult already and the chief gives me a smile.

For some reason, Malo's look make me flush. I resolve not to let that happen anymore.

Ignos serves as a distraction. He's badgering me with questions and ideas. Thoughts on how to wrap the Charre around my finger. Musings on what we can do when we have their loyalty. The things we can command them to build. That's where Ignos really gets strange, because the structures he's describing don't exist.

Not that I've seen, anyway.

We're walking through a vast valley whose sandstone cliffs rise up on either side of us. In the far distance is the vague outline of the volcano. Around that, according to our village traders, begin the vast fields and meadows that make up the bulk of Charre territory. Stories whisper about how it used to be forest, but the Charre took the trees for their own ends.

Several hours in, with Ignos getting close to straight over our heads, a call comes from the rear of our column. Malo leaves me behind and pushes through his own warriors to get a better look.

While I can't see over their heads, an expanding dust cloud from back the way we came makes it clear something's heading this way.

"They're running fast," Viera, appearing next to me, says. "Think it's your tribe coming after you?"

The question spins me for a moment. My village does have hunters. They could move fast through the jungle. I want to believe that Father has ordered an all-out attack to get me back.

"He wouldn't do that," I say, dousing the shock of hope in cool logic. "Father wouldn't risk the village for me."

I don't believe it until I say the words, but it's true. Father and Mother kept no secrets about the sacrifices of power. How they had to make decisions against their own interests if the village required it.

What choice would be more obvious than letting their entire tribe survive by losing a single girl?

The rest of Malo's force goes to set up. They form a staggered line, all twenty of them, and begin to pull out their bows and arrows. Their kukri. Viera and I move over to the side, to get a clear look at what's coming our way.

Whomever they are, they're moving at a full sprint. I see their bodies, obscured by dust, pounding forward with arms raised and clubs held high. Their skin makes it clear they're not Viera's kin, the colors of their tattoos clear they're not mine. This is a batch of Solare intent on their own demise.

"Stay back here," Malo slips to us with another warrior by his side. "We're not risking you on a pointless fight."

"Pointless?" the Charre warrior says. "For you, Malo, it may be. The rest of us still need to earn our lions."

"Not at the cost of the priestess," Malo fires back, and then he's gone; returning to the line with his kukri drawn and ready.

"Who are they?" I ask, because I can't believe a Solare tribe would leave the jungle for a fight like this.

"They wish revenge," the warrior says, and I can see the slight smile on his stone face. "We took what we needed from their village days ago. At the time, it was lightly defended. Now, we know why."

I can imagine. Hunters often take days to pursue valuable game. A single large boar, bear, or elephant could feed a village for a long time, but if you were gone when enemies came along, you could lose everything.

"Draw!" Malo's command rings sharp in the clear air.

As one, ten of the Charre warriors lift their bows and bend back their strings. "Aim!"

Their angles. Why?

Ignos is noticing that the Charre point their arrows low. To me, it's obvious: less likely to kill your target from their direction.

For the sacrifices. I see.

Again the gaps in Ignos' knowledge seem strange to me, but in the chaos of the coming fight, I can't focus on that. Instead, I see the Charre launch their arrows. They fly towards the gritty and grizzled bodies of tribesmen which I do not recognize, but know anyway as fellow Solare.

There's no sound when the arrows hit except for screams. Those that dodge strikes, whether through luck or by darting to one side, make shouts of their own. Pain and fury mingling together. It's enough to make me hold my breath.

I realize I want the Solare to win.

I know they won't.

The Charre quickly put truth to my thought. They wade forward in a line, exchanging bows for kukri—one in each hand—and, as the Solare close with their clubs and knives, begin a brutal dance. I've never seen a fight before, and I'm horrified by it.

The Charre hook their enemies with the kukri and throw them to the ground, or spin the Solare so that any retaliation swings well wide of its mark. Every time a Solare hits the ground, a Charre is quick to kick away their weapon or, if the Solare refuses to give in, if they try to push themselves back up, the Charre puts the blunt end of the kukri to work.

Malo stands out. He's easy to track with his lion skin, and the chieftain puts himself in the center of the fray.

Where the other Charre use their kukri as weapons, Malo wields his as limbs. He whirls and ducks, jabs and counters, turns a club swinging towards his head into a wild miss that leaves its owner open for a hard kick to the knees.

As short as the fight is, the Solare have time to realize they stand no chance against Malo, and by the end he is standing alone amid a pile of surrendering bodies.

Watch yourself.

Ignos whips me away from the spectacle and I see a Solare, one of a few still standing, cutting towards us. He's holding a black-glass knife, a sacrificial instrument turned into a desperate weapon, and I can see tears streaking his face as he moves. The Charre warrior guarding us shifts to plant himself in the Solare's path, and I wait for the inevitable end.

The crack shocks me to my core, and I feel my heart jump. I'm on the ground in an instant, hands covering my ringing ears. The Charre warrior joins me, though he's looking back towards where the noise came from. He doesn't see what I do. He doesn't see the Solare now on suddenly-red ground.

Interesting. There's more to your world than I thought.

I don't know what Ignos means by that. Instead of thinking about it, I follow the Charre warrior's eyes and look behind me. To where Viera stands, holding her gray tube, her pistol. Viera catches me looking, but this time there's no offered nod. No quirk of a smile. She's deadly serious, and so are the Charre warriors—Malo included—who stop tying their new captives to consider the threat.

"Translate for me, Kaishi," Viera says.

She's still holding the pistol. I didn't see what it did, but I've seen the results, so I nod.

"What you just saw can happen again. Will happen

again, if I want it to. You'll keep your hands off me, and you'll keep your hands off her, and we'll all make it to your city alive. Understand?"

She's realized you're her only hope of survival. Clever.

I say the words, and the Charre look to Malo for guidance. The lion warrior steps over the bodies and heads straight for Viera. There's a look to him that says harm is coming, and Viera sees it.

Raises the pistol.

Malo stops.

"Don't," I say, though I'm not sure who I'm saying this to. I only know that I've seen enough violence.

"Priestess," Malo speaks to me in Charre. "This Lunare is a risk. A danger. I cannot let her remain."

But you cannot let her leave. Viera has tied herself to you, now. And they fear her. She'll be useful.

"Viera," I say. "Promise me that you won't hurt anyone unless they come after you first."

"Only time I was going to use it anyway." Viera doesn't look at me as she says this, instead matching stares with Malo, who turns to me.

"Then anyone she kills is your responsibility, priestess," Malo says.

In my mind, I feel Ignos' warm approval.

At the back end of the section, a shorter walk than the first but still minutes, the four of them stare at another gate.

Soft red globes again.

"Cutters." Bas announces and they reach for the weapons.

"Wait," Sax eyes the mind scanner on the gateway's right side. "I have a better idea."

Before any of the others can comment, Sax turns around and jumps into the nearest pool. The light vanishes instantly beneath the surface, but the mask adapts. The suit covers Sax's eyes, and begins feeding a different type of visual information. Red-yellow glows wherever it detects heat. Sevora, swimming in their natural habitat.

Without a host, Sevora are small. One could fit in Sax's palm. They're thin ovals, with numerous tendrils coming out of their larger end. Each of those tendrils is coated in barbed flagella. Useful for climbing, tearing their way inside something.

If a Sevora could get inside Sax's head, he'd be its slave.

Its unthinking host. The Sevora know that too, and they swarm him. The mask makes it seem like Sax's whole world is covered in reds and yellow. But the mask is pulling double-duty here. The barbs can't pierce it, so the squid creatures flail at Sax uselessly for a second before realizing, while they can't take the Oratus, he *can* take them.

Sax swipes with his claws and grabs a pair of Sevora. Makes his way out of the pool.

Mind scanners are simple things. Looking for signs of a Sevora and that's all. They're not smart enough to know that the Sevora sitting in Sax's claw isn't where its supposed to be. So the scanner makes a chirp and the gateway blinks green. Slides up into the wall.

Sax turns and launches the two Sevora behind him, arcing them out over the pools. Doesn't wait to see if they make a splash or have a harder landing, because the seed ship suddenly lurches. A shuddering jerk, and Sax digs his claws into the floor to keep from falling over. Loud pops follow the shift; echoing their way along the section's walls and coming towards them.

"Go!" Sax yells as explosions follow the pops, breaking apart the section's wall around the gateway.

Vincere conditioning teaches them to follow commands without hesitation precisely for situations like this, where moments make the difference between life and a cold, long death. Sax leaps ahead, with Bas alongside him—Gar and Lan are already gone, but pairs wait for their partner—and they get through the gateway before it slams shut again. This time, not just with the standard door but with a second, thicker one.

On the other side, booms and bangs continue to ripple through the section they were just in. Tearing it apart. There's a gravity tweak then as the seed ship adjusts its rotation to account for the loss of mass. For the fact that the entire two sections Sax and the others went through have separated, taking the rest of the Vincere forces and who knows how many Sevora with them.

And leaving the four Oratus alone. One set against against a seed ship full of thousands wanting them dead.

Good odds.

As the price for leaving Viera her weapon, Malo and the other Charre give Viera its consequences: the corpse of the Solare fighter. Viera stares at it, then looks at me.

"When people die in Lunare," Viera says. "We cast them off the cliffs. Nature takes care of the bodies after that."

"There are no cliffs here," I reply. "Ignos asks that we burn our bodies, to bring his fallen back to him."

I'm hoping Viera will understand, because I'm having a hard time looking at the graying corpse. True, conflicts between Solare tribes often ended with dead, but they were marked by the stains and stabs of spears and arrows. This one, this one appears dead by magic. I don't want to turn him over, to see what Viera's weapon has done.

"Then we'll burn him." Viera doesn't have a fire to steal from, but it's not hard to gather enough scrub brush from the scraggly bushes littering the area. I help her, partly for the distraction of using my own hands.

Behind us, the Charre finish up with their captives.

Malo gives notice that it's a short time till we march again. He seems entirely willing to leave us behind.

"I don't think your Charre friend is happy with you," Viera says as we pile up the brush.

"I don't care if he is," I reply.

That's not true though. I do want Malo to like me, and not just because Ignos tells me his support will be important. For what, I'm still not sure. If my god demands it of me, however, who am I to deny his wishes?

"You don't?" Viera laughs. "The way you're looking at him says otherwise."

She takes the black-glass knife the Solare was carrying and begins striking it against a small rock. Every hit brings sparks that flash into our brush. No fire yet, though.

"Just how am I looking at him?"

"In Lunare, we have an expression for this. We call it 'shining' when one spots another they desire." Viera keeps whacking with the black-glass blade.

"You think I'm 'shining' Malo?" I feel my way around the word and instantly dislike it. It's not something the Solare would say.

"You might not know it yet," Viera replies, and as she does so, one of the sparks finally catches.

The brush goes up in orange, and suddenly there's heat on my face to match Ignos' burning light against my back. "But you are. Nothing to be ashamed of. He's wearing a lion. Enough to make anyone look at him twice."

I search for a long stick to bring the fire to the body and realize, here in the desert, that there are none. Only bushes. Small twigs. My attempt to storm away from Viera's questions ends in failure, and I look away from her as she stands. Try to find somewhere to go.

"We'll have to pull him over," Viera moves on from our conversation, though what she says repulses me.

I've never touched a dead body before, but Viera needs someone to pull the other hand, and the Charre aren't going to help. The Solare's fingers are cool to the touch—I imagine they would be colder if not for the Ignos' work—but they're easy to grip. I plant my feet and it's like hauling grain, or pulling on a cart.

Only this one used to be alive.

We get the Solare to the fire, but I'm not sorry we don't get to see the results of our work. Malo's pressing us to move, and I'm eager to find somewhere out of the heat. Viera doesn't say another word as we rejoin the march, and I wonder if she's thinking, looking at all the Solare captives that survive, whether killing one was the right move.

She staked out her power. See how the others watch Viera warily now? You ought to find something similar, so they see you as a threat.

I'm a Solare daughter without her tribe, in a place I don't know. I'm the opposite of a threat.

Remember the Cache. It can help you.

I'd almost forgotten about the bracelet. It's still on my wrist, the same green-brown it's always been. I ask Ignos if it can make something like Viera's gray tube appear.

It can do far better. We can use it to show the Charre, when the time is right, that they should not only fear you, but obey you. Then, you can prepare them for the coming of their gods. Of yours too.

Their escape is manifest in more ways than one: the section they've entered now, unlike the first two, is lit in creamy white, and it's clear the Sevora inside it aren't operating any sort of defense. Sax is stunned to see no weapons aimed their way.

No shouts or shots zinging into their masks. In fact, aside from their set, the landing is empty.

The rest of the section is not, though there are no glowing tubes and only one small purple-black pool that Sax can make out. The flat steps leading down from the landing hit what looks like soft blue rubber with even lines sectioning it into lanes. The rubber itself looks gouged, with deep scars crisscrossing its surface.

The track rings the entire section, and all the divisions within it. There are arenas with stacks of equipment— weights and bars. Target ranges where, even now, Sax can see a trio of Flaum sending hot lasers into thin hit slips.

In the center of the section stands a quad set of buildings, reaching three stories high and sporting flat roofs. Square, open-air windows dot them at precise intervals.

"I forget that the Sevora live here too," Lan says, and Sax agrees.

A Vincere station wouldn't be all that different, really.

"Why aren't they looking for a fight?" Gar asks.

"The separation is the last resort," Bas answers. "They would not split away a whole section unless there were no other option. So perhaps they think we were caught inside it?"

"We need to get to cover," Sax interrupts.

They have, somehow, regained the advantage of surprise and he doesn't want to lose it standing in plain view.

As they limber down to the track, then walk across onto the first pathway they find, Sax realizes there's no cover to be found. Thin fences separate the arenas, more, Sax suspects, for safety than for security. The barriers don't hide their massive Oratus bodies, and at least one of the Sevora must have seen them by now.

So why aren't they attacking?

"I'll take the lead," Gar says.

Nobody argues this and Sax puts himself at the rear, still puzzling.

"Go quick, straight for the gate," Lan says as they form their line. "I'm not sure what's going on, but let's take advantage."

"No." Sax thinks he has the idea. "Be calm. Move slow. Don't fire your weapons. Let's see how they react."

Gar, for once, listens. They walk, claws hanging loose with weapons sheathed. The experience makes Sax itch; he's not one for stealth. An Oratus is made for destruction, not sneaking. Intelligence gathering fell squarely into Flaum territory. When a group of the furry creatures—all, given by their precise motions and lack of chittering conversation, infected with Sevora—passes by them, it's all Sax can do not to reach out and tear them apart.

But it's that nonchalant passing that gives Sax the proof he needs to confirm his theory: the idea of hostiles this far into the seed ship is so strange that the Sevora believe the four of them are hosts. That the Oratus have been taken and they're simply moving about the ship like the rest of the infected.

What's more disturbing to Sax is that, if the Sevora think this, then they must have evidence. It's the greatest shame, the worst possible thing for an Oratus to allow themselves to be taken by a Sevora. If trapped, self-slaughter is a last resort. The preferred way is to die taking as many enemies as possible down with you. Capture... the thought has Sax opening his mouth to hiss before he remembers what they're doing and closes it again.

Never. Sax would die a thousand deaths before the Sevora take him.

The volcano's name is Tutio, Malo tells me. To the Charre, it's a symbol of their own survival. We're looking at the puffs of smoke rising from Tutio's snow-ringed top as we devour our last breakfast before making the final march to Damantum. The city's there, down the slope to my left, where the sands of the desert give way to brown, wavy fields.

"Survival?" I ask, because Solare stories say to stay as far away from Tutio as possible. The volcano has a habit of getting angry, and those who don't respect that anger tend to succumb to it.

"Yes." Malo speaks in his reverent tone again, the one that comes up every time he discusses Charre's god, Damantum, or, really, anything about Charre life. "Many times Tutio has burned Damantum to the ground. Razed our fields with its furies. You would think this a bad thing, right?"

"Generally."

"At first, of course, it is. People die in the fires, and those that don't might starve. Eventually, though, the Charre return. We build stronger walls and deeper trenches to catch Tutio's liquid flame. The fields that come back are larger and healthier than before. We grow, Kaishi."

This is a ridiculous view. No civilization grows stronger by having itself destroyed routinely. Yet another thing we will change, Kaishi.

I agree with Ignos, though I'm not so sure about his comment on change. Even if I get to some level of power where I can demand things of the Charre, I doubt I'll be able to get them to move their city.

No, we will stop the volcano itself.

Malo notices my mouth hang open and cocks his head. "Are you all right, Kaishi? Did my story disturb you?"

I get myself back. "No. Ignos is whispering some strange things."

"What is he saying? Can you tell me?"

I stand, shaking my head. I'm not going to start spilling Ignos' statements to Malo quite yet. Not till I understand them myself. The only reason I'm alive is that Malo thinks I'm talking to a benevolent god. If he thinks Ignos wants to dominate his civilization, that tone might change.

I wonder, then, why I care? At the start of the march, way back in the jungle, I'd been sulking. Dismal. If the Charre had decided at the end of that first day that keeping me along was a burden too heavy to carry, I'm not sure I would have fought them.

Now I see Malo watching me with a mix of questions and concerns, and I'm... not happy, but alive and glad to be so. Even if Ignos is Malo's main concern, it's nice knowing he cares about me. At least a little.

Viera, too. In the day since we burned the body, the Lunare has left my side only for natural reasons and when I've asked her to.

She's otherwise walking next to me, sharing stories of her homeland beneath the rocks. Her endless legends cover everything from massive monsters making new caves of their own to a week-long celebration when the snow melts and all of Lunare has more water than they can drink.

In short, I have friends. Not something I had back home, when people saw me as the priest's daughter. Someone to be respected, yes, but not befriended, lest any offense you caused brought the wrath of Ignos upon you.

Damantum sprawls in the distance ahead of me. Unlike my village, which spread haphazard through jungle clearings, this city is ordered. Wide avenues split rectangular districts, and the river circling Damantum is bridged in several places by arching stonework. To the northeast, the plains give way to blue ocean.

I focus on a sloped building in the center of Damantum. It's hard not to look at it, because the structure appears to be gold. Ignos blazes out from its surface, so that I find myself shading my eyes, trying to get a better look.

"The Vaos," Malo says, joining my watch. "It's the center of Damantum, and the greatest thing the Charre have ever made. Even Tutio dares not destroy it."

"What is it for?" I ask, and Malo looks at me with another one of those nice smiles.

"You, Kaishi. It's for you."

They've made it to the buildings and now Sax sees that these are rooms of a different type. Large, enclosed spaces with pitch-black floors, walls, and ceilings. He sees these through the building on his left, while the one on the right appears to have its windows covered by sliding shutters. Virtual training.

Complete blackouts in the room, and then projectors give the students whatever they're looking to study. Battles, sure, but Sax remembers even normal lessons buttressed by holographic trips to the subject, whether it was a place or the inside of a body. So many lessons before he earned his first mask.

They go past the buildings and all the way beyond a second set of fenced areas. One in particular draws Sax's eye: a large, mottled spire with various colored bulbs hanging from different heights. Pole-like creatures cluster around and on it. As Sax watches, the poles, through small holes, appear to sprout many-fingered hands that push them around or scuttle them up and down the spire. Tevens.

Supposedly, the hard-shell pole comes from secretions the creatures make, and each one's markings tell the secret of that Teven's ancestry. What Sax really cares about, though, is how something tastes, and Tevens are bland, and the pole shards scratch Sax's throat if they're not properly chewed. There is better food.

At the back of the section they cross the track again, make theirway up the steps, and there's another gateway. Red-rimmed like the others. Sax doesn't have a Sevora handy, and pulling out their cutters would ruin any hint of deception they've got going.

"I say we do it anyway," Gar announces when it's clear what they're all thinking. "Look at them down there. This isn't a military force. By the time we cut through, they'll barely have noticed."

"Except they don't know we're here now," Bas says. "If we can get through without them knowing, we could make it to the core undetected."

"Which isn't any fun," Gar replies.

"Sometimes there are more important things than your bloodlust," Lan says, and, after a second, Gar's tail twitches to the floor in agreement.

"So we need someone to let us through," Sax says. "A hostage."

"I've never taken one before," Lan replies. "Always easier to eat a captive."

Truth.

While they've been walking through the section, above the shouts and high-pitched squeal of laser-fire, there's been a constant undertone of pattering. Soft thuds on the ground. Looking from the landing, Sax identifies the source: a group of circular creatures bolting around the track.

Rotams. A bundle of double-kneed legs around a central round body. The scars on the track have an answer now: every Rotam leg ends in a hard hoof, one that has a retractable claw. Sax has seen Rotam charges before—they wheel up and around every surface, then roll over you, carving you to pieces in the process.

They're eyeless, and sense movement, and sound, through soft fibers coating their body.

Which means Sax can wait, down by the track, for the Rotam to pass by. As long as the Oratus stay still, they should be able to snatch the last one in the group without the others knowing.

The other three agree to Sax's plan and, as the Rotam circle the opposite side of the section, the set takes up their positions. Sax gets the first opportunity, as it's his idea. The Stim's still going strong—the effect lasts for hours—and so when the Rotam go by, Sax has no trouble reaching out and grabbing one a couple of meters behind the others.

His claws dig into the creature's body and he lifts it off the track. It struggles, but from the side, the Rotam don't have much in the way of defense. He sees Bas give him a congratulatory tail twitch, and then they're turning to head to the gateway.

Which slides open. Before it should.

"The Oratus continue to live up to their reputation," the voice, hissing and deep, comes from what Sax hopes never to see. An Oratus, standing tall and clad in black, shining armor. The plates and helmet make him look ridiculous, and must be more limiting than a mask, but the Oratus doesn't seem to care. "Now, it's time for the Sevora to live up to ours."

Around him pour out Flaum, all aiming weapons at the set.

There's noise from the track too—the Rotam that just passed by have turned around.

Sax knows they're pinned. Trapped.

Dead.

The gates of Damantum stand tall in Ignos' evening light. Gilded gold and peppered with obsidian, which Malo says is intentional. An homage to Tutio. Charre signs decorate the sculpted columns. Some I recognize, and others I don't. It's a reminder that if I'm to preach to these people, I have a lot of learning to do.

As we near the city, the warriors break off. Malo dismisses them, and they disappear. Going to see their families, lovers, and friends.

Malo stays near me, along with Viera, who's trying to look everywhere at once.

"A city full of enemies," Viera says when I ask her why she's so tense. "Any Charre would love to put a knife in my back."

I can't disagree with that statement. Most Solare would want to do the same.

We make our way to the gates, pressing through the crowds of traders and merchants shifting in and out of the Charre capital, and two guards approach. Unlike Malo and his warriors, these do not wear any animal skins and are instead bare-chested, sporting leather skirts and sandals. Each of them hold spears, and wears a red feathered mantle. They look at me for a moment, apparently decide I'm no threat, and turn their attention to Viera.

If the Solare aren't worth attention, the Lunare get double.

"What have you brought us today, Malo?" the lead guard says.

"A priestess," Malo replies, pointing at me. "She'll go to Jakkan, and you'll see her soon. She hears Ignos, and says he wishes to give us miracles."

The warriors don't believe Malo's endorsement. They crack smiles, hide their laughter. I'm about to speak up when Malo continues, "This other one is Viera. A Lunare. Be careful of the weapon she holds, as it commands deadly power."

"Deadly power?" Now the guards are interested. "We can't let her have it, then. Not if you mean to take her inside the city."

"You know the terms," Viera says this in Lunare tongue to Malo, and I translate when the guards stare and Malo looks to me.

"She says she won't give it up." I try to shrug, like it's just not going to happen, but I don't think they buy it.

"Unless you can make her?" Malo asks.

"I can't," I reply.

I don't want to try. There are certain things that I'm willing to risk for my friends, but disarming one of them in a place so obviously hostile? That seems like a bad idea.

Malo nods, apparently respecting my situation. Then he turns to Viera, who matches Malo's look with a defiant glare of her own. I don't catch it, but Malo darts forward, so fast, and grabs Viera's right arm. Keeps it away from the pistol.

The guards are almost as quick, and they have Viera restrained in moments. One of the guards untangles a rope from a loop on his skirt and ties Viera's wrists together.

Malo pulls the pistol, carefully, from Viera's holster. The Charre chieftain holds it in both hands, looking at it as though sight alone will reveal its secrets to him.

"Give that back." Viera struggles, but she's not making any headway.

"Tell her I'm sorry, but Viera can't be permitted to roam the city armed," Malo says to me.

"Stop fighting," I tell Viera. "You're only going to make it worse. They may just decide to kill you. How's that going to help?"

Viera looks for a moment like a rabid animal, caged and snarling, but as the ropes tighten the attitude fades. Her mouth soothes into a straight line. Her eyes are embers, and she directs their heat at Malo, who ignores it.

"If you're bringing them into the city, then she's your charge," the lead guard says. He holds forth the end of the rope to Malo, who takes it.

"I accept. She'll be taken care of and watched," Malo replies.

Then he turns to me, and motions me forward through those arched, yellow stone gates and into the city.

I want to argue. To say that Viera, now that she's unarmed, can be let free. Ignos stops me. Tells me that it's more important now to gain the trust of the city. Of these people. One Lunare isn't worth risking our dream.

Our dream. Not sure I ever wanted this, but now I'm

too far in to back out, and I can't deny a growing part of me loves the adventure.

So I walk forward. Into the most bustling city I've ever seen. It's streets are packed with people shuffling back and forth. Many carrying baskets and bags loaded down with fruits and meats, cloth and clay urns. Stands are set up all along every corner and open space, connected right to the small houses behind them where the owners can wake up and start selling until they pass out at the end of the night.

The sounds of bargains being driven, coins being exchanged fill my ears, along with the smells of a thousand cooking scents and spices.

There's an undertone beneath it all that I pick up too. Of refuse and waste. Still, Damantum feels alive. As if the city is awake and has a spirit far more vigorous than my village ever did.

"This is my home," Malo says as he leads me through the streets. "It is everything to me, as it is everything to the Charre What do you think of it?"

Do not insult it.

Like I need the reminder.

"It's overwhelming," I say. "I've never seen so much in one place before."

In truth, I notice, it is missing one thing: trees. There are so few. Damantum is all brown and sandy. Light-bleached and hot. What shade there is comes from the sharp corners of buildings, and not the leafy shadows of the jungle I love. So even as I take it in, I realize that Damantum is not, and maybe never will be, my home.

"You'll get used it in time," Malo says. "Everyone does. The treasures that are here, the experiences, the people. It all is a lot, I know. Eventually you'll start to see why this is wonderful. You'll fall in love, like I have."

Viera stays silent during our walk. Every time I think to ask her a question, or even look at her, Ignos yells at me to stop. At first I argue, but then begin to think Ignos' advice is right; Viera's not the only captive I see in the streets. Many are led about in groups with ropes chaining between all of the them in a line. Nobody looks at them. Nobody acknowledges their bowed heads and scuffing bare feet.

Would a priestess?

No, Ignos says, and I agree. I won't be able to help Viera if I join her in the ropes.

We reach the Vaos. It is gigantic. Tall and monstrous and beautiful and horrendous at the same time. As I saw from the volcano, the whole temple is gilded in gold. It shines and shimmers at dusk, a flickering multitude. Halfway up the giant stone slabs that make up the Vaos' steps, there's a wide square door. One haloed by a set of four burning braziers.

"That's where you belong," Malo says to me. "Go in there, and you will meet our high priest, Jakkan. He will help you. He will teach you what you need to know so that you can give us what the Ignos needs us to hear."

"Are you coming with me?" I ask.

"I'm not a priest, therefore I'm not allowed on the steps of the Vaos without permission."

I notice that Malo is right; despite the teeming masses of people moving through the courtyard around the great temple, many of whom stop to pray up to its altars, there are no bodies on the steps.

No one taking a careful walk up to the top. But at Malo's urging, I do.

I have to raise my knees high to get up, because the steps are not small. There are twenty of them to get to where the doorway begins.

Look at where you are. Already climbing above the mess. Keep moving, Kaishi, and we will make it.

When I reach the doorway, I turn to see if Malo and Viera are watching, but they're gone. Only crowds of people funneling by, a few casting curious glances up at me.

I'm alone.

There's only one way to go, though, so I look inside. It's a dark tunnel. Not a long one. Every meter, set into the stone walls, are small basins with candles flickering away.

I take hesitant steps.

The sound of the city dies away as I go inside, and a cool breeze carries burning incense. The Vaos opens up to a central chamber, and I can see at least four doors off of either side. Standing in the middle, his back tight and frail, is a man. A design inked on his back, in various dyes so as to create a beautiful rainbow collage, is of Ignos at dawn.

The golden orb and the multicolored bands of his blessings radiating out. As I watch, the man turns, unfolding his hands, which had been clasped for prayer, and grins at me. His right eye is milky white and there are gaps in his teeth, most of which are gold.

"Welcome," the man says, and his voice is strong and firm. Iron. "I've been waiting for you, Kaishi, supposed speaker for our god."

When Stim wears off, it's like coming out of a leap —everything speeds up and seems, at first, too real. Actions happen too fast. There's no time to think. Sax's body twitches in the room, one of the black ones, so that it seems like he's lying in the middle of blank space. The windows are closed, so there's really nothing other than Sax, the Sevora-stolen Oratus, and a quartet of watching Flaum.

"Yes, that must be painful for you," the Oratus says as it watches Sax breath hard, heavy. "Stim, I take it?"

Three Flaum stand in the corners of the room, each one pointing a two-pawed miner at Sax. He's fairly sure that, if he had the Stim and a moment's surprise, Sax could move fast enough to take out at least two before the third vaporized him. That would still leave the Oratus, though, and that's the most important target.

"Can you speak at all, or is the prospect of me existing so terrible that you can't even form words?" the Oratus continues.

In a situation where sacrifice is not possible and attack is ill-advised, gather intelligence. Sax knows his training, so he lifts his head, ignores the pulsing headaches leftover from the Stim, and talks, "You are an abomination."

It's a strong opening, and Sax feels better for having said it. At least, until the Oratus laughs.

"Am I?" the Oratus replies, then considers for a moment. "Do you know what? I might agree with you. Look at me, in this armor? And look at you, in that mask, all pure."

Sax isn't sure what to say to this, so he stays quiet. Lets his eyes drift to the Flaum and checks their attention. Right now, they're still riveted. That's the Sevora control, though, not the Flaum themselves. Through the mask, Sax listens for the sounds of the others, but there's no pick-up. These buildings are thick, likely jammed with electronics. Their signal might not get through.

"You're probably wondering why we haven't shot you yet." The Oratus paces now, circling Sax like a predator, those talons clicking on the black floor. "It's a tricky thing, getting a working mask. We don't have a single one. All of the Sevora. Not one. Can you believe it?"

Sax can. The mask is a second skin. It'll only come off if Sax forces it to. Every other way would break it, and when the mask is broken, it takes care of its own elimination. Now Sax knows what the Oratus wants, and when you know what your prey desires, you can set a trap.

"Are you offering a deal?"

"Yes," the Oratus pauses, stares hard at Sax. "Take off the mask, and I'll let you live."

"You'll just give me to a Sevora. I'll be like you."

"Like me?" the Oratus resumes his circling. "You'll never be like me. You live once, while I live a thousand times, in many bodies. But you, this one life of yours, will last longer."

"I only need to tear you apart a single time." Sax opens his mouth wide, shows all of his teeth. They gleam in the low light, razor weapons waiting for their chance to strike.

Every child has nightmares. They see ghosts. Figments of stories that whirl in front of their eyes in the dead of night or, sometimes, when they're alone in the jungle in the middle of the day. The man in front of me comes from those nightmares.

His eyes, wrinkled and bordered with dark ink, stare at me. His face, etched in deep lines, appears to have seen a century, and holds all of the wisdom that went with it. His head is clear. Shaved. His body, in front of me, is thin and wrapped in a fine cloth that he pulls idly up over his left shoulder.

Here at last I see some evidence of Jakkan's position: his robe has many colors, and dyes are rare in both Solare and Charre. Reds and greens interspersed with dashes of blue. It makes me think of running by colorful trees. Yet, the idea strikes me as wrong. The painting isn't quite right, the streaks not where they should be. Not natural.

I get the idea that Jakkan rarely leaves the city. The jungle, if he's ever seen it, is a memory and not a core of his heart like mine.

"You see me," Jakkan says. "Tell me, what do I look like?"

Be careful. This one lays traps with his words.

I hear Ignos, but there's something in the way Jakkan speaks that compels me to answer. It might be the fact that he seems to be holding me as the center of his focus. As if I am the most important thing in his universe.

"You look nothing like the warriors that brought me here," I say.

I adopt, without realizing it, the language Father uses to speak with the elders. Respectful, honest. "Yet I don't think your strength comes from your arms and legs, but from your mind."

I'm about to go on, when Jakkan holds up a hand. Palm towards me. "My strength comes from Ignos," Jakkan says, and I hear a hint of reproach in his voice. "All strength does. What he chooses to grant us is what we have. You, as a priestess, should know this."

I'm not sure if this is a question or not, but Jakkan doesn't let me answer anyway. He turns away from me, walks over, in short easy steps, to a mottled black pot which seems to be boiling tea over hot coals. The small alcove bears the black-ash stains of many fires. All this leads me to believe Vaos is not only Jakkan's temple, but his home.

"Tell me your story," Jakkan says as he pours himself a cup.

My story is pretty simple. A young girl happens upon a god who crashed down from the sky. I can't tell Jakkan that. This is the Charre high priest. I have to come up with something better.

Ignos is ready for me. His words come streaming through my mind and I find myself spinning a tale I wouldn't have believed if I'd heard it myself.

"I began the same as you," I say, stating the words as Ignos presents them. "Chosen, not by any man, but by those greater. In the middle of a fast and crowded world, where disease, wildlife, or the spirit of your enemy could make for a swift end, I survived. I grew. I began to learn what it means to serve Ignos. This, for the Solare, means placing your tribe before yourself. Your people before your own life. It's simple, but important, and it's what keeps our village strong.

"However, my tribe did not let me hunt, because I am not a man. Impossible walls kept me out. So I did what I could and wished for more. I assisted in the rites, I learned to craft the clothes we wear, I practiced making the food that would feed my family. In time, Ignos recognized my devotion and my wish, which led me to you."

After I finish, Jakkan hands me some tea and I take a sip. Warm with a fruit-filled aftertaste. Pleasant, after a day of walking in the heat.

"Kaishi, if I am to let you stand in front of our glorious people and preach, I must make sure you do indeed hear the words of Ignos." Jakkan, sipping his tea between words, turns and vanishes into one of the side rooms.

I hear a clanking clatter of things moving around. I stay still. Finish my own tea.

"You will take this medal," Jakkan says as he comes back into the room, a stained bronze circle hanging from a thick ribbon around his hand. "You will wear it, then you will go to the Pits, on the west side of the city. You will be found there, and you will be shown to a juar, which you will tame in the name of Ignos. Should you succeed, they will give you a different medal, which you will bring back to me."

"Tame a juar?" the request is so strange that I don't understand it at first.

Jakkan nods again.

Ignos senses my sudden fear, but I don't have time for his questions right now. Jakkan's still talking, and if I'm going to get out of this, I have to listen to every word.

"You may think you are the first one to come to me," Jakkan continues. "The first one of our people, or any people, to come and demand to stand on this great temple and say they hear from Ignos. So I've devised a test. If you are truly favored, then Ignos will intervene. The task will prove as nothing to you, and you will be back here before long, ready to show us all how wrong we are."

If the Oratus is intimidated by Sax's display, he doesn't show it. "This one said much the same." The Oratus taps the metal plate on his chest. "He made threats. Tried to hurt himself, to hurt me." He leans closer to Sax, who could swipe at him now, but that wouldn't guarantee the kill. So Sax feels hot breath on him and does nothing. "Do you know what happens when we take over your mind?

"You watch every moment. See out of your own eyes as you slaughter your friends. As you betray everything you are. This one is still here now. He is begging for you to leap at me and tear apart my throat."

Sax tires of listening. Tires of waiting for traps. Death comes for all Oratus at some time, and now it is his turn. So he bunches his legs and leaps. Sax knows he'll only have one strike, so he swings, in the air, and swipes right where the Oratus asked him to: at the vulnerable slit between the armor in the neck.

The Flaum don't fire. The Oratus doesn't flinch. Sax doesn't realize his mistake until he makes contact, his midclaws catching hold of the armor so his foreclaws can do the blood work. It feels like his every nerve comes ablaze with hot fire. The Oratus lifts Sax away, and Sax does nothing; all Sax can think, all he can do, is burn.

The Oratus throws Sax to the ground, and the mask, at least, blunts this force. It dulls the Oratus' kick a moment later too, sprawling Sax over onto his back. With a normal shock, Sax wouldn't be shaking now. Twisting and turning. The Oratus' armor seems to have melted away Sax's nerves. Left his body numb and unresponsive.

He watches the Oratus step over him. Sees the claws spread. There's a precise way to remove a mask, meant to be done only by the one wearing it. This Oratus knows what it is, no doubt he's ripped it from his captive's mind, and Sax is helpless as the creature leans down and pokes the claws on his four hands into Sax's palms. In the exact spots where, if Sax were to clench his own claws into his own hands, they would strike.

The mask peels away like a falling cloak; a brush of cool fabric along his skin, and it folds into a silvery pile at his feet.

"I didn't think that would actually work," the Oratus says as he bends over to pick up the mask. "A theory, stolen from this one's mind, and look at this. We have one, finally."

The Oratus runs a look at the Flaum in the room. "Carry him out, now. Let's take him before he gets his function back."

The three Flaum struggle to lift Sax and resort to dragging him across the metal floor, and then out into the open, down one of the pathways. Sax traces the lights on the ceiling. He knows exactly where they're taking him, and if he could snap his own neck, he would.

Some things are far worse than death.

The streets of Damantum flicker in the light of a thousand torches. Dancing shadows parade off of gold-glinted statues and homes as the city shifts into revelries. I walk down the the front of the Vaos, playing with the medallion.

So these are giant, murderous creatures? Kaishi, I say we leave the city. Find a small village and grow our legend there. Then, when we have an army of the faithful equipped with my miracles, they'll all come groveling to your feet.

I reach the courtyard and look to the West. The roads leading that way dim, though the noises coming from that quarter ring over those coming from the rest of the city. Taming a juar. A jungle cat, though not many remain in Solare territory; hunted and driven away. I run my fingers along my mosswrap, cool and dry around my shoulders. It wouldn't do me any good against such a creature.

Exactly my point.

So instead of heading west, towards the Pits, I go straight. Walk by merchants pulling their carts in the opposite direction; heading home. More than a few people catch my eyes as I move, drawn to the moss, or my roving glances as I try to take in all I can of the city.

I feel their eyes on my face and its Solare features. When they notice the medallion, however, all of them look away and never turn back.

Jakkan's task is known throughout the city, apparently.

Yes, go towards the gates. Though I might suggest hiding that medallion, or throwing it in some dark alley. It's conspicuous.

I reach the main road, which, during the day, had been crowded with stands selling everything I could imagine. Now there are fewer, but the number still gives me a moment of panic. So many people, so many options. My hands find the medallion, hanging around my neck, and grip it tight. The firm metal calms my nerves. One foot after another. I slide between the crush of people, focusing on what I'm here for than the multitude of things around me.

What you're here for? Go to the gates. Your life is too valuable to waste!

I ignore Ignos. Push the god's voice to the back of my mind, so that Ignos' words come only as a buzzing, far off conversation. No Solare god would advocate fleeing such a challenge, so this must be another of Ignos' tests. My courage and conviction are being called into question, and for one of the first times in my life, I can control my own actions.

I will not run.

Ignos has no reply.

I find a stall covered in growing plants. Vines wrap the entire canopy, with wooden tables draped in urns over-flowing with various leafy things. I go towards it, and barely begin to look them over before a short man appears, his long black hair tied on his head.

"I'm Zolin, and welcome to..." the shopkeeper trails off as he notices the medallion. Starts to turn away, but I put a hand on his shoulder.

"Please, why does everyone see this medallion and act strangely?"

"Because it's a sign of Jakkan's disfavor," Zolin replies. "You are stained by the high priest. Nobody would share in that."

"Stained? Jakkan gave me this medallion himself. As a sign I was on a mission from him."

"Then you're going to have a tough time of it." Zolin's still watching the medallion, like it's a snake that might bite him. "You won't find any help in Damantum wearing that."

"Fine," I reach to pull it off, but before I can even start, Zolin grabs the medallion and pulls it back down. Keeps around my neck.

"No, you can't take it off! Not unless the high priest does it himself. Any guard sees you try to remove it, they'll kill you." As if thinking he could be implicated in the idea, Zolin shoots rapid looks around the crowd.

Nobody's paying us any attention.

"So I can't take it off or I die, but you're not going to help me if I'm wearing it?"

Zolin rubs his hands on his face. Looks hard at me. "You're young to get that prize. What'd you do to earn it?"

I tell the short version of my story. That I'd come to Damantum after a religious experience and that I want to become a priestess. Jakkan gave me the medallion and sent me on a quest to the Pits to tame a juar. When I finish, Zolin laughs.

"Tame a juar? That's a quick way to the grave," Zolin says.

"That's why I'm here." I point at the plants. "I need some curare. Do you have any?"

"What would you need that for? You're not a doctor." Zolin's his left hand flies up to his tied hair, where it begins pulling on a loose strand and wrapping it around his fingers. "Unless you mean to..."

"I do," I say. "And bamboo. A small stick."

Zolin nods. "I've got those, but if you're planning what I'm thinking, you'll need to find something to do the dosing. I've not got that."

I see Zolin's eyes slip past me, across the avenue. "But you know somebody that does?"

"In this market? You can find anything." Zolin leads me around the stand, cutting a few leaves off of one particular plant and, using a mortar and pestle, crushing it into a thin liquid. "How'd you manage to learn about this beauty?"

"I'm not from around here," I answer. "We used it from time to time at home."

Zolin pours the liquid from the mortar into a small jar, caps it loose with a piece of wood. Then, from a rangy bamboo thicket at the back of the stand, where the reeds are nearly as tall as I am, Zolin cuts a section off. Using the same knife, Zolin cleans out the inside of the piece and then hands both things to me.

Then waits.

"I, uh, don't have anything to give you," I say when I realize what he's waiting for.

"Oh yes you do," Zolin says. "Here's what I'm asking. You make it past this, and I've got a feeling you're going to, you keep me in your prayers. And you come see me whenever Jakkan needs more incense, all right?"

I laugh.

"The needle?" I ask. "Where can I get that?"

Zolin points across the road to a stand that looks to be advertising hardier weapons. Jagged, curved swords and other big blades. At my hesitance, Zolin grunts, walks out from his stand and leads me across the street. Without letting me get a single word in, Zolin speaks to the surly blacksmith manning the shop and, in no time at all, comes out with a pair of sharp needles, each one an inch long.

"Now you've got the materials, but do you have the skill?" Zolin asks.

"You'll know if you ever hear from me again."

"I hope I do, Kaishi," Zolin says. "There's grim rumors coming about the Lunare, and I'm thinking this city might need a new kind of priestess. One as smart as our warriors are deadly."

Without the mask, the seed ship's air is cool. There's a slight breeze—the recyclers keeping things fresh—and Sax smells the burn of disinfectant in the air. A hallmark on ships; the chemicals do their work to keep disease, deadly in compact confines, to a minimum.

It's this familiar scent, more than anything, that brings Sax down from a raging panic as the Flaum carry him out into the section. The sterile sting is a connection to things not quite so terrible as this moment, and the smell jolts his mind to what's important.

Namely, not becoming a Sevora toy.

The Flaum struggle to hold the Oratus' weight, and Sax sways through the air as the small creatures shift back and forth. As a result, Sax, whose numb muscles have his neck and head limp, gets a clear look at the captive Oratus following him. Sax's mask is in those claws, and the Oratus is snapping commands at seemingly nobody, which must mean that armor of his has a communicator in it.

Ideas for escape come and go, but they all have a

common theme: Sax has to get his muscles moving again, or he's done.

It's a matter of trying. Like, after he's woken up in an awkward position, urging his legs to move. Flexing and loosening the muscles in his arms. At first, nothing happens, but gradually the feeling comes back. Twinging nerves burst like shocks.

Now the Oratus stops and watches as the Flaum maneuver Sax through a hard-railed fence gate. The ground here is smooth silver, spotless. Not scuffed with use like the rest of the section. As they move Sax around, he sees Bas, Gar, and Lan assembled in a line. There's a band of Flaum around them, holding rifles to the Oratus' backs. Captives all.

A new sound plays in the background. A burbling, shunting noise. Liquid current. Sax knows what they're doing now, and its confirmed when the Flaum swing him around to the side of a small pool full of purple-black ink. Not a birthing pool, but a hosting one.

Where the Sevora claim their victims.

Then, without fanfare, without a taunt, the Flaum throw Sax in. A fleeting moment in open space—the lower gravity hesitates before pulling Sax down—and then he hits the ink. The stuff pulls at him, sucking him inside and under the surface.

Before, in the birthing section, the Sevora were numerous. They gave off tremors as they swam towards him. Here, there's little indication. Sax guesses why when he feels the first tickles at the edge of his head. Only one in here. A Sevora that's earned its prized host.

The captured Oratus had said the armor and its electric shock was a test. One that had worked, for a while. One that, with the mask deflecting some of it, isn't able to keep Sax stunned long enough.

Time, and the relentless push of Sax's desperate anger, frees him from the shackles.

The Sevora tickles again. Trying to find a way inside Sax's mind. Unaware that it's no longer predator, but prey.

I f the market had been bustling with commerce, the Pits hum with death. I walk by the Vaos again to head towards Damantum's west side and leave behind the scent of incense for the harsh blow of burning flesh, of bloodstained air, and sweat's salty stink.

Yells echo down the alleys, punctuated with the roar of wild things. Crowds shift from those in traditional garb— the capes and loin cloths or skirts—to darker fare. Hair, on both men and women, begins to fall down around their shoulders instead of being held up in ties. Scars make their appearances. Grime is everywhere.

In the market people had met my eyes and looked away, here they don't notice I exist. All at once the buildings disappear and I'm pushing through a throng into a wide courtyard, cracked stones replacing the hard dirt beneath my feet. Crude wooden barriers divide the courtyard into four parts. Stakes nailed to others with bits of metal act as fences. Not enough by themselves to hold in a creature that wants to escape, but that's where the crowds come in;

people ring each of the arenas, raising fists and passing coins. Others share skins full of what, I don't know.

I'll protest one last time. This is foolish. Needless. You're risking my miracles on a stupid chance.

I am, and I am not. I know I could turn around and walk out of the city. Perhaps even scrounge or find enough help to make it back to my village alive. But what then? Wait out the coming attack, either from the Charre or the Lunare? What end is that?

You could gather your strength, find a better way. One that includes fewer claws.

There isn't time. I'm here, now. I can do this. I can use, for once, what the jungle has taught me, what me people have given me. In my right hand, hidden beneath my cape, I hold the bamboo reed with the needle, soaked with Zolin's mixture, inside of it.

I'm ready.

Yet, nobody here seems to notice the medallion. Not a soul calls out to me, or tries to guide me through the press of people watching the fights. In one arena, a pair of what appear to be slaves fight each other with clubs, bashing away though neither looks like they want to.

The next pit over holds a strange event: several Charre warriors, wearing their bear skins, face off against a single captive. The warriors appear to be taking turns—darting in and exchanging blows with a desperate, bloody prisoner.

"This one is the last of his tribe," one of the watchers is saying as I go by. "He took down two bears himself. The bunch of them are fools for getting in there with the man, I think. Why risk death and waste a great sacrifice?"

On the other side of the courtyard sits a stack of bamboo cages with rope tying the stalks together. Foxes, small bears, and larger lizards pace, growl, and sleep inside. Other creatures I don't recognize. One is huge, with eight thick legs and covered in short white hair, and its large, eyeless head dips towards me as it laps up some foul-smelling slop from a shallow bowl on the ground.

The juar waits at the end. Lazing on a mat, with a leg of some animal set before it. Dinner. Which is a good sign. The predator might not be hungry when I step into the ring with it.

I move closer to the cage. Look harder at the animal. Its tanned fur seems healthy, and when the jaur yawns, I see its jagged teeth, sticking out from its mouth at all angles, are long and sharp. We consider juar to be shredders, to be uncaring predators who will slash and snap at anything that moves. Or even things that do not—I've seen a coconut bearing the scars of a juar's rage.

Not every animal earns a caring treatment here, but the juar appears to be a lucky one. I come close, my face near the bars, and the big creature, standing taller than me, stares back with amber eyes. Slowly, I draw up my right hand.

"What are you doing? Getting a look at the competition?" a brash voice sounds right behind my ear and a thick arm claps down on my left shoulder. "Don't you worry, you'll get your chance soon enough."

I look and see a large, round man whose withering teeth and clawed face leer at me. "Been a while since Jakkan sent another one to the Pits. I thought for sure all the upstarts had realized pushing the head priest was a quick way to die."

"He gave me this." I, with my left hand, hold up the medallion.

The big man doesn't bother looking at it.

"I know who you are. Word's been spreading all night. You're the one that says she can talk to Ignos, right?"

"I can."

"Better get chatting, then, cause you'll be needing some help once those warriors get done with that poor soul over there. Soon as he's down, you're in." Then the round man turns, bellows something over the clamor of the crowd, and heads away.

I wheel back towards the juar cage. Bring the bamboo reed up to my mouth with my right hand while cupping my left in front of my face, as if to quiet a cough. I take a deep breath, and blow hard into the reed. I don't see the needle fly, but then, I don't need to. The juar yelps, hisses, and bats at its chest.

Not where I want the shot to hit. The neck would have been far better. The chest takes time to circulate. Too much time, going by the size of those paws.

Behind me, the crowd bursts into a frenzy of yelling and shouting. I catch enough words to know the cause. The bear warriors have finished their business. The captive is dead.

My turn.

The tickling becomes full on contact as the Sevora finds its target: Sax's aural cavities. Slight pricks of pain as the Sevora digs its barbed tentacles into Sax, and the moment's now. If Sax is going to survive, he has to act.

But slow.

There can't be any hint to those above the surface that something is going wrong. His left foreclaw moves, sluicing through the thick ink up towards his own head. The Sevora slips in—Sax can feel its body contorting, pressing against the inside of him. The barbed tentacles start to retract.

Too late.

Sax dips a claw into his own head, and when it makes contact with the Sevora, the parasite freezes. Sax does not. He pushes harder, feels the claw break the Sevora's skin, and pulls back. An explosion goes off in Sax's mind as the Sevora realizes what's happening and tries to fight. Tries to squirm inside Sax's brain. Its tiny tentacles are no match, however, for an Oratus arm, and Sax's claw is hooked enough to keep the wriggling Sevora on it until the parasite is out.

Without pausing, Sax pulls his claw down, turns his head, and shoves the Sevora in his mouth. Ink floods in too, but its designed to keep the parasites alive and tastes like nutrient soup. Good for washing down Sevora squid.

Sax doesn't even need to breathe in here—the ink carries with it the oxygen he needs to survive, so Sax waits a few moments. Figures it would take a bit of time for a Sevora to get control of its new host, learn how the muscles work. Sax does a silent count to a hundred.

Then curls his legs beneath him and pushes against the pool's floor. Surfaces slowly. With extreme control. How a Sevora would do it, hopefully.

The ink drips away from Sax and he's able to see everyone's stares, even the Flaum who ought to be paying close attention to the three deadly Oratus right next to them.

They're waiting to see what's come out of the pool. Sax dashes his eyes around, holds contact with Bas for just a moment so that she knows, and then he wades to land. Walks to the captive Oratus, who tilts his head in a nod towards Sax.

"Give yourself time," the captured Oratus says. "These bodies have many limbs. No need to rush." He turns to the other three Oratus. "You see what's become of your leader? The same thing that will become of you. Give us your masks, save yourself some pain, and join us."

"What is your name, friend?" Sax hisses. In a moment, his claws will be ripping apart that armor. Tearing off the head inside of it. Sax wants to know who he's about to end.

"Avan," the Oratus replies, and Sax can hear the question in his voice. "However, shouldn't you know that already?"

Sax replies with something other than words: his mid-claws stab forward, biting into Avan's hard armor, while his foreclaws swipe at Avan's head. A normal, trained Oratus would have seen the attack coming. Would have reacted in time.

Avan is not a trained Oratus. Avan's reaction is to jerk back. Or try to.

Sax tears at the helmet, rending its straps to pieces and ripping it off of Avan's head. He knows there's a chance Avan could trigger the electric shock again, send Sax into a numbed fit, so he's got to move fast.

Then he's not holding Avan anymore. Just an armor plate. Avan's backpedaling, a spiderweb of clasps dangling from his chest. Which is when Sax understands why Avan didn't try to shock him again: the mask. Avan still holds it in his claws.

The shocking armor didn't destroy the mask while Sax had it deployed, but a dormant mask is like cloth—easy to tear apart. As Sax tosses aside the armor—it's lightweight here in space—he catches hints of the battle apart from him. Skittering panic from the Flaum as they try to organize some sort of defense. Hissing anger from the other three Oratus as they rend that defense to pieces.

Surprise is the great equalizer, and Sax has it here.

That advantage dies with every second, though. Avan's already pulling for his miners, and Sax can't give him any more time. Without a mask, Sax is vulnerable, so he takes to the air. Leaps forward, all four claws extended and sharp.

Avan ducks away to his right, barreling through a fence to a sparse target range. Behind him loom the four core buildings of the section. Sax catches the ground, digs in those claws and bursts after Avan.

Part of Sax wonders where the other Sevora are? Four

armed Oratus and all this giant seed ship sends are a few Flaum? He expected battalions. Artillery. Real resistance.

It comes a moment later. With Sax bounding after Avan, his claws outstretched, shining, when the section's lights extinguish, plunging everything into darkness.

The caretaker, the man who'd grabbed me by the juar cage, takes me by my shoulders and guides me through a parting crowd to the fighting pit. Inside the wooden fencing, the gray stones are splattered with blood, spit, and spoiled food lobbed in from outside. The caretaker leads me inside the stakes, then looks at me.

"Tell me, priestess, have you ever fought a juar before?" the caretaker says, his voice saying that he already knows the answer.

I stare back at him, figuring I can use any hints he deigns to give me, and shake my head.

"It's not so hard as it looks. Nobody expects you to kill the thing, even Jakkan. The point is to live long enough. You do that, and you'll prove yourself worthy of the high priest's attention."

"How long?"

"Ah, see, that's the trick," the caretaker points across my pit to the next one. The one that had contained a pair of slaves. It too appears empty. "In another minute, someone will be entering that pit. Same as you did now. They'll be facing another juar. All you've got to do is outlast them. See?"

"Outlast them?"

"Juars need to eat, priestess. They like their food fresh. You want yours to go hungry." The man laughs as he walks out of the arena.

This is a savage game. Look for a way to run, Kaishi. It does us no good to stay.

Except there isn't anywhere to go. People crowd up to the fences, their faces wild and leering, full of drink and tossing coin back and forth. Taunts and jeers mingle with the odd shout of encouragement.

I try to close off from the frenzy. Fall into myself. I must be able to think if I'm going to get out of here alive.

The posts on the north side appear the weakest, and the crowd there is thinnest at the main passage. When you run, I would go that way.

Cheers rise up, coupled with an animal's harsh snarls. No, a pair of them. Now the crowds move quick, if only to get out of the way. I see the juar I'd shot in the cage, hissing at the end of a rope collar as the caretaker pulls it along. The rest of the leash leads away from the collar to the thick coil around the man's arm. The caretaker has slipped on a thick coat of leather that covers his chest, arms, and neck. Gloves woven in with gray metal wrap around his hands.

Protection I don't have.

A shout rings out behind me. My competition. In the other pit, pushed out into the open, wearing only a tattered robe and nothing else, stands Viera. She's whirling at the crowd, her neck and face red from yelling. Not that she can understand the Charre, or they her.

When Viera finishes her look around, she catches sight of me and stops.

"What're you doing here?" Viera calls across the pits.

"A test. Same as you," I reply.

Behind me, the caretaker leads the juar up to the side of the pit. The creature lopes over the low barrier into the arena with lazy familiarity, though its collar keeps the beast tight to the caretaker. I retreat to the far end of the pit as the caretaker slips the juar's collar over a thick post, tying the juar at a distance.

"This isn't a test," Viera yells back. "It's an execution."

"Only for one of us." I watch the juar as it watches me. I see, thankfully, my dart is already having an effect. While the creature prowls back and forth, its eyes look heavy and its breathing heaves.

Sleep will come soon.

"What do you mean?" Viera sounds frustrated. "I can't understand a damn thing they're saying."

"If you die, I live," I shout back. "Or the other way around."

A second set of growls comes out from the other side of the Pits as the caretaker leads a second, mangier, juar towards Viera's arena. This one's coat holds more gray, and it's gaunt. Decaying with age. But the creature lets none of its years show in its eyes, in its sharp claws that slash at any poor reveler that comes too close.

"It's insanity," Viera cries. "How can they do this?"

I have no answer. No demand from Ignos calls for pitting the unarmed against wild creatures. This is simple bloodsport. Pleasure at pain.

The caretaker leads Viera's juar to the corner of his pit, the closest one to mine, and then takes up the second juar's leash. Holding one leash in each hand, the man lifts the coils high and begins a sort of song. The crowd joins in, and while I can't catch all of the words, it sounds like a prayer. A blessing for the fight.

As they sing, I stare at the juar, at its big green eyes. My death lies in those pupils.

The song ends, but before the last note dies away, the caretaker lets the ropes fall free, gives the juars all the slack they need to get around the pits.

"How do I fight one of these things?" I hear Viera yell.

"Keep moving!" I reply.

I sidestep to the opposite corner of the pit, keeping my eyes on the juar across from me, who watches my shifting without comment.

Technically, nothing is keeping the juar in the ring. It could leap the barrier and tear into the yelling crowd, but it doesn't. Afraid, maybe, of the rope tying it to the caretaker. What the caretaker could do to it.

Watch out!

I jerk my eyes back and see the juar bounding towards me. The great beast takes one lope, then bursts into a leap at my throat. I do what I'd done in the jungle in games with other children: I roll. Fall on the stones and twist. I hear the juar strike the rock behind me. Claws tug on my moss wrap; the dried vines tearing apart. I don't pay attention to that, only to pushing off of the ground and running away.

Back along the juar's rope, towards the corner and the grinning caretaker beyond those wooden stakes.

Behind me, the juar tries a roar that starts strong and fizzles to a yawn. The crowd laughs, and one man calls out to the caretaker and asks if the juars had their rest.

"Plenty of it!" the caretaker replies. "They sleep all day as it is. This one's just got to wake up!"

The caretaker snaps his rope, and I see the crack wind to my juar and jerk its collar, stopping its yawn. The juar snarls back at the caretaker, then its eyes move to me. Slow, though. Not much longer and the creature would collapse. Behind me, the crowd around Viera's pit begins clapping and shouting. I want to look, want to see if the Lunare has fallen, but I don't dare glance away from my own monster.

The juar lunges towards me, ready to pounce again, and I tense. Ignos is screaming in my head to run, and I try to ignore the god's panic. No time for that now. The juar opens its mouth wide, long fangs sharp and white. Tilts its head slightly, locking on my face. Ready to lunge for my neck.

Ready to go for the kill.

I feel the stiff wood boards of the pit's border against my back.

Nowhere left to retreat. The caretaker, directly behind me, is laughing. The crowd hushes. They know the moment is coming, just as I do.

Those claws will be finding their mark.

The first thing Sax does when his vision goes black is drop to the ground. Lower his profile. What is dark for him will not be for others; Bas, Gar, and Lan still have their masks on and those will flip to show the infrared spectrum: greens and reds playing off of heat signature. The Sevora may have something similar.

Sax does not. His only immediate comfort is that Avan, without a helmet or mask of his own, is probably seeing the world as the same endless black as Sax is.

"This way!" Bas' voice rasps out from the nothing, and Sax traces the sound behind him.

Claws scratching against metal floors mingle with other noises—the moaning of injured Flaum, the clatter of larger things running through the section. The Sevora wouldn't have made this move unless they had a plan.

The Oratus must make their own quickly.

Bas meets Sax out of nowhere. She taps him on the shoulders with her tail, which Sax then grabs. She leads him along the path, and Sax has enough memory of the section to know where they're going.

If they can't tell where their opponent might be, they need to find ways to limit the options.

"The door is shut," Lan's voice this time. A higher hiss than Bas. "The control panel isn't responding."

There's a bang, followed by a second and a slight tremor as something hits the ground.

"That works too," Lan sighs.

There's a deep laugh that Sax attributes to Gar, and then Bas is moving again. Sax follows her, reading the movements in her muscles to duck beneath the door's threshold. He recognizes the feel of the place, the sudden absence of moving air, and the deadening of noise from outside.

They're back in one of the buildings. Ready to hole up.

"He took my mask," Sax states the obvious, reminding the other three that he's blind and unarmed.

"How?" Bas asks and Sax relays the details.

"Then they'll want the rest of us," Lan says after it's done. "Protocol says we destroy them. And ourselves."

"We're not at that stage yet," Sax replies.

The outcome isn't certain. Yes, they're likely trapped in a section with a seed ship's worth of Sevora getting ready to make an attack, but Oratus don't give in to despair.

"I won't be a plaything for some parasite," Gar says.

"Then don't be," Bas hisses. "The Sevora know our protocols as well as we do. They'll be expecting us to hole up, to guarantee that none of us are taken. So we do something else."

"We attack." Sax agrees with his pair. "Split apart. They'll need to restore some power to open the gateway, and when it does, rush it. Move quickly and focus on getting through, not killing them."

"What are we waiting for, then?" Gar asks, and they all agree.

No point in waiting for the Sevora to come after them. The Oratus are predators. Everything on this ship is prey.

The juar hesitates. I wait, but it doesn't jump. Instead, the juar opens its mouth wide and its tongue lolls off to the side. Relief runs through me like ice—the poison is taking effect.

The crowd laughs, and the caretaker shouts at the juar, cracking the rope again. I sneak a glance Viera's way, but people have filled in the space between us. I can't see her.

Pay attention!

I snap back to see the caretaker's managed to get the juar moving. Instead of looking at me, though, the creature snarls towards its master. It crouches, those big legs tensing, and leaps towards me.

Over me.

It blocks out the lights as its mass of fur and claws dives above my head.

The juar clears the wooden stakes and flies into the caretaker. The beast knocks the him over, clawing at openings in the man's armor. Biting at his face, trying to get through. The caretaker fights back, wrestling to throw the juar off, but the beast is too big, too agile, too angry.

You can either watch the man get eaten, or you can run, Kaishi. You know which one I'd choose.

Ignos makes a good point. I clamber over the barrier, unmolested since crowd is too distracted to notice me, and finally get a look at Viera's arena. The Lunare is sporting some deep scratches. Bleeding, but she's still standing. Her juar isn't even watching Viera anymore, but is staring, open-mouthed, at the caretaker's scuffle.

The crowd, meanwhile, begins to back away. Realizing, maybe, the juar may win the fight and come for them next. Some flat out run; dashing from the courtyard into the city streets. Some call for guards.

With a growl, the second juar follows its rope and joins its brother. Its teeth and claws sink into the caretaker's leather, tearing it to pieces.

"Come on, priestess," Viera shouts as she climbs over the barrier towards me. "I say we leave before anyone knows we're still alive."

The courtyard breaks into full pandemonium. Guards, holding weighted nets, run by us towards the juars. Care-takers of other pits join them. The rest of the crowd alter-nates between fleeing and calling for new bets, now that the stakes have changed. I'm splattered with someone's drink as I push through the Charre, and I see more fun than fear in these faces.

From one show to the next.

So when Viera's hand pulls me through the last of the mess, I'm relieved. We're out of the courtyard and back into the dark streets. At the first deserted alley, though, Viera stumbles aside. She leans against a house wall, away from the bustle. Torchlight sneaks in from the street, but most of what I see is shadow. Shapes in the stone reveal, upon a closer look, tracings of Charre animal gods.

"You need something for those wounds," I say, looking at Viera's body. Several deep cuts on her chest and arms bleed freely; long gashes with white puckering at the edges.

"Thanks for letting me know," Viera replies, but her voice is taut. "You don't happen to know where a doctor is in this city? Anyone that won't turn me in on sight?"

I shake my head. "I don't have any friends here. These are not my people."

Viera sinks against the wall until she's sitting in the dirt. "Isn't that just fantastic? Your people. I thought the whole point of you coming was to make these your people?"

"I'm supposed to tell them about Ignos," I say. "Then, if they believe what I say, they might help me."

"Any chance that belief is coming soon, and with medicine?"

What would Jakkan say if I went back to the temple with Viera?

What would the high priest do?

Viera groans. Jerks my thoughts back to her. Someone who protected me. Helped me.

I can't leave her here to die.

"Come on. I don't know a doctor, but I do know someone who may help." I offer my hand, and this time it's me lifting Viera to her feet.

I sling her arm over my shoulders. Together, we walk through the streets. Curious glances from the few Charre running the around this late, the imperious stares from guards on their way to the Pits. Most don't bother with a second look, and those that do see my medallion and quickly turn the other way. For once, I like being the outcast.

Unwanted and dangerous.

. . .

The Vaos towers above the surrounding houses and blazes with torches set on every step. A shimmering, fiery pathway to the home of the Charre's chief priest. An appropriate image, I suppose, for Jakkan.

Both of us climb, slowly, towards Jakkan's chambers. I don't know what I expect, but seeing Jakkan standing with a pair of other men wearing priestly ropes doesn't surprise me. The small boy in the middle of the room does.

Jakkan recites some sort of chant while the other two priests, using colored paste, paint the child in intricate designs. When we, with Viera leaving a bloody trail, walk into the room, all of them look at us, but none of them stop.

Jakkan, without breaking his recitation, catches my eyes and nods towards his water basin. There's a cloth there. I lead Viera around the ceremony, keeping as quiet as I can, and begin to wash the Lunare. Viera, for her part, sits on the floor and closes her eyes. Her breath rasps in and out. With torches flickering and a solemn prayer droning in the background, I focus on wiping the cloth back and forth, gently cleaning away the blood from her wounds, washing out the dirt and grime.

These are vicious cuts. If we were back among my friends, they could be healed in moments. As it is, you'll need to resort to stitching. Or cruder methods.

I look around, but there doesn't appear to be any needle and thread. No way to perform the stitching. Viera's cuts continue to bleed. If there's no way to stitch, to close the wounds, then what?

Fire, Kaishi. She'll hurt, but she'll live. At least for now.

There are plenty of metal instruments in the room. Ceremonial brands, irons. I take one, lift it softly as the priests continue coating the boy in swirling art. Patterns I recognize as the Charre Emperor's sigil. A helmet and a rolled scroll combining with the glowing orb of Ignos. The crest of the Emperor.

Who is this child? What is his purpose?

I'll ask those questions later.

I hold the brand in the torch flame, keep it there till the metal begins to glow a warm orange. Then, lifting it out carefully, I angle it towards Viera.

"I'm sorry. This will hurt." I whisper the words, though Viera looks like she's unconscious.

I press the brand close. Nearly brushing the angry red wound.

A light touch. Brief and then on to the next spot. We're trying to seal the blood, not cook her.

I go to work. Press the brand to the open flesh. It sizzles, smokes, burns and turns white-pink in front of me. Scarring and sealing. Viera's eyes shoot open, and she might have screamed except I shove the balled up, bloody cloth between Viera's teeth. Keep it there as I guide the brand along Viera's gashes. Scar them white. Stop the bleeding.

Keep the Lunare alive.

Without saying so, the four of them separate into their pairs. Gar and Lan leave first, angling to the left. Bas and Sax will go right, and then both sets will turn towards the gateway, approaching it from opposite angles. The unspoken side of this is that whichever pair draws the Sevora will sacrifice themselves, leaving the remaining two to complete the mission.

It is grim. It is required.

Sax feels no sadness as they leave the building, only urgency. Determination. A desire to find Avan and destroy the taken Oratus.

Sax holds on to Bas's tail with his foreclaws, though she provides him with a Flaum miner. Their own weapons are missing—taken after their capture and not present at the birthing pool. Flaum miners are too small for Oratus claws, so Sax holds it with both foreclaws. Awkwardly.

Back outside the building, the groans of the wounded have stopped. It's quiet, except for the clatter of Oratus claws on the surface. The sheer silence unnerves Sax. It's not in an Oratus to be quiet. They are destructive, not made for stealth.

"Do you remember our Enlightenment?" Sax whispers to Bas, a noise that sounds the same as air leaking from a pressure pipe—high pitched and static-y.

"How could I forget a dying star?"

The flares had been beautiful, a gift after the trials of their pairing. The two of them had watched from the radiation-shielded deck of the station called Nova, designed and used exclusively for viewing interstellar phenomena. The Nova would stay at this particular star until a solar storm destroyed it. Then a new Nova would be built wherever was deemed most beautiful.

Wherever would convince new Oratus that the galaxy was a place worth saving.

Oratus had three moments in their lives when frivolous things were permitted: the death of a pair, the Enlightenment, and Restoration—if an Oratus reached an age or suffered an injury that required severe medical attention. Sax has experienced only one of these, and the short time with Bas and an exploding star dominates his memories when he isn't fighting for his life.

Sax is fine with that, though. He doesn't want his senses to dull. His claws to lose their sharpness or his teeth to forget their taste for the flesh of his enemies.

But what brings him back to the Enlightenment now is the darkness. "Do you remember," Sax says. "How they closed the shield for a minute? How the whole room went dark and the only thing you could hear was your own breathing?"

"Your vents the loudest of all."

"I was excited." Sax grips tighter as Bas lurches up and over another fence.

"I felt it. You. Your heartbeats through your claws. It was the first time I understood what it meant to be a pair."

"A feeling that has never left me." Sax would say more, except in front of them, up steps that Sax can't see, an arch of green lights springs to life. The gateway. And, haloed in front of it, Avan.

By the time I'm done burning Viera's wounds, the ceremony behind me is over. Jakkan falls silent, and the two priests escort the painted boy from the chamber. Viera, after gnawing through most of the cloth in her mouth, simply passes out and lets me finish the cauterizing.

When I lift the brand away from the last cut, from the gray puckering flesh that, at least, no longer seeps blood onto the floor, I too feel like collapsing.

Nicely done. I'd even let you cauterize me. If I had a body.

Using fire to heal. I've seen it done before, though I'd never been a part of it myself. A desperate measure for only the most serious wounds. If there had been a poultice. If there had been needles, then perhaps I could have stitched her up. Bandaged the wounds and left Viera without that burn. But I don't know this city, and Jakkan offered no assistance.

"I see you have failed," Jakkan says when I set the brand

down. "I see you return to me with the same medallion you wore when you left."

"I did not fail," I reply, not taking my eyes away from Viera. "I survived the Pits. As you asked."

"I did not ask you to survive. I asked you to return with a different medallion. You have not done so, and therefore you have failed."

Jakkan's words are too much. After surviving the juar. After dragging Viera bleeding through the streets of a city I do not know, where people stare at me as if I am the enemy. As if I am not to be touched. Being told I had failed falls on me like a searing weight, and I push back.

I grab the brand with my right hand and whirl towards Jakkan, stabbing it towards his face.

"You can say what you like. I lived. I survived your trap." I take a step forward, and Jakkan stays where he is. The brand comes close to the priest's face, but he does not waver.

"Tell me," Jakkan says. "Did you accomplish what I asked?"

The brand feels good in my hand. Strong. Heat still radiating from the front of it. With a short jab, I could shove it right into Jakkan's eye. Or perhaps swing it at his neck. The priest looks unarmed. Vulnerable.

What then?

Ignos unleashes a cascade of thoughts: What would come after such a strike? The people of the city would not love me for killing the high priest. How could I say Ignos wants this to happen? Wants the Jakkan murdered in his own sacred temple?

"No, I did not," I say the words, but keep the brand up. My eyes strong. Not my fault I failed an impossible task.

"Then you learned something. Do not let your

emotions, do not let the moment carry you away from the facts at hand. A priestess must always, if she is to lead the people, be able to know what is right, no matter her surroundings." Jakkan looks past me to Viera on the ground. "Who is this woman?"

"She fought in the Pits with me. We survived," I launch into a quick version of the story that Jakkan hears without emotion.

Without reaction.

"You have led her here. Dripped her blood on my floor. Burned her wounds with a sacred instrument," Jakkan grasps the brand I hold, his hand touching mine on the cool end of the metal. "Do you understand the sacrilege that you have committed? To save a nonbeliever?"

"I made a vow to protect her, and she did the same for me," I say. "Ignos would understand."

Jakkan rips the brand out of my hand. Tosses it across the room, where it hits off of the wall to the ground. Gives Viera a dismissive look. "She will be fine for now. Come with me."

We sweep out of the chambers, towards the steps. I spare one last glance at Viera, who's still unconscious. Then I follow Jakkan all the way up to the top of the Vaos. He stops and rests one hand on the East altar. Waits for me to take everything in.

The view is incredible. Unlike anything I've ever seen before. The blazing of a hundred thousand torches lights up the streets like a glittering ocean in the dark. Above me, the stars fade against the orange firelight, as if Damantum exists in a world of its own, banishing the outside with the glow of its people.

"I always find Damantum more beautiful at night," Jakkan says. "When you have proof of all the life that is here. A Charre lit each of these fires. A Charre interested in preserving our city. Our livelihood, our civilization. So long as these torches are lit, Damantum will continue. Ignos will be worshipped."

"Why did you bring me here?" I say.

"I've inquired about you," Jakkan replies. "From Malo, from the warriors that journeyed with you. They all believe what you claim. To a man. They say you hear from Ignos himself. They say that you will take my place."

At this last, Jakkan looks straight at me. I expect an accusation, hatred or jealousy to show. Jakkan, however, keeps the same blank slate. He gives no hints to me as to what he wants, as to what he needs me to say.

All of my life, I'd been given little hope of power. Little chance of position. My destiny had been chosen by my sex. Standing on top of the Vaos, for once, I cannot tell where my own future lies. Options abound. So many paths to follow. And all of them could be swept away if Jakkan chooses to cast me down.

"I don't want your place," I say. "Ignos chose to bring me here. I'm only following his will."

"And his will must be respected." Jakkan nods at the medallion around my neck. "This first task proves that Malo was right. Ignos favors you. How many escape the Pits when faced with the juar?"

I don't know. Jakkan doesn't wait for me to answer.

"None," Jakkan says. "None."

"They said the one who lives longer gets to leave?"

"A ploy to get some fight from you," Jakkan almost looks sad, but then his face slides into the straight mask. "Should your friend have fallen, the crowd would have cheered your own death moments later."

"How was I supposed to survive, then?"

"You found a way." Jakkan says, as if that answers the question, then waves away my open mouth. "You understand my responsibility. The Emperor looks to me for Ignos' guidance. Therefore I must be sure that any who claims to speak for him truly hears his words."

"I escaped the Pits, as you said. Isn't that enough?"

"You may have his luck, but are you truly his vessel?" Jakkan says. "Tomorrow there will be a sacrifice. For the boy that you saw, in honor of his approaching manhood. In honor of his parent's life. You will perform it. You will conduct the ritual, and you will give us a message from Ignos. Do it well, and I will grant you your audience with the Emperor. More so, I will grant you a chance to join me. To lead the city into the light it deserves."

When the two of us descend, some hours later, after conversations of home and life in the city, Jakkan goes first. I follow, almost bumping into the high priest when he stops at the entrance to the chambers. Jakkan turns to me, a small smile on his face. "It seems the one you rescued has no wish to thank you."

I look around Jakkan and see only dried blood stains on the temple floor. Viera is gone.

Sax only has a moment to think before the gateway opens. In that moment, hope and hunger mix with the sudden light to push him forward. He bounds past Bas, clenches his legs, and leaps towards Avan's shadow.

The low gravity gives Sax plenty of lift, and he drops the miner as he glides through the air. He has no chance of hitting anything with it anyway, and the satisfaction of a laser is nothing compared to the visceral cutting of his claws.

The gateway doesn't wait for Sax. It shunts open, sliding up into the wall of the seed ship, and reveals a waiting Sevora force. More Flaum, because the standard-issue troops are always there, but what catches Sax's attention as he flies are the Slivers; worm-like things with gossamer wings that glow violet as they fly over Avan's head.

Each of the four Slivers has, grafted onto their many legs, heat stingers: small lasers that, individually, are nothing more than annoying. Together, the simultaneous blasts can overwhelm a target's nervous system. Send them twitching to the floor. Means the Sevora aren't giving up on capturing the Oratus after all.

The Slivers, though, didn't expect to see Sax flying through the air towards them, claws extended and ready to rend. He hits a Sliver before it has a chance to move, and Sax doesn't even have to bite—his weight alone crumples the fragile creature and they both plummet towards the gateway floor.

Avan, and his new Flaum friends, notice. And, as Sax crashes down into their mix, they scatter. Sax doesn't even get a swipe in at Avan before the captive Oratus is gone. Pressing through the Flaum and through the gateway.

Coward.

Sax would follow, but he's otherwise occupied. The Flaum are overcoming their own surprise, turning their miners on Sax. Sitting still means a quick roasting at the hands of their lasers, so Sax moves.

Surrounding an Oratus at close range is like being in a razor blade tornado: Sax darts at a Flaum near the gateway, while his tail whips towards the Flaum left of that one. He digs his claws into fur, then leaps off to another one. Red bolts flash where he was, coupling with the green light of the gate and the filtering blue aura of the new section beyond to create a washed out strobe effect.

Sax barely registers the faces. The targets. Without the Stim, he can't keep up with his own instinct, and simply responds to touch. To the tear of claw through cloth. To the thwack of his tail swatting another Flaum to the ground. It's a massacre, a chaotic frenzy.

Until sudden burning drives Sax down.

Dust motes dance in the light of dawn as I open my eyes and look out through the open archway from my room. One of four leading off of Jakkan's main chamber in the Vaos, the high priest had let me settle into the spare space. The mat on the stone floor suffices, though I prefer soft jungle ground where I don't wake with aches in my back.

Not that it had been a restful night anyway: Jakkan didn't spend any time worrying about Viera, but instead showed me the scrolls with depictions of Charre rites, told me to read, and then vanished into his own chambers.

I'd taken the scrolls and sat next to the fire. Read one after another. Familiarized myself with tales and odes, songs and prayers, some of which were known to me and others far different. The Charre rites are like relatives—their shapes and duties recognizable, their names changed. So similar that I started putting in Solare words where they didn't belong. Found myself sinking into the stories told around my village's campfires instead of the ritual tales in front of me.

I suggest you find a way to your bed, Kaishi. You're turning the scroll awfully slow, and as much as I like rereading the same words endlessly, it's become a bit boring.

But I had to learn. I shook my head. Tried to open my eyes all the way.

Not all of it, and not right now. I've read everything you have, and I'll feed it to you during the ceremony. However, I can't lift your arms. Can't speak from your mouth. So if you don't have the energy to manage that, then we're both going out the grisly way.

I supposed that if I was going to trust anyone to get a ceremony right, it would be a god. So I accepted Ignos' offer and stumbled to my chamber, collapsed on the mat and sank into a too-short slumber till, what seemed like moments later, Jakkan woke me with the breaking of dawn.

The high priest holds a new, beautiful cape for me. Weavers have speckled the cloth in oranges and blues. Expensive dyes. Colors only worn by those of noble rank, or that had given their lives to Ignos.

Jakkan himself says so, and he wears similar finery. Gold hoops hang from his ears and another ring from his nose. His hair is tied in a knot on top of his head with silver bands. His hands hold still more jewelry, which he hands out to me.

"Today these are yours," Jakkan says. "If this goes as you wish it, then tomorrow you shall have your own."

The earrings, speckled with rubies and sapphires, appear to be small depictions of Ignos. I slip them on, then comes the piece for my nose. A swooping golden band made to look like waves of light in early morning. Thus adorned, I wait for Jakkan, who had retreated to his chambers. This time he emerges with a couple of pots. Each one filled with dye. He sets them down in the middle of the room and then, nodding to me, goes to the far window.

This side of the Vaos looks out to the West, opposite where Ignos rises. On the mountains overlooking the city, I can see Ignos' dawn display: purple, brown, orange and yellow as the light glances off the peaks and the slopes below to paint the fields in Ignos' colors.

"It is the most divine part of the day," Jakkan says. "Evidence that the Ignos' will is truly beautiful. We must remind the people of that. Today you have a chance to do so. I will be there, yet you alone will speak the prayers. I trust you have learned what you wish to say?"

I nod, though in truth, I only have glimmers. Before, at the crashed ship and at my village, I had spoken from my heart. From Ignos' instruction. I've never performed a formal rite, much less a sacrifice.

A show, and little more. I'll send you the right words, and so long as you put enough spark into the right actions, they'll love you for it.

"You have performed a ceremony before?" Jakkan asks.

"No. I left my village before Ignos gave me the chance."

Jakkan actually looks pleased at this. "The first time you hold the knife is a moment you will remember forever. You become one with the teachings. You will feel the power of Ignos as you give the greatest honor to your sacrifice. Though I must warn you: do not let the blade fall from your hands, no matter how heavy it feels. Strike with strength and make a clean cut. Ignos will be watching."

A pair of other priests enter the temple, and I stand still as they apply dyes to my face. To my shoulders and the rest of my body. Coloring me like the blue and purple cliffs. Making me the very image of dawn.

. . .

By the time they finish, Ignos is high and already a crowd gathers outside. Their murmurs and cries of deals offered and taken buzz in through the front of the Vaos. I'm not sure what to do next, so I wait for Jakkan, who, eyes closed, appears to be muttering prayers to himself.

When his lips fall still, he nods for a second, then asks me; "You are ready?"

There is only one answer to that question. "I am."

The high priest leads me from the temple, out onto the landing where the crowd, so many thousands, begins to cheer. Jakkan holds his arms high and wide, as if embracing the chants. I follow his lead, holding my arms out and soaking in the stares. The strange looks. The mild hush that comes over the hustle and bustle as the people notice their high priest stands with another.

A woman shares his place. One, by look, not of their city or their people.

"Yes," Jakkan announces. "You have noticed that I do not take this stage alone. Beside me is a priestess. A voice of Ignos. She comes from far away, and Ignos has seen fit to pass his wisdom through her to us. Today, she will lead the sacrifice in his honor. Today we welcome this new priestess into our city. We welcome her wisdom, as it comes from Ignos himself."

The crowd stays silent for a moment. Evaluating Jakkan's words. Seeing through them, looking for the joke. Looking for a reason to disbelieve.

Now is the first chance. Tell them who you are. Strike the spark that will become the fire of their belief.

"My name is Kaishi, and I bring the heart of the jungle to this holy city. The gods have bade me bring their message to you. Ignos moves my lips and it is his words that pass from me to you. They are the words of our hope and salvation. They are the words that will bring Damantum to a new and brighter age."

Still the crowd looks wary, muttering to themselves. Until Jakkan, taking my hand in his and holding it high announces, "We honor Ignos, together."

That, at last, breaks the hold on the crowd. They cheer. Loud enough to rock the temple's foundations, or so it seems. My nerves go numb, my legs grow tight. My heart beats so fast I'm afraid it's going to burst. This, this is what my father must have felt every ceremony. This is what he had been talking about when he referred to the pulse of Ignos. His energy flowing through Father. Now, it flows through me.

Jakkan wastes no time and leads me up the steps to the very top of the Vaos. There are the twin altars, gleaming and wet from a washing earlier that morning. A pair of guards, wearing bear skins and holding their spears in one hand, stand ready. Another priest, with robes not quite as fancy as theirs, holds, on red cloth, a black-glass blade. Half as long as my arm, the mottled and jagged knife is like a shadow. Heavy, sharp. It will cut through bone as easy as through melon.

A different roar comes from below. The sacrifice has appeared, with an escort. Malo leads five guards, him wearing his lion skin. They lead their prisoner up the steps, and by the time he reaches the first landing, I recognize who it is. One of the Solare tribesmen, one of my own people that had been captured from the battle on the way here.

You can mourn him later. Do not let his sacrifice be a waste.

Now, at the foot of the Vaos, appears the boy. A man and woman, who must be his parents, form his escort. The trio marches up the steps, trailing the bowed head of the Solare prisoner. I watch, because what else can I do?

When Malo reaches me, he steps to my side and leans in close, "This is your ceremony, Kaishi. Take the honor Ignos has given you, and show it to them. We all believe. We all believe in you."

The two bear guards take the prisoner from his escort and press his back to the altar so that his head hangs off the edge. The son and his parents halt at the first landing. Beneath the part in the middle where the door to the inner chambers opens. I'm not sure why, until I notice a groove running down the center of the steps.

A funnel for the blood that leads directly to the lip of the doorway.

The blood from the prisoner will run down the stair, over the edge of the door, and onto the son. A blessing.

Do it. Claim what's rightfully ours, Kaishi.

Then Ignos speaks to me; a ritual prayer before the cutting. At first my words come quietly, but then my voice finds its stride as I recite the rite. Ignos feeds me lines, and I let them tumble from my lips. I call for honor, for blessing, for enlightenment. The greatness of the city and its people and the Emperor. At the end of it, I take the knife offered by the priest and hold it high so that Ignos catches its black-glass blade.

Then I look at the altar, at the man pressed against it. Malo, now, keeps a hand at the top of the prisoner's chest. The sacrifice's heart clear and ready. Someone has dabbed a line of red paint on the precise spot. The prisoner does not struggle. He knows, as do I and everyone else in that court-yard and on that temple, that in a moment the prisoner will come face-to-face with his god. Dying by sacrifice buys him honor, buys him a chance at a better life beyond this one.

The blade itself is heavy in my right hand. When I start to move my left hand over, so I can grip the knife with both, I see Jakkan shake his head. A priest or priestess cannot use two hands. Only one, and only precise cuts.

I place the blade against the prisoner's skin. My mouth says the words without my mind following. A last pledge to Ignos. A final call for his blessing.

I begin.

It's not the heat, or the pain that stops Sax, but rather when his foreclaws stop responding. When his legs go numb. Sax manages to look up and sees the other three Slivers have swung around. They're zeroing in on him, and the Flaum take advantage.

Their Sevora-taken minds orient the miners at Sax. Claws press in the triggers.

In their triumph, the Sevora forget to count. They don't look into the dark beyond the gateway. They don't see what's rushing towards them, mouths open and teeth glittering.

Bas gets there first. Sax sees her simply burst through a Flaum, her left and right sets of claws grabbing two more and bashing them together in front of her. The piercing fire in Sax's nerves begins to ebb, and he notices Lan, holding a pair of Flaum miners, taking easy shots at the Slivers, who have sacrificed their own dexterity to hover over Sax.

Gar, meanwhile, telegraphs his actions by way of scattered limbs and screeches. The Oratus prefers using his mouth to his tail, and any Flaum that can't run finds itself food. It's over in seconds, though Sax takes his time hauling up to his feet. His muscles spasm, and it's difficult to walk. Still, he's alive. Went right into a fight without a mask and came out the other side.

"How did it feel?" Gar asks, his face coated with evidence of terrible deeds.

"Dangerous," Sax says.

He could say more. He could talk about the thrill of knowing he was one well-placed shot away from oblivion. He could mention the blossom of fear—something he hasn't felt in a long time—when the Slivers shot him down, but the center of an enemy's ship is no place to share feelings. Gar sees he's not getting more and accepts it with a nod.

"Stupid, more like." Bas steps over the bodies to join them. "Next time, let the ones with masks take the lead."

"Odds would put our survival substantially higher than your own," Lan provides, with bits of Sliver wing hanging from her teeth. "Yet our own odds are significantly reduced should we lose you."

"I see your points." Sax gives them that, though he has no intention of waiting in the back during the next fight. No fun in it.

Together they turn towards the gateway and what lies beyond.

Much as Sax would like to take weapons, or bites, from the fight's left-overs, there's no time. If the Sevora decide to shut the door, they'll be sealed in here. So they lope to the other side.

The center ring of the seed ship is tall and thinner than the sections. It's also empty. A long wrap-around metal floor hugs the outside wall, providing a platform, one that is empty, much to Sax's disappointment. What's more interesting, though, is the gap between the platform and the ship's core.

It's open. A chasm that, when the four of them move forward to look, appears to vent directly into open space. The reason isn't hard to deduce: hanging above, suspended from a series of what seem to be large pipes, are ships. Small ovals, only a few times Sax's own height. They're hanging in rows of three, like teeth, with their points aiming straight down through the opening.

It's a seed ship, and they've found the seeds.

The hot soup sluices down my throat, thick and orange from the sweet potato. Across from me, Jakkan tilts his own bowl to his lips. Malo watches, sitting next to me. No bowl of his own. When I look at Malo's empty hands, Jakkan says, "This soup is for the priests. He will have his own soon enough."

"Don't worry, Kaishi." Malo throws me a smile. "It is my honor to watch over you."

It hasn't been long between the cutting of the knife and the pouring of the soup. Without looking at the sacrifice, I had spoken a final prayer and the crowd had dispersed. Returned to the ways of the day. Jakkan had then led me back into the temple, while the guards removed the body. At the base of the Vaos, the parents and their friends had celebrated the boy's ascension.

"You did well," Jakkan says, wiping away a stray trail of soup from his chin. "Your words were strong. Your grasp of the fundamentals appropriate. The flourish with the knife, they appreciated that. I do not think we should waste anymore time."

"Waste time?"

"Word came this morning," Malo says. "I've already spoken with Jakkan. It seems the Lunare are moving. Towards your jungle, and eventually us. Only they are doing something different this time; rather than killing the tribes they come across, the Lunare are pressing them into service, convincing them that the Lunare have the divine right to rule our world."

"How can they say that?" I ask.

"It doesn't matter. What it means is that we no longer have time for the voice of Ignos to perfect her training." Jakkan's sighing as he says this. "It means I don't have time to find out whether you are really telling the truth. You must prove yourself in front of the Emperor, and then in front of all our people."

"Prove what? That Ignos speaks to me? That he will tell us how to stop the Lunare?"

"We are creatures of Ignos. I said as much last night, and you saw as much today. Yet these Lunare wield magic that we have not seen. Strange devices. How do they have such things while we do not, if we are the chosen people? Our populace, even the Emperor, have begun to wonder if the Lunare are divine. If they are, in fact, what *you* claim to be."

"Jakkan knows Ignos' blessing. He can speak of his wishes. But words are as water against the hard stone of sight. See a man attacked by Viera's weapon, and your faith in Ignos' protection will be shaken," Malo says. "For those outside these city walls, especially, our hold grows tenuous."

They want you to be their tool. Take advantage of it, and when the time comes, we'll twist things around so that we're the masters.

"You want me to convince them." I follow Ignos' logic.

"You want me to speak to your people and tell them what? That the Lunare are not who they say they are?"

"Declare them abominations. Affronts to Ignos. Or they will be the end of us," Jakkan says. "Do not think we are playing games here, Kaishi. Do not think that I am doing this because I want to. You must convince the Emperor, convince the people that the Lunare are nothing more than miserable things to be swept away."

"How will my words prove more effective than yours?"

"Ask," Jakkan replies. "Ask Ignos for help. Ask for his aid. If you are lying, then he will not help you and your persuasion will fail. If you are successful, however, and Ignos' gifts convince the tribes to follow the Emperor, to rise up against the enemy, then you will have saved both our people and your own."

The bracelet feels cool and heavy on my wrist. Ignos has suggested miracles lay within it. Treasures that could bring salvation to the Charre. Maybe, to my people too.

"I'll do it." There's a refreshing finality as I say this, as I choose a path to walk. "Take me to him, and I'll do everything I can to convince the Emperor. If he'll even listen to a woman like me."

"He won't listen to you, but he will listen to Ignos." Jakkan finishes his soup and sets it aside. "Now. We will take you."

I drain my bowl as Jakkan and Malo stand up. Follow them outside the Vaos, down those golden steps still wet with the remnants of the sacrifice. Walk with them to the busy streets with their hardpacked dirt, under shining afternoon light.

We head towards the Emperor's palace. I can see it, north of the Vaos and at the end of the main road. While the temple is at the center of the city, the Emperor's seat borders a lake on the north end, both a position of honor and subservience to Damantum's god.

Malo takes up a position on my left while Jakkan moves to my right. The crowds make way for us. A lion warrior, high priest and, I hear the whispers, one whom Ignos himself speaks through. Nobody troubles us. Nobody keeps their eyes on me for more than seconds. If this is celebrity, I don't mind. It feels good to be desired. To be followed.

Father had always claimed such attention required respect, that one had to earn their presence in front of the crowd.

With the sacrifice, you did so.

I keep my head high, back straight, eyes forward. Ignos' approval warms my mind.

You're becoming what you need to be. We're seeing the Emperor, and soon you'll be by his side. Eventually, you will take his place.

Take his place? Even though I, being a Solare, don't quite hold the Emperor in the same reverence as the Charre, there are stations in life. The Emperor, according to Jakkan, is chosen by divine marking, by Ignos himself. Wouldn't taking, even desiring, the Emperor's place be a direct insult to the god?

Even gods make mistakes, Kaishi. Sometimes we have to correct them.

"You must never call the Emperor by his name," Jakkan says as we walk. "You must never touch him. Not unless he commands you do so. I would advise against looking in his eyes. Or even disagreeing with him, at least directly. Rather, frame your words with respect. Understand that he is chosen not only by Ignos, but also by

Damantum's people. He carries that weight in all that he does."

"Yet do not be afraid," Malo counters. "The Emperor is reasonable. He will listen to what Ignos' voice has to say."

"Malo." I suddenly want to talk of something else, keep my mind off the fact that, very soon, I would be in a room with the holiest person in the entire Charre empire. "Last night, I went to the Pits. Viera was there."

"I'm not surprised. I sold her off as soon as I left you. She's a fighter. I'm sure she did well."

"We escaped."

At Malo's look, I tell the story, and Jakkan interrupts every so often to illustrate why I had gone to the Pits in the first place. When I get to Viera's disappearance, Malo frowns.

"I take your expression to mean you don't know where he is?" I ask.

"A woman of her look will not go unnoticed in the city for long," Malo answers. "Especially one with those wounds. Wherever she is hiding, she will need food and water eventually. Then we will give Viera her reward." Malo's hand drifts to kukri hanging from his waist.

The clearing where the Emperor's palace sits is larger than the whole of my village. The palace itself could have contained our Tier inside of it. Sheer sides bleeding into a domed roof painted over with vibrant reds and yellows— core colors for Ignos. Charre prayers are carved into the walls, and many people passing by press their hands against them, muttering the same words to themselves.

A central arch leads into the palace, and two warriors, sporting lion skins like Malo's, stand guard with spears in front. The arch itself is unvarnished, beige stone without designs.

"To remind you, and all of us, of our own humility as we pass through." Jakkan answers my question. "Before we go before the Emperor, we must place ourselves beneath him, beneath Ignos."

"Incredible, isn't it?" Malo sounds swept away. "If Ignos does not love us, he would not permit this to exist."

At the entrance to the arch, after a brief inspection from the guards in which they make sure neither Jakkan nor I carry weapons, Malo puts a hand on my shoulder.

"I cannot follow you any longer. I'm not permitted inside."

"I'm going in alone?"

"Jakkan will be there."

"He's not a friend," I reply. "You are."

"Then know I will be with you in spirit." Malo laughs. "Besides, you are the messenger of Ignos, are you not? He speaks through you. With that, you are never truly alone."

How can they destroy all of the seeds? Sax is stuck on this for a minute until Bas, going past him down the metal platform, slaps her tail against the floor.

"They're not the objective," Bas says when Sax and the other two look at her. "We take the ship, they'll burn with it."

She's right, as usual, but Sax plays with his idea anyway. Bash the ships against each other and they might fall off those hooks. The gravity here is low enough that jumping up to them wouldn't be a challenge. Then they could run along the lines, torching one after the next.

It would be so much fun.

But Bas is right, so Sax follows her around the ring, looking for some path into the seed ship's core. The four of them break into a run when nothing quickly appears, because every second they spend here gives the Sevora time to regroup. Gives Avan time to figure out the mask.

They see three other gateways as they go around, all of them red-lit and locked. No paths to the central core, though. Seeds go the whole way around, minus some scattered gaps. It's hard to tell how many this one's launched, but Sax knows they'll have to hunt each of them down.

Every Sevora seed launches with a Cache, and every Cache has the specific steps to follow to bring the next wave of Sevora to power. Partly how they took over so much of the galaxy so fast—one seed ship seven cycles ago scattered Sevora around, and over time the planets they found became infested. Launched their own seed ships before anyone knew what was going on.

Now the Oratus and the rest of the free galaxy are so close. Take care of this ship, track its launches, and the Sevora would be done.

A galactic stain wiped clean.

"So what's the plan?" Lan asks when they find themselves back at their first gate.

It's easy to tell this one is where they came in, despite all four gateways being identical; the fight left plenty of splatter, and nobody has tried to clean it up.

"We have to get to the core," Sax says, though he knows this is obvious. "They must have ways of getting air and supplies to it, even if there's not a larger pathway."

"If you expect me to squeeze into one of those tubes..." Gar starts.

"We'll never fit," Bas says. "How about a different way? Punch in?"

"We don't have cutters with energy left," Lan reminds her, but Bas points up, towards the seeds.

"Use those," Bas says. "Take one, turn it and punch through the hull."

Sax likes the idea, but he doesn't know how to fly a seed, if they're even meant to be flown. Current thinking has the

Sevora identifying possible planets and shooting the seeds out straight to their targets on autopilot.

Sax has seen cracked seeds before, and knows that there's enough nutrients packed in there that, when frozen by the sheer cold of space, a Sevora could travel as long as it needed to.

The seeds, though, aren't the only ships on this giant craft. They didn't land in the docking bay, but crashed through the lab section. Which means the Sevora must have ships elsewhere—shuttles to move their forces around, fighters to defend the seed ship. Any of those might work, any of those could crash a hole in the core.

It's a desperate move, for desperate times.

The headaddress, ranging from teal to deep blue like the shallows leading out to the ocean, catches my eyes first when I enter the chamber. It sits on a cloth held by a servant; A thin man wearing only a simple cotton cape whose eyes track the floor as if it holds secrets.

Several others stand along with the man towards the back of the chamber, each one holding another treasure. Whereas the Vaos faces East and West, the palace angles north and south, so that light appears to climb in from the sides. This gives the Emperor, standing in the middle of the room, a haloed look. As though the glimmer comes from him.

Jakkan goes to the Emperor, shares a word too quiet for me to catch. The Charre's most holy person seems, to me, to be nothing more than normal. Unadorned, except for a beautiful feathered cape laced with gold, the Emperor looks no taller than my own father. His arms are thin, his face round. I see wrinkles clouding his cheeks, and his tight eyes glare at me, perhaps feeling my judgment.

"So this is the one I am supposed to respect," the

Emperor announces. "The one who says she can hear from Ignos himself. Who will tell me I am wrong to think of these Lunare as gods in their own right."

Before I can reply, the Emperor strides away from Jakkan, right up to me, and his hand darts out quick and catches my chin. With one eye narrowing, the Emperor sweeps his gaze over my face, his lips twisting into a sneer, "Jakkan, I believe you've brought me the wrong one. This girl is nothing more than a scared little Solare. Out of her depth. Send her back."

Stay firm. Courage, Kaishi.

"I'm not scared," I say to the Emperor's face, and I ignore Jakkan's sudden lurch. If the high priest wants to protect me, he's too late. "I'm not out of my depth, your holiness, but exactly where I am supposed to be."

"And where is that?" the Emperor says.

"Wherever you are. So that I can relay Ignos' words directly to your ears."

"I am the holy Emperor. You presume that you need to relay Ignos' will to me?"

Brief smiles cross the lips of the servants. I notice and doubt plays its part, twinging my nerves. I'm young. Not even a Charre. What right do I have to be here, addressing the Emperor?

You have me, remember? Now tell that gilded fool that you will help him repel the Lunare.

"I cannot make you believe me," I speak slowly, measuring the words. "But I can give you secrets. Gifts from Ignos that will let us turn back the Lunare. That will give you the chance to bring the Charre to a new era of glory. All in your name."

The Emperor's face shifts into a calculating stare and I know I've found the man's weakness. He scratches at his chin for a moment, "Give me an example. Some proof of what you say."

I will tell you how Viera's weapon works, and you will tell him. Repeat my words.

"You have seen the weapons they carry? The ones that spit fire?" I ask.

I remember too—the metal and wood magic, the cracking in the valley and the Solare dropping down, dead, into the dirt.

"I have held it," the Emperor replies. "My best engineers are working even now to unveil its secrets. Though I hear the Lunare have many more, and stronger, marvels for us."

"They have the same principle. A powder that, when lit, produces an explosion that propels a rock towards its target." I'm repeating Ignos' words as they come into my head, and yet, as I say them, I understand their meaning. How Viera's weapon works unfolds itself in my mind as I narrate its function. "Your alchemists could make this powder themselves, if they so wished, and many more things besides. While outfitting an army to equal the Lunare will take time, Ignos can give you enough to scare them. To break their claim of godhood."

"Did you hear her, Jakkan?" the Emperor asks the high priest.

"I heard her well, my Emperor. I think her council wise."

"Do you? I found it strange and desperate. A girl making things up to keep herself from the altar." The Emperor raises his hand, and, as one, the servants snap to attention. "I have not grown this empire by listening to the fanciful words of jungle dwellers. Of lesser tribes. You talk of miracles, but an Emperor must deal in realities. I—"

"Please, holiness," Jakkan says to the Emperor's back. "What cause have we to ignore Kaishi's advice? The people have heard her message and approve of it. If she is correct, and Ignos really can help us through her, then what have we to lose?"

The Emperor considers me, and I can see a twisting anger there, mingling with the slightest hint of fear. The Emperor, holiest of holies, believes me a threat. The realization travels up and down my soul like lightning. If the Emperor finds me dangerous, then my only future is under the knife.

He will change his mind. Everyone in this room heard your words. Everyone in this room heard the high priest support you. Not even the Emperor can kill one so obviously favored by Ignos without repercussions.

Speak what I say again, and we may yet get out of this alive.

I sink to my knees, press my forehead to the cool stones in front of the Emperor in his feathered, gold cape. "I swear to you, Emperor, that we will have the tools you need by the time the Lunare near. They will be awed by your brilliance, by the power of your people, and you will chase their armies to the ends of the world."

I don't look up until I feel the Emperor's touch on my shoulder. The servants and the guards relax. Looking down at me, the Emperor speaks, "You promise much, Solare, but Jakkan vouches for you. So I shall give you your workers. You shall have until the Lunare pass Tutio. If you fail, then your life will be given to Ignos, and Jakkan will lie beside you, his heart carved first."

Sax relays the crash-into-the-core idea to the set, and there's cautious agreement. Theoretically, Sax's plan holds up, though there's a lot of ifs. Still, nobody has a better idea, so Sax gets the vote to go.

"I don't know which gateway leads to the docking bay," Sax says after, and even Bas shakes her head.

"Why suggest it then?" Bas replies. "We don't have time to explore every section on this ship."

"Then we start with the closest one." Another bit of Vincere code: When in doubt about what to do, complete the simplest action first. Since nobody knows which way is right, they ought to go the first way they can.

Of course, the next gateway is locked. Sax glares at the black nub as it scans for Sevora and finds none. It's not intimidated. How to break through a door when they have no weapons? Above them, a rushing noise echoes from the pipes. All four Oratus scatter, on instinct, to minimize the impact of an attack.

Lan points her miner up, but doesn't fire because there

isn't any target. Sax traces the noise along the pipes to the nearest rank of seed ships, which start to shake.

They're being filled.

The seeds settle, and a steady, growing thrum replaces the rushing noise. Sax watches the seeds vibrate, and suddenly the row of three near them begins to steam. Loud whines echo through the ring as engines spin up, and the noise answers the question of why nobody's in here. If this happens regularly, Sax would lose his hearing, and shortly thereafter, his mind.

Then a seed drops. It's a slow thing due to the gravity, but the hook, with the piping running through the barb to the back of the seed, retracts. After a couple moment's fall to clear the hook, the seed's engine pulses into full ignition. Fire pushes back up towards the pipes, white-hot, and then the seed is down and gone, through whatever shield the Sevora put between vacuum and the ship's air, and out to space.

The second and third seed follow seconds later, and Sax is left with a ringing head and a dangerous idea. "We use the seeds," Sax says to the set, and they hiss in laughter.

"I want to see you fly one," Bas says, knowing full well Sax hasn't flown a ship in his life.

But Sax is ready. For once, he has a comeback to Bas and her knowing sarcasm. Rather than trust his words, though, Sax turns around and leaps. He goes high, up to the nearest seed, and hits it.

Sticks his claws into its shell. It's not cloth, but few things can handle an Oratus digging in, and he finds purchase.

"What are you doing?" Gar shouts from below.

"Aiming!" Sax edges his way around the seed, setting

each claw in before he moves the next, until he's gone halfway around.

The other two seeds in the row are behind him now, and in front, below, is the gateway. Now that he's listening for it, Sax hears the rushing noise, only this time feeding into a different part of the ring. The seed ship is launching again. Maybe in desperation, maybe because it can. Either way, Sax bets that these seeds will fire soon.

So he presses in with his claws and leaps, turning in the air, to the next seed. Catches himself. Now he has leverage. Sax, with his left claws biting deep into the second seed, leans out and looks at the three Oratus.

"Two more!" Sax shouts, a raspy, ear-splitting hiss. "Together, we can push it."

This hits the others like inspiration. Bas and Gar win a battle of glances and copy Sax's flight. They scramble around the first seed, and, with Sax descending to the pointed front of the second seed, get themselves in position.

"When it starts to fall," Sax says. "You'll jump. Gar, you go first. Then Bas. I'll go last."

The three of them are on the seed when the fluid starts rushing again. As Sax hopes, it's coming right above them this time. Burbling, roaring and flushing down into the seed. Sevora likely pouring in with it. Ready to launch and infect some unlucky world.

This one, at least, won't be getting to its destination.

"Ready," Sax says. Bas and Gar hiss in agreement.

The seed starts to shake. Both the one they're on, and their target. If it goes like before, the target will fall first, and that will give the Oratus their chance.

The right hook moves. It shakes, begins to lift off of the first seed and Sax doesn't have to say anything for Gar to know his time is now.

Gar leaps, pressing off with his claws and lunging towards the first seed as it falls loose from the hook. Bas follows. They both hit the seed as it starts to fall. The force of their leap couples with the low gravity to shove the seed towards the gateway, into prime position for Sax to make his own jump. He presses his legs, digs deep and angles towards the front point, that bottom apex of the seed.

And leaps.

He leads with his shoulders, trying to push every ounce of force he has into the seed as he strikes it. A loud roar starts in the ring; the seed's engines igniting. As Sax hits, he notices Gar and Bas dropping away, beginning their slow fall to the metal floor. Sax himself feels the seed rotate, their combined impact is enough to orient the craft.

Sax holds the nose as it swings up, and then he feels himself accelerate. The seed is moving, its engines launching the ship right towards the gateway.

Sax can't hang on. His momentum will send him right into the same spot as the seed. So he pushes off, down towards the floor, and away from the gateway.

Only it's too far. His momentum too much. He's over-shooting; falling into the chasm that leads to outer space. Sax twists in the air, staring down at the black emptiness beneath him. Nothing out there but cold death.

The noises of the second and third seeds beginning their own release rumble up, and then a shattering bang, a crashing crumble of metal and dust and sparks as the seed they pushed hits... something.

Sax can't tell, as he's drifted below the floor and all he can see are the launching seeds starting their path towards him.

"Flip your tail up!" Bas's voice, and Sax follows her instructions without thinking. That's the point of a pair –

you do what they ask without doubt because it will save your life.

He feels claws bite into his tail and it hurts, but Sax stops falling. There's a lurch and someone's pulling him back. He feels the heat as the next seed closes on him. Even if the seed doesn't hit him directly, its rockets will burn Sax to ash.

"Hurry!" Sax hisses.

There are honorable ways to die. There are deaths full of pride, like sacrificing yourself to harm the enemy. Giving your last breath to one more swipe of the claws. This would not be one of those. This would be sad. Pathetic.

The pull increases, and Sax bumps against the side of the chasm and then back over the metal floor as the seed brushes past behind him. The skin of his head puckers at the heat, his scales blister, but Sax lives.

It's Lan holding Gar, holding Bas, who pulls Sax back up. He lives because they work together as a set. He lives because the Oratus do not abandon each other. But none of them mention it. They don't have to. They all know their job and they do it.

Now they're looking at the wrecked hole where the gateway used to be. The seed ship isn't even there. It punched right through. Hard rock meant to last for cycles in space, propelled by rocket engines, is more than enough for an interior gateway.

On the other side, they see something Sax never expects. Something he didn't think the Sevora capable of.

Malo leads us back towards the Vaos as Ignos dips towards the horizon, but we've barely left the Emperor's presence before the high priest whispers in my ear, "Tell me of these miracles you wish to produce, and I will see the proper people informed."

Kaishi, the real power is yours now. Don't give it up.

"No, Jakkan." I stop in the middle of the street, forcing the high priest to do the same. Ignos is right. The Emperor put my life against the success of these miracles, and I will not leave their success up to Jakkan. "You will bring the people I ask to me, and I will inform them of the tasks myself. This is my duty to the Emperor, and Ignos works through me."

"Kaishi," Jakkan slides a smile onto his face. A warm one, understanding. "You must realize that you are an outsider. The artisans you need will not work with a Solare, no matter how much she says her words are those of Ignos himself."

"Then you," and I look at Malo, sharing him in my words. "And Malo will make them. Or I will tell the

Emperor his miracles have been lost because his own people will not follow his orders."

Jakkan's warm smile vanishes, replaced by a tight line. Malo, meanwhile, appears uncertain, looking at Jakkan and I. Even people passing around us glimpse the tension and give a wide berth.

"Your tone has changed, Kaishi," Jakkan says. "Have I not said that we must be allies here to save our civilization? That we must work together?"

There had been a time when a promise of friendship would have swayed my heart. My mind, even. Now, in the cold crush of Damantum's people, surrounded by buildings instead of trees, with the burning smell of forges instead of soft flowers, my soul keeps its clarity. I observe Jakkan's words like I would a strange insect, searching for their true intent.

I find nothing kind in them.

"Together," I reply, memories of the Pits and Jakkan's first, lethal task driving heat into my words. "Yes. Only as partners now, not with my body under your foot."

"He is the high priest, Kaishi," Malo pleads. "Second only to the Emperor himself. Please."

Jakkan nods at the warrior, his eyes still on mine. Waiting for me to break and submit.

You were beneath them, now you are equal. Soon you will be greater. We're nearly there, Kaishi.

"Partners." I don't smile. "Call me whatever you wish, but either we are equals, or this city can burn."

Jakkan sinks into a look I've seen before on Father's face; one of calculation. Schemes brew behind Jakkan's wrinkled, leathery skin. I see scenarios play out, each one twisting in the high priest's mind until he comes out ahead.

"As partners." Jakkan nods at last. "For the city, and our people, I will set aside my pride. As you have failed to do."

I ignore the bait. I have the status I want, now I need the loyalty. "Do you still believe in me, Malo?"

"If I did not, then I would not be here, priestess," Malo replies, though the words come less ready than before. A sign, perhaps, that the warrior is less than happy with my grasp of power.

A true leader cannot be overly concerned with the feelings of her subjects. They will follow you, and that is enough.

"Then here are the people I would see." I pull the list from Ignos, and I feel the Cache burn on my wrist as he calls to it. Images and formulas full of symbols I don't recognize pour through my mind and it's all I can do to keep from screaming right there. I think, without the sacrifice and its pressure to train me, I would have. "The city's best workers of metal and wood. Damantum's greatest jewelers and alchemists. Bring them all to me, and we'll begin the work needed to fight off the Lunare."

"I can see to that," Jakkan starts, but I cut him off.

"No, Jakkan. While Malo gathers the people, you and I have do something more important," I look down at myself, and then point at Jakkan's own robe and headdress. "I need clothes, jewels like your own. I must be more than a priestess. I must be what Ignos would desire of his messenger. Make me look the part."

The high priest does not dispute the argument. Instead, as Malo departs to arrange discussions with the city's premier artisans, Jakkan takes me on a tour of Damantum's markets. With the high priest at my side, the shopkeepers don't look away as they did before. Zolin, tending to his plants, notices with a start that I'm still alive. I give him a smile and he shakes his head.

First, I have to choose a color. As the Emperor embodies the blues of seas and shallows, and Jakkan uses the reds of blood and soil, so I need to choose shades that will set my soul into my clothes, hair, and skin.

It's not a hard decision.

"The luminous greens of the jungle," I announce to the dyers, whose stands are cluttered with pots containing all manner of colored inks. "I want to shimmer like an emerald, but with the mystery of a forest valley."

Second, a headdress. My crown. A band with feathers or stalks; straight threads of colors. Again, I'm drawn to my roots. The shades of the birds around my village: black and white and yellow. A burst of

orange and red for fruits and flowers. The craftsmen begin sticking feathers, dyed and not, into a band. The resulting arrangement, while holding the appropriate hues, appears jangled.

"That will not match your green cape," Jakkan whispers as we look at the initial attempt.

"Why should I care?" I reply. "I'm supposed to represent all people, Charre and Solare. Different colors seem the easiest way to do that."

"A fair argument," Jakkan says. "Yet, as one knowledgeable about such things, remember that the people see you as you are, not as you wish to be. They will wonder why you choose such a strange arrangement, they will ask why a messenger of Ignos seems so ugly, why her headdress stands so apart from the others Ignos favors."

Jakkan may have a point, Kaishi. This thing you have created is, shall I say, quite unappealing to the eyes.

I want to push back. Want to be stubborn, but Ignos'

voice meshes with Jakkan's appeals—which, this time, hold no trace of another agenda—and I back down, "You might be right. Let's try a bright green in the center declining towards black at the edges."

Even the craftsman is more excited about this than my first attempt, and the end product shows it. When I place the crown on my head and stare at myself in the still basin of water kept at the stand for that purpose, the headdress is a vibrant, verdant green. As if life itself has come from above and traced its way down to me.

"Beautiful," Jakkan says, and I think he means it. "Now, there is one place left for you to visit."

Similar to the dyers, the tattoo artists have bowls of various inks around their stands. Stones serve as chairs, with warriors and others sitting on them while the artists perform their work, creating intricate inkings of Ignos, lions, bears, and the Vaos.

Jakkan, shifting his cape so that I can see the elaborate design dominated by Ignos on his back, says, "Here you must pick your new body. Your old one will be given to Ignos. Open yourself to his wisdom, and let his words guide your tongue in the telling, and their hands in the painting."

I wait for Ignos to tell me what I should do. How I can transform my own body into a powerful message, but Ignos is silent. I sit on the stone, feel the cool, rough rock against my thighs, and think. Jakkan and the artist, an old, weathered man, stare at me.

If I have to choose for myself, then, there is one design fit for my body. One depicting the god that has brought me this far. That has done so much to change my life. I describe the details: The light green shades. A circular design with a wide set of eyes in the middle; an everlasting search for knowledge. Four arrows reaching out from the center, to look in all directions. At the angles, carved blocks to serve as the foundations that same knowledge created. At the end, a series of circles filling in the gaps: the travel of ideas from discovery to practice.

Ignos, a part of my mind, will now be part of my body as well. While I speak, the artist dips and pierces. Pokes and paints my skin. There is pain, yes, but I bear it, because there is no other option.

One step closer, Kaishi. One step closer to the salvation of your people.

I t's dark, but not total, and not sinister.

Rather, what Sax sees now is a luminous show that uses the shadows to focus the eyes on what they're meant to see. Which, in this case, are glorious fountains: arches of water spritzing back and forth over vast areas covered in what Sax can only describe as entertainment.

Tables, mobbed by Flaum, Teven, Whelks and other species Sax is not able to recognize from afar, blink and flash through various games. Pulsating beats clash and echo across the metal flooring, and every thud carries with it a multitude of cries and calls. Floating banners move back and forth through the space, illuminating with advertisements and movies.

"We found their fun," Lan says, and she's right.

Seed ships hold many thousands, and it now seems obvious to Sax that to keep even Sevora in a civil state, there has to be a way for them to enjoy themselves. A place to go when not on shift, a place to have fun. To cavort, to play games and remind themselves that all is not one battle after the next.

The Sevora need this because they are weak. Because they cannot handle the cruel reality of life.

Sax also sees the seed, or what remains of it. It's punched through the gateway and lies on the ground in front of them. At the bottom of the steps and further beyond, having, it looks like, bounced its way to its final resting place: burrowed into the side of what had once been some sort of lit statue, which is now sparking.

Sevora species gather around it, pointing and chattering. All of which means nobody is noticing the gateway or the four Oratus standing there, haloed by the bluish light of the center ring behind them.

"Let's use it," Sax says. "Keep moving. Remember mauling these Sevora isn't the objective. We need to get back to the outer ring, to the docking bay."

"If it's even in this section," Gar says.

"If it's not, then we'll try another," Bas replies.

"If it takes that long, I may have to eat some Flaum," Gar mutters as they start their walk.

Every foot fall onto the hard floor brings new assaults to Sax's senses. He sees Flaum in various states of intoxication. Falling over each other, or simply standing with glassed eyes and slack expressions on their faces. A reckless sloth that would never be permitted on a Vincere ship. Slivers alight on posts covered with purchase for their talons. They too seem exhausted. Uncaring of the four Oratus wandering in their midst.

Sax thinks he knows why.

They're so deep in the seed ship now. So far beyond the outside, that what are the odds of an enemy force making it here? It's far more likely that these four Oratus are taken, Sevora slaves like the rest of them. Though even if they weren't, Sax is fairly sure these creatures wouldn't mind. They are so far removed from real consciousness that Sax thinks they wouldn't react if he begins carving them up right here in the open.

So they keep going. Into and through the center of the section, which is a large square with a bursting sapphire fountain in the middle, one that seems to spray up different colored water. Around it, spread at intervals, are vast arrays of tables and chairs and nutrient dispensing machines. Most of the spots are taken with Sevora-hosted species happily munching away on whatever they can get.

"Fascinating, isn't it?" Sax knows the voice. Turns and sees Avan, no longer wearing any of his armor, watching them. The captive Oratus has apparently made his way out of the dark crowd. Avan spreads his claws wide, as if to show he means no harm. "Please, let me speak."

Sax sees, or rather feels, Gar twitch, crouch down into an attacking stance. They can't afford a battle here, so Sax whacks Gar with his tail.

"We're in enemy territory," Sax hisses as Gar snarls back at him. "You start a fight here, we'll never survive."

Gar keeps his glare hot, but lowers his claws.

Avan clasps his own in front of him. "You're right of course. With one yell, I could have a horde descend upon you. You would doubtless slay many, but you would be torn apart." He pauses, his vents taking in a long breath. "You and I both know the small fleet you have at this end of the galaxy won't be capable of taking down this seed ship for a very long time. How many more worlds will the Sevora infect before you bring it down?"

"Wherever you go, we will find you and we will end

you," Sax replies. He desperately wants to do as Gar nearly did: tear Avan's grin off of his face.

"I'm sure," Avan replies. "But what if I told you it won't matter? What if I told you that there are things you don't know. Things that would make your every action meaningless, if you knew them?"

"Why haven't you killed us yet?" Sax hisses the only question that matters—if Avan's tracked them here, then he could have shot them, stunned them or burned them.

He's done none of those things.

"Because I want to leave," Avan says. "I need a way off of the seed ship, and I need a way to survive. You are that way. An offer: I will guide you to a ship, to your chance at the glory you so desperately seek, if you will guarantee me safe passage back to your own vessel."

"How do you know we're looking for the docking bay?" Bas asks.

"Because you are on a seed ship. They hear everything. I hear everything."

Sax flexes his claws. "Then why are you talking to us now? Revealing your plan?"

Avan looks around at the loud, thumping surroundings. "They can hear everything, except for this place. Except for where there's so much noise that the recorders catch only garbled nonsense. Where it's so dark and difficult to see that it's hard to know what's happening."

"But we only came here by chance," Lan argues. "You couldn't have known that–"

"By chance?" Avan interrupts. "Who do you think triggered the seed ships to launch? Who do you think waited until you derived your plan and made sure the right ones fired when you were ready? Which, thank you for making it so much easier than I had expected. Crashing through the gateway with a seed ship? None of us saw that coming."

Avan has them. Sax knows this. They can either go with him, or fight him here and now. Though Sax can't tell, he assumes Avan's figured out how to put on the mask. Which means he's protected, to some degree. The four of them could likely make an end of him, but then their own deaths would come shortly thereafter.

Or they could trust the despicable creature and follow him to the docking bay. To where they wanted to go.

"I don't think we have a choice," Sax hisses. He waits for a denial, but none comes.

Though he hates the razor smile that pulls over Avan's face, Sax does nothing to erase it.

The meetings with Damantum's premier artisans and craftsmen are, according to the Emperor, to begin immediately. With my outfits determined, Jakkan leaves me back at the Vaos, which, he says, will serve as my home.

Kaishi, now's the time. The Cache. Use it.

The bracelet. Green and shimmering in the light. I run my fingers along its warm sides. It flashes, and I feel as though the light streams through my eyes and into my core.

The Cache stores our knowledge, Kaishi. Make miracles with it. Give your people what they need.

Using the Cache feels like reaching through my own memories, only the things I find are like nothing I've ever seen before. Pictures of creatures I don't recognize from any legend, places so beautiful and terrible they defy description. And things. Wonders that Ignos promises will change the course of my world. I begin to fall, diving through one after another. There is so much to see, and I want to learn it all!

Stop.

Ignos' voice pierces my frantic churning. The image in my mind shifts to something that looks like Viera's weapon.

The Cache holds too many secrets for any one person. Look for what you need, and you'll find it. Look for everything, and that is what you will lose.

From that point until, with night long descended, Malo returns with the first group of artisans, Ignos and I explore the Cache. We pick out miracles suitable for the Charre; ones that can built in the time, and with the materials, that we have. I choose several more too, ones Ignos thinks are beyond us, but that I believe will stoke the fires of our imaginations. Belief in the new powers coming to us.

Yes. You must think of the Charre, now, as your people. That is what they will become, soon.

Are they my people? The Charre, who took me from my home? I don't think so, but then, I can't afford to treat them as enemies. To do so means death. I know that if the Charre can push back the Lunare, then perhaps I can persuade them to leave my own village alone, to protect them.

So I stand ready to begin when Malo enters the temple.

First there are the metalworkers, and with them I show schematics. How to make the magic fire that Viera had summoned so effortlessly. How to make even larger weapons, ones that could shoot hundreds or thousands of projectiles in mere moments of time.

Not all of them are possible with Damantum's workshops, and even if the Charre had the material, knowing the plans and executing them are two different things.

Still, we speak, with Malo fueling us with tea throughout the night and into the next day. The metalworkers have their own ideas, looking at what the Cache provides, and leave with the coming of dawn to produce their own versions of Ignos' miracles.

I barely have time to blink before the next group arrives.

The woodworkers. I give them designs for boats and larger ships, even planes that will fly through the air. I show things that are so far beyond their greatest imagining, seeing my own legend building in their eyes. Creating a priestess that has all the answers. That has all the guidance for what is to come. The woodworkers leave like the metalworkers, with visions dancing through their minds and inspiration pouring from their mouths.

The doctors follow a quick lunch of peppers and pork. We go over detailed maps of cells and biology, though I'm disappointed to learn the Cache holds no diagrams of our own species. Regardless, in several hours of conversation, the entire medical practice of the Charre people transforms.

Word spreads of the miraculous priestess hiding in the Vaos. Jakkan begins functioning as my own assistant. Scheduling meetings, making sure I'm adequately cared for. Ushering in and out groups of all kinds. From writers to hunters, sculptors to warriors. All of them come. All of them ask for more. I, with Ignos in my mind, am only too happy to give them everything I can.

This. This is how you find your people. This is where everything you are becomes real. Where the Charre stop looking to the Emperor, and start looking to you.

I don't dare put that thought to words.

Not even the Emperor himself is immune to the rumors. On the third day, he calls for another audience. I go, with Jakkan, back to the palace. Back to see the Emperor in all his finery. Again he stares at me and issues warning after warning, threat after threat. He expresses fear and angst over the Lunare, who are taking their time in approaching. They are gathering up smaller tribes with their own wonders. Claims are spreading that the Lunare are the true gods. That Ignos favors them.

The Emperor throws us back to the streets with demands, ones that I plan to exceed.

By the fourth and fifth days, as evidence of my miracles becomes known on the streets, as the first objects coming from my teachings find their way to the Emperor, his opinions change. On the sixth, when the Emperor calls, he does not request Jakkan. This time, Malo asks only for me.

This time, I go to the Emperor alone.

With nobody there to help me, other then the voice of Ignos in my head, I promise the Emperor that I will deliver. That my wonders will be ready. That when the two of us go out to greet the Lunare, the sheer brilliance of the many inventions of the Charre people given to them by Ignos will not only bring all of the other tribes to their knees, they will bring the Lunare themselves to heel.

The Lunare, I promise, will realize their mission is a hopeless one. They will leave in fear. The Emperor will rightfully reign over all.

Rather than issue his customary defensive threats, the Emperor reaches behind him, to a servant who holds a small box. From it he pulls out a small thing that looks like a tube with a wooden leg on the end. Like the weapon Viera had held. The Emperor points it at the far wall. Presses back on the lip of metal sticking up from the top. And then pulls another small loop of metal with his finger.

The noise inside the palace is deafening. A loud crack reverberates from the stones and pierces my ears. I'm stunned, my head rings and I do all I can to stop myself from diving onto the ground or running away. Only the Emperor, watching me to see what I do, keeps me from it.

When I manage to look, I see a chunk of the stone wall is missing; crumbled on the floor. The Emperor stares at the device.

"Your miracles are more than just words," the Emperor says. "This, this is what we need. This will make the difference. We cannot, unfortunately, make enough. We do not have the mines. The forges. Yet."

"We will, your Holiness," I say. "In time, yours will be the mightiest nation ever known to man."

"Perhaps," the Emperor replies. "But will we have that time?"

I don't know how to answer, and the Emperor, placing the weapon back in the box, doesn't seem to expect me to.

"The Lunare have many of these. Some longer, larger. I am told they have whole roving monstrosities covered in large things they call cannons that, when fired, sound as though the sky is being ripped asunder. How can your miracles compete with this?"

"They can be better. They will be better. But we need time."

"Does Ignos tell you how to find that?"

Meet them. Go out, confront the Lunare face-to-face. Scare them. Take the wonders we have, and use them to buy that time. Every day, every week you get is crucial.

"We can't let them reach the city," I say. "If they do, they can disrupt our efforts. They can distract the people that are even now working to put these devices together. You are the holiest, Emperor. With me by your side, we can change the minds of the tribes that follow the Lunare. We can tell the Lunare they are no longer welcome, and show enough to prove it."

The Emperor's hand reaches up and brushes his headdress, fingers filtering through the feathers, "Ignos has seen fit to guide you this far, and I would be foolish not to follow the wisdom he shares through you. Perhaps it is time for us to reveal ourselves. Get ready, for tomorrow, we shall make for the desert and show the Lunare they never should have left the mountains."

With Avan leading them, Sax and the others make their way out of the entertainment section. Plenty of Sevora stare at the group of five Oratus, though they turn to their drinks quick enough after a glare or a wave of a menacing claw. Like the gateway in the central ring, green lights halo the exit from this section, further out from the core.

Looking back, Sax sees the broken gateway already under repair. The crashed ship already cleared. Entertainment section or no, the Sevora could move fast when they wanted to.

"Tell me," Sax says to Avan as the latter raises his head to next gateway's scanners. "How many Sevora are on this ship?"

"Thousands," Avan replies, not turning away from the black nub. The green lights blink and the gateway shunts open. "Enough to rotate crews around continuously. Those behind us are enjoying their time off."

"Even in the middle of a battle?"

"We have been at war constantly for cycles. If we hadn't

found a way to find joy in the midst of all the fighting, we would be a sad species indeed," Avan wraps his long mouth into a smile. "Although I suppose you Oratus don't quite understand that."

"The battle is our joy," Gar says.

"Yes. Of course it is." Avan waves them through.

This section feels more like a labyrinth, with narrow corridors between tall walls that stretch from floor to ceiling. Circular windows dot those walls, and, going by the large doors appearing every so often with keypads, Sax assumes these are the homes for Sevora living on the ship. Capsules for sleeping and little more.

On the sides of the structures, spidering out over the pathways, are perches on black metal poles. Slivers land on them, wrapping their bodies around the bars for rest. Yellow lamps hang from these perches like fruit from trees, spreading soft light across the cold metal floor. Every so often they walk through small plots of plants in cutouts between buildings, a brief concession to beauty in an otherwise efficient design.

The entertainment section held swarms of Sevora shifting around. Mobs of them cackling with laughter or sharing meals. Here, though, what Sevora they see—in the usual assortment of Flaum, Teven, and Whelk hosts—travel by themselves or in pairs. Rushing, always. As if being caught outside here would result in something terrible. Avan, who doesn't say anything as they walk through the district, seems to sense Sax's impending question and looks back at him.

"This section is currently under resting orders," Avan said. "Species are only to be moving through here in emergencies, which is why you're seeing worried looks. As you might imagine, keeping our workforce healthy is of paramount importance."

He points a claw towards one of the windows up above. "From the outside, these are designed to only cast light frequencies that promote sleep. On the inside, there are screens showing images that promote relaxation. A variety of substances are also available to help Sevora find the rest they require."

"You drug your own people?" Bas says. Sax flashes to the Stim he took at the start of this mission, but keeps quiet.

Avan turns fully around as they reach a point between buildings, where a single arch plant, its many pink curling vines twisting up and over each other, provides decoration. "To think that a species as oblivious as yours is besting us in this war... yes. We do. Neither Flaum nor Teven are natives to space, and they, being quick to mature and easy to dominate, make up the majority of our forces. In order to ensure the hosts get the required rest in an environment not conducive to such things, we use various means."

"Not only are you taking their bodies, but you are ruining them as well?" Lan says. "And you hope the rest of the galaxy will let you live?"

The rest of them hiss agreement—Sax too. Avan must be under the influence of his own drugs to think the Oratus would agree to share the galaxy with a species like this.

"You say that as if we Sevora can control who, what we are," Avan replies, taking Lan's provocation in stride. He spreads his four arms wide, expanding the claws. "We need hosts to survive. Few Sevora ever reach full maturation and the capability to breed—to do so requires space and protection, which we haven't seen for cycles. As such, we... copy ourselves. Grow new Sevora in tubes and pools. Yet still, we number far less than the ubiquitous Flaum, who pollute the galaxy with their trillions."

Pollute the galaxy. An interesting phrase, if not entirely wrong. Sax has seen more than his share of Flaum on Vincere ships, and they tend to be the first to come and rebuild worlds rescued from the Sevora grip. Flaum produce litters numbering close to a dozen or more. Enough so that pairs of Flaum could repopulate cities on their own in little time. If the species possessed the intelligence or strength to make their own attempt at ruling the galaxy, the Flaum would have little trouble achieving dominance through sheer numbers alone.

"You need to find the benefits," Sax says as Avan recommences their march. "Why should we let the Sevora continue to exist? What good do you provide?"

Avan doesn't have an answer ready. No eloquent argument or sharp comeback. After walking in silence, after they leave the capsules behind and come to the next gateway, only then does Avan stop short of the scanner and glance at Sax, his eyes burning.

"Who are you to play as gods, and decide what species live or die?"

I t's not long after the meeting with the Emperor when, back at the Vaos, two guards come in looking for me. They're wearing bear skins, and when Jakkan asks why they're here, they point to me. "We have information for the high priestess."

"High priestess?" Jakkan says, and while I pick up the surprise, Jakkan doesn't flinch.

"As the Emperor has decreed she is to be addressed," one guard says. I try to look at Jakkan, to say I have nothing to do with this, but the high priest doesn't look at me.

"Then address her." Jakkan turns back to towards a scroll he's reading.

"What is it?" I ask.

"We've captured a Lunare," the guard begins. "Hiding in the city. Apparently, she had made threats to a family, secured a room in their house. But she has since fallen ill, and now she begs for your help."

"Viera," I say, and I catch Jakkan's ears perk up at the name. "Where is she?"

"We have her chained at the foot of the temple," the

warrior replies. "We are ready to prepare her for sacrifice. It does not look as though she will live much longer, so we should hurry."

"Bring her in," I order. It feels strange to do that. To command someone.

You are powerful now. It is only right that you use what you've gained. And that what you've gained will change who you are.

"In?" the guard seems confused.

"In here. In this chamber. I made a promise to the woman, and Ignos will not see it broken."

At the mention of the god, the two guards stamp their spears and vanish.

"So your friend has returned." Jakkan's voice is heavy with warnings. "I would advise you to be careful. The Lunare are not well-liked in the city, as you can well imagine. Being seen helping one will not do you any favors."

"I can only hope that the miracles Ignos has given will buy me enough respect to help Viera," I reply, then, after thinking for a moment. "My tribe did not try to fight every one that came through our territory. There is a chance that the Lunare don't have to be your enemy. They could be valuable traders. Partners even. We just have to convince our people."

"Kaishi, it is not us you have to convince," Jakkan says. "It's the Lunare and their band of marauders. If they wish to trade and return to their mountains, we would gladly barter with them. What they want, however, cannot be traded. Only taken."

Before I can reply, the guards bring in their captive. It is Viera, though far paler, sweating, and unconscious. The problem isn't hard to spot: the wounds I cauterized, those white marks scarring her chest and arms, are red and inflamed around the edges. Rashes span across the front of her body.

Infection.

There are ways to cure this. Though none that you currently possess.

I implore Ignos to tell me more. I'd made a promise to Viera. Also, given Jakkan's increasingly askance looks, and the Emperor's other-worldly standing, I have few friends in the city. If there is any way to keep Viera alive, I want to use it.

Then here's what you must gather.

Ignos rattles off a series of ingredients. Instructions for how to blend and cook them together. To make a small pile of powder, stuff that I would need to keep on making until the infection subsides. I tell Jakkan, and I can see his reluctance to help me gradually gives in to the desire to see another miracle in action.

We dispatch the guards to find herbalists and glass workers, while Jakkan and I stoke a large fire. In the hours between the guards departing and returning, I lay Viera down, and use a cool cloth to wet her forehead. To try and calm the fever raging inside her.

Viera utters words in her own language, twisting and turning on the floor. Sweat drenches her, and her pallor grows. It's obvious that she won't live long.

"A sacrifice will not break your promise," Jakkan says at one point while I'm matting the cloth on Viera's forehead. "You made that vow to a living, healthy woman. Now, she's dying. You have the opportunity to honor her. You have the chance to have her depart this earth and go to the home she so obviously wishes to return to. Give her to Ignos, Kaishi. Gain the people's everlasting love."

Jakkan speaks wisdom. Get what you can from those you can use. Don't spend your influence on a lost cause.

I can't.

There simply isn't a part of me that can accept carving into Viera's chest and pulling out her heart. Not after I'd worked so hard to keep her alive. Not after she'd helped me from the juar pit.

No.

I will save her, or she will die in the attempt.

Using the Cache, I walk the herbalists through the process. The steps to turn these ordinary ingredients into medicine that will give Viera a chance. Metal, herbal leaves, the fermented alcohol that would otherwise be used to make honeyed wine, all of these and more are boiled together until they form a strange milky substance.

Then, I spread it on the infection.

We repeat the same process for three days. Each time I whisper to Viera that she will get better. That she will soon be up and running again. It helps me believe, if nothing else.

Caring for Viera does not, of course, take all of my time. I still work with Damantum's artisans, checking and advising them on their progress. Testing what they develop. Learning from their expertise and coupling it with the secrets the Cache provides.

Until the Emperor himself appears at the Vaos.

I've been turning away his messengers every morning, declaring that I cannot leave yet. It's one thing to tell a meek servant that I'm too busy working miracles to depart the city. It's another thing to see the Emperor in full regalia stride up and into the chamber, to see Jakkan fall to his knees and bow. I follow suite, if only because the Emperor's expression tells me my life depends, now, on subservience.

"I'm told the march to save my people waits on one woman," the Emperor's voice, in the close confines of these chambers, echoes off the walls. "I'm told that my priestess, the one that promised salvation for the Charre, lets the Lunare gather their strength, lets them draw closer..."

The Emperor strides, as he trails off, between Jakkan and I, over to where Viera lays on her mat, still unconscious, if not quite so pale as before.

"For this one. A Lunare herself—"

"A friend," I say, standing and ignoring Jakkan's muted gasp. "A friend who saved me when none of your own would. Who protected me as I now protect her."

The Emperor reaches to his waistband, pulls out a black-glass knife from a loop. His face is blank as he holds the knife out to me.

The implication is clear.

I refuse it.

The Emperor pulls the knife back slow. Gives me plenty of time to reconsider, but I stand firm. As Ignos says, I am powerful now. I have the weight of miracles on my side. And I choose to use that weight for what I believe is right.

"If you will not sacrifice this one," the Emperor says, and I'm relieved when he slips the knife back into his loop. "Then we will take her with us. The Lunare are at Tutio, and we have no more time to wait."

"Take her with us?" I'm too surprised by the statement to watch my own words.

"I have had a cart prepared. It waits at the steps, along with several priests to care for her." The Emperor looks at Viera.

"Then you planned for this from the start?"

"One Lunare is not worth risking my high priestess's support," the Emperor replies, but when I start to thank him, he talks over me. "Do not make me regret this. Prepare her to move, and let us save my people."

Ships of all sizes spread out across the docking bay, visible from the gateway as Sax and the others go through behind Avan. Rather than only a magnetic shield, as with the seeds, here a large, sliding set of metal plates act as an additional layer of protection. Each plate interlocks with the ones next to it through sliding latches. Even now, Sax sees one of the plates slide back and a pair of Sevora space fighters—dart-shaped things with a single, cylindrical energy cannon on the nose—jet out into the dark.

Sax estimates another dozen or more fighters sitting behind those two, though pilots didn't seem to be lining up to fly. The seed ship is in the middle of a pitched fight, where it has been boarded by an enemy force, and it hasn't launched all of its defenses?

"Why?" Sax asks Avan. "What are all of these ships still doing here?"

Avan keeps moving, heading down onto the vast flat section. Sax notices the Sevora has clenched his claws.

"There are not enough pilots," Avan says. "The war has

decimated our numbers. Whereas you can simply train another Flaum, we must first have a Sevora ready to take a host. Then, only after the Sevora has established control, can we begin training."

Avan leads them to a larger shuttle, an ovoid craft with no visible cannons on the outside. No weapons at all, in fact. Its sleek exterior, painted in the greens and whites of a peaceful ship, confirms the craft's purpose. That it sits ready, with a a set of four armed Flaum soldiers at the foot of the shuttle's metal legs tells Sax that their arrival here isn't unexpected.

Perhaps Avan would be making this trip even if Sax and the others hadn't gone along.

The shuttle loads through an elevator, rather than a more usual ramp. The platform sinks down from the middle of the shuttle on four thin poles which set themselves on the ground. The craft has three struts; one in front and two thick legs at the aft, and its engines point towards the bay door. Avan singles out Bas and Lan with his claws and tells them to get on the platform, which is too small to hold all of them at once. Bas catches Sax's eye, and he blinks twice at her. Affirmative.

They will go along with Avan's plan. For now.

A pair of Flaum, each holding a primed, heavy miner nearly as large as themselves, join Bas and Lan on the platform. Sax knows these weapons—a trigger, a big battery pack, and a wide nozzle. Capable of blasting hot energy in close quarters and guaranteed not to miss anything in front of you. If Bas or Lan want to attack, they'll have to kill or disarm the Flaum immediately, or be melted into char.

Once they settle, the platform shoots up into the belly of the shuttle with the whistling shunt of hydraulics. Moments later it descends again, empty. Avan waves Gar on, and two other Flaum join him. Sax starts to board the platform, but Avan holds up a claw. "Not yet. I need to make sure your friends won't get any ideas. Tear apart my soldiers and leave me down here."

Sax would have made the same choice had he been in Avan's place. The four Oratus, left alone with the Flaum, might have gone for an attack like that. Commandeer the shuttle. Though, Sax thinks, it would have been a short hijacking. Without a way to open the docking bay doors, Avan could have had other guards blow up the shuttle where it sits.

Which means Avan has a different reason for keeping Sax down here.

"Why now?" Sax hisses, turning to Avan. "We have the clear advantage. There is no reason for us to meet with you. To save your species."

"Sax, your friends would see me dead in a moment. That one, Gar, is particularly violent. You do not seem quite so bloodthirsty. Why is that?"

"I am disgusted by you," Sax answers as the shuttle's platform descends again, empty. "But you are not the objective. We won't risk our mission for one Sevora."

"Then, perhaps, you can see what so many of your species cannot. What I hope your commanders will be able to understand."

"And that is?"

"A vital piece of information," Avan says. "One that the Sevora learned by accident. From an unexpected host. Knowledge that, if broadcast widely, would be dismissed as slander. Propaganda. But if allowed to grow quietly, it could change everything. Reset the galaxy, and our places in it."

"A bold statement, Sevora." Sax follows Avan onto the

platform. "Given your imminent defeat, I'd think you would say anything to save yourself."

"I thought the same when I heard it," Avan replies as the platform rises. "Even in our dire need, we aren't ones to leap at false hopes. Except, Sax, I now believe it is true. The Sevora have sought confirmation, and have found enough evidence to make our claim more likely than not. And if it is true, Sax, then all of our species would be fools not to act on it."

The inside of the shuttle is a luxury that Sax has never known: lounging couches, with straps for any sort of acceleration, splay around a wide area bordered with shifting works of art. Images from other worlds, vistas of orange mountains and green oceans, captivate the other Oratus.

Their Flaum guards seem similarly fascinated, the miners hanging loose at their sides. Whatever this ship's purpose today, at one point it had served as the finest pleasure currency could buy.

"A jewel," Avan says of the shuttle as they rise into it. "Designed for different times, but now called to a mission far more important than its original owners ever envisioned."

As Sax looks around the shuttle, he feels the engines begin to rumble. The vibration churns through the ship, and everyone finds their seats. Sax winds up on the end, with Avan conspicuously choosing a spot next to him. Sitting on cushions like these, with a tail, requires contorting his body, and Sax winds his tail around his own waist to keep from sitting on it. The other Oratus do the same, though Avan's tail leaks out to his side, flopping off the edge of the couch towards the floor.

"Will you tell me what this is? The great secret you claim to have?" Sax asks Avan.

"So that you might dispatch me and deliver it yourself?" Avan gives Sax a toothy grin. "I won't take that chance. The words come from me, or from no one."

"If this was your plan, then," Bas says from across the ship. "Why try to kill us?"

"You aren't necessary," Avan replies. "I would be on this ship, heading out into the battle, with or without you. If I can save our seed ship from your claws, and help my own goals in the process, then why not do so?"

As Avan speaks, the shuttle lifts and burns out of the docking bay. Sax looks out the front window, into the laser show of the fight still underway. The four of them left the middle of the seed ship to find a way into the very heart, and now they have it.

Avan's promises are intriguing, of course, so Sax will see to it that the Avan will make it to Evva, but Sax also has a mission. One he will not fail.

Jakkan waits for me at Damantum's gates. The Emperor has assembled a vast train there, with soldiers standing in rows along with porters to carry goods. The Emperor is there as well, standing on his own chariot, to which are hitched a pair of large creatures. They're called, so I'm told by one of the guards, oxen. Bulky beasts with horns, most are used for field duty, which is why I haven't seen them throughout the city.

These two, though, sport mantles of blue and gold washing down from their massive horns, across their backs and spilling into tassels down their sides. The Emperor's chariot is opulence. Thankfully it's a cloudy day, or I'm not sure I could stand all the flashing gold and gems.

My spot, so I'm told, is walking next to the chariot. A place of honor, and as nobody else in the force—save Viera —is riding, I don't begrudge the opportunity.

We're leaving with a purpose: to convince the Lunare that a fight with the Charre will be costly, will be terrible, and is not condoned by either their god or ours. To that end, I see a series of woven crates supported with bamboo poles stretched across the backs of Charre workers. I open one to confirm my suspicions—inside are some of the weapons we've been making, waiting for their chance.

Crude, but the overall design should work. I would not be the one to pull the trigger, Kaishi. Let someone else see if it explodes.

I have no intention of fighting the Lunare. I'm not here for a battle, and, after the Pits, have no desire to start one.

"I have a gift for you," Jakkan says as we say goodbyes near the front gates. I wait, but he doesn't present anything. "Your spot. In the train. I've elected to stay behind in the city and give you my place at the Emperor's side."

"I don't understand?"

"I'm giving you the chance to supplant me," Jakkan spreads a warm smile. "I've seen it. During these last few days especially. You are truly one with Ignos, and you deserve your place at the Emperor's right hand. I will stay away to watch the two of you grow a great empire and will serve you as best I can. Right now that means taking care of our city and carrying on the work that you started. Destroy the Lunare, Kaishi, and bolster the Charre with their bones."

"Destroy?" I haven't heard Jakkan use such harsh language, but there's anger in those words. Pride too. "I think we're going to negotiate. To convince them to leave Charre alone."

Jakkan laughs. "With the Lunare? The Emperor is bringing you on this journey for a reason, Kaishi. To see that no civilization, no upstarts from the mountains, dare provoke us. They will either run, or the Emperor will see them crushed."

I'm stunned by the admission and can't think of anything to say. My expression only delights Jakkan further, and he leaves me then, staring after him as he gathers followers to wave at our march from the gates.

Come now. You can't really be surprised? What is the point of power if not to destroy your enemies and raise up your allies?

I've driven a knife through flesh and bone. My words have brought about at least one death. My hands are not clean. But those were my choices, and I knew the consequences. If Jakkan is right, then what I've been helping the Charre make will result in conquest, in fire and death.

Either you or them, Kaishi. Do not be so naive. Think of how far you've come.

I do, and feel like retching.

When the horns sound to march, I'm alongside the right ox and one of its large, brown eyes stares back at me. It's in shadow as the Ignos' morning light hits the other side of the beast's long head, and in its iris I see a warped reflection of myself. I'm wearing my finery; the green headdress and bright cape, my mosswrap is back at the Vaos, not fit for a high priestess.

I don't know who I'm looking at.

"You seem distracted," The Emperor, above me in his chariot and adorned in all sorts of glittering, blue and gold robes, says. "Are you not honored to be on this great and glorious march?"

"I've never marched with an Emperor before. It's overwhelming." I say something to say something.

The Emperor chuckles, then raises his right hand. At the signal, horns blow again and the column begins to march. Thousands of warriors with all manner of skins on their shoulders. Servants, porters, cooks and caretakers mix in. For the first time I feel what it is like to move with an army, to be a part of something so large and in motion. The thunder and rhythm.

It almost lets me forget what Jakkan said.

Almost.

After an hour without conversation, the Emperor turns back to Damantum and I follow his gaze, careful to keep my march steady. The walls stand tall. People are on top of them, still waving at the departing army's snake. "All of them believe in us, Kaishi. It can be hard to leave under the weight of so many expectations, but you will get use to it. Our mission demands it. Ignos demands it."

"Jakkan says you want to kill them." I can't keep from asking anymore. "The Lunare?"

"As they wish to own us," the Emperor replies. "I am the chosen one. There can be no other ruler. The Lunare proclaim themselves the divine people. How can I allow such a thing? How can my people keep their faith when such blasphemies stand?"

"So death is the only way?"

"If the rumors are true, the Lunare leader will offer another path to us, only to stab us in the back should we choose to walk it." The Emperor shakes his head. "They conquer through lies as well as force. Any negotiation will end in blood, one way or another."

After the rest of the morning bleeds away with footsteps, the troops at the front announce a halt. Other, friendly forces are coming. The new warriors resolve themselves into Malo and his band, returning from Damantum's outer villages, and coming back with foul news.

"They're falling before the Lunare," Malo explains to the Emperor while I listen. "Some try to fight, but give in when the Lunare spit their fire. Others don't even bother.

They bow and scrape. Trade freedom for their lives. Embrace Lunare's rule, and march with them."

After the briefing, I excuse myself from the Emperor's company and find Malo back with Viera, near the rear of the column and being pulled along on a small cart. Malo greets me with a soft smile. "So you found her."

"She lives," I say, and seeing the two of them together brings unexpected heat. "With no help from you."

Malo nods. "The woman is an enemy. She deserves what came to her."

"She promised to save me. Just as you did."

Malo hesitates, then reaches into his belt, unhooks Viera's weapon. Places it on the cart next to the Lunare.

"I hope she still can." Malo leaves before I can say another word, vanishing back into the press of troops.

That one is moody. Though I think he still means you well.

There are thousands of people here. I believe I can count on two of them, and one of those is still lying in a cart, eyes closed and broken.

When the horns blow to resume the march, I leave Viera's side and head back to the front.

"Tonight," the Emperor says when I've rejoined my place. "You will demonstrate your miracles. Make sure they work as Ignos demands. When we meet the Lunare, there will be no room for failure."

The movements need to be precise. Use every moment. Sax seeks out their eyes.

The shuttle coasts free of the seed ship, and as the craft leaves the sliding plates and their magnetic field behind, it lurches. The Flaum, sitting on the couches, jostle from side to side. Their hands leave the hafts of their miners to steady themselves. Sax sees Avan notice. Sees Avan's mouth open, his warning shout begin.

Too late.

Across the shuttle, Bas strikes at the Flaum on both sides of her. Two claws on her left, two claws on her right, each with three sharp razors raking at their targets. Going for the miners, for the hands reaching towards them. Lan and Gar do the same, as does Sax. A simple grab, clench, and tear. Now without arms of their own, the Flaum freeze in shock.

"What are you doing?" Avan finally finishes his exclamation.

The Sevora tries to rise, but unlike Sax and the others,

whose tails don't interfere with their legs, Avan's inexperience makes the action difficult. Unwieldy in the low gravity.

Sax springs towards the shuttle's ceiling, catches himself on the inside hull with his claws, then launches back down at Avan. As the captured Oratus makes it to his feet, Sax slams into him, knocking the creature to the ground. Each of Sax's claws pins one of Avan's, while Sax's tail goes over his shoulder and wraps itself around Avan's throat.

"Do not struggle," Sax says. "The shuttle is ours. You have no reason to die for it."

Though Sax keeps his eyes on Avan, he can hear the sounds from the cockpit. Panicked squeaks from the Flaum, and the subsequent orders from Lan to turn the shuttle up and around. Orders Lan finishes with a simple statement: if the Flaum and the Sevora in their heads obey, then Lan and Gar won't tear them all to pieces where they sit.

Bas joins Sax, holding a pair of the heavy miners in her arms and pointing them down at Avan.

"Why haven't you finished him?" Bas asks. "He is an abomination."

Sax tightens his tail around Avan's throat to keep the Sevora from getting any ideas, and looks at his pair. "He states that he has valuable information that could change the course of the war. I can't take the chance that he is not lying."

"We cannot take him with us. He won't sit quietly while we destroy the ship."

"No. Which is why Gar and Lan will take him to Evva. She'll decide whether his information is worth his life." Sax turns back to Avan. "I offer you this, Sevora. A journey to our side. A chance to tell your tale. Will you accept?"

"That is what we were doing, before you murdered my

crew," Avan says once Sax loosens his tail enough so the Sevora can speak.

"And that is what you will continue to do. Bas, ready one of the evac mods. We'll use that."

Bas hisses her dissent. "Reckless, Sax. We can guide the shuttle in. Its size alone guarantees damage to the seed ship's core."

Avan's eyes flick between them, wide, red, and shivering. Sax ignores him, "You heard me, Bas. Until the mission ends, I make the call. Ready the mod."

"What are you trying to do?" Avan asks, but Sax doesn't respond.

He watches Bas for a moment, making sure she actually goes to the evacuation module's door and begins punching in the commands to ready the craft. Bas does what Sax asks, though Sax knows he'll catch many mouthfuls about it later.

If there is a later.

"Gar, Lan," Sax announces. "You will fly the shuttle back to Evva. Make sure Avan gets a chance to tell his promised story. If it fails to justify his existence, I trust you will rend the skin from his bones. Now, you will bring the shuttle across the center of the seed ship. Bas and I will use the evac mod to make our assault."

The two Oratus greet the command with silence. Sax refuses to turn his head away from Avan—the body of an Oratus is a weapon, and Sax dares not it out of his sight.

"We will honor your command, Sax, even if we don't understand it," Lan finally says.

"You see, Sevora?" Sax hisses after Lan speaks. "We are loyal without control. Without giving up our bodies to your parasites."

"I am trying to save my species." Avan, for the first time, sounds broken.

"Until you convince me otherwise," Sax says. "It is my goal to destroy it."

Gar approaches then, trading watch on the pilots with Lan, and places a clawed hand on Sax's shoulder. Without speaking, the two exchange positions, with Gar holding Avan against the ground and wrapping his own tail around the Sevora's neck. Only when Sax stands and heads towards the evac mod, does Gar say anything, "You are taking my blood, brother."

"I shall spill enough for both of us, brother," Sax replies, as custom demands. The answer satisfies Gar, who focuses on his prisoner. Sax knows the Oratus won't move from that position until something blows him away or they land on the Vincere ship.

"The launch window is approaching," Lan announces from the cockpit. "Get ready."

Bas waits inside the cramped evac mod, the benches inside too small for her body. Sax joins her, squeezing into the opposite side. Their tails meet in the middle, looping around each other. Without any sign, any words or glances, Sax puts his claws out and Bas clasps them with her own. She accepts his apology, forgives the harsh words, and they promise to fight together through whatever is coming, all with a touch.

So it is with one's pair.

The evac mod has no windows. Shielded with thick metal to block both the heat from an atmosphere, radiation from outside space, and the inevitable impact a jettison from a crashing ship would cause, the evac mod serves a singular purpose: to get its passengers to their destination alive.

So when Sax shuts the door behind him with a simple press of the two-button control panel, the two of them wait for Lan to get the shuttle in the right position without worry.

They will have one shot at this. A speeding projectile aiming directly at the heart of the seed ship. Miss, and they will either crash elsewhere and be stuck in the same plight as before, or they could burn through the ship entirely and fall into the crushing gravity of the giant orange planet.

A shunt sounds. A moving of metal. The brief wail of an alarm.

No other clue announces the evac mod leaving the shuttle. No other sensations bleed through to the two Oratus that they are now in motion.

They fly in silence.

That night, as an endless number of campfires illuminate the desert around us, I gather with a group of Charre warriors, including Malo, to run a final test on what the Cache has given us.

Four woven boxes are arrayed in a half circle on the edge of the army camp, with nothing but sand on the other side. Nomis' light shimmers from above, mixing with the flickering orange to cast our shadows out beyond.

As the warriors watch, I go to the first crate and open its lid. Inside appear to be blades. The same black-glass that marks the sacrificial knives. Only these blades are loosely connected. A single long central fiber runs between them, flexible and twisting. It ends in a sturdy grip of wound rope, with a soft bulge on the underside. I take hold of it, and lift it out. It's long; almost twice my height, and the weapon coils around my feet. Despite the sharp blades, the device is light. Easy to hold.

"This is called a shard," I say, remembering the name from what the Cache told me. "You can whip it at your enemies, like this."

I heft the shard and snap it forward, cutting back with my hand at the last instant to crack the blades. They slash forward, biting through the air and clashing against each other, throwing sparks. Vicious, but not all that different from the kukri they hold already.

Until I use the trick.

I twist my wrist so everyone can see the small orb attached to the end of the shard's grip. "Here, however, is the secret. Squeeze this. A little bit of oil will leak down through the fiber and onto the glass blades. Then all you need to do is crack it again."

I do what I say. Squeeze the pump and sheen coats the rope's fibers. I crack the shard again. Sparks fly as the black-glass clacks. Only this time the sparks catch fire. Soon the entire rope, except the handle, is aflame.

"See how it burns, but the fiber beneath does not?" I say. "You can strike fear into their hearts. Over and over again."

I let the whip settle into the sand, the dirt snuffing out the remnants of the fire. The expressions on the warriors' faces are suitably impressed, though they're not amazed yet. An interesting weapon, but hardly a divine miracle.

I'm just getting started.

From the next crate, I pull out something very similar to Viera's pistol. A wooden stock in a metal frame.

"The Lunare will load a black powder into their weapons before they fire. This will give us an opportunity. Whether to strike with our hands, or with these," I lift the weapon, aim into the distance, and pull the trigger.

With a pop, the gun makes a loud noise. My shoulder rocks back, but I ignore the bruising, the brief bite of pain as the weapon kicks into me. No time for that now. "Rather than packing the powder into the weapon, we pack it into the ammunition. Press the trigger, you strike the shot and it explodes forward. Each of these can hold twelve at a time."

What I don't say is that the entire Charre army only has three of the guns. Their point, after all, is not to decimate an army but to show that a fight would be fruitless. Too costly for either side. At least, that's what I hope.

The third crate contains more miracles. Globes that, when tossed, explode into tremendous gouts of flaming fire and noise. Others that don't burn but spread noxious gas, causing people near them to descend into coughing fits and crying agony.

The very last crate holds not implements of war, but the stuff of peace. Ointments and salves. Medical tools that can repair even the most grievous of injuries. I want these for the Charre, yes, but also as a potential peace offering. A chance not to kill, but to bring two peoples together over mutual benefit.

I'm thinking too of my own tribe. How destroyed they would be if the Charre and Lunare made the jungle their battleground. How much better everything would be, instead, if the two factions made my old village a center of trade. Of peace.

Malo comes up after the demonstration, as the other warriors leave, chattering amongst themselves in excited voices. For once, he doesn't look at me like I'm something to be taken care of. I see the same level stare he gives to Jakkan and other warriors.

Respect.

"I never believed, when I took you from your village, that this would be the result," Malo says. "I thought, at best, you were a talented girl. That you had some inspiring prayers. Not that you would reshape our entire empire."

"I thought the same thing, but the Ignos knew better. He's used me."

"For the good of the Charre. The good of our people."

"Your people," I reply. "One reason I'm still here is because I know the Lunare will be worse for us. If I succeed, perhaps the Emperor will spare my people your brutality."

"You've become so hostile." Malo's face is curious, intent, concerned. "Why? What have I done?"

"It's more what you didn't do," I say. "You didn't warn me. You didn't guide me through Damantum, but threw me at Jakkan's feet and left. You did not tell me about the Pits. You claimed to support me, to believe me, but you tore me from my family and left me to live or die on my own. Should I be grateful to you for that?"

Malo takes a moment, stares at the campfires. "I didn't know what to do. I'm a warrior, not some father figure. Not a guide."

"It doesn't matter what you are. You shouldn't have to be trained to know when someone you call a friend needs help."

Malo says nothing. After a minute, with me waiting every second of it, the warrior mutters a goodbye and stomps off towards his warriors.

I go back to Viera, only to find that the two priests caring for her are ecstatic. Or at least, as happy as Charre priests can get.

"High priestess," one of them exclaims as I near. "Her fever is broken. The treatments, they seem to have worked. The infection subsided."

I push past the priest and kneel by Viera. Place my hand on her forehead. She does feel cooler. The red around her scars has faded to a more pasty pale, but the Lunare's eyes remain closed. She breathes lightly. Yes, she might live, but Viera is not healthy yet.

Not that I have time to worry. Tomorrow, according to the scouts, we meet the Lunare.

The impact comes in a shuddering crash. No lead-in. No warning sign. Just one second floating with a slight sensation of rapid movement, and in the next the evac mod bounces Sax into Bas. The mod crackles and rolls, the sound of rending metal making it to Sax not as noise but as vibrations. He feels the wreckage in his bones.

The small lights in the mod go out. Plunge the container, which has no windows, into black. Then a flaring red. A warning.

"You have a mask still," Sax says to Bas, who confirms it. "You can go."

"The vacuum will kill you."

"The mission takes precedence." Bas reaches out, runs a claw down the side of Sax's long, narrow face, "Patience, dear one. The ship will take care of us."

A risk. Most ships of any size have measures in place to keep a hull tear from destroying everything. Some could deploy electromagnetic shields across gaps, using pressure and magnetism to keep everything inside the ship from rushing out. Others use temporary sprays; sealants launched from repair robots to close a hole until more permanent measures could be used.

Bas would be hoping for one of those. The danger, of course, is that something else could find their evac mod in the meantime. Set up an ambush and blow the two of them away the moment they open the door.

"It's not worth the risk." Sax brushes Bas' claw.

"Tell me, Sax, would you not do the same for me?"

Sax opens his mouth to say that he would carry on with the mission. That he would put success above any one person. But no words come out. He seems unable to form the sentence. Bas hisses in laughter at the sight of it.

"A pairing is more than a single mission," Bas whispers. "You, Sax, are worth more alive to me than a thousand seed ships."

Sax adjusts his tail so he can sit back against the wall of the evac mod. Stares at Bas. Reaches out with his claws again and clasps hers. They might be trapped, but Sax will make the most of these moments.

"When did you know?" Sax says. "When did you know you cared about me?"

"From the moment I saw what lay behind the danger in those eyes of yours."

"What do you mean?"

Bas tilts her head to one side, "Most Oratus are weapons, Sax. They live and breathe violence. It's what we're taught to love. I do. You do. But we don't stop there, do we?"

"You're talking about Avan."

"I'm talking about many moments, Sax, when we chose a different path. When I noticed you could see other ways, that's when I knew you were the one I wanted. The one I needed."

Before Sax can reply, the lights in the evac mod flip from red to a deep blue. Pressure and oxygen. What vacuum had existed after the crash had been fixed by someone or something. They can leave.

"We'll come back to this, Bas." Sax reaches for the control panel that opens the door. "I wouldn't mind hearing more about how amazing I am."

Bas doesn't laugh. Instead she yanks Sax's arm away from the panel. "I go first," Bas says, pushing Sax, gently, towards the back of the evac mod. "I'm the one with the mask, remember?"

When the evac mod's door swings open, it reveals a sparking mess of wires, torn metal sheeting that had been a ceiling or floor, and flickering white lights. Bas pokes her head out, then withdraws back into the capsule.

"We're in a rounded area," Bas says. "Hanging at the top of it. There's a chamber directly below us. Can't see into it. This room rings it. Appears to be food, oxygen, and water, at least, piped in here from elsewhere on the ship."

"It's a sealed bridge," Sax says. Not unusual on massive ships or ones carrying precious cargo. Keep the captain and controls separate from the passengers to reduce the odds of a hijacking or, as in this case, attackers from reaching the place where they could control everything else.

"And we're inside it." Bas flashes Sax a toothy grin, then scrambles out of the mod and drops. Sax follows, drifting towards the floor. From outside the mod, Sax can see the circular section, as high as the other parts of the seed ship they've visited. In the middle, directly below their hanging mod, is a wide cylinder that almost reaches up to them.

The structure lacks windows and, in the white light cast from globed bulbs scattered along the ring's walls, seems entirely black. At ground level, the section appears to have a variety of amenities: Tubes opening to bins for water, counters for food, and one large waste pit that, Sax figures, would lead back to the seed ship's recycler.

Someone could live here indefinitely.

Sax hits the floor and balances on his legs, letting his claws dig small grooves into the metal. Something tickles his vents. A smell that doesn't belong in a place like this. Too much carbon in the air. As though he's stuck in a room with a bunch of hard-breathing Flaum.

"Do you smell that?" Sax asks Bas, who's loping around the central cylinder, looking for a door.

"Faulty electronics?" Bas replies as she moves, and Sax begins to circle the opposite way. The cylinder building isn't so large that they would run out of earshot. "From the crash?"

"Too natural." Sax goes around, but there doesn't seem to be any clear door. No lock, no sliding gateway. It's clear, though, that the command cluster they're looking for sits inside those walls. "Can we break through?"

Bas doesn't hesitate. She swipes a claw across the metal, sounding a shriek through the space. Her claws leave a silver line, but no tear.

They won't be getting in that way.

"Whomever is in there has to leave some time," Bas says, glancing at the food and drink receptacles. "We can wait for them."

Sax is about to answer, but the carbon smell smogs the air. Blots out every other scent. He focuses on it. Opens his vents and inhales. His body tells him the scent is stronger form above. Sax looks, and freezes.

A large shadow moves on the ceiling.

"Bas, we're not alone," Sax says, as the darkness falls towards them.

We only march for an hour the next day, and stop well before Ignos reaches its zenith, in a valley with Tutio behind us at one end and the sandy waste leading to my jungle on the other. The Emperor proclaims that the Lunare will come to us, and not the other way around, so we wait.

I try to make use of the time. Viera is still out, so once the column stops moving, I help the priests set her up towards the back of the forces. Then I work with the miracles, positioning the crates near the Emperor and making sure that the warriors who would open, who would show off their contents, understand how to use them.

The Emperor himself still has the small pistol made just for him. He holds it in his right hand, while in his left he carries a ceremonial scepter topped with a golden depiction of Ignos, each of its six rays sporting rubies, diamonds, and sapphires. It's glorious and majestic and I'm entirely happy to let the Emperor take the spotlight.

War, I'm learning, isn't my favorite thing. Too much

grit, too many orders, and the constant expectation of death hang over everything.

Around noon, dust appears on the horizon, growing closer as it sweeps into the valley in front of the volcano. The same brown cloud that I saw around the Solare tribesmen. This one grows faster, moves more quickly towards us. The ground tremors with the pounding of feet and larger things. Monsters I've never seen before.

The Lunare, astride their rolling, wooden and rock constructs in the center, are surrounded far and wide by the stamping march of other tribes. I can't look away from the Lunare... buildings. I don't know what else to call them. They look like boats, with a curved front prow, yet have turning wheels propelling them along the ground.

Large white, scaled beasts with no eyes and with many legs pull the things towards us, grappled to their tasks by thick iron chains linked to collars.

All too clear, as well, are the openings in the sides of the hulls where gray tubes poke out, pointing in our direction.

Fassoth. How are they here?

I don't understand what Ignos is asking about, and he quickly moves on. Tells me that it's important to avoid those creatures, as they're deadly when angered. Then he falls silent, as Ignos is prone to do.

"Look at how many there are," I say to the Emperor. "We're outnumbered."

"I did not bring all of the Charre with us for a reason," The Emperor says, sounding as unconcerned as he looks. "What will decide this conflict is not strength in numbers. They will not take Damantum, or eliminate my people with their weapons. They will take it by destroying our faith. The Charre will fall when they stop believing in me. In Ignos.

"How much of the force you see before you are Lunare? Not many. The cowards from the mountains hide in their toys. They rule by fear. When we show the tribes they have collected that the Lunare are nothing to be scared of, they will turn to our side."

Don't stay near him.

I don't understand Ignos's sudden warning.

The history of all things is splattered with the blood of heroes who led from the front of their forces. The Emperor, astride that chariot, makes a grand target of himself. You, next to him, are as likely to get hit by a stray shot.

"How will you be safe?" I ask the Emperor.

"Ignos will protect me. Even these tribesmen, who call the Lunare their leader, even they will turn against these invaders if they strike me down outright. The Lunare will know this."

Malo joins us as we watch the Lunare approach. Their boats stand three times as tall as the Emperor. There are three of them, each with a pair of the white, furred beasts, and they rise above the Charre forces.

I guess there are several hundred Lunare packed on and around the boats. Around those, however, are thousands of tribesmen. Gathered from the jungles and desert lands, forced or coerced into marching with these strange things.

It's not the war Father envisioned being the end of the Solare—the bows and arrows and spears in the jungle trees, but instead a facing off between forces armed with weapons he could never have imagined.

A Lunare steps to the fore of the center boat. Unlike the Emperor, he isn't clad in golden finery. He doesn't wear a cape or carry a staff. His face is smudged with dirt, which makes his silver helmet, shaped in a way that makes me think of mushroom caps, gleam. His uniform is simple cloth, and there is nothing about what he wears that speaks of leadership, except his stance. His tall standing, broad gaze, and the sheer respect with which all of the other Lunare direct him as the man levels his stare at the Emperor.

Silence fills the expectant air.

The Emperor taps his staff on his chariot's floor, and the oxen lope forward a pace, until they are nose to nose with the creatures Ignos calls Fassoths. He looks up at the Lunare leader.

"Should I go?" I whisper to Malo, beside me now, who shakes his head.

"The Emperor must be the absolute authority, high priestess."

I hear the honorific. Malo has called me priestess before, but always with a twist of kindness, like a friend. Now it comes with a harsh formality. Maybe I'd been too hard on him. Too difficult.

Remember what I said before. Now is not the time to concern yourself with his feelings. Instead, win this confrontation. Claim your mantle.

And then what? Ignos keeps pushing me towards more and greater things, but to what end? How much would I lose along the way?

End? This won't ever end Kaishi. We'll keep going and growing. First the Charre, then all of the tribes, and further and beyond until you'll have gone farther than you could imagine.

What if I don't want to?

Ignos doesn't answer, and my momentary reverie shatters as the Emperor raises his staff. The warriors bearing the miracles step forward. First, comes the one with the shard. He squeezes the handle and cracks the black glass against each other. Starts a swirling fire.

I hear the gasps around me, but the Lunare seem unimpressed. Two other Charre come forward, holding the rapid-fire guns. They aim up, over the heads of the Lunare, and fire two quick shots apiece.

Again there are gasps. This time, I notice the Lunare paying attention; eyes drawn to the guns.

"We have many more," the Emperor shouts. "Ignos gives us his vision and we manifest it."

The Emperor's words seem to move the tribes. The Solare and tribal men on the sides of the Lunare shift, glance at each other and up at their new leaders, who in turn look to their man in the center for a counter. My heart twists at the strange smile that comes over his face. If the Lunare leader has any doubts, fears or worries, I can't see any.

"A grand show for one who has so little. We come here not to see your playthings, Emperor, but to prove that there is a better life. That the Lunare bring paradise and providence. All of these tribes here know of what we speak. All that remains is for you to learn." The leader, then, runs his eyes over the front of the Charre army.

He stops on me.

"One woman among your troops, Emperor?" the Lunare leader cries. "And without a weapon?"

"A high priestess is necessary for Ignos to bless our journey," the Emperor replies.

"Bless? So you say *she* carries Ignos' words?" the Lunare crows.

Malo wraps his hand around my arm. "Be ready," he whispers.

"Ready for what?" I whisper back.

It's not like I can do anything, standing there with a

thousand troops at my back and a host of enemies in front of me.

"Through her, Ignos tell us your days in this land are over. That, to save the lives of you and your men, you should return to your mountains. Crawl back to your holes in the ground." The Emperor booms his voice now, and I understand they're talking more to the armies than to each other.

The Lunare reaches into his belt, pulls a pistol free, and points it at me. "Surely, if this high priestess has the protection of your god, I would not be able to kill her?"

"You have seen the gifts Ignos has given us." The Emperor makes no move to attack, no move to shift soldiers in front of me. "Is that not evidence enough?"

"Tricks," the Lunare announces. "Lies meant to twist your minds. Again I ask you, if I shoot this girl, will Ignos protect her?"

"He will find a way," the Emperor replies.

The Lunare nods. Keeps his finger on the trigger. Then swings the weapon towards the Emperor, and fires. The gunshot cracks loud; in that instant it's the only noise in the entire universe.

I don't see the bullet, but I do see the smoke. The Emperor slumps forward against the front of his chariot, and the oxen, frightened, turn to run. They trample away, rumbling down the line between the armies, the Emperor's body tumbles from the chariot into the dirt before me.

"Do you see? His god has failed him. Your true Emperor stands before you now. Follow me, and lead your fellows into the light." The Lunare raises his pistol high and waves it.

I stare with Malo and all the others. Aghast. How can the Emperor, the holy one, die like this?

The fight hasn't started, and the Lunare have already won.

Sax figures his instincts, those twitchy actions that come without conscious thought, are the main reason he's survived this long. They save his life again when his tail, along with Sax's legs, pushes him into a roll along the ground. Behind him, the creature dives out of the shadows.

Bas rolls the opposite way, so that when the two Oratus stand, the creature is directly between them. Which, considering it's a Fassoth, is less than optimal. The Fassoth is a nightmare to look at: its long, ridged, snow-scaled body bleeds into eight trunk-like legs, each ending with a splayed assortment of claws. Its head is a hard bulb, eye- and earless. White hair puffs out between the scales, thin and light. On their icy home world, the Fassoth hunt by crouching down, waiting for something to pass. Hiding in the drifts.

Most of the time, Fassoths serve in labor capacities. Strong and nigh tireless, so long as they're kept fed, Sax has found plenty of them on Sevora worlds, has fought more than his fair share. Never, though, in tight confines like this.

Never with only a single partner, unarmed. Still, if there's one guide to fighting a Fassoth, it's to keep moving.

So Sax goes. Takes a leap towards the creature's back. As Sax flies, though, the Fassoth twists, those hairs picking up the shifts in the air. It rolls as Sax soars overhead, gravity now acting as an impediment and keeping Sax in the air long enough so that, instead of striking the Fassoth's back with claws extended, Sax bombs directly into the creature's clawed legs.

Where the Fassoth's true terror waits. On the ends of each of those legs, in the center of the claws, sits a gnashing maw of sandy teeth. Rock-molded and gummed over time to form jagged edges. Sax is about to get caught by these things. Grabbed and chewed to pieces.

Until Bas, streaking through the air in the opposite direction, tackles Sax and pushes both of them back to the ground away from the Fassoth. Sax taps her with a claw in thanks. They separate, crouch and hold ready. The Fassoth squirms back onto its feet and shifts towards them. Sax sees the creature's rocky plates flex, pushing air in and out. Not too unlike his vents. Those are the Fassoth's weak spots. If he can get his claws between its armor, he'll be able to tear the Fassoth to pieces.

"I'll distract, you go for the back," Sax hisses.

"Flip it," Bas replies. "I still have my mask."

"That won't help against this."

"Stop talking and attack," Bas says as she charges the Fassoth. The creature, more than three times her size, takes the bait and runs towards her, all eight of its legs shoving along the ground.

Sax, again, goes for the air. This time jumping against the side wall of the ring and using his claws to dig in, to catch himself above the ground. Sax sits still for a moment.

If he doesn't move, the Fassoth will have a hard time knowing where he is. Will forget about him and focus on Bas, who, using her tail and widespread arms, darts back and forth. Creates as many moving molecules as possible. With so much motion, the Fassoth will have to guess where she is.

Bas begins to back up as the Fassoth slinks closer. When it thinks she's near, the Fassoth rises up on its four back legs, using its front four to swipe at Bas. She ducks and weaves, ignoring openings in favor of keeping herself alive. A pair of the Fassoth's limbs come in high, followed by its second two sweeping low. Bas, using gravity, twists through a flip in the air, the giant legss gliding just over and under her. Sax would marvel at the move, but his own time has arrived.

Normally, from here, Sax would open up with miners. Spray concentrated beams of energy to bisect the Fassoth, or shave off its legs and leave it incapacitated. Sax has no miners. Sax is unarmed, save for his claws.

They'll have to be enough.

Pressing off the back wall, Sax launches himself at the Fassoth. His angle comes in shallow, so that when he nears, and the creature begins to turn towards him, Sax twists and reaches with his claws. They slide across the Fassoth's back, feeling their way between the slats and digging into softer tissue. The pull turns Sax the rest of the way around as he crosses the Fassoth's body, and the Oratus plants his legs on the Fassoth's side, digging his claws in as the creature, having rotated the wrong way, begins turning back.

Sax presses off again, jumping away from the Fassoth towards the central building's wall. The move should have brought the Fassoth's attention back to Bas, who is trying to dance in, swiping at the legs. Fassoths aren't intelligent. It should obey its instincts. Go after the closer target. But this one doesn't. This one ignores Bas and spins to follow Sax. As Sax lands against the building, the Fassoth rushes him. Those legs propel the creature too fast for Sax to jump away.

So Sax doesn't. He hears Bas try a desperate roar, one the Fassoth ignores. Sax lets his claws slip from the wall and wraps himself in his arms, his tail, and prepares to be crushed.

The Fassoth barrels into Sax, smashes the Oratus into the building. Sax feels the Fassoth's sharp claws on the ends of its legs bite into him. The teeth cut Sax's skin. But the thing about low gravity is that it's hard to stop yourself once you get moving, and a Fassoth can get moving like few other creatures in the galaxy. It smashes into the central cylinder, its bulk carrying into the wall and pressing against it.

Sax figures the side walls are designed to stop lasers. To protect against cutting weapons and beams. The top and bottom of the structure, the most likely targets for a ramming like Sax and Bas had attempted with the evac mod, might be reinforced against a crash. The sides, though? Where would a heavy impact come from in a tight space?

The wall bends, twists and breaks as the Fassoth crushes through.

The impact flattens those trunk legs against Sax, crushing the Oratus into the Fassoth's underbelly, and, despite the claws digging into his arms, Sax fights back. He falls into the manic spirit hiding within every Oratus. The bloodlust. Activated, at times, with Stim, here it comes naturally. The stinging pain from the Fassoth's teeth vanishes, replaced by pure, unbroken fury.

Sax cuts, slashes, bites and lashes even as the Fassoth does the same to him. Until, suddenly, the creature whips

Sax through the air into the far wall. He slides along the metal to rest on the cold floor.

Across from him, Sax can see the center of the seed ship. With one of its walls destroyed, the rest collapse, the sides folding against each other and bending out across the ring. The Fassoth, with Bas digging into its back, writhes, but Sax has done the damage. Cut deep enough. These are death throes.

His eyes drift to the center, to the leader of the seed ship, the Sevora they had been sent to eliminate.

What he sees makes perfect, horrifying sense.

Panic is quick to turn to anger.

I see the Emperor's body before angry cracks split the air again. Directly behind me. Malo's taken one of the miracles from the Charre warrior. The one that can fire multiple rounds. Malo fires them all.

The shots strike the Lunare leader, still standing on the front of his boat, one after another. The first two tear the glee from the Lunare's face. The third and fourth knock him back into the boat. The rest of Malo's shots fire into the railings, causing the Lunare to dive away in a shower of wood chips.

As if Malo's attack is some hidden signal, pandemonium erupts: people fly everywhere. Charre warriors rush forward to safeguard the body of their fallen Emperor, while others charged into the Lunare ranks. The Fassoth rear up high and batter anyone that comes close with their legs.

The Lunare seem lost without their leader, calling for a retreat. A bass horn, a hollow rock the Lunare use as an instrument, sounds moments later. This triggers some training in the Fassoth, and they immediately wheel away from the fight, dragging the boats with them.

As for the Solare tribes, they don't know what to do. Leaders on both sides are dead. The Charre avoid them, instead focusing on any Lunare not in a boat, and those they pin down. Tie up and take captive.

Staying here is dangerous. You've played your part. Leave.

Ignos makes sense. I'm at the front of the line. If a focused fight breaks out, if the Lunare decide they aren't quite done, I don't belong in the middle it. So I take off. Push my way back through the Charre ranks as they press forward, Malo's ringing voice calling for a full attack.

Others join in with Malo's cry, echoing ululations for the destruction of their enemies. The sheer noise over-whelms me as I struggle away, bouncing off of bodies and squeezing by sharp edges until I reach the rear of the force. Near Viera, her cart, and the priests watching over her. They all stare at me. They have no idea yet of what's happened.

"The Emperor is dead." It's the first, the only thing I say.

The priests fall to their knees and begin to pray, and I let them send their quick words to Ignos before continuing. "With his death, the Emperor gave us a chance to strike down the Lunare leader. They are running now. We'll win."

"What is victory with such a loss? Without our Emperor, we have no one." One of the priests stands as he says the words, though he looks at me as though I have an answer.

"I wouldn't say that," the tone sounds foreign. Then I recognize Viera's voice, hoarse and tired as it is. "I'd say you have your leader standing right there."

The Lunare isn't yet sitting up, but her eyes are open, and she's managing a weak grin my way. I would have smiled back, if not for the frowns and hard stares of the rest of the priests.

Those are not the looks of rejection, but calculation, Kaishi. Stay strong, and they will accept you.

Ignos speaks endlessly about my climb to power. That I'll reach a point where I can save my people by leading those who would destroy them. As I look into the faces of the Charre around me, I realize that it's not me they believe in. It's not me that has the power.

The Charre believe Ignos speaks through me. Our god is choosing my body as his vessel.

You are. Be what they believe.

It's what Father did every day for the village. What my mother did every day for me. I can do it for them.

"Right now, our warriors are fighting and dying while we stand here." I turn as I talk, catching all of the priests, the ones who, through their capes and bangles, staffs and tattoos, speak to all that is holy about Charre and Solare people. "Come with me. Back to the front. Together, we can convince the other tribes to join us and push the Lunare away."

There's hesitation, but nobody wants to look like a coward in front of their god. They fall in line behind me, with me, and together we surge back towards the fighting. This time I don't have to push my way through—the warriors move aside for the priests and, with their blessing, for me.

The front itself is a mess. Bodies scatter across the sand and shrubs, Lunare and Charre and Solare all together. The worst of the fighting is over—the Lunare and their boats are in full retreat. The rest of the tribes stare at us, and with the priests giving me a stage of their own making, at me.

"Followers of Ignos," I yell. "You have seen your falsehoods laid to waste. You have heard the lies of the Lunare dispelled by truths. Our mighty Emperor has given himself to save you from their deception. I bid you not to pick up arms against your brothers, but instead to bare them against the true enemy." I point to the cloud of dust, the boats rising above it in the distance. "Chase them from your lands. From your villages. Reclaim what Ignos has given you, and his miracles will be yours."

As if to accentuate this promise, Malo hefts his gun high, so it's clear to everyone just what miracles would be finding their way forth. Just what this new priestess promises in exchange for loyalty. That is enough. One by one the tribes lay down their weapons, and fall to their knees. All of them, one after another, kneel before me.

Until I stand alone in a circle of thousands.

Even with Bas and the writhing Fassoth tangling in the background, Sax can't look away from the mangled mess in front of him. There were rumors, of course, of what happens when a Sevora reaches full maturity. It takes so much time, is considered so risky for the Sevora itself, that few bother to stay in their hosts long enough for the growth to occur. Instead, at the first sign of the change, the creatures retreat back to the birthing pools or other watery environments, killing their hosts in the process, and wait for new bodies to arrive. Sax has seen those remnants plenty of times; on ships, planets, and space stations that he'd snatched back from the parasites.

This host originally, it appears, had been a Flaum. Sax can see enough fur sticking out to discern that much. Otherwise, though, the thing in front of him resembles nothing he has ever seen. Mounds of discolored flesh pile on one another, fungal eruptions building on what had come before. They rise on stalks, taller than Sax himself at full height, out of what had been the Flaum's body. At the tops of these stalks, the domed tops mesh together with one another, forming an irregular canopy. From that canopy hang, in stringy masses, yellow, orange, and red strands that resemble the tentacles Sevora have while in their swimming, parasitic stage.

All of that is bad enough, but what spins the scene for Sax are the open tubes ringing a rectangular platform in the center, on which the Flaum's body lies. Each of the tubes has a small opening, no larger than the palm of Sax's hand. Red strands from the Sevora hang above many of those tubes, and the ends bulge out, as though something is stuck inside them. Because something is, Sax realizes. The bulges are moving. Independently.

Meanwhile, the orange and yellow strands loop and lift above the top of the Sevora, towards a long series of terminals showing everything from views of the battle beyond the ship, to graphs and meters that, Sax assumes, cover the seed ship's systems.

"Sax!" Bas's yell yanks Sax from his haze, and he sees his pair break free from the Fassoth's arms as the great beast collapses to the floor, twitching away its final seconds of life. "Are you alive?"

"For now," Sax tries to shout the reply, but his voice isn't up to it. The bloodlust leaves him like a breath of cool air, draining away Sax's strength with it. He's been cut, gashed one too many times. Sax can feel each and every bit leaking from his insides onto the metal floor around him. A tangy taste in his mouth. A blur at the edges of his eyes.

Bas appears in front of him, seeming to fall from above. She's jumped the center. Stayed well away from the Sevora. Smart.

"The Fassoth did its work well," Bas whispers, looking Sax over.

Nothing about her expression gives Sax hope.

"The mission, Bas," Sax replies. "Please."

Bas looks back at the Sevora, which seems to be ignoring them,

"I've never seen one like that before."

"You have to destroy it. It's the pilot, Bas. It's controlling this whole ship."

Knock out the Sevora, and perhaps the seed ship would fall into the gas giant's gravity well. A craft this large, no matter its armor, would hit that planet's strong atmosphere and tear to shreds. It's the one thing Sax could see working. Their one chance.

"Take the mask," Bas says and without waiting for Sax to reply, she presses her claws together.

The mask melts off of her and piles in front of Sax. He reaches for it, places his claws into the soft material. The mask flows up and around Sax, into his wounds, where it hardens. Acts as a salve, staunching the bleeding. Sax bears the pain, the agony of the mask sealing the wounds, with his eyes open and mouth taut. Bas has given him life, and he won't dishonor that gift by showing weakness.

"Thank you."

"It's not for you," Bas says, keeping her eyes on the parasite. "It's for me. When you're ready, I'll need your help."

"I'll be there." Though Sax can't guarantee that. His limbs are loose, weak, and the idea of getting up again sends a thin tremor through his nerves.

Bas rises to her full height and spreads her arms, claws glittering. That's when Sax notices the parasite hasn't been idle during their conversation. Orange and yellow strands have stretched from the stalks out towards them, angling towards the pools of Sax's blood on the floor. The strands fork, new offshoots poking out towards them. Growing fast.

Across the room, the Sevora envelopes the Fassoth's

body with more.

Bas begins with the close tendrils, slicing through the ones on the ground with her lower arms. With every cut, the strands retract. Draw closer to the mushroom mass at the center.

"Caution," Sax hisses at his pair's back.

Bas' tail twitches an acknowledgment, and she goes slow, swiping as the strands come into range. Better to be deliberate than risk everything with a creature neither of them understand.

As Bas approaches, one of the red strings, dangling over the tubes, begins to shake, the bulge inside writhing harder. The end of the strand peels back, revealing a slug-like creature with tentacles of its own for a brief moment before it falls down the tubes. A new Sevora.

At the sight, Bas leaps forward, towards the central mass, and strikes the soft heads with her claws. They dig deep, scattering and tearing away milky-white glops of the Sevora. At first, it seems as though Bas will rip apart the entire creature in moments.

But the Sevora isn't done.

Strands shoot up from the floor, over from the Fassoth's body, from everywhere except the red ones hanging above the tubes. While Bas works her way into the creature, the Sevora fibers wrap around her arms, legs, and tail. At first, Bas rips them away, her claws carving away a swath of the strands with a wide swing. The move, though, leave Bas' arms on her left side, and new strings rushed to fill the gap.

The Sevora pins Bas' limbs tight to her body. Bas bites at them, gnashing away fibers, until the strands fill her mouth, forcing it open. Sax knows he needs to move. Needs to help, but his arms and legs won't respond, and Bas is dying in front of him.

I carry the soup to Viera myself that evening. The Lunare lies in her cart, though her skin looks less like the color of death and more like warm milk.

"So did it work?" Viera asks when she sees me. "Did the Lunare run?"

"I thought they were your friends?" I set the clay bowl of soup in front of him.

"Friends change," Viera says. "Besides, none of them are as much fun as you."

"Fun?"

"Not every day you get to meet a high priestess. Not every day you get to run from juars in the Pits."

"Hopefully it's not every day you get so infected you nearly die." Viera shifts her shoulders, attempting to shrug. "It depends. You going to try to cauterize me again?"

I glance away, towards the fire. "Because of Ignos, we won't need to do that much longer. There are so many new things, Viera. So many discoveries waiting for us. We won't need the old ways."

Viera catches the change in tone. She takes a sip of the

soup and her expression fades into a blank slate. Waiting for me.

"Things are going to get more dangerous from here on." It's soothing talking to Viera, someone who has no standing in Charre world, who's as out of place as I am. "Malo tells me the city's elders, in Damantum, they'll pick someone new. Another Emperor. One who won't much like me."

"Like you?"

I nod towards where the priests are eating around their own fire. They keep casting looks at me. Not favorable ones.

"They don't like my power. Now that the fight is over, they're realizing what it means to have someone like me around. Someone who has a god whispering in her mind. How can they compete with that? Who's going to listen to them now?"

"Who cares? Tell them to get real jobs."

I laugh, and it feels good to break free. It only lasts for a second, though, before I remember that Father is just like those priests, and he did everything for my village. "The Charre need their faith. If I tear the priests away, then who will listen to the people? Who will hear their prayers? Who will perform their ceremonies and tend to their sick? I can't be everywhere at once."

Viera doesn't have anything for that one. I keep going, then, to spare her the need to talk. Let her take another drink or two of the soup.

"So I have to work with them. I have to work with Jakkan when we return. He's going to be my only chance to rally everyone to my side."

"Tell me something," Viera says. "You're from some small village in the jungle. Your father is the head of a tribe. You have a family. Why bother with this? You already won.

The Lunare won't come back for a long time. Why not just disappear?"

Because that is not who you are.

"Because Ignos will not let me." I hold my hands up to the coals. It's a chilly night, and the fire's warmth feels good. A little thing, but a normal thing. Good to have those every now and then.

"I don't think you get it. If they don't like you, then it won't matter which god is on your side. They'll find a way, and you'll die."

"I thought you'd protect me." I smile to take the edge off.

"Not going to be doing a lot of protecting like this." Malo interrupts by stomping near our little fire. A motion that kills any further conversation, and leaves both of us staring up at the warrior.

"Kaishi," Malo says, and he bows slightly. "I'm sorry to disturb you, we need your help. My warriors tell me one of the miracles isn't working. Perhaps Ignos will tell you how to fix it?"

I look at Viera. "You see, this is why I need the priests. Why I'll need so much help. Because I need to tend to my own miracles."

"Perhaps you need to make better ones then. Ones that don't break." I want to laugh with Viera again, but Malo's set face keeps me quiet.

The two of us walk through the camp, past fire after fire surrounded by warriors. Finally, we reach the outskirts, where a set of warriors are packing away the miracles. As we approach, they stop and look at me.

"Show her," Malo says. "You asked me to get her, now she's here. Show the priestess what you need repaired."

The lead warrior, a black bear skin over his head and

shoulders, reaches into a crate and pulls out the shard. He holds up to handle.

"It no longer burns."

"Have you refilled the canister?" I ask.

At this, the warriors all look surprised. A simple problem I've already showed them how to resolve before. So why is this an issue now? It shouldn't be.

"Is that everything?" Malo's as exasperated as I am. "Even I could solve that for you."

"No, chieftain. It is not everything." The warrior drops the end of the shard, and then suddenly cracks it forward, towards me.

The others charge with him.

Sax can't see Bas anymore. The Sevora has covered her in its fibers. Sax can, though, still see movement in there. His pair struggling. He has to do something. Has to get up. Sax sweeps his tail, mostly unharmed, behind him and pushes. Rises onto his feet. His claws slip on his own blood and Sax falls onto his side. As he tips, Sax tries to catch himself, and his lower left arm brushes something on his side. A slight bulge in the mask. On the ground, Sax feels for it. Realizes what it is.

The Stim vial. Bas never used hers.

Sax jams his claw into the bag, feels the liquid coat it. Instead of gently withdrawing, Sax scoops his claw out and sticks it, drenched with the drug, into his mouth. A small amount increases concentration, removes pain. A large amount can kill, can send the user's muscles and hearts into such overdrive that they simply explode.

Now, though, Sax needs all the strength he can get.

The Stim burns through his body. Unlike the Oratus' natural bloodlust, the drug doesn't drive away Sax's senses. Rather, his blurred vision vanishes, and he stands again without effort. Whatever damage the motion causes to his muscles isn't going to hamper him.

Not now.

He turns towards the Sevora, towards Bas. Sax can charge, can try what Bas did, but that didn't work. Bas shredded the domed growths, but there are too many of those fibers. Sax needs another solution. He scans the room, finds nothing, and then looks up. Back towards their crashed evac mod, still cradled in broken beams and metal plating up in the ceiling.

A ceiling that meshes with the outer hull.

Beyond the evac mod, Sax can see what has closed the opening behind their crash: a pale gray plastic. Just like the assault shuttles, the stuff acts as a temporary seal against vacuum.

Temporary.

Sax leaps towards the wall, digs in his claws and scrambles up the side towards the top of the chamber. Climbs along the ceiling towards the evac mod. The craft still hangs there, hatch open, as if waiting to be used again. So Sax does use it; as a foothold to rise up into the broken bits of rubble and splintered wires. To the seal itself.

Thin and opaque, the seal feels like a rock when Sax presses his claw against it, but when he flexes the sharp points on his hand, they bit into the seal as they would a soft wood. He can break it. Expose the chamber to vacuum.

Down below, the Sevora is ignoring Sax. Its tendrils, the ones that aren't wrapping around Bas, are concerned with the Fassoth. Continuing to devour the thing's body. No doubt the parasite assumes Sax has nowhere to go. That he will, eventually, become the Sevora's next meal.

Sax latches onto the hull with his legs and his mid-claws, digging the points deep. He will have to hold against the pull, at least for a little while. The Sevora must die before Sax can let go.

With his fore claws, Sax begins to punch at the parts of the seal he can reach. Small holes, not quite through to space. When he'd peppered the surface, Sax lets his tail hang down, then swings it up hard. His tail smashes into the weakened seal and punches through. A third of the seal breaks away immediately, and in front of his eyes, Sax can see the spinning orange atmosphere of the gas giant.

Cold, hard space.

Vacuum feels like a thousand hands at Sax's back, pushing him towards the opening. His claws, though, hold. The rushing air blots out any other noises—a deafening roar as atmosphere flees the ship.

Sax keeps focus on the next step: the seal must remain open. Tiny robots, like spiders, crawl out of slits in the hull around Sax. They scamper to the hole and, from canisters attached to their backs, begin to spray sealant. Attempt to close the hole.

Sax isn't going to let them.

With his foreclaws and tail, Sax scatters the robots. Sweeps them away in bunches. The seed ship will send as many as it can to the breach until it seals, and there would be millions of the things on a ship this large, but Sax doesn't need to fight them forever.

Sax risks a glance at the Sevora and sees a mass of strands. All colors, all rising towards him, like a plant growing at an incredible rate. They rise around the evac mod, which shifts in its cradle as the vacuum pulls at it too. In a moment, the strands will reach Sax. In a moment, they will wrap themselves around him, and his desperate attempt might end. Even so, this is his only option, and Sax can't give up now.

So he keeps swiping at the robots, keeps the seal clear, and suddenly the strands are flowing past him. They attempt to bend; Sax sees them twist as the vacuum pulls them past, but the fibers aren't strong enough. One of the Sevora's mounds blows by, a larger chunk.

The rest of the Sevora follows—the vacuum pulling the entire creature up and out, sucking it through the open seal and into space.

Something's missing. Sax sees the strands go past, but no Bas.

Where is she?

Sax tears his eyes away from the disappearing parasite and looks down again. Bas is there, clinging to the evac mod, looking battered, but alive. She meets his look, and Sax sees her mouth open, but the vacuum roar blots out any sound. Sax waves with one claw, stops sweeping the robots away. In a few moments, they'll complete the seal again. Sax and Bas will be safe. He watches the little things get to work.

Until a massive, white shape flies up from the ground, bounces off of the evac mod into the broken seal and splits it all the way apart, sweeping the spider bots with it. Sax feels the thing strike his back, knocking his hold away, and then Sax is through, following the Fassoth's huge body into the open black of space.

There are moments when time seems to freeze. When everything slows and I find myself aware of all the things that escaped my notice seconds ago. I see the blank eyes of the four warriors arrayed against me, all of them dead set on mine. I see their mouths carving into growls and shouts, which drown in the noise of our army's victory celebration. I see their arms reaching towards me, or drawing their kukri.

Behind them, the desert stretches to the dark horizon, shaded gray from Nomis' glow mixing with roaring fires. The light from those same fires casts an angry orange upon my attackers, giving them the look of the devils my father used to harangue our village about. Demons and monsters that would take those who failed to pay the proper respects.

As they come for me now.

I fall away, stumbling back from the four attackers and, tripping on a rock, landing on my back. I don't stop, but press my hands against the dirt, pushing myself further. Anything to keep moving. In front of me, the warrior with the shard casts its black, glinting death.

Malo's kukri catches the strike as the shard whips forward, knocking the attack aside. Malo follows his own block, setting his feet and swinging his other kukri towards the attacking warrior's chest. The hooked edge leaves a wide red gash as it cuts, and the shard-wielding warrior steps back, gets some space.

"What are you doing?" Malo shouts at the warriors, though he doesn't need to. The warriors themselves are answering his question on their own. They cry out infidel, blasphemer, assassin. Maker of foul things.

Dark names pour from their mouths as the four come for me. Malo's right kukri catches the shard as the warrior strikes, and the black-glass edges bite into the kukri's wooden haft. With a hard yank, the warrior pulls the kukri from Malo's hands. Two of the other warriors, their own kukri drawn, force Malo into a desperate defensive dance, with his single kukri working to deflect the strikes.

Leaving me with the last warrior, the brown fur skin nearly hiding his face as he moves toward me, kukri ready to strike.

"Stop!" I yell loud and clear. It's the only thing I can think to say.

The soft desert air carries my command above the singing and drinking, and my voice pierces the celebration.

My cry makes the attacker pause. He looks beyond me now, doubtless at all the others now bearing witness to their deeds. His death for this is certain. His hesitation slides into desperation, and then resignation. He takes a stride, raises his weapon, and then grunts as a thrown kukri embeds itself in his side, and then he falls.

Malo.

He's to the left of me now, and he's thrown his only defense to grant me a little more time; a few more pushes of my feet against the ground, scrambling away from my enemy. I hear my friend scream, angry and pained, as the other warriors find their marks. Malo disappears to the dirt, the two warriors beating him to the ground.

You must move. To the crates. They are your only chance!

Ignos is right. I get to my feet, spy the other three crates nearby, and run towards them.

"High priestess, submit," the shard warrior says, advancing towards me as I close on the closest crate. As I grab the lip and push it open. "You've been speaking the words of devils. And now you have killed our leader. The holiest one himself. As Jakkan said it would to be, so it is. Answer for your crimes. Reclaim what honor you can."

Jakkan. Why would the high priest say the Emperor would die?

At the bottom of the crate, lying there on cloth woven for its bed, is the weapon Malo had used earlier that day. Fit to fire rounds, with a new case of them already loaded. I pull the weapon out, straining to lift it, and turn as the warrior raises the shard.

"Jakkan is spewing heresies and twisting your mind." I'm talking as I try to find the trigger, remember how this one works. "Think! Who but Ignos could create devices like the one you hold, like the one in my hands?"

The warrior's eyes slide to the weapon. Cold and gray in the dark, then he glances back up at me. "Such things are not meant for man."

His arm goes back, the shard flies high, and I find it, the smoothed metal that gives the slightest bit as my finger brushes it. The trigger. I press it in.

The gun kicks against my shoulder again and again, and I ignore the bruising pain of every kick. The gun's point bounces further up with every round, with every ear-splitting shot and echo and crack.

Red blossoms in front of me, and the warrior collapses into the dirt.

You can let go now. It's done.

Only then do I realize the gun itself has stopped firing. It's only clicking its empty magazine. I'd fired all twelve rounds. Most of them, going by the looks of my aim, arcing high into the sky.

The fighting is over.

The other two warriors are being pulled away by Charre, disarmed and captured. Other bear and lion soldiers close in front of me, barricading me with shields and spears in case these four are merely the first attempt.

My warriors—as I've already started thinking of them—escort me in a phalanx back to the priests, to Viera and her fire where they set up a ring around me, facing outwards and glaring at all comers. My priests offer tea, clamber to sacrifice the assassins with the dawn.

I nod. I agree.

I think only of Malo.

For a life lived in ships, Sax has never truly been in space. Never experienced the creeping chill of the great beyond, the black void. As he flies, he can only think about one thing:

Bas.

Sax has her mask. He'll survive in vacuum for a long time, with the armor protecting him from cold and recycling his air. Bas, though, will live only moments. Sax can't rotate his body, so he turns his head, tries to look towards the seed ship, already speeding into the distance, already falling into an orbital decay.

"This is Sax, hailing for rescue." Sax makes the call without thinking; standard procedure if they are knocked free from a ship.

The mask's communicators aren't long range, but Sax can see plenty of action around him. The battle continues. Someone will hear, will track the signal. Sax sees it then. A speck rising up from the seed ship. Heading his way, though Sax knows it won't reach him. The evac mod. Floating free from the larger craft. Its smaller size means its orbit will last longer, it might stay up. There's a chance, Sax knows, that Bas is in that mod.

He chooses to believe she is. The hope makes the long drift through space easier, makes repeating his calls for rescue more urgent. It's about saving his pair now.

It seems like forever before a shuttle floats into view. Before another Oratus, this one tethered to the craft, grabs Sax from his endless orbit of the gas giant and pulls him inside. From there, a series of moments pass as Sax directs the crew to capture the evac mod before it descends too deep into the atmosphere. As the Flaum medical officer on the shuttle peels off Sax's mask and begins applying treatments. Numbing agents, stitches, and more. Sax barely pays attention. He stares at nothing, running replays of the last few moments on board the seed ship.

He'd seen her, Sax is sure. Clinging to the edge of the mod. Watching him. Waiting for the seal to close. Would she have had the time to get into the mod? Close the door before all of the atmosphere drained? If Bas hadn't given Sax her mask, she would have—no. That is foolishness.

The mask is the only thing that let Sax continue breathing that close to the vacuum, that allowed him the energy to finish the mission. Bas made the right choice.

The shuttle loads the evac mod through its tiny bay, meant more for landing craft than something like this. Sax pushes himself off of the medical table, ignoring the protests of the Flaum, and runs. The door to the bay slides open as Sax approaches, just as the pair of Flaum on the shuttle crack the hatch. The mod's entrance swings up, joints creaking, but Sax doesn't wait for it to finish moving before he dives inside.

He wraps his arms around his pair, careful to keep his claws from poking through her scales, and Sax carries Bas from the mod. Lifts her to the medical bay, and, when the Flaum waves at Sax to put Bas on the sole bed Sax himself had just left, Sax obeys.

Later, when Bas asks Sax what he'd been thinking at the moment, why he'd interrupted his own treatment to do what either of the other two Oratus were more than capable of doing, Sax replies that he wasn't thinking anything.

Instinct.

Instinct had saved his life, and now it had saved his pair's.

Low on oxygen, covered in strange pokes from the Sevora's tendrils, Bas goes directly from the shuttle's medical bay to the ship's hospital when they dock with Evva's commanding vessel. Sax, still weak himself, leans on Gar for support as he watches Bas, unconscious, receive precise attention from a swarm of robots. It isn't until one of the things, covered in arms and instruments, tells Sax that Bas will make an eventual recovery, that Sax feels the universe right its tilt. His ears stop ringing and, for what feels like the first time, Sax sucks a full breath through his vents.

Gar and Lan laugh, then. A happy hissing. Through the translucent wall behind them, a fiery bloom blossoms against the orange planet. The seed ship, derelict without its piloting parasite, crashes into the atmosphere.

Another mission accomplished.

I wake up surrounded by warriors and priests. Ignos rises as he has every day of my life to this point, but when he shines on me now, I'm told Ignos shines on an Empress. A woman who united the Charre and Solare. Who drove away their enemy. Who hears from Ignos himself.

Leaders from villages and tribes approach me in a train, each one bowing and offering allegiance. Malo is still clinging to life, so Viera stands near me, hand on her weapon. Surprise hits faces as people realize my closest guard is a Lunare, but right now I can't think of dealing with all of this alone. I barely know what to say. I thank them, and speak what Ignos tells me.

Ignos pushes, through me, for the tribes to pledge their loyalty. Not to the Charre, but to me. This too causes a stir, but when they remember the miracles, nobody questions it.

Part of me waits for Father. Did he join the Lunare as they swept through the jungle? Are the hunters of my village here in this gathering?

But they don't appear, and as the last leaders say their

vows and begin taking their forces home, I'm left at the head of a Charre force that, too, needs to be moving. The sooner we get back to Damantum, the sooner Malo gets better care.

The sooner, Viera says, we can deal with Jakkan.

The two of us spend the march back together, with me in silent consultation with Ignos while Viera spins tale after tale. The woman seems to have a hatred of silence, and now that her illness has returned her voice, Viera never lets it rest. I don't mind the stories of the underground, the dark caves and high mountain cliffs.

When Ignos lets me listen, anyway.

The god is busy. He tells me plans, things I must do to keep his favor now that I have the power to make them happen. First come pools full of a strange mixtures of plants and minerals. Housed inside buildings, if possible. Then will come forges and factories. Massive structures that will transform the Charre into a state unrecognizable from now. Ignos's vision is sprawling, but it is a vision.

I made my way here, to the top of a throne I never wanted, and guaranteed the safety of the Solare tribes. My plan is complete. Ignos tells me what comes next, and I'm grateful for it. After two days—the wounded make our return a slow one—the walls of Damantum appear. The first time I saw those walls, they struck me breathless. Now, it's unease. A nausea that I recognize from before the sacrifice, from when I first spoke as a priestess to my village.

Actions are about to be taken that I cannot reverse.

At midday we reach Damantum's towering gates. They're closed, and Jakkan, with a cluster of priests and curious citizens, stands on top, staring down at me.

Break him, Kaishi. You cannot allow threats to your power to stand. He tried to kill you. Us.

"Hold here," I announce. I don't want my first act as Empress to be an attack on my own city.

I walk out in front of my force, and only Viera follows me. The two of us are alone on the sallow grass, an easy target for an assassin, though I feel Jakkan would have to be truly brazen to attack in front of everyone.

"Jakkan," I shout. "Tell me why the gates of my city are closed to me?"

"The holy city does not open to heretics," Jakkan replies. "You know I cannot let you return, Kaishi. You know that the source of all your strength is a dark one. Without the threat posed by your supposed gifts, the Lunare would not have killed our Emperor. They would have been our allies. Instead, you drive us to war and corrupt the city and its people in your quest to rule."

"I do not try to rule," I answer.

Jakkan's words catch me off guard. It's a strange argument to make. Why would I have gone out to fight the Lunare, if it was my intent to take over? As I look at the people standing on the wall, and glance back at my own force, I realize Jakkan isn't talking to me.

Before I come up with an answer, the high priest repeats his accusations, going into even more florid detail about the many atrocities I will commit to secure my place at the head of the city. As he speaks, I see the conflicted stares of my own army, of the crowds on the walls.

Jakkan is trying to do more than prevent my entry.

He is converting my empire.

You inspired a village, a city, and an army, Kaishi. Do not let this fool stand in your way.

Ignos is right.

"Then tell me this, Jakkan," I interrupt. "You say the miracles, brought to us by Ignos through me, are the work of evil, yet they cast the Lunare from our lands. They avenged the Emperor. They save the lives of our people each and every day. How can that be evil?"

Jakkan opens his mouth to rebut me, but I keep talking. I understand the high priest's trick now. Establish momentum, draw the audience in, and let no one divert me from my course.

"Why did the Emperor, the holiest of holies, choose to bring me with him instead of you?" I scan the faces of the crowd as I shout, meet as many eyes as I can find. "Perhaps it was because you were disloyal. Because he did not trust you heard the true words of Ignos. You, who sent assassins to kill me."

By Jakkan's face, I know I am correct.

"Lies. Lies and slander cast upon me by this newcomer. She isn't even a Charre herself. She is a Solare! Not one of us!" Jakkan sweeps his arms high, beseeching the crowd. "Stand with me and cast out this usurper, this witch, who threatens to—"

A familiar crack echoes across the plain. The shot strikes Jakkan in the shoulder and the high priest lurches back from the parapet and falls out of sight.

Viera, her pistol drawn, shrugs at me. "Thought he was calling you an awful lot of names. Didn't find that to my liking."

Being placed on medical hold is, to Sax, the worst form of punishment. He'd let himself get hurt—mauled by a Fassoth, really—and, as a result, is quartered in the medical wing of Evva's ship. Healing isn't even the priority —Sax endures pokes and prods, injections and examinations to see whether exposure to a mature Sevora could result in something strange.

Which is why Sax isn't surprised when the door to his quarantine room opens without any warning. Consisting of a bed, table, and an Oratus-fitted chair, Sax watches the feed of the battle—now winding down, with ships either retreating or cleaning up scrap—playing on the quarter of one wall serving as a screen.

"Sax, you've been cleared," Evva, her crimson scales bright in the light, explains as she walks into the room. It's tight with both of them in here, and they swish their tails around until they find a clear landing space. "Bas, however, is still recovering, but we can't wait for her before moving. Thanks to the defector, we know now that this wasn't what we hoped for. There are still more

Sevora ships out there, Sax, and now we know where they are."

"Defector?"

"The infected Oratus, Avan," Sax catches Evva's glance behind them before she says his name.

Checking for eavesdroppers.

"There are cameras in here, commander," Sax says. "But nobody's going to check them if nothing irregular happens."

Evva stays taut, her claws clenching, but she continues, "He's been providing very interesting information that I'm working to verify. The implications, Sax, could be enormous, and I tell you this for one reason: I trust you, and few others."

"He wanted to save the Sevora," Sax replies. "What is he telling you?"

"That there may yet be a reason to stay our hand," Evva hisses. "Of course, he could be wrong, and if he is, I shall enjoy handling the execution personally."

"You're not going to tell me, are you?"

"Too many ears, Sax. But I didn't come here to talk about Avan. I have more mundane orders for you. We've learned about a seed that made landfall on a planet known to have intelligent, if pre-awakened, life. We rather the Sevora didn't corrupt the world entirely."

Sax sits back on the bed. Looks at his claws. "I'm not a cleaner. There are many others, less experienced, that could do this. Why me?"

Evva moves closer, sets a clawed hand on Sax's shoulder, leans in and whispers "Because I need you alive, Sax, for what might come next. Keeping you from the front is the easiest way to do that, and this assignment serves as a viable excuse."

Evva straightens and announces, loudly, "I know it isn't the assignment you wanted, but the fleet is moving quickly and we don't have time to wait for your recovery. This mission will be an easy way to ease you back into active duty. Bas too."

Sax, left with few options, stands as Evva moves to leave the room.

"I will complete the mission to the best of my abilities, commander."

"As ever, Sax. I honor your life." Evva bows as she says the formal words.

"It is my honor to give it." Sax bows in kind, and then Evva is gone.

D o I know what it means to be an Empress? To lead the Charre, not my own people, as I'm barely seventeen summers?

No.

But I have a god speaking through me. I have a bracelet full of miracles. And as I step outside the Vaos' chambers, an adoring crowd chants my name. Promises my every command will be carried out. In the days after my return, I presented small miracles furnished by the Cache to Damantum's elders.

One by one, I swayed their opinions with medicinal ointments, plans for new, personal miracles, and, in some cases, with gold and artifacts that Jakkan, who had met his fate under the black-glass knife, had left behind. When the time came to choose a new leader for Damantum, no one else even bothered to submit their name.

On my left stands my personal guard, a Lunare named Viera. Her old, ruined clothes replaced by the finest Charre cape and cloth. Green, like my own. On my right stands the leader of my armies, though Malo kept standing, for now, by a pair of lion warriors.

Together we stare over my city, over the walls to the vast fields where the changes are already starting. Black smoke rises, thunderous fires burn deep; new miracles being born.

All ours, Kaishi. All ours.

The black pool burbles, pops and churns in front of me. A pair of tanned, cloth-wrapped workers sweep long-handled poles through the same mix that had brought my god to me, keeping what's inside churning, bringing it closer to what we need.

Well done.

I'm smiling as I look around the chamber, walls lined with lit torches, and see a second pool slowly filling as more workers dump buckets of the mixture into a stone pit. Alchemists create each new batch of the mix; a blend of plants, minerals, and water.

My fellow gods will be happy. Proud of what you've made.

Ignos talks about his fellow gods a lot now, but that's not the only thing that's changed.

With the Cache, the people who call me Empress are crafting one miracle after the next. It's like watching a fire-burned jungle grow: something wholly different emerges from the landscape. My people, our world is changing. The words taste strange to me. *My people.* The Charre were, not long ago, enemies. Or, at best, adversaries to be wary of when they crashed through the jungle to my village.

Now, they scream my name when I walk the markets. They drink every word I preach. Take my every order as a dream.

Months ago, I was a sixteen year-old girl with no real future. A small tribe Solare waiting for something to happen. Now, I'm getting called by a pair of priests and told it's time to lead a ceremony.

I leave the pools, following the trail of torches up and out of the temple. When Ignos tells me that when they're ready, we'll use a device my metalworkers are making to send a message to where the other gods are staying. We'll tell them that it's time to come home.

When the rest of the gods arrive, then truly everyone will see as I have seen, will know what I know, and all of my people will be saved.

I don't know about that part, but not having to struggle for food, not having to carve out the hearts of captives and pray for rain, that sounds pretty good.

Still, I'm not an Empress of nothing. Evidence of my people's prowess is on display as I climb the hard stone steps into the Vaos' main chamber. The windows on either side let light in from precise angles so that a golden glow fills everything. Heat comes with it, comforting after the cool air underground. Incense, burning in several small vials around the chamber, hides the musk of a city in full growth.

There's something new hanging on the walls: three clear globes with black bases latched to the stone. I go to the first one and press a small round, raised area close to its bottom. The globe flickers, green sparks popping up from inside it. After a moment, they steady, keeping up a cascade that brightens the room.

"A sparker, Empress," says one of the ever-present priests awaiting my command. "A new miracle, though this one of our own making."

"Our own?"

"The inventor took what the Cache provided and made her own modifications, Empress." The priest bows deep. "She mentioned that if you wish it to stop, all you need is to release the button."

I do so, and the sparks die off immediately. "Tell this inventor to come here soon. I need to congratulate her."

Your people are growing up, Empress. I am impressed.

I smile at the voice in my head. Ignos doesn't talk as much these days. He is, he tells me, pulling and weeding through more of the information from the Cache. Once the pools are ready, things will move quickly and he needs to be prepared. When I ask him for what, he doesn't reply.

I like it when he talks to me. Ignos is the only one who truly knows, after all, who I am. Where I came from. He keeps our grand show going. Keeps my people from finding out who I really am.

I reach up and adjust the emerald headdress so that it fits more comfortably. The shawl on my shoulders is similarly green, a homage to where I came from. One of the few I allow myself. I can't be seen as a Solare. I can't be seen as less than the people I lead.

"They are ready for you." My lead general and commander, and my friend, Malo joins me in the chamber. To the lion's mane framing his face and shoulders, he's added a fine white and gold robe, a symbol of his rank. I think he looks better in the plain skirt of a fighter, but then, I come from a simple village. "Only adoration today, Empress."

"Don't call me that," I reply. "You know my name."

Malo quirks a smile. "I do. But now, especially right now, you have to be a leader. And a leader needs her title."

I don't argue, because he's right, as he is about most things. So I follow Malo as he walks ahead of me. As soon as he appears at the threshold to the great steps, their mottled gray stone sprawling in front of him, horns blow. A cheer rises up, one that continues and grows as I join Malo. As I raise my hands to the crowd.

Thousands throng into the square around the Vaos. For a moment I can't resist, and look up behind me at the twin altars, up those many steps. They glow in the noonday light of Ignos. Each of those altars holds a prisoner. Ones caught plotting against me.

Not every Charre likes the thought of me leading their empire.

Once, I'd wanted to end the sacrifices. I'd never relished holding the black glass knife, making the cuts. Ignos, though, warned me to wait. Told me that such ceremonies might be useful. He is right.

I walk up the steps, the crowd cheering behind me. Today, I'm grateful. I won't be wielding the knife. Instead, a pair of younger priests carry the burden. New ones in my order, and they'll be doing slicing.

I watch, and occasionally look over the sea of smiling, cheering faces, and this time when I speak the rites and prayers, I add new ones. I tell my followers to believe, to get ready, because their time is nearly here.

Ignos is coming for them.

Sax admits that this is one of the prettier planets he's ever seen. From space, the swirling whites layer over large swaths of blue give contrast with the brown and green continents. The colors of life.

And life mixed with the Sevora means danger.

"Briefing, how long have the Sevora been here?" Bas, his pair, asks the line of terminals in front of her rose-gold body. Much more fascinating than Sax's own gleaming gray, one of many reasons why Sax is infinitely happy Bas shares his existence.

They're standing in the bridge of their craft. A shuttle they've been squeezed into, seeing as Oratus are massive creatures. Four clawed arms, two taloned legs, and a tail, all covered in hard scales, makes for awkward seating arrangements.

Bas is talking to the shuttle, to a briefing program and the windshield's sudden shimmer starts its response. The program scans its available data for an answer, then flashes green as it finds one and molds it into a conversational phrase.

"Less than a single local orbit," the program replies in the voice of Evva, their commander. "By conventional measures, and the estimated technological level of this planet, you have enough time to interrupt the process."

Sevora move quickly to establish their foothold, to capture a race and build their infrastructure. If the planet is truly primitive, it can take longer. Sax, though, is more surprised at the look of this planet than anything. Atmospheric scans and visual data indicate a world rich in resources, with a hospitable climate.

It's surprising the world isn't already settled, inducted into the galaxy at large.

"Evva, why is this an unknown planet? We're not on the fringes." Sax addresses the program as if he's talking to his commander.

It's easier that way.

The windshield flashes red a second later. No logged answers.

"Transmit question," Sax says and the program beeps acknowledgment.

Evva's ship is a long ways from here. Light-years. The briefing programs use quantum tuning to leap the distances —micro changes in this shuttle's program shift the designated one on Evva's ship—but the process takes time. Every letter of Sax's question would be sent one by one, registered by Evva's program, and then Evva's answer, when she chose to send it, would be received by the shuttle in the same way.

It's why memory dumps are more efficient—simply spew everything about a given mission into the designated briefing program before leaping away and make it easier for the team to look things up.

Of course, this is only necessary because the Vincere forces split up. They destroyed the last seed ship—a mobile

Sevora breeding ground—and now Sax and Bas have to clean up a Sevora that escaped.

Which is why the Oratus have come; One Sevora, left alone, can rebuild the entire race. It's happened before.

From orbit, they spend revolutions scanning the planet and find the only real concentration of civilization is in a broad belt just north of its equator. An East-West stretch that covers a range of climates.

They pick up structures, movement, and even some signs of energy use. It's strange to see life so concentrated in this one part when there's a whole world to explore, but Sax isn't here to ask questions. Isn't here to learn why these people chose to do as they have. He's here to make sure they can continue to make their own choices.

And if they can't, he'll save them from that fate too.

The high, healthy stalks signal a great harvest is on the way. I point across a rolling hill, covered in yellow wheat, towards a roving herd of goats farther off in the distance. There are several dozen of them, roaming around a couple of shepherds. If I had a pair of the new telescopic eyeglasses our metal-workers are making, I could likely see the silver collars around the animals' throats, and the shock-buzzers in the shepherds' hands.

"Are they yours too?" I ask the man standing next to me, who laughs.

There's real joy in that laughter, a big-hearted chuckle that says more about the state of my people than anything else.

"No, Empress. I tend the crops, and they tend to the goats. In exchange, I give them food and they give me milk. It works for the both of us."

"It works for the Charre," Viera, standing behind me in her emerald leather armor, hand perennially on her pistol hilt, says. "Looks like you're having quite the year."

The farmer laughs again, dishes Viera a knowing look to

say he doesn't begrudge his own success. "It's been a wonderful year for everyone. Ignos has favored us, and the alchemists' fertilizer has made our stalks grow tall, hard, and strong. This season will be the best we've ever had. Not one in Damantum will starve."

"And none of your purses will be empty," I say. The farmer nods, but says nothing else.

Societies must either be desperate or thriving before they'll invest in something new. Be happy yours is on the latter side of that equation.

"Have we seen enough for one day?" Viera asks.

We've been visiting the major landholdings outside of the city. Crawling up and down the wide sloping hills and mountains that overlook the glorious metropolis that I now name my home. Damantum, city of thousands upon thousands, all of whom call me, whether they wish to or not, Empress.

I'm still not used to surroundings of brick and stone, and the chance to get out of the city, feel the wind in the wild free air instead of the stultifying smells of sulfur and waste, has been a treasure. One I'd rather not relinquish until I have to.

"Are there anymore?" I say, both to Viera and the farmer.

"Depends, Empress," the farmer says. "There's not many who wouldn't step outside to thank you. But most of us, especially as Ignos draws down, have to see about feeding our own families. Finishing our chores. Life out here doesn't wait for ceremony."

"You'll wait on your Empress just the same," Viera says.

"Of course, of course, I didn't mean to imply any disrespect," the farmer looks at his hands. Wrinkled and calloused, though he himself is not that old. "What I only mean to say, is my wife, my children, they will be missing me."

I shade my eyes, look to where Ignos is bleeding down towards the horizon. The act reminds me of the four guards standing near us. My Shadows, Malo calls them. A permanent part of my life, especially after Jakkan, the former high priest, hired assassins to kill me. Ferociously loyal, Malo says. Personally reviewed by himself. I trust them.

I trust Viera too; a Lunare traitor who, nonetheless, has helped me become who I am. As I look at her, what really holds my attention, what draws a frown to my face, is the pistol looped through a leather belt on her waist.

We are advancing through ages. Faster than you could ever imagine. Guns are a necessary evil. Simple, deadly. They'll keep you alive long enough to get to better ways of waging war.

Though, with the Lunare driven back, I don't know who we're going to be fighting against. It's clear my people don't either – there's been parties in the streets. Celebrations. Trade is booming with the jungle tribes and new routes are opening to peoples in the West and North. It's a good time to be a Charre. It's a good time to be an Empress.

They land the shuttle in the dark of night over the crater where the seed crashed. Bas found the site from orbit—a rippling, fresh pit where the devastation from the strike is still visible beneath new growth.

It's clear to Sax, as soon as the boarding ramp goes down, that the seed hit some time ago. It's already overgrown with small plants and ferns. Vines stretch around the mottled gray outside of the craft. A small nest of furry creature scatters as Sax claws his way to the ship.

Insects cluster around him, drawn by the shuttle's low blue lights, which provide visibility without being overly conspicuous. Sax brushes away the foliage. Confirms that the seed opened. Confirms that it's empty of the life-sustaining nutrients.

"It's been triggered," Sax says. "The Sevora is gone."

Bas, waiting at the top of the pit, doesn't seem surprised. "We detected plenty of evidence of life on the way here. Likely, someone stumbled upon it."

"It's been here a while, if the growth here is consistent

with other worlds," Sax replies. "Enough time for the Sevora to immerse itself."

The subtext: the two Oratus have to be ready for resistance.

They return to the shuttle, gear up with a pair of miners —heat-blasting rifles—apiece, and Sax grabs his black bars, the ones that, if needed, can cut through anything this planet would care to throw at them.

From there the Oratus head into the jungle. There's no trail, and the thick, snarled plants mean it's been some time since any thing has made its way to the crash site. So, instead, Sax listens. The sounds of the jungle crash over him in waves. The hoots of mysterious creatures, sharp, chirping calls of others, the whistling of wind shooting between tree trunks, making branches and leaves clatter their way from canopy to ground. It's a lovely chorus, even if it doesn't help Sax determine where to go.

But there's something else beneath the sounds—a low, consistent pulse that shakes his legs.

Music.

Bas hears it too, and they both glance at each other, their eyes acknowledging their shared intuition, then head towards the sound. It's slow going – the growth is thick, and the two Oratus commit to staying quiet. It's unclear what kind of resistance they might face, what level of technology. Best to surprise a potential enemy than the other way around.

As they close, the music grows louder, and now there's singing to go with it. Words Sax is surprised to find he recognizes. A cheerful song, of harvests and thanks. Of gifts.

"Sevora gifts," Bas hisses.

Sax agrees. They keep moving and Sax falls into the mystery of the hunt. The strange sweet zone where time dilates and all of his instincts come into focus. Where the slightest whisper of wings feels like the loudest thunderclap.

Which is when he notices they are being tracked.

Sax looks to his left and sees a strange species standing there. Counts two arms, two legs and what appears to be a head growing out of a sizable torso. Smaller than Sax himself. Though, going by the steady eyes staring back at him, this species is not afraid of the Oratus.

The creature holds a short spear, and it angles the weapon towards Sax. Shoves the spear, point first, towards the Oratus. Not close enough to hurt, and Sax recognizes the warning. Step closer, the creature is saying, and that point will make its way into Sax's chest.

Sax's mask would likely turn the spear, and Sax would, doubtless, be able to tear the creature apart. But if Sax can see one, there might be others. Starting an uncertain fight in the dark, risking their lives and health, would be a poor plan.

Though he wouldn't mind if the creature started one.

"What are you?" the creature says. Sax is momentarily stunned to hear the galactic common tongue spoken on this strange world.

It signals Sevora, and Sax tenses.

"Stop," Bas says as she senses Sax's plan. "No Sevora would ask what we were. It would know, it would react."

She's right. Sax straightens, and notices the creature has fallen into its own battle stance. One hand up to its lips, forming a circular gesture, and the other holding the spear, point toward Sax, low and ready to stab.

"We are visitors," Bas hisses. "Newcomers to your land. Who are you?"

"We? We are the Solare. This is our jungle. Our village. Why have you come?"

Neither Sax nor the warrior relax. Both ready to jump at each other's throats. Bas, though, let's her tail touch Sax's his own. Calm down, the gesture says, don't make enemies we don't need.

"We are called Oratus," Bas answers. "We come from far away. Beyond the sky. We are searching for another who came from the stars. Who promises wonders."

Bas' answer works. The creature steps forward, but as it does so, it raises the short spear's point up. "I'm sorry, but you are too late. Who you were looking for left long ago."

Sax straightens up as well. "The one we're looking for?"

The creature seems to remember something. Its face flicks towards the village. Towards the music and sound. "I'll take you. There are others here who would who would be better at explaining than I."

"We would be grateful," Bas says.

They follow the creature through the last bit of jungle. Along the way, they ask and the creature tells them what they are. Humans. Their tribe and people named Solare. Men and women, daughters and sons. The man speaks so freely and Sax doesn't understand why until their escort calls them gods.

Ah.

Sax does nothing to dispel the thought.

They head into a wide clearing from which rise a number of crude stone buildings and one strange, tall mass of wood, moss and rock. In front of it appears the rest of the tribe. The whole group of them dancing and chanting around pleasing pits of fire. Roasting meats, fruits and burning incense fill the six breathing vents stitching Sax's chest with smells.

At least for a moment, because all of it stops as soon as Sax and Bas come into the firelight. As soon as everyone stares at them. In the quiet, there in a clearing, Sax picks up rustling from around them. He looks, and at the borders of the village stand other humans, holding bows with arrows aimed at the two Oratus.

They've walked into a trap.

I put too many peppers on the fish again. The white meat is littered with the green circles, but I can't take them off. Not with Viera watching, her face already breaking out into a grin. So I take the whole thing, the fish, the maize, the peppers and the bits of cabbage and shove it into my mouth. With none of the dignity and refined class that an Empress ought to have. But we're alone, our only company a pair of flickering braziers.

It's the same chamber I used to share with Jakkan. In the Vaos, the grand temple in the middle of Damantum. I haven't made the move to the Emperor's palace yet, and I don't know if I ever will. There's nothing about that place that I like, and all it brings with it are bad memories. Ghosts. Not that I knew the Emperor well, but there's something about going into a dead man's house that feels strange.

Uncomfortable.

The heat builds in my mouth. I meet Viera's mocking stare and suffer through it. The tingling burn coats my cheeks and goes down my throat as I swallow.

Why do you do this to yourself?

I ignore Ignos. This is a moment for concentration. Some battles are won with weapons, some by smarts and sneakiness, but this, this will be won by fortitude.

"You want some of the goat milk?" Viera taunts.

I shake my head. The fire increases to an inferno writhing around my tongue. I don't say a word.

"You sure? I think I see a tear in your eye."

She's not wrong. I feel the moisture on the edges. I blink once. Keep my stare, my smile locked. Finally, finally the spice begins to die. I'm fairly certain I've scalded something, but I'm still alive. Haven't thrown up, haven't spat everywhere, haven't burst into sobs.

Viera notices the color of my cheeks fading away, because she sits back against the wall of the chamber and laughs. "Nice work Empress. Good to know you can handle your spices."

I open my mouth to answer, but it's too dry, too torched to form any words so I close it again and swallow. Then we both hear noise from the entrance. Footsteps approaching.

My quartet of Shadows stands outside, as ever, though the persons involved rotate in shifts. Even so, I'm not afraid. Anything that could best the four of them, would only get through to Viera and her fire-spitting pistol. Past that, I have my own small version, special made for me, stored in a small box at my side. A knife beneath my robe, tied around my waist on a cotton belt. Plenty of options.

I don't have to use any of them, because it's Malo that appears, still sporting the lion's mane, and pulling another groveling man with him.

"My Empress," Malo drops into a quick bow. "This one approached Damatum's gates not long ago. He claims he's from the jungle. From the Solare and that he's run all night to get here."

"A far journey," I say. "One I don't think is possible?"

When I traveled here with Malo, it took a week to make it from my village to Damantum. Hard marching during the daylight hours. That one man could make the same trek in two days?

"Tell her," Malo shakes the man with his hand. Then releases him.

The Solare tribesman falls to the ground, places his palms flat against the stones, and his forehead follows them. He speaks into the ground. "My Empress, I came not from the jungle. I am the tenth in the string. Together, we relayed the message along the route you yourself created."

"I created?" I ask.

Malo coughs. I look at him. "Kaishi, when you ordered us to keep up better communications with Solare and the surrounding towns, we developed a system of runners. Like this one. They're stationed all over Charre, stretching to the jungle east and to the cities west and north, so that as soon as one receives notice they run to the next station, ensuring rapid delivery of critical information."

"You could've led with that," I say.

"Sorry," Malo says. "The man's message muddled my mind."

"Then let him speak it." Viera waves a hand with fish in it, one she shoves into her mouth a second later. I notice there are far fewer peppers on her portion than mine.

The runner starts speaking to the ground again and Malo pulls him up. "Speak directly to the Empress."

The man's eyes dart to Malo, then back to me. I nod, give him a small smile. I've learned that the smallest gestures of kindness can make all the difference in keeping someone loyal. Appreciative. Helpful.

"I can only tell you what I've been told," the man blubbers. "They're saying that more gods have come, Empress. Strange creatures taller than any of us. Four arms and tails. They talk in our tongue." At Malo's look, the man revises. "I mean, the Solare tongue."

"You mean the Lunare," Viera interjects.

"Viera," I warn. The woman has a love of conflict, and I don't have the patience for it right now.

The Charre speak a different version of my home language, one that both the jungle Solare and mountainous Lunare adopted. Trade urges fluency in both, though I've noticed most Charre, including Malo, learn the barest minimum of their partner tongue.

"Keep going," Malo says.

The man inclines his head. "These new gods say they're looking for someone who approached a crashed —" here the man stumbles over a word, then figures it out: "ship. Someone who speaks of magic and miracles."

The man doesn't say it, but we're all thinking it. Me.

I know what this is. Who they are.

I wave away the man. Thank him for the message. Malo escorts him outside, then returns. Returns in time for me to relay what Ignos just spewed into my mind.

They're invaders. From another world. My enemies and the enemies of all you and your people stand for. They will destroy everything to get to you, to me.

I deliver those words to Malo and Viera, then relay Ignos' commands. When I say we're supposed to gather our forces, march, and eliminate them, neither Viera nor Malo seem particularly perturbed at the thought of war, but they're fighters, so why would they be?

"To be honest, Empress," Viera says. "It's been getting a little dull in the city. I love it, but I was thinking I might take another trip to the Pits soon so I don't lose my edge."

"You talk about life and death is if it's a game," Malo says to the Lunare, who sighs as soon as the Charre starts talking. "Every fight should be fought with honor. Dedication. If we must pull men from their families and send them forth, the men must know what we are after. What their sacrifice is for. Then, when we claim our victory, our soldiers can sing of their triumph for seasons." Then Malo shrugs. "It will help us gather volunteers."

"It won't be the size of our force that matters," I say. "But the skill. A small band of our most talented, fearsome fighters. Ones that can fire an arrow with pinpoint accuracy, or slip through the thickest trees without being noticed. Ignos thinks there will only be two of them, though each is worth a hundred of our own."

"A hundred?" This is the first time Malo looks surprised, and I detect a bit of eagerness too. "Then we will take four hundred of our best, and hope that is enough."

"Send the messages, and inform the armorers; we'll need more weapons." I stand, the food suddenly tasting dry in my mouth.

I follow Malo outside chamber, and as he leaves and descends to start the preparations, I climb up. To the very top of the Vaos. I can see Nomis in her shimmering silver hovering over the fiery, beautiful carpet that is Damantum at night. It's a wonder. One I don't want to lose.

I ask Ignos if we'll be okay.

There's no answer.

Sax readies to break for the tree line when one of the singers comes forward from the cluster. This one looks older, at least by the conventional way such things are judged. There's gray in his hair, his skin bears the marks of both battle and age. But his eyes are vigorous. His mouth is tight.

"Our chieftain," says the guard who brought them here, and he sinks down to one knee.

Sax and Bas do not.

"We are looking for someone," Sax hisses as the chieftain nears.

He's a meter smaller than the Oratus. Frail. Easy to break. It's clear this species does not elect their leaders by strength alone. Perhaps they are not as primitive as they appear.

"Someone who changed," Bas continues for him. "Someone who may have talked of strange things. Of other places, of miracles and magic."

Both Sax and Bas know these words, and know this speech. This is far from the first world, or the first species to be discovered in the process of eradicating the Sevora. Once the Sevora became known, the Oratus and others worked to spread as quickly as possible throughout the galaxy. To uncover as many places and intelligent species as they could and bring them into the galactic fold.

This did not always work. Some, too shocked by the appearance of such advanced weaponry, species, and ships, simply failed to adapt. Either slaughtered each other, or lost their own ways and became gears ground in the established order of the galaxy. Their cultures died, and all things that made them unique vanished in their assimilation.

Even that, though, is better than serving the Sevora.

Sax watches as Bas talks. The person shows the signs: there's not enough surprise, not enough shock. Not only at what Bas is saying, but at the Oratus themselves. Creatures three meters high, with four arms and two legs ending in three large claws apiece. Long tails and heads, with mouths full of sharp teeth. Sax's appearance alone should send these people running. That it does not means they have seen or heard fantastical things.

This tribe, this village knows.

"I have heard such talk before," the chieftain replies slowly. "It came from there." He points behind them, to the jungle and towards the place where the seed crashed. "And it left soon after."

"These words do not leave on their own," Sax hisses. "We need to find who carries it."

The chieftain tilts his head. "You need to find a god?"

Sax can't help it. He hisses with laughter. It's clear the village, these humans don't quite know what's going on. The chieftain backpedals a step, and the guard kneeling next to Sax jerks up, spear tight.

"That, humans, is an Oratus laugh," Bas says, and now

she hisses of her own accord. "What my pair means to say, is that what you saw is no god. A species playing tricks. Trying to turn you and your entire world into slaves for its own ends."

The chieftain shakes his head. "It wasn't a creature like you. The words came from the mouth of a girl. My own daughter."

Sax nods. The thing seems to understand the gesture. Good. "The Sevora take over the minds of those they capture. They look and sound like the ones you know and love, but they are not." Sax points to one of the cooking animals, turning on a spit over one of the fires. "Your daughter is like that creature there. An animal, roasting and waiting as a Sevora eats her life."

Bas hisses a chiding sound. A warning not to be too dramatic. To scare or anger these people.

The chieftain only looks sad. "How are we to trust you? You tell us that my daughter is taken by something like that." He points to the meat. Not quite what Sax had intended, but no matter. "You tell me, strange beings, that we should trust you. That we should give you answers. Why?"

Sax glances at his claws, slowly enough that it's clear to everyone what he's doing. "Because this creature must be destroyed. Because it is a threat, not only to you in your world, but to all the others."

Once again, the words fail to faze the chieftain.

"Your daughter," Bas says. She's better with these sorts of connections. "You say she spoke of a god?"

"She didn't speak of a god," he replies. "She was. She is. Ignos is within her."

Bas is about to reply, Sax is staring at his claws as they shine in the firelight. They're sharp, ready.

"Then we will take him out." Bas says.

Malo stands across from me, about ten paces away, with his arms crossed and a sardonic grin on his face.

"You're using that one again?" Malo says as his eyes track to my right hand and what I'm holding in it.

"It's the only one I'm good at," I say, though that's not strictly true.

I have managed to fire one of the guns, as we've taken to calling Ignos' miracles. I even hit the target.

The shard, though, has a more immediate feel to it. There's a weight, as I hold onto the rope grip, that the guns lack. Knowing that when I swing my arms, the interlinking glass shards will whip forward and slice anything in their way gives the shard a familiar feel. It's a weapon I can understand. One I can know.

It's an inferior tool. One you'll need to discard when the time comes.

Ignos thinks most of my choices are inferior, so his judgment doesn't bother me much. Instead, I square my shoulders to Malo, take one glance up at Nomis rising silver behind him, and settle into a slight squat. We've been working on positioning—keeping my knees from locking, resting on the balls my feet, ready to shove off in any direction.

Malo doesn't move. Stands there. Meets my stare.

"I'm ready," I prompt, but he doesn't shift.

He's waiting for you.

I see that now. The only weapons Malo has are attached to his belt; short wooden staves with vicious, sharp talons curling away from the tops. Kukri. The shard has a meter or more of reach on those things, so I take a slow step forward, then snap my wrist.

The shard slides up from the ground, blowing sand as it moves and curls towards Malo's face. Only after I make the move does it occur to me that I could kill my army's leader, and my friend. But Malo slides back a step, turns to the side, and all the surprise attack gets me is the tiniest of cuts on Malo's left shoulder. He keeps his arms crossed. Waits for my next attack.

"I don't want to hurt you." I let the shard settle back into the sand, then pull it back towards me.

"That is my problem, not yours," Malo replies. "What did you do wrong there?"

"I almost had you."

"Almost. What did you do wrong?"

I think, but I'm suddenly irritated. Malo should be focusing on the fact that I nearly shredded his arm off, not asking me questions. I'm about to bark that idea at him, when I see that he's not kidding.

There's a set to his face, to his body, still turned to its side, that says answering this question might be the key between my living or dying some day.

"I was too slow?"

"You were too direct." Malo faces me again, kicks at the sand. "Every move you made led right to the attack you planned. In a real fight, you cannot give yourself away. Feint, then come at me again."

"Won't you know I'm feinting?"

"Not if you do it right."

I take a deep breath. Look to my right, where the camp-fires of my army make a glittering constellation on the dark sand. To my left, where the valley wall begins to rise into a rocky brown cliff. Above, starlight peeks between a rare cloud drift, racing to catch Nomis' glow.

"I'm done for tonight," I say, loosening my grip.

I head towards the fire, making a quarter turn right and taking steps, the shard dragging in the sand behind me.

"We've only just started," Malo says, and I hear him catch up with me.

At his third step, I whirl. This time, I use my body, along with my arm, to whip the shard around. Its glinting blades slice through the air in an arc, whistling as I spin around. I get to see Malo's eyes go wide, see him fall and land on his back in the dirt as the shard whistles above. He and I both know that, in a real fight, I could crack the weapon back and send it slinging down towards him before the Charre warrior would have a chance to move.

"Surprise you that time?" I say.

Malo sits up slow, gives me a nod. "Much better. Though I would not expect that trick to work on just anyone."

"Only on you."

It's what I might have said, but Viera gets there first. She's striding towards us, and by the way she's shaking her head at Malo, it's clear she's seen what happened.

"The Empress alone has that advantage," Malo replies, starting to stand up from the sand.

"Does she?" Viera says. "Do you know why the Lunare win most of our fights, Malo?"

"Because your kind doesn't care about honor."

"Exactly."

"Now you're both annoying me," I interrupt. "Viera, what are you doing here?"

"Food's ready, Empress," Viera looks over at me "Didn't want it to get cold while you're out here playing in the sand."

"Training." Malo joins us. "There may yet come a time when neither of us can defend her, and Kaishi must fight for herself."

"With that?" Viera looks at the shard with the same skepticism Malo showed moments ago.

"I like it," I say again. "It's effective."

"You want effective, try these," Viera pats her pistols. "Instant gratification. No need to get up close. Especially when your enemy has breath like this guy here."

Malo sighs, then looks to me, "Tomorrow, Empress, I'd like to revisit this. Viera has a point—you must be able to feint away an adversary, not only your teacher." He brushes by us before Viera can come up with another insult.

"Why are you so hard on him?" I say to Viera as we watch the warrior go.

"Hard on him? Malo doesn't care what I say."

"I think you're wrong." I put my hand on Viera's shoulder, to forestall her opening mouth. "I'd like both my friends to stop behaving like enemies. If Ignos is right, if what we're up against is as terrible as he's telling me, we'll all need to work together."

"If Ignos is right, Empress, it might not matter."

Dawn finds both Sax and Bas tired. They slept through the night in shifts, one for four hours and the other the next.

Not that an Oratus needs a full night's rest to feel relaxed, but a little bit helps. The morning meal, full of the meat the chieftain labels pork, wakes them up somewhat. Followed by a warm drink of something called tea; a watery, herbal liquid that nonetheless kicks some part of Sax's brain into overdrive.

Then the young warrior that found them in the forest the previous night approaches, says he'll be the one to lead them east. Towards where the chieftain's daughter went.

In the bright daytime, the jungle is colorful. Full of moving animals and birds. Plants twisting in the breeze. Buzzing insects that find themselves unable to get through the masks both Bas and Sax wear, and the two draw jealous glances from the warrior, whose covered himself in sticky, smelly sap that's nowhere close to equaling a mask's proficiency.

They step across ferns and vines, and trails barely

visible until they are already upon them. At one point they hop across a series of stones to cross the shallow river.

Neither Bas nor Sax speak much during the journey. He's absorbing information, keeping an eye out for hazards. Bas is likely doing the same. There's no reason to waste words.

It's not until evening, with the young man never tiring, that they reach the foothills and the first sign of civilized life they've seen in a while. A hardened, deep-wood wall, appearing at the end of the trail with a wide gate, that extends as far as Sax and Bas can see through the crowded, foliage-filled space.

On top of the wall, as the planet's star slides towards setting, a pair of pale-skinned guards look down at them. Unlike their guide, who wears a simple mosswrap, these two wear deep green tunics, cotton clothes. Thicker than necessary, and it shows, based on the sweat that coats their faces.

"What horrors are you?" one of the guard shouts.

The other one says nothing but aims a wide-ended gray-metal tube their way. A primitive gun, though far beyond what they saw at the small village. Its presence is a sign the Sevora is here. A sign that the Sevora's influence is already spreading. The parasite is moving fast.

"They seek an audience with your leader," their guide shouts. "They came to our jungle last night, and so we brought them to you."

"With Avril? What gives them the right?"

Sax looks at the man. He's the same as the other members of their species. Soft, simple. And, Sax has no doubt, easily intimidated. He punches his legs and leaps. High up to the very top of the gate, where he digs his claws into the wood and clamors over. Now he towers over the one who'd asked the question.

Staring down at him, Sax opens his mouth ever so slightly, just enough to give a sure glimpse of all the teeth inside.

Sax senses the other guard aiming his gun and cocking its hammer, and Sax whips his tail. Knocks the weapon from the man's hand and sends it flying.

"We seek an audience with your leader because we want one," Sax hisses. "This Avril will meet us, or they will die. Along with all of you."

The man eyes slide from Sax's face to his left. Sax follows the look. On the other side of the wall is a sprawling tent town. Simple fortifications. Small buildings made of wood and cloth. Not a long-term settlement. A military camp. There are plenty of soldiers, staring up at them. Some are fishing for their own guns, but Sax isn't worried. Even if the bullets could pierce the mask, which Sax doesn't think they can, a few quick shots of his own miner would doubtless render them petrified.

"I can tell her," the guard stammers. "I can send the communication. If it's agreed, we'll let you in. Take you to Avril."

"You will take us to her now," Sax hisses. "She will not refuse."

The man goes even paler, to a shade of white Sax is not used to seeing in the living.

There's a bump, a scratching as Bas climbs herself over the wall. As she picks up the other guard and holds him aloft, off the ledge.

"We will speak to your leader, and we will do you no harm," Bas roars out to the assembling crowd. "If you attempt to hurt us, attack us in any way, we will slaughter all of you. And we will enjoy it."

That last seems to do the trick. Guns drop. Swords

return to sheaths. Just like that, the two Oratus have themselves a captured force.

"Where is she?" Sax asks the guard he's still holding in his claws.

"In our capital, of course," the man says. "Marilo, deep inside the mountains."

"Then you will lead us there. Now."

It has only been months. A single whole season gone. Yet home feels like another world to me. I see the Tier, standing only a fourth as high as the Vaos and infinitely smaller in width and grandeur. I see our stone houses, which felt so large to my old self and now seem as though they could all fit within a single Damantum court-yard. All of my childhood compressed into a fraction of the empire I now rule.

Whatever remains of the girl that left this village dies when I see Father.

When I last left him, he had looked down on me from the Tier. Watched, along with the rest of my village as I had gathered up my meager pack, my mosswrap and marched away with the Charre soldiers—Malo included—from my home.

Now he sees me at the head of great force. Sees me dressed in fine robes, with emeralds hanging from my ears and neck, wearing more on my body than the worth of his entire village. Father doesn't see his daughter anymore. That much is clear.

You have grown beyond him.

I wince at Ignos' words. There's a difference between knowing something and having it told to you. Father, and Mother beside him, lead a small band of our village's hunters; faces I recognize. People who once asked me to do errands, who ran with me through the trees during games. Now they stare at me with guarded faces, hidden souls.

They walk towards me as I stand on the edge of the clearing, with Malo and Viera by my side and several hundred Charre warriors at my back. Common Solare respect dictates a visitor should not enter a village without the permission of its elders, and, despite the ability of my army to raze my home a dozen times over, I hold true to that custom.

"Kaishi," Father says as he comes up to me. I see a flash of recognition as he notices Viera at my side—the Lunare had been trading in our village prior to Malo's arrival—but I cut off any further words.

I step forward, wrap my arms around Father, and pull him in tight. Release and do the same for Mother, who, I notice, enters into the embrace more willingly. She is only hugging her daughter, whereas Father hugs the leader of a rival empire. When I stand back, though, I notice both of them can't resist small smiles. Their simmering happiness warms my heart more than anything.

"They were here," Father continues, guessing at why I've come.

"Who were they?" I reply.

"*What* were they is the better question," Father replies, and I hear a cascade of murmurs make their way through the village hunters behind him.

Murmurs that only grow louder as Father describes a

pair of monsters, taller than any man and with four arms, a tail, and claws as long as Malo's kukri blade.

"But they are no longer here," Malo states as Father concludes his description.

"We sent them away. To the East." Father can't resist looking at Viera.

"You sent them to my people," Viera says. "Of course. Why not, when confronted with devastation, pass it on to somebody else?"

"Better our enemies than ourselves," Father replies.

"Then we will follow them," I say, trying to keep Viera in check. "Either we'll catch them before they reach the mountains, or we'll help the Lunare fight them off. It might even be a chance for our two empires to come together."

Perhaps, with both of your armies working together, you might win.

"Two empires?" Father asks.

The Charre, the Solare, and the Lunare. Three peoples, with the Solare stuck between more powerful neighbors. No one, Father included, could believe the Solare would survive should either the Charre or Lunare let the other have the jungle. Mutual fear keeps my old village alive. Ignos has been telling me the time for that is at an end—I have his guidance, and I should bring the Solare and their resources into my widening grip.

"It will be better, father," I say slowly, measuring his reaction to every word. "With Charre resources and the miracles Ignos provides, the Solare will be happier. Healthier. There will be no more fear."

"You would rule over us?" Father asks, and his voice is innocent.

Careful.

I don't need Ignos to warn me. This man is my father.

I've had a thousand arguments with him, watched as he dismantled the verbal parries of a hundred traders and visitors from other villages. Getting into a war of words with him is a choice I do not want to make. So I stop the fight before it can start.

"I *am* ruling over you," I say. "As your daughter, and your empress. When we turned back the Lunare, the tribes with them pledged their loyalty to me. As have the Charre people."

"As we have not." Father stands straighter.

"As you will do, now." I push hard iron into my voice.

The jungle goes still for a long moment.

"You know we cannot resist you, Kaishi," Father says finally, waving his arm back at the village behind him. "We are small, simple. All we have is our independence. The right to determine for ourselves what is right."

Which has brought them nowhere. You will make them better. You will make the world better, with my help.

"When the Lunare come again, what will happen?" I say. "Whose daughter will you give up next time to send them away?"

I can see those words hurt. My parents do not meet my eyes. Even Malo, the hardened warrior who took me from this place, glides a concerned glance my way. I don't back down. Don't look away.

"There is no other choice, Father," I continue. "You will join, as will all the other Solare. Together, we will make a better world."

He's not giving in. I see him put on a hand on Mother's shoulder, and I know what's coming next.

I came here to help Father, not kill him. So I speak first.

"You told me, when I left, not to resist. Told me that everyone here would suffer if I did," I speak softly, so that those behind Father have to strain to hear. "I'm telling you the same thing now. Join me, help me find the monsters who came here, and save your village. Save our people."

My words douse the fire in his eyes, and once his spark is out, Father nods. For the first time in months, his hands clasp mine, but I feel no love in their grip, only sadness.

They will understand, Kaishi, when you deliver them from their harsh existence. They will love you for it.

I hope, but I don't believe.

Ten humans guide them through the caves. Five in front and five behind. A ratio Sax is comfortable with, as the narrow caverns mean his tail alone could knock all trailing him to the ground while his claws deal with those ahead. Bas being beside him only means any attempt at resistance would be so futile, so useless as to be unimaginable.

Which the stance of their guards, their low shoulders and huffing, nervous breath conveys. Their fear fills the air, mingling with the cool, rusted scent of mineral water coming from the stream sharing their path. The trickle coats the stones on their right, occasionally pooling and then rushing onward again, further and further down.

The state of this world and the creatures on it leads Sax to expect darkness, and he's ready to switch his mask to an infrared spectrum as they descend past the point of daylight. Until he notices glows, of a blue and purple cast, coming ahead of them. The guards make no mention of this, but keep trudging forward. Sax refuses to ask questions, and his patience is answered seconds later when the source comes into view.

Mushrooms and moss, glowing on the rocks in patches. The stalks shimmer blue as they rise from the ground, from cracks in the stone or from the patches of dirt mingling in the crannies. The moss clings to the ceiling, a phosphorescent pink, its shine bright enough to give some idea of where they're going, if still too dim to lay out the path as clear as day.

"Cultivated?" Sax says to the guard leading them, the one he took hold of on the wall, as they pad along.

"Throughout Lunare, yes," the guard replies, a bit of pride making itself known. "They're the only way we get light down here, short of torches. You'd be surprised how many sticks you've got to burn to keep an empire lit."

"So you plant these things along your routes."

"Living beneath the rock doesn't come naturally." As if to illustrate the point, the guard steps carefully around what looks like a rubble from a fallen boulder. "Takes being clever, takes having the guts to deal with problems instead of hoping they'll get better. It's why the surface tribes can't handle us."

"If they can't handle you, then why are you still here?"

Bas touches his tail again, but Sax ignores his pair this time. If they're marching into a dangerous place, to confront dangerous people and demand the head of their leader, Sax wants to know all about them. What keeps these people going, what they're afraid of, and why they choose to live outside the light.

The cave breaks into a wide chamber, split in half by the creek, and wide-pointed stalagmites and stalactites rise from floor and ceiling like alien sculptures. Patches of the moss and mushrooms give the place a surreal radiance, and for a moment Sax feels like he's back aboard the seed ship, stuck in that nightmare world of flashing entertainment, where the parasites could forget the lives they stole from those who deserved them.

"Hard to leave home, I suppose," the guard says as they crunch through the room. "It's not like they've got it better up there anyway. Have to deal with storms, lots of bugs, dangerous animals. Down here it's quiet, and in the cities, always warm. Just saying that if we wanted to, we could take them."

Not if they attacked as poorly as they defended, but Sax doesn't say that. They're far from their shuttle now, and neither he nor Bas has any idea how these tunnels go together. If their guards decided to run away, the two Oratus would have a hard time finding their way anywhere.

"How long have you been here?" Sax asks. "How many cycles?"

"Cycles?"

They speak galactic common, but don't know about cycles? One tribe uses the most primitive spears, bows and arrows, while this one wields guns. The variances here are confusing. Nonsensical. Unless someone outside intervened.

"A standard length of time," Bas is explaining. "Cycles are marked by major events. Like the defeat of the Sevora, or the colonizing of a new system."

"I don't understand the words you're using," the guard replies. "But the Lunare have been in these mountains longer than I've been alive, my father and his father too. Longer than that, I'd imagine."

Long enough for natural evolution? Sax isn't a biologist, but there are certain trends between species in the galaxy; the Flaum have big eyes, furry coats and small bodies because they lived, originally, on a cratered world with little light. Cold, with meager food supplies. Couldn't have been too unlike these caves, yet the people walking the Oratus through these underground pathways, aside from their pale skin, look unsuited to a place like this.

Sax turns these thoughts over in his mind as they trudge along through more, and narrower, passages until they again open up into a chamber. This one, though, is far larger than the first. So big that Sax can't see the ceiling, the far wall. So big that it contains houses, streets, a whole town lit in blues and pinks from mushrooms and moss.

"You think this is big?" the guard laughs, looking at the two of them. "Gove is an outpost, nothing more. A spot to rest before we head on to Marilo tomorrow."

There's noise coming from the village, the sound of drills turning and hammers pounding. Smells of soot and cookfires cling to the wet air, and Sax notes the creek seems to run right through the center of the town. They continue on an avenue alongside it, and Sax is very aware of pressing eyes on him as they move. Their claws are causing a panic throughout, Sax is sure.

Gove's center consists of a rounded courtyard split in two by the creek. Twin walking bridges, with silvery rails over gray stone arches, connect the two halves. On either side is a cut geode, the two broken edges facing each other from across the water, made to stand on small pedestals.

Storefronts, with those mushrooms glowing in the windows, call out offerings for shelter, for mining gear and food. Yet there seems to be nobody here aside from the ten of them. Even the sounds of hammers and drills die away as the group of them move into the courtyard's center.

When the guard stops near the geode, when the other nine with him fan out around Sax and Bas, the Oratus already know what's about to happen. Their claws are ready. Their tails swish. These Lunare are about to make a fatal mistake.

"Looks like you two don't know caves," the guard says. "We've had runners going ahead of us the whole way. Gove is ready for you."

The guard raises his right hand, and Sax notices the fear that had gripped the man on top of the wall is buttressed by confidence. Something's given his courage back.

When the rumblings come, a chorus of them that echo from the floors and ceilings, Sax understands. From each of the seven streets leading into the courtyard, white-furred beasts stride up, each one mounted by a pale-skinned creature. Eyeless, strange and monstrous, the Fassoths tower above their apparent masters.

These things shouldn't be here. Not on a world so far from populated space.

Yet, here they are, and the Oratus can do nothing except surrender.

The object is unnatural. It sits between the trees, and on some of them, having crushed them to the ground in its gray bulk. Ignos tells me it's made of metal, and that it's pieced together part by part, which explains the thin lines running across it. Like scales, only squared and perfect. There's a bulb at the very front, with what looks like a transparent plate across it.

Glass. To see through, while providing protection.

I walk beneath the ship—what Ignos tells me it's called —and stare up. There's several meters between my head and the ship's bottom, and here I see the gray is scarred with black streaks. As if it's been burned. I see where the three struts, two in back and another in front, extend from the ship. The connections are large, circular.

Charre warriors, along with my old village's hunters, look at the ship with me. One of my old village's hunters had seen the craft some days ago. After the two creatures had arrived at my village, after Father had lied to send them away. Now I'm here, with Viera, Malo, and some of my force, to try and learn what we can about the new gods that have decided to visit our world.

Gods. It's not the name Ignos wants for them, but it's what the tribesmen say. What else, after all, could be so different? Could arrive in a craft so vastly unlike anything that we have?

I care about you. They do not. I will give you miracles. They will take your lives.

Good and evil don't determine what makes a god. I put my hand against the front strut, feel the metal and how hot it's getting in Ignos' light. The ship ruined the canopy here, and the light is so bright my left hand is ever-present above my eyes, shading them.

Doing that, I can see that the jungle isn't wasting any time in claiming the ship as its own; nests are forming in creases, bundles of leaves and branches. Ferns and vines are making tentative forays up the struts from the ground, wrapping around the ship's feet.

It's been here for some time already. Well more than a week.

"Kaishi," Malo says, joining me beneath the front bulb. "Can Ignos tell us what's inside? Or how to get there?"

I can't. This is not a door I can open for you.

At my shaking head, Malo sighs. "All this adds, then, is questions."

"It answers one," I say, and Malo waits for me to continue. "Why they came here. Look."

I point to the remnants of the crashed seed, the hole where I found Ignos so long ago.

"They didn't choose this place randomly." I walk to the edge of the pit. Push back encroaching memories, the moment when I couldn't feel my arms and legs, the sucking black ink. "They wanted this seed. They want Ignos."

"We knew they wanted you." Malo isn't impressed, apparently.

"But not me," I look down at myself. "At least, I don't think they want Kaishi. What they want is Ignos, the god inside of me."

Malo tilts his head. "Ignos is inside of you? Physically?"

"I don't know," I say. "When I came here, I found this. Ignos says it was his. So he must have come inside of it, right?"

I did.

"Why would a god need to travel inside such a small ship?" Malo asks, then turns back to the larger, newer one. "If these gods come in something so much larger, then perhaps we really are in trouble."

"Father said there were two of them. Do you think we could lose to so few?"

Malo shakes his head. "A season ago, I would have said no. Now, with what we've seen, with what we've unleashed? I don't know, Kaishi. I don't know if we have any place with warring gods."

I nod. Ignos had implied much the same. Which makes what I say next easier.

"Malo, if they've come here for me, for Ignos, and we can't stop them?" Malo picks up the tone in my voice, pays close attention. "I'll let them take me. Make them promise to leave the rest of our people alone. Then we'll survive."

"But you will not."

"The Emperor, when we faced the Charre, rode out in front," I say, remembering. "He put himself before his army, his people, knowing the risks. Knowing that his sacrifice would be worth it. I can do the same."

Malo puts a hand on my shoulder. "Then, my Empress, we must not fail. We will drive these gods from our lands and make them understand that we are not their prey. You will return to your city a savior, and the world you and Ignos envision will come to pass."

His touch, his words make me smile. "I hope so, Malo. I do."

We stay at the ship a little longer, but can't find any way inside of it, so when Ignos slips down towards the horizon, I make the call to return to the village. In the morning we'll march again. To the East, through the rest of the jungle and towards the mountains. Towards the Lunare.

Towards war.

S even Fassoths, and now seventeen guards. Sax estimates he and Bas could pull their weapons, down one or two of the large creatures with their miners before the others crushed them. Which would leave the Sevora free to continue its dominance.

No. A fight isn't the way. Sax loosens his muscles, moves his claws away from the bars clipped into his mask.

"You have us," Bas says, reading Sax's motions. "Though we never claimed we wanted to hurt you."

"It's not about what you claimed, but about what you are. I am Avril, and the Lunare you threaten are my people," the voice comes from the top of one of the buildings, and Sax notices, leaning over the flat roof, a female of the species. This is the first one he's seen with shock-white hair, with a face far paler than the rest. "Monsters, do you have names? Or should I think of you solely as nightmares?"

She's also the first one to look at them without fear.

"We are visitors," Sax hisses, and both of them give up their names. There's little risk in doing so—either this is the Sevora host, and they will all be dead shortly, or they are not, in which case the Oratus will leave and never return. "We are looking for a problem that chose to land on your world."

Sax and Bas perform an immediate assessment of Avril. The guards are paying her obvious deference, so she must be the leader. Yet, she hasn't ordered them killed, which any Sevora would do. Unless it's already started reproducing. Unless it means to capture the Oratus as well.

"I could argue that you are the problem," Avril says, not moving from her perch, and Sax sees a pair of shadows behind her. Other guards, most likely. "Didn't you disrupt my fortification outside the mountain? Haven't you forced my soldiers to take you here?"

"What we did is nothing compared to what will happen if you prevent us from completing our mission." Bas replies.

"Then persuade me. Now."

"Are you free?" Sax asks before Bas can say anything.

"Free?"

"Do you make your own choices? Are your people able to decide for themselves what to do with their lives?" Sax stays away from the irony in this, as he knows he has no such freedom for his own existence. Still, if he had a choice, Sax would choose to be right here.

Well, perhaps not right here, surrounded by death, but—

"I do. The Lunare do." Avril's curious now, relaxing.

"What we are seeking will change that. Will tear that freedom away and turn you into slaves. Husks made to serve its desires."

"If we met such a creature, we would destroy it."

"The Sevora do not stay in the open," Bas interrupts. "They slip inside your mind, they take you when you are not ready. They could be here, right now, and you would never know."

"They cannot be seen?"

"They live inside you." Sax scans the crowd as he says the words, and he sees the guards' eyes follow his.

Murmurs spring up, and uncertainty spreads. Questions leap to a dozen mouths and die, unasked, as Sax watches the guards assess their friends. Who among them might be one of this creature's pets?

"There must be some sign of this thing you seek," the woman says. "Or why would you be here searching for it?"

"A Sevora," Bas says. "First seeks to rebuild its own society. To create a world where its kind can flourish. You will know its presence by the sudden spark of genius. By the miraculous inventions of things unknown to your world."

These words strike the woman and her face slides into contemplation. It's a long moment before she speaks.

"Not long ago, a grand force of ours swept forth from these mountains intent on ending the constant strife that has plagued these lands. Warring tribes who never seem to tire of sending one another's children to the tops of altars. We prefer not to sacrifice our own, and thought to spread our more civilized ways. However, our force was stopped. Halted by an army with weapons they should not have had, beyond our own abilities. Weapons they did not have months ago."

"East of here?" Sax says.

Avril shakes her head. "West. The Charre empire. Ruled now, I'm told, by a young priestess. One who, as you say, came to power with a string of miracles. Who promises much, and then delivers."

The village elder. The old man. Either he lied or Avril is lying now. A Sevora tactic. If Bas and Sax did as Avril is suggesting, if they left and went all the way back west, they would lose so much time. Enough for a Sevora to devise an escape, or develop more lethal tools.

"We can make you an offer," Sax says, and Avril waits, letting Sax continue. "Let us examine you. Find you clear of the Sevora. If you are, then we will leave and look for this priestess you mention."

"And if I am not?"

"Then you will not feel anything," Sax replies. "Your death will be swift, painless."

"Yours would not be," Avril says. "Kill me here and so many will descend upon you, my people will grind you into nothing."

"Then let's hope it doesn't come to that."

Avril takes the words without emotion, but vanishes from the rooftop. Moments later she pushes open the front door of one of the nearby shops. Strides towards Sax, who looks down at her with toothy determination.

"What is your test?" Avril asks.

"Stand still," Sax replies.

He reaches behind him and grasps a thin silver bar attached to the back of his mask. Takes it forward and holds it next to Avril's head.

The guards around them tense, and the Fassoths lean forward against their saddles, ready to charge at the slightest command. With his right foreclaw, Sax turns the silver bar so that it's level with Avril's left ear. She's staring at him now, close, and he can see that her eyes are a kind of pinkish-red. A fascinating color.

Sax moves the silver bar so that it touches the woman's ear, and then he presses in on a slight indent a third of the way up the device. It hums, a frequency too high for them to hear, but Sax feels the vibrations. A Sevora would feel them all down its many nerves, shaking and dislodging the creature, spurring it to escape the twinging agony.

Nothing happens, and Avril continues to stare at Sax until he pulls the bar away.

"Tell me more about this force to the West," Sax hisses, and the corners of Avril's mouth curl up into a smile.

Several more marching days pass before the Lunare outpost's wooden walls fade in through the morning jungle fog. A barrier my force can easily pass by burning it down.

I hope we don't have to.

A pair of Lunare, standing atop the gate with their guns held ready, stare out at Viera, Malo and I as we approach. There's a chance they'll just shoot us, so a trio of Charre warriors, holding thick, long and wide shields, march in front. The cover isn't total, but makes the odds of a good shot low, and my line of archers with bows stretched and arrows ready ensures the Lunare would only get one off.

"We're here to talk," I shout, as the two guards say nothing at my approach.

"A lot of people just for talking!" the right guard replies.

"It's a dangerous subject," I say. "Where is the leader of this outpost?"

"Busy," the same guard replies.

"You know who you're talking to?" Viera interrupts.

"This is the Empress of the Charre. You'll treat her with respect, or I'll shoot you where you stand."

I'm at once annoyed and flattered by Viera's response. It's nice to know she cares, though I don't want a fight here if I can help it. I didn't bring the thousands upon thousands of warriors I'd need to assault the Lunare. It's a surgical force, with a single objective.

"I know perfectly well who I'm speaking to," the guard says. "And I'm not a part of the Charre Empire, so I'll talk to her as I damn well please."

"Viera," I say quietly, firmly. "Leave this to me."

I'm a little surprised when, with a slight bow of her head, my friend acquiesces and keeps her mouth shut. I take a breath, look back to the guard, who's now wearing a stupid grin. Like he's won a fight.

"Two things may have come this way," I begin. "They would have looked strange to you. Unlike anything you've ever seen. They were searching for me."

They've been here. The guards are giving it away with their glances. Even I catch the quick flash between the guards, a moment of blinked congress to decide how to respond. That they aren't clueless or confused tells me all I need to know.

"We've seen what you're talking about. Two of'em. Mean-looking monsters." The guard points over his shoulder, towards the mountain rising up behind the outpost. "We're leading them into Lunare right now. They wanted a chat with our own leader, Avril."

"A chat?" I ask.

"Don't know if it's going to be more than that," the guard says. "Point being, they're on the other side of these walls, which is a place you won't be seeing anytime soon. I'd take your army and go home if I was you."

I have two options: I can order an assault, attack the wall and, maybe, win. I'd lose men, but we prepared for this last night. Or I can back off. Wait to see what happens.

They are here for you. For me. Whatever they find in that mountain won't be what they're looking for. We do know, though, that they'll come back once they know you're here. We can use that. Prepare.

"Can you carry a message for me? From the Charre Empress?" I say to the guard, who shrugs. "To Avril, or to those creatures, if they can be found. Let them know that I'm here waiting for them."

"You want to stick your army in the muddy jungle, be our guest," the guard says. "I'll send your word along, and when those things tear you apart, we'll come right behind. Take what ought to be ours anyway."

I'm tempted to raise my hand. Let the arrows fly. But an Empress can't give into temptation. She has to think about her people first. That's what Father did, and that's what I do now when I order our band back—the three warriors holding the shields raise them up, casting shade over my back.

"You mean to have us wait?" Malo says as soon as we're under the cover of the trees. "Sit here while the Lunare plan an ambush, or a full-scale assault?"

"We can't march back, Malo," I reply. "Have our warriors set up camp. Start cooking fires. And rig defenses."

"So you do expect a fight here," Viera says, and she doesn't look too disappointed by the idea.

"Ignos thinks these creatures will pursue us regardless. So yes, once they realize the Lunare don't have what they're looking for, I think they'll come for me."

"Which is why we should return to Damantum," Malo

argues. "There we have strong walls and thousands who will fight for you. Coming this far was a mistake."

"Thousands who will die for me, Malo," I lean against a tree, its cool bark something I've felt too little of in my months with the Charre. "I can't take the chance these things would destroy Damantum to get to me."

"I think she's made her choice, lion man." Viera moves next to me and matches my stare towards Malo, who flicks his eyes at Viera.

"Kaishi, you asked me to lead your guards. Your armies," Malo's talking evenly now, the tone that says he wants my close attention. "I'm not the most experienced warrior we have, nor the most brilliant general among your ranks, so I can only believe you put me here because you trust what I have to say."

"Because you're my friend," I reply.

"Then listen to me now." Malo points back towards the Lunare outpost. "They are not going to sit while a Charre force rests outside their borders. We will wait for these creatures, and while we do, the Lunare will prepare an attack of their own. In one strike, they'll eliminate all of us, and our country will be left without its leaders. It's a dangerous mistake to stay."

The Oratus, the things that are after you, will not wait. Once they know that you are here, they will come, whether these Lunare are ready to follow them or not.

"Ignos says the creatures will come for us quick," I say. "We prepare, and we'll wait here for two days. After that time, if the creatures haven't made their strike, we'll retreat."

It's not what Malo wants to hear, but I'm still the Empress. I'm still his leader, and the lion warrior does not defy me. Malo turns away, shouts the commands, and my band bursts into activity.

My right hand lingers on top of the shard's handle, and I wait for death to come to me.

Daylight is far brighter after a long time spent underground. It only takes a moment for the mask to adjust the filters for Sax, shading his vision and allowing him to see down the front of the mountainside clearly, where the arrayed Lunare forces wait behind their wooden wall. Several Fassoths stand amongst the guards, hitched with thick ropes to towers that sit on large rolling wheels. Lunare soldiers clamber around on them, taking up positions, as if they expect an attack will come at any moment.

"The enemy is waiting right beyond our walls," Avril explains as she notices Sax and Bas watching. The Lunare leader journeyed back with them, and she's peppered them with questions every moment of the way.

At first, Sax splintered in some of his own, interjections about Lunare culture and methods, how they grew and developed under the mountains. Avril's answers, though, proved unsatisfying. Vague and full of unknowns, though Sax figures that her wandering explanations are as much because Avril lacks the knowledge as any desire to mislead the Oratus.

What continues to be clear, though, is that the Sevora have no place in Lunare society. None of the methods, the systems employed by these cave-dwelling people match what Sax sees in the parasites. They're clean, even if the presence of things like the Fassoths strikes Sax as strange.

When Avril took over the questioning, though, it became Sax's turn to evade. She wanted technical descriptions, blueprints and instructions for how to create the masks, the miners, for how to surf the stars as the Oratus do. Sax gave her only the vaguest ideas, the loosest sketches.

Bas contributed silence. It's not the job of the Oratus to bring new species into the galactic fold.

"Will they attack?" Sax asks Avril. "The enemy?"

"I'm told they've set up their encampment out of range, but close. Put up minor fortifications. They wouldn't bother with that if the Charre were going to move against us soon."

"So they're setting a trap."

"I wouldn't call it a trap," Avril says. "They're waiting for you. They respect you."

"How many?"

"Several hundred. It's not a large force."

Avril doesn't say it, but her answer makes it clear: these Charre have come only for the Oratus. To take Sax and Bas and end their threat. And the only reason they would know the Oratus are threats is if a Sevora told them.

"We will strike tonight," Sax says.

"Do you need support?"

Sax is about to say no, but Bas beats him to it, "We do not need anything, but, if you are prepared to offer it, distraction would make it easier."

"I think we can provide some." Avril points at the

mobile towers. "They have cannons. Loud, large, and perfect at getting attention."

They're almost down the mountain path now, stomping along the gravel rock. Ignos drifts in its afternoon descent, and clouds are chasing after it, promising rain. Better cover for their assault.

"Avril," Sax tries the name, but the hissing mangles it. "Why are you helping us?"

"Because without their empress, the Charre will fall."

Sax pauses, surprised at the lack of deception. No attempt to disguise her naked ambitions. Then again, Sax doesn't care what happens on this planet, or to this species. What's important is that the Sevora do not gain control.

"Does that worry you?" Avril asks, seeing Sax's hesitation.

"My mission has nothing to do with your power struggles," Sax says. "So long as we find the Sevora, nothing else matters."

Rain and darkness both fall soon after, with the clashing bangs of thunder and lancing bolts of lightning joining in. Sax and Bas assemble at the head of the Lunare force—with Avril watching from atop the wooden wall. It's a quick check to make sure both of them, freshly fed on fungal soups and jungle creature meat, are ready; masks tuned to lowlight vision, miners charged and operational, stim vials at hand if necessary.

Sax lifts his right foreclaw towards Avril, who lifts her right hand in response. Then the two Oratus leap. First, up to Avril's level. As they crouch, ready to scramble over, Sax hears Avril say, "Good luck, gods. I hope you find what you came for, and I hope I never see you again."

"Agreed," Sax hisses back, and then they're over the wall.

Both Sax and Bas catch the ground in a squat, then burst to the left. Out of the main pathway and into the trees. They don't go far before scaling a pair of thick-trunked, leafy ones. Climb all the way to the top, where the two of them poke out above the canopy, where the wind and rain pelt their masks.

From here they can see, even in this storm, the spotted orange glows of fires. At ground level, beneath the canopy, enough of the pouring water is blocked to allow such things. Not that Sax is complaining—a clear path to their target is all he can ask for.

Together, the two of them lope from one tree to the next, timing their leaps to coincide with cracks of lightning and the loud thundering rumbles. It's slow-going, but Avril asked for time to get those massive things moving, and it's better for the Oratus if they're not seen.

But these humans are not fools. Or the Sevora have instructed them well, as before long Sax leaps onto another tree and nearly winds up landing on one of them. The warrior is covered with bark and grime, though the rain washes it off in streaks. Still, in the night, he's mostly invisible, and Sax only realizes he's there when the warrior gives a shocked yelp.

Sax is on a thick branch, and his tail is already wrapping around the tree's trunk, a way of stabilizing him should the branch crack. Less than a meter away, on a second branch, crouches the human, already recovering from his shock and swinging his small bow and arrow to bear. Sax doesn't have time to pull a weapon, so instead he leans forward, towards the tree, and bites through the branch holding the man. Oratus teeth can cut metal, and the wood shreds like fluff in the face of those razors.

The man vanishes, crashing all the way down to the

jungle floor. He might live, but when Sax watches for motion, blocks out the rain and focuses the mask on the body, there's no sound.

"They have scouts in the trees," Sax says, the mask linking him with Bas and sending the words to her.

"Did you see one?"

"I did. He fell."

Bas' hissing laugh comes through the mask, and Sax can't help but join. Quietly, though.

Then it's on to the next tree.

Eventually, sputtering fires spread beneath them. Clusters of warriors, dressed more simply and sparsely than the Lunare, huddle around the flames. Lean-tos and small tents covered with animal skins dot the area, the little concession to shelter here. As Avril said, this is a camp, but it's not a settlement. Nothing here is made to last.

It's not hard to spot the quartet of guards in front of one fire farther apart than the others. The four stand at taut attention, with spears in their hands, looking outward. Even upward, but Sax and Bas—who is high up in a tree five meters away from her pair—are too far away to see in the dark. To Sax, the guards appear as bright green forms, and behind them, kneeling around the fire, are two others.

One is smaller than the other creatures. Avril and the other Lunare suggested the Sevora host is young. This size would fit.

A rolling rumble of thunder is followed, moments later, by a louder, more direct bang. Something breaks through the trees far to Sax's right; the Lunare plan to fire wide of the camp, to avoid hitting the Oratus.

Their targets don't ignore the sound. The warriors sitting beneath Sax burst to their feet, grouping together into parties and scrambling out into the forest. The four guards around their target shift in the direct of the noise, but don't abandon their posts.

"Well trained," Sax hisses.

"They will not pose a problem," Bas replies.

And now there's a fifth one, dashing from the ranks of scrambling warriors. The quartet parts for him. One more to take care of. And quickly; the Lunare are not committing to an attack—it's a distraction and nothing more. The Oratus do not have a long window.

"We cannot wait," Sax says. He hears an agreeing hiss.

The Oratus flings himself from the tree, towards the four guards, with claws outstretched and ready.

The second crack throws me to the ground. Not because it strikes close to me, not because it blew up the dirt at my feet or shattered the branches over my head, but because it flashes me back to the last time I fought a war, only months ago, in the deserts to the west, where bangs like these signaled my rise to Empress.

Viera's helping me up in a moment, and I notice that, in her left hand, one of her pistols is already drawn. My four Shadows spread out, forming a loose barrier between us and where the noise came from. Charre cries calling for groups to assemble, to march out in search of the enemy, ring out between the clatter of the rain.

"You're all right?" Viera says as I get to my feet.

"Fine," I say. "Just surprised. I didn't think the Lunare would attack."

"Me either."

Malo brushes through the Shadows, looking hard at Viera and I, making sure I'm not hurt.

"We're spreading out to engage," Malo says. "Though sending fire from afar isn't a normal Lunare strategy."

"They might be trying to see how we'll react, to draw us closer to their walls," Viera replies.

"My warriors know not to press that far," Malo says. "They'll stay well back of the walls, but if the Lunare can truly strike us from within their shelter, we'll need to move, Empress."

I start to agree with Malo when lightning flashes again, splitting the night apart in a wave of light. My eyes fly up to trace the bolt, and in that moment, I see a strange, unnatural shape in the leaves. I'm not the only one; the Shadows shout their alarm too. Viera pushes me behind her, drawing her other pistol. I reach for my shard, Malo pulls his kukri as the Shadows back closer to us, where they can fight as a unit.

They don't even have a chance. Bright blue bolts, things that I've never seen before, lance out like the lightning above and strike the Shadows from two sides. Four flashes, and my four guards are burning on the ground. I don't even have time to grasp what's happened before their attackers land on the forest floor in front of me.

I know immediately these are the things that Ignos fears. They match nothing except my nightmares, with their four long, clawed arms, swishing tails, and mouths full of gaping teeth. They're hissing now, too, a rasping roar that causes me to back another step.

Oratus.

"Uglier than I thought you'd be," Viera announces, then raises her pistols and fires both.

The shots strike the creature on the right, a gray-scaled menace, and it seems as though spiderwebbing cracks appear in the creatures' skin. But nothing else. No stagger, no falling to the ground or toppling backwards. Instead, the monster darts forward towards Viera, its two front claws tearing towards the Lunare's throat.

Malo jumps in front of the attack, his two kukri catching the creature's swings. The Oratus—I use Ignos' name for them automatically, like an instinct—has two more claws, though, and it uses those to grip Malo's waist and throw the warrior to the side. Viera's trying to reload, but she barely readies one before the pink-scaled Oratus is on her, using its tail to trip and then pin Viera to the ground.

Leaving me facing the two creatures alone.

"What do you want?" I ask, though I think I know.

"You are the Empress?" asks the gray-scaled one, speaking my language without issue in its rasping voice.

"I am," I say. "Why are you attacking us?"

The two Oratus glance at one another, then the pink one looks at me. "Sevora, do not try to lie to us. We know what you are."

"Sevora?" I've never heard the word in my life.

"You know what we are," the pink one continues. "I can see the knowledge in your eyes—"

"Ignos told me!" I cry, desperate to keep them from hurting Viera.

I can see Malo picking himself up from the ground, shallow cuts in his sides where the gray-scaled one had clawed him. In another moment, maybe, the warrior could take them by surprise.

"Ignos?" Now it's the gray-scaled one's turn to talk.

"My god," I say. "The voice inside my head."

"The one that came from the crashed seed?"

"Seed?"

There might be a way to survive this, Kaishi. Tell them the truth. All of it.

"It would have crashed down in the jungle. You would have found it, an oval, in a pit surrounded by rocks and burning things."

I catch Malo's eyes with my own, shake my head slightly to keep the warrior away. Based on how the gray-scaled one handled Malo's attack, I'm afraid another assault will only hurt Malo more. I'm ready to try Ignos' idea, so I begin to tell the story. I speak fast, treading lightly over details, and the two monsters listen to the entire thing.

"Mind loosening your tail?" Viera coughs. "Can't really breathe here."

I'm surprised to see the pink one listen, lift her tail slightly off the Lunare's chest. I'm not as surprised to see the grey one whip his tail suddenly, catch Malo's legs and trip him over.

"You're coming with us," the pink one says. "Now."

"Then we're going with," Viera announces.

"No," the gray-scaled one says.

"Yes," I say. "Or I'll fight you. And I don't think you want to kill me."

If they wanted me dead, after all, the two Oratus could have done that by now.

Again the Oratus look at each other, then back to me. Then the gray-scaled one takes a step forward, I see the tail twitch, and there's a sharp pain.

Nothing more.

They should all be dead. The three of them. One, the Empress, the young female, should be the first executed. Then the two with her in the hold, to be safe. Bas takes them for controls. To compare their natural, non-Sevora biology to the infected one.

A pointless experiment.

Sax and Bas had come to this planet to find the Sevora, and they had succeeded. One swipe of his claws and this would be dealt with. But Sax can't defy his pair so easily. Not there, in that stormy jungle. So Sax helps Bas take the three humans out. Carries them in a long sprint through the jungle, Stim packs—with Bas overcoming her distaste of the drug because of the necessity—serving to keep them moving even when exhaustion should knock them down. The scared

humans don't do anything—the razor claws close to their throats a constant reminder of the consequences.

Now they're in the shuttle. The three prisoners stuffed in back. The one with the pistols, the one that had fractured Sax's mask, hadn't stopped talking. Changing between threats and questions. Sax had wanted to shut her up, suggested that one human control—the silent, wounded warrior—was enough. Again Bas refused. Said that they should try to learn as much as they could.

She somehow thinks this is a key. That the Sevora can be taken care of if the Oratus can only figure out what makes these humans so special. Sax looks from the terminal and its briefing program to Bas. He's finished sending in all the information, which is transmitting through to Evva's ship.

They'll have to wait, in orbit, to see what Evva orders next. To see what the Oratus commander wants to do with this

new species. With this new problem. "You think I'm being too soft," Bas says, reading his mind. As always.

"We began, Bas, as an answer," Sax growls—he can't keep his frustration away. "We are the solution to the Sevora problem. And yet, here we're sparing one? We're taking a species we don't know? A species we care nothing about? Instead of completing our mission?"

"Shake the bloodlust from your eyes, Sax. Our mission is to rid the galaxy of the Sevora problem. Not kill them all."

"It's worked well so far."

"Has it?" Bas steps over to the console, switches from the briefing program to the standard data repository on every Vincere ship.

An encyclopedia of worlds, races, history. All there for reference as needed. Sax knows what she's going to pull up, watches anyway as she presses through the screens and gets to a narrative for their very own race.

A brutal history displays on the windshield, outside of which the blue-green planet spins to the left as they continue their orbit. It's a graph, mostly. A timeline covering all the major events that resulted in the two of them being here now.

"Look at all the fights. Look at all the times we meet the Sevora above one world or another. We throw everything at them for cycle after cycle. Chase them into one inevitable end after the next and then they come back." There's a heat in Bas' voice that Sax hasn't heard in a long time.

Bloodlust, the common Oratus drive to kill. It's the culmination of their passions. A mixture of instinct and love that comes together to make the Oratus into the pure devastation they ought to be. Yet in her voice now, Sax hears that same drive.

"How many times have we made it to what we said was the last seed ship. The last Sevora. Only to win and find the Sevora have already moved. That they're already growing. Then it all starts again. Billions and trillions of lives burned away. Including our own."

"Our own?" Sax looks at his claws. He still alive, so far as he can tell.

"What have we done, Sax? One trip on the Nova? One dying star? The rest is all battle. The rest is all blood and gore and claws and tearing. Risking our lives in this endless fight. Those three back there? The humans? If they hold the key to blocking Sevora control, then we must learn from them. Find out how to end this."

"What if you're wrong?" Sax replies. "What if the Sevora is lying, if it's clever, and it leaves the human to infect us? Then what? Is it worth risking everything for this?"

"I think so."

Sax rises to his full height. Bas matches him and they lock eyes.

"We are made to be weapons, Bas. We're not scientists.

We don't research and design the galaxy. We're not meant to be more than swords to cleave through our enemies. We have one here." Seeing no sway in Bas' face, Sax adjusts course. "Let's compromise. If the Sevora has the creature under its control, then it's a risk. Even if it is resisting the Sevora, who's to say for how long? We can kill the infected one now. Complete the mission. Then tell Evva about the other two. They can be studied. More can be gathered from this planet."

"How long will that take, Sax? How many cycles more?" Bas isn't budging. "You don't even want to try."

"I don't want to lose us," Sax says. "I don't want something to happen that doesn't need to. We've almost won this war, Bas. Let's not lose it now by risking ourselves." He's not making a dent with her, so Sax again ups his offer. "We do this, Bas, and I'll request time. You know we've earned it. Evva will give it to us. We can go back to the Nova or somewhere else. See some of these wonders that we've been missing. And let those who know what they're doing, deal with these. The war might even be over by the time we come back."

This last overture works, though Bas accepts it with a heavy flaring from her vents and a narrow-eyed nod. She still believes, Sax knows, this is the wrong decision. But there are measures, degrees to this. Letting a Sevora break free and take over either one of them is a risk they can't take. So Bas agrees.

They'll eliminate the infected one, and keep the others for research.

The transition to the shuttle's cargo bay means squeezing through stacks of supplies. Crates and containers full of nutrient goop and Stim. In the back, using straps to keep material stable when landing, are the three prisoners. They're tied, sitting in a line with their backs to the wall.

"What do you plan to do with us now?" the talkative says. She told Sax her name was Viera, but Sax has trouble forming the word. "Finally decide to off us? I see that mad gleam in your eye. You take us prisoner and then you kill us in cold blood."

"Not you," Sax says. He points at the infected creature, who's just coming back to consciousness. "That one."

There's no point in waiting anymore. Sax raises his right foreclaw, ignores Viera's sudden shouting. The third captive, heretofore sullen and silent, catches the mood and adds his own protests to the mix.

But there's one sound Sax cannot ignore. The sharp ding of a received transmission. Sax pauses. The noise rings throughout the shuttle, making sure it's heard throughout the ship. There's no way a response should come this fast. No way Evva should be responding. He left a long message. One that describes everything.

Yet, as with every official communication, because of the transmission time, Sax must start with the most important information.

That a new species has been found, one the Sevora do not seem to be able to control.

"Sax," Bas starts.

"Yes," Sax sighs, and he lowers his claw. "Let's see what she has to say."

The reply message is short. No doubt because Evva thinks Sax is going to do just what he's planned. Minimize the risk. Remove the hazard.

"Don't kill her. Take her to Cobalt station, at these coordinates."

The orders are succinct and clear.

A list of numbers follow. Ones easy to plug into the shuttle's navigation system. The station is a single leap away, though it's not one Sax knows. Regardless, the infected one lives.

For now.

Waking up after getting smashed in the head feels awful. A pounding pain that greets my opening eyes. I'm not exactly upset about the distraction, because what I'm looking at doesn't make any sense. It's not the stone, yellowed walls of the temples I've known. Or the green and leafy jungles I've walked my entire life. Instead it's a plurality of colors twined together with hard gray. Large cubes are stacked around me, striped labels bearing words that I can read: Nutrients. Water. I shake my head.

Jumble my brain back into place.

Ignos mashes words I don't understand. Apparently waking up just like me.

"Are you awake Kaishi?" It's Viera talking. A cool waterfall of relief cascades through me as I realize both she and Malo sit nearby. "How are you feeling? Alive?"

"I think so," I reply.

They haven't killed us yet. Why?

I don't have an answer for this question. I'm too busy staring around. Other boxes surround us in this dark space and green lights glow in globes on the ceiling. Dim. There's a thin breeze going through, though the air lacks any of the flavor I'm used to. It's plain, stale. No scent of anything. My ears catch a study churning sound that I feel in my bones. Unnatural and constant. Things moving around me and underneath.

I fight the urge to panic, if only because Viera and Malo are looking at me with concern, and if they are stable, if they are not shrieking and yelling and crying, then I can't be either.

"Where are we?" I ask.

"I heard them call this the shuttle," Malo replies in Charre tongue, though he's learned more of mine and Viera's language in the last month, mostly, I think, because he's tired of not knowing what we're saying about him. "After they, um, knocked you out, they took Viera and I. We couldn't fight back." Malo looks away, and I can tell he's ashamed. He failed as my bodyguard.

Failed as the leader of my warriors.

"You tried," I say. "You stood up for me. You fought for me against something you had no hope to defeat."

No hope is putting it lightly.

I flash back anger against Ignos' comment. No hope to defeat them? Then why? Why weren't we prepared? Ignos had to know this was coming.

Nothing I could've done would have saved you. I was trying to move your people forward as fast as I could. We ran out of time.

This strikes me as weird. Ignos is a god. He can control time, and everything else. How could there not be enough? How could we not be prepared?

Because I'm not the only god. Because there are others

who seek to fight me. And they do not wish me, or you, to succeed.

"You all right Kaishi?" Viera says again. "Is Ignos still talking? I would've thought he'd shut up about now, seeing as he's done nothing to help you."

"I'm trying to figure that out myself," I say. "He's not making sense."

"Gods seldom do."

All at once the green globes shift to red, and a low tone echoes throughout the shuttle. Words, words I am recognizing yet don't understand play out. A hissing voice calls for preparation. Says we will be leaping soon.

Leaping?

It's best if you close your eyes. It's easier that way.

As if I'm going to follow anything Ignos says now. Not after what he's done, or rather, what he didn't do.

So I keep my eyes open, and regret it.

It's as though the universe tears. Everything in front of me and around me and inside me seems to twist and shift and strain. To pull apart so far until I feel like the distance from my right hand to my left is a thousand kilometers. I'm at once everywhere and nowhere, in pain and in paradise. Then I snap back. Like a runner hitting a rock. All my senses go numb and ajar at once, so I can't feel anything except that I'm out of place.

Stay calm. It will pass.

I become aware that Malo and Viera are shouting. Tears are streaming down my face. It's a matter of retaking control of my own body. Putting myself back together again, as if I were a tree that lost all its leaves and now has to reattach them to my branches one by one.

"Stay quiet," I say to Viera and Malo. "Focus on yourselves. Find your pieces, and pull them back together."

I don't know if they understand what I'm saying, or if they even hear it, since they're still yelling incoherent nonsense. I keep talking to them anyway. Soft voices. They don't have Ignos in their heads. They have nothing telling them that it will pass, that what's happened is not fatal. But, together, the three of us bring ourselves back from the edge. Until, with Viera's face red and slack-jawed, and Malo gasping for breath, we're okay.

We're alive.

"We'll be docking shortly," the voice of the rose gold one. I recognize it, though I'm not sure where it comes from. "Congratulations. You managed to survive a leap."

Her hissing laugh echoes through the boxes.

obalt hangs like a spiderweb in a dark corner of space. There's not even another star nearby. They're all twinkling in the distance. But then, that's par for the course with Amigga researchers. Their projects are all so secretive—they tell the

Vincere it's to avoid contamination—that they build their stations away from the habitable parts of the galaxy. Where no one knows what they're doing.

Amigga inventions appear, though, as if by magic. New ships or devices, methods for terraforming worlds or curing them from the same gone wrong. Sax knows all of his weapons, the mask, came from Amigga pursuing their own ends and passing along the benefits to the Vincere and the rest of the galaxy.

What everyone also knows, though, is that the Amigga choose what they pass on to everyone else. What they keep for themselves... well, Sax has no time for speculation.

Evva's orders are clear. Now that they've completed the leap, the briefing program picks up more from the commander. Sax plays it, with Bas listening nearby.

"I presume you saved the specimens. Deliver them to the station. Make sure they're taken care of. The Amigga there will handle the tests. Will look to see if there's anything we can glean from it." There's a burst there, static. When Evva's voice comes back, it's something different. Less ambient noise. She's changed locations. "Sax, Bas. I'm talking directly to you to now. Avan, the captive Oratus you brought back to me from the seed ship? I've had a chance to look into what he's saying. There may be some truth to it, and some of his assertions concern the Amigga. Stay alert. If something goes wrong, save yourselves first. The specimens if you can."

And that's it. A warning with little detail.

"That's not like her," Sax says. "Something has Evva mixed up."

"Or someone's listening to her." Bas always has the more reasonable ideas. "Either way, we're here."

The station is a long, flat triangle. At the far point, there's a sphere, large and round. The station's core. Where the Amigga stays. The other two points are closer to them, and as they draw near, a white rectangle opens in the base wall. A docking bay. One large enough to accommodate several shuttles.

Which means *Cobalt* expects, or expected, some traffic, though the bay appears empty now. The initial part of docking with the station is tricky—in order to generate some gravity, *Cobalt* spins around the lone point and its sphere. Bas pilots the shuttle and has to first match *Cobalt*'s spin velocity, then guide the shuttle closer and closer to the station. Sax watches as the white-blue glow of *Cobalt*'s inside draws near, a searing scar against the otherwise black background.

"Why are we going here?" Sax says as Bas switches the

shuttle to its automated landing procedure. "If Evva thinks the Amigga might be a risk, then we should leap somewhere else. Back to the main Vincere fleet, maybe."

"She didn't say she had proof," Bas counters. "I don't think we scrub the mission on a hunch, especially with its potential."

The shuttle glides in, firing the microjets to keep from hitting the floor and ceiling—the empty bay means they aim for the open middle, so sides aren't a concern. A thick red light flares as they enter, telling Sax that the whole bay isn't pressurized. No fancy electromagnetic shields here. Instead, the bay is clear. No loose things that might get yanked out as vacuum comes in.

A heavy airlock door, twice as tall as Sax and three times as wide, sits at the back wall, no doubt leading further back into the station. The inside of the bay is all white-washed. Not the standard Vincere military gray but gleaming pearl. Even the lights are white. Spotless, sanitized.

Sax finds it blinding.

The microjets make the landing easy, and the struts pop out beneath the craft without a problem. Behind them, the top and bottom of the massive bay door come together to seal away the cosmos. The red light begins a slow shift towards green as oxygen pumps into the room; making sure it's safe to breathe.

"It's an older station," Sax looks up from the console, where he's been digging into the encyclopedia. "Around since the start of the eighth cycle."

"So why did Evva send us here then?" Bas replies. "With what we might have, we should be at the best."

"If you were suspicious of the Amigga, if you didn't

trust those in power, would you send us to the newest and the best? The Amigga getting the most attention?"

Sax surprises himself with the thought, but it fits: way out here, on this older model station, they would be far from prying eyes. The Amigga running *Cobalt* might not be part of Evva's concerns, might simply want to run its experiments out here in the dark, alone.

Except there is somebody here. Even though like bar isn't all green yet, there's motion in the docking bay. Sax catches it as it moves, and he can't categorize the thing. It's blue and globular. Resembles an Oratus, though it is very clearly not that. It has no defined features. No eyes, no mouth. Its skin is perfectly smooth, as though made from a mold. It waits near the shuttle, staring at them through the windshield.

"What is that?" Bas says.

"I don't know, but I'm going to be ready." Sax moves to put on the mask, safely stored on equipment racks in the back of the bridge—designed to ensure the Oratus piloting the shuttle are never far away from their weapons.

Even though it's damaged, the mask still serves its purpose. It wraps over his claws in his arms and his torso and legs. Covers Sax with a seal mostly intact. Enough to provide protection, enough to hold the weapons he brings. Bas does the same with hers. When the bar outside in the bay flashes green, they give no thought to the prisoners, to the specimens.

They lower the landing ramp.

The thing moves towards them before they even reach the bottom. Holds out a gel-claw toward Sax. A traditional Oratus greeting. Both should Oratus give claws, clasp them tight. Follow with a touch of the heads to one another. A symbol of kinship, of shared purpose.

But this creature is no Oratus. Sax stares at the claw until the thing retracts it.

"Welcome, Oratus. I am Dalachite, and I see you've met my familiar," Dalachite's booms out through the station's intercom. It's deep and gurgling. One unused to speech. "Clever aren't they? My own invention. Looks just like you."

"This thing is an abomination," Sax says in reply. "Nothing about it is real."

He doesn't know from where the Amigga, as that's clearly Dalachite, is watching him, so Sax addresses the familiar.

"Well then, I'm afraid you'll need to overcome your prejudice. My familiars are everywhere on the station. *Cobalt* wouldn't run without them. But tell me, do you have it? The specimen?"

So Evva, or someone, has been in contact with the Amigga.

"We do," Sax says. "One of them, we believe, is infected."

"With the Sevora. Yes. It's exciting, isn't it?"

Sax almost laughs at how different his idea of exciting is from Dalachite, but swallows the urge. Remembers Evva's private words, and asks, "What will you do with them?"

"That is not your concern, Oratus." Dalachite picks up a note of haughty irritation, as if Sax is playing at things far beyond his understanding. "You are here as my guest. You are completing a mission. I invite you to do so now. If you will give me your captives, please."

Bas goes back into the shuttle. It's an unspoken move, a tacit agreement between the two of them. Bas seems to understand the specimens more than Sax does, so she'll go bring them out. In the meantime, Sax keeps his eyes open for weapons. Any sign that this might be some sort of strange ambush. Anything that might lend credence to Evva's warning.

There's nothing. Only the blank blue of the familiar.

"How long?" Sax asked. "How long have you been on the station?"

"Since *Cobalt* was born," Dalachite replies. "You must understand, Oratus. Amigga do not travel. We do not move or take other jobs. We simply are, and we build our homes around us. *Cobalt* is as much a part of me as any organ. As my skin and bone."

That answers that. Sax can't think of anything else to say, so the two stand in silence until, with the clanking claws on metal, Bas reappears leading the three specimens behind her.

Almost at once, the blue familiar changes. The claws sink back into center mass, which shrinks down before limbs pop out again, only this time in the shape of the specimens. The tale disappears, and the legs soften. Five small flagella form on each foot, each hand.

"Delightful," Dalachite says. "It is been far too long since I had a new species to play with. Look at these. Fingers and toes? Yes. This will be fun."

"This isn't about fun," Bas speaks now. The humans are all too afraid, or struck silent by the world around them. "This is about solving the war. This is about finding a cure for the Sevora infection."

"Of course it is. Of course that's what I'll do, but first things first." The familiar, despite not being the source of Dalachite's voice, looks at the specimens. "Let's get all of you settled. Please, follow the familiar."

That's it for pleasantries. The blue thing ignores Sax completely and instead beckons the humans to follow. They stare back at it, not quite sure what it wants, until the familiar waves them forward again. Bas tells them to obey, and then the humans do. The infected woman tailed by the other two. One brown and one pale. Sax and Bas watch them go, watch the door out of the bay open and shut behind them.

"Is that it?" Bas says as they stand alone in the docking bay. "Do we leave?"

"You heard Evva," Sax is talking now through the mask, staring at Bas so the slightest whisper sends between their two masks like the clearest shout.

"So then we stay." Bas looks fine with this idea. "We stay and watch. Make sure the Amigga does as it should."

Sax agrees. He has no desire to see the humans survive. But the image of that blue, false Oratus lingers in his mind. If he finds an excuse to destroy it, he will.

verload. That's the only way I can describe it. So many new things, so far beyond anything I'd ever thought of.

They strike me one after another. First comes the shuttle. Standing up, leaving it through a strange metal ramp. Something that makes unnatural sounds as I walk upon it. My legs, my arms feel light, and with every step I feel as though I might float away. Instead, as I walk, I force my feet down, every time I hit the ground it's a victory.

Where do I walk into? A place unlike any I've ever been before. A pure glow pours from above, and yet somehow it seems lifeless. At first I think that it must be Ignos, but then I look up, as we walk out from beneath the shuttle, and see that no, like inside the creature's ship, there are globes at in the ceiling producing these rays.

The floor is a glossy black. So shiny that I can see myself in it. The only break in the alabaster walls comes from a strange green line that seems level with the glass covering on the front of the shuttle. Malo and Viera, like me, stay quiet. There's nothing we can say that is relevant to the moment. There's nothing here that makes sense.

We're clinging to our sanity now.

This is a space station. This is what it's like to live outside your world.

Ignos is muted. The explanation is perfunctory. It's not hard to see why. I'm still angry at him. Still incensed that the god of my people can keep such things from me. That he could leave us so unprepared for what was coming. I'm starting, now, to wonder what kind of god he is. If Ignos is not all-powerful, then what is he?

I'm a guide. Your friend. The only way you'll get through this.

In that, Ignos has a point. He at least seems to know what's happening. He seems to understand, and urges me to follow when the strange blue creature waves us forward, and when the pink-gold monster seconds the command, I do.

The floor is cold on my bare feet. My skin breaks out in goosebumps as the chill air plays upon us. None of us were wearing much back in the jungle. It was the summer season. So here we are, in thin cotton capes and wraps, freezing.

We head towards the door, which is plenty tall and large for all of us. We could walk abreast if we wanted to, though something compels us to stay in single file. We're moving towards a destination, not walking for conversation, and all of us are in our own worlds.

There's magic when the door opens. In one moment, a collection of pressed silver boards stands in our way. In the next they do not. It shoots up, I think, but I'm not sure as it happens so fast. A hallway lays beyond, with branching paths and more white globes glowing in the ceiling. There's nothing on the walls except that same sterile white. I wonder if, perhaps, we died in the jungle and this is the beyond. An unknowable blankness.

You are very much alive, Kaishi. Do not forget it. Or you may not be for much longer.

The blue thing, which looks like a child's drawing of her father, leads us through. Once in the hall, its arms begin to wave, and a voice erupts out of the air. I see no mouth, I see no speaker, but sounds come through the air nonetheless. Speaking in our common tongue, and I worry that Malo will not be able to understand.

"Welcome to your new home. Welcome. It's a place where you shall find how small your old life really was. Here you will learn, here you will change. Here you will provide a great service to the rest of the galaxy." The voice gets excited with itself. Like a priest winding up towards a grand conclusion.

Only I don't like what it's saying. I've heard promises before. I've heard people both great and small talk about all kinds of wondrous things that would be coming to me. I've seen how, more often than not, those promises turn out to be lies.

The thing notices my skepticism, because the blue creature stops and turns towards me. Though it has no mouth, I hear words again, coming from everywhere.

"I see doubt in your eyes," the voice continues, and I detect wounded pride, like a hunter whose prowess I'd questioned. "Do you really think that you will be hurt here? You are prizes. You are miracles. You are my most treasured possessions."

"Possessions?" That's Viera now.

"Oh yes. You're on *Cobalt.* I am Dalachite, and you're in my home. You'll stay here as long as I need you." The blue thing spins on its heel then and continues walking.

"I don't like that word," Viera whispers as we move.

Hallways branch off of where we are. Closed doors leading I don't know where, but we go past them all. Deeper.

"I don't believe it," I say. "We might be somewhere else, but we are still ourselves. It does not own us. Doesn't have control of our bodies or our minds."

"Not yet," Dalachite says. "Up here on the right are your quarters. Each one of you has a room, and you'll ignore the rest. It may not be everything that you want at first, but we'll be working together to make it as you like. Follow my familiar and it will see to your comfort."

In turn, the blue creature leads us down a short hallway with six doors, though only three have green circles above them. At the first one, the blue man points to Malo.

"You first now. Come on." Dalachite issues the command pleasantly, as if telling us to smell a pretty flower.

"He doesn't understand you," I say. Malo's looking at me, and while I don't see fear in his eyes, I see wariness. Confusion. I translate for the creature, "It wants you to go inside."

"Should I?" Malo asks. "I'd rather stay with you."

"I don't think we have a choice. Not now."

Malo accepts the order of his Empress. He steps past me, follows the familiar's outstretched arm, and goes inside the room. The door shuts behind them as soon as he enters. We repeat the process at the next one, with Viera stepping inside, and the Lunare promises to come see me in a minute.

Now we're at the last one. My room. The door opens as the familiar approaches, and inside I see what looks like a bed. It's not a mat, it's not stuffed cloth full of cotton. It's huge, and appears to be some sort of silvery mass within a metal frame. The rest of the room is taken up by a wide black screen on one wall. On my left, across from the bed, is what appears to be a table.

"I know it seems spare," Dalachite says. "But you will be spending much time here. Sleep, as your species requires. A place to spend the occasional bit of time between sessions. You'll come to like it."

"What happens next?" I ask the familiar, because even if Dalachite's voice doesn't come from it, I need to look at something.

"Next? Next we discover who you are. How you fit together in the universe we know. Then, perhaps, some sleep. Some food."

"After that?" I say because everything Dalachite described sounds unimportant.

"Then we find out what to do with that thing inside you. The parasite that can't seem to control your mind."

And my world falls apart.

I f the Oratus are going to stay on *Cobalt*, they'll have to find a way inside. They're looking at the closed door out of the docking bay. Sax wants to take his claws to it. See whether the door can handle an Oratus raking its metal. But he doesn't. This is a research station, and in the hierarchy of his galaxy, the Amigga stand apart. They are neither above nor below the Oratus but equal.

Therefore, Sax cannot go tearing up the station. Not unless he wants to pay the consequences.

"They'll kill you," Bas reads his mind, says what he's thinking. "You damage this place, the Amigga itself might do it. Or Evva, once word gets back to her."

"That's the problem," Sax says. "They put weapons in a place where weapons don't belong. How is it my fault if I do what I'm made to?"

Sax walks over to the door. Takes five long strides, and each one sending tingling shivers up his legs as the claws click and resonate on the metal floor. It's a sensation that he's become use to. Living in space will do that; carpet is too expensive, too unnecessary. The door has a red light over the top. A standard make for these stations. For Vincere ships. Red means locked, green means open and blue means only for the right person. Sax guesses there's not many people on the station, so blue doesn't show up much.

"Sax." Bas' caution isn't necessary. Sax won't attack the door. Not yet, anyway.

Instead, he raises one hand, clenches his claws together to form a fist, and is about to knock when the door swings open. It's too late though: Sax's fist is already flying forward. The blue familiar, still looking like a human, appears in precisely the wrong position.

Sax smashes the familiar's face.

It's like punching water. Sax's bony, scaled knuckles drive ripples in the familiar's face, and it blows apart. Blue ooze showers the hallway, Sax, and everything else. The mess lives, though, only for a second. The goop reverses direction, comes together, racing back towards the familiar. Rivulets returning to their owner. Sax watches a line slick its way down his leg to the floor, race over and absorb into the familiar's foot.

"Now that wasn't very nice," Dalachite says. "I don't know what they're teaching you Oratus now, but it used to be we didn't greet our partners with fists to the face."

Sax opens his mouth to make an excuse, but the Amigga tramples on.

"Not that it matters. In fact, you performed a valuable service. I've always wanted to see how my familiars would handle a strike I didn't deliver to them. And look, they're brilliant! Bio matter. I've made it myself, right here on *Cobalt*. It will always come back; electrical pulses, you see. They connect the cells, and when they're close, the energy spurs them to knit back together!"

Sax can't argue with Dalachite's results: the blue

familiar is collecting itself, and already looks as though Sax didn't touch it.

"I didn't mean to," Sax grits out the apology, then moves to what he wants to say. "We're staying, at least for a little while."

"Good, good. Upon reflection, I've reconsidered my earlier position." Dalachite's enthusiasm hits Sax wrong. Why would the Amigga want them around? The answer comes a moment later, "I have many experiments that need testing, and, as you might imagine, not many find their way out to this far corner of the galaxy."

"Isn't it your choice to be here?" Bas asks, stepping up to join Sax.

"Of course, but it comes with its costs. As I said, though, there'll be plenty we can do. Also, with those other specimens, it might be useful to have you around. Extra security."

As if this thing needs extra security. Sax isn't stupid. He figures Dalachite has more than one of these familiars. Those hands, watery though they are, look like they could hold a weapon if they had to. Maybe this is what Evva was talking about, maybe this is what she meant when she said to stay ready.

The familiar leads them down the hallway, and they take a swift right instead of going straight. They walk through a wide room, with several tables. Clearly a dining hall, and meant to hold far more than the zero occupants it has now. Bas asks the obvious question, "Where is everyone?"

"Like I said, *Cobalt* is an old station. The research I perform doesn't require much in the way of extra crew, so why pay for all the nutrients? Why pay for the extra facilities? We disembarked the last batch of scientists a cycle ago.

As you can probably tell, it's been lonely. I'm happy to have you here."

Sax is unimpressed with what he can see of the food stores. The same sort of nutrient goop they have on the shuttle, and it's not even the flavored kind. This *is* an old station. He starts tell Bas that maybe they shouldn't stay here all that long or they might go crazy, but then notices the familiar is staring right at him. Even without eyes, Sax can feel the thing's attention, and it makes his tail twitch.

"The experiments, friends. There are things I've been trying to train with my familiars. You see, they are my first and last line of defense. They are also my greatest project. Yet, sparring against myself is somewhat limiting. Would you mind?"

"Would we mind what?" Sax says.

"Training my familiars? The design, I mean. A little bit of exercise will teach them quite a lot. Think of it as a way of paying me back for using my station. For eating my food."

"It's a leap to call this food," Sax says.

"And it's a leap to say you're pleasurable company," Dalachite replies. "We're both making compromises here. So let's do the best we can, shall we?"

Sax glances at Bas, and his pair shrugs. "Both of us?"

"Oh no, just one of you. For now. This familiar will guide the other to your quarters."

"I'll unload the shuttle if you want to take the first round," Bas says.

Sax knows that means Bas is going to go and get herself armed. Get ready to blaze to the rescue if Sax needs it. It's an easy ask to accept.

Then the familiar is guiding him back out of the mess and into a deep maze of hallways. The first thing Sax is going to do when he gets a moment is pull up the map to this place and memorize how to get from here to there. He doesn't like being lost. It makes it all too easy to fall into a trap. Or an ambush.

The familiar leads Sax into a large room. Cavernous, even. Unlike the other rooms, light green padding covers the floor and walls.

There's a cabinet in one corner, and its shaded red. The standard color for aid. This isn't just a sparring room for familiars, this is a training area for many things. The blue familiar walks to the center of the room and then shivers. Its hand and feet grow and droop. Its chest and shoulders shrink.

The familiar's limbs pool on the ground, split apart, and then build up again into another person. In seconds, there are two familiars standing in front of Sax, each one slightly smaller, shorter, and thinner than the first.

"Aren't they wonderful?" Dalachite says. "Of course, I'm going to have them use this new form. An Oratus takes up too much mass. They would be quite small."

"What do you want me to do?" Sax says. "If I even touch them, they break to pieces."

"To start with, how about we get an idea of their speed. Try and track them." There's a lilt to Dalachite's voice that tells Sax it has full faith in its creations.

That the Oratus will fail, and fail badly.

The Amigga is wrong.

The two familiars jump back from Sax, going in opposite directions and running towards the walls. Sax watches for a moment, gets the lay of their lines, and makes tracks for the closer one, heading toward the wall to his left. It's strange chasing something that has no defined body, that appears to be liquid moving in a mold. But then, Sax has encountered many strange creatures in his life.

Every one had a weakness.

When the familiar reaches the wall, a breath ahead of Sax, it doesn't stop. It doesn't press back, or turn and cower at the oncoming Oratus. No, it starts running up the surface. Its feet suction to the sides and the familiar heads directly above Sax. The problem is, Sax can jump. Far. He presses his legs and leaps, four claws outstretched, straight towards the familiar's back as it climbs the wall. Sax is ready to grip, to sink those claws in and start to tear.

But there's nothing to grip onto. Sax simply passes right through the familiar and explodes it into a raining shower of blue gel. The familiar's pieces splatter down to the room's floor while Sax manages to catch the wall with his talons and digs his claws into the soft surface.

The Oratus twists his head around. Stares at the puddles beneath him as they gather and form again.

"Not fast enough." Dalachite sighs. "Something to improve for future iterations. Still, let's keep going."

"Keep going with what?" Sax says, hanging from the wall.

"Based on the speed of your movements, it's unlikely my familiars will be able to dodge or outrun you. So let's change the game. Why don't we try a little bit of combat. Put you on the defensive for a change."

"Oratus don't go on the defensive."

"If you say so."

Beneath Sax, the familiar he'd exploded reforms into its human-like shape. As Sax watches, both of the familiars go over to the red cabinet and open it. Inside, Sax can see the shelves that had once been used hold aid kits, bandages, or emergency medical supplies.

Now, though, the cabinet is full of danger; miners, and weapons of a more personal nature.

Each of the familiars pick out sharp blades, nearly a meter long. Ones that curve upwards, towards the wielder, the closer they come to the tip. The familiars turn back to Sax, set themselves apart, and wait.

Giving Sax one chance to look at his options.

Then they rush forward, their steps synchronized, and hit the floor at the same time. Sax is on the wall, which is good, as he's out of the reach of those swords. Until he remembers that they can climb. The two familiars reach the side beneath Sax and, again, start running up the wall towards him. Both of them raise the swords high over their heads to deliver what looks like a strong overhead smash.

It's almost like they don't realize the Oratus has a tail. Before they hit striking range, Sax twists and sweeps his tail across the wall, slicing through their fragile bodies. At the sudden loss of cohesion, the whole watery mess tumbles down to the floor.

One of the swords lands point first, sticking up like a monument to the defeat.

Dalachite doesn't say anything this time. It doesn't have to: the familiars show that the fight isn't over. The blue liquid pulls together, now as one, and rises into a full Oratus shape. Four arms, two legs and the tail, though the end result is smaller than Sax. The familiar picks up the blades, one in each of its two foreclaws. This time, it keeps its distance.

"So it's a coward now," Sax says to the room, hoping the Amigga can hear.

"It's learning," Dalachite replies. "Every time you defeat it, my familiar will adapt."

It'll have to adapt a lot before it poses a threat to Sax. He detects a slight twinge in his stomach. The fight is so boring that Sax is getting hungry. Time to finish this. "You want me to attack?"

"I want you to treat it as an enemy," Dalachite says. "Because, be assured, that's how it's treating you."

Fine.

Sax digs his legs into the wall. If the Amigga wants to see how Sax treats his enemies, it's in for a show.

Taken as a whole, revelations haven't spiked my life regularly, which is why I'm still reeling from the last few months. I've been torn away from my family, shoved into the highest points of a rival civilization, and then stolen away by things spawned from the darkest nightmares in less time than two seasons. Through it all, I'd had Ignos. Either directly in my mind, or, before that, as a source of strength when nothing else worked.

Kaishi?

Is it all a lie? My father's belief? My tribes' faith that the world we live in is presided over by a just, if uncompromising force?

You need to calm down. Think. Listen to me.

The sacrifices. So many people. So many hearts torn out on the stone slabs. All of it for nothing. I can't—

STOP!

I blink. My world shifts back from hazy tears. They blur the blank walls, and the otherness of my gray-white prison threatens to jar me back into despair.

It's true, Kaishi. I'm not your god.

Perhaps it's the frankness of the admission, or maybe, like a boulder on the edge of a slope, I'm about to lose control anyway, but the words bend my confusion towards anger. I have a target.

So I fire.

It's not words I send after the thing in my mind but indistinct heat, torching rage and betrayal. Shot after shot of broken trust and shattered spirit. If this thing had been standing in front of me, I would be screaming. As it is, I clench my hands so tight that I feel my nails biting into my own skin. I don't let up.

Ignos—I know, now, that's not its name but I can't think of another at this blind-fire moment—recoils. Whether I'm actually causing it pain, I don't know. I don't care. It needs to know what it's done. How it's ruined everything.

Have I, though?

Of course it has! Look at where we are? What we're doing?

You saved your people, didn't you? Your tribe?

Yes, that might be true. But the way—

Your work forged an alliance between your own people and the Charre, did it not? And the miracles I gave you? Won't that ensure their strength for seasons to come?

Ignos hammers me with logic, and I struggle to keep up my raging. At home, in the jungle and surrounded by friends and family, I would have brushed aside those arguments, would have pushed and fought and scrabbled until my point was made. Here, though, where I'm on unstable ground, Ignos' words stabilize. Present the possibility, the proof that, perhaps, I'm not a complete failure for trusting some strange creature from beyond the sky.

I realize my panic, my tears and anger are not because of my people, my family or the Solare.

It's all about me.

A knock on the door comes through muffled, light, lifeless. Without the chords of real wood. Still, I look towards it and the act helps keep the clouds at bay.

"You can come in," I call.

There's a moment's hesitation, then a reply comes through, "I don't think I can, actually."

It's Malo and I'm up in an instant. The door sits in its frame; a raised pearl band looping around an entry twice my height. Compared to the openings in our family home and even the great Charre buildings, it's massive. There's no handle. I try pushing on it, but the door doesn't react.

"Do you know how to open it?" I look around the door as I ask the question.

There's a black nub to the right of the doorway; a protruding half-sphere that seems to stare at me. I touch it with the tip of my finger and it's hard. Cool and smooth, too smooth for natural rock.

"When I approached my door, it just opened," Malo replies. "Can you see anything?"

It's me.

I pause.

The door. It's detecting my presence and is locking you inside.

Makes sense. Why wouldn't Ignos continue wrecking my life?

There is a way past it, of course.

I wait for a list of requirements. Some elaborate ceremony I must perform to placate the black nub.

No ceremony. Ask. Ask the Amigga that runs this station to open the door.

I don't know what an Amigga is, so I assume Ignos is talking about the blue creature.

Dalachite, Kaishi. The voice that's always listening here. Ask it.

So I do.

"Dalachite, I don't know what you are," I say to the air, and as I speak, I hear Malo ask what I'm doing and ignore him. "But can you open my door? I don't know how."

"I can open the door for you," Dalachite says. "But, were I to do so, I would need your assurance, your promise that you would not attempt to leave."

"Leave?" I reply.

"Your chamber. You must stay inside unless my familiars come to take you."

"What? Why?"

"Oh, it's very simple, really. You see, I have much to learn about you. There are two ways I can do that: either I take you, leaving you intact, and we learn together—that's what I would prefer—however, if that becomes too dangerous, if there's a chance the Sevora inside your head could leave or infect another, then it's safer to paralyze you. Extract those components of your nervous system that allow you to move. Then, I will learn what I can."

I recall the blue familiar. It hadn't held a weapon, hadn't seemed threatening. Yet, the ease with which Dalachite speaks of hurting me...

They can do all it says and worse. Listen to it, Kaishi. Our chance will come later.

"I won't leave," I say to the voice.

A second later the door shoots open, and Malo steps inside. Without waiting, he wraps me in a hug, and I return the gesture. It's nice, feeling those arms around me. Nice feeling some support of any kind, really. Even though, beneath Malo's wiry muscles, there's tension.

The same fear tightening my bones.

"Where are we?" Malo whispers the words, but they're a question I can't answer.

"Far from home," I give the only reply I can. For now, it's enough.

"Home," Malo squeezes hard, then releases and steps back. "Do you think we'll see it again?"

"I think you might," I say. "Dalachite keeps talking to me like I'm some sort of experiment. Something that's been discovered. I don't think it's going to let me go."

We will make them.

"I won't leave you," Malo says. "You're my Empress."

I laugh. I can't help it. "Malo, I'm a lie. A fraud. This thing, this thing in my mind? It's not Ignos. It's just another creature. It used us."

I can tell by the way Malo's face screws up that he doesn't understand.

"You see that blue thing out there? The one that led us here? And the two monsters that took us from the jungle? It's like them," I'm shouting now but I don't realize it. "It's from somewhere else. It's inside me and it's talking to me and it's pretending. It wants us to do things for it, Malo. It doesn't care about our people. Just itself."

Mutually beneficial, Kaishi. What helps me help you. Do you see that?

I ignore Ignos. It's not hard now. Before, pushing it away felt like I was rejecting my own god. The core of my childhood and my tribe. Now, now it's like batting away an annoying fly. I do it without a second thought.

"It doesn't matter," Malo settles his face into a straight-forward stare. "You're still you. I'm still me. We'll think of some way to get out of this."

"You're still you," I say. "But I'm about as far from me as

I've ever been. I left my family. My people. All for this thing in my head."

"But you still have friends. You have me."

I hear a shunt from the hallway, and before I can deliver another surly, annoyed crack to Malo, Viera appears. Her eyes crisscross between Malo and I, and then her mouth curls into a sardonic smile.

"I see it let Malo out first," Viera says in Lunare.

"Talk so Malo can understand," I reply to Viera.

"Only saying that it's nice to see you two," Viera replies in Charre.

Suddenly there's tension in the room. I don't know why Malo only replies to Viera's words with a curt nod. It seems like we should all be sticking together. That we're so far from what we know, that the three of us are all any of us has left. So I try to cut it.

"I'm sorry," I say to Malo. "I'm torn right now. But you're right. We have to help each other. If we want to go home, we'll have to work together to find a way."

Be careful what you say. Or rather, how you say it.

I make the connection: Dalachite, the voice that comes out through the walls, it talks in the same tongue Viera and I use. But the Charre, Malo, their language is different. The voice might not understand it, might not know what passes between our lips. I warn the other two to stick to speaking Charre, and there's no argument.

"We know one way off of the station," Viera says. "That's the way we got here."

"I remember how to get back to it," Malo says. "If we can get there, perhaps we can figure out how their... thing works."

We fumble for the words. For a way to describe the

ship. I realize I'm still wearing the answer. I looked down to my bracelet, the Cache. It's still on my wrist.

"I have this," I say and nod at the artifact. "It can help us, but I need time. Time to learn how to use it, to understand this station."

"Then we'll give you time," Malo says. "However much you need. I will defend you."

"Defend? I'll be happy if we just don't die." Viera looks back down the hallway. "Speaking of dying, one of those blue things is on its way back. Guessing this meeting is about over."

Viera isn't wrong. A few seconds later, the Lunare steps inside the room to make way for another blue familiar. It doesn't even look at either my friends, but points at me with a smooth aqua finger.

"Time for your first session, specimen. Please, follow the familiar," Dalachite says over the speakers.

I feel my friend's nervous stares, but they can't do anything for me here. Dalachite said it prefers me alive, so I have to trust that I'll stay that way.

At least for a little while.

A long leap carries Sax over the familiar's head. Above the swords that could swing and catch him mid-flight. Sax rolls as he hits the ground, using his tail to push him along the somersault to the far end. Near where the red cabinet sits ajar, gleaming with weaponry.

He hears the familiar's feet along the ground, though it's a sad, soft pounding. Not true Oratus claws. Sax could use his, but those swords have reach. Instead he darts for the cabinet.

Sax reaches in and grabs a pair of short miners, spins around as the familiar closes, and pulls the trigger. The familiar should blow to pieces. Energy should glance out and pierce that silky smooth blue skin and burst it into puddles. But when Sax pulls the triggers, nothing happens. There's a quick click, but the deadly rays don't come. The familiar continues moving forward, sweeping those swords up and sending them crashing towards Sax.

So Sax does what he can and throws the miners up to

block. The swords strike with a loud shrieking noise as they cut into the metal weapons. They don't get all the way through; the blades catch on the bottom half of the barrels. Sax feels the jerk and gets an idea.

With his foreclaws, Sax throws the miners to the left. The swords, caught within, yank out of the familiar's grasp and fly along with them. They hit the wall, but Sax isn't seeing that. He's already moving forward, his mid-claws taking swipes at the familiar.

The weakness of Dalachite's creation is made plain. It tries to intercept Sax's attack. Tries to catch Sax's claws with its own. But there's no strength there. No solidity. Every one of Sax's claws runs straight through the familiar and tears apart its arms.

Rends its legs. Until the Oratus, or what was supposed to be one, is yet again a splatter on the floor.

"Do you know what your issue is, Amigga?" Sax calls to the voice, blue slime dripping from his mouth after an eager bite. "Your familiars don't have weight. Enough reality. You want to fight something like me, then you need to give your familiars bodies that work."

There's nothing for a while. The familiar cells flow together into a pool and stay there. Sax, bored at the silence, goes over to where the miners and swords sit and picks them up off the ground, separates them. Takes a closer look.

The miners are standard issue, if, like so many other things on the station, somewhat out of date. They lack the power of Sax's own weapons; unable to punch through heavy walls, like the seed ship gateways. The swords, meanwhile, are nothing better than training weapons.

They're missing the capability of the ones Sax has used before. A slot in the hilt to allow the blades to retract and extend. Wiring for heating in case the blade has to cut through metal. A feature that would have, should have let the weapons carve through Sax's improvised defense.

Minutes pass and Sax goes to the door, but it's not open. He can't find any way to make it so. He tries calling out to Dalachite, but receives no response. For a moment Sax wonders if he's going to die in there. Starve out, or suffocate as punishment for the insult he's delivered to the Amigga's creations.

"I'm sorry," Dalachite announces with no warning. "I had to deal with another matter. I see you've made short work of my experiment."

"Short work is an understatement."

"Yes. But my familiars are new. You have had cycles to develop and refine. I will not be discouraged. Neither is it fair to expect an Oratus to fight like a robot, or punish you for your success. I'll unlock the door, and you may proceed."

"I'm doing this to be nice, Amigga," Sax says. "I'm not your prisoner, or your plaything. Next time, let me come and go as I please."

"Of course, Oratus. Of course."

The door shunts open and Sax leaves the training room. Heads back down the hallways, this time using his vents to guide him. Smelling the scent of cooking food. Of nutrient paste heated up into its edible state. The smell of Bas; a sweet, strong scent that says his pair has been busy too.

When he comes to the kitchen this time, Bas has an array of colored bars spread out on the table. Nutrient goop starts out as such: a soft spongy liquid, but when heated hardens into a cracker. One packed full of vitamins and energy. Stimulants and steroids to keep muscles strong in space, where such things, with little gravitational resistance, fall into rapid decline.

"I've unloaded what we need," Bas says as Sax enters. "Found our quarters."

"I won." Sax waits for Bas to congratulate him, but his pair only laughs, a short hissing sound.

"Are you expecting an award? I'd have been more insulted had you lost to something that Amigga made."

Sax would agree, but the fight is sticking with him. How quickly the familiar changed and adjusted holds a headache in Sax's mind. So he tells the narrative to Bas. Explains the back and forth. Describes how the familiar could split, and how it could use the weapons.

"The miners weren't charged this time," Sax finishes. "But they could've been. They will be one of these times. I have no doubt. Dalachite is going to try to kill us."

"If that's as you say, then we're outnumbered," Bas replies. "You and I can kill an army, but not one that keeps coming back."

"Unless we eliminate the source," Sax replies.

"Not yet," Bas says. "Not yet, Sax. We can either kill Dalachite now, and render this whole trip worthless, the specimens unexamined and our potential solution to the Sevora problem unexplored. All for a hunch. All because you're afraid. Or, we prepare."

Prepare. This makes more sense. Hope for the best, be ready for the worst. Common wisdom.

Sax has an idea for that.

"Did you happen to find where the humans are?"

"Yes," Bas nods to a side of the kitchen, where a console sits in the wall, its black screen displaying nothing. "The blueprints for the station are on there. Maps. I think I know where they are."

"Then after this, I'll see to our preparations." Sax sits

down at the table, wraps his tail around his waist, and begins to bite into the flavorless, crunchy, bars.

They're better than the blue familiar ooze, but not by much.

The room is spherical, with a small platform extending out from the door into the middle. There's nothing there, on the platform, except for the shiny pearl metal that covers everything on Cobalt. The familiar directs me out to it anyway. The voice hasn't talked much on the way here, as if it's become distracted by something.

I make the walk to the platform in silence.

Ignos, though, keeps talking.

This is an immersion chamber. They'll test—

Stop it. Be quiet. I'm still reeling from learning what Ignos really is, and every time the creature buzzes my mind, I start to panic. Worry that Ignos is going to manipulate me again. Tell me something I want to hear that helps its own ends.

On the platform I can look around me. It's not an exceptionally high sphere, though I think it's tall enough for one of the Oratus to stand where I do. Certainly more than twice my own height above and below. The paneling, though, catches my eye: interlocking rectangles, and the lines between each of them pulsate in different colors. Waves of yellow and orange and blue and green cascade around the sphere. It's mesmerizing, unnaturally beautiful.

I hear the door shut.

I'm trapped in this room, and for the first time since getting on the station, I feel hungry. Biological needs. But all of that quickly goes away when the lights go out and plunge me into darkness.

"This is meant to give me an idea of who you are. How your mind and body operate," Dalachite says these things with a falling edge, as if it's reading a script while doing something else.

I don't have a chance to ask what that is, because novas appear in front of my eyes. A series of wild flashes and I'm about to stumble back, when I realize the platform I'm on has changed. My feet were on smooth metal, they're now locked. Bands have come over them, sealing me down. It's uncomfortable, and I feel like I could break my legs if I try hard enough, but the bands keep me stable while the world explodes around me.

That's the only way I can describe it. Bright lights burst one after the next in a myriad of colors. After a few seconds of this I shut my eyes, squeeze them tight and try to make it go away. Even behind my eyelids I can see the splashes until they stop and darkness returns.

When I open my eyes, I see nothing, but now I feel a breeze. Wind picking up, though I'm not sure where it's blowing from. The air whirls around the chamber and it gets very cold. So cold that I shiver and my teeth chatter against each other.

"Stop," I try to say, and my words gasp out as steamy breath in front of me.

As if Dalachite is listening, the wind slows to a crawl,

then stops entirely before starting back up in the opposite direction. This time, hot. So hot. I begin to sweat as it feels like I'm standing in the desert, underneath the burning heat of Ignos.

It's still black.

Before I can breathe, before I can say anything, the air stops and the room equalizes its temperature. Back to the same cool nothing as everywhere else on the station. A small circle appears in front of me. A light. It begins to move. I follow it around with my eyes, as there's not much else I can do standing there on the platform. I wonder at the point of all this is, but I'm trapped and I'm scared and I don't know what else to do, so I watch.

The circle goes too far left, to the point where I cannot follow. My head turns and then I twist my body to track it until I can't rotate anymore without snapping my hips apart. The dot hovers at the edge of my vision, then swings back and does the same in the opposite direction. Then it centers directly in front of me. Grows brighter, so bright that again I squint and then it dims suddenly and disappears.

In the dark in front of me images appear. Things I don't recognize. Strange vistas, orange and green. Churning oceans with strange white ice formations arcing across in the background. More and more flash in front of me, staying only for a second or two.

Until one. One that makes me gasp. One that makes tears come to my eyes. It's a grove of trees, with vines hanging from their branches, sloping towards a fern-covered ground. In the back, almost hidden, I can make out a small river flowing by. I've not seen the exact place, but it feels to me of home. It is so much home.

The picture fades away to nothing.

I hear clanking and grinding machines, a word I've

come to know from Ignos' inventions. I feel things running along my body. Cold, metal. Poking at my skin and I try to reach to brush them off, but as I do so something grabs my arm. More bands. In the dark I cannot see, but they feel to me as if they're coming from the same place, the same platform that is still holding my feet.

Pain. Brutal sharp and brief. It travels from my arm down my body to my legs and back up again. As if testing each and every part of me.

"Very good, Kaishi," Dalachite says as the pain fades. "You are a fascinating specimen. Something I never expected to see. I have one final test for you. One last thing. So if you would please, relax."

"I," but that's all I can manage. My body is exhausted, my mind burns after what's just happened, and all I can do is slump into the metal holding my arms and legs.

The door opens, and footsteps come towards the platform. I turn my head to look, but as I do so the door shuts again and anything coming close is shrouded in dark. A moment later I feel chill fingertips touching my head. Only these are not the fingertips I know. These don't have the rich texture of human hands.

These don't have the warmth of a human's body. No, these are lifeless and slick, like being grabbed by a drop of water. They hold my head straight. I feel something long begin to sneak into my ear. It keeps going and going and going and fear pours out of Ignos, so much that I'm nauseated by it.

A twitch and a vibration and I'm aware, for the first time, of what Ignos *is*. There's a frenzy in my mind. In my head. As though thousands of skittering feet are running between my ears scratching and grabbing everything they can. The sensation is followed by a throbbing aching blast that would have me on my knees if I were capable of falling.

Then it's over. The object withdraws, foot steps recede. The door opens and shuts again.

The chamber lights come on slow, and once the whole room is cast in that same alabaster white as the rest of the station, the restraints pull away.

I fall on my knees, plant my hands on the cool metal and cry.

Sax leads the humans, who call themselves Viera and Malo, through the last hallway to the training room. It wasn't hard getting Dalachite's permission for the exercise, as the researcher wants to learn about the specimens as much as Sax wants to train them.

"So what are you?" Viera asks as they walk. "I understand you came from the sky. From wherever this place is."

"I did not come from here," Sax replies. "I live, if you wish to call it that, far away. On a ship much larger than this station."

"Station, ship… I'm thinking these mean different things to you than they do to me. I'm guessing you don't paddle your way around?"

"Paddle?"

Malo, the other one, mutters something Sax can't understand.

"I'm not joking." Viera says. "It's a question. Rather than sit silent like you, I'm trying to figure out what's going on here."

Sax glances from one to the other. The humans exhibit courage in the face of danger and unknown circumstances. A healthy sign. Sax gives them a quick lesson on space travel, on how leaping creates folds in the universe to take a ship from one end to the other, and by the gradual glazing of their eyes, knows when he's said enough.

"Another thing," Viera says as soon as Sax falls silent. "The other one, with pink scales? She comes from the same place as you? Is she your sister?"

"We are called Oratus," Sax says. "The 'pink one' is my pair. My mate for life."

"Yeah, we humans try to do that to," Viera shrugs. "Always seemed too much trouble to be worth it."

Sax stops. Presses the tip of his tail against Viera's chest and turns to look at her. "I don't care about your society or your species, except as it can help us stop the Sevora from infesting the galaxy."

"So would you say Bas is the nice one?"

This is wasting too much time. Sax doesn't answer, but lopes on.

When they reach the training room door, the light above already shines green; Dalachite following through on its promise. Sax leads the way in and gestures with a single foreclaw towards the center.

"Stand there till I say otherwise," Sax orders with a sharp hiss, and then he heads towards the cabinet.

Inside, much the way he left them, are the two damaged miners, a collection of smaller arms, and the swords.

Where to begin.

With a visceral lesson, obviously.

Sax grabs two small miners and turns back to the humans.

"Watch," Sax says and raises the miners, aims one at each of the two humans, and pulls the triggers.

Azure bolts flash out for a split second and strike each of the humans. They both twitch, then fall. Collapse without a sound onto the floor. Sax laughs, then walks over and stares down at the two humans.

"Do you see?" Sax hisses. "These are stunning miners. Packed full of energy, they will overload your nervous system and fry your mind for a short period. Useful, because stunning shots use a relatively small amount of power. Which means you can fire over and over again."

To demonstrate, Sax points the weapons at the humans and, just as Viera and Malo start to move their eyes towards the Oratus, Sax shoots them a second time. "These will not slow down a large creature at all. They will not keep anyone, even at your small size, paralyzed for long. So it's best to use these in an emergency. To buy yourself time, or to surprise someone expecting something different."

Sax replaces the stunning miners in the cabinet and pulls out one of the heftier weapons. One not broken. He strides back to the middle the room. Viera and Malo are blinking now, coughing. Trying to find their nerves.

"This a full miner. It can fire like so," Sax pulls the trigger and bright red flashes out and digs into the side of the room.

The laser light burns into the padded walls, leaving the metal beneath clean.

"Quick, lower powered shots still capable of doing plenty of damage to the right target. Or, if you don't mind burning through your power, you can use it like this."

Sax adjusts where he places his claws, causing a different set of small colored circles on the side of the miner to illuminate a deep red, and he pulls the trigger. This time, instead of a single flash, a steady stream of molten energy shoots forth. The frothing red beam torches the padding, disintegrating it as the beam moves. Sax keeps blasting for a few seconds, careful to shift his aim so as not to actually burn through the room's wall to the other side.

"Now that's a weapon," Viera says from the floor.

Or rather, tries to. Sax catches the words, interprets the meaning, but the sound is more a squeaking rasp than anything. Her vocal cords still not working the way they should.

"Both of these will help you should you need to fight," Sax says. "Later, you'll have the chance to fire all of these. Learn how not to blow yourself to tiny, tasteless ash."

Sax goes and gets the swords. By the time he gets back to the center of the room, both Malo and Viera are standing again, though neither looks particularly thrilled.

"They don't stun too, do they?" Viera nods at the swords as Sax walks up.

"They don't have to," Sax replies. "Why stun when you can kill?"

Malo says something to Viera again, and the human shrugs.

"Do you not speak our language?" Sax asks.

"Little," Malo replies.

"The man has his own tongue. He understands most of what we're saying, just not how to talk back." Viera explains. "I'll translate."

Malo repeats what he said a moment ago. Viera replies with a curt line, then turns to Sax.

"Malo says that killing is wasteful." Viera shrugs. "Can't sacrifice a dead human."

"Sacrifice?"

"Right. You win a fight, you take the prisoner, then carry them to the top of some temple or somewhere, take out their heart and ask your gods for stuff." Viera talks as though she's describing the dullest dirt in the galaxy. "You monsters do something similar?"

"We eat our prisoners."

True enough for these humans, anyway.

Viera laughs, tells Malo, who proceeds to look ill, which only makes Viera laugh harder.

"See, Malo has a deep love for his people," Viera continues to Sax. "He has this idea that they're the chosen ones. That they're going to wind up ruling our planet. And, I suppose, this galaxy you keep talking about."

Now it's Sax's turn to laugh. Viera points at the Oratus, then says another series of words to Malo. The human warrior, for Sax can tell Malo's profession in that way a fighter can see himself in another, doesn't appreciate whatever Viera says. He pushes away his friend and holds out a hand to Sax.

"Think he wants the sword," Viera says.

"That much is clear." Sax gives Malo the blade. The warrior turns and points the tip of it at Viera. "I believe you have insulted

him."

"Believe I did," Viera replies, shaking her head. "We would have wiped his civilization away if Kaishi hadn't found a creature with all the answers in her head. Guessing Malo is still feeling sore about that."

A rivalry, with a deeper anger to it. These emotions are dangerous. Not something Sax wants to contend with if, or when, he needs these two fighting alongside him and Bas. Best to purge such feelings early. He holds the second sword out to Viera, who takes it and spins the hilt in her hand.

"You'll find gravity is lower here than on your home world," Sax says. "Your moves won't have quite the same speed. Swing light and learn from each other."

Sax steps back until his tail touches room's wall and waits. Viera looks at her sword, then over at Sax. "What are you wanting us to do? Whack away?"

Sax nods.

Malo says something then, and Viera sighs back at the warrior. Spreads her feet and sets the sword in the middle, with both hands on the hilt. Malo bends his knees slightly, leans forward and holds the sword at a flat angle. There's time for a single breath. Viera makes the first move. Steps into a sweeping cut at Malo. But the gravity is low, and the momentum from her lunge is too much to stop.

Viera floats as she tries to swing, tumbling forward. Malo, looking to take advantage, swipes up his sword for an overhead cut, but that motion too brings Malo up off the floor just a bit. Enough to throw him off balance and together the two of them fall gently to the ground in a crumpled heap.

Sax can't help it, he laughs; loud hisses ringing through the chamber.

The two fighters untangle themselves, once again taking up their positions. Viera lets words fly, and Sax catches the name, Kaishi, of the third human. Interesting. Perhaps she is the real center of this conflict.

Malo relaxes his guard, opens his mouth to unleash some retort, when Viera charges. She doesn't even lead with the sword, instead she bends her right leg and shoves off, throwing her left foot into a kick that catches Malo's face. The warrior flies back, bounces into the wall. The gravity gives Malo enough time to catch himself, plant his hand on the ground and kneel, looking up towards Viera, who's laughing.

"This gravity thing. It's great," Viera says to Sax as she hops, goes a meter in the air and sinks back down.

Malo yells something full of heat, and then he's on his feet rushing forward. Viera touches on the ground just as Malo arrives, the charging warrior swinging his sword in a crossing slash, with enough control not to send himself spinning. Viera manages to block the swing, angling Malo's weapon down to the floor. Viera follows the guard with a left-hand slap, again to Malo's face, and the warrior staggers back.

"Don't get angry now, Charre," Viera says. "There's a reason the Lunare were winning before Kaishi intervened. You're out-dated. You're all pathetic."

Sax can see something though. It's in Malo's eyes. In his bearing as the warrior stands back up. Viera continues to fling insults, though Sax thinks Malo isn't hearing them anymore. He's in the fight, as any true warrior should be, and this kind of fight ends only one way.

Sax needs to stop this now. This isn't a training exercise anymore.

"I mean think about it. Your army spends all this time working with sacrifices. Slaughtering defenseless people on top of Tiers or your giant temples? How is that helping you?" Viera gestures with the sword. "Know what? It's not. Not at all. I wouldn't be surprised, by the time we get back, to find we have all of you in chains working our mines."

When Malo attacks again, he gives no signal. Only a slight tightening of his arms. Then Malo launches himself. Pushes both feet into the ground and dives forward with his blade pointed straight at Viera like a missile. A move impossible in higher gravity. One Sax suspects Viera has no training for. No preparation. No idea how to defend. She swings the sword, tries to block, but Viera is too slow.

Malo strikes, dives the point deep into Viera's chest.

And Sax fears he's killed a human.

I step through the halls. A familiar guides me. Its blue hands reach out and hold mine, pulling me along as I try to fix myself. I'm reaching through the stories of my childhood, the ones about our god Ignos, about humans and animals and survival and triumph that provide examples of how to deal with this sort of trauma.

I find nothing.

There's no Solare story for this. No legend or tale told around the fire that says what to do when you find out how easy you are to break. I was poked and prodded on that platform. Tested and torn. My body made to dance for some unknown reason, for some creature I don't know or understand.

Which brings me to a question. Which gives me a way forward.

"What was that?" I ask the familiar—my first words since I left the platform.

"I'm getting to know you," Dalachite replies from the walls around me. The familiar keeps us walking. "The start of a long and fruitful relationship for both of us."

Fruitful.

Long.

I'm not sure I'll last through more of those.

As if it's reading my thoughts, Dalachite continues, "These first conversations might be difficult. Painful, even. But that's natural. What discoveries happen without such hardship? Where would we be without the willingness to endure strife to gain what we need?"

"I don't see you enduring anything."

Careful, Kaishi. This one has the power to kill us at any moment it chooses.

Which might be a relief. In any case, I've said the words, so, while we walk, I wait for the voice to respond.

"I'll forgive you that one, specimen." Dalachite chooses not to use my name. "What I've endured is beyond your comprehension. What I have lived through, sacrificed for the good of the galaxy, is so far beyond your short trial that it doesn't bear mentioning. Go now, recover, and know that you have much more to give before you can claim yourself a martyr."

I don't want to be a martyr. I don't care about the galaxy —something I didn't know existed until hours ago. I just want to go home.

Then fight your way back.

I will.

We're not heading back to my room. I only notice—as most of the hallways look the same—because we've been walking longer than it took to get to that terrible platform.

"Where are we going?" I ask, but the familiar doesn't stop and Dalachite doesn't respond.

Eventually we reach another door and the familiar opens it with a blue palm on a black box to the door's right. A whoosh and its open. I freeze. A creature stands on the other side. The pink and gold one. Outside of the jungle, of the panic that consumed us all that night, I can see how beautiful those scales are, even as clenching fear tightens my throat.

Is this another test? Has Dalachite decided it's my time to die after all? But the creature only stares at me for a moment, then gestures at a high, silver table. On it, piled like small buildings, are stacks of thick, colored bars. Oranges, browns, yellows—it's like a warm-colored rainbow. The familiar, I notice, disappears as I step in and shuts the door behind me.

"They will fill you up," the pink gold creature says once we're alone, its voice a soft hiss. "Provided, of course, your body functions like ours."

"My body 'functions'?"

It's not a term or phrase I've heard before, but I'm thankful for something to take my mind away from the tests and terrors I've been through.

"Yes, functions. Surely you know and understand that all things are a product of what lies inside them. The ever present motion churning to keep the those eyes of yours blinking, that mind thinking." The creature's voice is a mix of hisses and growls. It sounds strange in my ears, but then so does everything else on *Cobalt*.

"How does yours function?" I ask.

"I am Bas, an Oratus. As is Sax. We are living weapons," Bas says. "We exist to enforce the laws of the galaxy. To keep it stable, harmonious and peaceful for those who live in it."

"That sounds like a speech," I say.

"It is," Bas laughs, a sort of half hiss, half snort. "Now, sit down. Eat. We can't have our prize specimen dying on us."

I follow Bas' orders. Or rather, try to. The table doesn't have chairs, and it's far too tall for me to eat at. The colored bars sit at the level of my eyes, and I'd have to reach up and over to get to them. I do notice, though, that there are gray-shaded plates in the floor alongside the table. I walk over to them, and glance at Bas, hoping she'll give me the answer.

"Simply sit." Bas provides. "They will rise to greet you at whatever height is most appropriate."

I do so, bend my legs and my knees, as if I'm going to sit down. Something rises from the floor, forms a perfect mold, and pushes me up to meet the table. The nutrient bars are now perfectly positioned for effortless snacking.

"That's neat," I say.

Because it is.

"Try them. When you're done, you can use the facilities there," Bas points to a small door off the kitchen with a green frame.

I devour three of the bars—hunger rising in me at the food, even if it tastes dry and dull, to demand I stuff myself full. After, I use what Bas calls a lavatory, a strange experience where, once again, smooth shaping molds move to accommodate my needs without my asking. Eventually I rejoin Bas at the table, where she hands me a large bowl full of water and bids me to drink.

"You and Sax have strange names," I say after I take a full gulp, with some of the water splashing over the sides onto the table.

Bas doesn't pay any attention to it, so neither do I.

"Stranger still to give them and not receive one in return?" Bas says to me and I blush.

"Kaishi," I say. Bas smiles at me, which, with her rows of sharp teeth, makes me twitch.

Bas watches me take another drink, and when water

splashes again, this time bouncing off of the edge of the table onto my clothes—still the cape and robe I've been wearing since we left home—she laughs a second time.

"I usually drink from something smaller?" I ask, nodding at the bowl.

"I'm sorry, Kaishi. It seems *Cobalt* is not ready for your presence," Bas replies, spreading her claws in what I think is a shrug. "I'm sure Dalachite will strive harder in the future to accommodate your species."

It's an admonishment. I can tell that much by her tone. Still, I shelve my pride to ask other, more important questions.

"What is this place?" I ask. "A station? What's Dalachite?"

"A creature you don't know," Bas replies. "If we are the weapons of the galaxy, Dalachite and its brethren are its mind. Amigga run stations like this, control our governments. Lead teams searching for scientific discoveries, and determine what we should do with them."

"You obey them?"

"I enjoy slashing my claws through an enemy, exploring a new world, or diving into a battle to see it won," Bas replies. "The Amigga like none of these things. So we make ideal partners."

"And one of them runs this station?"

"One of them *is* this station. When an Amigga chooses a home, like this one, it's built around them. They are literally embedded inside so that they can see and sense everything. It's why we brought you here."

"So it could study me."

"So it could find a solution," Bas reaches over and rests a claw on my forehead. I should jerk back, but I'm too tired. If this Oratus feels like killing me, I won't have the energy to fight back.

"You mean the thing inside my head. Ignos." I decide to stick with the name. Ignos hasn't offered a new one, and I don't care enough to change it anymore.

"What you carry is the galaxy's greatest enemy, and we will do anything to stop it."

She doesn't know what she's talking about. Her kind, and these Amigga, they are the galaxy's true demons. They rip apart any who think differently, who stand before them. Do not trust them, Kaishi. Do not, or you will wind up their toy to twist and turn and poke and prod until you are nothing.

Bas tilts her head at me. Watches my eyes. "It's talking to you, isn't it?"

I nod.

"Sevora, I know you're listening." Bas is talking to me, and yet not. "Do not harm this one, or I will taste you between my jaws. And I will chew slowly." Her eyes narrow on mine. "As for you, Kaishi, know that you have friends on the station. Those who will protect you."

I'm about to thank her, then I remember that Bas and Sax brought me here, want Dalachite to test me, and I say nothing.

The door opens behind me, the noise saving me from an awkward silence. A familiar stands in it, gesturing at the both of us to stand and follow. Dalachite's voice crackles around us, "A specimen has been wounded. Until the situation is contained, please return to your quarters. Immediately."

Viera is light in Sax's midclaws. Barely heavier than a furry Flaum. The weight means Sax outruns Malo, leaving the warrior behind as he dashes through the hallways. Dalachite already knows what's happened, and panels in the floor change green in front of Sax to guide him towards *Cobalt*'s medical bay.

When he needs to move, Sax can be very, very fast: His claws bite deep into the floor, leaving scratches but propelling Sax forward in long heaves. His tail catches lips in hallway intersections and pushes Sax in the right direction. Even his foreclaws, empty, grab what they can and push.

All the same, Viera is losing a lot of blood. It splashes and leaves a brutal trail. Sax feels the thick, hot liquid on his skin, and he resists the urge to lick it away. To take a small bite of the specimen so vulnerable in front of him.

His mission is to protect, not destroy.

There are three familiars already in the medical bay when Sax arrives. All of them looking vaguely like humans, or Flaum. Two arms, two legs and at various heights. The number of blue figures stops Sax. It confirms what he fears; that Dalachite has far more familiars running around the station than it's let on thus far. Any or all of them could come after Sax with swords or miners.

But that's not important. Not right now.

What's worse is that *Cobalt* is old, and its treatments out-dated. The medical chamber is a single large room with a split bed in the middle. It's large and wide, with thin lines visible where, if necessary, the platform can break apart to hold multiple patients. Right now it's as one, and it's where Sax lays Viera.

As the human body hits the bed, lights above Viera grow bright. Machines and equipment wheel forward from the corners the room under their own power. They stop at the optimal length for Viera's mass and width. Programmed to optimal efficiency. Except nothing happens. Viera groans, and the deep gash beneath and to the left of her neck continues to leak.

"We have no protocols," Dalachite says overhead. "There are no standards for this species. No commands to follow."

"It's a carbon-based form. Scan and repair," Sax hisses.

"Why risk damaging the specimen further?" Dalachite replies. "If it dies, then we can still harvest it. We can still learn. Or you can try to save it, ruin it with some ill-conceived attempt. Then what would we get? Nothing."

The mission is protection.

Sax steps forward to the split bed, towers over Viera. There's one common rule when dealing with injuries like this, and that is to stop the bleeding. Then restore fluid and blood, if possible. Sax barks the orders. The familiars don't move, but the machines, programmed to respond to vocal commands, leap to action.

The bed itself flashes blue beneath Viera for a second, running a scan of the human's anatomy. Immediately after, a robotic bundle of thin spindly arms, each with a different tool on the end, bursts into activity. Reaching forward with a dozen different tiny appendages to snip and snap and sew until the gash disappears under a cascade of stitches.

Another mobile rack with various bags of hanging fluids and drugs, shifts near Viera, adjusts itself and aims a syringe. It stabs Viera's left forearm. The syringe pulls back some of Viera's blood and, like the bed, flashes blue for a microsecond. The bags shift on the rack, one with a deep crimson coming forward and slotting into the tubing leading down to the syringe. Synthetic blood.

It's strange that *Cobalt* would have the necessary fluids for a new species, but Sax is glad of it all the same. Still other robots tend to Viera's needs. They dive down from the ceiling to clip away clothing, to measure heartbeats and breath. To make sure that he's warmed with heated rays from above and below.

Sax watches with the familiars. Old medicine. On a modern ship or station, Viera would be dunked into a bio-tank and regenerated through its mixture of nutrients, nanobots, and living cells ready to substitute for what her body could not do for itself.

Cobalt is an old station, and old methods must suffice.

Malo bursts into the room, finally. Sax notices the warrior is still carrying his sword and, before Malo can make another move, Sax reaches over and tears the weapon from him. Malo barely reacts, his eyes on Viera.

"Alive?" The warrior asks.

"Too soon to tell," Sax replies. "Your attack was good. A clever move."

From the horrified way Malo looks at him, it's clear the

warrior can understand Sax, even if he doesn't quite know how to speak in common tongue.

But Sax isn't a much of a talker anyway. They settle in. Stare at the buzzing machines.

Watch a human's life creep back from the endless abyss.

Bas ignores the familiar, brushing by its blue, protesting arms. She says she knows the way to the medical bay. But after the third turn, after we see our first splotch of dropped blood, two familiars come out of the hallway ahead of us and block the path.

Point us back.

"Both of you to your respective chambers please," Dalachite says. "There's been an accident, and while cleanup is underway I would appreciate it if everyone kept themselves out of this mess."

It isn't a request.

The familiars split Bas and I, the pink-gold Oratus giving me one last wave of her claw as our familiars lead us in different directions. We make our way quick back to the rooms I suppose, now, belong to Viera, Malo, and I. Both of theirs, I notice, have glowing red lights above their doorways. Locked, or absent.

I'm shuttled into mine without comment, and the door shuts behind me as soon as I'm inside. It's strange being alone now. The fun mystery and excitement of being somewhere new has worn off. So has the fear. I replace it with grim determination. Acceptance. This isn't where I want to be, but if I'm going to leave, I'm going to escape, and to do that, I first have to stop denying that I'm here at all.

So I look around my room. Try to find something useful. There's the soft, raised bed that is obviously for sleeping. Something which I haven't done since arriving on *Cobalt* and which, my fuzzy brain is telling me, I may need soon.

But not yet.

Elsewhere, other than the blank pearl walls, there's a black screen on one side and a small door that opens to my own... what did Bas call it? Lavatory. I look in there now and notice there's a strange thing in the ceiling in a compartment to the left of where the lavatory's primary business is conducted.

It's a lattice of holes. There's a button on the wall beneath them, that, when I press it, I find it's not just a button but also a dial. If I turn it to the left, it begins to glow red. Turn it right, it glows blue. When I press it in, stale-smelling water sprays down from the holes. I realize the dial, here, controls the temperature: red makes the water hot, blue makes it cold.

I've been chilly since making it to the station, so I take off my ragged cape and enjoy a few, fleeting moments underneath those hot drops. When I press the button again, some time later, I'm blasted with dry air from all angles, from vents with holes so tiny I didn't even notice them before. At the end of it, I'm clean.

I'm about to pull my old clothes back on when I notice, behind the bed, a new cabinet is open. I'm not sure why, whether someone came into my room while I was in the lavatory or if the opening is automatic, but bright blue—like the sky back home—clothes are in there. At least, that's what I think they are, but when I pull the top one from the pile and set it on the bed, it seems to puddle together.

It's a mask.

There's awe in Ignos' words.

I've never actually seen one like this.

But what is it?

The Amigga prefer things activated by touch. So place your hand on it. See what happens.

I do so. Lay my hand flat on the blue... I want to call it fabric, but it's clearly not. Too smooth, too lifeless. Yet when I touch it, like the Cache did so long ago in the jungle, the mask grabs onto my fingers. Pulls itself up my hand, arm, and eventually over my entire body. Even my head. I close my eyes as the mask rushes over them. There's a sense of fleeting pressure, and when it's gone, I open my eyes to clear vision.

I'm suddenly warm. Perfectly so.

When I look down at myself, it's though I'm clothed tight. A form I've never seen before, but one that fits my every angle, and makes me colored silver-blue, like the familiars in bright light. Even my hands appear gloved. Like a Lunare, clothed to stay warm under the mountains.

The thought interrupts my fascination like the crack of Viera's pistol.

One of my friends is hurt, and here I am, playing in my room. Forgetting all about them.

If you want to learn what's happened, use the console.

I stare at the screen on the wall to the left of the door. It's blank and dark.

Remember, Kaishi? Place your hand on it.

I do so, laying my right hand flat against the screen. It leaves an impression, and when a leaf-green line begins to outline my finger-tips against the screen, I jerk it back. The illustration vanishes.

Leave it there. It needs to know who you are.

I stare at my hand for second. Who I am? How is this thing going to know from my hand, who I am?

It looks for signals. Etchings in your palm, the heat of your hand. The mask gives you to it. That's how the console knows it's you and not Malo. Whether you're an Oratus or an Amigga.

I still don't quite understand, but I press my hand again to the screen. Once the green tracing finishes, the black fades away to a soft white background similar but not quite matching the tone of the walls. Against it are colorful symbols. One is a shifting spiral. The other appears to be a circle suspended in an oval shape. Another is a jumble of letters mashed into a square, and so on and so forth they go. There must be dozens of them.

A knock interrupts my exploration. This time, when I look towards the door, the light flashes green and the door parts to reveal Malo on the other side.

Only it's not the Malo I remember. This one, my friend, is covered in blood. He holds a crumpled up set of clothes in his arms. I know the uniform. The robe. Viera's.

"Is she alive?" I ask, and when Malo nods, I sigh in relief.

"I nearly killed her, Kaishi," Malo says as he enters the room. He holds out the clothes as if I'm supposed to take them. As if they're mine now, somehow.

"How?" I reply, and Malo tells me.

"It was for my people," Malo says at the end of his story.

"At least, that's what I thought. She mocked us. The Charre. But what are mere words in a place like this? When all we have is each other?"

Malo's face is the picture of anguish. He sits on the side of my bed and stares at the console, though I don't think he sees it. "Do you know why we were out in the jungle, raiding Solare tribes?" Malo's not expecting me to answer, so I don't. "Because we wanted to know what the Lunare were doing. We wanted to know what they wanted from you so that we could get it first."

"To keep them from having it?" I say.

"No. So that we could try to buy a better life for us. From them." He leans forward, presses his hands against his knees, then forces his eyes to me. "You saw what they brought to the field. You saw those strange creatures. The rolling machines of war. They were going to crush us, Kaishi. Wipe us away if we stood in front of them. So I was searching for a way out. A way to save our people, and I found one."

"You found a lie."

"Be that as it may, it worked. Now I'm here, but I don't think the wounds are closed. I lost myself in my hate, Kaishi. Which is less than you deserve. I'm not worthy of you, of serving you or my people."

Malo rises suddenly. Brushes by me as if he's going to leave.

"Am I still your Empress?" I say.

There's a long heartbeat.

"You are my Empress," Malo replies, facing the door.

"Then as your Empress, I command you to stay. To help me and Viera. To be my sword when I need it, and my shield when I don't. Do you accept?"

Malo stiffens, but there is no hesitation.

"I accept, Empress."

Without another word, Malo strides from the room. The door shuts behind him.

I'm left alone with Viera's bloody clothes.

Bas comes into the med bay covered in a destroyed familiar's blue spatter. Sax takes one look at the evidence and bares a toothy grin.

"It tried to keep me away from you," Bas explains. "It failed."

On the table in the middle is the human. Still being monitored, still being worked on, though the intensity of the machines dies down as Viera gets further and further away from losing her life. The three familiars stay, staring at the human, and so Sax and Bas will stay too.

"The Amigga wants to let her die," Sax says. "Take her for parts."

Bas does a slow pan through the room. "Not a terrible plan."

"I put her in this mess. A training accident. Not the way for a warrior to go." Sax clicks his claws against each other. "Besides, I thought we wanted them alive?"

"Insofar as they serve our needs," Bas replies and then goes on to relay the details of meeting Kaishi. How she thinks the human is definitely not captive to the Sevora and may actually be coming to hate the thing inside her mind. "She smells of sadness. Not quite despair, but not far from it."

"She needs an objective," Sax says. "Something to aim at. Something worth living for."

They both turn back to the human on the bed.

"Do you think they pair like we do?" Bas asks.

"That one mentioned something like it. It sounded awful."

"You can't judge other species by the greatness of your own, Sax."

Yet, Sax feels he can. It's justified, in fact. For how else can Sax measure who he is, what he is, without bench-marks? Without seeing just how far below him everything else is?

The predator must know his prey.

"I need to send a message to Evva," Sax says after several minutes of buzzing medical machines. "She needs to know what we think."

Bas is about to reply when the three familiars turn as one and look at them. "You disobeyed me." Dalachite's voice comes from above. "You shattered another of my familiars."

"It was fun," Bas says. "And it can remake itself."

"Not if you walk away wearing it," the Amigga contin-ues. "When I ask you to return to your quarters, I expect you to do so. This is my station and you will follow my requests."

"Those requests sound more like orders," Sax says.

Without really thinking about it, he and Bas separate by a meter. Enough room to maneuver should the three famil-iars get some idea. Though they're all unarmed, and Sax still holds the sword Malo brought with him. If any fight breaks out, winning would be quick and easy.

"Call it what you want, so long as you obey," Dalachite says. "But it's time, I think, to rest. This one's life is well in hand. She's breathing, her heart is beating."

"How do we know you won't kill her as soon as we leave the room?" Sax replies.

"Because I'm not a monster," Dalachite says. "Besides, I can learn as much by watching this one heal as I can by killing her. See how her cellular structure reforms. What her body does to combat potential infections. All you've done is change the parameters of my studies. Not ruin them."

"Do we trust it?" Sax asks his pair.

"I'm not sure we have a choice, unless we intend to fight every familiar on the station." Bas waves a claw at the three blue creatures in front of them. "Let's go. I'm tired as it is."

They leave the med bay. Head back towards their quarters, except halfway there, Sax pulls off. Goes towards the docking bay. When Dalachite asks why, Sax says that they left a number of supplies on the shuttle. The excuse pays off, and Dalachite doesn't talk anymore. It's a quiet walk the rest of the way.

Sax acts normal as he goes up the boarding ramp. Heads to the bridge, where the console and transmitter lie. There's no way to cover what he's doing here, so Sax has to hope Dalachite is busy with other tasks and isn't watching through the windshield.

Staring at the bay's bright green light beyond the glass, Sax presses the button to record and begins to speak. He leaves a long message; shares what's happened on the station. Explains how he believes Dalachite is threatening him. That Sax thinks this will fall apart sooner rather than later.

When the transmission ends, Sax leaves the bridge.

Grabs a token crate of nutrient goop. Heads back through the twisting hallways, towards the quarters. Makes it to the last one when Dalachite finally speaks.

"Suspiciously few supplies, Oratus," the Amigga says.

"Had a craving for our own food. But tell me, Amigga, do you ever sleep?" Sax replies. "Are you always spying?"

"Always spying, Oratus. Always seeing."

"Then I hope what you saw met your expectations," Sax says.

There are any of a dozen formal goodbyes. Ways to say good evening and good night. Sax uses none of them. None are worthy of this encounter. None are worth dispensing on Dalachite and its blue creatures.

Bas already has her mask off and is lying on the large soft sponge that serves as an Oratus bed. Their limbs tangle with each other on the reddish, soft surface. The sponge is cool to the touch, and it bends and folds around them. Their claws puncture it, but it heals around their points so Sax feels surrounded by a thick glove.

As they do every time they sleep together, Sax sends his tail out along the base of the sponge where it meets Bas'. They wrap around each other, and their claws dig through the sponge to clasp.

And the pair sleeps.

I'm sitting on the bed. Wearing the mask and wondering how to take it off. It doesn't seem right to sleep in such a thing, not that it isn't comfortable, but I feel as though it's monitoring me. Measuring what and who I am every second and modulating appropriately. It's a strange feeling, and not one that will lend itself to dreams. Dreams I think will already be hard in coming, considering where I am.

I believe you can take it off.

I ask how and Ignos doesn't reply. Apparently it doesn't know. I glance at the Cache, still tight on my wrist. Again I see a bright green flash and it's as though I'm in a giant forest of information. Pictures hover in my mind's eye, and the Cache attempts to search for what I'm thinking about: the mask. All it finds, though, are fuzzy descriptions. Hunches and speculations about how they work.

While I'm in, I focus on the term 'Amigga' and the Cache obliges. No pictures—apparently, whatever created the Cache hasn't ever seen an Amigga in the flesh—but plenty of text. It's full of adjectives: scientific, aggressive, impersonal and focused. There's a curious sentence about the Amigga having more to do with the current state of the galaxy than any other species, but, when I try to dig further, the Cache comes up empty.

So I blink it away and turn to the only other thing in my room that might hold answers: the console. Its screen is still on. Full of those dizzying icons. Ignos wakes up and begins explaining them to me. I focus on the knowledge databases, like the Cache. Using one, I pull up a map of *Cobalt* and look at where the medical bay is, where my platform room stands. Memorize what I can of it, even though half the terms are unknown to me.

I pay particular attention to the route from my room to the docking bay. To our escape.

From there, an icon that looks like a spinning circle with numbers and dashes catches my attention. I tap it and see a log of events. Simple, laid out one after the other to the dates themselves, all aligned under what the log call "cycles". The log shows ten of them.

A cycle can last a long time, depending on what happens. Hundreds and thousands of your Earth years might pass from one to the next. Or only a dozen.

Dalachite built *Cobalt* in the eighth cycle. Deliberately at distance from the rest of the galaxy—a term I don't understand.

You and all your tribes are but an infinitesimal part of everything, Kaishi. Yet, you may be its most important discovery since the beginning of the cycles.

Because of Ignos, or so that's what Bas said.

Yes.

There's a small burst of frustration from Ignos then, as if the admission pains it somehow. Nothing I can do about it, though, so I look back at the time-line.

Cobalt, after completion, went along at first without anything noted. Tests were assigned and completed. Staff stayed and morale reports showed that things were happy. All recorded in brief, bland updates. The first blip occurs not long after the station was built. When half the staff departed the station. There's a short note indicating the scientists were superfluous and were removed to decrease supply expenses. From then on, every entry marks more and more scientists departing. The notes, though, change to indicate the removals were due to increased efficiency.

The mystery isn't hard to solve: the familiars slowly replaced everyone. I glide over the remaining notes of staff departures and successful experiments, until I come to the very last one:

The last of us are leaving, not through our own desires, as we have spent all our lives here, but because Dalachite has decided we are no longer relevant. Its blue 'familiars' are everywhere now, watching our every move, haunting our footsteps. We Flaum may not match the Amigga's intelligence, but we are living beings; we have souls, we have dreams and desires. The familiars have none of these. That Dalachite finds this an advantage is obvious.

One is opening the door even now.

I bid you goodbye, Cobalt, and may your master drown in the void of its creations.

I tap away from the timeline. The only thing on this station, then, are the three of us, Sax and Bas, Dalachite and its familiars. Elsewhere on the console I find, finally, instructions on how to remove the mask. The creature that appears on the screen to demonstrate makes me stumble back; it looks like a tall, brown-furred mouse with a longer, naked nose. Yet it's clear what its small claws are doing. So I try it.

I spread the fingers in my hands, then press them down against my own palms. It feels like stepping out of the shower; the mask slides off me and clusters on the floor in a bundle like when I first found it. I set it aside, crawl into bed. Say the words that make the lights go out.

A second later I turn lights back on. The darkness without them is absolute. Total. Like in the chamber with the platform. My heart races. Chills and sweats mingle across my body. I take a few seconds. Long deep breaths.

You can dim them.

I say the words Ignos tells me, and rather than vanishing, the lights quiet to the level of dying twilight. A soft, orange glow. Low enough for me to sleep, bright enough to keep from triggering my fears.

Though I wonder why Ignos keeps helping me.

Because you are still my only way to survive.

How can I trust it?

You have to choose to. I can't make you. But I will always try to help you. Because without you, I am nothing.

I have to trust Ignos won't hurt me. I can't get it out of my head anyway. It's with that knowledge that I fall asleep. Slowly, waiting for dreams and nightmares.

The nutrient bars are the same this morning as they were the day before. Not that days have any real meaning on *Cobalt*—the lights here shift to simulate day and night, but there aren't seasons, calendars to keep track of.

Sax is grateful for the protein. For the energy. Especially when the familiars show up again. They look at him, at Bas with their blank blue faces. There are two of them this time, and when they point to Sax, he's not surprised.

"Another exercise?" Dalachite says. "I've made some adjustments. I think you'll find it more interesting this time."

If there's any lingering animosity from yesterday's events, Sax doesn't hear it. As if the Amigga has moved on, chalked it up as a squabble not worth mentioning. Sax is fine with that. He's made his transmission to Evva, and there's plenty of weapons for the Oratus in their quarters. If things get worse, they'll be ready.

"Do you want me to go this time?" Bas says.

"I would much prefer him," Dalachite interrupts. "I'm

calibrating the familiars, and so I need a consistent source subject. One whose styles I can analyze and then see how effective my tweaks have been."

"What kind of tweaks?" Sax asks.

"It would ruin the purpose of the demonstration were I to tell you ahead of time. The whole exercise lies in how well they, and you, adapt."

Sax, beneath the table, sneaks his tail beneath Bas and delivers two quick taps to the bottom of her own tail. He stands up, looks at the two familiars. "Fine. Now that I've got a full stomach, you'll have all the advantage you need."

"To win?" Dalachite laughs.

"Oh, you'll lose," Sax replies. "Just more slowly."

The two familiars lead him through the hallways and back to the same training room. It bears the scars from Sax's gunplay the night before, burns Dalachite does not acknowledge. This time the two familiars go to the center of the room and turn back to Sax.

"Another chase, like yesterday?" Sax asks.

"I think it would be the perfect place to start," Dalachite says. "Whenever you're ready."

This time the familiars don't even move. They stand there, watch Sax. He looks at them. Both familiars are the same size. Both have the same two legs and arms. Neither one capable of outrunning an Oratus. Neither one wearing any sort of weapon. How is this going to be any different than before?

Not that it matters. Sax bares his teeth, clenches his legs, fakes towards the one on the left, and then lunges at the one to the right.

His clawed feet pump into long leaps, and Sax catches the familiar with his midclaws, cuts it to pieces. The familiar explodes in a tremendous blue spray.

Something bites Sax's back. A micro stunner's tingling burn. If Sax wasn't wearing a mask, he'd be in a lot more pain. As it is, the spot in the middle of his spine feels like a lit candle is being held up to it.

"So you're cheating today," Dalachite says as Sax whirls around to see the other familiar. Rather than running to the wall as it did on the day before, the familiar sprinted right to the cabinet. Cut behind Sax after the Oratus went right, and armed itself.

"You're one to talk," Sax roars. The micro-stunner could damage the mask, if Sax let it. "You said this was a chase. Not an attack."

"The battlefield changes constantly, Oratus."

The familiar fires again. The bolt strikes Sax in the chest, burning, but otherwise dispersing through the mask's defenses.

If that's how the Amigga wants it, then Sax will play its game. He darts towards the second familiar, this time using his feet to dance to the right. Towards the door and the wall around it. The familiar tracks and fires another shot. This one misses. A little too slow. Sax angles slightly left, jumps, uses the gravity to hit the padding above the door and spring off so that he's flying towards the familiar at a diagonal angle.

The familiar can't get the miner aimed quickly enough and Sax smashes it, presses the familiar back against the cabinet where his claws rend it into goo.

Any taste of victory dies when Sax hears the door open behind him. Turns to see four more familiars walk in. These are not empty-handed. Each one holds another sword. Not an old model from the cabinet either. These are newer. They shine with circuitry. With buzzing edges. Made to cut right through metal, or through a mask.

"Well done, Oratus. You've exceeded my expectations. However, you've also tried to undermine my station with your little message. I'm sorry, but our experiments are over."

Sax reaches behind him, pulls a pair of miners from the cabinet. The broken ones from before. He takes a quick glance back, sees the working one that he used with Malo and Viera, but it hasn't been recharged. There's one sword still left though. So he takes that. The four familiars advance slowly, each one holding its blade in front of it, level towards the Oratus.

Sax sinks to crouch, drops the broken rifles and holds the sword in his left foreclaw. The four familiars march in a line, which means the ends are the weak spots. Sax doesn't want to get trapped against a wall, so he feints to the right. Away from the familiars and towards space. Then he uses his tail, grabbing the inside of the cabinet, to yank himself back left. Sax claws the up the wall and jumps. He's not going for an attack this time and soars high over the row of blue heads.

The familiars all turn to follow him as Sax lands on the far end of the room, plenty of clear padding between him and his enemies. As Sax hits the ground he bursts forward, charging right at the center of the line. His legs and midclaws scramble on the ground, pushing faster across the room. The four familiars prepare their swings. Sax rolls. His right claws bite into the padding hard. Pull Sax towards the door. Towards that side of the line and out of the range of the two left familiars swinging down towards where he should have been.

As Sax spins, his tail lashes over his shoulders to catch the head of the closest familiar, the one on the end of the right side. The blow doesn't break it, but sends the familiar reeling back.

Buys Sax a second.

Which is all he needs.

Sax completes the roll, he catches himself on his legs and darts forward at the next familiar. Its blade sweeps to meet him, and Sax catches it with his own. But where the familiar only has one weapon, Sax has many. He presses the familiar's blade up and sweeps beneath it with his midclaws.

The familiar breaks apart, and as Sax's skin is pelted with blue goop, he catches its buzzing sword with his tail as it falls to the ground, and flips it at the next familiar. The sword spins end over end, slicing right through the familiar's liquid middle. Which leaves only two.

No, four. Sax counts quick. The other two are back near the cabinet. The ones Sax tore apart earlier. They're grabbing the small, stunning miners.

So that's it then. Sax sees it all in an instant. The familiars putting themselves back together. They'll keep coming, keep hacking away at him until Sax inevitably makes a mistake. Until he gets too tired, or simply misses something.

He notices a red glow above the only exit.

Sax won't leave this room alive.

The opening door shocks me awake. The lights rise from their dim glow to bright scalding white, and as my eyes come into focus I see the blank head of a blue familiar standing there. Staring at me, or at least I think so, though I can't see its eyes.

"Time for our next session," Dalachite's voice says.

I get out of the bed and the familiar watches me as I put on the mask. It's the only clothes I have now, and the mask feels better than my old robe and cape. Fewer scratches, less dirt. It warms me up to the perfect temperature. The mask is also, aside from the Cache, the only real possession I have. It's a comfort to have it close.

I follow the familiar down the hallway, noticing that both Malo and Viera's doors are red-locked. I don't even know if Viera is out of the med bay, and when I ask I receive no response. Part of me wants to stay back, to resist the familiar just to see what would happen, but Ignos tells me not to.

Making Dalachite angry is only going to hurt you more.

This time we go to a different room. There's no platform, no spherical wall, but instead a single long shelf on one side and, on it, a tank full of greenish water. There's nothing else in the room, though I can see some scuffing on the floor. As if furniture had been here at one point, and now moved. There's another familiar in the room, near the tank. It waves me over. As I go, the familiar that led me shuts the door and, I notice, moves to stand in front of it.

I know what's going to happen.

I don't.

When it does, I want you to remember that I'm on your side. Remember that I want the best for the both of us.

I know that. I don't necessarily believe it, but I trust it when Ignos says that its own survival depends on me. It's in my head after all, so if Dalachite decides now is my time to die, it seems likely Ignos would go with me.

I get near the tank. The familiar directs me to the center so that I'm staring across the water. The tank itself is about a meter wide and nearly half a meter deep. There's nothing in it, aside from the liquid. I don't see fish or anything swimming, no plants growing.

The familiar shoves me in.

Not all of me. Just my face and my head. The familiar holds me down and pushes me beneath the surface. I start to shout, to scream, but then I realize I don't need to. I'm still able to breathe, and it's not hard to know why. The mask. It's doing the work for me. So I stop struggling and wait to see what's going to happen next.

I don't have to wait long. The familiar holding me down doesn't relax his grip, but, through the blurred walls of the tank, I see the other familiar come close. He reaches beneath the shelf, and comes back with a shiny silver device almost as long as my arm.

This may hurt Kaishi, but it will be worse for me than for you.

The familiar reaches over with the device, pushes it beneath the water. I feel the ripples as it comes close and I know exactly where it's going. Now I struggle; my hands and arms jerk. I try to kick with my legs, but the familiars are strong. Stronger than me, anyway, and they ignore my attempts.

Stop it, Kaishi. They will only hurt you.

They're going to do that anyway. Ignos, though, is insistent, sad. So I let myself relax. Shut my eyes. Feel the silver piece slide into my ear. The mask coats my skin, but there's something about the device. Something that makes the mask recoil and creates a hole. Ignos starts to tell me, and I catch the word electric, before all is lost.

Before, in the first session, I felt it when Ignos experienced pain. When it thrashed and turned and writhed in my mind. This is similar, only not so random. It's as though Ignos is caught in a net. Stuck on the end of something, and the thrashes are focused. They prickle the right side of my head and my temple burns, and then I feel it. A rushing, slimy thing, leaving tiny scratches across my ear as it moves.

There's a sudden pop. A vacuum. My ears clearing and then I'm being pulled back. Out of the water and away from the tank.

"Look at it," Dalachite's voice comes into the room.

The Amigga doesn't have to tell me, because I can't look away. In the tank is something both small and terrifyingly large. A narrow, sloping body nearly transparent, so that I can see the small batch of organs inside. The very top seems to fray into a thousand strands: long, stringy things that stretch out through the tank as the water shifts. That drift all the way to the edges.

"That is a Sevora," Dalachite says. "That is what is inside you. What is telling you the things that you should do. That is whose demands you've been following."

The thing about nightmares is that they're often scarier when you can't see them. When they travel through the shades of dreams waiting to spring upon you, and you know that they're there but you don't know what they are. Here though, here I'm seeing Ignos in the flesh. I'm seeing the thing that was inside me.

I know then that when I slipped into the black ink in the jungle, this came into my mind.

"There's something very special about your species Kaishi," Dalachite says. "Something that we have not seen before. Something the Sevora did not expect. Do you see all those fronds there? They wrap and ensnare your nerves. They splice into all that you are and take you. Twist you and turn you into a puppet. But this didn't happen with you, did it?"

"I could hear it. We could talk to each other."

I remember of course. I remember after I woke up. With Ignos my head. When it complained about how it couldn't move me. How I couldn't move my own legs until it gave the control back. Why?

"That is why the Sevora are the enemy of the galaxy," Dalachite continues. "They take intelligent races and subvert them to their own ends. A true evil. A parasite. You, and the rest of your species, may hold the secret to preventing that."

"What secret?"

"Somewhere in that body of yours is the reason that Sevora is unable to take you over as it would any other species. It's my job to find out what that is."

I'm afraid to ask but I do anyway. "How?"

There's no answer, at least not a verbal one. But I find out soon enough. The familiars take hold of me again and bring me back to the tank. Press me under the water. My eyes are open and I watch, they even let me tilt my head enough to see the Sevora. To see Ignos.

It doesn't swim so much as bob, until the strands flutter. They move as one, waving back and forth and pushing the Sevora towards me.

When Ignos touches my head, I feel its stringy tentacles. They press against the mask and then bounce away. The Sevora can't, doesn't try to go back inside. But instead it sits there, hovering near my head.

I should be horrified, I suppose. Should be screaming or panicking. I'm not. Partly because, I think, I know it's Ignos there. I know that it's had so many opportunities to hurt me and hasn't. Not directly, anyway. I also have no choice. I can't fight these familiars.

Not alone.

Part of me, too, is curious. The silver thing comes back into the water, guided by a familiar's hand, and approaches my ear. This time, when it punctures the mask, I can feel it moving around, almost touching the sides of my skin. The mask recoils from it, and the space gives the Sevora a chance to shoot forward into my ear like an arrow. The trailing edges of its tentacles crawl once more into my mind.

Into me.

This time, I know what to look for. I feel a second consciousness tap into mine. The tingle in my nerves as they say they're no longer sending messages just to me. When my head pulls out of the water moments later, I hear Ignos.

I'm sorry, Kaishi.

He's never going to be able to beat these things.

Sax runs around the room, jumping and leaping and rolling. Making precise moves when he needs to take out the two familiars that keep trying to get the micro-stunners. The four with the swords chase, but they're slow. Sloppy.

Sax is going to get sloppy too. His muscles are already burning. His mask bears scorch marks from near misses. He's going to make a mistake and die beneath a familiar's blade.

How is he going to get out of here?

Sax takes another flying leap up the wall and then from there jumps onto the ceiling, latching on with his claws. The familiars with the swords head to the sides and begin their weird suction run up towards him. Sax has only seconds to breathe. Meanwhile the two stunner-wielding familiars are re-assembling themselves from the latest thrashing. There's nothing else in the room, except the glowing red light over the door.

The door.

It's metal, too strong for Sax to break through with his claws alone. There's more than claws in this room, however. More than micro-stunners and swords. He glances at the cabinet. The one miner still in there. Half-charged from his show time with Malo and Viera, but even half should be enough to blow a hole in the door. Weaken it for Sax to get through.

Now that he has a plan, Sax wastes no time. He skitters along the ceiling, towards a sword-wielder reaching the top of the wall and turning upside down. Sax meets him, and as the familiar swings his sword, the Oratus bursts forward. Sax gets beneath the strike and slams the familiar into the wall. They both fall, the low gravity and padded floor letting Sax hit the bottom without injury, though his claws mean the familiar can't say the same.

The other sword-wielders drop themselves, and while they're doing that, Sax gets a free run at the cabinet. Jerks it open, grabs a rifle and turns face-to-face with a pair of micro-stunners. They fire, and the two blasts catch Sax right in the chest. The stunners burn, searing hot and a strange wave of numbness spreads through Sax.

He can't give up now or he'll get hacked to pieces.

There's a thing that happens with Oratus. When they're desperate, angry, when they're fighting for their lives. Sax calls it the bloodlust, and it wraps him up in fury now. Pushes away the burns, the aches, the exhaustion. Sax surges, takes another two blasts and then he's through the familiars. Bashing them to the ground and throwing the stunners across the room.

A pair of sword-wielders is next, and Sax sidesteps them. Does a quick jump towards the center of the room and swings, in the air. He aims the miner at the door. Pulls the trigger as he floats and unleashes a lance of azure energy that strikes its target. The door's center-right side glows orange before curling and blackening away from the beam, which sputters out a moment later.

Older miners suck power like a Fassoth sucks food. Sax has forgotten how many power packs they used to carry.

The third sword-wielder catches Sax from behind, nearly lops off his tail, but Sax feels the air moving as the sword comes and only suffers a gash instead. The Oratus turns and, with a single bite, obliterates the familiar's head. Swallows the goop. Sax isn't sure if it'll make him sick, but he knows the stuff won't be going back to reform the thing.

The two swords that he had dodged are closing in. They stand between Sax and the door, but Sax doesn't have time for this. He turns the miner sideways and whips it at the right swordsman. The familiar moves to block, but Sax follows his own toss with a leaping jump. Catches the rifle as the swordsman blocks, and uses the added momentum to shove the blade back into the swordsman's own body.

Sax bowls it over and continues towards the door. The last swordsman turns to give chase, but it's too slow. Sax barrels into the weakened door, which blows apart as the Oratus hammers into it. Sax rolls into the hallway, scrambles on the floor and launches himself down the corridor. He hears Dalachite's voice. Calling to him, laughing at him. Ordering him back to the room.

Sax ignores the sounds of his prey.

He heads towards his quarters. This time there are no green lights telling him where to go. No familiars pointing the right direction. Sax homes in on one thing and one thing only: the smell of his pair. The scent of her guides him through the station, and when he opens the door to their quarters, he finds Bas already armed. She takes one look at the gash on Sax's tail and the burn marks covering his skin and hisses. It's not a laugh, it's not a greeting. A low, angry, fiery rush of air snarling out between her teeth, lips, and the vents lining her chest. A sound Sax has only heard a few times before, a sound reserved for him and those who dare cross her path.

"I'm going to kill it," Sax answers.

"We're going to kill it," Bas replies.

"Secure the specimens," Sax argues. "Secure the shuttle. Make sure we can get off the station."

"You want this, don't you?"

She knows him so well.

"I need this," Sax says.

The prey has been annoying him since they landed here. The familiars are strange abominations. Unnatural. Now Sax can act on it. He gets to put this high and mighty slime into its place. His eyes move to the locker above the bed. There lie a pair of small rifles, and the black bar swords that he prefers.

The Amigga began the fight, Sax will end it.

I'm walking back to my room when my two-familiar escort pushes me forward with more urgency. There's no answer to my startled ask, no explanation for being shoved through the halls. Pressed through doors that shut behind us, closing off passages as we pass through them. I wind up back at my room. No chance for food, drink or anything else. The door closes and I hear the familiars pad away.

Something's wrong.

I gather that much. What's more concerning is that the console is dark and doesn't react when I press it. I'd hoped it might have some information on what's happening in *Cobalt*, but no luck. Left without options, the curious furor dies away, which turns my attention to my own head, and what's inside it.

Do you find me disgusting?

Yes. There's no other answer. Not only does Ignos look terrifying, it's inside me. Always there. I now know those long skinny tendrils are wrapping themselves around my body and connecting to my nerves. How am I not supposed to be disgusted? How am I not supposed to be scared?

Knowledge, Kaishi, is the antidote to fear. You fear me because you don't understand what I am. Let me change that.

I don't protest, so Ignos goes on. Tells me the Sevora's story.

The Sevora woke in the distant past. Ignos doesn't know how many cycles ago, and as I don't really comprehend what a cycle is, I don't press it. All it knows is that they exist deep in the caves and caverns of a rocky world. One covered with marshland on the surface.

The Sevora there swam through the waters, occasionally finding and devouring creatures that shared their space. Some grew to full maturity, and embedded themselves on the ground beneath the vast oceans and swamps and birthed new generations. Ignos itself has never reached that stage. Will never, if it has any choice.

Because once you mature, once you burst forth the next generation, you die a long death.

Not really though. Ignos and I have different definitions of death. For it, for most Sevora, death means the loss of new life.

After a Sevora matures, it can no longer take a new host. To travel and to see what else the galaxy holds. Mature Sevora grow into their home. Like Dalachite and this space station. Once the maturation cycle triggers, everything else stops.

I pester Ignos to get back to the story. As interesting as Sevora genetics are, I don't need more nightmares. I won't be sleeping as it is.

Ignos heads back to the timeline, to the first instant the Sevora had any inkling of their true abilities. The moment came when intelligent life first visited the planet. A flash in the sky similar to what I experienced back home.

A ship crashed in a shallow swamp. Bands of furry creatures, ones Ignos calls Flaum, emerged. The same ones that I'd seen in the console's videos of how to put on a mask. They stumbled around the swamp, unsure of where they were, and the Sevora took advantage. Stole one, then the next and the next until the entire ship had been made captive. For the first time the Sevora had thumbs and fingers, and ideas for them to steal. They took that knowledge, they took the crashed ship and made more.

And spread.

Their growth happened unheeded for a long time. Ignos is boasting at this point. Diving into a lustful, wistful history that makes it clear this is what Ignos wants to return to. The Sevora infiltrated societies, cities, whole planets and grew to enslave them all. Taking each and every sentient creature's mind and turning it to their collective will.

Until the Amigga found them. Sent the Vincere to carve them back. Since that point it's been a continuous, bloody conflict. The Sevora, however, need captives. Need bodies to host. The Amigga and Oratus, along with all other species, don't have that problem. The lopsided numbers mean the Sevora have been in gradual retreat since the start, and now they're almost gone.

Ignos is looking for sympathy, but, as a Solare that's experienced my people's own decline, I don't have any to spare. Doesn't help that the Sevora live by using others. I'm repulsed by the thought of being a guest in my own body. Hard to get motivated to help a species like that.

Yes, we use species. We take their ideas and expand on them. Enhance their technology, purify their societies of problems both physical and cultural. We stop violence,

Kaishi. Crime. Hate. It all goes away. No Sevora, no host starves or wants for medical attention.

I think we can have that without losing freedom.

Then show me where.

I can't. Yet.

Ignos doesn't give up, though.

You and I are connected to the same nerves. If I feel pain, you feel pain. If I feel pleasure, so do you. The species we take, they live and continue to live great lives. It's like watching something on a console, but experiencing the joys of it. The successes. There's no failure, there's no death.

Then why are we here on this station, if the Sevora are so wonderful?

My question goes unanswered for a moment. Ignos eventually comes back slow. Cautious.

We are here because the galaxy does not understand us. Because it sees us as a threat. As enslavers, rather than liberators.

What am I then? How does Ignos see me, someone whose will, whose mind it can't take?

An anomaly. But also, perhaps, an answer. You present a choice to the galaxy, Kaishi. You present the hope of an equilibrium. If we could give the option to a species, the choice of a life lived without stress or fear or worry, or one with all those things but with true freedom? Then perhaps the Sevora would not be hated quite so much.

I don't see how anyone could choose the former, but Ignos laughs.

You've seen the Pits of Damantum, the desperate person who wishes for something better. Who is at the very end of all of their dreams. Who, given the choice would abandon what little their freedom has given them and instead choose comfort, happiness, peace.

I'm about to continue the conversation when there's a knock. My mask lets me connect with the door and shunt it open. Malo's standing outside, his cape and robe torn and ragged, but I'm drawn to Viera, hanging on Malo's shoulder, tired, pale, yet still launching a sharp grin my way.

I can't help it. I scream a little in delight, run forward and hug the Lunare, then the Charre. Tight. Both Malo and Viera return the squeeze, and when I step back, they both look at each other, then at me with small smiles.

"I apologized," says Malo in Charre tongue. "Viera says I'm better with a sword than she expected."

"You're lucky," Viera adds. "Do that thing again and you'll wind up with my blade in your side."

Malo shakes his head, looks at me. "What I've learned, painfully, is that it's just us here. No matter how terrible Viera might be, it's better to have her than to lose her."

"Come in," I say. Partly because I've noticed, in the hallway, there are two familiars standing at the end of our section. They're watching us with their blank blue faces, and it's causing twitchy chills.

Malo and Viera step inside and the door shuts behind them. I keep the conversation in Charre, hoping Dalachite can't make sense of what we're saying.

"Tell me," I speak to Viera. "Tell me what it was like?"

"Unpleasant. A sharp pain, and unconsciousness, and then the slow-growing sensation of a thousand things happening to me. I flickered in and out what must've been a dozen times. Imagine opening your eyes and seeing strange metal limbs coming towards you, pulling back, poking and prodding your skin. Looking to the left and seeing a tube leading from your arm to a strange bag full of red fluid. I'll have nightmares about this forever."

"She showed up at my door," Malo says. "Moments ago. Like this."

"The familiars brought me. They said I should get some rest, but since when have I followed orders?"

"Certainly not mine," I say.

"Obviously. I'm your adviser, not your servant." Viera clicks her teeth. "And as your adviser, I'm wondering, when do we get out of here?"

It's a question I've been pondering since the first session. At once I'm fascinated by everything around me. I want to know more, to understand and grow into this wide universe, but I'm getting the feeling that every moment on this station puts me at risk. Dalachite doesn't, after all, seem all that interested in my health, which makes my answer easy.

"As soon as possible. I don't think Dalachite is going to let us leave alive."

I tell them about my sessions. I tell them about Ignos. They're stunned, but Viera is the quickest to shed her astonishment.

"There's a creature in your mind that's played off as a god? Can't say I'm surprised given what we've seen. Doesn't matter anyway, its answers still worked. Its machines did what they should do. So long as its in your head and not mine, lets use it."

My eyes flick to Malo, to see how he's taking it.

"You're still my empress," Malo replies, bowing his head. "There's more to that than having a god in your head."

Not exactly satisfying, but I'll take it.

"Here's what we need to do," I say. "Get out of here. Find a way to the docking bay, and then I can use the Cache, and Ignos, to learn how to pilot the shuttle."

"You think that thing will let us walk out of here?" Viera

asks. "Because I'm betting it'd rather have us chopped up to bits so it can study every one of our insides."

You need weapons.

I pose Ignos' question to the pair.

"The training room," Malo says. "There is a whole cabinet full. I'm sure we could use some of them."

"Because that's what I want, you holding a sword again." Viera says.

"What if I promise to only attack our enemies? Cut up those blue things?"

"I'd be okay with that. So long as I'm at a distance."

I look at both of them. They nod back at me. The plan is set.

We're getting off this station.

It doesn't take Sax long to encounter the first sign of resistance. Only a few steps out from their quarters, with Bas heading in the opposite direction, and Sax sees a familiar move in front of him from another hallway. It's unarmed; hands by its sides. Sax, with deadly weapons encircling his waist and embedded in the mask, keeps on moving. *Cobalt*'s a large station, it'll be a long hike to get to the center.

"Please," Dalachite's voice pours into the hallway. "Before you come to kill me. Before you decide to end all that this station has been built for, I'd like to show you something."

"You've shown me plenty already," Sax hisses.

The familiar doesn't move, so when Sax is close, he opens his mouth. Makes sure that wherever Dalachite is watching from, it can see those teeth. See what will be tearing through his creation.

"Not this. You haven't seen this before, I guarantee you." What stops Sax is the Amigga's voice. Not the words that it says. But rather the tone.

There's no worry in it. No fear. Only a sly, tantalizing tilt.

"What?" Sax can't resist.

"Follow." Dalachite doesn't say anything else, and the familiar turns and heads down the hallway, in the same direction Sax was going anyway.

Sax follows.

They go by the kitchen, and Sax isn't surprised to see the door locked shut, red light glowing. In fact, all the other routes seem shut. Even the lights begin to dim as the Oratus walks, until Sax is following a blue familiar through a dark maze, with sole ceiling lights launching spots of brightness. It would be creepy if Sax understood that emotion. Instead, he keeps his claws ready. His mask scanning for hidden anything.

Monsters are scariest in the dark, and there are few monsters worse than Sax.

A green light bursts out of the black, and there's the whooshing sound of a door opening. The familiar turns to Sax and points into a room that has just appeared from a blank section of wall.

"What you're looking for is in here," Dalachite says.

"What I'm looking for? What I'm looking for is you."

"No, no you're not. What you're looking for, what everyone is looking for, are answers. The reason you're here."

Sax slow blinks at the familiar. He's always known why he's here. To eliminate the Sevora. And after them, anything else that poses a threat to the order of the galaxy. There's no other reason. There's no grand mystery.

"You're wrong," Sax says. "I know my purpose."

Laughter comes through the invisible speakers.

"You only think you do. You're part of a grand

construct. A game that's been played since before your pathetic race was made."

Sax will enjoy devouring this one.

Again the familiar gestures. Sax goes into the room. He's curious. He doesn't care what Dalachite says, but if there's a threat in here,

Sax prefers to neutralize it. If there's not, he's got the weapons to break his way out.

Nonetheless, as he goes by, Sax turns, and with his midclaws, splits the familiar and shreds it to pieces. It'll reform, but the move brings some satisfaction.

As soon as Sax is inside, the door slams shut behind him and lights spring up. Spotlights around the edges of the ceiling, focusing on the center of the room. The space is large, square, and the middle floor is a series of metal grates, with dozens of small holes. On top of those sits a platform, rising a meter from the ground. Flat and sleek and silver. On it, being dissembled by a set of four familiars, are two Flaum. From the smell, they're fresh bodies.

"The next thaw," Dalachite says. The familiars take pieces and put them into bags, drain fluid into the holes in the floor using small suction tubes.

"What is this?" Sax says the words aloud and in his mind at the same time. It's clear there's a dissection going on, but why? What secrets could the Flaum, a species that has to have been torn apart over and over and over again for cycles, still hold?

"Do you see this?" Dalachite says. "This is what science is. Continual learning. Reaching forth and finding new discoveries. Perfecting those discoveries that we have already made. You see my blue familiars, yes?"

Sax feels an itchy anger. A growing desire to take apart the things in front of his eyes. The horrendous show that he's watching is terrifying, wrong. What is happening on this station?

"Every piece of these Flaum has been preserved. Every part of them will go to my algorithms. Will live on through my familiars."

"Live on?"

"Do you ever wonder, Sax, how I make these familiars?"

Sax doesn't answer. He knows Dalachite's going to explain anyway, and it does.

"I take the cells of the living, spin them and turn them into what you see before you. Yet, they are imperfect. Still so much work to do. So keep going, Sax. Keep going and you'll see."

A door opens on the far side of the room. Beyond the platform. Dalachite means for Sax to keep going. His claws twitch; they want to tear. But Sax resists. As Bas would say, this is about the mission, not the moment.

Sax walks on, around the display and out of the room to the next one. Which is exactly like the first, except a single crucial difference: This platform is on solid, hole-less ground, surrounded by medical machines holding bags and tanks and containers full of what, Sax doesn't know. All of them are pressing, poking, prodding a shape in the middle. One that is the familiar's blue, but also yellow and red in spots. As though true flesh is growing over the fragile familiar goop.

"Everything must grow, Sax. Everything must evolve on itself. It took so long to make the familiars. To get them to the point where they could replace my staff and my robots in the simplest of duties." Dalachite continues on.

Sax can smell a wide range of chemicals. Alcohols, glues, stinging scents of life. The strange ozone iron smell of blood. He takes a step closer to the center platform. Yes, that is hair. It's sprouting from a couple patches on the familiar. Patches that are brownish-blue. Patches that look almost like skin.

"There are always initial imperfections. First models. The ones you see everywhere, demonstrating my concept. Setting expectations for what comes next."

A green light blinks on and another door shunts open. Further.

Sax goes. He's aware this is a show. He's aware of what's going on here, that this isn't for Dalachite's benefit, but for visitors to the station. To those who are invested in its progress. Why else would the Amigga bother with this?

The third room holds something different entirely. It's thin and long. The wall to his right is one large screen. One that immediately lights up and begins to play a short sequence. Creatures slide onto the screen, each occupying their own space.

Sax recognizes the Flaum, the Whelk and the Teven — the strange, pole-dwelling creatures. All of them have green circles around their images. There are others, all with red X's. But there are two missing entirely. His own, the Oratus, and the new ones. The humans.

"As you can see, I have a long way to go. The project is incomplete. In many ways."

At the far end, another way opens. Sax keeps moving. He can't stop now. He's curious in spite of himself. He's angry in spite of his curiosity. The next room holds another platform, but this one is empty. The spotlights angle towards the silver center, leaving the sides of the room in shadow.

"Come, Sax. Won't you help me? Won't you be my next great experiment?" There's a sudden catch over the speakers, a frustrated sigh. "Unfortunately, you're not the only troublemaker on this station. Do enjoy yourself, Sax. I'll be back soon."

This has gone far enough. Sax takes a step towards the center of the room, scans for the doorway, and his mask pings a warning. The bright lights are blinding, they keep Sax from seeing into the dark sides around him. So Sax has the mask switch to infrared viewing.

They're everywhere.

At least a dozen, maybe more. Hugging the walls and now walking towards him. Familiars. Sax can't make out the details from the blobs of orange and reds he's seeing, so he backs up. His tail hits the platform, and Sax climbs on it as his claws draw the pair of black bars from the mask.

With a squeeze, each bar jets out a meter-long blade, nano-sharpened to shear through the thickest armor. The familiars continue to close, and Sax waits. Once they step close, he'll be able to cut them all down.

And they do. A crashing wave coming at Sax from all angles. He begins to cut, to whirl and slash. Green and red fills his vision, and he feels their hands, pulling, beating, tugging.

An endless avalanche.

The three of us leave my room in a line. We head towards the two familiars standing guard. They look at us, and I expect Dalachite to ask what we're doing, but no comment comes. Viera leans on me, and instead of going right to the familiars, I suddenly veer left into her room.

There, I do what I did in mine and open the compartment above her bed. Just like in my room, a mask is there. I help her put it on and then we go to Malo's and do the same. They ditch their ratty old clothes from a world that no longer seems quite so real. One of jungles and daylight and desert and rain. Now we're in this one. Home of metal and bright lights.

Our new outfits—the masks cling to our skin like silver, seemingly as we command—elicit no reaction from the familiars. Viera, still leaning on me even with the mask, speaks first. "Left something of mine in the med bay. I'd like to go get it."

"You left nothing in the med bay," Dalachite's voice

says. "Now please, I'm busy with something else. Return to your quarters."

My eyes drift to Malo, and he takes charge. We don't have any weapons, but then, neither do the familiars. They stand equal our height, and their bodies are strangely similar to ours. That doesn't mean they know how to fight. That doesn't mean they're human.

Malo jabs the familiar nearest him in the stomach and then, using the momentum of the swing, curls into a back-handed elbow into the familiar on the right. Both stumble back. Both appear, otherwise, entirely fine. They straighten, and again bar the path forward.

"I don't want to hurt you, but you have no right to leave your rooms. You are my subjects. You will stay until I call for you." Dalachite's voice is hard.

"I think we'd rather leave," I say.

You have to rush them together. Push through.

In Charre, I say what Ignos suggests. We charge right for the center, between the two familiars. Malo leading the way, Viera second, with me last. I'm guessing Dalachite won't want to hurt me. That it'll be restrained, slower, with me than the others. Malo angles forward and lowers his shoulder as the familiars move to cross their arms.

Malo's a strong lion warrior of the Charre. He does not bend. He does not give. He pushes and shoves and he cries out for his god. I push Viera behind him and the Lunare stumbles, reaches down and uses her hands to push herself back up from the floor, and so when Malo hits those crossed arms and breaks the familiars to the side of the hallway, we're right behind. Ready to rush through.

I feel blue hands grab at my back. They miss.

We're running. Viera and I follow Malo, and I'm working

to keep Viera on her feet. Her breathing is shallow, labored. I see sweat break out underneath her mask, the strange clothing doing what it can to wick it away. She's even paler than before, when the fever drove her to the brink of death.

"Stay alive Viera. Keep moving." I say.

"Don't worry Empress, I won't fall apart on you. Not completely, anyway." Viera replies.

Doorways shut along our path. As they close themselves off, the lights dim. Until suddenly we can't see anything anymore, except for single train of bright spots leading us forward. We stop, and I turn around, expecting to see the two familiars following, but they're nowhere.

"Since you persist, I will show you what you want to see. Show you where you need to go. Follow the lights, my subjects, and you will find your answers," Dalachite says, its voice booming out around them.

"Do we follow?" Malo says.

"I don't see have any choice," I say. "But let's be ready. Because I'm guessing this doesn't lead us to the docking bay."

We move forward, Malo still in front, Viera in the middle and me in back. It's a slow walk, and I use the time to pester Ignos with questions. Try to get some idea of what's going on, but its not sure.

The Amigga will try to capture you. That's all I can say.

I could figure that out for myself.

The lights eventually lead us to a sealed door, red light glaring at us. I reach and place a hand on the metal, but it doesn't open. The mask fails to unlock it too, finding no connection.

"We followed the lights." I say to the air.

"You did. You did. If you would please wait just a

moment, there are preparations that need taking care of," Dalachite says.

I look at both Viera and Malo. "I don't think this is going to end well."

"Can't give up hope yet, Empress," Viera says. "We're still alive, aren't we?"

"For the moment," I reply.

Malo hammers his hand in the door twice more. "Open it up. Kill us if you're going to, or let us go."

To my surprise, the door does what Malo says. It slides up and open. In the room, which is brightly lit by an array of spotlights, is single large gray platform. On the floor beneath it are metal plates punctured with dozens of small holes. It all glistens, as though it's been washed recently.

"Now if you would please proceed, the three of you, onto the platform. We can begin." Dalachite's voice echoes off the walls.

We walk inside and the door shuts behind me. I turn, but the only panel is dead black and unresponsive.

We're trapped.

He fights himself into a corner. They keep coming at Sax, even though his blades are whirling, cutting every new arrival into pieces. They keep coming because they know his swings will slow, he'll start to miss, and eventually they'll pull Sax apart. As if that's not enough, Sax notices the familiars getting larger as the ones he cuts absorb into the next wave. It's a futile onslaught getting worse by the second.

Blue hands grasp at Sax's face and arms. They scratch and pull until Sax bites or slashes them away, buying micro-seconds of reprieve before the next familiar fills the gap. There's no way he survives if this keeps up. No way Sax can win an infinite war.

So, in those micro-seconds, Sax searches for a solution.

There are two doors in the room. The way he came in, and another, to his right. With a wall of familiars standing in between either choice. He ducks another couple of punches and retaliates by slicing off the arms that threw them.

The crush continues.

Both doors have red-glowing lights above, and Sax doesn't expect Dalachite will open them. He'll have to use his miners. He has two attached to the mask, around his midclaws. Sax grabs one with his left while doing a wide, clearing sweep with the blades held by his foreclaws to get some space. Prepares to take a leap, and then does so.

Unlike the training room, this one doesn't have a high ceiling, and the shallow angle lets blue hands grab at Sax's legs and tail, and they pull him back into the mob. Sax waves the swords as he gets pulled down. Cuts away his attackers, earns himself a new clearing as he hits the floor. He's surrounded, though, so he can't stay there.

Sax scrambles back towards the platform, the one place where he can get a clear shot.

His legs power him forward, and Sax uses the one midclaw he has free to grab the lip of the platform and pull himself up. Or tries to; more hands grab his tail and yank Sax back the other way. He spins, bringing the swords to bear, but the familiars are ready.

Some get cut while others duck the swings or dance back. Then they dart forward again before Sax can recover, pin his arms. Grab the blades themselves even as the edges slash into their skin. Blue goop spatters everywhere, an ocean of it, but the living slime swims back towards familiars the moment it hits a surface.

Sax stays focused. The door. That's the objective. He angles his miner towards it with his left midclaw and pulls the trigger. The short blast, a white-blue bolt, lances through the familiars and strikes the door, burns a hole into it. Then grasping hands rip the miner away. Three familiars grab it and even Sax's midclaw isn't a match for that much strength. The familiars kick the miner back through the onslaught as they swarm forward.

Sax gnashes his teeth, kicks with his legs, slashes with every free claw he has, but he's being buried and he knows it. A trio of familiars presses Sax to the ground, and he catches sight of his stolen miner, lying on the floor beyond his feet. Too far away to grab, but it gives him an idea.

Sax darts his head forward, taking a bite out of the familiar pinning his right midclaw to the ground, and fills his mouth with blue slime. Uses the moment of freedom to pull the other miner from his mask, angles it down along his own body, and, with blue fingers stuffing his mouth, pressing into his eyes and the vents along his chest, pulls the trigger.

Sax doesn't even see the beam, but he hears the result.

A white, boiling heat washes over him. The mask isn't able to deal with it, and Sax feels the skin of his tail and legs burn as the protective shield melts away. Bright flashes and roiling orange flow through Sax's vision. The infrared goes completely red and white, so Sax blinks back to normal spectrum.

Turns out shooting one miner into the battery of another makes a miniature apocalypse.

The lights are gone, and instead all Sax can see are streaks of scattered flame clinging to the walls, to the floor and ceiling. The blast scattered familiar remnants every-where, the goop turning into bubbling black with the heat. Dark smoke and charred smells fill the room.

Sax stays low, forces his legs, which screech at him with pain, to move. He scrambles over the flames, towards the door he shot open. There's no familiars left. Or if there are, they haven't reformed, and with the flames devouring every trace of leftover goop, Sax doesn't think they're coming back.

Sax throws himself at the door, which doesn't present

an obstacle; it just falls away, weakened by the miner shot and the subsequent explosion. The hallway is cool, clear, brightly lit. There are no doors off of this one. Just a long corridor heading, Sax knows, towards the station center. Towards where Dalachite lives.

The Oratus slumps against a side, the cold white bulkhead serving as support. Takes a breath. Then another and a third as smoke wafts out overhead.

This one is going to hurt. Most of Sax's tail is numb, his legs too. A look along his body shows his gray scales turning black. He'll need a long time in the healing tanks.

But that's for later. Now there's the mission. Dalachite still lives.

Sax pulls himself to his feet. It hurts, but the muscles still respond. Badly burned, yes, but not severed. Not melted into nothing.

Fury pushes the Oratus forward.

The door barely closes before there's a loud bang somewhere nearby. The three of us stare at each other, and Dalachite, which had been finishing its command for us to walk to the center platform, cuts off abruptly. Leaves us in silence.

"What do you suppose that was?" Viera says.

I don't know, but I don't say that, I just stare at Malo, who's looking at the far door.

"I think it's the other ones. The creatures who brought us here," Malo says. "The one, Sax? He doesn't like this place. He doesn't trust those blue things."

"If he's trying to destroy this station, then I'd rather us not be on it," Viera says and I agree.

Which means we have to find a way out. The door we came through is still unresponsive. Same thing with the other exit. We walked in here, and now we're stuck.

"Dalachite wants us to get on the platform," Malo says. "Maybe we should?"

"Following its orders already got us here," I say. "Following them again would just make things worse."

"No, no," Dalachite's voice bursts into the room. "It will not make them worse. No worse than they already are. Rather, it will give you purpose." His words have heat in them now. Anger, rage even. "You'll get on the platform, and you'll lay there and you'll wait. You'll wait because that is what subjects do. That is your job."

We look at each other. "I'm not going to," I say.

Careful Kaishi. This is not one creature you want to anger.

"What the Empress commands, I do," Malo says.

"This isn't an ask. It's not a request. It's an order," Dalachite says. "One I'm willing to enforce."

The far door, not the one we came in, shunts open suddenly. Standing there this are a pair of hideous creatures. They are brown and patchy, and where the fur is not, there are blue streaks. The same smooth skin of the other familiars. Their eyes are blank and black, and wisps of hair fall from them onto the floor.

They're unstable. Strange.

"What are—" Viera doesn't finish the sentence before the two of them grab Malo and haul him to the platform.

Viera is too hurt to react, but I step forward, and snatch at one of their arms and try to pull, but it doesn't move. I've felt the other familiars. The blue ones. They're strong, but not mountains. I had a chance to resist their strength, but these, it's like trying to pull a stone. As though the flimsy blue has been buttressed by taut muscle.

"Do not struggle, subjects." Dalachite's words are followed by Malo hitting the silver platform.

As he does so, one familiar reaches underneath and pulls out a long silver rod. I'm trying a kick and the familiar takes the blow without a care, then turns and pushes me away onto the ground.

It places the rod over Malo's struggling legs, and the rod snaps. Flexes itself around Malo's thighs and squeezes tight. The other familiar places a second rod around Malo's chest, trapping his arms to his sides.

Viera and I look at the odds as the two monsters turn towards us. There's no question of us fighting them. Not with Viera was weak as she is, not with me unarmed. Dalachite calls for us to surrender, and we do so.

The familiars direct us onto the platform with Malo, order us to lie against each other in a row of three.

"Now I'm sorry you had to witness my experiments," Dalachite says. "They're not quite ready yet, as you can see. However, some unexpected difficulties are forcing me to use extra measures."

Wait for an opportunity, Kaishi. The Amigga is distracted. We'll have a chance.

I understand what Ignos is saying, and the familiars haven't wrapped us in metal bars like they did Malo. Instead, when the familiars reach beneath the platform, they bring up clear, rippled tubes that slink down into the holes in the floor. Each one has, on the end, a long, sharp needle. It's not hard to guess what they're going to do with those.

"I didn't think you would hurt us," I protest. "We're your subjects. Your prize experiments."

"Oh you are," Dalachite replies. "The most interesting subjects I've studied since the start of this station. Perhaps in my entire existence. However, I must put *Cobalt* ahead of any single test, any single specimen. That means you three will be worth more to me dead than alive."

"You'll never learn everything about us," I'm saying it frantically,

I've no idea if it's true. No idea what the Amigga is capable of.

"Little one, you must remember, I have your shuttle. I have its records. I can simply send someone to gather more of you. Bring back as many humans as I want. Now, do close your eyes. It will be easier that way."

The familiar gets close. I'm clearly the first choice, as one of the brown patchy nightmares lines up at my head and another at my feet.

Viera tenses, and I feel like she's about to pounce.

"Don't," I say. I speak in Malo's language, and hope Dalachite still can't understand. "Wait for my move, then you go."

Viera nods slightly.

The familiars, tubes in each hand, bring the points towards me. The needles glisten in the bright light. Stabbing straight for my legs, my arms. Centimeters away when I move.

In the jungle, playing games as a child, we rolled around. Somersaulted underneath knotted vines and low branches. Played tricks and tags on each other. So it's second nature for me to kick my legs up, bring them to my chest, though I feel the slight scratch as a needles catch the bare ends of my feet. I keep rolling back and press my hands on the side of the platform. Feel the needles of the familiar behind me scratch my shoulders, but I ignore the sting. The mask blunts some of it anyway.

I press off.

I don't so much hit, as fall into the familiar standing behind my head. It drops the tubes as we both fall back, and I strike it high enough that it overbalances and collapses to the ground. The other one is rushing around the platform when Viera kicks out her left foot, hits the familiar in the leg and trips the thing. It falls hard, and then Viera, lacking mobility, rolls off the platform on top of it. Lands on the familiar and starts punching.

I slip off of mine, grab the tubes from the floor, and try to avoid glancing at the red wet on the needle points. My familiar starts to get back up and as it does so, as it turns its brown patchy blue face towards me, I jam the needles into it.

Deep.

The tubes start to shake as the needles dig all the way in, and I realize I've kicked off some mechanism. The familiar lurches back, but I've put the tubes in far enough that I see little metal wires spring out from the tops of them. The wires grip into the familiar's skin, holding the needles steady and then I watch as the stuff that makes the familiar begins to drain through the tubes, filling them with blue slime. The familiar begins to shrink down before me as the tubes drain its very life away.

That's what would've happened to me. My blood, my muscles, skin and bones, all of it sucked away into *Cobalt*'s bowels.

"This is very unexpected," Dalachite's voice comes over as Viera continues to struggle with her familiar. "All of my experiments are going rather wrong today."

I ignore the thing. Scrabble across the floor to where Viera's fighting. Towards were Viera's getting thrown off her opponent and slammed against the wall. Towards where Viera's crumpling in a heap. This familiar doesn't have its tubes anymore—it dropped them on the far side of the platform—so I've nothing to stab it with, nothing to grapple with, except my own hands.

Which prove ineffective.

The familiar doesn't hesitate. It grabs me, crushes me

tight in its arms and holds me to its chest, and then I feel it run. We dash towards the far door that it came in, which opens as it nears, and then shuts behind us.

As it closes, I hear Malo shout my name.

And then there's nothing else.

Sax lurches down the hallway. Slow. He doesn't remember this from the map. No idea where he's going, but there seems to be only one way, so that's where he heads. All Sax knows is that *Cobalt* is a long, triangular extension from a sphere in the middle. As long as he's heading towards the center, he'll get where he wants to be eventually.

The hallway ends in a rounded door with a glowing red light, as per usual. Sax raises his claws, the only weapons he has left.

"Don't," Dalachite says. "You've damaged quite enough of my station already. If you want through, I'll open this."

Sax doesn't care to reply. He doesn't have the energy, the focus to taunt. He gives the creature a moment, holding the miner towards the door, when the light flashes green and it opens. On the other side is what's called a band room. A chamber that circles the center of a station to without walls in between. Rare to have, and costly, but if you need the space, this is the way to do it.

Dalachite is putting that space to good use; stretching

out in front of Sax in either direction is a long chain. Large plastic bars move, pulled by what Sax guesses are programmed magnets, in a slow loop across the wide, flat silver surface. Each bar spans the width of the room, and Sax can see their tops are grated with fine steel. The bar bottoms are coated with small nozzles. Nozzles that, as the bars move, squeeze out the same blue stuff that makes up the familiars. They're layering the slime on the silver floor, which is divided into long thin sections going perpendicular to the plastic bars.

Sax realizes what this is, what's going on.

The layering bars create familiars. A couple dozen at a time or more. The dripping goop builds them into beings. Sax doesn't even have the energy to move. To act. He simply watches, mesmerized, as the bars go around and around and around and then the wave is done. The whole line pauses for just a second, the bars sliding up to the ceiling, which parts and allows a new batch of goop to refill the bars.

There's a soft buzzing sound and a slight stinging smell fills the room. Current; strong electricity. Evidenced further by the twitching familiar forms. After the sound dies, each one sits up, slowly. Then stands, rising off the silver platform. They all turn and look at Sax.

"There you have it," Dalachite says. "The source of my servants. Nothing so brilliant to one who's seen the galaxy, I'm sure."

Except Sax hasn't ever seen anything like this, and he knows why: if this can be everywhere, anywhere, then what need would anyone have of other species? The Amigga, *this* Amigga, could run whole worlds with these things.

Sax asks the one question still burning in his mind, "How do you control them?"

"Simple, really," Dalachite says. "Consider the Sevora. Consider how it places its own commands into a target's nerves. How it supersedes the host and sends its messages throughout. All I've done is take a bit of Sevora into my own self. All I've done is splice my own genetic material into all of these. They are my familiars, after all."

"Sevora can't communicate through air," Sax hisses back. "They need to be inside you. They have to capture you."

"Do they? If the Sevora ever truly looked at themselves, they would know that everything they do is biological impulse. That everything they share with their hosts comes via signals. Specific frequencies, specific micro-volts. It's not hard to send those same signals throughout the station. It's not hard to convince a staff of willing followers to set up a mechanism for you to do this, especially when they don't realize it's going to be their own end to do so."

"Then you are no better than the parasites we're fighting," Sax says.

"I don't believe I ever claimed to be," Dalachite says. "The real fault of the Sevora, of course, is that they failed to establish their power before we realized they were there. I won't make that mistake. The Amigga won't make that mistake."

"You already have," Sax says.

He may be burned, he might be exhausted, but Sax still has four clawed arms and a mouth full of teeth. He sets about using them.

These familiars barely know what they're doing; their movements are slow and jerky. Sax tears through them like grass. Shreds them to pieces and then makes sure to grab the bars as well, gouging up the room's wall to the great metal things. His claws take time to cut through the thick bars, but

Sax slashes every one of them in two. It takes time, moving around the band, but at its center, *Cobalt* is a much smaller station than at the outskirts.

Every bang of the bar pieces hitting the floor is a victory.

"Now I want to see you make your army." Sax glares around the room, unsure of where the cameras are.

"First I welcomed you to *Cobalt*. Then you tricked me, lied and sought to destroy my creations. Now, again, you rip apart what you don't even know. You, Oratus, are the single greatest example of our failure." Dalachite is howling now. "Because of you, my own progress is set back cycles. Do you know how long it will take to repair this? To bring back those familiars that you burned?"

"I don't care." Sax is hunting for the next door to the station's core, but there doesn't seem to be one.

"You don't care? How like an Oratus. How like you to disregard all science just so you can pursue your tearing of flesh and drinking of blood—"

Dalachite continues to rage, but Sax tunes it out. There must be away from here deeper into the station. The Amigga has to feed. It can't seal itself off entirely. Sax clomps across the silver printing floor to the far end. Scans the wall. Flips the mask to infrared, and there. He sees it. Behind one section, a different color. Lower air pressure, cooler temps. Sax moves over to it, stares at the plate. Now that he's here, he can pick out the lines. A disguised sliding door, but why?

Dalachite falls silent. It must realize what Sax is looking at. "Do you know what Oratus? Do you know what you have forgotten in your quest to destroy me?"

"Do tell," Sax says. He takes his claws and jabs them into the wall, points first. The metal resists, but not for long.

It's too thin, not made to withstand an Oratus strike. Sax breaks through and begins to tear it asunder.

"You forgot that you're not alone on this station. You've forgotten your pair. Your humans."

Sax keeps ripping and tearing. Bas can take care of herself. The humans, though, aren't as capable, and if Bas is guarding the shuttle, then no one is be helping them.

"I will do whatever is necessary to keep you away from me, Oratus. Even if it means destroying my most prized subjects."

"Do you have them?" Sax asks.

"They are screaming beneath my knives even now," Dalachite says. "But, if you agree to let me live, if you agree to leave the station, I'll let you have them. I will let you all go."

The metal door falls away, the shreds of it revealing an older, darker hallway leading farther. Sax sees other entrances off to the sides. Storerooms, most likely. The food and drink Dalachite needs to survive.

Except, the humans.

Sax is so close now, but if he kills the Dalachite, or if he tries and the humans die, then it's as Bas says, the mission fails. Their chance at peace fails.

"Do we have a deal, Oratus?"

It's dark in the room. For a moment. Then, as the familiar drags me along with one arm, the entire wall to my right lights up in white. Strange shapes begin to populate the space. The first one is brown, furry. Like the familiar dragging me, only without the blue patches. Next to it appears a strange slug-like creature, and a third, long and straight, with what seems like a shell covering its body and little arms and eyes popping out of holes. Several more appear, one rounded with what looks like many small feet jutting from its central circle.

This one, unlike the first three, is shaded red.

I'm looking at them because I can't think of anything else. I'm breathing fast, my heart thundering as the familiar pulls me along the floor. I'm panicking, even though I've been in life or death situations before, and I know why: the sacrifice at the top of the Vaos, the fight with the Lunare, I understood where I was and what was happening. Here, nothing makes sense. The familiar has no place in my society, in my knowledge of the universe.

It does now.

Ignos isn't helping.

We're halfway along when a thunk echoes behind us. A pounding on the door. Viera, unless Malo found a way to free himself from those metal bars. Either way, the noise makes the familiar glance back. Over my head and away.

Fight back.

I do it almost without thinking. I catch Ignos' suggestion, its attempted command of my muscles, which goes nowhere but into my mind. I plant my left foot and throw my shoulder into a falling twist. It's a heavy move, but the familiar is a heavy creature. Stronger than me, but it's not expecting my attempt. Its feet slip as I swing my body and its grip falls loose as it curls around. The momentum sends the familiar right into the great white display, which it hits, and the screen shatters. The entire thing flickers and dies as the familiar, body still sticking out towards me, twitches while sparks fly around it.

I stand up slow, stare at it. Wait for the familiar to get back up and come after me, but it doesn't.

Don't wait. Go.

So I do. I run back to the closed door we came through, but the light is red and I don't see way open it. The mask doesn't help me either. I look back at the familiar, but it's still stuck there. Not moving anymore.

There'll be others. Is there another way out?

There is. At the end of the hallway, visible in the screen's sputtering light. An open door, though I can only see shadows through it. Still, with nowhere else to go, I head that way. Run down the hall, past the familiar's body, and into another room. There are no lights here, and the white that I see is coming from what looks like a broken door at the other end.

Mounds of blackened liquid sit throughout; curled

and burned onto the floors and ceilings. Some of the piles glow orange in parts, radiating heat. The room smells of smoke and char. It's a place of death, and I don't stay there.

I move into a long hallway, and stop on the other side of the door. At the other end is the creature that took me, the Oratus. It's standing large, though I notice there appear to be black burns all over the lower half of its body. Sax takes a limping step towards me.

"Stop." I say.

Not that I think I can command it to do anything, but it seems hurt. Less deadly than before.

"Where are the other two?" Sax asks me, his voice a hissing rasp.

"Behind me. Locked in another room." I think for second. "Can you free them?"

"They're safe?"

"For now." I guess I don't know that for sure, but there hadn't been any familiars in the room I left. Hopefully, it's stayed that way. "But if we can get back there?"

Sax shakes his head. "You are the most important, and the Amigga is the greatest threat. We go back. Now."

The Oratus turns a slow circle and I stare at its long tail. Forearms, those glistening claws. There's a faint glimmer between its lower torso and its upper, and I realize that it's wearing a mask. One that's only half there.

I can't believe I'm saying this, but you should follow it. That Oratus is our best chance of getting out of this alive.

Follow it? It's going away from my friends. I can't leave them.

If you help it take care of the Amigga, your friends will live. It's the only way.

The only way. How often had I heard Ignos say that?

Talk about destiny. Plans. The sure route to achieving my hopes and dreams.

"I'm going back for them," I say down the hall as I turn around.

"If you do," says Sax to my back. "I'll die. You'll die. Every one of the people you know on Earth will be taken and used by this creature to make more of those familiars. This is our chance. Do not be a coward."

I look at my hands. They are still a girl's hands. Weathered by jungle years, yes, but otherwise young. I don't have many battle scars. I don't have decades of courage building me up to this moment. How am I supposed to help a deadly creature like Sax fight Dalachite?

Not everything is won with strength. Sometimes, just an open eye and a willingness to take advantage is enough.

Then I hear something I don't expect. Is a low rasp, as if the Oratus can't quite believe he's saying it either.

"Please."

You must, Kaishi. Help him.

I flash back to the sessions, stuck on that platform while strange images flare in front of my eyes. Feeling Ignos crawl in and out of my head as Dalachite and its familiars force the Sevora to move. The sheer panic moments ago when a nightmare thing drags me away.

"If we are going to kill this thing, let's do it fast." I meet Sax's eyes, let him know I'm not scared. "I want to save my friends."

The human girl is courageous. Sax is happier than he would've thought to see that. He won't be going into the Amigga's chamber alone. The last encounter with the mature Sevora on the seed ship floats fresh in his memory. How easily things could be turned against a single person. How crucial a partner.

Sax wishes it could be Bas here instead of this little human, but he'll work with what he can get. They head back to the ruined familiar factory, and when Kaishi asks Sax what happens here, he tells her.

"This is where the familiars are made."

"Were made, I think."

Sax waves his foreclaws at the destruction. "This is what *I* was made for."

The two of them cross the floor. Head towards the next door. Metal shards litter the entryway.

"I thought we had a deal, Oratus," Dalachite's voice booms out of somewhere.

"The deal required the humans to be captured," Sax replies. "As you can see, they are not."

"One, perhaps. But the other two—"

"Will survive," Kaishi says. "They're warriors and they know what they're fighting for."

"And just what is that?" the Amigga counters.

"Humanity," Kaishi replies.

Sax isn't waiting anymore. He goes through the door, Kaishi behind him. There are two sealed doors on the sides of the next hallway, and one circular, large one at the end. Dim light makes it harder to see than before.

As they pass by, the first door shoots open. No light locks on these. Perhaps there's no need, this deep in *Cobalt*. Regardless, it's easy to see what's inside. Boxes of stored supplies. Apparently lifted back in here right off the ships. Nothing that concerns Sax and the human, so they go on to the end. The other door, on the right, remains closed. Sax almost checks it, almost tries to see if it opens, but they're so close now. Too close to waste time on distractions.

Sax turns to Kaishi as they stand outside the door. "When it opens, I don't know what we'll find on the other side. Stay composed. Stay ready to move. I'll draw its attention, and you find ways to help where you can."

Sax knows the mask is only covering his upper body. His head. There's plenty of pain from his legs, but he's got enough left to do this. Enough left to brave the Amigga. The door isn't locked: at a touch from Sax's claw on its surface, it shunts open. There, in front of them, is a vast room.

Twice the size of the seed ship's center. Catwalks ring the chamber, extending from the door and looping around the middle. The walkway in front of them extends to a platform in the center. On it rests the Amigga. Part of it, anyway. Dalachite itself extends from its core to the edges of the chamber. It looks less like a living creature and more like a synapse. A central cluster of organs and tissue with numerous branches spitting out towards the sides, to ports and terminals where they've immersed themselves.

The lighting is intense and multicolored. Glowing from hundreds of terminals showing all manner of different data. All of them connected with hard Amigga fiber to the creature's main core. *Cobalt* is part of the Amigga, and the Amigga part of the station. Destroy one, and Sax would likely destroy the other, at least in any functional sense.

"So you made it here. Congratulations." Dalachite sighs. "You've ruined my experiments. Destroyed my familiars. Rendered all the progress I've made over so much time meaningless. Are you happy, Oratus? Are you happy you've defied your masters?"

"No," Sax replies. He's noticed Kaishi staring open-mouthed at what she's seeing. He needs to buy time for her to get composed, to be ready when the fight breaks out. "Defying orders doesn't make me happy, but using these claws to rend you and your creations to pieces will."

Sax takes a step forward. He's promised to draw fire, and that's what he'll do. He scans the room for weapons, hoping the mask will pick out any that he can't see first. But there's none. As though Dalachite, living on a research station, never considered that one day it might be attacked.

"Do you know who your commanders really are?" Dalachite says, and it's disconcerting to Sax to see the creature talking to them, but hear the voice come from all over.

The Amigga has no mouth. All the other Amigga that Sax has seen, without their own stations, use mobile suits. Mechanical accessories and prosthetics to make their way around. Those have clear speakers. Those offer clear targets.

"I know who they are." Sax is content to let Dalachite talk, and stops his advance.

Sax uses the seconds to plan a strategy. The first goal is simple – sever as many connections as possible. Make it so Dalachite can't access *Cobalt*'s systems. So that, at the least, the Amigga can't set *Cobalt* to self-destruct while they're on it.

"We are your commanders, Oratus. The Amigga. We created you, we own you. And you shall obey." As Dalachite says this, there's a shunting rumble throughout the station. Sax hears a whine behind him, and he whirls in time to see a Flaum, an old chocolate-colored one coming into the room behind Kaishi, with white fringes on his fur, holding a miner.

The Flaum fires.

The blast catches Sax in the stomach. There's no impact from a laser, no force, but the burning, searing bolt set Sax's nerves aflame and he stumbles back along the catwalk and then off of it. He bounces down and hits a pair of the Amigga's thick, trunk-like connections, before rolling to a resting place the very bottom of the sphere.

I see Sax fall. Turn and look at where the blast came from. The creature is about my size. Fur the color of mud with ashen fringes, and weathered, bat-like face. It's wearing a loose uniform with faded colors; greens and browns. It levels the stubby, thick weapon at me, but doesn't pull the trigger.

"Now Kaishi," Dalachite says, its voice coming from speakers around the sphere, so that it seems to echo from everywhere. "You know I don't want to hurt you. You know you have so much promise. Yes, yes this foul Oratus damaged me. Set us back. But you and I, we can rebuild the station. You can join Coorvin here and make it whole again. Set the universe on its rightful path."

I don't hold much with what Dalachite says. It's already tried to kill me multiple times, and the monster itself looks so crazy and terrifying that I'm having a hard time putting together coherent thoughts.

Ignos, though, helps me.

What you're looking at is the Amigga's caretaker. Every

Amigga has to have one, once it gets settled. After all, look at it. It can't move. It can't even feed itself.

Coorvin, which I gather is the furry thing's name, stares at my face. I see glimmers of intelligence in those beady black eyes, but the mouth doesn't move. It shot Sax, so I can't regard it as a friend, but then, attacking it might mean I wind up the same as the Oratus—charred at the bottom of the chamber. So I hesitate. Decide to fall back on what I do best: ask questions.

"What should I do?" I say aloud, ask it of Dalachite, of Coorvin, and Ignos.

Coorvin replies first, in a hoarse, light rasp. "Help me."

"Yes, help him," Dalachite says. "Say the word, Kaishi. We can even spare those other specimens. Your friends. You'll all be together here on *Cobalt*. You'll all work with me. You'll never want or need for anything ever again."

I'm not picking up that vibe from Coorvin. That all his cares are gone and he's living a blissful life onboard *Cobalt*. There's pain in his tight face. Like he's struggling with something. So I take a step towards him.

Kaishi, what are you doing? Don't antagonize–

I push Ignos away. The Sevora isn't human. The Sevora hasn't seen this look before. But I have. I saw it in the eyes of the sacrifice on the top of the Vaos in Damantum. I saw in Viera's eyes before she passed out as I cauterized her wounds. The look of someone waiting to be rescued, of someone needing another's help.

I can't resist that.

"What is he?" I ask the Amigga. "Coorvin?"

"Oh, he's a Flaum. My caretaker. Implanted, of course, to make sure I can influence him as necessary. I need him less, of course, with my familiars, but I've made sure he's lived a long and fruitful life. And I may need him yet, until

I'm certain the familiars can handle ever duty without issue."

I move closer to Coorvin, and he turns his weapon towards me, that wide black barrel aiming squarely at my chest. Ignos screams at me, telling me to say something, to do something.

So I step quick. Past the point of the weapon. Coorvin starts to twist, but he's slow. I lay my hands on the barrel, grab it. The weapon's still warm from the shot fired at Sax. Coorvin tries to move it away from me, but I'm stronger than he is. Stronger than an old Flaum. It's not hard to pull the weapon from his hands.

"Kaishi, what are you doing?" Dalachite says. "You must understand, hurting me will not help you. You'll still be stuck on the station. Be a prisoner here forever. Without me, you'll never leave. You'll doom Coorvin too—he'll never get more food. Another chance to go home."

I swing the weapon around, point it at the Amigga. "You weren't going to let us go home anyway."

Dalachite quivers, ripples moving up and down its skin and the connections to the walls. Strange purple lines illuminate up and down the thing's body, and a wet sheen drips out from those lines to coat the creature.

"You could just come close, Kaishi. End your struggle now. Find peace. I'm not above mercy for my subjects."

The Flaum, behind me, makes a move. Tackles me. Coorvin isn't heavy, but he's enough to throw me off balance. I hit the laced metal floor and the weapon bounces from my hands, rolls off the edge of the catwalk.

As Coorvin grabs for me, I kick him away, my foot connecting with his face. Coorvin staggers back, puts his furry hands up to his head, closes his eyes and shakes back and forth. I climb to my feet.

Hear Dalachite's laughter.

"Now you've lost your weapon, Kaishi. What are you going to do, beat on me with those fists of yours? I'd like to see you try. That is the one thing I would've changed about your kind. But they didn't ask me. No, no they did not."

I don't know what he's talking about, and Ignos feels just as confused. Still, I have to find some way of destroying this thing. Then I remember. I glance behind me, the door to leave the chamber is still open. I back through.

"Running away? Or have you decided that you truly belong on the station?" I hear Dalachite ask as I go.

I don't reply.

Inside the hallway, I see the second door, one that didn't open when we first came through, has slid aside to reveal spare accommodations. Where Coorvin had been hiding. In the room to the right, the supplies still sit. Crates bearing names and terms that I don't recognize. No weapons, no solutions here.

I head back to the broad chamber where Sax claimed the familiars were made. It's not far, and there, split into pieces, are the metal bars with the nozzles. The things Sax said created the familiars. I take a piece. It's taller and longer than me, but I'm able to lift it. Either I've become stronger since coming here, or there's something else going on.

I run back down the hallway, carrying it before me. Like a spear; a weapon I know how to hold.

No, Kaishi. Don't.

No time for new plans. I use the metal bar like a spear. Dive right into Dalachite's chamber, keep my feet pounding on. Coorvin recognizes what I'm about to do—I see his furry head jerk, his paws reach towards me, but he's a second too slow. I thrust the metal head right into the glistening, mottled Amigga skin. The spear bites into Dalachite, and I hear it scream.

A scream that changes, quick, to a gurgling laugh. I try to pull back on the spear, but it's stuck. Before I can react, the Amigga twists its body, rotating itself and the spear, with my hands around it, so that I'm lifted into the air above the creature. I notice, then, that the spear is smoking, melting down into the Amigga.

Its skin is coated in absorbent acid. It's how they eat, Kaishi.

"Clever, so clever you've killed your self," Dalachite chuckles through the speakers. "The Amigga would never make a species smarter than us. Always with weaknesses. Always with flaws we can exploit."

Make a species?

I try to climb to the top of my makeshift spear. Feel the jagged edges cut into my hands as I grip my way to the top. The bar creaks as the Amigga continues to melt it away. I risk a glance down; it's only a meter now to that glistening, burning ball of flesh. The remnants of the spear, as they disintegrate, spread out beneath me in a pale yellow spot.

"But at least it worked. At least they succeeded," Dalachite continues to talk. "Do you know how long we were tried? How many species failed us?"

Another moment, another half-meter closer. I think if I time it right, as soon as I hit the Dalachite's skin, I can jump. The mask should protect me that long. I hope. I adjust, widen my stance as I hold onto the top of the spear. Get ready.

"It's been a long time since I've had fresh meat. A milestone, as well. I imagine it's the first time any Amigga has tried human." Dalachite says as the tips of my toes dangle just above its shimmering skin.

There's a bright flash. Blue and white, iridescent. It burns and boils up through the Amigga. Turning the brown and green skin of the creature black and orange as it fries and bursts its body into flame.

My spear creaks and breaks at the heat, and I plunge into the boiling inferno.

S ax is dying.

There's a hole burned into, through his chest. A miner at close range and a damaged mask is a mortal equation. That he's fading out of existence, the left of his two hearts torched to nothing, isn't what bothers the Oratus.

It's the thought of a mission unfinished. A goal left standing.

Which is why the clatter of the miner as it slides down the sphere towards him sparks dim, blurred life in Sax's nerves. His eyes break through the veil of pain and he sees it, black and dented and scraped but there. Within reach of his right midclaw. The only noise he hears is a ringing, aching echo. The only smell the spicy char of his own scales.

His midclaw moves in a jerk. Sharp, short. Sax's energy comes like that now. Spasms. But it's enough for the razor points to find their grip. The miner is made for Flaum, though, which means Sax doesn't have points for his claws. The trigger is shaped for a finger—rounded and large. With another yank, Sax pulls the weapon close to him. The metal is cold. So cold that it takes Sax a second to realize it's not, in fact, the metal he's feeling but the icy chill of his body shutting down. His legs are lost to him. He can't move his tail. It's like a lit room gone suddenly dark—Sax has no grasp of things he once knew so well.

But he has a grasp of one thing. Sax moves his right foreclaw, wraps it around the close part of the barrel, then, with both claws, swings the weapon up so that the butt of it rests against Sax's chest. This brings with it a rippling sensation as the miner bends and bursts his blistered scales. There's a spike of pain, and Sax can feel himself wanting to pass out.

To slip away.

He returns to a memory, his first formal training, when Sax is standing in a line. There are five other Oratus, four to his left, one, Bas, to his right. They stand on a long, flat plain on a planet whose name, now, blurs to nothing. It's all rock and dust anyway, a place long abandoned by any life of note and now used, thanks to its breathable atmosphere, as an Oratus base. Their school. Their home.

Along either side of the tanned, rocky plain are set tall, black pillars. Nubs extend from some, acting as hubs to smaller pillar spokes. Twenty in all, and they hum with the audible pulse of power. Their teacher, an Oratus with blue-green scales, raises a foreclaw, then drops it. As he does so, Sax, Bas and the others, break into long, loping strides. Until they pass the first pillar. It's a cacophonous, destructive sound. Ringing pulses that make Sax's nerves vibrate like a ringing bell. He keeps moving, because there is no alternative. There is no choice for an Oratus. No other way.

The next pillar launches stinging bolts of electricity, ones that strike him with numbing force. Then there is fire, cold, noxious gasses and worse as they pass through the Thrashing Wheels. Together, the Oratus struggle through.

They push their way to the end. And when they get there, helping each other to stand, the blue-green instructor is there, and he points back the way they've come.

Again.

And again.

And again.

Sax steadies the miner with his left foreclaw—his left midclaw, too close to the miner's blast, has, like his legs and tail, vanished from his consciousness. He rests his head back on the hard metal floor. It's not hard to make out what's above him: the latticed catwalk, and through it, the brown bulk of the Amigga. There's motion too, sliding through the grease-blur of his eyes; what looks like silver, stabbing forward towards Dalachite.

The human. Kaishi.

The species has more courage than Sax expects. More than their weak, squishy bodies suggest. But she doesn't know that you don't fight an Amigga up close. Stay back. Fire away. Now she's caught. Dalachite's taking her weapon, and Kaishi herself.

The development doesn't change Sax's plan. Just means he has to adjust his aim. Doesn't want to hit the human. So he lowers the angle of the miner. Off-center now, but a burn like this ought to be enough. Sax presses down with his right midclaw, pushes and holds the trigger in. There's no kick—a miner runs on energy, and there's no recoil there. The blue-white bolt that comes out, that keeps burning, is beautiful. Grand and spectacular and Sax would watch it for infinity if he could.

The miner melts through the catwalk, hits the bottom-front part of the Amigga. The liquid coating the creature's skin superheats, bursts into its own flame that spreads across the entire creature. Dalachite's connections to *Cobalt* shrivel and blacken, burning skin falling around Sax like volcanic rain.

Sax realizes he's still holding the trigger and lets go. The world seems dark for an instant when the bolt vanishes, then it's replaced with an orange glow. Like the familiars. Fire, enemy of space existence, seems to be a hallmark for Sax on this station. He wants to laugh at this, but the act is exhausting, so he lays there instead.

Watches.

The catwalk, loosened as its connection with the outer ring falls away, begins to crumble. The burning ball that had been Dalachite rolls off the slant, falling towards Sax. Slowly, of course, as the gravity here is a bare fraction of what it is even elsewhere on the station, where Cobalt's spin keeps down and up in existence. Falling after it is a shape he knows; the human. The flames curl around her, skin unburnt, and Sax is confused for a moment before he remembers her mask.

She'll survive. The specimen.

Bas will be proud of him.

urning searing bright and black. That's what I fall into. That's what should kill me in my slow, twisting descent. I reach with my arms, my legs, trying to find some purchase as the world ignites around me. I close my eyes and expect pain, but feel none of it. A slight warmth, like Ignos on my skin. No puckering blisters, the torching pain of the fire.

The mask.

As I roll off Dalachite's carcass, popping and bubbling as everything inside the creature bursts and boils, the mask keeps me insulated. Instead, I see the blue and red and white and orange flickers as they roast the monster around me. The catwalk we're resting on groans, then snaps and collapses and I fall further still. Down towards the vents and terminals that make up the spherical walls of the room.

Dalachite's limbs, those long stretchy things going from its body to the outer sides, shrivel up, disintegrate into ashen clouds. I realize somewhere in this that I'm screaming, but the crackle and pops of snapping metal, the hissing whispers of cooking skin drown out my voice.

I manage to twist so that I'm looking where I'm falling, and catch myself on the sloped side of the sphere. The terminals are smooth to the touch, with the only purchase coming in the small gaps between the screens.

I slide, slow, towards the bottom. Blackened bits of metal and things I don't recognize tumble around me. Cling to the mask, to me.

Then it's done. Everything settles. Burning bits of viscera and debris litter the bottom of the sphere. I pick out one thing in the middle of that. A large body. The Oratus, Sax. He's lying there, his right claws holding Coorvin's weapon, dead silent.

I see the broad burn in his torso, and other wounds scarring his skin. The creature has had a tough time of it. I don't know what it takes to kill one of these things, but it certainly looks like Sax has met that mark.

"Are you alive?" the voice comes from above. Coorvin, the strange fur-covered thing, the one who'd been holding his head, seemingly incapable of speaking, stares at me from the ledge by the door.

Where the catwalk had once connected, a memory marked by a jagged set of torn beams and bars.

"I don't know," I say.

Because the truth is I don't know what's happening. I can feel myself breathe, I can feel the side of the sphere through the mask, and I think, maybe, I'm not in danger.

You are. Without Dalachite, Cobalt will slowly die. You need to get off the station.

Ignos jerks me back. It's still in my mind, and it's speaking clear, but leaving the station means getting out of here, back to the shuttle.

"Do you have a way to get me up?" I ask Coorvin.

The little creature looks around, then back at me. Shakes its head.

"Can you jump?" Coorvin asks.

I haven't considered making a leap for the ledge. Everything seems to float here, so I might be able to make it. To attempt that, I'll need to get to the other side of the sphere. Back over towards Coorvin. So I walk, one foot after another, stepping over the broken, twisted bits.

Stepping over Sax.

I notice something, staring down at those gray scales, at the vents that line his chest. He's shuddering. His claws twitching slightly. Is the Oratus alive?

It doesn't matter. Leave him.

Ignos had sent me on the quest to find and kill the two Oratus. Claimed they were a mortal threat to me and my friends. Yet Sax saved my life. He destroyed Dalachite before it devoured me, had tried to help Malo and Viera.

Before I really think about it, I bend over, grab the Oratus' claws with my hands and pull. Sax is like a large log. If we were home, I'm sure I couldn't move him, but here he slides ever so slightly along the smooth metal, dragging ash with him as he goes.

"Coorvin, I need help," I shout. "He's still alive."

This agitates the furry creature, who watches as I pull Sax close to the upward sloping side. The part of the sphere beneath the ledge. I'm almost there when noises begin to ring out; sharp clanging sounds unnatural and strange, and when I look around, I can't find the cause.

"Alarms!" Coorvin shouts. "Without Dalachite, Cobalt's systems can't work. We have to leave now!"

"Not without the Oratus!" I reply, and ask Ignos what 'systems' Coorvin is talking about.

There are countless ones that may need constant mainte-

nance. That sound might mean something simple, like a familiar asking for an order. Or something worse, like an oxygen drain that needs repair before vacuum sucks us all away. Or a course correction before a speeding piece of space debris cuts the station in half.

That doesn't sound good. I look at Sax, limp. If Coorvin can't find something soon, I'll have to leave the Oratus. He helped me, but Sax is also the reason I'm here in the first place.

I see a way, if you're determined to save him.

A way?

The Oratus drug themselves before fights. It's disgusting, but it works. Looks like this one still has his, attached to the mask there. It's a small box, singed on the outside. Down by Sax's waist.

I lean over, pry open the top with my fingers. Inside is what looks like a clear container with a black, smooth seal, one I need a way to pierce. The answer strikes me in the form of a jagged piece of metal. I grab it, stick the piece down through the seal until it's coated with the strange substance. I pull it out. It looks smeared, like tree sap.

I think they eat it.

I hold it near Sax's mouth, but it's closed tight.

I've seen, growing up, wild animals and people playing with them. The creatures would bite without warning, snap and slash, even if they were asleep seconds before. I know what lies behind Sax's lips: all those rows of terrifying teeth, and even if Sax doesn't mean to, he could bite my hand clean off.

But if I don't find some way to wake him up, he'll die.

I begin to push, to pry. Sax's lips are squishy, but, with a bit of force, his jaw moves. Like pushing aside a thick branch. I see the rows and rows of teeth, and in the back, a long twisting tongue curled up on itself.

I stick the metal in, rub it on the tongue. I try to be careful, but the metal is small, I'm nervous, it slips in my fingers, and I see a line of red where it cuts. Sax's eyes fly open, and I jerk back. Fall over and hit the side of the sphere. Catch myself, and watch as the Oratus spasms.

Sax is blinking rapidly, his throat making short hissing noises, and then Sax spits the metal out.

We both lie there, breathing for a moment, then the Oratus looks at me.

"I cannot move my legs," the Oratus hisses, and bits of blood drip from between his lips as he does. "You have to pull me."

"I don't have the strength," I say.

"Use the Stim," Sax replies.

There's a banging from above. It's Coorvin, and he's dragging a box of supplies. He drops it, and it floats down to me. Comes to a rest on the floor of the sphere. Before I can ask what he's doing, Coorvin runs off again. I turn back to the Oratus. His claw is resting on his Stim pack, and I watch it break the seal, digging deep, glistening when it comes back out.

"Come closer," Sax says.

I don't want to. I don't know what that the drug is going to do to me, but what are my alternatives? Dying here?

So I crawl on my hands and knees to keep from sliding on the metal. Sax sticks the claw towards me, holds it steady, and I lick it. The same way I would a stick of sugar cane. The same way I might get the last bit of juice from a split melon. The stuff tastes sweet, it pops in my mouth.

And then I'm a new human.

Sax watches the human take the Stim. He's not sure how the creature's body will handle it. It's a small dose, barely enough to see an Oratus through a quick fight. Yet these species, if the Amigga's tests are right, only have one heart. Their bodies are smaller, fragile. The last thing Sax wants right now is for Kaishi to explode. For her muscles to twitch too hard and fast and snap or spin out of control. He's seen that before with Flaum, ones who thought they could find an advantage by overindulging in Stim's power.

Other Flaum had to clean up the mess that experiment left behind.

Kaishi's eyes blink rapidly for a few seconds, then close as she shudders, but she appears to stay alive. There's another crunch as a second crate falls, piling against the first. Sax understands what Coorvin is doing: creating a ladder, steps of the sort that the Oratus and human can use to climb out of the sphere. Kaishi, with the Stim, will still need to push Sax up.

"Now pull," Sax says. "Drag me to the boxes, and then lift me up."

Kaishi nods at him, and then reaches out, grips his forearm, and starts to drag Sax. The Oratus helps when he can, using his tail and his midclaws to push himself along. Together they get over to the two crates Coorvin has dropped as the Flaum pushes a third one off.

They're resting on each other, with the base pushing against the bulk of the collapsed catwalk at the bottom of the sphere.

Kaishi uses the crates, gripping the one and then another, and pulling herself, and then Sax after her, until they're on the top of the stack. Now they're only two meters beneath the ledge where Coorvin stands, watching them.

Sax plunges his claws into the flat faces of the terminals on the side in front of them. Shatters their screens, punctures the gray metal slates, and tries to climb, but even with the Stim, his arms quiver; he can barely hold himself up, which means lifting is out of the question.

Beneath him, Kaishi pushes. Thrusts Sax up until the Oratus manages, with one outstretched lunge of his foreclaws, to grip the edge of the ledge. Coorvin scrambles over, grab's Sax's right foreclaw with his hands and tugs. The power is so pathetic that Sax wants to laugh, but every little bit helps.

"Climb me," Sax hisses down to Kaishi, who, after hesitating for a moment, obliges.

She jumps onto Sax's tail and clamors up the Oratus' body. Sax takes a foot to the face without whining. Without biting it off.

Restraint Bas would admire. Kaishi gets up on the ledge, turns and looks at him, holds out a hand.

"If I reach for it, I'll fall," Sax hisses.

"You have a better idea?" Kaishi replies.

"My tail," Sax says. "Get ready to grab it."

Kaishi lies down, chest on the ledge. Coorvin moves near her, hands at the ready. Sax swings his tail from left to right, back and forth, going farther and farther, building momentum, and then, moving right, Sax lets his left foreclaw loose, allowing his body to swing with the tail. Kaishi and Coorvin pull as Sax swings around, scraping Sax's chest against and over the edge of the ledge. Sax clamps down his right foreclaw and midclaw as Kaishi and Coorvin dash and hold his tail and pull the Oratus the rest of the way onto the platform.

He's up.

Which leaves room for the next crisis.

The alarms are deafening now, and coming in a thousand tones and beats. What terminals remain are flashing reds and yellows. *Cobalt* itself seems to be shivering. They can't stay here. Sax pushes himself onto his tail. He still can't feel his legs, and he looks down to confirm they exist. Kaishi and Coorvin place themselves beneath his midclaws, supporting the Oratus on their shoulders. Together the three of them walk from the sphere and leave Dalachite to its final resting place.

They trudge along the hallway, through room where the familiars were made, and two of the chambers beyond. Until they come to a sealed door, next to a now-ruined screen Sax remembers showing the progress of the Amigga's experiments.

Sax has enough strength for this, with the Stim still pulsing through his blood. He takes his four claws, drives them into the sides of the door.

"Pull me!" Sax hisses.

Kaishi and Coorvin shove the Oratus hard, and Sax

adds what he can of his own muscle. The claws rend the metal away, and the door falls towards him to show, on the other side, two humans. One, Malo, is still wrapped in bars on the table. The other, Viera, holds the remnants of another bar like some sort of weapon, eyes wild and ready to swing.

"Kaishi, you're alive!" Viera yells.

But the human's face turns as she sees Sax collapse, eyes closed, to the floor.

I pick Sax up again, Viera helping Coorvin and I. We drag him to Malo's body, and though Sax seems barely alive, we uses his claws like knives to cut the metal keeping Malo tied down. The Charre warrior springs up and replaces me under Sax, sharing the burden with Viera.

"What happened?" Viera's asking, and I say I'll fill them in as we go.

The walk through the station is slow. Every so often we come across familiars; leftovers, plain blue, standing silent and eerie. Not reacting, not moving or noticing us. We pass by the kitchen, and there's no food ready to serve. No sign of violence. We don't go back to our quarters—nothing there worth grabbing. Only to the docking bay. To the shuttle, to our escape.

Evidence of the failing station manifests in flickering lights, in locked doors sealing passages and glowing red—an indicator of unstable pressure. The sounds echo back and forth down the hallways, chiming off of each other in a haunting dissonance that makes me wish for the natural jungle cries of my home. I knew what those meant, these noises are alien, and frightening.

Sax, limp and staving off death, hisses strange things. Stuff about power supplies and unstable reactions.

"Do you know what he's talking about?" I ask Coorvin.

"Like all stations, *Cobalt* demands modulated power. Most of the time it can function on its own, but Dalachite has been making so many changes, the station might not be able to survive without its guidance. *Cobalt* might be breaking apart."

"Kaishi, we should leave him and go," Viera says, her breath is faint. I'd forgotten that she almost died not that long ago.

"He saved me, Viera," I reply. "Hurt himself trying to save us. We're not leaving him."

"Honor demands we help," Malo adds.

That keeps Viera quiet, keeps us all moving until we get to the docking bay. Until we get to the ruin. Slumped against the shuttle is Bas, two miners in her mid-claws, resting amid a horde of burned and broken familiars. Charred lumps of blue goop mark the end of a tough fight. Bas has her share of wounds; She's bleeding from cuts, and her plenty of her pink-gold scales have been knocked off, damaged. Yet as we enter, she raises one miner towards us.

"Does he live?" Her hisses are weak, tired.

I step forward. "He's alive. He saved me, and we killed the Amigga."

Bas gives me slow nod. "I could tell when they stopped coming."

"What happened here?" Malo asks.

"Had to keep the shuttle safe. It's our only way off the station."

Take it. I can tell you how to fly. Leave the Oratus. They'll kill you as soon as they recover.

I blink.

They took you before. What do you think will happen now? They won't let you go. They'll take you somewhere else. Somewhere worse than here.

I feel sick all of a sudden. Torn. My eyes find Viera and Malo's, and they're waiting for my decision. Waiting for me to help them bring Bas and Sax into the shuttle.

But I think Ignos is right. Either one of them, Sax or Bas, could kill us all by themselves. Or take us to another station like this one. I remember the sessions, remember the pain the terror.

I can take you home, Kaishi. All of you.

"Coorvin." I look at the Flaum. "Are there other ways off of the station?"

"There are several evacuation modules," Coorvin replies. "But I don't know why you'd want to use them with this shuttle right here."

You see? No need to take the risk.

"Come on, let's move," I say. Viera and Malo go to lift Sax, but I shake my head. I hear a sharp hiss, and see Bas has her miner trained on me. "I'm sorry. You can try to kill us now if you want but we're leaving in that shuttle."

"Kaishi?" Malo asks. "What are you saying?"

"Ignos is right. There's a risk, Malo. The Oratus brought us here, they won't let us go. If we want to head home, then we can't bring them with us. Coorvin says there are other ways off the station. We don't need to take them."

"I can't let you leave," Bas says. "Not with that thing in your mind."

She raises the miner, pulls the trigger, but nothing

happens. It's empty. Bas doesn't even look surprised, just defeated.

"I'm sorry," I say, and then Viera, Malo and I head towards the shuttle. Up the boarding ramp inside, which, with Ignos telling me how, I shut, leaving our kidnappers behind.

Sax can't protest as the humans walk pass him onto the shuttle. He watches, his nerves flickering, trying to establish contact with his legs. The shuttle ramp slides up, and not long after a hum fills the air as the shuttle's engines turn on.

"You let them go," Sax says in a burst of breath to Bas.

"The miner was out of charge," Bas replies.

"You had another."

"To do what?" Bas, still resting against the shuttle strut, says. "Hurt them? Kill them?"

"Keep them here?" Sax says.

"They wouldn't have gone with us willingly. They would've died, and then this would all be useless. We know where they're going. We can follow them."

Bas makes a good point. If they're going back to the human's planet, they'll be easy enough to find. To track down again. But that means the Oratus have to live long enough to do so.

The shuttle shakes and the struts begin to move. Bas falls to the ground as her support pulls away. She drops her miners and drags herself towards Sax. Who, himself, with the help of Coorvin pulling him along, heads towards the door out of the bay. They have to leave before the magnetic shield lowers for the shuttle. Before vacuum sucks them into the space.

Whomever flies the ship isn't an experienced pilot: the shuttle goes up slowly, gets a meter or so off of the ground before doing a lazy turn around. Plenty of time for Coorvin, Sax and Bas to make it to the door and back through. To slam it shut and seal them in the hallway.

There's a familiar standing there, staring at them, unmoving.

"The evac modules are this way," Coorvin says.

The Flaum doesn't seem perturbed in the least that Kaishi took the shuttle. Then again, he's spent so long on the station, Coorvin might just be happy to leave, no matter how.

There's a low rumble, a churning beneath the continual blaring of alarms, as the shuttle rockets out through the bay.

"We're in deep space," Sax says. "There's no habitable planets around?"

"You know what it was like with Dalachite?" Coorvin says, his voice high and jittering, yet somehow solemn. "That thing dominated the station. Drove away the staff and replaced it with familiars. It experimented on all of us, and it nearly took my mind. Now I'm free to go find some-place new. To get off the station. The evac mods give us a chance, so I'm going to take it. You're welcome to come with."

"Then let's go," Sax hisses.

They head through to the station towards the evac mods. The smell of ozone and burning electronics fills the air. *Cobalt* is falling apart without Dalachite, its heart and soul.

"What did the Amigga want?" Bas asks Coorvin as they go.

"Dalachite wasn't the only one looking for these things," Coorvin shudders as he speaks, as he walks. "They communicated. All of the Amigga. The familiars are a test, a way to remove the need for us."

"Us?"

"Species are unpredictable, Dalachite told me. They need, they want. Familiars have neither of those things. They will obey without question, and on a large scale."

"Then why not machines?" Sax hisses.

"I don't know," Coorvin replies. "I didn't really have conversations with Dalachite. More like it ranted at me."

They reach the trio of circular doors, each one leading to its own evac mod. Coorvin takes them to the one on the left, punches the panel, and the door slides open. Inside are a pair of benches and a lot of bound packages full of rations and water. Medical supplies. Enough to last for quite some time. They head inside, Sax and Bas working to arrange themselves in the least painful way possible, breaking into the packs of healing salves, bandages and beginning to patch themselves back to life.

"Ready?" Coorvin says.

"Launch us," Sax hisses.

With a few quick presses, the mod is shut tight, and a second later they blast off into space.

I stare into the black infinite and realize I have no idea what I'm doing.

Beneath my hands are a string of terminals not too unlike what I saw in the Amigga's chamber. Screens displaying graphs and what look like maps. One scrolls a message full of names I don't know or understand. From someone named Evva. Ignos tells me to ignore it. To ignore everything except for a single screen on the far right side. I have to step over there to reach it, as it's clear the shuttle is meant for longer arms, larger bodies. Malo and Viera, behind me, stare around dumbfounded.

I can't imagine what this would be like without a voice in my head explaining everything.

This is the part we need to use. It sets the leap trajectory. A folding of the universe around the ship to move us where we need to go.

Then again, maybe having a voice in your head doesn't help all that much.

I'm going to give you a series of numbers, and you need to enter them precisely as I tell you.

Part of the display holds a series of circles with numbers inside, going zero through nine. To the left of the number pad is what looks like a glowing sphere of bright points. Things that, if you shot them in the night sky, would resemble the stars Ignos says they are. Ignos reads off the numbers, and I don't know where he's getting them from, but I enter them anyway. Press my finger on the little circles representing each digit. As I complete the entry, the stars in the display begin to shift. To zoom in and narrow until one isolated region is represented. It's clearly a map, though of what I'm not sure.

The galaxy, Kaishi. What lies beyond the sky of home.

A home we're going back to. I turn to Malo and Viera. "I've entered the directions Ignos gave me," I say. "We're going home."

You should strap in.

I look around. There's no clear way to do that. No seats, or anything to hold. The bridge holds only tiled metal floor and terminals.

You have to hit the button first.

I glance back at the display, and the number pad has transformed into two square blocks of color. One green, the other red.

The green one.

I touch it, and there's a pleasant sounding chime. The broad window looking out to the black grays out, and then a giant number 10 appears. It begins to count down. The floor beneath my feet and the ceiling above my hands rotates, and shiny black webbing dangles from above, while thick bars slide over and across pairs of tiles on the floor.

You must step between them.

"Put your feet underneath the straps," I say, stepping into my own.

When I slide my foot between two of the strapped tiles, a bright green light flashes, and then the strap restricts until it almost hurts, pinning

my foot to the floor. The same thing happens with my other foot when I shift it in.

Above me, the netting slides down. It fits to me; molding around my back. I feel something click behind my feet. It's almost like I'm standing in a hammock, a comfort I sometimes had back home—thick mossweaves hung between two trees.

The counter reaches zero.

"This is what we did before, isn't it?" I ask Ignos.

It doesn't have time to answer. The universe warps and splits. My stomach slides into and out of itself, my head bursts with ringing confusion. The gray in front of me turns a broad white, then a rainbow of color splashes across, as if I I'm spinning quickly through a room of flowers. It fades just as fast, turns back to black. To a star-filled expanse, one giant, entirely tan circle in front of us, wisps of gray scattered over its surface.

I'm breathing hard, but coming back from this leap is not the disaster of the first. I'm ready in a few seconds. Even Viera and Malo aren't crying. Aren't panicking, though I notice Viera's fists are clenched tight against the netting.

Is this it? Are we home?

Of course.

CLARITY'S DAWN

THE SKYWARD SAGA - BOOK THREE

My home appears from nothing in the dark. A great brown and white circle hanging against an endless black expanse with bright lights twinkling, like holes in a leafy canopy. I stare at it through the front windshield of the shuttle, my mouth open. My eyes blink and see that my home is still there. When I left it, when I'd been taken from it, I thought I would never see its jungles, its oceans and mountains again. I thought my family, all that I knew, was lost forever.

Yet here it is again.

Are you happy?

Ignos, who I once thought was a god, what is now strange creature living inside of me, sends its words in the same way I might think them. Wisps of feeling, images and emotion passing through me. Am I happy?

Yes.

The shuttle will guide itself. Take in the view. Relax.

I don't have much choice anyway. The bands locking around my feet and the netting clinging to my back, the things that kept me stable during the leap, do not retract.

I'm stuck, as are my two friends, Viera and Malo, behind me. That might be a problem if we had anywhere to go, but right now we're transfixed by what's going on in front of us.

The brown circle is growing larger, closer. In between the drifts of white, which Ignos tells me are clouds, I see black specks cut across the view. Some larger than others, some appearing, like the birds of my home, to fly in formation.

Are they others? New Oratus, new creatures coming to take me away as soon as I land?

No. Those are my friends.

Ignos had mentioned, when I first found it in that crashed rock months ago, that its friends would follow. Its job was to prep Earth for them. These other gods would rescue us from hardship. Solve our problems and bring us to a new era of happiness and peace.

So why, why does this strange knot start to form in my stomach as I stare at the growing brown mass. As the specks define themselves into strange shapes. Some, like the planet, are circular. Others are jagged, made of lines and cutting edges as they zip around.

"Whatever those are, they're coming closer," Viera says.

She's speaking about a set of three things off to our left. I can see them because, from the twin wings on their sides, bright red lights glow towards us.

"I can't move," Malo adds. "Can you, Kaishi? Can you free us?"

I ask Ignos the question, but the creature doesn't respond. It's staying silent now, and my unease grows. "I don't know how."

"Better hope these are friends, or we're in trouble," Viera says.

"Ignos says they are."

"Forgive me if I don't trust that thing," Viera replies.

I watch as the three ships outside slide around us. To the point where, when the ships leave my view, I can still see the slight glow of those red points. The world in front of us has grown to fill the visible space. Parts of the brown shade differently. Large circles. Ripples in the earth, which I assume must be mountains. Others look like deep divots. Craters, perhaps.

What I don't see are jungles. What I don't see are oceans.

Are they on the other side?

Ignos doesn't answer. The shuttle begins to shake, and suddenly the edges, then the entire windshield glows white and orange and red.

"What's going on?" Malo says. "Is Ignos telling you anything?"

Everything will be fine.

Ignos' words carry condescension, the same sort of kind dismissal that my parents used to give me when I was small child. An answer that says Ignos does not trust me with more.

As quickly as the fire picks up it recedes, and now icy particles begin to form. Strange crystalline formations grow on the glass. From hot to cold to melting again almost as soon as they form. All I see now is foggy gray white.

"I don't know what's happening," I say.

"That makes three of us," Viera replies.

In a past life, before, I would've prayed. Prayed to Ignos, the real god, not the creature, to deliver me from harm. And for the first time, for the first time since that strange night in the dark of the jungle when I saw the light of the ship that bore this creature to me, I pray. Pray to god I no longer think is inside me, one that I hope is around me. Is guiding me.

Malo hears my words and joins in. It's a simple, common ritual. An ask for forgiveness, for courage, for guidance. For protection and love.

"Here's hoping that works," Viera says when we're done; the Lunare doesn't join us in the prayer but she's happy to reap the benefits of it.

For a moment, it seems like we do. The gray breaks and beneath us I see something I can recognize; the tall spire, snow-tipped, of a mountain. Though this one, unlike the rocky gray against the green jungles of my home is almost all black. Around it, at its base and stretching for as far as I can see, there is no green. Only whites and grays and blues and reds. Only buildings. Arcing and toppling on top of one another, stacked and merging. Split by long cylindrical tubes that circle and divide them like veins on a fern frond.

The knot in my stomach grows to full panic. Because I know now.

This is not my home.

The shuttle drops lower. We swoop along the mountain, and in the shimmering reflections of the tall buildings I can see that we are still being followed, tailed by the three craft that met us above the sky. But these are not the only things joining us in the air. Whereas my skies were filled with birds, these are full of objects of all sizes. They zip and dart everywhere, filling the blank spaces the same way fog or locusts might at home. I don't understand how none of them hit each other, and Ignos replies with a single word:

Automatic.

I don't know what it means. I don't know what any of this is. I don't understand what I see as I look inside the buildings that we pass, as I see strange devices, odd lights of pinks and yellows. Wide halls with groups of creatures I could never before imagine standing or moving. Talking or, in some cases, appearing to fire strange weapons like the kind the Oratus had on *Cobalt*.

Beneath us, the tubes seem to split everything, I see more shapes, several that look like Coorvin, the furry and big-eyed guide we'd left on the station. Called a Flaum, I think.

Below us, the travelers rocket by in small pods, sitting as they're shot along to whatever end. Beneath them, on the surface, there are red-lined roads. Paved in stone. Red brick that appears molded without crease. Walking feet, claws, or stranger things cover the surface as hordes of creatures meander back and forth. It's a sight that should fill me with wonder but instead twists me with dread.

"Where are we?" Malo says. "This isn't home."

No, it isn't.

I ask Ignos if it lied to me.

I never did. I let you assume. If you went back home now, the Oratus would simply take you again. I can't let that happen. I can't let you fall into their hands.

What I do is my choice.

No. Not anymore.

The shuttle takes a sharp right turn, coasting us above a broader avenue and underneath a series of archways that glow red as we pass beneath them. The ones in front shimmer a pale yellow, the same that I've seen on insects warning you not to get too close. I realize these arches are guiding us down, towards a wide gaping hole that appears to lead into the ground.

"Don't know what that thing inside your head is telling you, Kaishi," Viera says. "But I'm not inclined to trust a word it's saying. Wherever this is, it's not home. Whatever these things are, I'm betting they're not our friends."

"We can't do anything now," I say. "Look and learn. Try to figure out what we can do."

You can accept it. You can understand that your place in a larger galaxy is here. With us.

My place is with my people.

Kaishi, you have no people. All you have is me. All you have is what the Sevora will give you.

As I look forward, as we dive through the last of the arches and into an all-consuming dark beneath the ground, the only thing that breaks the my numbing shock is the cool wet of tears.

Time is a fluid concept. For Sax, at least, the definition of passing events is constantly in flux. Local time, measured by wherever he just happens to be. Galactic time, long ago shifting to measurements in cycles, grand events marking shifts in civilization's power and goals. And, of course, his own biology. The rate of cellular decay and regeneration in his muscles and tendons and organs. This last is most apparent to him now, sitting cramped with Bas, his pair, and the old speckle-furred Flaum Coorvin in an evac mod hurtling through space.

"Do you know what it would mean for us to die out here?" Sax hisses all of a sudden.

He does this more to break the silence, one that's been steadily growing in the eternity since they've launched from *Cobalt*. Since they've escaped from a space station hurtling towards its own ruin, whether by rogue asteroid or by internal power failures.

"I believe, in an environment such as this, were our bodies to fail we would drift, largely preserved, for a long while," Coorvin muses, his large black eyes staring off at nothing. "I don't believe there's enough biological matter in here for us to decay properly."

"Exactly," Sax says, though that's not at all what he meant, but it fits anyway. "We would lose our chance at honor. At victory. At solving the reason why."

"Why?" Bas hisses a lighter, cleaner note than Sax.

Like most things between the two, Bas is better, more beautiful.

"Because we don't know yet. We don't know why that Amigga cared so much about the humans. I don't know why fassoths were on the human's planet or how the technology we saw there came to exist. Its relation to the primitive structures is all wrong."

"An inquisitive Oratus?" Coorvin says. "I thought all of your kind were brutes. Bred for war and nothing else."

"I was," Sax says. He looks at his claws, the gray scales bleeding back from translucent pink and gray points. Four of them, one set on each arm, and two more talons on each of his thick legs, currently tucked in beneath him along with his tail. "I deserve to be in the midst of the enemy, tearing and shredding and slashing. Yet here I am sitting in this cramped prison waiting to die. Such a space makes you think. Makes you wonder."

"Evva will tell us," Bas says.

She's serene, with her pink-gold scales, leaning back against the front bulkhead of the mod. This one has no windows, though there's nothing to see. All they're doing is hurtling through space. A single set of emergency beacons flaring, but who knows if anything is nearby, who knows if anything ever will be. They could crash into an asteroid, a planet, and not know it until it happened.

This does not bug Sax in the slightest: If he's going to die an insulting death, he'd rather it be a surprise.

"Do you know that Dalachite thought the Oratus were the worst things in the galaxy?" Coorvin says of *Cobalt*'s now very-dead master, and now his white-tuft, black-furred face turned to look at them. "A failed experiment, it called you."

"Experiment?" Bas opens her eyes, yellow with black vertical slits. "What did it mean by that?"

"I don't know," Coorvin says. "It never elaborated. I didn't ask. Not my place, and not my interest."

"Which is?" Now Bas is as eager to carry the conversation as Sax was to start it.

"To find the answer, of course. The key to peace in the galaxy. That's the whole reason *Cobalt* was built. Why all of us signed up for the project."

"All of us?"

"Most left before you came," Coorvin said. "Took positions elsewhere as Dalachite changed its plans. As it became certain that the only way to survive was to eliminate everything else."

"It failed." Sax says.

"It came closer than you think," Coorvin counters.

But before that Flaum can continue, a buzzing noise breaks out inside the mod; the communications array sparking to life. Moments later a wet voice pours out amid static. High-pitched and drenched, like a river rushing through words.

"Hailing the mod, hailing the mind. Looks like you're going in the right direction. Care to tell us why? Seeing as we are here for *Cobalt* and *Cobalt* appears to be in a state of, can I say, disarray?"

The three of them meet each other's eyes. Then Coorvin jumps to respond.

"This is Coorvin, we evacuated the station. Critical power failure. Requesting pickup."

There's a burst of static and then the voice comes back. "Power failure! Well that's just downright bad. Guess we'll have to be keeping these supplies then. Maybe a delivery, sell them. Who did you say is in that mod, just you Coorvin?"

"A couple of others," Coorvin replies.

"We're closing in on your location, would like to know a bit more about those others if you wouldn't mind, Coorvin. You know how I dislike surprises."

Coorvin released the small button on the transponder. "Plake. She might kill us if I tell her what you are."

"Why would she?" Bas says. "We haven't done anything to her."

"You're Oratus. She's Vyphen."

That explains it. Sax rests his head back against the bulkhead. No Vyphen would willingly rescue an Oratus. It's hard to have much sympathy for the species that drove your own to ruin. That removed its sole reason for existence.

But then, the Vyphen didn't vanish. They discharged, streamed back into civilization, and found a new set of needs and wants. Did what other species had for cycles— found new desires that required certain means.

"She likes money, yes?" Sax hisses after a moment.

"She's a runner. Of course."

"Then tell her. Tell her we can pay her more than she'll know what to do with. Bas and I are respected. High up in the Vincere. They'll pay for our return."

The evac mod shakes. Something's docking with them. The transponder buzzes again.

"Coorvin, as you'll be able to tell unless that Amigga's stripped all your senses, we've docked with you. Going to open the door in a moment. Provided, of course, you tell me just why you're being so secretive. And, while you're at it, maybe explain to me why *Cobalt* decided to explode. Amigga generally don't let power failures take out their stations."

Coorvin looks at both Bas and Sax. The Oratus nod at the Flaum, who squeezes his eyes shut tight for a moment, then presses the transponder button.

"It's a pair of Oratus, Plake. I know what you're thinking. I know this isn't what you're hoping for, but they say they have money. They came in an official craft, on military business. They can pay you."

Just buzzing static. Then another thunk, a bang on the door.

"I see why you were trying to hide that fact from me, Coorvin. I really do. You think that I'm going to let two monsters onto my ship? You really think so?"

Sax reaches across Coorvin, presses a claw on the button. "Captain Plake, this is Sax, of the Vincere, third letter rank. I've never done anything to hurt the Vyphen. Never done anything to hurt you, your ship or your crew. My pair and I are only requesting transport to the closest station, and will pay you well for it. If you like, we can stay in your cargo hold. Out of your way. You'll collect a good sum for our delivery."

Sax releases the button, turns back to Bas, as he can here her amused hissing laugh.

"Never knew you could be so diplomatic," Bas replies.

"When I have to."

"Interesting," Plake's burbling bursts from the communications array. "I suppose I could bury my hatred for you for a little while. We're not too far from another station now, a place where you should be able to secure passage back to where you need to be. But when I open the door, it's my ship and my rules. You'll follow them, or I won't hesitate to melt you into slag. Nothing would make me happier."

"She sounds like a fighter," Sax says.

"She's efficient, and very protective of her ship." Coorvin replies.

There's a whistling noise of pressurizing air, and suddenly the outer locked door twists and shunts out away from the mod. Reveals a trio of creatures, all of them holding miners, and all of them pointing right at Sax and Bas.

"Coorvin, out you come," a pitch night-furred Flaum, with a small miner in one hand, beckons for Coorvin to jump out.

Coorvin doesn't wait either, scrambling out of the mod. Sax is slightly insulted, but it's not like the Flaum owes either Oratus anything. It's because of them he's no longer on the station, even if that means Coorvin's outside Dalachite's clutches.

"You two," hums a deep red Whelk, a slug-like beast that stands two meters tall, though its short, stubbly arms are no match for Sax's claws.

It holds a large weapon, no, Sax sees now: the miner is meshed into the sides of the Whelk's body. It's not the only modification showing on the slug; some sort of strange helmet with a cybernetic eyepiece rests on the Whelk's domed head. The Whelk's skin, a sliming crimson, shimmers as Sax looks at it.

Whatever they're dealing with here, this isn't an ordinary merchant ship.

"Time to come out, and you're gonna do it slow. As I say." The Whelk's voice comes from a slit it breaks in its skin, and the smattering of sounds come from undulations deep within its body. It's a strange noise, but it works."First the pink one. Slow and easy."

Sax wants to protest. To argue and demand that he go before his pair, the better to let Bas know if they're going to be facing a surprise execution. Yet, the last thing he wants to do is antagonize their would be rescuers, so Sax stays quiet as Bas climbs over him. Her tail, ever so briefly, wraps around his own and gives a slight squeeze. Then she's gone, out through the circle and beyond the red Whelk. Sax sees the other Flaum peel away, the black-furred creature already chittering at Bas.

"Now you. You were the one that talked, right? The one that said cash for delivery?" The Whelk sounds smug as it says this.

Sax feels his claws clench. Forces them back open. Keeps his arms low.

"I meant it," Sax says. "Deliver us, and your captain will get her money."

"How much you think she'll get for one instead of two?" The Whelk says. "Or dead instead of alive?"

"You'll get one shot," Sax hisses, leaving his mouth open so the Whelk can see just how many teeth are waiting to bite. "You'll get one shot, and then I'll tear you in half. Then I'll tear the rest of your crew to pieces. I'll find your captain and I'll stuff her back in here with what's left of you, and shoot her into space. One shot. Better kill me or all of you are dead."

The skin beneath the Whelk's helmet changes, a streak

of pale blue forming against the crimson in the shape of a nasty grin. "Glad we got the threats out of the way. At least I know you're actually Oratus. No Sevora come would bother with a speech like that. Come on, get out of there. The captain might hate you, but I know what you do. As one warrior to another, respect."

Sax follows the Whelk's lead, clambers out the evac mod and into a wide cargo bay. He notices first that this isn't some small shuttle, this is a serious ship. A freighter of size, and one that's currently hauling a ton of what looks like foodstuffs. The crates tower around them, with the broad doors for unloading closed to his left. Beneath him, Sax can feel the engines hum, the vibrations of the ionized gas pushing the ship forward. No doubt they'd be leaping soon.

Beyond the crates, the ceiling of the freighter begins to slope down and then spreads into three separate portals leaving straight, left and right.

"Don't think you'll be getting the grand tour though," the Whelk says as Sax looks around. "Captain Plake wants you restricted to the right module. Luckily, it's a good one. Kitchen, entertainment. Plenty of space for your big bodies."

"Thanks," Sax says.

"Don't thank me," the Whelk replies. "Thank her."

The Whelk points with his fixed cannon by Sax, over the top of the crates to the straight-away portal, which had just opened to reveal a feathered, smooth-skinned yellowish creature, with two long legs, and a pair of feathered arms that extend to circular, webbed hands with nubby fingers. Large round eyes, rising up over the top of her head, rotate towards Sax. Her mouth opens, and Sax can see, even from this distance, the folded curl of her tongue.

"Agra-Red," Plake announces, her voice just as gurgling

as it sounded through the transponder. "Get them locked away. I want to leap out of this dismal patch of space and kick these two off my ship before I decide to kill them."

"Plake's a wonder, isn't she?" Agra-Red, the Whelk, laughs and nudges Sax forward with the edge of its miner.

Delightful.

*V*imelia.

Ignos sends me the name as the shuttle passes into a large cavern beneath the ground. I can't even see the end of it, as the moment we leave the tunnel, a light, bright and white, opens above us and tracks the shuttle, sliding just ahead and guiding us towards an empty space. It's a blinding shine, and the light washes out anything outside that I could see. The engines slow down and stop as the shuttle lowers itself to the ground. Struts extend and the whole thing settles with the slightest of bumps.

Vimelia is my home.

"Does this mean we can get out now?" Viera says, and I see that her netting is gone.

The straps holding Viera's feet to the ground retract and in the second mine do as well. A short, quick snap, and then I stumble forward, suddenly free. My legs are stiff, my knees hurt, but I can move.

The Sevora did not begin here, but this is where we have gone. Where we live.

I catch myself on the terminals, the screens that used to show a map of the galaxy, now dead and blank. I don't understand. This shuttle belonged to the Oratus. To Sax and Bas. Why did it come here?

Because you told it to. Once it arrived, my friends guided it down. Do not be afraid, Kaishi.

"Do you know where we are?" Malo asks me, and as he says the words, he puts his hand on my shoulder.

That's the first touch I've had since we left. Since I learned that I took my two friends to place so far from home that it doesn't even exist in our imaginations. I almost break right then. Almost collapse at the idea that we've come so far and yet are nowhere near where we need to go.

Tell them.

"This is where Ignos, where its kind live," I say, though I can't quite bring myself to turn and look at Malo and Viera as I talk. "When it told me what numbers to press, it sent the shuttle here."

"The creature tricked us," Viera says. "Seems like we ought to get it out of your head and underneath my boot."

"For once, I agree with the Lunare." Malo's voice is angry, resigned. "It's betrayed you, Kaishi. We can't trust it anymore."

"We didn't have a choice," I say. "We don't know how to fly this thing. We didn't know where to go—"

I want to keep going, to pour out my frustrations one after another, when a whooshing sound from behind us, towards the middle of the shuttle, draws me away. Closes my mouth. Viera and Malo don't hesitate though. The Lunare steps back, near me, and puts her clenched fists up near her face. Malo does his own version, settling into a crouch and keeping his eyes straight ahead.

I see it then. Something that looks much the same as

what we left behind. Only instead of gray or pink gold, these scales are a strange faded yellow, and many have black around the edges, a few are even missing. The Oratus still stands tall, and it's flanked by a pair of very real, non-fuzzy Flaum that stomp into the shuttle behind it. Whereas Sax and Bas didn't seem to wear any clothing, this one sports strange black metal pieces. Bracelets around its wrists and ankles. When it looks at me, with burning green eyes, I get the sense that it sees possibility.

"Please, put yourselves at rest," the Oratus says. "I am Nasiya, leader of the Sevora. Which one of you is the master?"

"I am," I say, stepping in front of Viera and Malo.

No sense having them take the blame, get hurt if there's an attack.

"You entered the code to come here?" Nasiya replies in the harsh hissing voice Oratus have.

"Ignos told me what to enter," I reply.

This only seems to confuse the creature, and its eyes narrow.

"Told you?" The Oratus doesn't turn around, but I can tell it's not speaking to me when it says, "We confirmed that there are no weapons on the ship, yes?"

"Of course," a brown-furred Flaum replies. "The scan showed that even though this is a Vincere ship, there is at least one hosted creature among these."

The Oratus centers its eyes on me again. "One hosted creature. I see three. Though, much to my chagrin, I know not what you are."

Answer him.

I don't know what to say. Part of me doesn't want to say anything. Wants to push back, demand that we be taken home. Part of me wants to fight, to resist. But we've been fighting for so long. It feels like an eternity since we left the city, Damantum, on the march to stop the Oratus invaders. In truth, I don't know how long it's been.

I do know that I'm tired. My head hurts and my bones are weak. I need food, sleep. And the last thing I can do right now is struggle.

"We are humans," I say. "From a planet called Earth. Ignos came to me, and lives inside me now."

Things happen quickly. Nasiya triggers some invisible signal. His shape, those pale yellow scales, fuzz and then vanish entirely. I barely process this before the two Flaum beckon us forward and push the three of us out of the shuttle.

As we go down the ramp, I see a dozen slug-like creatures standing off to the right holding what Ignos calls instruments. They sweep up the ramp after we leave it, and sounds of ripping metal, shifting crates, and loud yells pour back to us.

Now that I'm in the bay, I get a better view of the giant space and notice it's packed with other ships, some coming and going, those lights popping up to guide them. The Flaum lead us through the dark, though I'm not sure how the Sevora hosts can see the where they're going, until I start stepping along the ground. Low green circles appear— it seems the ground itself changes color—directing me where to go.

It reads me, Kaishi. Vimelia connects to me the way I connect to you.

The three of us follow the Flaum, with more walking behind. If they carry some form of weapon, I can't see it, and once the threat of our execution dies away and my pounding heart slows, I actually start looking around. We pass from the large cavern into beautiful hallways. Or at least, they appear that way to me. The walls are coded in waves of shifting color that change as we pass by. A section may start as swaths of bright blue and morph with a wave of green that fades into pink and yellow as we leave it behind. I ask Ignos what it means.

Just as you have your paintings, the Sevora have ours. Much of our history is told through patterns of light and how they change. It is a language, it is a story. One I will tell you someday if you like.

The hallway ends in a long chamber with a wall full of circular doors. Lines of species stand in front of them, stepping in through those openings as others step out. We go to the largest one, on the far right. It's the only one without a line, and also the only one with a red line around the doorway. In between each of the circles, screens display messages warning of closures, delays, and news full of terms I don't understand.

"When it opens," the lead Flaum announces in its squeaky voice. "The three of you will move in first. You will take your seats on the far side as best you are able. We will follow, and when we are secured, we will proceed."

As if waiting for its speech to end, as soon as the Flaum quiets, the circular doorway shunts open and reveals a strange pearl disk waiting for us. The three Flaum in front of me part, and wave us through.

"Guess we're riding this thing?" Viera asks.

"I suppose?" I say. "I don't think we have a choice."

"You mean we're prisoners again?" Viera replies, and I can't help smiling at her sarcasm.

Humor is like a cup full of cold water right now; refreshing and vital.

"We will do what we've done before," Malo says, and I notice he's switched to the Charre tongue.

It works here, as it did on *Cobalt*. The Flaum escorting us stare around at each other, confused. They don't know what Malo said. We have our secret, and I shake my head slightly to warn them not to use it. Not here.

I lead the way, walk through the circle door—warning Malo to watch his head—and step onto the white disk. Around us is a cerulean-shaded transparent tube. Every so often black lines mark the seams between pieces, the seals holding it together. I can see ahead of me that the tube curls up and slightly to the right. Away from the bay.

I'm about to ask where the seats are when the disk shivers and, seeming to arise from nothing, three individual chairs mold up out of the surface. They're barely wide enough to fit me, and Viera and Malo squeeze into theirs, all of us arrayed in the line, at odd angles. As soon as we sit down, like the straps on the shuttle, more pearly stuff leaks up from the floor and wraps itself around our arms and legs. Three Flaum get in behind us, and this time I see that the chairs are indeed flowing up from the disk, making the plat-form itself shrink in the process. Some form of amorphous material, forming itself to the needs of the riders.

"While we are en route, try not to speak," the lead Flaum warns us, though he doesn't explain why.

There's no signal, no sign. One moment we're sitting on the platform in our cramped chairs and the next we're shooting up through the tube. Rising upward at a velocity I've never felt before. Far faster than dashing through the trees. Wind blows my hair forward, dark strands slashing across my face. I close my eyes.

No. Keep them open. Look.

I do, then. And I'm glad. What I see around me is beyond anything I've seen before. From the shuttle, up above, the city seemed false somehow. Unreal. I couldn't reach out and touch it, I wasn't level with the buildings and the swirling, swooping structures. But here, as the tube rockets us out of the cavern and into the day, I'm stunned at built beauty rivaling the jungle flowers of my home.

Glittering structures of all heights and all colors rise up around us. Some resemble shapes I've seen on Earth: squares, or tall towers. Others rise as triangles or sloping domes. Thin spires that lead to cubes raised high in the air.

Next to us, on either side, other tubes rise up and glide in parallel, then cut away or up or down. New ones join our track. We shift, though I don't really feel it aside from a slight jolt in the scenery. All I know is that we're moving. Going somewhere.

The Flaum in front of us don't seem to react. Their eyes pin to me, Malo and Viera. They're so serious. I don't know why, seeing as were surrounded by marvels.

In Solare legends, we talk of the great cities of the gods; gold and silver and jade everywhere. Whole palaces built of gems that sparkled with an infinite shine. If I could have chosen a place that described those tales, Vimelia would be it.

The Sevora cannot choose the qualities of the species we take, but we can choose what we create. Express ourselves through the worlds we make. What we wish we would see around us. Vimelia is a representation of what we wish to be.

Beyond the buildings I see a tan sky cluttered with moving specks and shifting forms. All shapes, from the angular angry things that escorted us in, to larger floating barges drifting through the air. Others rocket up from the surface, screeching towards the sky before vanishing. There's so much motion everywhere that it almost makes me dizzy. The jungle, aside from buzzing insects, was often still.

I try to take a breath, to ask Viera and Malo what they think, what they see, but when I push air out of my lungs it doesn't want to go. The words emerge and die instantly. Squeaks amid the constant roar of wind. That's why they warned us not to speak.

The platform twists and swirls through a series of interlocking gates and I sense a sudden fall, though I don't see it, and we slow to a crawl as we pass beneath a series of large, metal loops. The sky vanishes for a long moment and we're plunged into dark.

A switch station.

Then we are out again, this time moving in a straighter line. I can see the switch station behind us, and from the outside, it looks like the Amigga; so many tubes looping in from everywhere. Platforms shoot in from all angles and sides and then back out again in different directions.

We're nearly there. You should know, Nasiya and the others want to help you. Help us. You have to trust them.

Ignos ruins the magic of the moment by bringing back reality. How can I trust them? How can I trust any of these things?

Because you have no choice. Because you are far from home and the only way back rests in us giving it to you, Kaishi. You are not an Empress, you're not a young girl with the protection of her tribe or her father. You are alone and you are in danger. So let us help you.

I don't respond. Not directly, anyway. Ignos can read my emotions, scan my thoughts. I can't hide anything from the creature, but at least I can ignore its responses. So I do, and I watch the movement until the platform begins to slow. Until the sky goes dark and we move under a white awning. Then our ride comes to a rest. Once the Flaum rise, their seats once more flow back into the platform. Like a melting candle.

The three creatures move to the circular door, which shifts open as they approach. Two more of the slug-like things on the other side, bright green in color and holding miners of their own.

"We don't need more escorts," the lead Flaum says, loud enough for me to hear.

"There's been an alert," one of the slugs says, its voice a staccato hum. "Clarity's Dawn. Nasiya wants these three protected. Heavily."

Clarity's Dawn? I don't know what that means.

It's not for you to worry about.

"That was about the craziest thing I've ever seen," Viera says as we stand up. I almost fall as the chair vanishes beneath me, but Malo catches my arm and holds me study.

"It's amazing," I say. "Did you see all of those things flying through the air? We could do that someday. Back home."

"You two, stop talking," the lead Flaum growls, turning back to us. "Follow, please. And stay silent. There'll be time enough for talking later."

"No need to get snappy," Viera murmurs, but the Flaum doesn't hear her.

We follow them, out away from the tube onto another landing. This one isn't as crowded, but whereas the species in the cavern came in all types and clothes, from rags to armor to metal and further, these all seem to sport the same greenish orange clothing. Many of them, whether on fur, smooth skin or something else entirely, wear a simple square badge with an orange circle overlaid on a pale green surface.

The symbol of my people. The orange is us, a strong line against outsiders. Protecting the life contained within.

Beyond the loading area, we walk into a tall, wide hall with sloping sides reaching up to a vaulted roof. I'm reminded of the Vaos, the grand temple in Damantum, though in its material and design this Sevora building is nothing like it. Rather, I feel the same grandeur, a pulse of power resonating here, just as it does back home.

As we walk, I feel the eyes of a thousand things watching me. Some friendly, curious. Others angry or threatened.

"Do you think we're wanted?" I ask. "Some of these are looking at us like we're enemies."

"I sure hope so, seeing as they took us here. Seeing as it's your buddy that put the code into the shuttle." Viera's scanning the crowds, and I see her hands drift towards her belt, though there's no weapon there.

"She didn't have a choice, Viera. None of us did. None of us do." Malo, always defending me. Even when I don't deserve it.

At my friend's words, the Flaum leader jerks his head back towards us and snaps his furry fingers. His point made, Malo quiets and I say nothing. Instead we watch and walk through one mesmerizing room after another until at last we find ourselves at what appears to be the top.

It's an enclosed room, with clear see-through walls all around. The floor appears made entirely of the same white stuff as the platform we rode. The Flaum direct us to the middle of the room where, as we stand, a table rises. Only this isn't a rectangle or square, it's a circle forming around us. Trapping us inside. Small chairs grow beneath us, forcing us to sit.

The Flaum back away towards the door we came in, and then leave entirely.

"I think I could jump over this," Viera says.

"There must be a reason we're here," I say. "So don't do anything stupid."

"She's talking to you, Viera," Malo says.

"I'm talking to all of us, myself included."

There's a flicker. The fuzziness, and then again the pale yellow Oratus appears near the back window. It stares at the three of us for a moment, passing its gaze from one of us to the next.

"Welcome to Vimelia. Welcome to your new home."

There's silence for a moment, and then Viera says what we're all thinking, "Home? This isn't our home."

Nasiya looks at my friend. Spreads its teeth in a grin. "You are unhosted, yes?"

"If you mean that I don't have one of those slug things in my head like Kaishi here, yeah. I'm unhosted."

"Then you've yet to understand. You will see soon enough that Vimelia is yours. All of you will. I'm very excited that you've come. Very excited that you've decided to join us."

"We decided nothing," I say. "We were tricked. We didn't want to come here."

"Fortune sometimes happens upon those who don't expect it." Nasiya throws away my remark. "In a moment, your meals will arrive. Then, you'll be shown your quarters. Tomorrow, your true tour of Vimelia will begin."

We don't get a chance to ask it questions; Nasiya fuzzes out and vanishes, leaves us in the white room alone.

Nasiya has never been much for words. It prefers action, as you will see.

I shake my head. I don't care about Nasiya. What I do care about, though, is getting off this planet. Getting back home.

But even those concerns fall away when the door

behind whisks open and the Flaum walk back in, our guards followed by other Flaum wielding trays instead of weapons. Sitting on the silver serving platters is stuff I recognize from Cobalt. The same strange pastes Bas served me on that cold metal station.

As the Flaum come into the room, the table and chairs surrounding us melt down to the floor. New ones rise up, more adequately spaced for a meal. A large, flat saucer surface, with rounded stumps for chairs whose tops are just large enough for us to sit on. When we don't make an immediate move, the lead Flaum, the black-furred one that's been leading us the entire way, waves with his rifle towards the setup.

It's not difficult to interpret what they want.

As we sit, the other Flaum place the trays of paste in front of each of us. Then brown bowls with blue specks are set next to those, filled with a clear liquid. It looks like water, but none of us touch it until one of the serving Flaums pantomimes a drinking motion.

"Think it's poisoned?" Viera says, in our secret Charre tongue, as we pick up the bowls.

"They have easier ways to kill us," Malo replies, then takes a long drink.

We both watch. He might choke and collapse. Turn purple. Or, for all I know, sprout fur and morph into a Flaum.

Ridiculous. It's just water.

As if I trust Ignos now. But after a few breaths, and Malo taking a second drink, I decide to follow. My throat's been dry and scratchy for a long time—we didn't exactly get many breaks on *Cobalt*—and the cool water feels delicious and silky on my throat. Heavier than the rivers back home.

Vimelia's water comes from deep beneath its surface. What you taste is the planet's own flavor.

"How do you know what we can drink and eat?" Viera asks after her own sip. "Or does everyone run on water and roast pork?"

"This room," says the lead Flaum. "Scans what you are. The flakes of your skin, the breath you exhale, the heat from your bodies. We form a chemical composite, an estimation of what you require to survive, and provide our best guess."

"Guess? So there's a chance you could kill us?"

"There are always risks with new species," the Flaum's chitter gets low. "Usually it takes a few accidents to get a perfect calibration."

"I'll try to help—you have any actual meat here?" Viera pokes at the nutrient goop with her finger. The yellow slime shivers at her touch.

"Meat?" The Flaum looks back at Viera. "Only an uncivilized worm would eat raw animal proteins."

"You're calling me a worm?" Viera replies.

Before the Flaum can clarify, a black square on its belt shifts to a bright green color and emits a single, bright chime. Without another word, it and the other Flaum turn and leave us alone in the room. The door shuts behind them, and we're alone.

I try a taste of a blue-green ball on the tray. It's mostly flavorless, a hint of mint, yet I feel what I'm eating is incredibly healthy. My stomach thrills as I swallow the bites. Yet I don't like the texture, the lack of nature in the ball. It's not from home.

But you live. Which is, after all, the most important thing.

Viera and Malo struggle like me, with hunger's desire pushing us through the motions. We use our hands; shovel the stuff into our mouths. I'm not surprised we didn't get any tools. Things that could be used as weapons.

"Tastes like dirt," Viera says.

"I agree," Malo replies. "I'd hoped we had seen the last of this on the station."

"I'd eat anything from home again," I say. "Even those peppers you gave me seem like miracles."

I smile at the memory and where it leads; the idea that, someday, I'd be eating another fish tortilla, spreading those peppers on the white soft meat and take a slow bite. Feel that heat rushing up and down my throat.

Truly, it's only when you leave home that you appreciate it fully. Yet you will find plenty to like here. Give it time.

We barely clear the trays before the Flaum come back in. This time there's no talk as they wave us up, and the lead Flaum ignores questions about where we're going. Directs us back to the tubes. There we board another platform, which takes us on a whizzing journey through the city. The skies have turned from bright beige to a soft orange, and I can make out a glowing, large orb on the far horizon that stretches like a mountain.

This is as low as our star will go. We have a strange orbit here, and no true night unless you go beneath the surface.

The heat of a jungle day flashes through my mind at the thought of endless light and I don't understand how Vimelia isn't melting?

Because of what we sprinkled throughout the atmosphere. Reflective dust gathers and pushes back the light and heat. Carefully controlled. Before that, all you see lived underground. In the cool dark.

The platform stops at a long and tall building that looks like sculpted emerald. I wonder why for second until I remember the badges. The life.

Yes. These are the quarters where you will stay until you join us.

I don't want to know what that means. We follow the Flaum off the platform and through a short tour into a long and wide chamber. On either side, going up many stories, are long walkways with doors, ones with the metal bars, and no curtains.

"This is a prison," Viera says.

"We don't know that," I reply.

"Even if it is, we don't have a choice." Malo kills the conversation.

The Flaum take us up a twisting stair to the third level and then out onto a landing. From here I can make out that many of the cells are occupied. Behind the bars, shapes lurk, and some press their faces, their snouts, their eyed tentacles towards us.

More Flaum stalk the walkways looking back at their charges. Two or three on each level striding back and forth. Some carrying food or other things they pass through the bars to the intended recipient. It's like a small city, although it's clear there's one thing not on offer here; freedom.

You'll get that when your friends are hosted, when you agree to help us.

We reach three cells in a line. They're empty, and the only thing inside is the same white floor as anywhere else.

The lead Flaum taps his right claw on the side of the gate. When I realize what's happening, I try to count out the sequence but it's too long, too fast. The bars rise towards the ceiling, and then another Flaum pushes me in. The bars come down, and then the other Flaum push Malo and Viera on to the next one.

As they walk away, Malo throws me a worried look and I try to reply with confidence I'm not feeling. I tell myself there's nothing we can do here now anyway, best to go along. Best to wait for another chance.

"This cell is tuning to you," the lead Flaum says to me through the bars. As he finishes the words, the white floor flashes blue for a moment before settling back into its pearly color. "It's designed to make furniture. Think of what you want, and it will give you what you need. It will not give you weapons, tools or other means of escape. I recommend sleep, if your species needs it."

The Flaum turns and walks away, leaving me alone in the cell.

Go ahead. Use it.

Following Ignos' instructions, I think of a bench, a simple chair there in the corner near the door. In a second something rises up and forms the wooden bamboo construct —though it stays the alabaster color—on the floor. It looks right for me. So I sit in it. Strong and solid. I imagine my small cot bed from my palace. It forms in the back corner, blankets even coming out of the stuff, although, when I press my hands to them, they feel more fake, artificial than what I'm used to. Not real wool.

When I put my hands on the bed, I remember the bracelet on my wrist. The Cache. Before Ignos can stop me, I open it and dip deep inside looking for answers.

And find many.

The crimson Whelk slithers its legless self in front of Sax through the bays. Leads Sax and Bas through the maze of cargo towards the front of the ship and the three different doorways pointing to separate modules. Agra-Red seems happy to talk about the crew, the ship, and Sax is more than happy to let it. Pays to learn about your enemies.

"So you see this place, built courtesy of Plake herself. Took the ship as a prize when her captain retired and the others fought for it. None of'em are left." The note of pride in Agra-Red's voice isn't hard to catch. "From there, she built her crew in the usual way."

Agra-Red pauses, intentionally waiting for a question. So Bas asks one.

"And what's that?" Bas hisses.

"Go to the most worthless pilots you can find, hire them, wait till they rob you, and then go find the right ones," Agra-Red shakes its head as it says this, the lack of bones causing the motion to make the entire creature ripple. "I've been doing this a long time, and you wouldn't believe the number of sob stories I've heard from captains who feel they've been cheated somehow. You hire wrong, you'll get wronged."

This continues until they reach the front, and then Agra-Red gestures towards a ladder to the right, ascending out from the cargo module to the rest of the ship. Agra-Red, and Whelks in general, can't climb, so it settles into a small mold-colored platform. When Agra-Red gets on it, the platform rises faster than the Oratus can climb.

Speed is important on a ship when spare seconds fiddling with rungs could mean the difference between an explosive decompression or a stable repair.

"Since then, we've been running scrap, food supplies and more to everywhere we can find. Because, and I don't figure you Oratus know this, there's not much left to the galaxy these days except sending cargo."

"What do you mean?" Sax asks. "Most of the galaxy is safe. Most of it's inhabited."

"Inhabited by what?" Agra-Red replies. "Boring, normal people? Ones content to live on the dirt rather than scorch the sky? No. You Oratus took the war, took the meaning from my life. From all of ours. Now you have two choices. You hire on like me, run cargo and count your coins and wait for a better life. Or you get desperate, capture a bit of excitement playing pirate until your life catches up with you and you wind up slagged, floating above some planet forever."

"You take a grim view of the galaxy," Bas says.

"You know my name? Agra-Red?"

The Oratus nod.

"My home and my color. I'm still around, but Agra itself? Bombed into nothing. The Sevora established a foothold and now it's just gone. Haven't found a single one of my friends or my family that survived. Would you be happy tilling dirt or tending a bar if that happened to your home?" When Sax and Bas don't have a reply, Agra-Red laughs, a sick thing with more than its share of ruefulness in it. "Ah, I forget. You monsters don't have homes."

Sax could correct the Whelk, but doesn't. It wouldn't matter anyway.

Agra-Red leads them through a short hallway which opens into a broad, spectacularly filthy kitchen. Stuff, like half-eaten nutrient packs, crates, bags and bits and pieces of paper and other trash lay about everywhere, with a thin cylinder in the center of it all, as though someone's been trying and failing to toss the garbage inside it.

"Welcome to your space," Agra-Red says. "Oh yeah, that there's Engee. She makes these messes."

Sax doesn't see what Agra-Red is pointing at until it moves. Sax thinks the cylinder is a waste bin, but now he sees it's a Teven, only instead of the usual sandy-colored shell, this one is metallic. Black and silver. With a bunch of things he mistakes for trash hanging off the shell's various holes.

"I'm being kicked out?" Engee exclaims, the sounds coming hollow through the holes, like a whistle. "But I'm in the middle of something."

"Not anymore," Agra-Red says. "We picked up refugees. They need a place to stay. And it's yours."

"Plake gave them this?"

"Captain's orders. Get out of here."

"At least you could be nice about it," Engee replies, and then trash can moves. Waddles close to Sax. He can't make out the Teven itself inside, at least until a small arms shoots out from one of the holes into one of the tools hanging off the side and lifts it up. Sax notices the hanging things aren't just garbage, but are some sort of attachment. The Teven sticks it towards them and Sax sees a strange red eye, one that a quickly flashes green. "They're not hosted. No Sevora in either of them."

"That's too bad. Here I thought I was gonna have myself a couple roasted Oratus." Agra-Red deadpans.

"You're expecting us to stay in all this garbage?" Bas says to the Whelk.

"Not my problem," Agra-Red replies. "Plake says we're leaping soon so if you want a comfortable ride, I'd find a seat."

Agra-Red and Engee head out of the room, slapping a wall panel on the way that shunts closed a door. The two Oratus are alone, stuck in a disaster area. Sax sweeps his eyes over the mess. Buried under some mounds of wrapping looks like some old crash chairs. Things that could be used, if needed, to ride out a leap.

"I wonder where Coorvin went," Bas says as she starts picking through the junk.

Most of it looks like scrap metal; parts torn off of other things collected here in a giant jumble. Some are set aside, on top of the table the Teven was sitting at when they came in. The beginnings of a project, something long and cylindrical. A weapon, or maybe an engine. Sax isn't much for gadgets unless he's using them.

"That Flaum took him," Sax replies. "Coorvin seems to know them."

Bas rakes her tail, sweeps the jumble from the table and moves the clutter onto the floor. It falls fast, which tells Sax that the ship is using magnetic gravity. An electrical charge run through magnets in the base of the ship. Keeps things tugged towards the center. Doesn't work so well on living creatures, but then, Sax and Bas are used to keeping them-selves stable in unstable places.

"How long do you think Coorvin lived with the Amigga?" Bas hisses as she and Sax clear junk away from their seats.

There's a net across the back of the wide chairs, and they each pull it on. Slip their claws through the gaps and watch the stars spin from the small viewscreen on the wall.

"Long enough to go insane, I think," Sax says. "Or nearly. He doesn't smell normal."

Which, for Flaum, meant fear. Skittishness. Sweat and shedding fur. At least when Oratus come around.

"How should we get back to Evva?" Bas asks.

"We could take this ship if we wanted to," Sax replies. "Except I haven't seen evidence of a crime. We would need to declare it a military necessity. Or get them to do some-thing criminal."

"That shouldn't be too hard."

"Then we confiscate it, fly this ship wherever we need to go."

"Where is that?" Bas says. "To the center? Right to the Chorus and the main Vincere fleet?"

The question catches Sax by surprise. Why wouldn't they head back to the Vincere? Why wouldn't they head back, rejoin the war against the Sevora?

"Are you suggesting there's elsewhere we should go?"

"We just killed an Amigga, Sax," Bas replies. "Yes, it was self-defense, but the Chorus doesn't look favorably on those that kill its own. Going back might just put us in a cell."

Sax waits. It's not like Bas to start a perfectly logical explanation without following it up with something more interesting. Besides, self-defense would play well. A deranged Amigga, left alone on the edge of the galaxy, gone insane with its own experiments, tried to kill both Sax, Bas, and three specimens that could mean an end to the bloodiest conflict in recorded history?

Sax feels he has an argument.

"But most importantly" Bas finishes. "I don't think Evva is there."

Sax is about to ask why, when Plake's voice booms over the ship's intercom. An announcement, a call to say that the ship is about to leap and they should all get ready for it. From there it's a quick countdown. Sax takes deep breaths with his vents. It's weird not being on the bridge, weird being surrounded by all this random garbage as the universe tilts sideways and he spins through the cascade of sensations that come with the leap. That come with the tearing and repairing of his atomic structure.

At least it's quick. Mere moments and then Sax blinks from one part of the galaxy to another. It's a physical cost, and a mental one, but thus far Sax hasn't had any lasting effects and he's done hundreds of the things. So long as you know where you're going, leaping isn't that bad.

In seconds both Oratus are out of their webbing. A few more after that and they're both standing by the door. Waiting.

"Don't know whether you're getting any ideas," Plake's voice comes over the intercom. "We're not letting you out of there until we're docked. I don't like randoms running around my ship in the best of times, and these aren't those. Sit tight. We're coming in on *Scrapper Station*, and once we get there you can get off and leave me alone."

"So much hate for the species protecting your lives," Sax growls, though he doesn't think the intercom is sending anything back to the captain.

"It's not hate, Sax. It's caution." Bas says. "*Scrapper Station* isn't a civilized place. We're not going here because she wants to turn us over to the Vincere."

The Whelk, Agra-Red, is right about one thing—when the Oratus imposed their version of order on the Vincere, they displaced the ragged cluster of species who'd made generations out of serving the grand vision of those twelve Amiggas making up the Chorus. Cast out and uncared for, the sudden influx of pilots, mechanics, soldiers and support staff began forging their own destinies in a galaxy that, so long as they weren't being too violent, didn't spare a thought for them.

Sax hasn't been to many of these outposts—the ones he's visited are those that fell to Sevora incursions, and he left most of those drifting ruins—and he's not thrilled to visit another. The dirty room they're in now serves as an accurate impression for what they'll encounter on *Scrapper Station*; trash, both of the physical and mental variety.

"If the Vyphen betrays us, then we'll make sure she regrets it," Sax says, taking up position just outside the door and looking back to Bas, who seems content to lounge in her chair.

"Murder doesn't go unpunished, Sax."

The words twist Sax for a moment. He's been a sanctioned killer for the entirety of his existence, given permission to do whatever is necessary to advance the Vincere's, the Chorus', agenda. The species on this ship, on the station, aren't Sevora. Aren't enemy agents. Unless Sax feels his own life is threatened, he doesn't have any standing to slaughter Plake and her crew.

"I don't like this anymore," Sax sighs through his vents.

"You'll recall I suggested killing the humans back when

we left Earth," Bas replies. "We could have left them to Dalachite, departed *Cobalt* and we wouldn't be here now."

"That perversion deserved its end."

The ship shudders as it begins its docking phase. The magnetic gravity decreases to prevent interference with *Scrapper Station*'s own systems, and Bas, with a flick of her tail, sends a pile of gray-metal tiles floating through the air.

"We'll find a way to contact Evva from the station," Bas says, her eyes tracking the chips. "She'll know how to get us back home."

The two of them share the space for a while longer, feeling every part of the docking process in the freighter's shakes and folks. It takes far longer to dock a ship of this size than it does the shuttle Sax and Bas used to fly—the freighter's too large to simply fit in a bay. Instead, *Scrapper Station* uses a series of arms to 'catch' the ship, once the freighter matches the station's velocity, and then it extends a long tube to the passenger airlock.

When that tube connects, the door to the Oratus' room shunts open, and for the first time Sax is face-to-face with Plake. The Vyphen is half Sax's height, and her red skin shimmers beneath the thick white and yellow feathers running along her back and arms. In low gravity, and on the small world the Vyphens called home, Plake could fly.

Not that it would help her escape Sax's claws in tight quarters like these. By her eyes, narrowed and deep green, Plake knows this. But she doesn't crouch away, flinch, or clench her webbed hands when Sax glares down at her.

Plake has the respect of her crew, and Sax begins to see why.

Agra-Red and one of the black-furred Flaum stand behind Plake, both with miners trained on the Oratus.

Backing up their commander's courage with the firepower it deserves.

"You'll follow me," Plake says. "They'll follow you. Let's go."

As they leave the room, Sax hears the churning, banging, shifting noise of unloading cargo. He throws a look over the railing and back down the deep bay. Bright white lights pierce the soft yellow of the freighter's illumination, showing where the robo-skiffs are working. Grabbing crates with their magnet arms, floating with them to the bay's cargo airlock, where, after pressure's drained, the skiffs would take their goodies across a short expanse to the station.

"I thought those were meant for *Cobalt*," Sax says to Plake's back as they move.

"*Cobalt* doesn't exist anymore," Plake replies without turning her head. "Figure that makes them mine to sell."

"Does the Chorus agree?"

"Who's going to tell them? You?"

Sax bares his teeth, though the Vyphen can't see it. He doesn't need Bas' tail tap to keep his mouth shut this time.

The connection tube doesn't give them much more than a view, through thick glass, of the station. It's enough to tell Sax why *Scrapper Station* has its name—built in the aftermath of a thick Vincere-Sevora battle, *Scrapper Station* looks like someone swept up a bunch of junk and glued it all together. There's no semblance of organization, no planning —the station shoots out in all directions, with jutting points and nodes veering out into space.

There's no planet near here, which means no gravity grabbing all these lanky parts. Only asteroids, stocked with valuable metals and the reason for the fight in the first place. As they walk, Sax can see small mining ships blasting to and from tiny bays, grabbing platinum and gold from spinning rocks and returning it. A big refiner craft, like Plake's freighter, is doing its own docking procedure. It's shaped like a cylinder, and the raw ore will be loaded into one end, refined during the trip, and the cleaned product will be ready on delivery to whatever crafters want it.

"There's more here than I expected," Bas says.

"None of you know what's going on in the galaxy you're trying to protect," Plake replies. "You see all those little guys? Grabbing the metals? They're supplying you with all your weapons. One run at a time."

"Would you rather we focused on this station than the Sevora?" Sax cuts in. "We're keeping you alive."

"By destroying *Cobalt*? Didn't think it was the enemy."

Sax doesn't have an answer for that. It would be easy to say Dalachite tried to kill them, that it was performing strange, reprehensible experiments, but the galaxy depends on its hierarchy and the Amigga stand at the top. Undermining their authority goes against everything Sax, and those who fight in the Vincere, stand for.

So he marches in silence until they're through the tube, passing through a dented door—evidence, perhaps, of a few desperate entry attempts—and into one of *Scrapper Station*'s arrival areas.

Rather than the cluster of species mingling their way back and forth, dealing in promises both physical and not, the wide room stands deserted except for a trio. Two of them, crag-like Lutos, hold large miners in their black-dirt arms. The single-eyed, mud-coated monsters don't talk much, and Sax is surprised to see any of them outside of their molten puddle of a home planet.

"Just as you promised, Plake," the voice comes from the

third, the only species capable of talking, a yellow mound with a pair of stalked, bulbous eyes. "I'll take them."

The Ooblot says the words. Sax is ready to dodge, but the fire doesn't come from in front, from the Lutos. No, the searing pain, the numbing shock that sends the Oratus down into black strikes from behind.

The Cache spills Vimelia's past out to me, and I'm surprised at how similar it is to our own. Ignos gave the impression that its people were ordered, were *above* us humans, but they fight and struggle as much as we do, even if they've exchanged spears for words and lifetimes sentenced to darkness for our sacrifices atop our Tiers.

I find out, too, that they're losing.

The slaughter of the Sevora at the hands of the Vincere and their Oratus—I remember Sax and Bas and wouldn't want to be the target of their deadly claws, much less an army of them—is a saga that seems to go on forever. I wind up turning away from the Cache's litany of battles playing out in my mind for fear of being lost among the swirling ships exploding into mini novas.

The shift brings me to the Chorus, and the Cache begins to struggle; Brushing up against the edges of its knowledge feels like grasping at a fading memory—there's tantalizing wisps of possibility, but nothing concrete.

Nothing beyond the sure sense of more Amigga, and their power over everything.

And hate. Such a feeling of it that I get angry. I'm not *with* myself and yet my thundering heart races my lungs in a sprint towards exhaustion. These things, these terrible Amigga are the reason the galaxy is in so much pain, the reason for all the death, destruction, and war that's tearing species after species apart.

"Kaishi!"

It's not Ignos breaking apart the Cache's hold on me this time but an actual voice. One I recognize as the fog of relentless knowledge clears away.

"We have to go, Empress," I parse Malo's words now, and turn around, towards the bars.

What I see doesn't mesh with the reality I left behind. The lighting's all wrong, for one. I'd jumped into the Cache with a bronzed orange glow filtering through the top of the prison, but now it's a brighter white. Though that only serves as a backdrop for the characters looking in at me:

Malo and Viera star front and center, both looking mostly like I last saw them, though Malo's wearing a warning on his face, while Viera shakes her head and looks confused. Glancing past them, it's not hard to see why.

A bluish-green creature lurks between the two, hunched over and wearing something I can only call a cloak, though with the way it catches and turns the light, which makes the creature flicker, it's clearly more than anything my father wore to our ceremonies. In its hands are a pair of small miners, both angled ever-so-slightly towards Malo and Viera. Its swamp-green eyes, though, are locked on me. By the time its mouth opens, and the long, pink tongue inside it shivers, I'm already moving to what's going on behind.

Where are the guards?

Ignos echoes my own question, and I wonder if the constant flashes of blue and red behind my friends have anything to do with the conspicuous absence. The blasts come from down below and up above, accompanied by occasional shrieks of pain or howled words I don't understand.

"Kaishi. Focus." Malo's command yanks me back.

"I'm here." I move towards the bars, though they're still closed.

I'm still trapped.

Don't. They mean to destroy you. Ruin any chance you have of peace.

Which doesn't mean much to me. Ignos has to work on its tactics—I've been torn away from my family, my empire, and all I've ever known and exposed to things I could never have dreamed of. Peace is nothing more than a joke to me now.

I make it to the bars, and as I do so, I see the creature's tongue uncurl from its mouth. The slathering pink tendril snakes its way around two of the bars and, as I watch, it shivers. The creature tenses.

Kaishi, you must listen to me. They mean you harm. These are not your friends!

There's a creaking snap and the two central bars of my cell bend inwards and then break in two. It's not much space to get through, and the jagged spikes of the broken bar ends keep me careful, but I make my way out to the balcony.

And look onto chaos.

What was, when we entered, an ordered set of routines is now a cascade of blown-open walls, frenzied firefights, and more than one up-close tussle between things I can't name. Even Ignos is too stunned to respond.

Then I feel the creature touch my arm. It's a cool, sliding sensation, like grabbing a jungle vine coated with morning dew. I shiver, and it grips me.

"You've taken too long already," the creature says, and its voice is a burbling brook, a rushing river. "My friends die now for your delay. We leave."

It's a command, not a question, and the thing pulls me away from the conflict playing out elsewhere. I stumble as it tugs, but my feet are well-versed in running and they find their steps quickly. Malo and Viera follow, though the creature doesn't pay them any attention; one of its black pupils is locked on me, the other ahead towards dangers unknown.

A few shouts harangue our run as we pass by unopened cells; those too unlucky to be part of the breakout. The creature pays them no mind, and I can't afford to as we're running now. I'm still wearing the mask from *Cobalt*, and it coats my feet as they stamp on the hard, smooth floor.

Fight back! To run with this one means death!

I can't help but hesitate at Ignos' words. The parasite hasn't ever tried to kill me, after all, even as it pursued its own ends.

The creature feels my pull, turns and glares at me. Its mouth comes to a point, and I realize there are a set of four tiny nostrils over the top of it, ones that flare at me now, coating my face with hot, sticky air. Then it cocks its head to the side, as if listening to a sound I cannot hear.

"You're the hosted one," the creature says.

"Yes, there's one inside me," I reply, though the creature doesn't seem to need the confirmation.

Ignos yells at me to run, thrashes in my head enough to make me wince. A gesture the creature notices.

"For the moment," the creature reaches into one of the

many pockets of feathers coating its body, pulls out something I recognize: a long, thin metal fork.

"Hold her," the creature says to my friends.

I barely have a chance to react before Malo and Viera each grab an arm. Pin me back against them.

"Sorry, Kaishi, but neither of us has any love for that thing you've got with you," Viera says.

They used my miracles the same as you.

"You lied." I speak the words out loud without realizing.

The creature raising the fork pauses, then gives me a blink before continuing. Its feathered arm reaches up towards my head and I close my eyes, taking, for a moment, a chance to escape from what's about to happen. Ignos doesn't let me. It thrashes. Tickles and scratches my mind.

I'm your friend, Kaishi! Don't forget that I want you, your species to survive. Don't—

The connection breaks like a dry branch—a snap and then Ignos is gone from my mind. I feel it, though; gripped by the fork and pulled out from my ear and, with a wet splat, onto the floor next to me. The creature doesn't waste a moment; its tongue shoots out, wraps itself around the ghostly gray shell of Ignos and brings the parasite to its mouth.

"Don't," I say as Malo and Viera let my arms drop. "It's helped me. It brought us here."

"It's not coming with us." The creature replies, and it jerks its tongue a little farther into its mouth. "These things have no right to live."

"This one does." I reach into the creature's mouth, and as I grab Ignos, the creature relaxes its tongue.

I pull Ignos free—it feels both brittle and squishy in my hands, like a soft melon—and hold the Sevora. Ignos doesn't try to pull itself up my arms or scramble away from my hands. The life of the creature that tricked me, pushed me into a destiny I did not want, quivers in my palms.

"It gave our people freedom," Malo says behind me. "For whatever else its done, the creature deserves mercy for that."

I nod. Then look over the great expanse from one side of cells to the other. The fights still rage, though I notice things are moving towards a retreat. Sevora guards, those furry Flaum moving in formation, are advancing, pushing back the motley squads of species I can't name.

"We must go," the creature says, and in its tone I gather the seconds remaining in Ignos' life are dwindling.

So I turn and throw the thing that's brought me here. That rescued my tribe from certain death and brought me to the heights of power. I aim with purpose, towards a group of Flaum advancing two floors below, miners keeping up a steady stream of fire. I see enough to know Ignos makes it across the gap, but before I see the result, my parasite and savior is gone.

Any chance I have to reflect on the moment is taken when the creature pulls me again, snarling that we're running out of time. Instinct takes over while my mind drifts in my suddenly quiet head as we sprint through dark hallways and down stairs.

Eventually we hit a landing covered with red-glowing runes that I can't understand. The creature seems to think there's another stair and wheels around, and we follow, only to find a thick sealed door blocking our path. The only other way is a broad, wide entry spanned by four arch-ways. I can see bright beige sky out the other end, but when I take a step, the creature grabs my arm and pulls me back.

"There's nothing that way but death," the creature

warbles, and then turns back to the door. "This shouldn't be shut."

"Don't know what your plan was," Viera says. "But that door isn't moving. Don't think we're going to like being on the other end of those miners either."

The Lunare steps up next to the creature, inspecting the door, and I take the chance to fall back near Malo.

"It's gone, Malo," I say, and the warrior knows what I'm talking about.

"Better that it is."

"You think so?" I look up at his face, and see its set in that too-serious way Malo has. As though he's about to deal with a cataclysm of terrific proportions, and only the most stoic of expressions can see him through. "Ignos helped us, a lot."

"A fruit, when ripe, is delicious. When rotten, poisonous. Ignos only helped you, I think, because it helped itself at the same time."

A bang ripples through the stairwell, from above. The creature stops staring at the door, shakes its head, and turns back, looking past Malo and I to the archways and the open air beyond.

"We're going to try for it," the creature says. "You're going to follow me, fast. Don't stop for anything, even when your body tells you it's going to die. Or you will."

Malo steps in front of me, but I pull myself around him, go up to the creature. Its deep green and black eyes meet mine, and when I extend my hand, its warm, rubbery grip meets it. The brilliant feathers streaming down the creature's arm make a pretty wing, though I wonder if its quite big enough for flight. Certainly the creature's body is far larger than the eagles I know back home.

"We go together," I say to the creature, and to Malo. "Come on, you two."

The arch is split into sections by thin, dark rock bands—I can only see where those bands end because the pieces in between begin to glow a hard yellow. At the sight, the creature lunges forward and we do our best to keep up. It goes under the arch, padded feet flapping against the ground and I, with my hands on Malo and Viera's, follow. As we pass beneath the arch, I notice the next three are lighting up like the first.

"Don't stop!" the creature cries.

I don't see anything that's going to prevent me; there's no wall, no rope around my ankles or armed guard. But there is, as I pass beneath the arch, a prickling sensation that crawls over my skin. Like getting lightly scratched by thorns all across my body. I think the mask I'm wearing blunts, but doesn't stop the sensation.

We don't stop.

Out the other side of the arch the feeling disappears. Arch number two, apparently cued, shifts its glow from yellow to a sickly orange, like a sunset trying to fight through clouds. The creature doesn't pause, but keeps going.

"Didn't like that," Viera says as we keep after it.

"It wasn't that bad," I reply.

"Then why have it at all?"

I can't answer that, because we're going through the second arch and the orange glow makes itself known immediately. Like diving into a hot bath, it's an instant change from the cool air of the hallway to a scalding rake across my body. I feel like when I was young, dared to dart across a fire, and my leap didn't carry me far enough—the flames licked me then as they seem to now.

I don't see fire. I feel it. The puckering of my skin, the air that I breathe stinging my throat. The mask lets me get just enough to keep going, keeps me from passing out.

We keep going, the three of us, and then we're through. I feel Malo begin to let up, feel myself suck in mouthfuls of air, and I know that I would give anything for water in that moment.

"You cannot stop!" it's the creature, and it's still moving towards the next arch, which is shining a crimson red.

"This thing has lost its mind," Malo says. "It wants us dead."

"We don't have a choice." I keep moving, push past the pain in my legs, force myself onward.

When the creature enters the third arch, there's a burst of light and it takes a moment for me to realize that its feathers are actually on fire. The tips burn as it moves, and its blue-green skin glistens as it hardens, chars.

Then I see nothing because my own eyelashes alight. My hair burns, along with the robes I'm wearing, though I notice those only as curious after-thoughts, a sort of addition to the sheer chaos of my own nerves as the mask barely keeps my skin from melting. Yet, as hot as this is, as scalding and brutal, I drift back to the endless series of struggles I'd braved to get here. All the dangers, all the near-deaths. A little bit of fire isn't going to stop me. Not now.

My right hand, singing its pain, nonetheless tells me when Viera falls. I can't see—I've closed my eyes to keep the heat from melting them—but I reach and feel the Lunare on the ground. Grab her searing shoulder and pull. Feel Malo pulling me ahead.

When my left arm leaves the arch, its like falling into the cold ocean. Immediate ice, comforting and cool. Every piece of me that follows is a rapture, an ecstasy that doesn't slip back to aching pain until all of me is out, until I've dragged Viera's burning self into the gap between arches.

I start patting the Lunare immediately, batting at her with what remain of mine and her clothes, and then a pair of webbed hands join the effort, and we get the small fires put out quick. Viera's still conscious, but she's shaky as she rises back to her feet.

"Can't do that again," she says, and her voice is scratched, harsh.

"You won't need to," the creature replies.

It pulls out the small miner I'd seen it holding earlier. Then draws the other one. The last arch is glowing a purple-black. I can't imagine what could be worse than what we've already experienced, and the thought of braving something else makes me shiver.

The thing hurls one of its miners towards the last arch. As the weapon reaches one of the glowing sections, the creature aims and fires its other miner. The shot strikes the thrown weapon as it nears the top of the arch, exploding the projectile in a blast of bright white and green flares. The top of the arch crumples and crackles with a bang, and chunks of it fall to the ground in front of us. Sparks pop and sizzle from the severed remnants.

"Couldn't you have done that earlier?" Viera says.

"Only have two miners," the creature replies, bearing its new scars without complaint. "Had to save them for the last arch. The one that would've killed you had you tried to go through it."

"Just about killed us anyway," Viera mutters as the creature steps over the wreckage and through the apparently safe arch.

We follow, and the thick doors to the outside recoil like a fan, pressing back into each other through to the side as we near. The hall opens into a vast courtyard; a tiled expanse marked by large smooth patches where, it's not hard to imagine, some of the many ships shooting through the sky might set down.

The creature waves us forward, and we leave the doorway, taking all of five steps before we notice the forms pressed against the building behind us. Flaum, ten of them, in all manner of browns, blacks, whites and grays. They're holding miners, and they point them at us, though most aim at the creature. They look just like Nasiya's Flaum, our guards from earlier, except for one thing: the badges on their chests. Not the green and black circle but instead a blue and yellow mixture. Colors racing together like paints dropped on a stone.

My eyes flick back to the creature, and it's hesitating. Its hand is on the one miner it has left, but I don't believe it's going to fight. It would be stupid, impossible. If it tried, I have no doubt we would be burned to oblivion.

"Don't shoot," I say. "Nobody needs to die here."

A bit of the Empress is still left in me, even without Ignos. I'm still trying to save the lives of my subjects, all two of them.

"If the Dawn goes, then we won't need to shoot anybody," one of the Flaum, a speckled white and black one, says.

Its miner, a thick and long rifle, points directly at the creature, who proceeds to heed the warning, to drop its own weapon onto the stone with a loud clatter.

"They're yours, then," the creature says. "I expect a thank you."

"You'll get one, when we're finished with them."

The Flaum never flinches. Never takes the miner away. Not until the creature, without a look back at us, bounds away across the stone and vanishes through a wide gate in an outer wall.

I notice one of the other Flaum tapping something into an armlet on his wrist. I keep my eyes on it, even as the rest the Flaum fan out around us. Encircle us, and aim their weapons outside.

"From one prison to another," Viera says.

"We'll find our way out of the next one too," I say. "We just need to stay together."

Malo grips my hand, strong. Calm. What I need him to be right now. The emptiness in my head remains a terrifying vacuum, and I wish I could ask Ignos what these badges mean. Who these things are. Ignos, though, isn't here. It might be dead, and I don't dare slip into the Cache's knockout knowledge now.

I feel the air before I hear the sound. A rush of blowing wind, bringing with it smells I don't recognize. Unnatural ones; chemicals and burning things. I follow the Flaum's stares and look up in time to see an elegant, bizarre craft descending down towards us. It's a long, flat surface curved around the sides and bottom; a shallow oval. Like the badges, it too is painted in bright blues and yellows, and also reds and blacks all mixing together as if the thing simply exploded out of a rainbow.

"You have a weird sense of style," Viera says to the only Flaum that's spoken, the speckled one.

"We stand by our principles," the Flaum replies. "All things together, all things inseparable."

"What you want with us?" I try to ask, but the Flaum ignores me.

No, the Sevora that controls it ignores me. I can't forget that we're on a world of parasites. That all of these things have, like Ignos, a controlling monster inside of them.

We don't have a choice, so we follow the Flaum over and up the ramp, into the craft. The floors are white, the same pearl as the tubes and elsewhere and it's not long before we feel it mold around our feet. Keep us tethered to the ground and stabilized. The same thing happens to the Flaum, though most manage to keep their weapons angled our way as the ship ascends back to the sky. As it moves, the plain walls and ceiling fade, turn translucent, as if I'm looking through smeared glass.

Frenzied movement outside keeps my attention as we fly away from the prison. Larger ships are moving towards where we just left, and I see more than a few smaller craft take tentative slides towards our ship before breaking off. Small dots that I assume are more troops descend from the larger, blocky ships and stream towards the prison like ants.

Part of me hopes the creature escapes, the other part isn't sure.

The ship arcs over the city, higher and higher yet not quite into the black of space. I feel the craft accelerate, move fast and burst away from where we were.

"Where are we going?" I yell to the speckled Flaum, as none of the others have shown any interest in talking.

"To safety," the Flaum replies. "To another part of Vimelia, where Nasiya won't be able to find you."

So Nasiya doesn't know about this. Interesting.

Back on Earth, in Damantum, I'd had a bit of experience playing politics. In the weeks after the Emperor's death, after my own ascension, I'd come to know the various factions of the city. Come to taste their squabbles and grow irritated with their endless demands, most of which had little to do with aiding their people and much more to do with hurting those they feared. Or thought were their enemies.

There's something else I learned in those weeks: that divisions, turmoil, can be exploited.

The flight doesn't last long. While it's hard to tell time on a planet that doesn't seem to have a true night, I think it's less than an hour. Just as my feet start to hurt, and my knees quiver at staying the same position, we descend. It's a straight down drop that leads to a gentle landing on a wide pad, like the prison. However, unlike the metal constructs and bustling buildings of the city we were in, this place is lush and green.

It's not hard to see why: small discs covered in nozzles buzz around every meter of open space, sending long sweeping arcs of what looks like water on to groves of flowers, trees, and grasses. Long thin tubes trail from the discs back to some underground reservoir. It's a bigger, more wondrous garden than anything I've ever seen. Plants, or least I think that's what I think they are, spiral up and around and grow out in all directions. Some appear to be solid glass, while others look to be pulsing, like a heart soon after it's freed from its human prison. A grove next to me shoots silver trunks straight up stories into the air before, at the top, bursting into a fluted nova of pink and red flowers. Others, dome-shaped, open every few seconds and release a tingly blue spray into the air. As we walk, escorted by the Flaum, I catch some and think of mint and jasmine.

There's music here too, though I'm not sure from where it comes. Or if, really, it's music at all. It's almost like a chant, a low rhythm that nonetheless rises and falls to some beat and measure only the player knows. I find my feet matching its echoes as we move along a wide, white gravel path towards what I think is a building far too small for such a magnificent display.

It's a singular tower, though not much taller than my

village's Tier. And not much wider either. As we draw close, the speckled Flaum holds up a hand and we all stop. I've learned that signal by now. The Flaum waves in front of us towards the tower and as he gestures, I see the air around the tower shimmer. Like peeling back a shroud, the tower elongates and grows wider and wider until it's the width of what the garden lets me see and maybe more. It grows higher until its taller than the trees of my jungle. Taller than several of them stacked on one another.

"We keep our strength hidden," the speckled Flaum offers without our asking.

The door, however, stays the same size and so, with three Flaum in front and three behind, we walk through in a line. What we come to is not a place of power like the throne room in my old palace, but instead a ringing mess. A chaos of shouting voices, a crowd of Flaum and other species of all kinds and names I don't know yelling and screaming and buzzing at each other. Every once in a while I see something fly through the air; small rocks aimed at someone across the wide room.

The floor gently slopes down so that whomever is the object of all the shouting stands at the middle. Up above balconies ring the vast space, and there even more species lean over the edges, haranguing in their loud voices. I've never heard such a roar, so much clashing of tongues, and my first thought is to put my hands up to my ears and press, closing my eyes. To quiet, just for a moment, the noise.

At first I think I've been too effective. The shouts all die away, and then I hear nothing. It's only when I open my eyes do I realize that faces of every shape and color look towards me, Malo and Viera. As if interpreting a signal, the speckled Flaum waves us forward, points to the dais in the middle, on which stands a great, blotched orange slug.

Unlike the slimy things of my home, this one has arms, this one wears clothes, and this one grins at me with toothless pride as I make my way through the crowd towards it.

"Here we have our prize," the slug thing warbles as we draw close. "The very thing Nasiya sought to keep from us. The proof of our position, of the necessity of peace."

Bas isn't here. It's the first thing Sax notices, it's what he focuses on. A pair finds his pair.

The room is a circle, and he's not in the middle but bunched up on one of the sides. A pair of the mud-like creatures are sitting in the center, playing some sort of game on a table. They look over as Sax begins to stir.

"Wake up? Almost too late," the one speaking gravel is a clay color, the other one a brown mud. "Boss say to kill you in an hour."

"Oratus too rare to kill. Boss was joking." The mud one lurches up from the seat, bits of itself sticking behind it.

Bits that will regrow.

Sax blinks a few times. Reasserts his vision. Pushes his vents to inhale and test the air; clean, but not so pure as on the ship. Space stations, even the ones with the best recyclers, have too much air and too much smell to handle to get the same quality as a small vessel. And *Scrapper Station* doesn't have top-tier parts. What Sax gets is the scent of booze, of chemicals and sweat. More than a little bit of blood. Makes his claws tingle. Makes them want to add to it.

But if there's one thing he doesn't want to fight, it's these two. Whatever body lies beneath that rocky exterior is going to take a lot to get to, and there's more than a little chance of his claws breaking off as Sax tries to dig through that thick skin. So Sax sits up instead. Glances around the plain art in the room; vistas pulled from various planets and stuck around, without any unifying theme or purpose. As if someone simply grabbed what they could find and threw it against the wall. Like *Scrapper Station* itself.

"Where's Bas?" Sax hisses.

There's no headache. No lingering pain. They gave him meds, made sure the Oratus wasn't too badly hurt. Which means they're not thinking he'll be a captive for long. They want to use him.

"Fine," the clay one says. "Awake. Working."

"Doing what?" Sax says.

"Business," Brown says. "Your job too. Keep people honest."

"We're part of the Vincere," Sax replies. "We're not your tools. We're not your peons, your employees, your guards. You'll let us go, or when the rest of the Vincere arrive, you be blown to particles so small nothing in this place will get any use out of you."

They laugh; a low rumble, like boulders falling and clashing against one another. Perhaps, Sax thinks, that's because that's what it is. Rock and earth grinding together. Sax is starting to believe, though, that his threats are losing power. He hasn't managed to get a single one to work lately. Dalachite on *Cobalt* certainly didn't care, neither did the Lunare on Earth, or even the Sevora on that seed ship. The Oratus aren't what they used to be.

"Save threats for boss," the clay one rumbles. "You, us, the same. Stuck."

Sax can't help but wonder if this is what they've been fighting for. All those Oratus that have given themselves, all the Flaum and Whelk supporting them, for these lumps of rock who can't do anything more than spout nihilistic nonsense. Stuck. Not for much longer.

"Take me to this boss," Sax says, not bothering to address the clay one's remarks. "I'm guessing he'll want to see me."

This time it's the brown one that takes the lead, "Us give tour, first."

Sax waves a claw. Doesn't object. Might as well see if there's anything worth knowing about *Scrapper Station* before he tears it apart.

The two Lutos lead Sax out of the room, and instead of another long, featureless hallway, the room opens right out to a wide floor. It's a big space, connected to others by half-closed walls with sloping doors. Mirrors drape those walls, casting back reflections of gambling tables and video displays. And those entrapped by them. The sounds of laughter and curses, cheers and jeers echo. Sax is in a place he despises, a place that thrives on chance and making odds against those who choose to partake. It is the antithesis of what the Oratus believe; that preparation can make victory certain.

Like a magnet for his eyes, Sax feels his gaze slide to the right, to a cluster of rollerball tables—where the contestants all take turns pitching colored orbs against a vast target board. The scores change depending on where the balls lands, and whomever happens to find themselves with the highest one wins while the others lose and, of course, the house takes a cut. A little bit of skill, a lot of luck, and Bas looks like she's had about enough of it. Sax's pair looms over the bundle of Whelk playing at the tables. Their liquid-like bodies fling the balls one after another, and Sax is compelled to go over there, but the the rock monsters grab his arms and lead him on.

"Later," the clay one rumbles. "You both stay, anyway."

Bas gives Sax a slight nod, and that's all Sax needs to know. She's safe, bored but okay. Which means he can focus on his two escorts, and where they're leading him.

It turns out the gambling hall isn't all that big. One more small room and they're out, back into the basic interior of the dilapidated station. Sax can still see all the marks where different plates were welded together, pieces scrapped from various wrecks forced into place. A habitat made with the ghosts of others. The core of *Scrapper Station* is a large open space dotted with tables, benches, people hawking goods and an endless swarm of species in transition from hopeful to hopeless and back again.

Gravity here comes from the spinning, and Sax can feel it in his talons as they grip the metal. A slight shifting, as if his stomach were in a wind tunnel. In here, outside the gambling hall, they're in the center, where the gravity's the strongest. Spokes shoot away from this core in all directions.

"How many live here?" Sax asks to gets them talking, revealing something, maybe, he can use.

"Thousand," Clay says. "More free here, than working for Amigga."

"Hah," Brown replies. "Your idea to come here. Now we're stuck. Watching baby Oratus."

"Baby?" Sax hisses.

The Lutos don't answer and the conversation's over.

They take a walk around the core, with the rock monsters pointing out the way to residential spokes, bars, restaurants, docking bays and the cluster of other services. Medical, waste, manufacturing are all bundled together in their own spokes. *Scrapper Station* seems a little too well ordered for a place way out here, without an Amigga to run it.

"Ooblots manage things," the clay one says. "Bosses' sisters."

That explains it then. Ooblots are always organized, dedicated. Weak and cowardly. Sax has never met one himself, not counting just a few hours ago. Never wanted to.

Now the Lutos are telling him it's time. Back to the gambling hall, through a door on the far end. Sax tries to catch another sight of Bas, but she's not looking; busy with some dispute. Her claws ready. Sax wants to watch, both in case he needs to help, and because there's something about watching his pair work that's entrancing. But he doesn't get the chance. He's ushered through and this time there is a short hallway. To the right and left Sax can see the rooms where security is monitoring everything. In the back is what he's expecting; the lush luxury that Ooblots are known for.

There's a couple of eye stalks standing from the creature as it sits on a velvet red couch. Like a Whelk with an added helping of liquidity, the Ooblot puddles himself around the surface. The skin that Sax thought was yellow is, on closer inspection, closer to gray with plenty of golden blotches from radiation—too much time on *Scrapper Station* and its poorly shielded hull.

"Sax, right? I am D'Rascale, what do you think of my little enterprise?" The Ooblot says, and its voice is a slap-smack of liquid thwacks as the Ooblot hardens and softens its body, throwing parts of it against itself to make the words.

"It's a pile of garbage," Sax replies and bares his teeth, just a little.

"Honesty. I can appreciate that. We all can, especially

in a place like this, where lies often travel farther than the truth," D'Rascale doesn't get up, doesn't wave for Sax to move anywhere.

Just stares at him with those two large round eyes set in those stalks.

A long breath of silence. The two Lutos still have hold of Sax's arms, and the grip is tighter now than it was outside. They think he's going to attack. That he's going to fly into some sort of rage. Sax wants to, but his pair is out there. He wouldn't be doing Bas any favors by getting himself killed here.

"They tell you?" D'Rascale asks.

"I don't have time for games," Sax says. "I don't have time to work for you. An Oratus is not security guard, a janitor, or whatever else you have in mind. We are warriors, we belong at the front. You will hail the Vincere, and you will let us go until they arrive. In exchange, you will be rewarded."

The Ooblot swings a tendril out wide and, as if by magic, a small servo robot putters over and hands D'Rascale a small drink. The Ooblot places its newly-formed appendage over the lip, and from the center of its "hand", a pipe-link tube emerges and descends into the liquid, sucking it up with a slurping noise.

Sax eyes the beverage. The last thing he's had to eat or drink was back on *Cobalt*. He was too distracted on Plake's ship, and now his body, sensing a chance to feed itself, awakens.

"It seems you do need something," D'Rascale says, its left eye rotating on its stalk to focus on Sax's face. No, beneath his lips, where, Sax realizes, a bit of saliva has snaked itself out and is making its final escape towards the floor.

Sax catches the drop in his right mid-claw. He's not an animal.

"Your Vincere, if you are so necessary as you claim, will no doubt come for you," D'Rascale continues. "Until they arrive, we can strike a deal. You work for me, I feed you." A dwindling pause. "Your pair agreed to it."

"Liar." Bas would never agree to something like this. Would never accept servitude, no matter the price.

"She mentioned you might react this way. But here's the truth, Oratus. You're stuck here and you have two choices: either you work for me, do as I say and reap the benefits or I have these two throw you out an airlock so you can have the death you so obviously wish for."

"Is it me that wishes for death?" Sax hisses and then hurls forward, jabbing with his foreclaws and slipping their sharp edges beneath the Ooblot's slippery body. With his tail batting back the two rock monsters, Sax lifts the creature above his head, then tilts his mouth up and opens wide, so D'Rascale can see just how many teeth will be cutting into him.

But the Ooblot seems unfazed. D'Rascale takes another drink from the glass, still held in its sucking hand.

"This is why you'd be such a good fit here," the Ooblot says. If being an inch away from death has any effect on the creature, Sax doesn't see it now. "In fact—"

There's a shout, then another and a crash from outside the room. Back towards the casino floor. Back towards Bas

Sax doesn't hesitate; he drops D'Rascale block back on the couch, turns and barges his way up through the door. Down the short hallway and onto a casino floor that's broken into chaos. Tables are overturned, species are running wildly, and Bas in the middle of it all, her pink-gold tail thrashing what looks like one of the Whelks away from her and sending it flying. Two more slug creatures try to pile her to the ground while another tears the end off of a bar chair and begins to bring it over.

Begins. Sax provides the end.

He takes two long steps and then presses his talons to the ground and launches himself over the large bar in the middle of the floor. He clips some bottles, sends a few glasses tumbling, but the Oratus makes it across in time to catch the advancing Whelk in mid-swing. His claws dive into the gel-like surface of the slug-creature's skin, digging and scooping and gripping and then he's throwing the Whelk away.

What should have been a mortal wound for most species hardly fazes the Whelk, and it catches itself on the floor, rolls, and then it wriggles its way upright. You want to kill a Whelk, you have to pierce an organ or cut them all the way in half.

This one, though, with its yellow green skin and wild eyes, doesn't come charging back. It hesitates, and in that moment Bas turns the odds even further against the slugs. She throws the two things off her—both slamming against the wall next to the rollerball tables—and rises up behind Sax. Now faced with two ready, angry Oratus, the four Whelk decide they've already lost enough and run from the room.

"I want them banned," D'Rascale says, its voice slapping as it slides into the room. "This is the third time those four have decided to end their night damaging my floor. Look how much business I've lost. If it weren't for the two of you, it might've been even worse."

Sax is about to reply that he was just protecting his pair when D'Rascale holds up a flat hand. "I'm not asking for a commitment right this moment. Take a breath, have some dinner. Then tell me if you'd prefer to die, or work." The Ooblot gestures back to the room he just came from; apparently that's the Oratus' temporary refuge.

As much as Sax wishes he could tear D'Rascale apart, he realizes a good choice when he sees one. If he's hungry and tired, then Bas probably is as well. A chance to talk in private, a chance to be away for a moment from people that want them in servitude, would be nice.

"Take him up on it," Bas hisses quietly. "For once, put your pride aside and give us a moment."

Bas settles it. Sax isn't going to go against his pair. He's far too tired for that.

The Lutos don't say a word as the two Oratus retreat to the refuge of the room. The servo robot brings them water and food. Nutrient packs, but also some fresh grown vegetables. Sax stares at the leafy green, likely produced from hydroponics here on the station. It's such a rarity that Sax overlooks his usual distaste for things that aren't bleeding and instead delights in the crisp crunchy flavor.

Only after they've consumed several pounds of food apiece do the two Oratus settle back on the red couch and look at each other. There's no more avoiding it.

"We can't stay," Sax says. "I won't work for him. I won't work for anybody."

"We've been taking orders our entire lives Sax," Bas replies. "What does it matter if we're taking orders from an Ooblot instead of Evva?"

"You just said it yourself. It's not Evva. It's not the Vincere. This isn't who we are."

Bas turns her rose-gold head away, stares at the mirrored walls. Clicks her claws. "We're weapons, Sax. And weapons are wielded. We've just changed hands, is all."

Sax is about to reply. To snarl and suggest they break

their way out right now. Clearly, what Bas needs, is a real fight, not the dusting they had a moment ago. Something to remind her of who she is.

A crackling from an intercom breaks his momentum.

"Sorry for disturbing you, but I feel there is something you should know. It's coming in off the broad waves." The Ooblot doesn't say anything more as a screen descends from the room ceiling. It turns on to reveal a familiar face.

Evva. Reddish-black scales. Next to her, a long list of apparent crimes.

It takes a while for the sound to arrive, for the broadcast to begin to play, and as with anything transmitted over the relays, it's a grainy, simple sound. But Sax doesn't need fancy audio to discern the words.

Evva, traitor to the Oratus, to the Chorus, plotter of dangerous crimes and spreader of false rumors, is declared a danger to the galaxy. Any who see her should take all precautions and contact the nearest authorities to ensure this stain on our society is dealt with.

The Whelk calls itself Jel, and it escorts us out of the chamber when the cheering dies away to fast conversation. Jel, however, brings its own conversation with us, warbling away as we wind through yet another nest of halls. I should feel claustrophobic—most of the buildings of my childhood were open constructs without these narrow corridors—but I'm struck by the art on display.

The Solare, my tribe and kin, use paints from flowers, fruits, and crushed rock to illustrate our history on our towering Tiers, tattoos on our skin, and dyes on the furs and mossweaves that make up our clothes. A form of expression we've refined over many generations. One I find beautiful.

And yet.

These hallways *ripple*. That's the only word I can think of for how the streams of color dart and dance with one another as we walk. They aren't images, really, but abstract bursts in constant motion, twirling and mixing and splashing their bright reds, yellows, and blues all across the space. I've seen screens now, both on the shuttle here and the space station *Cobalt*, and these appear more natural, not the product of glowing light.

"Each and every one represents a race in this galaxy," Jel shifts its speech suddenly, its big, bulbous head shifting towards me. "Their dance is the same one we perform even now, coming together and apart again."

"It's beautiful," I say, and know the words are inadequate.

"Notice how they never break one another?"

I'm about to answer when Viera does for me. "That's what you're all about, right? No war? Everyone plays nice?"

Jel nods, or maybe bows; it's difficult to tell when the Whelk's head essentially molds right onto its body. Jel slithers on and we follow. This time, when the Whelk resumes its speech, I try to listen.

Nasiya's faction, Jel says, are called the Hasir. They run Vimelia, and their constant agitation for Sevora independence, war and pride is the source of their power and the Sevora's overall decline. The Wem, of whom Jel is the elected leader, would see treaties. Would see reconnecting with the galaxy at large.

The words become a jumble as more species and organizations tumble out of Jel's mouth and, despite myself, I tune Jel out again and focus on the more visceral differences I'm seeing between here and Nasiya's buildings. First and foremost, the Wem seem to be fans of yellower, softer light. The glow suffuses everything, though I'm never quite sure where it comes from. As we leave the swirling paints behind and enter what appears to be some form of dormitory, the gold bricks that make up the place have their own luminescence. I brush my hand on one of the shining stones and glance at my fingers; they're coated with a fine dust that, like a far off star, twinkles.

Every breath I take, too, brings with it flowery perfume from the gardens outside, smells that take me back to the jungle, and ones far different from the sterile efficiency of the Hasir buildings. A constant, soft breeze keeps the air moving and the temperature cooler than I'd like, but not so cold that I'm uncomfortable. Viera looks right at home, while Malo, like me, rubs his arms as we move.

"Not all the Wem stay here," Jel is saying, gesturing with a stubby green arm up at the rows of rooms. "Most who do use this as a temporary refuge, to get away from the chaos of the city."

"Or to hide from a crime?" Viera asks.

I give the Lunare a sharp glance, but Jel's laugh cuts any embarrassment.

"If necessary," Jel says. "We try to keep as much of our work out of the grime as we can, but sometimes change requires a sleight hand."

"And gray morals," Viera adds.

"You will starve on virtue alone," Jel acknowledges. "Still, we are not Clarity's Dawn. We do not seek to destroy, only change."

The title tickles a memory, but before I can ask a question, we're moving again. The rooms, unlike the cells in the prison, open onto vine-wrapped balconies, and a pair of waterfalls trickle down on either side of a wide, tan platform that we board. At ground level around us, tall trees rise, sporting long tendrils ending in bright pink blooms. As soon as Malo steps on the platform, Jel does something I don't catch and the platform begins to rise.

Viera snares Jel in conversation and I take the opportunity to slide near Malo and ask him what he thinks.

"In these last days, Kaishi, I have seen more wonders than I thought possible," Malo says, but his voice carries caution with it, and I note that he's speaking our tongue, not the so-called common language used by every species we've seen so far.

"But?"

"Everyone we've met appears to want to use us for something. I can't believe these 'Wem' will be any different."

I chew on that for a second. Malo's right, of that I don't have any doubt. Nobody, not even my father and my tribe, would treat visitors with so much hospitality unless there was something they believed they would get in return.

"Malo, I'm starting to believe that's what our lives are," I say. "When we were young, we had to obey our elders, our superiors, and, above them, our gods. This isn't all that different."

The platform continues up, past the rooms and still higher, above the top of the chamber and into a tunnel bordered on all sides by those glowing bricks.

"There's a difference being told what to do by your parents, by the people you trust, or the gods you worship. They, at least, care about you. These things? Kaishi, I feel they would throw us away in a moment if we were of no use to them."

"You think they could throw us away? You? Warrior of the Charre?"

I mean the words to bulk up Malo's spirit, bring a laugh or a smile to his face, but all I get is a grimace.

"I couldn't protect you back on Earth. I didn't save you on *Cobalt*. Why think I can protect you here?"

"Because you promised me," I reply. "And my general doesn't break promises."

That, at least, gets a rueful grin. A small nod of thanks.

The ceiling parts above us and the platform breaks out into the open air. We're on top of the huge building, on a spire that rises over the main roof. Glass encircles us, and I can see, around the sandy ground, the circular garden spreading out around the structure. Beyond the green, buildings rise up, though in a more patchwork fashion than the concentrated metropolis we first landed in.

"Vimelia's city never truly ends," Jel says as we take in the view. "But it does quiet from time to time. We chose this place precisely because it sits beyond the clamber, because it forces us to see natural beauty. Remind ourselves that we strive for nature's harmony, not a forced structure."

"How?" I ask. "You talk about taking over the Sevora, about changing what your species, but how? The Hasir, and Nasiya, seem to have so much more than you."

"The Sevora blow like a leaf in this eternal wind," Jel replies. "A strong gust in our direction could, in one stroke, give us the planet. I hope that gust will be you."

"Never been a gust before," Viera says. "Do I wave my arms like this?"

The Lunare sweeps her hands from side to side and I roll my eyes. Malo looks away, shaking his head. Jel, though, says nothing, and Viera, seeing nobody appreciating her jest, settles into a humph.

"No, there is one thing that must happen before we go any farther," Jel says, and by the sudden weight in its tone, I can tell our happy tour is at an end. "We have members who have earned their chance to make a difference. Earned a chance to try. Earned a host such as yourselves."

There's a heavy silence.

One I break.

"You want to infect us."

"This is the Sevora home, human," Jel says. "To be here, you must be one of us."

"Ignos couldn't control me," I reply, the thought of another creature in my head injecting acid into my voice. "Your Sevora won't get what they want."

"One test does not make a thorough experiment," Jel replies, and I notice now that its two hands have slipped beneath its strange robe. It's not difficult to imagine a miner or two hiding beneath those folds. "Either we will prove you are not all you claim to be, and gain a new host species, or we will have the guides in place to ensure you know what to say and when to say it."

"Not happening," I say. Malo shifts behind me, getting ready. Viera, too, faces Jel, her hands loose. "I'm not letting any of you in my head ever again."

I have no idea if Jel understands my words—the Whelk sits there, its gooey mass playing about like a line of drippy tree sap. Malo and Viera take up positions on either side of me, and now it's the three of us on one side of the platform, and Jel on the other. Viera, who a moment ago had seemingly been the best of friends with Jel, wears the hardest expression of us; pure loathing etches into her face and I'm very glad the Lunare's with me instead of the other way around.

"Again?" Jel asks. "I didn't know any of you had the joy of being a host before?"

"It wasn't intentional," I reply.

The platform judders, then begins to descend back into the building. For a moment, I think our shot at escape vanishes with those glass walls, but we don't have any tools to break them with anyway.

"And now you are *unhosted*," Jel says the word the same way I might say 'diseased'.

"We're free, if that's what you mean," Viera speaks up. "We're staying that way too. So find another way to prove your point, or let us go."

The glowing bricks again surround us, locking the tension into that little platform.

"The Sevora will never listen to one that isn't a part of us," Jel says, and it tucks its arms back beneath the robes. "It would not have to be a permanent situation, but at first, it will be necessary."

Jel makes a certain sort of sense—I don't think the Solare or the Charre tribes back on Earth would listen to Viera without me or Malo vouching for her. But there's a wide chasm between supporting someone and letting a creature infest your mind.

"Necessary for you," I say. "We have no stake in your fight. All we want is a ship off this planet and back to ours."

Viera shoots me a look and I realize I've made a mistake. Given away something we need, and by the way Jel quivers —a motion which sends a side of my stomach twisting—the Whelk caught it.

"Ships can be arranged," Jel replies slowly. "Our planet is, however, engaged in a long-running, costly war. Sparing a vessel to take you home would require resources. Would need payment. I think you know how to deliver that."

The platform keeps moving and scenarios play out like lightning in my mind; if I agree with the creature, we submit, and they stick their friends inside us. If things go well, and Jel's faction gets what they want, why would they bother letting us go? If it goes poorly, then Nasiya has us all killed or stuffed with his own Sevora.

I don't have to look at Malo and Viera to know they've reached the same conclusion.

"Take it," I say in the Charre tongue. "Jel's our only way out of here."

Malo moves faster than I think possible; he dives forward, his shoulder slamming into Jel's bulk while his hands scrabble for its arms, trying to keep them from drawing whatever the Whelk has in its pockets. Jel utters a surprised warble as it hits the bricks going by, and almost gets its left arm free before Viera arrives. The Lunare tears the small miner from Jel's grip and places the weapon up close towards Jel's huge head.

"Or," I say. "You can give it to us to be nice. That's what friends do, right?"

The platform sinks beneath the bricks and back into the large dormitory. The first chance we'll have of being discovered, and it's a chance we immediately lose: there's plenty of creatures walking across the balconies, waiting for the platform, or chattering with one another. It only takes a single loud burble from Jel before plenty of types of eyes turn our way.

"I'm thinking we'll be running from this one," Viera says.

"We use the hostage." Malo adjusts his grip and his hands dig deeper into Jel's apparently soft skin.

"You're only hurting my host," Jel says, its voice suddenly tight, and I wonder if Malo's squeezing the thing that allows the Whelk to talk. "You'll only kill the Whelk. You have no leverage, except a surrender."

"Throw it," I say.

The platform's just about at the highest floor of the dormitory, the one with the fewest gawkers on it. We'll be dead or captured if we stay here in the open—I learned that much in the jungle.

Malo obeys, giving Viera a moment to shift back to my side, and then, with Jel protesting, he shoves the Whelk forward against the platform's railing. The Charre warrior grunts, squats, and starts to lift Jel over as the platform settles onto the third floor landing.

We're out of time.

"Cover us!" I shout to Viera, and I dash forward, planting my hands against Jel's body as Malo lifts the squirming Whelk over the railing.

Jel's skin is cold, clammy, and altogether disgusting— like grabbing a rotting fruit from a puddle, but my shove is enough to tip Jel over the edge, toppling the Whelk off the platform and down towards the ground floor. It strikes with a wet splat, and I turn away from the carnage. Part of me notes that I've just killed another species for the first time, and I quash any guilty thoughts by reminding myself that the Whelk lost itself to the Sevora long ago.

"Take another step and I'll shoot you. And you. Several times." Viera's threats accompany Malo and I off the platform and onto the wide balcony that wraps around the level.

A pair of confused Flaum, hands empty and wearing the same robe Jel worse, face us. Those badges are there too, the painted ones. If these Flaum, or, really, the Sevora controlling them, have any courage, however, it vanishes when they look down to see what's become of their leader. Both of them slide against the wall and wave us by.

We go.

We have no plan, no idea of how to get out, but we move. My feet pound against the hard floor and I throw glances at every room we run past, looking for some way down or out. Mostly, I have no idea what I'm looking at. One has a series of nets hanging from the ceiling. Another a pool of purple-blank ink in the ground, and the third looks like a miniature flower garden, though many of the blossoms have been eaten.

"What are these things?" I say without realizing it.

"No idea," Viera huffs in front of me. "Is it bad that I kind of want to stay here and figure that out?"

"It's your choice." Malo replies from the back.

Shouts follow us now from below, and I've no doubt the platform is moving down to the ground to pick up someone armed with more than fear. We're almost at the end of this side, and I'm hoping that something shows up soon or this escape attempt is going to be real short-lived. Already, looking back, I see a half-dozen Flaum pouring off of the platform and starting after us.

We hit the back wall of the level and there's nothing there. Another room on our right, and the balcony continues around in a long U that will only bring us to the people we're trying to avoid. I hear a pop, and see Malo's holding a miner now too. Another small one, just like Viera's. His shot goes wide of the approaching force, but they duck down into cover.

"They're not shooting back," Viera says as she presses me down behind the railing.

"Because we're only valuable to them alive," I reply, my eyes stuck on Malo's miner.

Idea.

"Give me your miner," I tell Viera, and the Lunare hesitates. "I said give it to me."

This time I inject my best empress tone, the one that suggests all sorts of terrible things if I don't get what I want. Viera, understands and hands over her weapon without complaint. As soon as I get my fingers around the hilt, I turn and, yelling Malo's name, throw the miner across the space between us and the Wem guards.

Malo gets it.

Aims.

Shoots.

Everyone's watching my thrown miner, the guards with confused disbelief, and thus everyone sees Malo's shot miss and bury itself into the side wall splitting a pair of rooms. I'm about to panic as one of the guards catches the miner with its furry Flaum hand, aims it back at us —

Malo fires again.

I can tell he doesn't miss because everything flares staccato white for a moment and there's a rippling sound, like a massive scroll of paper being torn again and again. Heat washes over me in waves as I fall back against the wall, away from the balcony. My nose stings—who knows what I'm breathing in, but it's not natural.

When the fire doesn't die right away, when the bangs roll over us in waves, I realize this isn't what I expected. I'd thrown one miner, but our whole level is shaking.

Oh wait. The guards. They must have been carrying their own weapons.

I open my eyes slow. Blink away the smoke. Look to where the guards stood a moment ago and there's only charred remnants of a balcony there. A concave divot splits the gap, those glowing bricks looking awful black now. I can't see any sign of the guards and I don't look too hard because I'm going to have enough nightmares as it is.

"Let's go," Viera says, and I'm only too happy to jump up to my feet, but hesitate when she goes back by Malo, towards the gap.

"Wrong way?" I venture.

"You just gave us our stairs," Viera points and while I wouldn't go so far as to call the wreckage 'stairs', there's definitely a jagged, ruined pile of debris leading down to the second level.

"It's a path," Malo agrees, and amid shocked yelps from the survivors below, we get moving.

Viera's ladder is a messy mix of shattered brick, twisted balcony railing, and torn things that, I'm confident, were worn not long ago by living, breathing,

Slaves.

The word sneaks into my head and stays there. None of those creatures came after us on their own, none of them controlled their arms and legs and tails or whatever they had. We killed them and it hadn't even been their choice to be there.

I pick from foothold to handhold, smoke and fizzy mist floating around me, and resolve never to let a Sevora in my mind again.

"I don't think we can pull the same trick a second time," Malo says as we assemble on the second level.

The piled debris block us from the platform, and there doesn't seem to be a stair in sight. But I realize we don't need one. Stretching up around us are strange, tree-like things; looping deep green trunks covered in bright pink flowers. Compared to a jungle tree, scaling one of these would be easy.

Down below, what Wem still in the dormitory are scattering, apparently the threat of death means more to the Sevora than it does to us.

"Just like home, Malo!" I shout, then take a step and leap through the air into a tree.

I catch myself one of the long thick branches, and immediately scramble down a limb of softer-than-wood material, placing one hand and foot after another towards the ground. I can't take time to look back up to tell if Viera and Malo are following, so I just move. Climb to the ground. Waiting for me when I step away from the ridged blue-green are a pair of gray-uniformed Flaum, who throw nervous looks at each other as I face them.

Yet they come towards me, holding nothing but their own claws.

"I'm not coming with you," I say to them.

"It's not your choice to make," the left one replies. "How you come with us *is*. Either unharmed, or otherwise."

I drop into a stance, extending my left knee and arm forward. Wait. They rush me at the same time, splitting themselves just slightly. I wonder why they don't use miners, and then assume all their weapons were blown to pieces with the actual guards.

I duck and weave around their swings. Flashback to games in the jungle, to exercises with Malo and the other Charre troops. I curl around one claw, slip under another. The swipes are slow, clumsy. These aren't soldiers, but I focus on evasion, on staying alive long enough to take advantage of some other chance that comes my way.

Shouts ring from behind me; Malo and Viera making my same journey down the tree, joining the fray. Malo grabs one of the Flaum from behind, wraps his arm around the creature's neck and then flips it over his back shoulder, throwing the creature to the ground. Viera has less luck, perhaps not as accustomed to hands and feet brawling as Malo.

So when the Lunare tries to do the same, she's not fast enough and the Flaum has time to react, pushes back from the Lunare, and moves to rake his claws across Viera's face. I interrupt with a kick to the center of the Flaum's back. One that sends the furry creature straight into Viera and knocks them both to the ground. Viera rolls as they fall, and pins the creature beneath her, delivering a pair of knockout blows when they settle on the floor.

Then we're running again. Out through the dormitory, into the hall. After decimating the guards and the two Flaum, nobody else seems to have an appetite for a fight. The hallway's empty, and at the far end, leading back towards the chamber where everyone had been yelling before, I see some species vanish. This time, I barely spare a glance for the swirling paints that, minutes ago, so enchanted me.

The great chamber is cavernous without anyone in it. As soon as we enter, the doors behind us slam shut. In fact all of them do except for one. The door where the Flaum force initially brought us in, the one leading out to the garden and the landing pads.

"Wonder which way they want us to go," Viera says.

"I suggest we take it," Malo says. "Every second here is more time for them to set a trap. Or worse."

"Then let's move," I say, and punctuate the remark by dashing towards the door.

Once again we're under the white-beige sky, running towards the giant garden. As we leave, our exit slides shut behind us. Locks us out of a place I never want to be again. Ahead, I see that the shuttle that took us here is gone, and so it's a plain blank stone courtyard leading to the garden. We run across it, not sparing a second for conversation. All our breath goes to our lungs, to our feet.

It occurs to me that we have nowhere to run to. Nowhere to hide, nor to go.

I wave at Viera and Malo to stop as soon as we get a little ways into the garden, when we're surrounded by strange looking plants that, now, seem more eerie. Their jagged edges and strange flowers loom over us, the ground under our feet is a prickly, sticky sort of soil. A green fuzz instead of grass or leaves. A tilted rush of homesickness infiltrates my mind and I push it away, an act I'm getting better and better at as home becomes a place I'll never see again.

"I don't want to keep running without a plan," I say to my friends.

Viera and Malo, for their part, are holding up reasonably well. All of us have a few scratches, tears and cuts we received from the fighting or garden thorns, but we're standing, alive.

"Getting away from here seems like a pretty good plan," Viera offers.

"To where? Back to Nasiya?" I say. "Even if we knew how to get there, they won't be happy. We'd wind up back in that same prison, or worse. I'm sure they wouldn't mind sticking a Sevora in our heads either."

"Can we find the creature? The one that broke us out?" Malo says.

"Oh yeah, the one that dumped us right off to these monsters?" Viera replies. "You think it will do anything different the next time?"

"No, it had to give us up," I say. "At least it tried to rescue us. Give me a moment and I'll try to find its group in the Cache. I think they called it 'Dawn'?"

"This garden is not the place to do your digging," Viera says and glances up.

Not that I need the sight of the shuttle to tell me it's coming. There's plenty of whining, whooshing noise. Probably that same Flaum crew, returning to end our troubles.

So once again we take off running. Dashing through the plants for what seems like forever. What pursuit there is, we never see. We just go and go and go, and I lose track of where we are. The plants eventually give way to dark metal structures, to broad streets and thousands of eyes, most of whom watch us, their gaze pushing us down dark alleys and into corners where we think we can fight.

Where I hope we can be safe, though I know we aren't.

The only thing to do is take the Ooblot's offer. D'Rascale wants them to do nothing more than roam the casino's floor, looking imposing. Sax finds a flash of his teeth, a single raised claw is all that's needed to defuse most fights well before they start. Any that aren't convinced take a single whack of his tail to fall in line.

The monotony gives Sax time to turn over Evva's accusation. Time to decide what's gone wrong, to know who to trust, and he comes up with blanks., There's no real reason why, he thinks, the Amigga would turn on such a decorated Oratus. No real reason to brand her a traitor and want her dead.

Then again, she's escaped. Evva's on the run, which means she must have known this was coming. Is that why she told Sax and Bas to safeguard the humans? To not trust the Amigga?

There's only one certainty in all of this—Sax and Bas won't find anything on *Scrapper Station*, so they need a way off.

And one presents itself when Coorvin wanders into the

casino. The Flaum looks notably heavier than when he was on *Cobalt*, and his scraggly gray fur is a more full silver. His eyes are brighter, and the Flaum doesn't shrink away when Sax notices he's there. Doesn't do anything more than smile when Sax clomps to tower over him.

"You're still here," Sax says by way of a greeting.

"Plake decided her crew could use a rest," Coorvin replies. "And she's still holding most of the food meant for *Cobalt*. She has to find a buyer, and there's going to be more options here than flying around at random."

"How close is she to finding one?"

Coorvin shakes his head. "I'm the new one on the crew. They don't tell me much, and, after so many cycles with the Amigga, I'm fine being left alone."

"Listen, Coorvin," Sax says. "We need a way off this station. To the Chorus, or one of the closer worlds."

"You're asking me to help you get closer to the Amigga?"

"I'm telling you," Sax hisses. "There are bigger concerns than your feelings here."

Coorvin, though, slants his eyes towards Sax, crosses his furry claws in front of his chest. "Sax, I'm not the one you want to be ordering around. I'm back in relatively polite society, and I'll be treated like it."

"I don't have time for that," Sax says. "How can we get passage on your ship?"

"There have to be easier options?"

"We don't have money," Sax replies. "Which means we need connections."

"So your plan is to try and get back on board the ship with the captain that sold you into this position in the first place?"

"My plan is to get that captain alone, and use my claws

to convince her of the necessity of my position." Sax leans in close to Coorvin. "I saved you from that monster, Coorvin. All I'm asking now is an opening. Some information that will let Bas and I try to solve our problem."

At this last, Coorvin relents. "This is what I get for waning to throw a few chits on the tables. If you want to start a dialog, go to the Junkyard's Rest—Agra-Red and a couple of the others like to go there after their shifts are over. Get them on your side, and maybe Plake will relent."

"Thank you," Sax replies, then straightens, walks away from Coorvin.

Wouldn't be smart to clue too many in on his relationship with the Flaum. *Scrapper Station* would have a lot of people interested in what the Oratus were doing, and Sax wants no part of their meddling.

He'll have enough blood on his claws already.

D'Rascale has them working opposite shifts, so that there's one Oratus present on the floor at all times. At first, the Ooblot thought he could confine Sax and Bas to their quarters when not working, but a sufficient show of Sax's teeth convinced the slime otherwise.

So it's not long before Sax gets his chance to investigate the Junkyard's Rest and the rest of the station.

Outside the casino is *Scrapper Station's* nexus—the large central ball around which the rest of the station spindles off of in various spokes. Cheaper to build a station like this and have it spin to generate some gravity than any other method. Even stations on the fringe of civilization, like this one, have some standards: every spoke is dominated by a particular type of purpose. From the Nexus, Sax counts seven of them, with two explicitly designated for living areas. Two more for docking bays and shipping.

Which leaves three for general commercial and entertainment, along with the space already used for the Nexus. The central ball consists of four main avenues that criss-cross the structure, meeting up at various points. Sax walks towards the closest one, tracking the species he's seeing. Looking for the ones that might be disposed to a bit of chemical relaxation, and, thereby, interrogation.

That proves to be a difficult challenge—*Scrapper Station* is a far fling from the Amigga-run domains Sax is used to. Most of the people here, regardless of their species, look like they're clinging to life. Many wear motley rags, or patched together bits of garbage. Those who look nicer tend to display miners and other weapons out in the open. Sax didn't notice this in the casino, where automated scanners force everyone entering to disarm themselves.

It's a side of the galaxy Sax hasn't seen before.

But, despite the appearances, the species are stopping in the various stores, whether buying weapons, scrap, or any number of other goods. Including ones outside the bounds of legality, something Sax would have reacted to until the Amigga's power lost its hold on him.

That, Sax supposes, is the most glaring lesson of this dive into the rest of the galaxy. He's never held much love for the Amigga, for their distant and seemingly arbitrary demands, but he can understand working towards galactic peace. Some sort of prosperity. But this? This can't be the ideal. What the Oratus and Vincere are fighting for.

On his left, Sax passes by one of the large lifts to the residential spokes. Three separate elevators made to shuttle people up the spoke and out to the fringes, pulled by thick cables. A cluster of Teven gaggle together outside of them now, chattering about some sort of business deal. Sax doesn't care, moves on.

The first sign he has of Junkyard's Rest comes courtesy

of a pair of Vyphen, looking haggard and tired, arguing about where to stop in for a sniff. Sax isn't familiar with the term, but among the list of locales, Sax hears the name he's looking for. At the same time, the Vyphen realize that he's listening.

"What're you standing there for, big guy?" the closer one asks him, a blueish creature with wilting yellow feathers. "We're not causing any trouble."

"I'm not here for you," Sax replies. "But I'm looking for the place you're speaking of. The Junkyard's Rest. Tell me where it is."

The two Vyphen look at each other, then the blue one turns back to him. "Up the third spoke. Ride it all the way to the end. It's the only place there."

Sax gives them a single nod, then moves on. He's seen the fear in their eyes, the tensing of their muscles.

It makes him smile.

Sax despises low gravity that increases the further he gets from the Nexus. The feeling that when he lifts a claw that it's not going to come down right away, that his leg will keep on rising until he puts forth effort to stop it. Even though the air is recycled and purified, Sax feels like he has to work harder to keep it down, to maneuver his body out of the lift and into the only possible option at the far end of the spoke.

The Junkyard's Rest.

The entrance is a wide, flat square that appears to have, at one point, been used as a freight exit. Too big for normal people, the bar has since filled it with glowing holograms displaying the prices of various specials and menu items.

None of which Sax is remotely interested in.

To help with navigation, all around this level and, Sax is sure, inside the bar as well, are posts coming up a little over a meter. He uses his claws to grab one and propel himself into the bar past a pair of nervous Flaum bouncers. As if they'd ever try and stop an Oratus.

Inside, Junkyard's Rest proves a slave to its name, and Sax wonders if its design has as much to do with the low cost of, well, scrap. Tables and chairs of every height are bolted to the floor and are made from random parts. Sax can see long benches carved from the wings of old fighters, while turtle stools for the fluid bodies of Whelk and Ooblots look like they've been made from rocket nacelles.

This all goes with the bar too—itself a long counter covered in polished scrap and serviced by robotic arms. Cameras project options down onto the tables, where patrons touch the hologram of what they want, and it's soon after flown to them by delivery drones.

Aside from conversations, the background is home to a low synthetic pulse beat, the sort of noise that doesn't cause unstable effects for some of the more sensitive species.

And then there's the Junkyard Rest's crowning achievement: a giant window along the very end of the spoke that looks out into the floating debris field around *Scrapper Station*. Lit by the reflection from the surrounding planet, the debris serves as endless entertainment as they bounce and clash with one another, occasionally interrupted by a passing ship.

What Sax doesn't see, though, is his target. Agra-Red isn't here, and Sax is drawing stares. He'll have to do something soon, or the wrong sort of attention is going to come his way.

So, for the first time in his life, Sax goes up to a bar.

Not a soul comes to serve him. Who would? He's a big, gray-scaled weapon that's still bearing plenty of scars from the burns on *Cobalt* and cuts from so many earlier battles that they all blend together to create a horrifying story.

It doesn't help that Sax keeps flashing his teeth at anyone who looks at him. There's a protocol to be followed here—namely, that prey should understand their place, and Sax considers everyone in here prey.

"You want something?" says a voice.

Sax looks for the source and doesn't see it, only row after row of bottles, box after box of stimulants, and plenty of inhalable packs.

"I'm using a speaker," the voice says, and then Sax sees the holes, right there in the countertop in front of him. "If you're going to order, use the menu in front of you. If you're not, I'd ask you to—" Sax manages to find the speaker, a beefy Flaum behind the bar, who meets Sax's eyes and gulps hard. "To, uh, take as much time as you need."

Sax turns to the menu, a litany of options projected on the surface in front of him. Most of them are unappealing: injections meant to swim throughout a Whelk's body, targeted to stimulate and numb various nerve centers, coatings that, slipped down a Teven's central core, would drive the creature into oblivious ecstasy.

Sax scrolls through the options, writing off each one in turn. He's not here to distort his mind, the very idea of which nauseates him. At last he happens upon the very end of the list, populated with less dangerous things like water and nutrient goop. He picks both of those.

Behind him, Sax feels a stool begin to rise up out of the floor and, with his left leg, he kicks at the thing until its mechanical brain gets the idea that Sax has no desire to sit.

Then he resumes his observation. Still no sign of the Whelk, though Sax knows he's only been in the bar for a few minutes.

Those minutes stretch, and Sax orders one water after another, goes through several light meals of nutrient goop, and notices an ever-expanding clear area around him as patrons decide the potential danger of being near an Oratus isn't worth a close-up look.

Not that Sax minds.

He watches the junk spin in space, traces the trails of ships leaping in and out of the system. It's peaceful in its own way, and Sax starts to understand why people might prefer these sorts of places. A chance for meditative nothing in a crowded universe.

"You're not who I expected to find here," says a confused voice, one Sax recognizes.

His hunt is over.

Agra-Red stands looking at Sax, a straight line spread across his wide, crimson face, shadowed as ever by his helmet. The Whelk's embedded miner is still there, but Sax notices the battery pack powering it has disappeared—a seeming concession to the rules of the place. Behind the Whelk stands Engee, whose sticking a single eye out from the top of her carapace and turning it around.

"I'm here for you." Sax isn't a fan of subtlety.

"Really." Agra-Red sidles up to the bar next to Sax, then half-turns towards Engee. "Get whatever you want, I'm buying."

"You don't have to," Engee replies, but joins him at the bar anyway, sitting to his left.

"She modded my miner," Agra-Red says to Sax. "Boosted the power enough that it'll burn through even your scales."

Sax looks at himself. The scars. "Already had that happen enough times."

"You're still alive, so obviously not."

Agra-Red eyes the glass of water on the bar in front of Sax, laughs, then punches in an order for some drug Sax doesn't know.

"I need your ship," Sax says.

"It's not my ship." Agra-Red replies, turning to Engee. "You order anything yet?"

"Can I trust you not to leave me here?"

"I'll get you back. Provided this one here doesn't tear me apart."

"You're going to tear Agra-Red apart?" Engee pokes her eye-stalk around Agra-Red's slug body.

"Not yet," Sax replies.

"See? He's friendly." One of Engee's tiny arms shoots out from her carapace and slaps something on the bar in front of her.

"Friendly. You ever been called that, Oratus?" Agra-Red says, turning back to Sax.

"By my friends."

"Where are they?" Agra-Red does a show of looking around the bar. "Not here?"

"Working. The job you sold us into."

"Again, not my call. You're confusing me for Plake, Oratus. Take up your issues with the captain, not the crew."

Sax flares his nostrils. His long tongue sweeps the back of his teeth inside his mouth. Whelk make for terrible food —they're sticky, and they tend to fall apart into jelly after they're dead. Still, he wouldn't mind eating every last bit of this one.

But that wouldn't get Bas out of the casino. Wouldn't get them off of this station, to Evva.

"We need a ride, Agra. We'll pay for it."

"With what? Last I recall, you didn't have anything to pay with. That why you're drinking water?"

Sax blinks. Payment. He'd... never actually paid for anything in his life. Always on Vincere assignment, always covered by their contracts.

He has no way of buying all the food he's been eating.

"I know that look," Agra-Red says. "You're lost now. What're you going to do? Murder everyone in the bar when they come to collect the tab?"

"You'll pick it up for me," Sax says slow.

"And what would prompt me to be so generous?"

"You're buying her a drink for fixing your weapon," Sax says, then raises his foreclaws. "You're buying me a meal for letting you live."

Rather than looking scared, or threatened, Agra-Red jiggles its body and laughs.

"I'll give you this one, Oratus, you truly do believe you're frightening."

Sax feels his eyes narrow, but again Bas comes to his mind and he forces himself to relax.

"Yet," Agra-Red continues, the Whelk's eyes rolling towards a bowl of powder a robotic arm places in front of it. "If you really want a ride, there's something you could do to get yourself on Plake's good side."

"What?"

Agra-Red leans over the bowl, its mouth expanding to wrap around the lips of the entire thing, and, with a slurping sound, all of the powder flows up out of the bowl and into the Whelk.

"There's a restaurant, Nova. Residential spoke two. Plake has what they want, but they don't want to pay her what she needs to make for the trip to be worth it," Agra-Red says. "Make them change their minds, and I'll help you get your lift. We're going back Core-ward after this anyway."

The Whelk is changing from its reddish hue to a purple color as the powder spreads through the thousands of spidery veins running along the slug's mass. Agra-Red's pupils dilate, itsmouth goes slack, and Sax figures this deal is done.

He's never played the part of blackmailer before, but recently his life's been full of firsts.

Sax stands, and when the one bartender looks from his safe space on the far end, Sax points to Agra-Red with his left foreclaw. The meal debt is passed.

Sax turns, is about to make his way out of the restaurant, when curses, angry ones, billow from behind him.

He wouldn't have turned, wouldn't have bothered, except the panicked, slurred replies come from someone he knows.

Sax wheels around to see a pair of Vyphen standing over Engee, who, given her stumbling state, has taken hard to her drink of choice. A pair of other beverages, blue and green ones, now littering the ground at the foot of the bar tells all the story Sax needs.

Engee's alternating between apologizing and the kind of uncontrollable laughter that shows she's a long way from her normal self.

The Vyphen, though, don't seem interested. Their own elliptic eyes are bloodshot, and their feathered arms reach for the Teven, who falls over as she tries to back away.

Agra-Red, for its part, is slumped over on the bar, unmoving as its skin shifts between purples and reds.

There might be more than one way to get a ride on Plake's ship.

The Vyphens back away in a hurry when Sax moves to stand over Engee, who's tiny legs have her scrambling back beneath him.

"Have a problem with this one?" Sax hisses, low and with a single raised lip—just enough to show off his teeth.

The Vyphen, though, take the moment to recover and find some spine to stiffen. They both meet Sax's glare with their rubbery faces, their bulbous eyes angled right as the Oratus. Sax realizes they're the same pair from the Nexus, the ones that gave him the directions here. They're so divorced from reality, though, that Sax doesn't think they'd recognize themselves in a mirror.

"Nothin' you need caring about," the right one, a blue-gold looking creature whose feathers are tight-trimmed. "She spilled our drinks, we're just looking for a bit of payback."

"Yeah," the left one, a mottled brown and green, whose own feathers are experimenting in a variety of angles, adds.

"Then I suggest you order your next round, and have her and her friend pay for it," Sax replies.

The Vyphen cock their heads at him. As if this is a ludicrous request.

"You're not hearing what we're saying," the blue-gold Vyphen says. "*Scrapper Station* isn't one of your military bases. We don't follow your laws. We're free to do as we like here, get what we're owed."

"Yeah," seconds the other one.

Sax unfurls all four claws, watches the Vyphen track those sharp tips. He bets they're imagining how painful they could be. Better make the consequences a little more clear.

"Thanks for letting me know," Sax says. "This Teven is mine. If you hurt her, then you'll owe me, and I'll take my debt the same way you're taking yours."

The Vyphen glance at each other. Then the blue-gold one puffs up his feathers, makes them stand on end like it's some sort of display. It's a rapid pop, and large enough that Sax doesn't see the second Vyphen pull a small miner from a holster hidden by his wild feathers.

The weapon comes out, aims towards Sax, and then the Vyphen simply disappears in a flash, a bright red one that leaves a molten pile of flesh and a cluster of falling, burning feathers.

Sax traces the blast back to the bar where Agra-Red is sitting, still looking droopy, but with its heavy, modified miner aiming towards where the Vyphen stood.

"She really gave it a boost!" Agra-Red laughs, then looks down at the weapon. "Added just enough reserve juice for a surprise shot too. Turned him right to slag. Excellent."

The blue-gold Vyphen dances a look between Sax and Agra-Red, then books it for the exit. Nobody bothers to follow.

Sax pads forward, sniffs and picks at the Vyphen's remnants, then grabs the small fallen miner. With his tail, he boosts Engee so that she's standing again.

"Miners aren't supposed to be fired inside!" the bartender's squeaking from his hiding space, but it's the kind of half-warning that nobody pays attention to.

The rest of the bar doesn't even seem to care—after a moment making sure they're not the target, Sax hears all the conversations come back, the music start playing again, and life return to normal.

A horde of small robots squeeze out of some vents and start dissembling the Vyphen's body, carting its pieces off to some recycler that'll, no doubt, turn it into some sort of food or energy.

Can't waste anything in space.

Especially opportunities.

"Did you not see what I just did?" Agra-Red replies

when Sax offers up his defense of Engee for the ride. "I'm the one that took care of the problem. You're lucky I can handle my grotto snuff."

"I would have cut them apart."

"After that one had shot you with the miner? Cause I didn't see you doing it before. And they say Oratus are so frightening." Agra-Red turns back to the bar. "Get Nova to buy the good, then we'll talk."

An impossibly dense array of lines and circles stretches out against black nothing in front of me. I focus, and I'm falling as the lines rush around. They expand and zoom in further and further, twisting into different and more specific shapes until they lock, with the corner I'm standing in holding center place. Then, with a little push from my mind, a bright blue line traces from where we are to an enormous oval that dwarfs my little hideaway.

"Kaishi, we've got to move," Viera's voice shakes the Cache's map away, and I blink back to the buildings and the thrum of ships flying overhead.

Leaving the Cache is always a disorienting experience, like waking from a deep sleep. It takes a minute for my body to regain control of itself, and I realize that I'm cold. I shouldn't be—I'm still wearing my mask, and Vimelia doesn't seem like a cold planet—but chills run through my veins nonetheless.

I've felt like this before, in Damantum, back when I had

the high priest Jakkan's medallion around my neck. Back when everyone watched me, wondering who I was and why I had been so marked. No hiding then, and no hiding now.

"They're getting closer," Malo, leaning around the edge of the giant bin that we're crouched behind, says.

We scrambled from alcove to inset, ducking out of sight whenever someone started to notice us. Anyone here could work with the faction we'd just escaped, anyone could work for Nasiya. I have to keep checking the Cache to make sure we're staying on target. This bin—I don't actually know if it opens—is a giant rectangle jutting out from the side of a many-stories tall building with sides of sculpted, shining copper.

I suppose the reason it's back here, hidden from the street, is that the bin is a stark gray, mottled and marked only by the giant pipe coming into it from a port in the building's wall.

"Who's coming?" I ask.

"A pair of those slug creatures. They're wearing our enemy's colors." Malo states.

No worry, no concern, just straight fact.

Our enemies. I suppose that's what the Wem are now. Two major factions on this planet, according to Jel, and we've antagonized them both. I glance out the other way of the L, a way which ends in another short alley between the copper building and a neighboring, muddy brown tower.

"Then let's go," I say.

We form our line, with Viera in front, Malo in back and me in the middle. It's how we've been getting closer and closer to the spaceport, where the Cache is leading us. Assuming, of course, that we can even find a ship like the one that brought us here, and that we could find out how to fly it without Ignos in my head. A question we'll have to answer if we make it that far.

For now, having the hope is enough.

We go through the small alley, which curls to the right, back towards the main avenue. A place we try to spend as little time as possible. There's not that many people in the streets—most are in the tubes or the ships flying above, but there's so many windows and so much movement it's impossible to know when someone's noticed us. And, as the only humans on the planet, we're pretty noticeable.

"Did you find it?" Viera says as we head towards the main road.

"I always do," I reply.

"Are we closer?"

"Every time."

We reach the end and Viera freezes at the edge of the buildings. She's holding our only miner, which looks small in both her hands, but I can tell by the way her muscles tense that she's seen something she doesn't like. Malo immediately flattens himself against the wall behind me, getting his feet in position to spring, ready to dive towards the creatures pursuing us.

"They're everywhere," Viera says. "They've got one of those big ships floating there in the middle of the street. Flaum leaving in groups."

We can't fight them. We can't outrun them. There's only one other option.

"We need a distraction," I say.

"I can sacrifice myself," Malo volunteers. "I head out there, catch their attention. You two can run."

"No," I reply. "Nobody's sacrificing themselves here."

There's movement back from where we came. The

sound carries on the slick stone ground. Slurping, squelching pops. Some language I don't know. But it gives me an idea nonetheless.

"How many?" I whisper to Malo and nod back the way we came.

"Only two, and inattentive," Malo says.

"Then there's our answer," I say. "Let's take them, and maybe we'll find something to use."

Nobody questions the plan. We retreat back down the ally, take a left and almost walk right into the two Whelk. One's a bright yellow, like Jel, and the other a putrid green. Neither is looking forward, both appear in some argument with one another. They turn just in time for Malo to smash his fist into the green one's face, for Viera, wielding the miner like a blunt object, to batter the yellow one. I, meanwhile, grab at the miners pasted to their skin. The weapons are partially inside the Whelks, as though sinking through their gelled exterior.

The Whelks take the hits, and actually begin to laugh. That's what I think the gurgling noises mean, anyway, given the wild expressions on their faces as Malo and Viera bring punches and kicks. Every hit shakes them, ripples through their the jelly skin without leaving a mark.

I dig my nails and press my hand into the yellow one's skin, get my index finger on the miner's trigger. The Whelk realizes what I'm doing, and its short arms reach for me, but Viera grabs the thing's gooey wrists and forces the attack wide.

I pull the trigger and the miner fires, most of it still inside the creature. Its bright red laser melts the Whelk, turning its slimy body into a sizzling wreck. It's not what I'm expecting and I stumble back, my hands still holding the trigger, and I keep it together enough to point the miner at the second Whelk. The red bolts keep going, burn through the green one and cascade against the side of the copper building, leaving charred, broken bits sprinkling to the ground. Malo and Viera grab the Whelks' miners once I stop firing mine, and we're armed.

Which is good, because we can hear the pounding feet, the yells of coming reinforcements.

I'm about to run towards the main street, a tactic that's likely going to get us killed, when that bin catches my eye. The giant pipe running into the top of it has to lead somewhere—the bin's too small to hold something for a pipe almost as wide as I am tall.

I take my miner and shoot at the bin's side. The bolts hit the bin's walls, which break apart like paper. The super-heated burns make a wide hole, and I find what I was hoping for.

Damantum had a rudimentary sewage system; a series of stone canals that wound below most of the buildings to the sea. Seems plausible here, in this improbably huge city, that they would need some way to move the waste from the host species. The Sevora, from what I've seen, like things clean. I haven't seen a speck of trash anywhere, nor any of the usual smells of living things.

I smell those now. Horrible scents, burning my nose and making me cough, but they mingle with hope. Because there's a way down through the straight pipe. A way out.

"That's not where I want to go," Viera warns. "And if we get stuck down there, they'll catch us anyway."

"They'll catch us for certain if we stay up here," I say.

Malo brushes by me before I can head into the pipe, which is dark and wide, though there appears to be enough muck clinging to the walls that it won't be a difficult climb.

Even in our masks, the filth clings to our clothes, our hands and feet. There's little light, and the rays sneaking in through the hole above dim and vanish quickly. But we keep moving, because what other choice is there?

The pipe begins to curve, like a sloping J until it evens out going horizontal. Here the muck is deep enough that it comes up to my knees. We trudge along anyway.

"I haven't been this blind in a long time," Viera mutters. "Though I'm not sure I'd rather see what we're walking through."

"Does this remind you of the forest at night?" Malo asks me as we trudge.

"The forest is alive, it sings and cries," I say. "This, this is silent and dead."

Yet even as I say that, I know it's not true. Things shift in the muck. My skin feels the quiver, and I wonder if it's like back home. If there are strange insects burrowing deep, devouring what we leave behind. I blink my eyes, even though there's nothing for them to see, because such thoughts only distract me.

Far behind us, the noise of someone being brave enough to attempt a climb sounds. They're moving slow. Whoever's after us isn't all that thrilled at the path we've chosen.

Eventually the tube widens, until a much larger opening appears, and I see, courtesy of a few lines of low yellow lights casting their glows, that we've ventured into some kind of central chamber. Other tubes pour out, like ours, into this one, sending their sludge in slow spurting movements.

"One of the worst things I've ever seen," Viera says. "Here I thought we were in the land of greatness. Where miracles would be everywhere. And yet, I'm still surrounded by crap."

"This is the true nature of this world," Malo says.

"More importantly," I say. "We're alive. Now we just need to decide where to go."

We've made it to the edge of a large tube, one that descends too deep for me to see.

"Don't suggest that we climb down this big thing," Viera says, peering over the edge. "I can't see where it leads and I don't really want to."

"We've come this far. We'll keep going. Whatever it takes to get home," Malo replies.

"Do you have any emotion?" Viera fires back. "Do you think about whether you enjoy something or not? Whether you like the life you lead? Because I can't get a read out of you. You're just a statue that—"

"Viera, stop it," I interrupt. "Do you think here, of all places, is the time to have this conversation?"

Viera shrugs, but she does stop talking, which I count as a victory.

"I do agree with you though," I say. I join Viera at the edge and look down; it's a gulf, deep and dark. "I'd rather not make the jump."

No lights, except a small yellow trio around a single tube on the far side. One that, like ours, is gradually dispensing muck into its larger brethren.

"Do you think that's a sign? Do we go that way?" I point at the lights.

"If we follow those lights, the Sevora after us will take the obvious route too," Malo says. "But then, we don't really have another way to go, do we?"

"Not unless you want to take a dive down there." Viera nods towards the depths.

With our direction settled comes the hard part: how do we get over to the other side? There aren't ladders, handholds or anything else I could see that would serve to let us clamber way around and across. We'll have to find something, and that's when I notice Malo holding his miner.

"Sometimes," Malo says. "You have to make your own way."

He raises the miner, leans out over the edge, and begins to stitch red bolts into the sludge covered side of the central pipe. Every shot from the miner carves a small ledge into the pipe's metal side; charring off the sludge and burning a line. The warrior holds the beams long enough to create a foot hold, then shifts, eventually going through all the power in both of his miners. By the time the weapons sputter to nothing, we have a semicircles worth of black jagged metal and charred chunks of crud waiting to test our weight.

Viera goes to take the first step and I grab her arm, pull her back.

"I'm the lightest," I say. "You should let me go first. The ledges are most likely to support me."

"And what if they don't?" Malo says. "You'll fall. Maybe die."

"If I don't we all will. For once, let me take the risk," I reply.

They look at me like I'm being stupid, but they don't understand how annoying it is to be held back. To be protected all the time. Besides, there's a chance that I'll find something on the other side to help them get across. It makes sense for me to go first. It makes sense for me to risk myself for the group.

The first ledge, a lip of curled, black metal, sits half a meter beneath where we stand. With Malo holding my right arm, I step onto it. I rock my foot into the notch, testing its strength. When it doesn't break apart, I step with my right leg. Plant both feet. The ledge holds, for the moment.

"Let go," I say to Malo, and he hesitates. "Do it, Malo."

My friend releases my wrist, his finger slide apart from mine and I'm free. That sensation alone almost sends me off the ledge, which is barely big enough for the front of my feet. I flex forward so that I fall against the outer wall of the large pipe. My hands dig into the sticky sludge, give me some traction even at the cost of knowing what my fingers are digging into.

"The next one is slightly up," Viera calls to me, as if I didn't know.

I take a look at the next ledge, and then count the rest. Eighteen burned-out cliffs carved by Malo's miner along the outside of the central tube's wall. Eighteen careful jumps to make; keeping my feet planted, my weight shifted. Any missteps would send me falling down into some infinite black. And, knowing what we've been walking in, I'm not sure I'd want to survive should I slip.

"Just go slow," Viera says, again giving the obvious tip.

I reach with my left arm and place it against the wall above the next ledge. No handholds, just muck. But it's better than sheer metal. I bend my legs against the ledge. I make the short hop, but as I do so I feel the first ledge beneath me break away, those charred bits crumbling down to the bottom. And as I land on this one, it too starts to bend and snap.

I have to move.

I flash back to the jungle, racing through the trees, and I move in the same way I used to when I was a child. I bound quickly, planting and jumping, oftentimes only getting one foot on the black charred edges. I hear Malo and Viera yelling, at first, and then they fall silent as they see me leap from one to the next. As they see me survive.

Left foot shove, right foot catch, my hands pushing off and steadying in equal measure. I don't even count, my every focus on the next jump. And then I'm landing, before I realize it, in the haloed tube on the opposite side.

I splash through a pile of muck and catch myself, kneeling in it, but breathing hard and too tired to care. Every single one of Malo's blasted platforms is gone. Every single one disintegrated into the depths.

"I'm never doing that again," I call back across to them.

"I'm with you," Viera replies from the other end.

Our voices echo around the tube and for a moment I wonder if we're giving ourselves away. But there hasn't been a sound from back behind us for a long time. Whatever's after us either gave up, or assumed we went a different way.

Speaking of, I turn and look into where I made my way. It looks just like where we came from. No equipment, no clear way to get Malo and Viera across. Even though I have miners, we're not going to try the ledges again. So I turn back to them and say I'm going on alone.

There's immediate protest. Malo warns about my safety, Viera, about theirs. About being left with nowhere to go. To which I say, "We have to find some way for you to get over here. Unless you can fly, I don't see another option."

I think we all know that, so after some more grumbling, the pair of them calm down. Take up their positions on the tube and settle in. While I turn to face the dark, and start walking. This is the first time I've been alone, truly alone in so long. Nothing in my head, no friends, or protectors. All that's here in this foul-smelling waste is me and the muck.

The soup in the bottom of the pipe sucks at my feet with every step. Every breath makes me want to choke on the heavy smells clinging to my throat. Bangs and rumbles echo around me, and the only light I have comes from those small globes, little points of white casting small circles against the endless dark.

There's only one direction to go, so I trudge on. Think about Viera and Malo, trapped back on the edge. Any Sevora force finding them would have them trapped, and likely have them dead, or captured.

I surprise myself by laughing at the thought of Viera with a Sevora in her head. What sort of arguments she would get in, debates she'd have with the creature. Would she do the opposite of what it wanted just to spite the thing?

The sound of my own laughter rings loud through the tunnel, and at first I'm fascinated. I've never been somewhere with a true echo, and this carries and carries.

Until something different comes back.

It's a grizzled grind, a shuffling of something large and stiff shoving aside the slop against the metal sides of the tube. And it's coming towards me.

My instincts tell me to run, to hide, but there's no place to do either. So instead I wait, hands clenched and defiant. The first thing I notice is a new glow. One that shines brighter, with long lights splashing across the walls in front of me. It moves, growing closer until it rounds a bend ahead and I'm hit with a blinding force of white.

My eyes try to shut, but I'm not fast enough. I step back without thinking and slip in the liquid and fall, splashing in the slime as the thing draws closer. The white blots out everything, and it grows and grows and I raise my hands to shield my eyes but still tendrils of bright squeeze through my fingers and stab holes in my vision. I might be saying something but I don't know because the growling, roaring churn of the monster is so loud as to render my ears useless.

It stops.

There's no rumble anymore, no grinding. Just the gentle lap of the muck around me as it roils with the settle of the Beast. The lights dim and narrow into to a soft yellow, leaving iridescent halos in my vision, the same type I'd get for staring at Ignos for too long.

"What are you supposed to be?" The words have a leathery ring to them, like the splat of slick skin against itself, like instruments I once heard in the jungle, played by hitting sticks against covered, dried melon shells.

Yet it clearly says words and just as clearly says them in the same common language that all these creatures seem to use. My language.

"I don't know," I reply. "But I'm a human."

"Human? Haven't heard that name before. Admittedly, I haven't left these tunnels for more than a cycle now. Seems plausible the slugs above might have found one or two new species since then."

"Slugs above?" I try to pick myself up, but I'm still a little blinded, and as I rise my hand slips and I splash back into the mud.

"Here, little thing, let me help you. Stay still."

I'm alone, stuck in the slop, half-blind and terrified of the thing in front of me, but with no options, I do as the voice says. I stay still. There's a metallic whine and I feel, courtesy of dripping drops from above, something slide over my head, reaching behind me to settle into the soup. The noise begins again after a moment's pause and I feel first the liquid and then something hard press against my back and push me forward so that I'm sliding along the bottom of the tube. I yelp, ask what's happening but all I get is a soft laugh, a kind of willowy chortle.

"It won't hurt you. Just settle in."

My legs slide across the floor of the tube, and in a moment I'm underneath the front lights. The goop slides away as I'm shoved up a small ramp. The metal piece pushing me slams into place and I realize I'm not in the tube anymore. At least, not directly. Dim red lights spark up, and I know I'm in the belly of the monster.

All around me are scattered piles of junk. Or at least that's what I think they are, seeing as I'm not sure what any of it is. There's tangled ends of netting and string. Broken pipes and things that look like they may have been miners once in some distant existence but have now become rusted relics. While my first thought is that this place is immense, I find, as my eyes adjust, that it's rather small. Half as tall as the tube. Maybe four meters wide.

A swishing slither from above tells me I'm not alone.

"I'm coming down," the voice says, and, like on *Cobalt*, it's coming from speakers around me.

Something in the top opens, and a square of light—the same yellow that the rumbling monster shines from its lamps—projects on the floor and a moment later a creature plops down.

It's a strange thing, almost like a water droplet trying to hold its shape. A milky white skin, and two long stalks, that, towards their tops, form large dual-pupiled eyes. The creature, though, is tiny. Maybe half as tall as I am. It stands, if you want to call it that, in the small space without a problem.

Then it moves towards me by shuffling its skin around and around. Like a jungle snake from back home, though this looks nothing like anything I've seen on Earth.

"Never eyed one like me before?" The creature says, and I confirm that it's the skin rippling together that's making the noises, waves crashing along its creamy surface.

"No," I say. "What are you?"

"Oh, well, I'm an Ooblot. You know, the things that usually travel in threes?"

I shake my head.

"Well, I suppose I don't know you. Seems reasonable you might not know me. But then, I have to ask, what are you doing down here?"

I tell the Ooblot my story. Spill it out because the Ooblot seems content to listen, and right now I'm desperate for a friend. Desperate to find some way to rescue Viera and Malo. This Ooblot might be my answer.

"Good thing you're not still hosted," The Ooblot says when I'm done. "The Beast would have picked that up, you know. These lights glow red for a reason. A specific frequency, makes a host eye's twitch. The Sevora can't stand it."

"And if I'd been hosted? What would you have done?"

"The Beast isn't just a junker. It's a burner too. I leave that latch closed, flip the switch, and then you fry."

"Then I'm glad I'm not hosted."

"Aren't we all. Then again, Clarity's Dawn wouldn't exist if we hadn't had our time with the slugs. Have to know your enemy before you can fight it, right?"

The name rings a bell. Ignos had warned me against it. But the other thing, the feathered, cloaked creature that had saved us from the first prison here had claimed to be part of Clarity's Dawn. So maybe they weren't all bad.

Also, the Ooblot claimed not to be hosted. That, right now, would have to be enough.

"I need to help my friends. They're stuck on the other side of that big cylinder behind us," I say as the Ooblot's many eyes look over its junk trove. "Can you get them across?"

"Get them over the main channel? With this thing? How far can you jump?"

I shrug.

"Guess we'll find out."

The Ooblot rolls away from me, back underneath the square light where it dropped, and says, "Follow me right on up and we'll get to finding your friends."

The Ooblot quivers and then its entire body mass squelches down, expanding into a puddle with the two eye stalks, and then it *pulls* up and launches through the hole.

"Come on now, you can climb up here." The Ooblot's cheerful voice echoes from the upper level.

I blink once or twice, confirm that what I just saw is not some sort of illusion, then take some tentative steps. It's nice walking on metal again rather than the thick muck. I do notice, though, that what I thought was rust on the pieces of junk around me is instead dried dirt, the same mud from the tube. Seems like this Beast is meant to gather whatever the Ooblot happens to find down here.

"Do you have a name?" I call as I move towards the hole.

I stare up, again shielding my eyes against the bright light, and a pair of curious stalks appear, looking back at me.

"T'Oli," the Ooblot replies. "That's what you can call me."

"I'm Kaishi."

"What a cool name. Much better than mine. But then, we Ooblots aren't exactly known for creativity. If you want processes, though, we are your species."

The eye stalks vanish; T'Oli's waiting for me to come up there. I stand tall, reach up with my arms, and I barely get over the lip into the upper level with the tips of my fingers, one hand on the left and right sides of the square opening. There's no way I'll be able to pull myself up with my fingertips. I'm about to say so when I feel a soft, warm glove surround the fingers of my left hand. The glove suddenly hardens, locking my left hand in place.

I yelp, and immediately T'Oli comes blubbering back, its eye stalks showing again.

"Don't worry, that's just me. We Ooblots have what we like to call a certain finesse. An ability, we say. We can harden ourselves—as stiff as metal if we have to."

"You've trapped my hand?"

"It's hardly a trap if I'm willing to let you free whenever you ask. I thought having the grip might make it easier for you to get yourself up here."

I try, and while my left arm lifts me slightly, my right hand slips off the lip. "I don't think that works."

"Swing your right hand over here then," T'Oli says.

"Can you let go for a minute? I need to shift."

The seal around my hand softens and I slip free without an ounce of stickiness. I take a second to stare at my left hand, but it looks normal. No cuts or tears, no blotches or change in color. Looks like whatever the Ooblot's doing, it's not hurting me.

So I put both my hands on the left side of the opening, a little apart. Like climbing a tree. This time, T'Oli covers both of them and locks me in. I still don't have a great grip, but I'm able to pull myself up, high enough for my head get over the lip. But it's not enough—with my hands stuck and T'Oli in the way, I can't lean forward. My muscles are burning and in a second they're going to give out.

Before I can ask for help, T'Oli rolls forward, its upper body sliding over the hardened lower half. It rolls into my face and I close my eyes. I feel T'Oli transition to rock, the whole of it clinging to my shoulders, face and hair, and then the Ooblot starts to pull.

I wind up going up, then over the edge, facing down and resting on T'Oli's body the whole way. Until my entire chest is clear of the hole, and then T'Oli liquifies itself and slides out from under me, leaving me gasping for air against the hard floor.

"What was that?" I said after a take a few cautionary breaths.

"An Ooblot pivot," T'Oli states. "Turn myself into a lever and pull. Really not all that special. Do it all the time."

"Sure..." My voice trails away as I look around.

Where we are, on the second floor of the Beast, looks like the shuttle we took away from *Cobalt*. There are a few things that the Oratus called terminals; screens blinking with various diagrams and bars and numbers. Data that I'm sure I could understand if I had time to study it.

My eyes, though, are drawn to other things. For one, what's playing on the ceiling above me. Now that we're both out, a metal grate slides over the hole to the lower level and, as it does so, the light shining down dims and lines illuminate all across the ceiling; neon blues and purples, sketching out what's obviously a map. The dim light pulses gently now in the same red glow as the ones below.

"The map's my own design," T'Oli quivers. "Put her together based on what I've seen done in some of those paintings they have around here. You've seen them, right? The ones with the shifting walls? This one tracks our position, shows it on the ceiling. True, I can pull up there in the screen, but that's no fun."

"I thought Ooblots weren't creative?"

"Get stuck in this thing long enough and anyone will get the urge to do something different."

I can't argue with that. Even though I've only been here a few minutes, the cramped ceilings and close walls are making me nervous. I'm a creature of free air—jungle forest or hillside plains. *Cobalt*, the shuttle, and all the narrow corridors on Vimelia do more to make me homesick than anything else.

"So where are we?"

"See that light? That's us. The lines are the tube system around here, and if you watch while we move, they'll change."

The mention of movement makes me remember that Vieira and Malo have been on the edge of that cylinder for a while now. They might be in trouble even as we're standing here. T'Oli catches the panic on my face and, even as I start asking about my friends, slides over to the terminals and presses itself against the wall. All of the Ooblot sluices into cracks and crevices, hardens against levers and buttons that I don't even notice are there until T'Oli is grasping all of them.

"How?" I whisper.

"This is designed only for Ooblot. No Sevora Flaum can drive this thing, can hit everything at once. It'd take an army of the critters and this place isn't big enough for'em. Best way to ensure nobody steals it," T'Oli says.

"There are thieves down here?"

The thing's motor starts up and its metallic rumbling begins and then we're rocking forward.

"Some," T'Oli says. "Where Clarity's Dawn is those of us who escaped our hosts and want to do something about it, there's plenty who don't care; the injured, the ones no Sevora wants to keep? They get discarded. The worst, though, are the ones that want their masters back. That try to hurt us to prove they're still worth keeping."

"What do they eat and drink down here?"

"All depends on your standards," T'Oli replies. "The lower those get, the more options you have."

With most of its body immersed in the controls, the only part of T'Oli that's talking to me is two eye stalks and a small oval of cream smashed against the central terminal. When T'Oli quivers, the voice it produces now is a much higher pitch than before.

I step up beside T'Oli, look out towards the tube. The Beast's bright lights are shining and guiding us. Now that I can actually see it, the tube's insides are steely gray and caked with what must've been seasons and seasons of muck and grime. Who knows when it's last been cleaned, or what disgusting things I'd been walking through.

I try to think of something else.

The Beast moves quick and before long were back at the vast central cylinder. And there, across it, I see Malo standing watch while Vieira, curled as far up as she could to get out of the dirt, seemingly sleeps.

"Can you hear me?" I say.

A moment later a light blinks green on one of the terminals.

"Now they can," T'Oli chirps.

"Don't worry," I say, unsure of how to announce the fact that this giant machine monstrosity is not, in fact, an enemy. "It's me, Kaishi."

I can tell from the confused looks – Viera startles and almost falls into the muck – that they don't understand. So I try again.

"I'm inside this thing, it's like a moving building. Like the ships we were inside before."

"Are you okay?" Malo shouts back.

"Fine, and I found a friend. We're going to help you get over."

"Is it another Sevora?" Viera asks.

"No such thing, and I'll thank you not to call me that." T'Oli burbles.

There's a large *chunk* and the Beast emits the same metal whine it did when it pulled me in. Through the glass I see the metal grate that must've pushed me not long ago extending into the tube. It's wide and flat, and slotted with holes. Like the nets we use back home—big enough to catch what T'Oli wants without bringing the slime along.

The grate extends out meter after meter and then stops. There's another quick ding and the grate rotates until it becomes flat.

"We use this as a lift to from time to time," T'Oli explains. "The thing is, Clarity's Dawn doesn't have a whole lot of machines, so we get the most out of what we have."

"It's too far," I say.

There's a good three meters from the edge of the grate to where Viera and Malo stand.

"I did say you'd have to jump," T'Oli replies.

"It can't go any farther!" I yell to Malo and Viera. "Do you think you can jump it?"

"No!" Viera yells back.

Malo, though, squats and stares. Straightens. "I think—"

There's a bright flash from behind them. Red, and it echoes along the tube until the light floods the main central chamber, then keeps on going past us. Rolling behind the light is a rumbling noise that sounds like thunder.

"Echo bomb," T'Oli says. "We gotta move. That light means the Sevora are bouncing sounds around here, trying to gauge what it hits. Guess you three are really valuable."

"Hurry!" I shout.

Malo says something to Viera that I can't hear. I lean forward and watch as Viera argues, sighs and shrugs. There's a bang as a second cascade of red comes through and both Malo and Viera turn their heads to look back on the tube. Viera's hands again grab at her waist for miners that aren't there.

"Just hold it steady," Malo yells our way.

Malo backs up, Viera kneels down, and, shaking her head, leans forward, gets her knees in the muck and presses her hands onto the hard tube floor at the very edge.

Malo runs. He clomps at first up towards the side of the tube, building up speed, then swings back to the middle— kicking up sprays of slop—and plants his left foot on Viera's back. Squats and leaps, flying forward towards the metal grate.

I catch the moment: one sprawling second of Malo, Charre warrior, floating through the air with hands windmilling, legs splaying as he flies towards the metal grate. My breath catches in my throat and comes out in a rush when Malo clangs against the edge and, his fingers gripping into the holes, pulls himself up. Malo lays there for a second before springing back to his feet.

"Your turn Viera," Malo says.

But she doesn't have the boost. There's no way.

"What are you doing?" I say.

"Being stupid," Viera calls back.

Now the light behind them is white. The same sort of running light that the Beast has. They're out of time.

Viera takes the steps, running hard, running fast, plants her foot at the edge of the tube, and it slips. She's jumping, but it's not far enough. Her hand stretches out and Malo slides to the edge of the grate and leans.

And catches Viera's wrist.

Malo's dangling there, holding on with his left hand. His feet—every toe slipped through the holes and holding—brace while his right hand reaches, scrabbles to pull Viera up.

Then the Sevora arrive.

I f the Junkyard's Rest looks every bit the workmanlike bar, Nova fails in its attempt to be a restaurant of class.

Sax's experience with these places is limited—Vincere craft aren't known for their upscale dining options—but he doesn't have to look hard to see the many cracks in this operation.

Nova is nestled among a residential spoke, surrounded by the slim apartments every space station provides. Sax guesses, from the sizes and number of doorways, that this spoke is the lesser of the two *Scrapper Station* offers.

That opinion is seconded by the lighting, which strives for the bright blue of a healthy planet but settles for a hazy yellowed version instead, as if someone had released a cloud of mustard in the sky.

Nova announces itself by a spinning, bursting globe over its front doorway, a design that casts alternating white and sapphire-blue balls to the outer edges of its spiral.

The light show continues inside, where tables, chairs,

food pits and other layouts meant for specific species dazzle Sax's eyes with their constant effects.

How could anything survive in here without going insane?

"Interested in grabbing a seat?" a young Flaum, looking entirely bored with everything, asks him as Sax walks into the place.

"Looking for the owner," Sax replies.

"She's in back," the Flaum says. "But if you're going in, you'll want one of these."

The Flaum points to a basket of what look like rubberized bandannas.

"Those are?"

"Easier if you just try one on," the Flaum, who's showing no signs of fear at the sight of Sax's clawed, scarred, monstrous self, tosses one of the black things at him.

Sax catches it with a claw. Stares at it. It looks just like a strip of clothing.

"You've got eyes, right?" the Flaum says. "Put it over them."

"Is this a trick?"

"Nah. It's part of the show. Twillo bought a whole container of these on a whim, which is why the restaurant looks so bad."

Sax hesitates, then figures that it's unlikely the restaurant would have some method of incapacitating an Oratus right at its entrance, waiting for him.

So he slips the bandanna on. The rubber seems to come alive as it slides onto his head, growing to match his dimensions and settling over his eyes.

Which changes everything.

Now the glaring lights aren't blinding, they're mesmerizing. They don't simply spin on the backs of tables and chairs, but seem to lift off and glide through the space, and when Sax takes a step, it's like he's walking through a world of stars.

"Pretty neat, right?" the Flaum says. "Bet this place would be doing better if Twillo could get people to put these on first."

"How?" is the only thing Sax can think to ask.

Beyond the floating stars, Sax can see streaking comets, the occasional bursts of light too—as if one of the stars happens to go supernova.

"Different spectrums, projections and mirrors, I think," the Flaum says. "Don't really know, but it's cool." She hesitates while Sax takes another long look around the space. "You, uh, still want to go find Twillo?"

Sax gives an absent nod. He might be a murderous weapon hellbent on getting off this station, but he'll take a moment to appreciate something beautiful.

Nova's back is nothing like its front—trading enchantment and effects for the usual dirty gray drudgery of a space station kitchen. Species—mainly Flaum—run dishware and ovens, burning the solar energy the station gets from refracting mirrors on its hull. They spare Sax glances, and he gets some satisfaction from their twitches, but the staff otherwise holds to their duties with remarkable determination. He'll have to tell this to Twillo.

Or at least, that's his plan until he actually sees her, in a small office hiding beyond the kitchen.

"You've got a guest, Twillo," the Flaum announces, then vanishes.

Twillo, though, responds more like what Sax would expect. As soon as the door shunts open, as soon as Twillo catches sight of Sax, of what Sax is, she bursts upward, cups her limbs into her and launches towards the far corner, tiny wings flapping furiously. When she makes the corner, her four limbs spring back out, their sticky fingers spreading like webs against the corner's sides and locking her in place.

"Been a long time since I've seen a Quib," Sax hisses, then steps into the office.

He looks up at Twillo, whose round ball of body is changing colors rapidly, trying, no doubt, to find the perfect shade of old metal gray to blend in.

"I can see you," Sax continues, then reaches up with his right foreclaw, almost touching Twillo, who presses herself back. "And I could touch you, if I wanted to."

The words have a deflating effect on Twillo, who stops her fluttering and shifts to a dull yellow color. As they slow down, her wings—solid, thin strips of flesh—settle against her sides like a layered blanket.

"I'm sorry," is the first thing Twillo says, her voice high-pitched and vibrating, coming from the small proboscis extending between her four tiny eyes. "The last time I saw an Oratus, they were tearing apart my home."

"It wasn't yours any longer." The Quib's home planet had been overrun by Sevora, and not all that long ago in galactic timescales.

Only a cycle had passed since the Oratus had cleansed every last life from that planet. That the Quib still existed at all was due to the ones that had been offworld at the time, and the ones the Amigga had grown afterward.

"You can't lose your home," Twillo replies. "I take it with me, wherever I go."

"Lovely," Sax says. "But I'm not hear to talk about your home. There's a Vyphen, Plake, who's trying to sell you some food. I want you to buy it."

Twillo ruffles her wings. Keeps her limbs tight. "Why should I care what you think?"

"Because this claw can carve you into pieces before anyone could, even if they would, help?"

Twillo's four little eyes dart to Sax's upraised foreclaw.

"What does that matter? I have a restaurant on *Scrapper Station*, one of the worst places in the galaxy. Killing me would be doing me a favor."

"And the people that work for you? What would they do?"

"An Oratus appealing to compassion?" Twillo's laugh sounds like a monotone buzz.

"Then what can I appeal to? Why won't you buy the food?"

"Because I can't!" Twillo shoots back. "The Ooblots control this station, and they determine who I can buy from."

"They don't like Plake?"

"I don't know!" Twillo says. "They just told me I couldn't get anything from her, no matter how good it looks. Have you seen the nutrients she has? I think they were meant for an Amigga!"

Sax settles back against the door. Closes his eyes for a moment. He's well past his sleeping point for this shift, which means he'll be tired while Bas is off. And it doesn't look like he'll have an answer for her yet.

"There's nothing you can give me?" Sax says, and he hates the resignation in his voice.

"You want to go to the Ooblots, you'd better have something to offer," Twillo replies. "They don't give away anything for free. Anything."

Sax flexes his claws again. Ooblots are hard to kill, though. They have a nasty habit of turning to rocks as soon as they're threatened.

"I like your decorations," Sax hisses, then turns and leaves before Twillo can respond.

With his time almost up, Sax heads back to the casino, already knowing he'll need plenty of stimulant to get him through this shift.

Twillo's remarks, though, give him a plan. Next time he's off—after some necessary sleep—he'll march to wherever those Ooblots running the station have set themselves and figure out some way of getting them to buy Plake's food.

Sax hisses at the thought, causing a few species wandering past him to look over in alarm. There's too many webs here, too many connections. It should be straightforward—Sax provides a service, namely, not wiping Plake from the galaxy, and in return she gets to keep her life and receives a little payoff from either the Vincere or Evva, whomever they happen to find first.

Sax turns this over in his head until he reaches the casino, at which point all thoughts of Plake, her ship, or the Ooblots vanish.

The casino itself is packed. Species jam themselves into every cranny, some climbing on others, just trying to get a look towards the middle. Even so, Sax doesn't have much trouble pushing his way through—nobody wants to annoy something with this many claws.

Around the central bar, punctuated by plenty of broken bottles and sprays of powder, stand Bas facing off with D'Arscale and two of its Luto guards. Around them, scattered throughout the casino, are the ruins of a fight—broken furniture, sprays of blood and other things. The telltale burns of miners.

What Sax notices first, though, what narrows his eyes into a red-flint haze, is that Bas is bleeding. She's cut and beat up, and while her claws are still ready, held wide and sharp, it's clear she's tired, wary.

"Here he comes, to add to this disaster," D'Arscale announces as Sax pushes his way through. "Maybe you can get your pair to see reason."

"They attacked me first," Bas replies.

"Even so, slaughter will not be tolerated in my business," D'Arscale says, then the Ooblot swivels an eye stalk to take in the crowd. "Though perhaps this will serve as a lesson to everyone that my staff is not to be toyed with."

"This was an ambush," Bas hisses, her claws clenching. "They wanted me dead."

"Welcome to *Scrapper Station*—everyone's wanted dead by someone here," D'Arscale replies. "But we have to cling to the semblance of civilization anyway."

"Where are they?" Sax interrupts.

"Oh, your pair took care of them well enough. This station's down five residents today, all thanks to her."

Sax strides over next to Bas, they touch their noses for a second. He smells no fear on her, only exhaustion, and Sax takes a deep breath through his vents.

Calm.

"They want to imprison me for defending myself," Bas whispers. "Even though they came at me with knives, attacked my back, I'm the one who pays for it."

"I believe they paid for it well enough," D'Arscale gestures at several spatters of drying blood. "And you can bet repairing all this damage will cost me plenty too. I thought having Oratus would help me, would keep me safe, but you both attract more trouble than you're worth."

Imprisonment on *Scrapper Station* would lead to one of two things: being sold off the station for a profit to whomever wanted them, or being jettisoned out an airlock if a buyer couldn't be found.

Neither is an appealing option.

D'Arscale waits, with his Luto guards, while the murmuring crowd looks on.

The Oratus make their decision with a tap of their tails on each other.

To call what happens next a fight would be an insult to the word—Sax and Bas leap, together, at the Luto guards and before either can pull a weapon, both Oratus have their tails wrapped tight around the Luto heads, leaving no illusions about what would happen should their victims struggle. Luto might be rock, but smash them against each other and they'll break apart easy enough.

Eight claws and two slicing mouths turn towards D'Arscale, who reacts in the same way all Ooblot cowards do; by turning itself to near-solid stone.

"That will not save you," Sax hisses.

It would buy D'Arscale a bit of time—as long as it takes Sax to throw his Luto away, pick up the Ooblot with his tail and start smashing it against the ground.

"Then let's negotiate," D'Arscale replies, the flapping words coming from the tiny section of flesh it's left open for this purpose.

The Ooblot's voice is small, meek and pathetic.

"You threatened us," Bas replies. "Under Chorus rule, such an act gives us the right to eliminate you at our discretion."

"Though not discretely," Sax hisses.

"I get it, I get it," D'Arscale patters. "But what will that get you? More guards will be here soon, and will you fight the entire station? Even you both could not manage that, and if you could without dying, what would you get?"

"Freedom." Sax and Bas rasp the word together.

"Yes, until your own army comes to eliminate you. Until someone else here stabs you in the back, slices your scales while you sleep. Poisons your next meal. Nobody wants an Oratus in charge."

"Then what is your offer?" Bas says.

"I'll let you go. Let you see my sisters, who can help you get what you really want."

There's a moment where Sax considers whether eliminating this Ooblot would really hurt their negotiations with its sisters, but the sheer helplessness of the creature is killing Sax's bloodthirsty drive.

"How do we know you'll keep your word?" Sax says.

"You've got an awful lot of witnesses."

Sax glances back at the crowd, and several dozen pairs of eyes stare back at him. To make sure they get the point, Sax gestures one claw towards them, edges out.

"You'll back us?" Sax asks.

His question is answered by a parade of nods.

"Then we have a deal," Bas says.

With the prospect of violence gone, the crowd dissipates fast, with some even returning to the tables and gambling machines, while D'Arscale's mix of robots and staff cleans up the mess.

"I'll take you myself," D'Arscale announces, thawing itself.

Sax and Bas release the Lutos, who stumble back, massage their necks and smooth their fur.

"You two useless mooks can stay here," D'Arscale says to them before rotating its eyestalks towards the Oratus. "Follow me."

The Ooblot rolls itself out of the casino, Sax and Bas following. If one Oratus drew attention wandering the station, two of them with one of the Ooblots catches every stare in the place.

"We're celebrities," Bas jokes as they walk. "I've always wanted to be a star."

"How bad are you hurt?" Sax asks.

"I'll get through this," Bas hisses. "It'll take some time to get my perfect pink back, though."

"I don't care about that."

"Sometimes I wish you did," but Bas laughs, then, when D'Arscale sends a stalk to look, switches to a hard glare.

Sax, meanwhile, blinks. Appearance? Why should he care about that? Bas is a glorious killer who can wield words as well as her claws. The color or condition of her scales means so little...

Sax is still turning the remark over when they reach another bank of lifts in the middle of the Nexus. Only it's not multiple, just one large platform, with only one apparent option.

D'Arscale approaches the large glass gates, and they remain closed as it nears. Then, abruptly, another face appears, one that Sax recognizes:

The blue-gold Vyphen from the Junkyard's Rest.

"What did the sisters do to deserve the punishment of your visit, D'Arscale?" the Vyphen warbles.

Sax waits for recognition, but the reptilian shows none. It's a mystery that's solved a second later when Sax notices a camera's black nub above the door. The two Oratus are standing well back from D'Arscale—at the Ooblot's suggestion.

Now Sax knows why.

"Eneks, let me up. I don't need a reason to see my sisters," D'Arscale replies.

"But you have one."

The doors don't move.

"Are you really pushing me on this?" D'Arscale's injecting plenty of ire into its slapping speech.

"Yes." Eneks, for his part, doesn't seem to care.

"This would never happen on a Vincere ship," Bas whispers to Sax.

"Because we don't have any Ooblots to deal with," Sax replies, and Bas hisses a quiet laugh.

"It's about security. I need more for my casino, and for the station in general. Too many fights, too much killing. It's hurting business," D'Arscale says the whole thing in a rush.

Eneks finally changes his distant skepticism, though, and manages a large sigh. "That, D'Arscale, might be the first thing you've ever said that I agree with. If that's what you're coming up to argue, I'll let you through."

A moment later, the glass doors slide apart and D'Arscale slithers through. As soon as the projection disappears, D'Arscale waves at the Oratus and they dash forward, diving through just as the glass doors slam shut behind them.

"What happens when we get up there and they see two Oratus?" Bas asks.

"I'm sure you'll be able to solve any problems." D'Arscale answers.

"Any solution's going to start with you." Sax settles into a crouch as the elevator begins to move, ready to spring as soon as the doors open.

Malo's still holding Viera by the wrist when the grate begins to move back towards us. It pulls along a pair of long metal bars that serve as runners and retract along with the grate. Malo looks like he's about to fall, and my white-knuckle grip on the terminals isn't helping him.

I turn around and dash back to the hole in the floor and ask T'Oli to open it. The Ooblot does so, the barrier shunting aside as it issues some command from the Beast's terminals. I slip down to the red-lit lower level, and look out as the grate comes closer. Malo's slid his shoulders forward, brought his right arm to double-grip Viera's wrist. Doesn't look like he has the leverage to pull her up, though.

Across the tube, a squad of armored Flaum crashes into view, their fur covered in patchwork armor and their hands holding miners. The first one points towards my friends, and the Flaum aim their weapons.

Malo and Viera are easy targets.

I have to change that.

I grab one of the pieces of junk, and throw it. It's heavier than it looks, but it flies over Malo and Viera as the grate pulls closer. The piece of scrap doesn't make it across the tube—falling through the air and into the pit. But what the junk does do, for one instant, is stop the charging Flaum. They watch the rusty miner to make sure it's not a risk. It buys Malo and Viera a moment.

"T'Oli, turn the grate!" I shout.

The Ooblot follows the order immediately, turning the flat platform up so it acts like a shield. A shield that exposes Viera directly to any fire.

"Now reverse," I continue. "Go backwards!"

The Beast rumbles to life and sprays muck everywhere as its treads take the machine back through the tube. With the grate retracting, and the Beast retreating, Malo's over the muck. He drops, landing in the goop with a splash. Viera follows a second later.

The Flaum, meanwhile, seem to be setting up on the other side of the large tube. Why aren't they shooting? Why aren't the Sevora gunning us down?

Oh that's right. They want us alive.

Malo and Viera run around the receding grate, dive into the Beast and join me. I barely have time to say hello before T'Oli's voice bursts over the speakers. "Looks like they brought bridging cables with them. We're in trouble."

"Can't you outrun them?" I ask.

"This thing isn't meant for racing," T'Oli replies.

"How slow is it?" Viera whispers to me. "They're all on foot."

"I didn't think it was *that* slow."

The three of us scramble up through the gate back to the second level, where we see why T'Oli's not confident in our escape: the Flaum brought more with them than just miners. They've launched a pair of thick ropes across the central tube, and each rope is deploying small fibers that stretch across the gap between the two cables, making a bridge.

But the real surprise comes when the Flaum start to run. They don't move like anything I've ever seen; each one twitches their feet and they lift half a meter off the ground. When they pump their legs, the Flaum burst forward, free of the muck.

"You've never seen mag boots before? These guys can move. No friction, all speed," T'Oli's burbling sounds awfully casual, considering the wave of death coming for us.

"How do we fight back?" Malo asks.

"We don't," T'Oli replies.

The Beast shudders to a stop and I'm about ask what T'Oli's doing when it starts up again, only this time going forward. Back towards the central tube, back towards the Flaum.

Seeing the Beast come at them, the Flaum open up. Bright flashes of red and blue as miners unleash destructive energy against the front of the Beast. The bolts splash against bottom of the machine, and I can see little parts of the terminal start to shift yellow and red.

"How much can this thing take?" Viera says. "Because you're not really avoiding anything."

"She's a strong one. She'll take a hit or three," T'Oli says.

As we approach the central tube, the Flaum begin to back up and spread out, some retreating onto the bridge and others using those boots to push themselves up the sides of the tube around us. Their miners continue to unleash molten energy into the Beast, and I'm noticing new grinding sounds coming from its engine, but the Beast keeps on churning.

Right onto the cables.

"We're going to fall in, you moron!" Viera yells.

"That's the point." T'Oli's casual dismissal is the only thing keeping me from full-out panic—if the Ooblot, self-professed member of an organization the Sevora hate, isn't worried, then why should I be?

And then the Beast's engine sputters to a halt.

We're most of the way onto the bridge cables, hanging out over the edge of the abyss. Yet the Flaum's ropes are holding, and we aren't falling.

"That's not good," T'Oli says as the engine whines down to nothing.

The Flaum notice too and hold their fire, start to ease in back across the bridge. I can only imagine the ones on the sides are looking for ways in.

"So what now? Surrender?" Malo says.

"We can't," I say. "I'd rather die than go back to the Sevora again. You think they'd give us any more chances to get away?"

"I need you all to run, when I say so, and push against the right side." T'Oli's command catches us.

"Run?" Viera's saying. "Clearly you've got the wrong idea about how big this place is."

"Do it! Now!"

It's the loudest I've heard T'Oli yell, its skin hammering out the words, and we jump to follow. All three of us rush to the blank metal wall on the right side of the Beast and push. At that same moment, there's a bang from the back of the Beast that shunts the machine forward a meter or so. Our weight, plus the burst, sends the Beast teetering to the side of the cables.

I see the world turn sideways out the front glass, the Flaum's mouths drop open, and then we're falling.

My stomach shoots up as my nerves freeze and my mouth opens into a scream. The lights outside vanish as we plummet, dropping us into darkness.

We land. At least, that's what T'Oli says. I'm battered, bruised and bloodied, having slammed against the floor and walls as we bounced off of the main tube on our way down. But in the end, we plunge deep into a huge pool of soupy liquid. The Beast itself doesn't float, and its crumpled body is slowly sinking down.

Muck leaks through the sides of the machine. Seeps onto terminals, drips from the ceiling, and even sprays Viera from a corner, coating her in brown awfulness.

"If we keep the swamp out for a bit," T'Oli says. "We'll be all right."

"We'll be all right?" Viera says, backing away from the sprays. "The fall didn't kill us, so now we're going to drown instead?"

"You asked for an escape. That's what I gave you," T'Oli replies. "Might be bumpy, but you're alive."

Malo lurches to his feet and catches my eye. We both move to a couple of leaks and press our hands, grab whatever's loose and push it against the creeping liquid. Trying to keep the Beast sealed for as long as we can.

"What happens now?" I ask T'Oli we descend further and further into the dark.

"Wait and see. We either get lucky and someone's paying attention, or we don't, in which case it's been a real pleasure meeting all of you."

I'm sure my eyes are as wide as Viera's, who finally notices what Malo and I are doing and joins in our efforts to keep the sludge from completely filling the Beast.

"At least we'll die free," Malo says.

"I was hoping we wouldn't die at all," Viera replies. "Guess I'm the optimist here."

"Ignos takes everyone eventually," Malo adds. "Now might be our time."

"Would you all stop being so glum?" T'Oli interjects. "The only reason I drove off those cables is because it seems like the Sevora really want you. And if they want you, then Clarity's Dawn could probably use you too. So shut up, and keep that muck from making my poor junker too dirty."

T'Oli's words keep us quiet for a minute, until I point out an orange glow from beneath us. It rises up, past the Beast's splintering windshield and I see it's a circle, wide enough to be the entrance to another tube. As we pass, the orange lights flare and the door—a sequence of eight curling plates—slides open. The muck's too thick to see what's on the other side, though.

"Hold on to something," T'Oli advises.

There's a sudden burst of pressure and all of us are thrown forward into what's left of the windshield, towards the suddenly open tube. I don't see it, but I can hear the door slide shut as the Beast passes through. What I do feel, what I do see, is the Beast slamming to the floor of a square room as the liquid sludge drains away through metal grates.

Hurting all over, I pick myself up. Look out at the deep red lights glowing in here, just as they did in the Beast's lower level. T'Oli said those lights give away if someone's hosted. Guess this would be the way to see if whomever owns this room had trapped anything they didn't want.

"This isn't exactly the front entrance, but we're walking into the only place on Vimelia we are allowed to be free," T'Oli says. "And please, please tell me that you're worth it. Because my baby's going to take a long time to run again. I don't think you appreciate the sheer horror of cleaning all the muck out of this thing's gears and grinders."

T'Oli's barely finished speaking, and I've barely finished figuring out whether any of my broken bones are broken – thankfully none – when a wide door at the far end slides open. It's big enough to admit something like the Beast, and it's lit with soft yellow lights. Another crew armed with miners comes out, only instead of the Sevora's endless Flaum squads, this is a motley mix up of species. Some I've seen, some I haven't.

"You get yourselves down and out of here. Sure they'll be wanting to talk to you." T'Oli punctuates its sentence by opening the grate again.

"Do you trust it?" Malo asks me before we move anywhere.

"I don't think we have a choice."

"At least this thing hasn't tried to kill us yet, or enslave us," Viera adds. "Though, somehow, I'm still hurting all over."

"I'd tell you to get use to it, but I bet you already are," I say.

"The day your warriors scooped me up from the jungle," Viera nods to Malo. "Was the last good day of my life."

The three of us drop down and climb out of the Beast, with T'Oli turning the grate so that we can leave.

It feels wonderful to be walking outside of the muck for a change. My feet step freely, though nothing's changed about the smell. My mask is covered in gunk, Malo and Viera are much the same. We look more like swamp creatures than humans.

"So you found your way to us after all," says the watery voice of the lead figure, who I recognize as our would-be prison escape-artist even beneath his armor. "I wasn't sure you would ever get down. Jel isn't one to set people free. Not ones she can use."

"We had to work for that," Viera replies before I can. "May have left our mark on her home too."

At the creature's tone, the other five members of his team loosen their grip's on their miners. I notice they don't relax entirely, and they're still spread out, giving themselves plenty of space should things turn sour. Trust doesn't come easy on Vimelia.

"The name's Rackt," the creature says. "Welcome to Clarity's Dawn."

Rackt takes us out of the room, while the rest of his crew follows behind. T'Oli announces it's staying to clean the Beast, and there's a lot of resignation in its pattering voice. Given the mess we're wearing, I don't envy the Ooblot.

Beyond the initial room—something Rackt refers to as an airlock—we pass into another tube, albeit one generally free of muck. That doesn't mean it's clean, though: junk litters the corridor, and the yellow light that looked so inviting from the outside dims and flickers along the ceiling as we walk. There's a sharp smell that burns my nose, a sour taste that lingers on my tongue and buzzes in my throat.

Malo and Viera, for their parts, keep quiet. I figure, like me, they're trying to take everything in.

Some part of me wishes Ignos—the creature, not the god —was still in my head. The Sevora could've told me more about Clarity's Dawn, whether to trust them or not, how the faction had begun, and where Rackt is taking us. Instead, I'm forced to ask Rackt, who falls back a step and walks beside me.

"The name tells our story," Rackt says. "A group of Sevora outcasts, left behind by their masters, came down here and found it to be better off working together than separate. Over time, enough like-minded species started what you see."

"And now you're fighting back?"

"Now we're trying to survive," Rackt says. "If the Sevora ever stop fighting the Vincere and the Amigga, they'd have the attention for us and we'd be wiped out. We're hiding in a bunch of tubes, human. We have nowhere to go, no way to get off this planet."

"So what do you want us for? You said, back at the prison, that saving us was a big cost for you."

Rackt pauses, gives me a straight look. "There are few known species that the Sevora can't dominate. Mine, the Vyphen, the Ooblots, who are rare, and, now, yours."

"And?"

"We can't let the Sevora tear you apart. They'll find a way." Rackt glances at his webbed, feathered hands. "That's why the Amigga pulled us from the war. Why the Oratus took our place."

"But the Oratus can be captured by Sevora," Malo says, now that we're all standing around Rackt and listening.

"Oratus are living weapons, bred and taught only to kill Sevora," Rackt replies. "Vyphen, we're different. Not as hardy, not as blind. The Amigga prefer species they can control, even if it comes at a cost."

Rackt gets moving again, but I don't let the conversation die.

"Which is it?" I press the Vyphen. "Did the Amigga get your species out of the fight because of the Sevora, or because of you?"

"You don't miss much, do you?"

"I've found my survival depends on it."

Rackt lets this go another few paces. Gives me a chance to get a better look at his feathers, which shimmer in the light. At first I think it's because the Vyphen are beautiful, but then I notice inconsistencies—patches where the gray and black feathers are dull. It's not the lighting, it's grease and grime. A glance back at the others confirms this—Clarity's Dawn isn't living in luxury.

Rackt did say they're trying to survive.

"We got tired," Rackt says finally. "All of the species did, not just us. Have you ever fought a war for generation upon generation? We'd get close to wiping out the Sevora only for them to appear, again, on some other world, with some other species subverted to their will. Eventually, the idea of peace started looking pretty good."

"But the Amigga didn't want that?"

"You're talking about the ruling species of the civilized galaxy. The Sevora won't submit to them, which means the Amigga aren't going to stop till they're annihilated. Now, with the Oratus, the Amigga just might manage it."

We reach the end of the corridor, where a wide set of doors trundle open at our approach. I look for a keypad, the same thing as on *Cobalt*, but all I see is a little black nodule towards the top of the circular door.

"Wave," Rackt mutters as we pass through, and makes a half-hearted gesture with his right hand towards the nodule.

I copy him, though I don't know why. A second later, I forget about it anyway.

The space holds a small underground city. A chamber that extends far back, down, and up. A platform leading to stairs sits in front of us, and, when I peer over the edge, I see row after row of bedraggled tenants, ramshackle dwellings made up of rusted bits of metal, shallow fires and even small sections where green things grow, with lamps glowing overhead. Species shuffle along makeshift avenues—places, it seems, that are clear only because nobody's dumped anything there yet.

But for all the grime, there's beauty here too. Many-colored lights are strung up between the larger dwellings, casting purples, reds and blues into the dim cavern. Laughter and the murmur of constant conversation bubbles up to us. The smells, too, mingle dirt and sweat with the meatier scents of cooking food. It reminds me of Damantum, of an urban life.

Our doorway is one of many. Haloed portals ring the chamber, some large and some small, all with stairs or ladders leading to them.

"Here we are, our home beneath the rock," Rackt says as we stare. "This is where the resistance lives. This is where the only free souls on the Vimelia survive."

Rackt leads us to the stairs, which are far larger than the ones I'm used to. These are wide and long, and dotted with little beads. At first I think the bumps make them uncomfortable step on, unlike the smooth steps in Damantum's temples, then I notice the mask around my feet grips to them. Useful, maybe, if I needed to run up and down.

"So tell me what your world is like," Rackt says as we descend.

The question sparks a waterfall. Words pour out of me, descriptions that turn into memories of my home village in the jungle, the desert plains, and the sprawling city of Damantum. Of family and sacrifice, of windswept mornings and nights deep beneath a forest canopy listening to the haunted calls of distant birds.

Rackt takes it all in as we go back and forth down the endless array of switchback stairs.

"You know how long it's been since most of these people have seen the sky?" Rackt says when I'm done. "Most, by far, were born here. Grown in Sevora vats only to live out their lives in in servitude until by chance or by neglect they managed to escape."

"I'm sorry," I reply. "I didn't mean to offend—"

"No, no," Rackt says and gestures with his feathers towards the mass of scrabbled shelters. "You should tell everyone what you just told me. Tell them that there's something better than being stuck at the bottom of a sewer. Tell them that their struggle can get them something new. Can find them something beautiful. Because right now all we have is anger. Frustration and rage."

"That only works for so long." I remember when the remnants of the Solare tribe attacked Malo's troop on our way to Damatum; they gave into their vengeance and were slaughtered for it.

"It's nothing to live by."

We reach the bottom, where I feel a thousand eyes on me as we move. The settlement isn't gridded like a city, and the paths that exist seem be formed at random. Junked hovels linger on either side of us, littered with species lying about, working or cooking or simply staring at us as we wander around various states of desperation.

From what T'Oli had been saying, I expected something more from Clarity's Dawn. I expected some sort of thriving society, an organized army. But this, this isn't even on the level of the worst Solare tribes.

Everyone here is falling apart.

I don't say this, not only because Rackt's fellows with their miners are still behind us, but because I know I could wind up in the same pen. I have nothing here, and the only reason I'm not dead is because I happen to be human. I'm exotic, a bargaining chip between species that want to use me.

We continue until we cross most of the settlement towards a giant shuttle wing. When we approach, I can see the wing's not alone. A few species linger around it and they look like they're chatting. What stops me, causes Malo to run into my back before he notices, is the creature in the center. The one that seems to be directing those around it with jerky waves of thin metal arms grafted to its body.

An Amigga.

It's not much like Dalachite, *Cobalt's* master – it hasn't spread itself throughout, linking veins to terminals. Rather, it's settled into what looks like a rusted metal chair. Those robotic arms look grafted onto its body, which is gray and patchy rather than the red and brown of *Cobalt's* master. Tufts of frail hair spurt from various parts. A single mechanical lens grafted onto its face twists and focuses on us as we approach.

"So you found them," the Amigga's voice, like Dalachite's, comes out of the vent in the bottom of the chair and sounds metallic, toneless.

"T'Oli did," Rackt replies. "By accident, it seems. They managed to find their way to the upper sewers, where they were trapped in the muck when T'Oli happened upon them."

"Our small band survives on luck, I'm glad to know it hasn't run out." The Amigga shifts to us. "You can call me Sapphrite. And you are?"

We introduce ourselves in turn, each of us cautious and suspicious. Sapphrite does nothing until we're done, when it gives us a slow stare.

"I'm not the first Amigga you've seen," Sapphrite says and I shake my head.

"The last one wanted to use us," I say. "Wanted to take us for parts. To make something else."

I'm not sure how Sapphrite could show surprise, but the zero reaction it does display only drives further daggers into my perception of the species. That the Amigga don't seem to regard operating on someone as evil tells me all I need to know.

"That should tell you why you are so important," Sapphrite replies. "It's been a long time since I've seen another world, since I've spoken with the Chorus, but the Amigga are always working on the next thing. The new thing. And nothing prompts discoveries like an injection of fresh genes."

"Well, that's creepy enough for me," Viera speaks loudly. "I'm sure you'll tell us all about what you want to do with our bodies, but I, for one, am covered in crap. I'm exhausted, starving, and in dire need of cleaning. So maybe this can wait? If you aren't going to kill us right now?"

"Yes, your needs are plainly evident. No need to fear, however. Now that you're here, you don't have to worry. Rackt, if you could show them to the Bunker?" Sapphrite says.

Strange, I don't feel tired. At least, not yet. All of the new things we're seeing, the people and creatures we're meeting, has me riding the same wave that kept me awake the very first night after Malo took me away from my village. But we're all dripping and dirty, and hunger, as if spurred by the idea, starts gnawing at me. It's been a long time since we had any real food, since the white room in Nasiya's tower up above.

Thinking of the Sevora leader turns me to Ignos. Is it still alive up there? Has it found another host?

"Kaishi, come on," Malo whispers.

Rackt leads us away from the wing but not back towards the tents. Instead, we head to a series of rooms built into the back side of the chamber, behind the wing. This space is cleaner, the globe lights here don't flicker much. A few species, older Flaum and Whelk, mainly, stare at us as we pass by, then turn to terminals.

"Most of Clarity's Dawn is made up of refugees," Rackt says as we move through the hallways. "Most have small skills, things like cooking or selling. Making supplies or other gear. There are other ones, like me, that have a more military background. That plan the raids."

"The raids?" I ask. "Like when you rescued us from the prison?"

"Exactly," Rackt says. "There's not that many of us, so we have to pick carefully. We need to understand exactly what we're doing, and get in and out before the Sevora can marshal their forces. All that planning happens here in the Bunker."

Rackt shows us to our quarters, a shared room for the three of us. The facilities aren't luxurious, but there's something of a shower, which dumps smelly water that's at least not brown. It feels incredible to clean myself off, to be refreshed. To remember every minute of existence isn't spent caked with dirt and grime. Isn't spent smelling of my own sweat and desperation.

After, there's a bowl in front of each of our small bed rolls. In the bowls are, for once, not nutrient goop but what looks like actual cooked food. I don't recognize any of it, but the collection of thick, colored petals seems plantlike, so I devour it anyway. It's sour, juicy, and one, a bright orange circle, packs a lot of tangy spice and I appreciate it. A little spark at the bottom of nowhere.

"The water's good," Malo says.

Each of us has a bottle, and when I try it I don't necessarily agree with Malo – the water itself is flavorless. It's been boiled, which means it's probably been through less than sanitary places. Then again, so was most of the water we drank in the jungle, and we didn't die there.

So I guzzle it down.

"When are they coming back for us?" Viera says as we finish, after each of us moves to our small beds, knowing nowhere else to go. "Because I am about to pass out right here."

"I can take first watch," Malo volunteers.

First watch? Here? Of course, these people may not be friends. We just met them, and Rackt made it clear we're meant to be used. Targets in their game. So I tell Malo to wake me up in a few hours—not that I know how he's going to track that time without stars or Ignos glowing overheard.

That question doesn't keep me up long: as soon as my head hits the pillow, I'm out.

There's so much green. It's not what Sax expects when the doors open, when they reveal a domed expanse with a view of starlit space. Soft grass splays out in front of them, broken up here and there with larger plants, and tables lined with the ladder-like structures Ooblots prefer to use as chairs.

A number of UV drones buzz through the area: floating bars that emit light and travel around making sure each and every plant gets the requisite amount before moving along.

Sax has seen things like this before—usually if the Vincere were called into some sort of celebratory experience as symbols of Amigga military might. Wealthy owners would point and cheer as Sax and his fellows marched out, and he'd look at all the worthless bags of meat and wish he could get back to his ship.

He feels the same way here. This isn't a place for him, for Bas. But at least there isn't a miner pointing in his face—the only one there to greet them is the blue-gold vyphen, Eneks, who looks less than thrilled to see two Oratus standing behind D'Arscale.

"I thought you said you needed more security," Eneks says, his eyes lingering on Sax.

It's clear the Vyphen recognizes him, but Sax isn't mentioning the bar.

"These two are the reason," D'Arscale replies. "They destroyed my casino."

"Self-defense," Bas hisses. "Your own clients destroyed your casino."

D'Arscale doesn't dignify that with a response, and after an awkward moment, Eneks leads them away from the lift and through the garden.

Beyond the flowers, there's even rows of growing produce. Vegetables and fruits. Sax bets that none of this ever makes it off this level to the rest of the station.

"Your sisters have a nice place," Sax says to D'Arscale. "Why do you have to stay in the casino?"

"I choose to."

Eneks burbles a laugh.

"We're not here to talk to you, Vyphen," D'Arscale says.

After the gardens, they come to a sprawling, if flat building. Too short for Sax and Bas to enter, the space is barely a meter tall. Enough, though, for an Ooblot to slide under and maybe enjoy. It's plenty wide, though. About a third of the level.

Then Sax catches what the roof is doing, and he's actually impressed. A translucent roof—giving those inside the building a perfect view of the stars overheard. Here, the Ooblot's home has the same, and Sax can follow the progress of the two sisters by the changing of the cream roof as shifts in and out of view.

Stuff like this is expensive, and *Scrapper Station* doesn't scream luxury. These Ooblots must be running some other game here to afford these things.

"I present to you, the Sisters," Eneks says a moment later, stepping to the side, keeping an eye on both of the Oratus.

"You're gonna love them," D'Arscale mutters.

Malo wakes me some time later—in that dark room, I have no idea how long it's been, though judging by his sallow eyes and my own relative alertness, Malo held out a long time before nudging me. He mumbles something about no interruptions and collapses onto his own bed.

I blink for a minute in the dark. The last time I'd held a watch we'd been back on Earth, out in the open. There, at least, you could watch a fire burn or listen to the sounds of nature. Now I have only the omnipresent hum of machinery to hear and nothing at all to see.

Which leads me at first to my imagination, and then to the thing on my wrist. The dull emerald bracelet Ignos had given me. The Cache. It holds, theoretically, all the knowledge the Sevora put into it. I could search its archives and learn more about Vimelia, about the Sevora and, maybe, Clarity's Dawn.

The problem with the Cache, though, is using it is more like diving into an ocean than reading a page. I'd be immersed in its information, and unable to tell if someone decided to come into the room.

So no, I can't betray Malo and Viera.

Instead, I pace. Practice my silent steps, rolling my feet along the cool metal floor. I listen to Viera and Malo's soft breathing—and the latter's gentle snores. I run through the names, whispering them aloud, of all the people in my old tribe, wondering how many of them are still alive. How many of them remember me.

I wonder what my parents think happened to me—last I saw them, I told them I was going to stop the pair of Oratus that'd gone tearing through the jungle looking for me. When I didn't come back, did they assume I died out there?

Eventually, though, boredom rises again. There's been no sign of anything at the door, no message or word from Sapphrite, Rackt, or anyone. Anyway, they said we were safe here? That we would be their key to their plans?

That they wouldn't hurt us.

So I raise the Cache, look at it, and at my stare and with my focused thought it flashes in my eyes a brilliant green and I'm lost.

First I look for Vimelia, the Sevora, and I embrace their history of conflict. Discovery plays out around me—their first encounter with a crashed Flaum ship, the taking of hosts and slow growth off of their planet and into the wider galaxy. Even as these events play out, however, I catch one constant refrain overriding everything:

Fear.

I press the Cache on this. On how fear relates to the Sevora and scenarios swirl: fear of discovery before they as a species are ready, fear of losing a valued host, fear of their own weakness. And, too, fear of their own irrelevance.

For the Sevora, according to the Cache's records of

thousands of debates, writings, and more from their own historians, have never been able to answer the question of why so many other species are self-sufficient while they are linked, inexorably, to the taking of others.

I rise back out of that despairing pit and instead try to find traces of Clarity's Dawn. When I do, one thing dominates all else:

Sapphrite, the Amigga.

The first and only Amigga ever captured by the Sevora, and done so early in their ongoing wars. The scattered bits about Sapphrite's capture reveal that, like Dalachite, Sapphrite had been found on a lonely outpost running all kinds of experiments.

I'm about to dive into the recording of Sapphrite's capture when my perception shakes. The Cache goes hazy. The words blur and then disappear entirely and I'm back in our room. Only now we're not alone.

Sapphrite is waiting for me to break out of the Cache, and it's by itself. Staring at me. The room itself remains dark, and, so far as a glance tells me, Malo and Viera are still asleep.

"Come with me," Sapphrite says.

There are any number of reasons I should say no to this, but the reason I agree, why I follow Sapphrite out of that room is that, to me, I'm still the Empress of the Charre. I still have a people, even if they're far across the stars, and those people deserve an Empress who tries all she can to keep them safe.

I can't do that by hiding in the room.

Sapphrite's chair goes slow, which I don't mind as it gives my eyes time to recover from the dark room. We wind through the Bunker's corridors and back out towards the wing table. There's nobody waiting for us, and Sapphrite keeps on going. Down into the tents.

"You have a Cache," Sapphrite states.

As the Amigga caught me using it, there doesn't seem to be a reason to lie, so I just nod. Sapphrite doesn't respond and I remember the Amigga, and it's facing forward now. Guiding us through the piles of refuse and sleeping bodies.

"Yes," I say. "The Sevora gave it to me."

"It is a dangerous tool," Sapphrite says. "I've known many who have lost themselves in one. Knowledge can be as intoxicating as any drug, and if you forget your body while you slide through a Cache's endless troves, they can be fatal."

I get that the Amigga's probably making conversation, but I'm not in the mood for pointless chatter.

"Where are we going?" I ask.

"Nowhere," Sapphrite replies. "I want you to take in this place, the species that are suffering here, waiting for hope, so that when we ask you, you'll say yes."

I'm not so cold that I don't see what Sapphrite's talking about;. For all the small cook fires, most of the species here look gaunt and tired. Sickly or old. Fur, when present, is patchy and the slug-like bodies of the Whelks bear a number of crusted, calcified patches.

"The Sevora could crush you whenever they wanted," I say. "It's not that they can't find you, it's that they don't care."

"Not enough," Sapphrite agrees. "We used to be stronger. We would hit the surface often, cause chaos. Try to get off a message to the Vincere with Vimelia's location. But we never succeeded, and now we've lost many, while the Sevora only get better at keeping their hosts contained."

"So what are you going to do?"

"If the Chorus learns about Vimelia, they'll send a force here too strong for the Sevora to survive. We need to get the location of this world out, Kaishi. You can help us do that."

"And what do we get? Malo, Viera and I?"

"You get to go home," Sapphrite says. "You get to forget about this world, this fight. Go back to the life you used to know."

I laugh. It's a cynical bark, but I can't help it. Forget? I would never, and I wouldn't want to.

"There's no going back once you've had a voice in your head," I reply. "Once you've seen and felt what we've seen and felt."

Sapphrite doesn't argue the point, but the Amigga does turn itself around. We're at the foot of another stair, and I realize there's no elevators in this chamber. None of the doors have ramps leading to them. The Amigga must have someone carry it, or else it's been stuck down here for a very long time.

"Perhaps not, but you can try." Sapphrite starts puttering back through the tents, and I have no choice but to follow.

If there's one thing I've learned since Malo took me away from my tribe, it's that charity is rare. Sapphrite's offering us a getaway, but it has to have a reason. Dalachite didn't care at all about anything other than itself and its experiments. I can't expect Sapphrite to be different.

"What's your reason?" I ask Sapphrite as we trundle by a trio of sleeping Flaum. "Why help all of these people?"

Sapphrite doesn't stop. Its metal arms hang limp at its sides as it rolls along. "The Sevora ruined everything I worked for. Destroyed my research, prevented me from completing my life's purpose. Bringing about their end by the force of my fellow Amigga would be the sweetest revenge."

"That's it? Revenge?"

Now the Amigga stops, rotates the chair so that it stares at me fully with its single eye. "I am going to die, Kaishi. On this planet, I cannot access the therapies that allow Amigga to continue on indefinitely. Riddles we solved ages ago are now coming back to tear apart my body. An Amigga may be killed, but dying? Of natural causes?"

It's expecting me to share in its bafflement, its head-shaking denial of a process that's taken every Solare and Charre for as long as humanity's existed.

"Amigga don't die?" I finally manage to ask.

"Not that way. Not unless you're cut off," Sapphrite hisses out a sigh through its speaker. "Which I have been, for far too long."

When we get back to the wing, Malo and Viera, along with Rackt and several others, are waiting for us. My friends don't look particularly thrilled as I approach with the Amigga, and I can guess why.

"Nice job keeping watch, Empress," Viera says to me as we walk up. "There's nothing I like better after a long sleep than waking up with this thing in my face."

She nods towards a purplish Whelk. The slug-like thing, for its part, does what I think is a shrug by quivering its body and rolling its eyes.

"It's my fault," Sapphrite takes over. "I asked her to come with me, so that she could learn, so that she can help you to understand why you'll be going back up to the surface."

"I know why we'll be heading back up," Viera replies, her spitfire returning with her energy. "To get off this place and head home. Right, Kaishi?"

Malo doesn't say anything, but by his straight look, I know he's wishing the same thing. Sapphrite, apparently done for the moment, only stares at me and waits.

"They want our help, Viera," I start. "And they're going to give us a chance to go home, yes."

"The way you're saying that makes it seem like there's a catch."

I didn't serve long as Empress—not before being removed by a pair of angry Oratus, anyway. In that time, though, I learned to recognize an audience. To understand I'm not really delivering a speech to one person when I answer a question, but to everyone.

"Clarity's Dawn needs help," I say. "They're going to lose this fight, and soon, unless we help them turn Vimelia into a target for the Vincere. Sapphrite has a plan, and part of that has us ending up with a ship and heading home, but we can't just leave on our own." Now I quirk a small smile at Viera. "Not least because none of us knows how to fly one of those ships."

There's a beat, then Viera throws a theatrical sigh out into the air. "Fine. What's this plan?"

"It's going to take some courage," Sapphrite says. "But I think you're the perfect trio to pull it off."

One violet, the color of approaching twilight, and the other a bluish white, like a new dawn. The Sisters emerge from their house like a pair of particularly smooth liquids, minus their eye stalks, which orient on the Oratus without surprise.

They both form up, standing, or rather, sitting at half a meter in height. Sax and Bas stare down at them, and Sax prepares to tell his story.

"Brother," the blue sister starts. "You've once again caused a problem. We've already removed you from this level, stripped you of administrative rights."

"What else can we do?" says the violet one.

"I have an idea, Sister," the blue one replies.

"What's that, sister?"

"These two, they are looking for our favor, yes?"

Four eyestalks rotate towards Sax and Bas, and the Oratus nod.

"Then here's my plan," the blue one says. "Kill our brother, and we will listen to your proposal."

"What?" D'Arscale flaps. "Kill me?"

"You've become a liability," the violet one says. "I agree with your plan. Oratus, do you agree as well?"

Sax looks at Bas, who bares her teeth. D'Arscale has done nothing to deserve their mercy, done nothing but deserve its own demise.

"We agree," Sax hisses.

D'Arscale tries to run, its liquid body squirming back while its eyestalks turn into that hard Ooblot cement.

Sax catches him with his tail, wraps it tight around D'Arscale. Looms over the Ooblot, then turns back to the Sisters. "How?"

"However you wish," the blue one says. "We're not monsters."

So Sax does it the kind way—asks for the nearest airlock. There's one on this level, ready for rapid escapes— so together the six of them cross the garden to it. Eneks places a feathered hand on the center of the circular door, which chimes an affirmative as it opens.

"This is what you want?" Bas asks as Sax grips the Ooblot with all four claws.

"Our brother has caused far too much annoyance to be left alive,' the blue one says.

"It continues to forget our birthdays," the violet one adds. "Among many other insults. D'Arscale is simply not worthy of the Ooblot name."

"You're evil!" D'Arscale thaws itself long enough to patter out a series of harsher invectives, none of which seem to phase the Sisters in the slightest.

"Do you see?" says the blue one when D'Arscale at last falls quiet. "No use keeping such a thing around."

"Do it," the violet one says.

With that debate settled, Sax throws the struggling, helpless D'Arscale inside the airlock. Eneks shuts the door, and with a second press opens the portal to the cold void of space.

Sax is certain D'Arscale is screaming, but they hear no sound as the Ooblot is sucked away into the infinite nothing.

With that taken care of, Sax turns to face the Sisters and, at their prompting, tells them about Twillo, about needing Plake's cargo purchased so that Sax and Bas can secure a ride off the station.

"You don't like it here?" asks the blue one, who introduces itself as L'Reneo. "*Scrapper Station* isn't paradise to a pair of Oratus?"

"It's not built for us," Bas throws in a much more diplomatic answer than Sax would have managed.

"Like most of civilization, it would seem," the violet sister, N'Ollene says. "Yet we must continue anyway, even if our efforts displease the mighty Oratus."

"Your sarcasm isn't necessary," Sax hisses.

"Oh, but it is. We can't hurt you physically, so words must be our only weapons," N'Ollene replies.

"Why hurt us at all?" Bas says. "We want to leave, you can facilitate that. Do so, and you'll be thanked."

"By who?" L'Reneo says.

"The Vincere," Sax says. "They're looking for us."

The Sisters swivel their eye stalks towards each other. Hold the stare for a second, then swivel back towards the two Oratus. For his part, Eneks seems to be enjoying staring out that airlock after the disappearing bit of light that is D'Arscale's vacuum-frozen body.

"Then we can make a deal." L'Reneo quivers as it says this.

"I don't want any more deals," Sax hisses. "I'm tired of deals. Tired of wandering around this station and talking to people who are, somehow, connected to everyone else."

"Oh, but you'll like this deal," N'Ollene says. "It's right in your department. Your expertise, if you will."

"What?" Bas says.

"You want a way out, and we want a particular person removed." L'Reneo shifts its eye stalks towards Eneks. "Our friend's brother was recently killed in a horrible attack on this very station, by a Whelk. A red one."

"Kill the Whelk, and we'll let Twillo purchase your provisions." N'Ollene adds.

"But the Whelk works for Plake—if we kill him, she'll never give us her ship." Sax shakes his head.

"Then perhaps you'll just have to kill all of them and take her ship for yourself." L'Reneo says. "*Scrapper Station* demands justice for our slain resident, Oratus. Deliver it, and you'll get what you want."

I'm exploring the tents with Malo as a way to relax, to see and explore among the colored lights, sights, and sounds of species abuzz. I don't think the details of Sapphrite's plan have made it out to the public, but anyone could tell there's major movements going on—for one, the Bunker is flooding with people going in and out. The various airlocks leading away from the settlement open and shut constantly, as Clarity's Dawn agents, engineers, and runners send messages and materials to where they need to be.

Viera's off with Rackt, who's promised to find her some miners and make sure she knows how to shoot them. Malo's happier with the jagged blades they have scattered around —most seemingly broken off from scrap—so he takes on the role of my protector as we wander.

"In a lot of ways, this feels like my home," I say as we shift past a quartet of Teven huddled around a cook fire. "Everyone living, working together to survive."

"There was no existential threat back home," Malo replies. "All of these species know they could be dead in a moment if the Sevora above decided they were worth the effort."

"You don't think we felt the same way about the Charre? The Lunare? Either of you could have crushed us if you'd chose to."

Malo shakes his head. "We never had an interest in conquest. Plenty of land to the West for us. Raiding your tribes was more about keeping our soldiers ready, confident. About gathering honorable sacrifices."

"Well now I feel better."

We pass by a ramshackle shop that's glowing with blue light. I look inside and see racks and racks of small cubes against the walls, most of them pulsing. They're hypnotizing, and I step in, reach for one to see how it feels, when something long and furry grabs my arm.

"Unless you're pure energy, better not touch those," it's a rasping voice, quiet and harsh. "They'll burn right through your skin, melt your bones and turn you into a smoking puddle."

I follow the arm and see it's linked to a three-limbed, monstrous thing with what looks like a half-mouth sticking up and out of a wide torso. As if a Flaum and Amigga had been smashed together, without much care for how things fit.

"Keep your hands off her," Malo says, stepping between us.

"Meant no harm," the creature's mouth twists and snaps as it talks. "Just trying to keep your friend from killing herself."

"Thank you," I speak quickly. "For the warning."

I don't see any eyes on the creature, yet it clearly knows where we stand, as it's oriented towards us, and its central arm—the one that grabbed me—hangs ready to reach out again. The other two limbs, its legs, end in what appear to be massive, but thin feet.

"What are you?" Malo asks the question, which I'm thankful for, even if it comes off as rude.

"An accident." The creature doesn't seem the slightest bit embarrassed about this. "A Sevora mistake. An old one, too. Tried coupling different species in one of their vats, and when it didn't work out, they tried to have me killed."

"You escaped?"

"Freed," the creature scrapes a laugh. "The Sevora scientist that grew me thought it'd be cruel to burn me down. So it let me go in the sewers instead, like that's some kind of mercy. Fell my way down here and look, a useless split-breed keeping watch on batteries. What an achievement."

"So these go in the miners?" I nod towards the cubes.

"Everything else too," the creature replies. "We siphon off what power we can from up above. It's not much, but it keeps this place warm, the filters running and our weapons with enough juice to cause some damage."

"You don't seem that excited?"

"What's there to be excited about? That attack Sapphrite's planning?" Again the creature falls into its hacking laugh, which is starting to annoy me. "We've done hundreds of those. They cause some chaos, but the Sevora always drive us away. Then they come for revenge, but their factions keep anyone from committing too much, so we nurse our wounds and wait to try again."

"You can't win a war that way." Malo glances at me, his eyes moving towards the exit. "There has to be drive, a willingness to keep fighting until the enemy is gone."

"Or you've made peace," I add, taking my own step away from the creature.

"Peace. There's a funny idea. You think I'm down here because I declared war on the Sevora?" The creature follows us as we step away from the glowing cubes. "No. They wanted me gone because I reminded them of their own failures. I'm a stain to be wiped away, not something to be bargained with."

We reach the edge of the shop and keep going, both of us making half-hearted goodbyes.

"To them, we're nothing!" the creature calls as we head away. "Nothing!"

We make it to a quiet spot with a few scattered boxes between a pair of larger tents. A string of glowing green lights gives the clearing a calming ambiance, which is what I'm looking for after the encounter with the strange battery keeper.

"Looks like the jungle, doesn't it?" I say to Malo as I head for the box.

It's not exactly a comfortable chair, but just sitting for a moment gives my mind a chance to reset. To breath in the smells and wind them around thoughts. So many of them on the edge of familiarity, so many entirely new.

"I don't know what jungle you lived in, Kaishi, but the one I remember didn't have lights like these," Malo sits down near me. I notice he's picked up a broken bar of metal from somewhere and holds it like he used to hold his spear.

"It hasn't been all that long," I say. "But it feels like forever since we've left home."

"The flow of time is driven less by the passing of days and more by experiences," Malo replies. "At least, that's what our warriors would tell novices when we trained. Their point, I think, is that we would forget the hours in their monotonous lessons and remember the results."

"Did you?"

"I'm still alive, so I suppose so."

I nod towards the metal stick. "And you've remembered to always keep a weapon handy."

"I don't need to remember that, Empress," Malo looks at the staff as if it's the most valuable thing he owns. "These adventures have taught me that every moment I'm without one, I'm vulnerable."

"You're a good soldier, Malo," I say, and throw him a smile to take the edge off what I say next. "But you could be a better friend."

"A better friend?"

"You're so serious. Always about the mission, keeping me alive, or watching for the next threat. Not every danger comes from the outside, you know."

"Are you okay, Kaishi?"

"Look, Malo, let's not ask about me for a change. What about you? Are you okay?"

This question seems to have Malo confused. "I'm fine, Empress."

"No, that's not what I'm asking. How do you feel about everything we've been through? About what Sapphrite's asking us to do?"

Now he gets it. Takes his eyes from mine and sweeps them along parts of the settlement we can see.

"There's nothing I've lived that could have prepared me for this," Malo starts. "It's one surprise after another, which I'm able to handle. What's harder, though, is seeing all of the constructs I've lived with torn away. I once thought the Charre were the best people alive, and now I know we're nothing next to all of these others. If they wanted to, the Sevora could destroy us. So could the Vincere. I have no doubt that Clarity's Dawn, bedraggled and lost as they are, would make a mockery of all our warriors and their years of wielding spears and shooting arrows. In short, Kaishi, I feel pointless."

In Malo's words I hear my own thoughts crystallized—we, humanity, are being reduced to bargaining chips by races far stronger than our own. We'd gone from masters of our own destinies to pawns in a game I can barely conceive, much less play.

But then, here we are, immersed in a band full of rebels, refugees, and refuse who won't accept that their role is one of servitude, that their destiny is decided by others.

"We have to take it back," I whisper the words at first. "Our agency, our choice."

"How?"

"We start here. With Sapphrite's plan. We start by speaking up. You've led a hundred raids. I've been sneaking around jungles and since I could walk. And Viera…"

"Viera's unpredictable, but always in our favor," Malo finishes for me.

"Exactly. This might be the home of Clarity's Dawn, and this might be their idea, but if we're going to carry it out, then humans are going to have a stake in it."

Just saying the words helps. My blood pumps harder, my smile feels more confident than it has been at any point since we've left Damantum.

Malo grabs my left hand hard. It's been a long time since I've felt his grip, warm and rough. There's a lot packed into his touch, and I meet his look not as Empress, not as a Solare chief's daughter, but as a friend finding strength in another.

Once again, Sax finds himself wishing for the simple clarity of a Vincere mission. A commander, an objective, and a horde of evil Sevora to destroy. Instead, he and Bas set off down the lift, back to the station proper, in search of Agra-Red. Though what he'll do when Sax finds the Whelk is a question he can't answer.

Back in the Nexus, Sax takes a step out of the lift, looking for the way to the docking spoke, when Bas taps his shoulder with her right foreclaw.

"Sax, before we go on, I need to take care of... myself," Bas looks down at the cuts and gashes, her bent scales.

As if the act of recognizing they're living, breathing creatures breaks a spell, Sax feels his own crushing exhaustion weighing in. They need a place to sleep, they need medical supplies. And neither can be had for free. Still, they first go to the only infirmary on the station, a place labeled only by a glowing bright green circle—that universal sign of health.

Inside, a pair of cheery Teven tell Sax and Bas that the cost of treatment by the medical robots, and staying in one of the recovery rooms, will run far more than either Oratus has to give.

Sax is ready to return to the tried-and-true flashing of his claws, but Bas stops him with a tap of her tail.

"We don't have payment," Bas says. "But we do have influence."

"What kind of influence?" the lead Teven, one with an unusual striping black and purple carapace, replies. "We don't need more space, and the Sisters would never replace us."

"With your customers," Bas hisses, and she looks at her claws. "We'll bring you more, plenty more, if you fix us now."

The Teven, their eyes peeking through the holes in their long shells, stare at the claws, then so a short dance with their limbs beating on each other's shells.

Sax always hates secret languages.

"How many fights are you planning to start?" the lead Teven says.

"Many," Sax replies.

"Hopefully not enough to take apart the station?"

"No." Sax has no idea what it would take to destroy *Scrapper Station*, but he's reasonably confident things won't come to that.

Though Sax and Bas have left their fair share of wreckage behind, *Cobalt* included.

"Then, if you can guarantee at least five other customers, I'll waive your repair and rest fees."

It's a deal. The Teven don't have Oratus-specific care rooms—there are so few of the species outside of the Vincere that it wouldn't make sense—so Sax and Bas separate. Each of them take one of the largest rooms available, normally meant for heavy Whelk.

The rooms themselves are clear, cream. Tiled across the floors and walls. Sax isn't sure why until hoses blast him with water from all sides. Only it's not just water—the stuff clings to him, seems to squirm across his scales.

Nanobots.

The little things nip and bite, knit and sew Sax's body back together. Sax doesn't think he has many new injuries, but then he feels his legs tickle, tear, and grow.

They're repairing the burns, grafting and splicing new skin and scales right there.

Well before the nanobots are done, Sax is ushered out to a recovery room, a tranquil, silent box looking out into space and the stars. Again, no Oratus chairs here, but Sax makes do with a large couch. A serving robot hovers over with nutrient drink, and Sax takes a long sip, feels the nanobots whir away, and drifts into a long-sought sleep.

The *Mobius* waits for them in Docking Spoke One. Sax feels better than he has in a long time—though the Teven remind them when they leave of their promised "referrals".

Not that Sax cares—if they don't have to carve up a half-dozen people, then he's fine keeping his claws put away. The Teven can't exactly do much to enforce their end of the deal.

Docked, the *Mobius* looks like it belongs here. Every part of the ship seems to be meant for something else. The outside is a dozen different colors, all of them pitted and scarred from space debris. Engines, weapons, and living modules spring off the large cargo core at various angles, such that Sax thinks Plake must give her crew freedom to do what they like to her ship.

"It'll never win a fight in heavy atmosphere," Coorvin

says, stepping down from the ship's ramp towards them. "Plake, though, says she belongs in deep space. Doesn't ever want to take this thing to another Amigga planet."

The little old Flaum steps over, looks at each of them.

"Did D'Arscale send you here?" Coorvin finally asks.

Sax decides the Flaum doesn't deserve to be sent to the Teven.

"D'Arscale is enjoying a scenic tour of local space," Bas grins wide. Her rose-gold scales glitter in the bright docking bay light, shined enough by their recent repair that Coorvin even winces a little.

"Ah," the Flaum replies. "So this is... a social call?"

"Have you heard of the Sisters?" Sax asks, and when Coorvin shakes his head, Sax fills the Flaum in.

"Plake's not going to be happy if you kill Agra-Red," Coorvin glances behind him, back up the ramp. "The Whelk's been her muscle for a long time."

"Which is why we're standing here, in the open," Bas says. "We want a lift off of the station. Plake has a chance, now, to give us that, either with Agra-Red or without him."

"Why don't you try one of the other ships?" Coorvin nods behind them. "There's at least a dozen more docked."

If Sax has to explain all the twisting events that led to them being here, one more time, he's going to start murdering everything in sight.

"We have no money," Sax leaves his summary short. "We need leverage with anyone who will take us. The Sisters give us that leverage."

"I think you'll find the Sisters won't give you as much as you need," Coorvin says. "But I'll get Plake and you can make your case to her."

The Flaum vanishes back up the ramp.

"If they attack us," Sax says. "I'll take the Whelk."

"Trying to protect me?" Bas replies.

Sax hisses a laugh, "I think Whelk are tasty."

They're not waiting long till Coorvin reappears, with Plake in tow. The Vyphen's not looking thrilled to see them, though her expression changes, as does all of them, when the space station's alarms begin to go off.

"Vincere vessel approaching!" announces a voice that Sax recognizes as Eneks. "Anyone that wants to run, your time is now. *Scrapper Station* accepts no liability for any consequences of your attempted escape!"

"Guess that means you should run," Sax says to Plake, who laughs.

"Why? You going to try and get revenge? I was just selling my cargo for a good price."

"You sold us into slavery."

"Hardly," Plake's rubbery mouth slides into a frown. "D'Arscale said you'd eventually be released to the Vincere, that he'd take any blame for keeping you."

"D'Arscale is an icicle now," Bas replies. "Which means—"

Plake waves her feathered arm. "Stop. I don't take threats from Oratus. Your way out is here. Take it. You can try to implicate me if you want, but I saved your damn lives. Feel like that's worth an even trade for mine and my crew. You Oratus are all about honor, right?"

Sax feels the Oratus are more about highly efficient slaughter, but honor works.

"We'll let you go," Sax acknowledges, and together the two Oratus turn to leave the twisting mess of demands from the Sisters, from Plake and Twillo behind.

Guess the Teven definitely won't be getting their payback now.

The docking spoke clears rapidly after the Vincere

arrival is announced. Ships scatter off the station, leaping away to anywhere other than here, anywhere they won't be trapped and inspected and, without doubt or mercy, eviscerated.

What fascinates Sax, though, is that the Vincere vessel, a light frigate with plenty of fighter support, doesn't make any moves against the smugglers. Doesn't make any attempts to enforce the police action that is the reason for its existence. All it does is stay near the station and launch a single shuttle, an oval-shaped, unarmed transport craft that floats over to *Scrapper Station*.

Sax and Bas watch the entire thing play out on one of the several giant displays within the Docking Spoke that show everything happening around the station. Ships are representing as little diamonds, the points showing their headings, while the frigate is designated as a big red circle. The red, according to a wide legend on the right, a glaring reminder of its likely hostility.

The shuttle shows as a bright blue diamond—a harmless designation—and, as it nears the station, a number six appears inside its shape.

"Betting that's our ride," Bas says and Sax agrees, so they head to bay six and wait.

The shuttle lands shortly after, tall struts untangling themselves from the base of the craft and, with magnetic jets burning silent, the shuttle settles onto the bay floor. Rather than a ramp, a platform descends from the craft's center, plenty wide for four Oratus, though this one only holds two.

Ones Bas and Sax recognize: Gar and Lan.

And they're ready for war; loaded with miners, wearing masks, and casting their heads about for trouble. When they center on Sax and Bas, Gar looks disappointed.

"Guess we scared away all the prey?" Gar says as the two Oratus bound over.

"There's plenty back in the station, if you're hungry," Sax shrugs.

"That's the not mission," Lan says.

"It never is." Gar looks mournfully at his claws.

"What is the mission?" Bas asks.

"You."

I resist reaching for my scalp, scratching at it. Drawing attention to what's there. The ride, though, is boring—a slow crawl up the tubes towards the surface in a mostly-fixed Beast.

T'Oli is back at the controls, its hard-white form navigating the Beast around bumps and ridges as we scale the walls. The machine's treads bite into the tube's sides and allow it to climb. To bring us closer to death.

Malo and Viera sit next to me, strapped into a trio of hard slats that explore new dimensions of discomfort by pressing into seemingly every nook of my back at once.

"Made for Ooblots," T'Oli said when we climbed in. "We fit everything, so everything fits us."

So to keep myself from going insane at the pinching, I think about how, in other tubes all throughout here, Clarity's Dawn is sending all they've got into this fight.

Or rather, they will. We're going in first. Start with a surprise, one that the Sevora won't see coming, and that ought to give us a real shot at getting out.

"Anyone think this has a chance?" Viera says as we ride.

"It has a better one than sitting down there," I reply. "And at least, this time, we get what we want."

"Right. Because instead of being kept out of the fighting, we're bait instead. Just what I was hoping for."

Sapphrite's plan had called for us to act as a draw, a distracting target for Sevora while the real work went on elsewhere. Clarity's Dawn would keep us safe, Sapphrite said, and then deliver us to the spaceport after.

Problem is, I'm not a fan anymore of 'after', of 'trust'. There isn't any guarantee that Clarity's Dawn won't use us as pawns after the mission. So instead, Malo and I made some recommendations. Swapped some places.

"This gives us the best chance of escape," Malo says. "We're in control of our own destiny now, rather than someone else."

"I believe I'm controlling your destiny right this moment, Malo," T'Oli notes cheerfully from the controls. "Could turn this thing right around, or stop it and let us all plummet to a messy end."

"But you wouldn't do that, T'Oli," I acknowledge the joke. "Because that would hurt your Beast."

"True enough," T'Oli replies. "Did I tell you how long it took me to clean her out?"

"Yes," All of us reply in unison.

"It was a monster job, is all I'm getting at."

I reach for my scalp again, catch Malo's eyes and pull my hand away. I haven't seen him make a single twitch towards his own black hair. Suppose that warrior discipline comes in handy sometimes.

"Did we decide who gets to fly our ship when we steal it? Assuming we get that far?" Viera asks after another few minutes of trundling.

"I've got the Cache. I'll use it."

"So you're going to fall into one of your trances right when we're running from a bunch of angry enemies?"

"Do you have a better plan?" Malo asks, leaning around me. "Are you equipped to fly one of these things?"

"I grew up with gadgets under the mountains," Viera replies. "I can figure it out."

"Then we'll call it when we get there," I say. "There's only so far a plan can go, anyway."

"You just don't want me to have any fun," Viera pouts. "Get stabbed by Malo, captured by Oratus, imprisoned by Sevora, the list goes on and on."

"But look at what you're wearing? Doesn't that count?"

Viera's sporting a new set of synthetic armor over her mask, though its mismatched colors give away the fact that it's a blend of other sets. After all, Vimelia doesn't exactly have human-sized gear, seeing as they didn't know we existed. What I'm really focused on are the pair of shiny miners, scrubbed clean and bolted onto latches around Viera's waist. There's a chance the Sevora might take them away, but if we're lucky, she'll keep them.

"Guess you're right," Viera glances down at herself. "I did get the best outfit." She looks over at us, does a theatrical head shake. "Kaishi, what are you even wearing? A robe?"

It's a simple, brown-green sheet. With the mask on underneath, I just need something to keep the Sevora from recognizing I'm coated in the mask's invisible shell. If there's one thing I'm not concerned about right now, it's fashion.

"And Malo? Did you fall into a fire?"

He's sporting the thickest set of all of us, mostly because Malo's got the frame to support some of the same gear given to heavier Flaum. Like Viera says, though, most of it's blasted-black, a relic of prior battles and hasty repairs.

Rackt told Malo not to bet on it holding up in a fight, but they didn't have anything better to offer, so Malo took it.

T'Oli drops us near the surface, though there's still plenty of muck for us to slog through before getting to one of the wide ladders up.

"At least I felt clean for a day," Viera says as the brown stuff once again clutters up our clothes and the stench overtakes any pleasant memories my nose ever had.

There's a reason for this, though—if we're going to be convincing as survivors who've scrounged in the Vimelia sewers, we can't look refreshed and clean. So we're properly filthy by the time Malo pushes open the surface hatch and we find ourselves once more in the chaotic wonder of Vimelia's streets. Admittedly, I'm a fan of seeing the beige-white sky after so much time underground. Just feeling a true breeze and knowing that I'm not trapped inside something sparks energy and a smile.

"Don't know how you manage to live this way," I say to Viera as I stretch out my arms.

"It's what we know," Viera replies. "And it's not all bad —hard to sneak up on somebody in a cave."

Viera's looking past us and we turn to see a pair of Whelk wielding what look like long, thin tools operating on a panel embedded in the side of the tall, shimmering green structure we've emerged next to.

Only the Whelk aren't working anymore—they're staring at us with slack faces. I give them a wave—we are, after all, supposed to be caught—and finally once of them reaches for a circular device in a pouch around its body. Pulls it out and begins yammering into it.

"Suppose we just wait now?" Viera says.

"That is the plan," Malo replies, though he edges closer to me. He's still got that staff with him and I'm glad for it.

The goal might be to get captured, but it's not to get killed.

We don't have to wait long, however, before the Sevora announce themselves through a whirring roar. Above us, a narrow shuttle makes its way between the buildings and, out of a pair of opening bay doors, a squad of twelve armored Flaum—bearing Nasiya's emblems—drop down.

At first I think they're all going to fall and crush themselves on the ground, but their boots flare up as the Flaum close and they wind up floating just above the surface.

I recognize the primary one—black with white tufts—as the one that greeted us when we first touched down on Vimelia. It's obvious the Flaum hasn't forgotten us either, as he doesn't take any chances.

"Keep your limbs raised and clear," the Flaum barks at us as his troops go through the whole surrounding song and dnace.

We're relieved of our weapons in short order, then to my surprise, we're walked out of the alleyway and along the main streets. Shuttles and other craft buzz above and alongside us, stopping ever-so-briefly to get a look at at the strange new species.

"Why aren't we flying?" I manage to ask the Flaum after we've taken a few steps.

"You're close enough to walk," the Flaum replies.

"Close enough to what?"

"Nasiya demands no more chances," the Flaum replies. "Even if you can't be directly controlled, you will be influenced. You're receiving your masters today," the Flaum says, and there's a hint of pride in his voice.

That's when I realize that T'Oli wasn't taking us to a random drop point—no, this close to the surface, T'Oli deposited us next to a Sevora Host Center. Probably not it's actual name, but that's what I'm choosing to call the massive, long and flat space the Flaum guide us to.

Unlike the other buildings, this one is a painted a sky-blue and, atop its flat surface, has a long series of winding spires that tilt towards each other and bind together around the center of the building.

"Unity," the Flaum says as we approach the doors. "No matter what divisions exist among the Sevora people, these spaces are sacrosanct. All who enter here do so to enrich their lives, and those of their hosts. Be thankful that you are going to receive one of the greatest gifts the Sevora can give."

"I can't wait," Viera mutters.

The way Lan says the words triggers a soft alarm in Sax's mind—there's caution there, wariness. Suspicion.

"You're here to rescue us?" Bas says.

"To see if you're still on the good side," Gar replies. "Or if you're with Evva."

"What happened to her?" Sax heads off that conversation, twists it. No sense in revealing his allegiance this early, with this little information.

"Stole a shuttle, vanished with a prisoner." Lan nods back towards the very shuttle they came in on. "Like this one. Any guesses as to who the prisoner was?"

"Avan." Sax's answer isn't a guess.

Gar nods. "Never would've thought the commander would fall for a Sevora. But I guess losing your pair messes you up."

"If I ever lost you," Lan says to Gar. "I'd... probably be more relaxed."

"You'd be bored, and you know it."

"She doesn't love Avan," Sax hisses. "Evva would never."

"Save it for the Amigga," Lan says. "If you know anything about her, where she might be—"

"They haven't found her yet?"

"Not yet," Gar says. "But they will. She's the top priority now. They're taking resources away from the Sevora to find her."

Why? Sax wants to ask this too, but he's getting the feeling that Lan and Gar are doing more than just picking two lost Oratus up from a rogue station. Neither one seems relaxed, both keep their midclaws on their miners, as if expecting an ambush at any moment.

"What's going to happen if we get on that shuttle?" Sax asks.

"If?" Lan replies.

"You heard me."

"You'll be debriefed. Asked about Evva. Prove that you're not on her side, and I'm sure they'll let you back in."

"Who's they?" Bas hisses.

Now Lan and Gar tense for a moment. Clear. The kind of movement Sax would expect to see from someone who hates their situation but who's trying to pass it off as bearable. The kind of movement he's seen from people who need rescuing.

"The Chorus sent Amigga to every cruiser," Lan says. "To preserve the loyalty of the fleet."

"They've interrogated everyone, even the Flaum and Whelk." Gar adds. "It's stupid, but once you're clear, it's over."

Sax wonders what'll happen when the Amigga find out he's burned one of their number to an ashen crisp. He thought the Amigga on *Cobalt* had lost its mind, but there's no guarantee any others would see it that way. Which means he and Bas could be going into a trap. But if they try to stay on the station, then... they couldn't survive here either. Sax sees only one option: try to find Evva. Right back where they started.

"What if we say no?" Sax asks.

"No to what?"

"Getting on that shuttle with you. Going back to the Vincere."

That stiffens their spines. Tenses their arms. Sax lets his teeth show just a bit. Feels Bas' tail touch his, wrap its end around the tip of his own. She's with him, whatever comes.

"That would be a dangerous choice," Lan says finally. "They would order us to bring you in. By force."

"Do you think you could?" Sax counters.

"Sax, I've always wanted a good brawl with you," Gar rasps. "But not here, not like this."

"Then let us walk away," Sax replies. "Because I'm not getting on that shuttle. The Vincere isn't what it was, and I'm not liking the new look."

In a flash, Lan and Gar have their miners raised, pointed at Sax.

"Bas, don't be like him," Lan hisses. "You don't have to pay for his choices."

Bas laughs. "The thing about pairs, Lan, is that I do."

It takes a long moment to pull the trigger on a friend, on someone that you've ridden with into the bleakest of fights, the deadliest of environments. Whose life you've saved and whose saved your life more times than either of you remember.

Sax and Bas use that moment—they both slide to the side, turning and flicking their tails at the miners Lan and

Gar are holding. Batter the weapons away from the claws and send them clattering to the floor.

Gar springs at Sax, claws outstretched, mouth opening in a wide, hissing roar. Sax, body angled aside from Gar, catches and throws the oncoming Oratus pass him. Feels a cut across his midsection as Gar's talons go by.

Gar, though, smashes into the ground, rolls against the wide door leading back into the station and, digging grooves into the metal floor, turns himself around and launches back at Sax. The two Oratus are nearly the same size, and Sax can see the blind bloodlust has taken Gar's senses.

It's going to be a raw brawl.

So Sax jumps forward, meets Gar in mid-air and the two crash to the ground, rolling and snapping and clawing at each other. It's a rush of instinct—a flash of claw here, glistening teeth biting there—and at the end of it, when Gar winds up on the bottom and kicks Sax off, both of bleeding. Both are grinning.

Ready for the next round.

"Never took you for a traitor," Gar hisses as the two circle each other.

"Always took you for a bloodthirsty maniac," Sax replies.

He wants to see how Bas is doing, help her, but looking away from Gar for even a second could prove fatal. All Sax has to go on are hissing sounds behind him, the crash and rumble as heavy bodies crash into things.

"You were right," Gar laughs, and then the Oratus launches—

No. A feint.

Sax bites, though. Jerks forward to meet a leap that isn't coming as Gar reaches behind his back and pulls another miner from his mask. Aims, fires. Sax has a split second to move and doesn't clear the shot, which powers into his left leg.

It goes numb. Not the burn of a killing laser, but the blue ice of a stunning shot.

"You want us alive?"

"The Commander thinks you might know where Evva's heading, what she's after." Gar raises the miner again as Sax keeps limping, trying to get towards a long rack of batteries. "Personally, Sax, I'd rather not kill you."

"I'm not getting on that shuttle, Gar," Sax hisses.

He gets close to the batteries—there in case a ship's dead and needs a burst of energy—when Gar fires again. Hits Sax's back, and now almost everything's lost feeling. Sax falls forward, his head jutting against the rack.

"Don't think you have a choice," Gar says, though the Oratus doesn't move closer.

A smart move. Keep your distance when you've only got a small miner and a big target. Stunning's an imprecise science. Better to overdo it.

Gar raises the miner again. Aims for Sax's head.

"Sleep well," the Oratus hisses.

And Sax, with the flickering connection in his left fore-claw, throws a battery at Gar as the Oratus pulls the trigger.

A bright blue-white burst engulfs the universe for a quick moment and Sax's eyes dazzle in the light. His mind goes fuzzy, and the only thing he does, for longer than he'd like, is lay there and try to reconnect with the rest of himself. That much super-charged electricity could have killed him, probably would have if Sax wasn't an Oratus. If he didn't have two hearts and layer after layer of thick muscle, protective scales, and a half-mask catching what it can of the blast.

Gar, though, fares worse. The battery, freed from its

enclosure and nearly to the Oratus by the time the trigger depresses, catches Gar with the full force of its fury. The physical push of the blast has knocked the Oratus on his back, but what's more evident is that Gar has no control of himself at all. His body is a wriggling mess as synapses run wild. The other weapons on him short circuit too—exploding or melting with a variety of pops and sparks, burning through the mask or melting into boiling puddles on the floor around him.

Not that Gar's stuck there for long—Sax, whose head is lying on the floor staring at his distressed former friend, sees Lan dash into view. Sees her scoop Gar up and lope away from the broken remnants of his weaponry. She pauses for a moment, turns back and looks towards what Sax believes is Bas, though he can't turn his head to look.

"You're broken now," Lan says. "You're on the wrong side."

"Did Evva ever do you wrong?" Bas hisses back. "Did she ever send us on a bad mission, or leave us to die? Why would she do this now, unless she had a reason?"

"Our job, the whole reason we live, is to support the Chorus. Do as they say, fight as they command." Lan keeps backing towards the shuttle, Gar in her arms. "Turn your back on them, and you've denied your reason for being."

"Your reason, maybe," Bas says. "But not ours. Go back to your ship, Lan. Tell them what's happened. We'll be here when you return."

"We won't come back alone. You'll be outnumbered. Captured and hauled before the Amigga as traitors. As dishonorable a death as you can imagine."

"Fighting for what we believe? You have a strange notion of honor." Bas appears in front of Sax, kneeling over him. Sniffs him quick, then reaches beneath Sax with her claws and lifts him up.

Lan and Gar get on the platform, which rises up into the belly of the shuttle. Bas doesn't stay to watch, lugging Sax from the docking bay, towards the lifts out of the spoke.

"We're going back to Plake," Bas hisses as they move. "Her ship is our best shot at getting out of here now."

Sax tries to agree, but his mouth doesn't work. So instead he lies in his pair's arms, and hopes the next fight won't come too soon.

"Why should I help you again?" Plake says, this time on the *Mobius*.

Coorvin led Sax and Bas up onto the ship, where Agra-Red waited with its new heavy miner in hand. Apparently Plake didn't want to be seen talking with the two most-wanted Oratus on *Scrapper Station*.

"Because of what we'll bring you," Bas says.

Sax is slowly recovering—he's able to control his own breathing now, and he can use his muscles to keep himself upright, if not walk with any stability. Still, he tries to look strong, even as a bit of drool escapes his numb jaw and plops down to the floor.

Plake eyes it, then looks up at Bas, "What's that, besides a ton of angry soldiers?"

"You said you hate the Oratus. The Amigga. That you want to see them beaten."

"Lots of people wish for the impossible, doesn't mean I'm trying to make it happen."

Bas breaks into a quick story about Avan, the Sevora traitor that promised galaxy-changing secrets. About how Evva's escaped with him, about how if Plake helps Sax and Bas reunite with their commander, they might be able to... do something.

"You don't even know these secrets?" Plake laughs. "Avan might be playing all of you. Another Sevora trick to get deep into our society."

"The Sevora was sincere," but even Bas can't put much force in this one.

"Look, Oratus. I don't like you. I'm not going to risk my crew and my own life on your crazy idea, which may be nothing!" Plake nods at Agra-Red. "Get them out of here. With any luck, the military will take care of them and leave us alone."

"Mistake," Sax manages to rasp. Weak, but it's there.

"Oh, he can talk now?" Plake shakes her head. "Too late. Leave."

Agra-Red doesn't give Sax another chance to argue. Forces the both of them out of the ship, keeping its miner trained on them the entire way. Then, once the two Oratus are on the floor, the ramp raises up and seals them out.

"That didn't go as I hoped," Bas says as she pulls Sax out of the bay. "There's only one other place we can try."

The Sisters let them in, let them up the lift back to their beautiful garden. Now, though, the Oratus frigate wipes through the viewing window every so often, spoiling any sense of peace. Rather than taking the Oratus to their building, the Sisters, with Eneks and a couple of armed Flaum that Sax recognizes from the casino, greet the Oratus immediately as they come off the lift.

"Your circumstances aren't good," L'Reneo says.

"Not good at all," N'Ollene adds.

"That's why we're here," Bas says. "For help."

And by the way the Sisters eyestalks swivel, by the

rapid clatter of their Ooblot forms, Sax knows they're in trouble.

Getting your feeling back is like waking from a dream—gradually, reality filters in. Your feet get their traction, your talons passing along the usual edge as they dig small cuts into the floor. Your vents open wider and wider, and you can actually feel the air rejuvenate your muscles. Your tail twitches when you want it to, and your four claws start to open and close on command instead of by nervous whims.

Sax gets all this back in time to hear the Sisters laugh in Bas' face, in time to see the Flaum guards pull their miners up while the lift doors behind them shut.

"The Vincere's offered good terms for you," L'Renee says. "We hold you here, they come get you, and *Scrapper Station* gets forgotten about for a long, long time. Know what it's worth not having to deal with Vincere inspections?"

"They wouldn't," N'Ollene says. "They're not one of us. Not normal people."

Sax squeezes Bas' shoulder slightly, lets her know that he's back, most of the way. She keeps holding him, though, because if there's one thing to keep hidden, it's an Oratus surprise.

"So if you'd follow our friends to the airlock, there, we'll be keeping you safe and sound till they come pick you up," L'Renee says.

"A nice ride home," N'Ollene adds.

The Flaum gesture with their miners and Bas pulls them both along. Across the garden towards the airlock. Every step brings another iota of feeling back, every step makes Sax a deadlier weapon.

The Sisters order the two Oratus into the airlock, with Eneks again stepping up to open the door. It shunts ajar, leaving a gleaming cream tube waiting. Stepping into that tube means death, a slow and awful one once the Amigga find neither Sax nor Bas knows where Evva is. And death by torture, death in captivity is not one Sax will stand.

He pushes off of Bas, sending her flying to the side and uses the momentum to pivot and leap at the first Flaum. The furry guard fires, but the shot's hopelessly wide of the crouched, scrambling Oratus.

The Flaum doesn't get a second one.

Sax turns from his downed target to see Bas splitting apart the other guard's miner, a scorch mark on her right shoulder. The Sisters, meanwhile, are running away with Eneks, rolling across the grass towards their building.

It's a futile effort.

"You'll stop, or you'll die," Sax hisses as he catches up to them, the Flaum's miner in his right midclaw. The weapon's not made for Oratus hands, but at this range, accuracy doesn't matter so much. He'll just spray lasers until they submit, or burn.

They choose the former, huddling up together and staring at their new captor. Eneks fades from his blue color to a sickly purple, and picks at his feathers while his bulbous eyes blink. Sax isn't used to having hostages. The normal Oratus position is that an enemy is better off dead, preferably eaten. Not captive.

The Sisters, apparently, can see his hesitance.

"What will you do now?" L'Renee asks. "Keep us here until your Vincere comes anyway and takes you away?"

"Or will you shoot us and wind up the same?" N'Ollene adds.

"We'll do neither," Bas replies, stepping up beside Sax.

She's not wielding a miner, but there's also no sign of the Flaum she tangled with. Either it's as dead as Sax's, or she's chased it off. Either way, the odds of the Sisters and their Vyphen pal making it away alive are growing dimmer.

"This station must have some defenses, yes?" Bas asks.

"Nothing major." Eneks hazards a reply. "It's not meant for fighting."

"But to ward off pirates? Certainly a place like this is a raid target."

Again the Sisters squirm, patter towards each other.

"Speak so we all can hear," Sax says.

"We have weapons," L'Renee says. "But they're not for you to use."

"Never anyone but us," N'Ollene adds.

"You'll use them, then, to shoot the next shuttle they send," Bas says. "We'll get them to send it, and then you'll destroy it. And everything that comes after."

The Sisters laugh. Eneks even looks confused.

"You think they'll leave? The Vincere will never go away if we fire on them. They'll simply attack in greater and greater numbers until there's nothing left of this station."

Bas shrugs her claws. "That's your future. This is your now. Either you take us to the weapons and fire them, or you die here. If you want, you can blame the attack on us."

There's not much debate after that. The Sisters roll off across the garden, with Eneks and the Oratus following. Until they reach the building, which is far too small for any Oratus to enter. The Sisters, though, scramble inside before Sax can react.

Bas grabs Eneks before the Vyphen can try to run, leaving Sax to make the obvious threat. Either the Ooblots do as they've agreed, or their beloved servant becomes a messy stain in the middle of their garden.

"We're not running," L'Renee's voice comes from inside the building. "The only way to arm the station is in here."

"Where nobody else can get it," N'Ollene adds.

"Hold him?" Sax asks Bas.

"He's not going anywhere. Right, Eneks?"

The Vyphen shakes his head, feathers ruffling wildly. Sax takes the cue to jump on top of the building, where he tracks the Ooblots through the translucent roof, watches them shift through one room after another until they get to the back, to a small room where, after Sax digs his claws into the ceiling and pulls it off, he can see an array of terminals.

"What did you just do?" L'Renee protests.

"He's ruined our home!" N'Ollene says.

"Making sure you do as you're supposed to," Sax replies. "Tell them you've caught us. Have them send the shuttle towards the airlock."

The Sisters do as asked. It's Lan's voice on the receiving line, and she says a pickup will be on its way shortly. If both Lan and Gar are on that shuttle... getting ambushed and blown up in space isn't a good Oratus death either.

Sax flicks back towards Bas, whose still holding Eneks and looking bored with it. He has to protect her, just as she protects him. Sax tells the Sisters to go ahead, to arm the weapons.

He's going to start a war to save himself.

The inside is long, wide, and unbroken. And I recognize it. These are the same pools Ignos had me making back in Damantum—frothing purple liquid with textured lips to allow for easy in-and-out access. Only where we were building two or three, here there are easily a twenty, if not more.

The space is crowded too—all sorts of species are being herded around by Sevora-hosted Flaum and Whelk. Everyone's being pushed into various lines, though our Flaum guards keep us away from the rest of the throng and take us to the far end.

"No common Sevora for you," the Flaum leader continues. "You'll be receiving the best of hosts, experienced and capable. You should be honored."

"It's never an honor to lose your freedom," Malo replies.

"Then think of it as sacrifice, if you prefer," the Flaum replies. "What you're doing here is only going to help your people. By submitting to the Sevora, you will save them, either from yourselves or from the rest of a hungry, brutal galaxy."

"Is that the pitch you make to everyone?" Viera asks.

"Because it's not very good," I add. "You should try talking up the miracles you'll be giving us. How we'll never starve, how we won't need to worry about making our own choices, how we'll never have to want for anything ever again."

The Flaum stares at me for a moment, trying to decide if I'm joking or being serious.

"Or can the Sevora not grant all of our wishes?" I finish.

"We will change your wishes, and then grant them," the Flaum replies.

That's clearly enough talking for him, as he turns and heads along the outer edge of the pools, and his guards push us along after him.

As we go, I look to the right and see a lanky Teven slowly walk towards a pool, its tiny limbs sticking out from the long reed serving as its central body. It hesitates about halfway across the pearly flagstones and a Flaum comes up behind it, reaches out with a clawed hand and pushes the Teven forward.

The Teven whirls at the touch and for a second I think it's going to mount some kind of resistance, but then the Flaum raises his miner and the Teven decides not to risk its life in the face of the laser cannon. It turns, wades into the pool and disappears beneath the purple waters.

"How many do you take every day?" I ask the Flaum, because I'm realizing if I don't talk, then I might panic.

"Thousands across Vimelia are exchanged every day," the Flaum replies, once again falling into his boastful tone. "Whether we're recycling old hosts, integrating new ones, or trading rom one Sevora to another to better match needs, the Sevora are always in motion."

I first met Ignos in a crashed pod outside my tribe, deep

in the jungle. When I approached its ship, thinking it was a rock, it opened and, inside, was an inky liquid much like what I see in these pools. I went in, and gained what I thought was a god, what was in fact a creature determined to spread its parasitic race across my world. Here, though, the event seems so commonplace. As if giving up everything to another species is as normal as cooking breakfast or running through the trees.

It twists my stomach into tight knots, and I take a hard swallow to get my breath back. Feel Malo's hand touch my arm lightly and breathe easier for it. I'm not alone this time.

There's no line for our pool, and as we approach, the Flaum asks us who ought to go first.

Malo volunteers immediately, but I shut him down.

"Let me," I say. "I've done this before, and I know what to expect. If something's wrong, I'll be able to deal with it."

"Nothing will go wrong," the Flaum says, nodding across the hall. "This is the most common thing we do. It's the very core of who the Sevora are. Now, get in and submit."

There's not much in the way of ceremony for entering a Sevora pool. The Flaum don't care if I keep on my clothes—I don't know if they realize I'm wearing a mask—and they don't blow horns, flash lights, or do anything other than watch me with their hands close to their miners.

Malo and Viera watch me too, of course, though their faces are etched with concern. Even though this is part of the plan, we all know it's not going to be pleasant.

The flagstones are cool to the touch, and everything glows somewhat in the clear light filtering in from the roof, which is a translucent cover that provides a frankly amazing view of all those intertwining spires. Not for the first time

I'm surprised at how much beauty these terrible things can create.

I get up to the edge and look into the purple. It's too dark to see below the surface, the water quickly getting to the level of a deep twilight. There's clearly current too—either that or the Sevora themselves make the ripples caressing the surface.

"Get in," the Flaum barks from behind me. "Your master needs its host."

Apparently that's the cue. I take the order and step forward, expecting there to be a step but there isn't one. It's just a cliff. I overbalance, send out a yelp, and splash into the pool.

That's me, always dignified.

I try to swim, but the liquid is heavy, pulling me down. As though I'm trying to shove against the same thick muck that coated the sewers. Every stroke tightens my muscles and leaves me sinking, to the point where I wonder if I'll just drown in here.

The thought dies a swift death as I feel a tickling touch around my head. I try to lift a hand to brush it away, but the ink is too thick down here, too heavy. I can't even get my arm up that high. Not that it matters anyway—Sapphrite's big design gets to work before the probing Sevora can realize my mask is blocking it.

The sign comes when the ink around me starts to shift color, to bloom into a sickly orange as the coating on my hair reacts with the nourishing chemicals in the ink and grows. Spreads its viral haze through the pool.

At once the tickling touch vanishes—if Sapphrite's creation works, that same virus should be devouring the Sevora now, gobbling up the thin-skinned parasite and spreading from this pool to the others.

Of course, the mask protects me from the virus too. Its protection is what made Malo, Viera, and I such perfect vessels for the delivery. As it is, though, I'm stuck at the bottom of a massively growing collection of voracious cells, and I can't lift myself out.

There's a shift next to me and I see the Flaum guard's gray-metal stick slash through the thick orange like a black line. I'm able to get my hands around it, the mask protecting me from the rough edges, and I feel myself start to rise.

Like a parting film, the orange gives way as I reach the surface to total chaos. Shouts pour in through the mask, coupled with far-off bangs.

Clarity's Dawn is beginning their part of the deal.

Malo grabs my arm and pulls me the rest of the way out, and I get my first look at what's happening to the rest of the pools.

Sapphrite said the bacteria would spread fast, hopefully fast enough to outrun any seals the Sevora could enact. Right now, more than half of the pools are turning orange as the stuff eats its way through the pipes that apparently connect them all.

Sevora-controlled guards are running around in a panic, heading for panels or just fleeing entirely as captive species realize they have a sudden chance to be free.

"They will seize their opportunity," Sapphrite said back down below. "They will fight back once they've seen what's coming for them."

In this case, anyway, the Amigga is right. After seeing what waits in those pools, and with the guards distracted, Teven, Whelk, Flaum and others rush either towards exits or towards their captors, angling to pull miners from their hands.

But not all of them. Some simply stand still, looking around, vacant-eyed and lost.

"We've got to go," Viera says, and I turn away from the scene to see my friend with both of her miners drawn, picked up from a pile of taken tools and weapons meant to be directly returned once a Sevora has taken control of their new host.

There's only one exit from the building that I can see, and it's crowded with bodies and the flashes of miners, though whether the attacks are coming from Sevora or not, I can't tell.

"Not that way." I point back behind the tubes, towards a set of maintenance doors, where some of the Sevora guards had disappeared. "They won't be expecting us to head through the back."

At first, at least, nobody stops us. With Viera leading and Malo watching behind, the three of us break around the long pool towards those doors. They're smaller than human entries, smaller too than the ones on *Cobalt*, which must have been sized with Oratus in mind. These are simple squares about two meters high, plenty tall for a Flaum but Malo has to duck under as we head through them.

That the doors open straight away surprises me, until I remember that the Sevora operate by absolute authority. Why bother with security when everyone on the planet ought to be under your iron-fisted control?

Beyond the door I expect to find hallways, but instead it's another open area, and what I see is horrifying: rows and rows of stunned species clumped together. Bodies of Flaum, Whelk and others piled on one another, though they're all seemingly still alive. Still breathing, though they barely move.

"You're a host for so long, you don't know how to be

free," Viera says, and even her light voice carries lead at the sight.

"This, this is what happens?" I say the words knowing neither of them can answer, knowing that I'm seeing it all spread before me.

There are shallow pools on this side too—much smaller, and many of the bodies are clustered outside of them. Where the Sevora must evacuate their hosts before heading to the other side for new ones. No secret why they'd want to keep these pools hidden , either—any captive looking at these bodies would get a very different idea of what it means to be a Sevora host.

And that's when I realize why some of the Sevora guards went this way—there are so many listless souls here that if someone roused them to fight, they could overwhelm this whole building and more.

"Hundreds and hundreds of them," Malo whispers.

"Come on," I finally muster. "We can't just watch or the Sevora will realize we're not taken. Let's go."

The shot fires—a blast of bright white hot energy streaking out towards the approaching Oratus shuttle. Just when it's about to hit, the white bolt diffuses into a series of thin crackles and scatters around the ship without any apparent damage.

"Dispersion shields," Bas hisses. "They suspected."

"How could they not? Two Ooblots catching two Oratus?" Eneks says. "Especially ones like yourselves?"

Sax watches the shuttle continue its approach, heading in towards the garden's airlock. If the ship had its shields running—something that drained plenty of energy, and not worth doing if you didn't suspect an attack—then it followed that whatever waited inside that shuttle would be strong enough to take Sax and Bas by force.

"Fire again," Sax orders, and the Ooblots carry out the order.

Another white bolt lances out, another white bolt dissipates into nothing.

"You only have one cannon on this station?" Sax says.

"Only one that we're willing to use," Eneks replies. "Try to kill us if you want, but if we make enemies of the Vincere, then we are most definitely dead."

"We need to run, Sax," Bas says. "Back to Plake, maybe? Force her to take us away?"

Sax is shaking his head before Bas is done talking. He's had enough of negotiations. Enough deals and dancing around. There's only one way he wants to get out of this—Sax wants to fight, to win, to get back who he is.

"Eneks, where is the nearest communications array?" Sax hisses and the Vyphen points towards another room in the Ooblot's short building.

"What are you doing?" L'Renee asks.

"It can't be good!" N'Ollene adds.

Sax clomps over the roof, tears off the cover of the room with his claws, then steps into the space. The terminals are set low, but Sax can still tap the screens, still open a channel to the oncoming shuttle.

"This is Sax, your target," Sax rasps into the speakers inset in the terminal's base.

"You're wanted for suspected rebellion against the Chorus," the voice that comes back is watery, a Whelk. "You're ordered to stand down and await our arrival. Any further attempts at attack from the station will be returned with lethal force."

"Torching an entire station for two Oratus seems brutal, even by our standards," Sax says.

"We follow our orders, unlike you."

"I follow my conscience." Sax cuts the communication. Flips the channel to broadcast through the station. "*Scrapper Station*, the Vincere is declaring that anyone on this station who does not submit for an interrogation, who does not give themselves up and face whatever crimes they may be guilty of, will be shot dead."

He takes a breath. Looks back at Bas, who gives him the nod.

A lie that might cause many to die.

A lie that might let the Oratus live.

"We've chosen to fight back. Any who stand with us, who want to survive, find your weapons, form up, and find your courage. *Scrapper Station* will not bow to oppression!"

Inciting innocents to rebel isn't something Sax has ever done before, and being up in the garden, away from those same people, makes it hard to discern what effect he's had, if any. The key, though, is that he added an open channel to that last broadcast, sent it flying out into space.

To the Vincere frigate, to the shuttle.

If there's guilt to be had in potentially setting up a fight between people who could have avoided it, Sax kills it with the sure knowledge that anyone on *Scrapper Station* is likely avoiding lawful work anyway. Everyone here has something to hide, someone to scam, and a willingness to do whatever it takes to survive.

What he's betting on is that they'll do enough to buy Sax and Bas some time to find a way off of this station.

"At least we'll keep our promise to the Teven," Bas says as Sax returns to them.

"Yes, I'm sure they'll be thrilled when the entire station is burning because of your actions," Eneks sighs.

"You've killed us all!" L'Renee shouts from her terminal.

"Only if you let them," Sax says. "It's either fight or die now, Ooblot."

"Then we fight!" N'Ollene announces. "Fire, Sister, and fire again!"

This time, it's five white bursts lancing forth from the station, and now the shuttle tries to move. It jockeys up and down, so that only three of the shots manage to splash across its shields, with the last punching through and glancing off the shuttle's armor.

"Aim for the frigate," Sax says. "Keep it away from the station. We'll handle the shuttle."

"I don't like this," L'Renee replies.

"But we'll try," N'Ollenne adds.

Sax and Bas lope over to the airlock as the shuttle screams in for a hard docking. Two Oratus against who knows how many. Sax still has the miner he took from the Flaum guard, but that's hardly enough artillery. They check around the airlock, looking for vulnerabilities, for places to set up in cover, but the bushes won't block any lasers, and the airlock is wide enough to let the troops stream through.

"Our only chance is breaking the seal," Bas says as they study the airlock, looking for hope.

"We don't have the weapons to do that," Sax replies.

"But we do," Agra-Red's voice comes from behind them. The fiery whelk's assault miner, built into its body, has a full set of batteries lacing from the weapon and around Agra-Red. Black, the burly female Flaum, stands next to him, along with Plake, each holding oodles of their own weaponry.

And they're all aiming at the two Oratus.

"What do you think, Plake?" Agra-Red says. "We blast them, the Vincere lets us all go?"

The Vyphen captain brushes her purple-red mouth with an iridescent feathered arm, then shakes her head. "Feel like that option's already gone. These two have torched all of us. That's what happens when you fire on a

Vincere ship. They'll just raze the station rather than take stock of who's innocent and who's not."

Sax is trying to find a vulnerability, but unlike the useless Flaum guards from earlier, Plake, Black, and Agra-Red are keeping their distance. They'd have more than enough time to react, aim, and fire before Sax could leap to them.

"That's the point," Bas hisses. "We told you. There's something bigger going on here, something that ends if Evva gets captured."

"Big enough to damn everyone on this station?" Plake says.

"Yes."

The Vyphen puts on a show of considering, but Sax bets she's already made up her mind. He's thinking if Plake really wanted them dead, she'd have shot them in the back. Not even given him or Bas a chance to respond.

"Here's what I'm looking at," Plake starts. "The rest of my life spent running nutrient goop and stopping in dives like this one, or a short burst spent trying to hurt the bastards who've turned the Vyphen into cretins like this one."

She nods at Eneks, who manages to look both offended and embarrassed at the same time.

"The Oratus torched my homeworld," Agra-Red says. "I've got no love for them. No love for you two, either, but it sounds like you might give me a shot at doing some real damage." It twists, aiming the assault miner behind Sax. "Besides, I need more excuses to play with this thing."

Both of them look at Black, who's wielding a snub-nosed gouter, hooked to a big tank on her back. She looks at the Oratus and shrugs.

"Coorvin says you're on the good side, and I trust him."

There's a loud thunk from behind them, followed by the whirring and clacking sounds of locks sliding into place. The shuttle's docking.

"Now get out of the way, you morons, or I'll fry you too," Agra-Red waves the tip of its miner, and both Sax and Bas break to either side of the airlock door.

Eneks dashes to the airlock's control panel, glances back at Plake, who shakes her head.

"Not until they're inside,' Plake says. "We've only got one shot at this."

Sax watches through the glass into the white cream of the airlock. Instead of a real window opening to space, there's now a tunnel lit by small globes of light. A tunnel that leads back to the shuttle, to the force coming to take them all.

Though, going by Agra-Red's manic grin, Sax thinks the Vincere's going to have a harder time than expected.

The first Flaum troops pour into the airlock, and they're ready for almost anything. They've got miners, they've got armor, and they're moving like a trained squad. What they're not expecting, though, is a mad red Whelk with a giant cannon waiting for them.

At Plake's nod, Eneks opens the panel and, as the airlock door shunts aside, Agra-Red opens up. A cascade of red bolts pours forth, punctuated by a rising whine as the weapon's pumps keep working to churn gas through the miner's ionizing batteries. Agra-Red keeps the steady spray moving back and forth, and, beyond the panicked screams of trapped Flaum, there's a new sound: vacuum alarms. Agra-Red's pierced the shell leading back to the shuttle, exposing everything to open space.

At the first hint of the pull, the airlock slams shut of its own accord and Sax doesn't even move a centimeter. The

Flaum, and anyone caught in the tunnel to the shuttle, isn't so lucky. They're blasted out into space, and Sax can see their flash-frozen figures spiraling away into the black.

"Seal it," Plake says.

Black steps forward with her gouter and starts a spray of heavy green liquid. It splashes around the airlock, letting loose plenty of steam as the plasma burrows into the metal. The cooling comes rapidly, with the green settling into a deep gray and hardening around the door, eventually encasing the entire entrance.

"They can break that," Sax says.

"But they won't," Plake counters. "Not when they have plenty of docking bays to use."

There's a crackle, then L'Renee's voice echoes over the station's broadcast system, "They're launching additional shuttles and fighters. *Scrapper Station*, get ready for imminent assault!"

"Show them what a bunch of scuzzy lowlifes and vagabonds can do!" N'Ollene adds.

They don't waste time hanging around the airlock. All five of them—Eneks retreats back to the Sisters—head to the lift, hustle in, and take it down to the Nexus.

"Never expected you to come to our defense," Sax says as the lift chugs lower.

"Never wanted to," Plake replies. "You forced our hand."

"We meant to."

"That's not what you're supposed to say."

"Thank you," Bas hisses. "Now, we have to leave."

Agra-Red laughs. "Leave? After you've got them all riled up?"

"Even if we manage to hold back this assault," Bas says. "They'll be calling for reinforcements. The station will be destroyed, unless we get away. Unless we claim responsibility."

"Compassion? From an Oratus? I didn't think you had any," Plake says, then sighs. "And I suppose you're planning on us to take you?"

"Yes."

Sax isn't much for subtlety.

We make it all of ten steps. We're next to one of the feeder pools, a quartet of Whelk standing, looking at us with nothing going on in their eyes, when there's a yell from further down the room.

"The humans came this way!" The Flauma's voice is hard, angry and bright. "Leave these, get them!"

It looks like the Flaum's group is busy shooting freed, confused species and tossing them into piles. Summary executions for potential problems. Seeing it makes me feel sick, but I suppress the revulsion when I see the ten Flaum turn our way.

"And now we run," Viera says.

Part of me wants to stay and fight, because it's clear the sort of end coming to all of these innocents. Clear the Sevora are choosing harsh security, that they're treating these species as products rather than people. But we're outnumbered and outgunned, and if there's going to be this much death, then the sacrifice ought to be for something.

Viera fires a few shots from her miners, though I don't see if any hit. I'm looking around, trying to find an exit, and locate one along the back wall; a series of arched doors similar to the ones in Nasiya's tower, the ones leading to those tubes and the white platforms.

"That way! Through the arches!" I shout as I break into a run.

In the jungle, I used trees for cover, whether to hide or to dodge thrown rocks, fired arrows. Here I do the same, only instead of trees, I use the ambling forms of stupefied Flaum, of clustered Tevens just beginning to flex their arms and legs outside their carapaces. The Sevora Flaum fire away, and they don't care where their miners burn. Species drop around us as we run, many without a sound. Maybe they're so divorced from their own feelings that they don't even recognize pain.

Bolts that don't hit a bystander zing into the walls and floor around us, leaving scorch marks or bubbling tile.

A shot lands right in front of me, exploding a chunk of the floor, and the hot dust blasts my face, the mask blunting the temperature. I stumble, though the mask filters away the dust, then feel Malo's arm on my back, pushing me forward.

"If we stop, Kaishi, we die," he says, and I want to tell him I know but can't find the breath.

The air is sick with burning flesh, with the electric zap of molten metal and discharged batteries and my mask doesn't clean out the smell. My ears ring with shouts, the whine of energy being spent, and the constant rumble of explosions outside the building.

But we make the arches. Me first, with Malo just behind, and Viera continuing her stream of wild shots. I notice the armor on her has a few burn holes, but Viera's still moving and we don't have time for first aid anyway.

All the arches funnel into a back, smaller section that in turn feeds into those same platform tubes.

"The middle one!" I point as we run towards the only platform already there and waiting.

The rest of the station is empty—apparently nobody wants to visit the birthing pools when everything goes wrong. Lasers continue to splash into the walls behind us, but the pursuit seems half-hearted. By the time we reach the platform, there's nobody even in sight.

"Anyone know how to use this thing?" Viera asks as we stream through the doors.

"No idea," I say, turning to the control panel anyway. "But I'm guessing anywhere is better than here."

There's no buttons, only a screen with a maze of icons. It reminds me of the console on *Cobalt*, and I wish Ignos were here to tell me what they all meant. Lacking the Sevora, and lacking the time to dip into the Cache, I tap one that looks like a flying ship.

The doors slam shut. I step back onto the platform and sit in the chair that forms to match my size.

"We're alive," I manage to say to my friends, and then the platform rockets away.

Our ride launches us up and away from the birthing pool building, and what I see sears into my mind: across Vimelia's vast cityscape, towers of smoke rise from all over, like black, billowing trees from a silvery desert.

Unlike our first ride with the Flaum, this platform expands a transparent film around us as we get up to speed, and I find my breath isn't stolen away by the rapid air. Apparently the Sevora build their transport by grades—ones going to and from the birthing pools get a better class of ride.

"Sapphrite wasn't kidding," Viera says as we zip through the air. "Clarity's Dawn is going all out on this one."

"Did you see how it looked down there?" I reply. "They were starving, and it seemed like only luck was keeping them alive. Rather than wait for the Sevora to end them, better fight on their terms."

"Better to die for something than because of someone," Malo adds.

The tube swoops us out and around the large sculpture heading the birthing pool building, and we get a good look at what's happening outside the main entrance, where most of the prisoners are scrambling.

It's just as bad as the way we went—a firing range of Sevora guards lays waste to unarmed, panicked prisoners trying to pile their way out of the building. A one-sided lightshow.

"That's so horrible," I can't keep from saying.

"Ignos wanted you to join that? No thanks." Viera glances at her miners. "You should have let me stomp the slug when Rackt took it out of your head."

"Maybe so."

The platform, mercifully, keeps moving and soon the slaughter disappears out of sight behind taller buildings. It's still hard to tell where we're heading, so I tell the other two that I'm going to slip into the Cache.

Even with all the excitement, triggering the Cache and its emerald flash pulls me away from our zipping ride and into the infinite, cool nexus of data. Immediately a giant map of Vimelia fills the space around me, and our current location shows as a blinking dot in a translucent blue city.

The Cache traces out our current path, and it goes right from where we are towards a large oval that, with a mental question, the Cache identifies as the spaceport.

With our side of Sapphrite's mission done—all we had to do was poison the birthing pools—our only goal now is to get to the spaceport, find the shuttle that Rackt is supposed to have waiting for us, and get out of there.

I shake away the Cache and announce to Viera and Malo that we're going where we're supposed to. Settle back in and watch out the front.

Filling the air now are more and more of the Sevora shuttles that dropped the initial group of Flaum that met us when we escaped the sewers. Nasiya's emblem blazes on some, Jel's on others. Both factions, it seems, are coming together to stop Clarity's Dawn.

And I realize I don't really care anymore. Not about the Sevora struggle, not about Sapphrite's wish to live forever with the other Amigga, or whether these creatures devour each other in their murderous politics. No, all I want is to go home.

Which is why I almost scream when the platform slows, then veers from its straight path to go down, right towards a tall, egg-shaped building beneath us. We shuttle through an opening in the top, big enough to only fit our single plat-form. The floors we pass by are dark, skeletal, as if this building is still under construction.

Eventually, the platform settles at the base, where, indeed, are piles and piles of materials.

There's also a set of five creatures standing, waiting. One strides forward as the platform's bubble recedes and our seats fall away beneath us. As the creature comes closer, I recognize the shape. Like Sax and Bas, but smaller, and its scales are a dull gray. Several flake off even in the steps towards us. But the claws on its four arms shine sharp enough.

"Kaishi. I hoped I would see you again," the creature says, and even with the rasping hiss of an Oratus tongue, it's one I know.

Ignos.

"You have a new body," is the first thing I can think of to say.

We step slowly off of the platform into the dark skeleton of the building. Above us, papered window frames filter brown light coming down from the sky, and a dozen open doros along the street let in the noise of the fighting. I smell dust, the twinge of chemicals.

"A host, Kaishi. That's what we call them," Ignos, ever teaching me. "But this one is a failure."

It does seem to be falling apart. Like it's old, or dying. Why would Ignos call that a failure?

"What do you mean?" I ask.

"There's never an end to our conflict. The Amigga aren't going to stop until we're all dead, which means we need to crush them first. To do that, we need better weapons. We need perfect ones," Ignos glances at his claws.

"So you're making Oratus?"

"They're too hard to capture, but take the DNA from the few we have and maybe we can do what the Amigga did, what we've already done to so many other species. What we'll do to you."

"Yeah, enough of this," Viera announces from beside me. "Now that you're not in her head, it's time to do what should've been done a long time ago."

She draws her miners as the four Flaum guards around Ignos draw theirs. Viera's hands are faster than Flaum claws, and she has the half-second advantage of knowing just what she's going to do. So her lasers hit first, sending a pair of Ignos' guards burning to the ground.

Ignos, though, doesn't sit and watch, but leaps towards me instead.

"You have to give yourself to us," the Sevora hisses as it flies towards me. "The Sevora need you!"

Malo's metal staff catches Ignos in a wide swing as the creature gets close to me, and Malo slams Ignos down into the ground. The Charre warrior is wielding the staff with both hands, and he raises it up, twists the point, and gets ready to stab the parasite that'd shared my mind.

"Malo!" Viera yells as she comes out of a dive, dodging counterfire from one of the remaining Flaum.

But not both.

The second, last Flaum's aiming at Malo, and it pulls the trigger as the Charre warrior stabs with the staff. The bolt flies true, taking Malo in the chest and sending him stumbling off of Ignos.

Malo falls at my feet. I want to check on him, but the Flaum is moving its miner towards me now, so I fall back on my training and dive forward, scooping up Malo's dropped staff and getting Ignos' much larger body between me and the Flaum.

Another series of lasers flashes around us—Viera, getting back to work.

"This isn't you, Kaishi," Ignos hisses, standing back up, a motion that sheds more scales. "You're not a fighter. You're a leader, a friend."

"And what are you, Ignos? I thought you were my friend." I hold the staff ready, watch those claws.

"I never claimed to be anything other than I was. I gave you miracles, the tools you needed to save your people. All I ask in return is a chance, a chance for my own species to survive."

"Not by taking over the very people you helped save!"

"There's no other way!"

Ignos jumps at me after its roar, and I dance back,

batting at a claw with the end of the staff. I'd seen Sax and Bas move, and Ignos seems jerky, unsure of how to manage the limbs. Of course, if it's only had the body for a few days...

I press the attack. Roll off my back foot and dart into Ignos' reach. The Sevora tries to adjust its long swings—claws slashing to where it thought I'd be, but can't seem to move them fast enough. I drive the center of the staff up and bash into its mouth, , then, as Ignos backpedals, bring the staff down to my waist and shove it forward like a spear.

The point sticks into Ignos' side, punching through thin, fragile scales. Sick, thick blood oozes around the wound, and Ignos clutches at the staff, looks at me with those yellow Oratus eyes.

"Perhaps I was wrong," Ignos mutters.

"You were wrong about many things," I reply.

Ignos yanks the staff free, letting more of the body's blood flow, and holds it in its right midclaw.

"There's an advantage to being a host, Kaishi," Ignos says. "You only feel what you want to feel."

The Sevora steps towards me, and then a bright flash comes over my shoulder, strikes Ignos in the Oratus' wide chest, and drops the creature to the ground.

"Come on, Kaishi," Viera says, running up next to me. "The thing was evil anyway."

The lift lands in the Nexus and the five of them exit into a sliding crowd of chaos. Species run back and forth, some alone and others in groups. Some carrying weapons, most looking for places to hide. Asking for escape mods, or how to surrender.

Sax doesn't care to tell them that the Vincere won't take prisoners. Not here, not anymore.

It's a quick sprint through the Nexus to the spoke where the *Mobius* is parked. Even in their various levels of panic, the crowds make way for the hulking Oratus and their heavily-armed friends. More than a few tag along behind them—presumably going for their own ships and figuring to be where the firepower is.

Which proves to be a good decision for everyone when the Sisters announce that the first shuttles have landed.

The docking spoke itself is a long, wide hallway with neon-lit numbers hanging outside large, arched doors leading into the bays themselves. Beneath the numbers are the names of the current occupants, and Sax can see the blazing blue of #6, and beneath it, *Mobius*, far down the spoke.

Most of the bays, though, are empty. And most of their doors are opening.

"Too late," Black says. "Cover?"

Two choices—either they press through, try to make it to the bay, or sit back and fight it out with the coming forces. The problem with the latter is the Vincere has more troops, more weapons than they do.

"If we play it safe, we're dead," Sax announces. "I'll go for your ship, and we'll come back for you. Cover me."

He tosses Bas the miner he still has from the Flaum, then Sax breaks for the wall.

Agra-Red and Plake take up the task of covering fire, along with a bunch of *Scrapper Station* scoundrels, and unleash lasers at the groups of soldiers pouring into the spoke. There's not much to hide behind in the hallway—a few crates here and there, some battery racks that everyone stays well away from, so the firefight quickly degenerates into a blinding murderer's row.

Sax goes up the right wall, using his claws to pull himself along. Space station walls aren't designed to resist Oratus claws, so he slices his way along in a rapid scramble towards the soldiers.

Shouts and screams grow loud, then a stray shot strikes something combustible and an explosion rocks the middle of the spoke, smoke and fizzing energy filling the air. Sax can't see anything except the flashes of those not deterred by the fact they can't see their target. He keeps moving forward, keeps his vents closed as long as possible—who knows what terrible gasses are getting blown through the air now.

It's hard to hit an Oratus in perfect conditions, much

less when Sax has a wall of gray hiding him from view. Sax climbs over the blue glow of Bay Five, and not long after finds himself above number six. He drops to the ground, is about to head through the doors, when he realizes they're closed.

Sax dashes to the control panel along one side, slams the button to open, but all he gets is a simple error message. Locked. So instead he taps the intercom, tries to talk through.

"Who's calling?" It's Engee, the Teven.

"Sax. Open the bay door."

"Where's Plake?"

Sax hears a noise behind him. The smoke's too thick to see what it is, but this far down the spoke, it's not likely to be a friend.

"She's busy. I need you to help me rescue them."

"How about you tell me where she is, and we'll get them first."

Sax hisses, raises his claw and is about to slam it against the panel, when a miner bolt crashes into the wall next to him.

"Tricked me once, Sax," Gar rasps. "It's not going to happen a second time."

Turning your back on an enemy is the last thing Sax wants to do, especially when that enemy has four sharp claws and a pair of talons. But the *Mobius* has to get in the air, or one of the lasers still flying through the smoke is going to hit Bas.

"Go up to Bay One. They're right outside the door," Sax manages to say before a pair of claws dig into his shoulder and throw him away from the intercom.

"Talking to someone?" Gar hisses, diving back on to of Sax, teeth snapping at Sax's throat.

Sax, pushing Gar back with his own foreclaws, manages to get his tail between the two of them and pushes up with the strong muscle. His tail shoves Gar up and off of him, through the air and into the smoke somewhere back up the spoke.

The Oratus hops to a crouch, scans the mist. There's still plenty of battle noise, though he's seeing fewer flashes coming back this way. The little band of roughs was never going to last long.

Gar drops from above, and Sax only gets a split second warning from the sudden curl of the gray smoke. Sax tries to leap right as Gar crashes into him, and that centimeter of distance means Gar's talons only dig a long gash down Sax's neck instead of piercing his head. Without the solid landing, Gar has to catch himself on the ground, which puts him at perfect level for Sax's tail to crack into him.

This time, Sax's smashing blow sends Gar into the Bay Six door, and Sax doesn't let his former friend set himself. Sax bounds forward and, in a single long leap, pins Gar. With his left foreclaw, Sax drives Gar's neck back against the metal, the tips of his claws pressing in on Gar's scales.

"You never did care enough about your surroundings," Sax hisses.

"I'm not the only one," Gar rasps.

A wash of blue light hits Sax, and he feels all sensation drop away, all things fade into a numb nothing.

Malo's still on the ground when we turn to him, and he's sporting a deep burn in his chest. His eyes are closed and his breathing comes ragged.

"Can we lift him up?" Viera says, and I move to try.

The warrior isn't light, though, and it takes both of us to even get Malo off the ground. As we lift him, Malo's eyes jerk open and he gasps.

"Don't move me!" Malo says, leaning on us. "It's too painful."

"It's either that or you get to stay here with all these lovely bodies," Viera replies.

"We're not far," I say, though it's only a guess. "It's no worse than when Jakkan's assassins attacked us back home."

Malo closes his eyes tight for a second, then nods.

"One step at a time," I say, and then we move.

Viera keeps one miner drawn in her right hand as we creep forward. I manage to sneak a look at the rest of the Flaum, at the smoke still rising from their bodies.

"You're deadlier than I thought," I say to her.

"Apparently I have to be around you," Viera replies. "Seems we get into all kinds of trouble."

My hand, on Malo's waist, feels his sweat, his shaking skin. I don't know if he's going to make it out of this, but I'm going to do my best to try.

We exit the egg-shaped building and find ourselves on a broad street. Not too far away, I can see the gigantic oval marking the spaceport, the place where we landed after Ignos first tricked us to traveling here.

"It's not far, Malo, not far," I whisper to him.

"Just keep going," Malo replies, his eyes still shut.

So that's what we do. With the continuing chaos throughout the city, nobody bothers stopping to see what's going on with three struggling species moving slow along the ground. We pass beneath huge buildings, under swooping walkways and tubes, many of which still have platforms shuttling people from one place to another. Even an all-out attack from Clarity's Dawn apparently doesn't shut down Vimelia.

"Did you see Ignos?" I ask Viera as we move. "The body it was using seemed like it was falling apart."

"Maybe they only had an old one." Viera doesn't sound the least bit curious. "Or the thing was sick. I'm not complaining, either way."

We carry on for a few more steps. Malo's getting heavier, but I'm not going to leave him, so I dig deep, push through the soreness in my shoulders and the pressure on my back and keep going.

I'm still curious how Ignos managed to grab us, how it redirected the platform to ambush us there at the bottom of the building. If it was planned, why only go with a few Flaum? If it wasn't, how did Ignos find us so fast?

"Kaishi, do you remember when the Emperor died?"

Malo says, his voice soft, weaker than I've ever heard it.

"You led our forces. Won the fight."

"I slept," Viera adds. "It was glorious."

"I thought I was doing it for revenge, to honor his sacrifice," Malo continues. "But I think we all knew, even the Emperor, that it wasn't him we were fighting for, but for you and what you were giving us. If we lost you, then we would lose everything."

"You mean, if you lost Ignos," I reply.

"No, you. For whatever else you are, Kaishi, you're kind. You care. If Ignos had found a warrior that didn't hold back, who just wanted to conquer, then we would all have lost."

"Quiet, Malo," I don't want him to die mid-sentence, especially now that we've carried him this far. "Try to save your strength."

"Not like Kaishi needs the praise anyway," Viera says. "She knows she's great."

Malo manages a half laugh, then falls silent again.

The spaceport is larger, closer now. There's no grand entrance, but instead a series of tunnels with arched openings leading down. In front of the closest opening, I see a familiar face and wave my arm.

Rackt and a pair of Clarity's Dawn Whelk scramble over to us and take a look at Malo.

"Can you help him?" I ask the Vyphen, whose packing a trio of miners, one larger in his hands and two smaller ones like Viera's on his belt.

The Vyphen glances at one of the Whelks, who pulls a pack off his gooey back and sets down near Malo, pulling a tube of some fluid and spreading a clear liquid over the area of the burn.

"It's a bad one," the Whelk says as he spreads the gel. "He needs better help than we can give him here."

Then the Whelk pulls something out of his pack—a little jar that I recognize.

"Stim?" I say as the Whelk sticks a needle through the rubber lid of the jar, pulls it back out coated in the sticky stuff.

"You've seen it?" Rackt asks.

"I've used it," I reply. "If we live through this, I'll tell you about it."

"Speaking of," Viera's eyes are tracking behind us, and while the Whelk gives Malo a dose of the energizing drug, we see a shuttle lift off from back the way we came, near the egg structure.

The craft wobbles in the air, then tilts its nose down and begins to speed towards us.

"What do you want to bet that's Ignos?" Viera says.

"No deal," I reply. "Let's get out of here."

I turn, and help a suddenly awake Malo to his feet. The Whelk throws his medical pack around his body and then we start to scramble for the entrance. My feet hit hard on the tile, and I feel Malo's hand tight in mine as we go.

"This, what I'm feeling, isn't natural," he says as we run.

"It's saving your life," I reply. "Don't complain."

"Not complaining, just surprised."

The entryway looms before us, an arch with a glowing red frame dotted with those black nodules. The ones I've come to realize can let others see you from far away.

Yet another thing I'll be glad to leave behind on this rotten world.

A gradual roar grows behind us and I don't have to look to know it's the shuttle. Air pushes us forward faster, and we make it past the threshold, the beige sky getting replaced by brighter, unnatural white lights. Which flicker as that rumbling roar gets so loud, so close—

"It's crashing!" Viera yells. "Dive!"

And we do as everything collapses, burns and explodes around us.

Somewhere in the tumble I lose track of Malo's hand. We're rolling through falling rock, bouncing down the slope until, finally hitting the bottom, I roll to a rest.

The mask keeps me upright and uncut, though it does nothing about the bruises and twisted ankle I'm feeling after that roll. Still, I'm the first one up, and I'm staring back at the collapsed entry and seeing carnage.

The front nose of the shuttle, gray and shattered now, is nearly touching me. Its wings are gone, and behind and around it, the entire tunnel has collapsed. Stone, sparking lights, and an unknown amount of pipes are bent and bursting around the craft.

The bodies of my friends, of Rackt and the medic Whelk—I don't see the other—are scattered around me. They're mostly still, or moaning. There's a sharp hiss, and the front of the shuttle, the glass shield, pops off and falls aside to the ground. Climbing out, its claws scraping against the side as it drops down, is Ignos.

Its Oratus body is bleeding from everywhere. There's a black scoring on its chest from Viera's blast, and the deep gouge from the staff looks like it hasn't sealed. Yet Ignos is standing there, staring at me with an open mouth full of razor teeth.

"Sevora can push past the pain, Kaishi," Ignos hisses at me. "We can bring a body to heights it could never achieve otherwise."

I'm shaking my head, even as I hope my friends can get themselves up. "You're killing it."

"This one? This one never really lived in the first place. From a tube to being my host, it wouldn't know what to do with freedom if it ever tasted it." Ignos steps towards me, its claws clacking against the docking bay's floor.

"That shouldn't be your choice to make."

"Yes. I could have left you alone. Let your tribe, all your people die in the name of freedom," Ignos doesn't stop. "Instead, I saved you. You owe me a debt, Kaishi. One you can repay right now by coming with me. Joining me."

"To do what, Ignos?" I cry. "What can I do that your Oratus body can't?"

"Save my species!" Ignos lunges forward with the last word, and I try to back-step.

Even with the mask, I'm not quick enough. Even weakened, the Oratus has too much strength. Ignos catches me, whips its tail behind my legs and trips me onto the ground.

It looms over me, and for a moment there in its yellow-black eyes I see something other than malice. And I reach for it.

"You don't want to kill me," I try to say.

"I don't," Ignos replies. "Yet, if you won't come willingly, then I have no choice."

"But if you hurt me, hurt us, you won't get what you want?"

"Look at this," Ignos glances at its claws. "It's not perfect, but it's close enough. And with time, we'll perfect it. I don't need you alive to get what I want."

Ignos raises its right foreclaw, and then it's no longer on top of me. There's a flash, and I see a mad ball of limbs. Black hair that I recognize.

Malo. His fists are flying, and connecting, until Ignos gets a claw into the man's back, bites in and flings Malo off of him and into the smooth docking-bay wall.

In the moment between Malo hitting the wall and Ignos getting back up, I realize we're far from the only people in the spaceport. Behind us, farther into the vast space, plenty of craft are coming and going. Their punctuating rockets add a peppered background noise to the continuing rumbles of far-off demolitions and the closer fizzle of sparking pipes.

There's bystanders too—species I'm assuming are controlled by Sevora, Flaum and others, staring at us from a safe distance.

An audience that scatters as soon as Viera gets up to a crouch and sends a few warning shots their way. Sends one over at Ignos too, which hits just over its ducking head.

"Gotta run, Kaishi," Viera curses as she half-walks, half stumbles over to me.

"We can't leave Malo," I reply, though I'm weaponless.

"No problem, you get the warrior, I'll take care of the slug," Viera raises the miner and advances on Ignos.

But she doesn't get there. One of those shuttles I assumed was leaving the spaceport zooms over towards us, blasts over the heads of the fleeing spectators and clomps its gear down next to me. The shuttle's shaped like a diamond, with the massive rockets glaring out one end of a smooth, pinkish shell.

"You all better get in here right now, or you're going to lose your ride!" T'Oli's voice, blasting out over the speakers. "Sapphrite told me to get you off this rock, but it didn't say I had to kill myself to do it, so you've got one chance!"

"Have one thing to take care of!" I shout back towards the ship, though I have no idea if T'Oli can hear me.

In any case, I run towards Malo's limp form. I'm not leaving him.

Ignos, with Viera working towards him, turns and runs. The battered body can still move with all six claws and talons pushing in concert. Viera tries a shot, misses left as Ignos juts beneath a resting spacecraft and keeps going.

I'm getting close to Malo, calling his name, and I don't like that he's not moving. There's a chill starting in my spine that I don't like, a reality growing I refuse to acknowledge.

He's a meter away when a bright flash splits the docking area, lancing ahead of me into the wall and shattering the rock. It's followed by a second shot, a red color, that slags the floor in front of me, turns the metal floor into molten soup.

"They won't miss a second time!" T'Oli calls.

"Kaishi!" Viera yells, heading towards T'Oli's ship. "Get him and go!"

I jump over the damaged floor, then dive towards Malo as another flash lights up the world ahead of me. Strikes the wall where Malo's lying, blasting rocks, metal, and worse all over him.

I start to scramble forward when pink metal slides in front of me, cutting me off from Malo's body. A door is open in the bottom of the craft, a thin ramp sliding down from it. My right foot plants and I jump, getting over the ramp and heading right towards Malo's body when something catches me, grabs hold of the robe I'm still wearing and pulls me back onto the ramp.

"You can't save him, Kaishi," Viera says, pulling me up the ramp.

"We can! He's right there!" But even as I say the words, I feel the pink shuttle shake as the Sevora defense pours their next attack into it.

"Malo gave himself for you, Empress, don't let it be for nothing," Viera says, and in that moment I stop fighting her.

I'm not stupid—going down for Malo means killing T'Oli, Viera, all of us. So I turn, I turn away from the warrior that'd stood by me for so long and leave him to die.

N o connection. He's in a void. No, there's something. A spark. He can hold onto it. Push. Harder.

Sax manages to open his eyes a narrow slit. It's barely enough to see.

But he has to start somewhere.

There's netting all around him. A forest of it. He must be in one of the shuttles, which explains the line of terminals in front, and the pair of Oratus working them. The cockpit window shows pure black space. Stars. The occasional laser flash arcing past them into oblivion.

Sax should feel the vibration from the engines, but he can't. Should be able to taste the tang of recycled air, but his vents now operate on instinct alone, on reflexive nerve action. No conscious thought required.

His mouth doesn't work either.

This must be what the Sevora feel like in a human's brain.

Gar twists his head around, looks at Sax. Spreads a toothy grin, "Looks like our friend is waking up."

Lan twitches her own head around, then snaps it back forward. To the terminals, the radars and flight controls.

"Stun him if he moves."

"His legs and arms are clasped," Gar shrugs. "He's not going anywhere. Though I suppose I could take a few bites if we want to be sure."

"Until they prove he's helping Evva, Sax is still Vincere. We shouldn't hurt him more than we have to."

"Sounds like a gray area to me."

Lan doesn't bother fighting further, which is like her. Keep Gar from going too far, but letting him go far enough. Sax tries to get more control, tries to find his own nerves as Gar steps away from the terminals. Heads over to him.

"We're almost to the frigate," Gar rasps as he squats down near Sax. "Don't know where Bas went. Didn't think she'd abandon you, but we always thought you two were a strange pairing. Maybe she's taking her chance."

Sax tries to glare. Only succeeds in closing his eyes enough for everything to go hazy gray.

"Don't like that thought? You'll have plenty of time to stew on it. The Amigga'll roast you for a good long time, make sure to get every useful morsel out of you." Gar wiggles his claws in front of Sax. "Then what do you do with a good weapon gone bad? I'll suggest a few things."

Something causes the shuttle to shake, because Gar suddenly leans to the side, sweeps out with his tail to stabilize himself.

"What's happening out there?" Gar looks back at Lan.

"We're being chased." Lan replies.

"Obviously. By who?"

"I don't know, but I can guess."

Sax manages to push his eyes back open and sees Lan swing the shuttle to the right, replacing the starfield with the solid pearl-white shape of the frigate. It's a beautiful, ridged feather of a craft, with sharp edges fanning out to provide the many docking points for fighters, shuttles, and other ships. A vessel Sax would have been proud to serve on, not long ago.

One that, if he lands on it now, will mean his death.

Getting hit with a stunning miner is like receiving a massive shock. The blast overloads the nerves, fries their connections and leaves them in a withered state, unable to send information until they recover. Depending on the shot —Sax is sure this came from a heavier miner than the one Lan used earlier—and the shielding—Sax wasn't wearing a full mask—the stun could work for hours or minutes.

There's another factor, one harder to quantify—will. Need. Desire. Sax can't make his nerves heal faster, but he can try to push movements through to his muscles. He can tell his claws to clench, his mouth to bite, his tail to swish, and while none of these get through intact, the Oratus starts to twitch.

Which gets Gar moving to the weapons rack—a literal spot to store miners against the wall while the shuttle's in motion. Sax can't turn his head enough to see what Gar's grabbing, but he's thinking he has a couple of seconds until his world goes black again.

Gar comes back into view. Aims the miner directly at Sax's chest.

"They say this doesn't damage muscles," Gar rasps. "Only the nerves. Not that it matters for you."

The shuttle rocks again. A warning light blinks on and loud ringing tones fill the cockpit.

"Thought you could fly one of these things?" Gar yells, looking back over his shoulder.

Sax pushes harder. His tail swishes.

"This isn't a fighter!" Lan replies.

Gar shakes his scaly head, turns back to Sax, then seems to get an idea. "Lan, open up a line to'em. Tell them if they hit us again, Sax dies."

"The Amigga won't like that!"

"We'll be dead, so it doesn't matter!"

Sax has to agree with Gar on that one. The conversation, though, is buying him a bit of time. More swishes. His eyes are fully open now. The air tastes stale—not much of it in here, but the fact that Sax gets any flavor at all is good.

"All right," Gar raises the miner again. "Time to sleep."

Sax sees Gar's claw depress the trigger, and Sax puts all his effort into one thing: a roll. His back shifts, his claws and talons, clasped together, swing Sax back into the netting, which sags deeper into the shuttle. And Gar's shot, a blinding bright blue, strikes right where Sax should have been.

Then the net rebounds, pushes Sax back to his spot.

"Nice try." Gar glances at the miner, confirms its still got energy. Raises it again.

"Gar!" Lan shouts suddenly. "They're—"

And the rest of her words vanish as the shuttle's roof cracks and breaks apart.

The ceiling over Sax's head shifts from its boring light gray to a red, then orange and white color. Pieces of the structure start to fall and again Sax pushes himself to roll away from the liquid drops of molten metal. Gar dances back too, forgetting about his captive and aiming the miner towards where the hole is forming.

Towards where, as the shuttle's hull peels back, Agra-Red's manic, helmeted face shows. Just behind the Whelk is the billowing beige of a docking tube, one that must be sealed against the shuttle's non-melted hull. Necessary to keep everyone from being sucked away in the vacuum.

Sax briefly wonders why Plake's ship would have the equipment necessary for this kind of raid, files it away under things to consider when he's not in a life-threatening fight, and resumes kicking and pushing himself along the net towards the shuttle's side.

"Give it up, Gar! Lan!" Bas' rasping shout rings into the shuttle. "You're trapped. Surrender, and you'll leave with your lives!"

"They're countering the thrust," Lan says to Gar. "The shuttle's engines aren't strong enough to keep us going forward."

"Tell the frigate to blast them off." Gar aims the miner through the hole, but doesn't pull the trigger. If Gar breaks apart the tunnel, Sax and everyone else will be sucked into space. For once, the Oratus shows restraint.

"And chance that they'll hit us?" Lan says. "I'm radioing the fighters. They'll be better."

"Anyone shoots at us, and we'll blow your ship," Bas says, still not trying to come down through the hole.

Their threats continue back and forth while Sax works at his bindings. They're hard clasps, energized iron. He can't get his tail around for leverage, but there's something he does have, something designed to get through just about anything.

Teeth.

Sax brings his claw clasps up to his mouth as Gar shouts something back at Bas. Slips the thin edge of the circle tight on his right foreclaw past his lip, and nibbles. Feels the points of his teeth echo pain, but he tastes metal too. Progress.

He's most of the way through the link—and Sax's teeth are grinding down—when Gar ups the risk.

"If you come down through there, Lan's going to blow the shuttle. Or I will," Gar hisses. "We're not going to lose. Either allow us to land, or we'll all going to die."

Sax isn't sure how Gar thinks its possible for the shuttle to dock now that there's a hole in its ceiling, but Gar's true meaning is clear; they're not surrendering.

"Lan," Bas shouts. "You know this isn't right! You know we're not the enemy!"

Lan, still by the controls, doesn't respond. Instead, she's tapping away at something. Sax doesn't know what, but the sooner he can free...

There. The clasp doesn't spring loose, exactly, but the strength holding it together, keeping Sax's right foreclaw from slipping free, vanishes. Sax, though, keeps still for a second. Makes sure Gar's attention is still on the tunnel, on the potential attack from the *Mobius*.

Then Sax slips his claw free and, using its razor points, skewers the central control box keeping the clasps together. They drop off, and in the same motion, Sax swings his legs up and frees those too.

The stun isn't all gone, so getting up feels a little like a dream—Sax can't feel every nerve ending, and only knows his muscles are doing what he wants them to by what he can see—namely that Gar and his miner are at eye-level now.

And Gar doesn't miss Sax's move either. The Oratus audibly growls, swings the miner towards Sax.

"Too late," Sax says.

Gar's about to reply when a bolt lances down through the hole. Blue and bright, burying itself into Gar's shoulder. It's followed by a second and third, putting the Oratus down hard. Sax walks over to the paralyzed body of his former friend, snags Gar's miner off the floor of the shuttle and aims it at Lan.

"Step away from the terminals," Sax says to Lan. "Choose. Now. It's us, or them."

Lan looks at Gar. "We're not perfect, but we're loyal, Sax. To the cause, not to any one commander."

"I don't think there is a cause, Lan," Sax hisses back. "It's only what the Amigga want. You're a pawn in their game."

"Maybe that's what we're supposed to be," Lan replies. Then she points at a hatch towards the back of the shuttle. The craft's sole escape mod. "We'll go that way."

Sax flips the miner's switch without thinking, changes it from stun to kill. Every bit of instinct is telling him not to leave these two alive. Not to give them another chance.

"If you take him, if you leave," Sax starts.

"Next time, there's no mercy." Lan picks Gar up from the shuttle's floor, and heads to the escape mod. Taps at the panel with her tail to open the door. "Sax, you're choosing the wrong side."

"I'm making a choice, Lan, which is more than what the Amigga will ever let you do."

Lan does nothing more than nod, then she slips inside with her pair, seals the door, and blasts away.

Bas drops into the shuttle after Sax announces the all-clear, and she helps her pair head back up, through the short docking tunnel to the *Mobius*. Disconnecting the boarding seal involves the same superheating method—after Agra-Red seals off the tunnel behind a hatch, a gout of energy melts away the seal and the tunnel retracts.

And Plake immediately sends the *Mobius* into a spiraling whirl.

"Fighters, lasers, they're all coming!" the Vyphen captain shouts over the ship's broadcast system.

With both Lan and Gar free and away, the frigate and the fighters have no reason to be cautious, and apparently any information Sax and Bas have isn't worth letting them get away alive.

"Turrets?" Sax asks Agra-Red as the whelk moves towards the front of the ship.

"None made for you," Agra-Red says, sliding onto the platform and riding it to the *Mobius'* second level. "Oratus are too large, too ugly for our guns."

"Too ugly?" Bas says, but the Whelk's already slipped away into a gunnery hatch.

"Funny, coming from a Whelk," Sax rasps.

The two of them head up to the bridge, where Plake is busy guiding the *Mobius* through one dive and twist after another. Sax and Bas grab onto some crash netting and watch while the universe spins and slides. Laser fire flashes around them, and the *Mobius* rattles as shots find their mark.

"Leap away!" Sax says.

"If I stay still for a second, we'll be burned to ash," Plake shouts back, slipping the ship into a dive back towards *Scrapper Station*.

Sax gets a proud moment when he sees *Scrapper Station*'s still sending hot energy out at the Vincere's fighters and retreating shuttles.

Retreating.

"We actually drove them off?" Sax says.

Plake laughs and Bas shakes her head. "They only wanted us. After they realized you'd been captured and I was on this ship, after Engee crashed it through Bay One, they started to retreat."

"But the station will survive?"

"Sentimental, Sax?" Bas says. "I didn't think you cared for it."

Plake guides the *Mobius* beneath *Scrapper Station*, using its spokes as barriers to block the fire. There's less of that too, now that they're out of the frigate's range. Sax begins to think they might make it out of this one alive.

"They don't deserve to die for us," Sax replies.

Though even as he says the words, Sax knows he'd give all of *Scrapper Station* up for their cause over and over again. And as Plake sets the *Mobius* in a level line, looking to leap, he knows they might have to.

"Where are we going?" Sax asks as the short countdown appears on the cockpit glass.

"A place to hide," Plake says. "So we can figure out how to find your friend."

Then the stars bend and warp, like Sax does himself, and they're gone.

As T'Oli careens out of the spaceport, I get one last look at the bodies of Rackt, the Whelk that escaped the crash, and even Ignos, whose Oratus form is bearing a pair of new blast wounds.

"You shot Ignos?" I ask Viera, numbly, who's standing behind me while the boarding ramp closes.

"It tried to kill you. It killed Malo. It deserved to die, Kaishi." Viera turns away from me and walks back into the shuttle.

I follow her, taking a glazed look over the room we've entered. The gray-metal walls and ceiling look like the very first spaceship ride I took with the Oratus where they'd kept us tied up in the back. Where we'd suffered through a leap among boxes and boxes of nutrient goop.

There aren't many crates here, though—instead, there's a number of wide creamy circles that, when we approach, grow out furniture to match our bodies. Chairs, couches, and small tables.

It's too much, and I've no interest in sitting down anyway.

"I'm going up," I tell Viera, who collapses onto one of the couches and doesn't appear the least bit interested in what I'm doing.

Up, in this shuttle, means a wide pearl stair with dual bronze hand-rails that, as soon as I step onto the first step, shift to match the height of my hands. I don't think I'm going to need them until the shuttle shakes again, throwing me to the side and forcing me to grip tight to one of the railings or be thrown back towards Viera.

"I'd sit down, cause these Sevora don't seem to want to let us go."

T'Oli's order is enough to push me up the stairs. I'm not going to wait for death—like Malo, I'm going to face it. See what's going to end me. So I press my legs down and power up the stairs between volleys, get forward to a narrow cockpit that must be in the shuttle's pinkish nose. T'Oli's spread itself around the various switches and knobs, so that it looks like the whole control panel is covered in a white plaster.

"Thought I said to sit down?" T'Oli's sole fluid patch, with its pair of eye stalks, flaps at me.

"I'm not," I state. "Are we going to make it?"

"Depends," T'Oli says. "On whether they can shoot straight."

From the cockpit, I can see the rapidly-approaching edge of space. The beige sky is fading towards a deep blue and then black. T'Oli keeps the shuttle weaving, so that the view jerks and twists as we fly. Flashes punctuate the movements; lasers biting off into the space beyond us. Which, I realize, is far from empty. Even up here, hordes of Sevora shuttles and other ships blaze around like wasps, heading who knows where.

"They're all panicked because Sapphrite's broadcasting

Vimelia's location to the galaxy right now," T'Oli says, and I'm stunned at how calm the Ooblot is. "Going to gather up their things, I bet, and make a run for it. They'll have to hope the Chorus doesn't have anything nearby to catch the signal."

"How long will they have?" The opportunity to talk about something so pointless and unrelated to what just happened is, somehow, necessary.

"Depends. You assume nobody gets away, assume that the Chorus has nobody in any neighboring systems, and you've got a long time." T'Oli laughs, then. "But then, you've also got us."

The shuttle rocks again, and I think I hear T'Oli issue some sort of Ooblot curse, which sounds like a mix between scraping rocks and gnashing teeth.

"Sorry 'bout that," T'Oli says. "Got a little distracted."

I decide maybe being quiet till we're out of danger is a good plan, and when T'Oli mentions that we'll be leaping in a few moments, I take the hint and go back down. Viera's still staring silent into a vague distance, so I take a seat and drift.

I first met Malo when he appeared at the base of my village's temple to Ignos, our Tier. He tore me away from my family, from the life I'd known every waking day to that point, and declared that I could be one to lead his people. He'd had confidence in me from that very first moment. Believed that I could do great things, and when I'd needed his help, Malo had done what I asked without hesitation.

Somewhere during those thoughts, T'Oli pops the shuttle into a leap. Like with the others, I'm twisted, turned, folded and frayed, but through it all I keep Malo's face in focus and run through our memories.

"Kaishi," Viera's voice jars me out of the reverie. "I need you here. Now."

I blink. We'd just come out of our leap, and T'Oli hadn't said anything yet. What did Viera need?

Around us, the shuttle's glossy white furniture sits sterile and dull. On the ceiling, around us, the walls have faded to a translucence that gives easy vision to the dark space and sparkling stars surrounding us. I'd call it beautiful if the word could come anywhere near my lips at the moment.

"Malo didn't attack Ignos so you could mope," Viera says, though the red around her eyes says she's been doing some of her own moping during our journey home.

"He didn't need to," I reply. "Ignos wouldn't have killed me. Not if I'd gone along with it."

"Which wasn't an option."

"Wasn't it, though? I'd already had a Sevora inside my head. I know how to control them. You both could have escaped."

"We wouldn't have left you," Viera sighs as she says this. "Because, stupid people that we are, we both agreed to get you back. We swore ourselves to you."

"Like you can't break that oath."

"Kaishi, everything's changed. I don't know what's going on anymore. Sometimes I think the only way I'm holding on is precisely because of that oath, so don't take it away from me."

"As if I'm worth protecting anyway." I glance down at my hands. The ones that couldn't even save my most cherished friend.

"Stop it," Viera's annoyed now. "No Empress gets to talk like that."

She's right. I know she is. I take a big breath, shudder

out the exhale, and look over at those stares. Time to go and see where T'Oli's taken us.

"Sorry, Kaishi, but it looks like we're a little late," T'Oli cheerfully announces as I join it in the cockpit. "You see all those shapes around your planet?"

Earth, in its sparkling blue beauty, appears marred by a dozen dark gashes cutting across its surface.

"Those are Sevora ships. My guess is they took the coordinates off of whatever shuttle you rode to Vimelia."

"They can't have been here too long, though," I reply. "We didn't stay on Vimelia more than a few days!"

"If you're lucky, that means they'll only control *most* of the planet by now," T'Oli quips. "Anyway, seeing as your home's a loss, where should we go now? Rackt and some of the others were supposed to have a plan, but they, uh, didn't look too alive when we left."

"We're not going anywhere." There isn't any question of that now. "Take us down, T'Oli. Take me home."

"Might not be your home anymore, Kaishi."

"Then I'll take it back."

THE SPEAR

A SKYWARD SAGA SHORT STORY

S he doesn't know what's happening, that much even Malo can see. He's keeping an eye on the young woman because they're taking her family. Her whole tribe. The warriors would find themselves under a black-glass knife. The women and children... well, that depends.

The Charre have uses for them. Plenty of work in the city and fields for those willing. Ignos would accept those who were not.

Malo keeps a tight grip on his black-glass spear, and a stern expression on his face. Jakkan won't tolerate compassion. Ignos, the high priest says, demands duty, demands that every sacrifice be taken seriously.

But, if Malo's being honest, he's worried the girl's going to try something. She's old enough to have spirit, and her face is making that telltale shift from shock to fear to anger. The desperate look that comes when you've nothing left to lose.

There are twelve... huts, Malo decides, though the ramshackle nature of the plants and sticks holding them together gives evidence that this isn't an old village. A case bolstered by the number of people he sees: most of the men must sleep outside, or on top of each other.

He hears Jakkan call for haste. The priest wants to be out of the jungle by nightfall, where the starlight will show any ambush. And because he's listening to the screeching call of his priest, Malo almost misses the moment.

Almost.

The girl twitches forward, unsure of the action even as she commits to it. She's lunging to the remnants of a cook fire, one still sporting what would have been a meaty feast. A large carving stone, a crude version of the knives the Charre forge in Damantum, is her target.

She manages to get her grip on it, just as Malo reaches her. It's a moment's decision: to kill or stay.

The former wouldn't be questioned, though the girl's death would be regretted as a sacrifice lost. But Malo's seen enough pain today, so he drops his spear, takes her wrists in his own hands, and doesn't flinch when hell itself turns to look at him.

"Don't die for nothing," Malo says, and he manages to stop himself from finishing the Charre phrase.

"I'm already dead," the girl replies and she tries to shake him.

"Tell me, who are yours?" Malo asks, eyes flicking towards the captives.

He wants to offer hope. A chance. It's a lie—he won't be able to save anyone from death or labor, but if it lets the girl's anger drain away, then it's worth it.

The question pulls her attention and he watches her look towards her tribe. They're bunched together, surrounded by Charre troops wielding their own spears and, in his colorful, feathered robes, Jakkan, who is pointing here and there, sorting the sacrifices into those more honorable than others.

"Him," she relents to hope, nods over to a smaller group, the ones tasked for a quicker death.

Not a prized captive, then. Malo can't tell which of the men she's referring to, and the afternoon is bright enough—Ignos is glaring today—that the sheen blurs all the prisoners' faces together.

"Your father?" Malo asks.

She nods again. More importantly, her grip on the knife relaxes.

"I'm sorry," Malo tries.

A miscalculation. She's not grieving yet.

"Sorry? You're the ones taking him from me," her voice says she hates his words. "You came here!"

"I don't choose our targets," Malo protests. "Our priests demand sacrifices, noble ones. Your father will go to a great destiny."

Now she starts to struggle again. Malo pins her hands against the flag of the knife, takes a quick glance and sees a few faces looking their way. The girl doesn't know the danger she's in—show enough spirit and Jakkan might decide she's sacrifice material after all.

"Don't," Malo switches tactics. "Think about what you want. Revenge?"

That's the word that gets her to stop. It's up to him to go.

"If you fight now, you'll be taken in a moment. Do not, and you'll have a chance, someday, to avenge him."

He's not sure why he's saying this except that he, right now, can't bear to see another fighting spirit die. He just can't.

She too seems to recognize the moment's futility, and drops the knife.

"Where will I go?" she says, not really asking him.

Malo has no idea. There are other tribes in the jungle, many, but they might do the same to her what Jakkan's going to do to these men.

He must have thought too long, because she slips free from his grip and makes her break. He notices too late—she's vanishing into the trees already—that she's scooped up his spear along the way. Leaves him empty-handed, standing over the cook fire.

"She took your spear," Jakkan says later, as they're about to march from the village.

"I did not think she could, high priest," Malo replies.

"Clearly, you underestimated her," Jakkan says, then turns to the group. "Warriors, the time has come to deliver Ignos' wishes to his altar."

Malo gets up from the stone he's used as a momentary confessional, but feels Jakkan's strong, gnarled hand grab him before he's gone a single step.

"I said 'warriors', Malo," Jakkan whispers into Malo's ear. "Without a weapon, without your spear, I don't think you qualify."

The first thing Malo notices when all of his fellow Charre are gone is just how noisy the jungle really is. The constant buzz of insects, hooting birds, and the growls of other animals. The breeze rustling through the leaves playing alongside a distant river's gurgle. It's a symphony far different from the planes in which he lives, where the wind is often the sole source of music.

Even with the breeze, though, Malo's still feeling the heat. Sweat drips everywhere, including onto the food he scavenges from the now-empty village. Jakkan took the men, and the remaining women and children left, presumably to head for another tribe before even less friendly raiders find them. The hasty packing means Malo has more than enough for an improvised trip into the jungle's heart.

Yet gathering what he needs takes time, and it was a late start, so when Malo takes his first steps beyond the village clearing Ignos is already gliding towards his rest.

Trails go cold. Trails in the jungle especially so, with all the movement and growth. Malo has a few snapped branches and twigs, broken ferns to mark where the girl entered the forest, but not long after, the signs fall away. The ground stops feeding him impressions and the plants refuse to give him any answers. Either she stopped and simply vanished, or she knows how to hide her tracks better than he knows to look for them.

"Which is more likely," Malo mutters to himself.

He keeps replaying that moment; she'd been quick, and he'd been happily surprised at her decision to run. So much so that he had lost his most treasured weapon. What was he thinking? Why even bother to save the girl? If she wanted to die right then and there, who was he to stop her?

Malo slides his hand to the kukri on his belt. It's a knife as long as his forearm, sharp and with a slightly curved blade that gets fatter as it reaches the point. Useful for hacking away at people, or at the vines crowding his path, as he starts doing now. The jungle only gets thicker as he leaves the village and what pruning they did behind.

He pauses as purple twilight sets in. Brushes away a cloud of insects from his face, sighs as they settle right back. The son of a city stonemason and a weaver has no business here. But he wanted more, and for the Charre commoner, more meant either the priesthood or the military.

Malo found out quick, in front of smaller congregations, that he had no gift for sweeping speeches. No soft empathy to guide a struggling member through their trials. What he *did* have was a knack for the kukri, the black glass spear, and delivering of punishment to his enemies. What started as schoolyard brawls progressed rapidly to a deadlier art.

One that helps him not at all in the thick forest. There's nothing to kill here.

Nonetheless, he soldiers on. Towards that gurgling river. Since she ran off without supplies, Malo figures she'll have to seek water and food from somewhere.

It's nearly dark by the time he makes the river, where he startles off a pair of boars who've been drinking from its current. The river's a wide one, and the waters froth over brown and green rocks on the bottom. Not deep, and easy to cross. Malo looks up at the sky—which is actually visible over the swath the river cuts through those trees—at the stars beginning to peek out.

It's getting too dark to forge through the jungle, and this is as good place to camp as anywhere. Preferably not, though, on ground level. Malo looks for a tree to climb.

But the jungle here is full of reedy, smaller trees stretching with minimal branches high into the sky. Not easy to scale, impossible to sleep in. So Malo settles for the dirt. Brushes away the sticks and stones and leaves until only black, moist sand sits beneath his feet. Malo takes a small bed roll from his pack and lays it out. Gathers some of the brush and, using a scrap of flint and his kukri blade, strikes a flame.

There's a chance the fire will draw someone to him. Malo hopes that someone is her.

Nothing comes. Malo eats a bit of the leftovers he stole from the old village's cook fires, drinks some of the water from the river after boiling it in the small clay bowl he keeps wrapped in the bedroll. Makes plenty of noise doing all this too.

Still nobody comes. Malo says a prayer to Ignos, asks the great god to forgive his foolishness, asks for Ignos' blessing and redemption. Then, despite the pestering bites and nibbles of curious critters, Malo lets his fire trickle down as he falls asleep.

And wakes up with a sharp point pressing against his neck. It's cool and hard, and as Ignos has not yet returned to the sky, Malo can't see whomever's holding it against his throat.

"Why did you follow me?" The voice whispers, and he knows in an instant it's the girl.

"I need that back," Malo replies. He hasn't moved from his bedroll, but his hand inches towards the kukri on his belt. The short knife would, at this distance, be just as effective as the spear.

"After all you've taken from me, you're coming to ask for something else?" She says and there's plenty of bitter venom in her voice. "I should kill you."

"Why haven't you?" Malo says, because he's hoping that he can buy another second, another inch for his hand to creep.

"Because I want to find your friends. I want my revenge." She stands up suddenly, loosens the spear from his neck and stamps it once against the ground.

Malo hears the rustling ferns, and is blinded by sudden,

uncovered torchlight. As he adjusts, Malo finds himself surrounded by women and older children. All of them are armed with a fool's medley of rocks and stone carving knives. A few bear crude swords and spears. One has a bow and, Malo counts quick, four arrows.

"Your people took ours," the girl says, and it's clear from the way they're looking at her that they think she's the leader. "We want them back. You can find other sacrifices."

"What do you want from me?" Malo says, sitting up and staring at the stern faces around.

"Show us where your force is going, and we won't kill you," she replies, then leans in close. "Right away."

Knowing what she wants and who she has helping her has Malo concerned as he looks over the angry eyes staring out in the dark. The group comes in all shapes and sizes, from weathered to fresh spring, scarred and thin to large and soft. Not one of them looks to him like a warrior. Not a one of them looks like they can hold their own in a pitched battle, even if all of them are tough in their own way.

Malo thinks his own mother is as tough as they come, but put a spear in her hand and she would be as lost as any of these.

"I can take you," Malo says at last. "I can lead all of you out of here, away from your homes and the land you know to go after my friends. After Jakkan and his soldiers. But what we find at the end of that road will be all of you dead or taken." He pauses to let the words sink in—an effect he's learned from Jakkan's many speeches. "Or you can choose to stay. To rebuild your lives and accept the course that Ignos has given to you. At least that way you'll have a chance."

He's hoping to see some expressions change. Hoping another voice will rise up in synchrony with his and calm them down, persuade them to a better course of action. Instead, all those eyes to shift to the girl and wait. She, for her part, shakes her head.

"I'm not making a deal with you," she says. "We tried that. We tried to negotiate with you. That brought us nothing but sorrow. So now this is what we're *telling* you to do. Bring us vengeance."

There's not a wavering soul among the two dozen that stand around him. Malo opens his mouth—he's about to start again. Because as much as he wants his spear, as much as he wants to return home, he does not want to see all these people die, and that's what will happen. Either here or upon an altar. But before he can say a word, a small voice from the back begins to sound a prayer. As if this is some secret signal all the others join in and they drown out the jungles noises with a sacred ritual of the Solare people.

Malo's heard it before, though only from captives as they're marched away from their homes. It's a defiant oath, an acceptance of their current hardships and the promise, with the help of their god, that they will be strong. That they will rise above, in this life or another, to claim their salvation. It's a powerful song, sung there in the night.

Their voices rise within them and he realizes he's saying the words too. She notices, the girl, but she doesn't stop.

None of them do.

Morning dawns with Malo starting awake, not even realizing that he'd fallen asleep. All he recalls are the burning torches and the voices rising in one prayer after another, songs and chants that slowly died as people settled into bedrolls or the soft sand and collapse into slumber.

Malo's so tired from the march that he didn't make it long, there in the warm shelter of the glowing torches.

He's not the only one awake now. She's up, for one. Filling a small urn over by the river. He gets himself up. Scoots off his bedroll and goes over to meet her.

It's a nice morning, cool yet without Ignos focusing too much of his attention on them. Just enough of the god's rays shine through the leaves and scatter rainbows along the still-gathered mist that fills the jungle in the nearly morning. Beyond the river it's quiet; only the ever-present buzzing of insects provides accompaniment Malo's approach.

"You know our prayers," she says as Malo squats next to her.

"Your people and ours are neighbors. It wouldn't be smart of us not to know," Malo says.

"Us." She nearly chokes on the word. "What about you? Did you feel it last night? What makes the Solare who we are?"

It's true, Malo can't deny it. There's something about a small group singing courage to themselves and their god that he doesn't get in Damantum, where thousands upon thousands throng for daily prayers. Where his voice is washed out by so many others rather than rising in concert.

"It is different," Malo gives her that much.

"It's all we have now," she says. "My father used to tell me the Solare only survive because of Ignos. That we have been torn apart so many times we should have died if not for his graces."

"Then you should know Ignos wants this," Malo dares to say.

"That he wants you here?" She says. "Why else would your priest make you search for simple spear, of which there must be so many where you're from. How would you have followed my trail—I tried to hide my tracks—without Ignos guiding you?"

"So that I can stop you," Malo says. "Suicidal vengeance is not what you are your people need now."

"They're not my people," she fires back. "We are together. And you will do as we say, because you owe us that much."

She's made a judge of his character, a good one. Malo knows he can't refuse. Because she's right, if they want to throw away their lives like this, if they want to end their suffering in one hopeless battle, who is he to deny them?

"If you want to catch them, you will have to move," Malo looks at the water. It's so peaceful and empty.

Damantum is surrounded by river-ways. Malo would go to their banks when he had time, sit and watch boats flow up and down with their catches, with their crates of things for trade or sale. Refuse from a crowded city swirling in the eddies. Here, though, the water is unsullied. Pure, clear and beautiful with the reflections of the trees above showing on its surface.

He wants to hold on to the moment, but she keeps going.

"I'll get them up," she says, then catches him by surprise with a slight smile. "I just realized, what's your name? I need something to call you."

"Malo," he offers.

She says her name is Naila, and then she's off, the water swishing in her urn.

Later, Malo's backtracking through the jungle, only this time not alone but at the head of a strange force. In daylight he gets a clearer picture of what Naila's army looks like. There are a few young boys in it, the oldest maybe twelve seasons. Not hardened at all. Mothers and sisters. Wives and daughters. There's not a hopeless look among them. Not an ounce of fear. Despite their lack of training, weapons, and chances of success, they're determined.

Which is something.

For part of the walk, Malo allows himself to think that maybe, maybe they'll earn a place in Damantum. Maybe they'll get something besides an execution.

"You need better weapons," Malo says to Naila. She's staying next to him at the front of the column. "Most of what you have won't hold up in a fight. Not for a second."

"I know," she says. "We need food too. We have to go back to our village. There's some things I doubt your force found."

Malo supposes it's possible. They weren't there to loot

place, after all. A sacrifice is more valuable than any gem, any treasure. Besides, Jakkan wouldn't want to sully the honor of those he's taking by desecrating their town as well.

"You ever use that?" Malo says as they walk.

She's still holding his spear, though her grip is oddly placed towards the back end of its haft.

"Not all of us have swords and knives," Naila says. "I fought with sticks, and staffs. Bamboo branches long and thick. This is not so different."

"Try to hit someone over the head with this, and you'll find it doesn't work so well," Malo replies. "This is a short spear, you should be holding it further up if you want to strike. Jab, not thrust. Strike and dodge."

Naila glances at the weapon as they trudge over a bed of ferns and wildflowers. "It doesn't matter," she says. "Ignos will be with us."

"You'll be saying that when you die if you go on as you are."

"We're stronger than you think."

"It's not your strength that I'm worried about," Malo says. "It's your weapons, your training, what this group will do the first time they get into a real fight."

"We'll surprise you."

"Where did your village come from?" Malo says during a break.

The entire crew is gathered in a leafy clearing made, apparently, when some storm had toppled a large tree. They're sitting around it, perched on the trunk and squashing small plants as they devour a lunch of fruit and edible roots foraged along the way.

"We were part of a larger tribe that outgrew the land it

had, so we elected to leave."

"Outgrew?"

She gestures. Vines and trees, and the screams of birds in the distance. "Does your home look like this?"

Malo shakes his head. Describes Damantum and its tens of thousands, its endless fields overflowing with fruits and vegetables. Its pens swimming in animals ready for slaughter. There are the poor and the starving, yes, but on the whole, Malo thinks the Charre keep their people living, and living well.

He's expecting Naila to acknowledge that, to state how much better the Charre have it, but instead he only gets a small smile.

"You think you have everything," Naila says. "But what do you do when you want to be alone? When you want to run through the trees, or swim in a pool?"

"There are pools in Damantum," Malo counters. He doesn't say you need to pay for them, and that they're often cramped and crowded.

"And trees?"

"Some."

Naila donates him a nod. "We can go in any direction here. My family, our friends, we grew tired of where we were, so we chose to leave. Set up our own village, made our own laws. Freedom, Malo. Have you ever known it?"

There's a rigid series of steps from Malo's birth that brought him here. Choices, made by his parents, teachers, priests and leaders. Few made by him. Malo's not naive enough to see no value in that, knows there's quite a lot he's gained from that structure, but when Naila's asking him if Malo's created his own life, if he's known freedom, he has to shake his head.

Not her kind, no.

Ignos is sliding well into afternoon by the time they make it near the village that has become the source of Malo's frustrations. He and Naila lead the column, but he's the one that holds up his hand for them to stop as they head into the last batch of trees before the clearing.

"There are shadows moving beyond the tree line," Malo whispers, wincing at the conversations springing up among children and their mothers, one sister to another behind him.

"You don't think it's branches moving in the breeze?" Naila replies, but she crouches next to him anyway, hiding her face behind the leaves of a fern.

At Malo's headshake, Naila gives a quick, sharp whistle that immediately culls the crowd into silence. They drop to the ground too, and most draw what weapons they have and hold them ready. It's an impressive maneuver, and one that gives Malo the slightest bit of hope that this force isn't going to be a complete mess come real combat.

"Let's get close," Malo suggests. "Just you and I, though."

Naila nods, exchanges a quick glance and palm-up wave of her hand with the woman behind them, who passes the signal down the column. Then she taps Malo on the arm —they're clear to move.

Malo walks by rolling his feet; placing his heel first and then gradually sliding the rest of his foot to meet it. The motion is slow, but keeps the impact light. No snapping twigs, and crackling leaves are muffled by the gradual breakup of their fibers. Naila, who's proving to be a lot more than the villager he imagined, catches on quick and the two shift their way to the very edge of the trees without a single sound breaking through the jungle's ambient rustles and cries.

The village has four main houses, and each one is squat and square. One is recent stone—Malo can tell because the rocks themselves aren't scarred from weather or painted over—and the rest are thatched bamboo and other branches. In the middle stands the humble beginnings of a Tier, only about a meter high and built upon a single large slate stone. Standing next to it and watching his hunter move is the clear leader, marked by the plumes of bright red and yellow feathers around his neck.

Malo bets that if the man turns the necklace over, each and every one of those feathers would be pure black.

These aren't Charre warriors. Not a follow-up raid from Damantum—which would be odd. No, these are Solare.

"They're from our old tribe," Naila confirms Malo's suspicions with a whisper. "Probably coming to trade, and now they think we've left it all behind."

"Doesn't look like they mind." The leader is standing over a small pile of crude weapons, tools, and Malo spies a couple of bracelets on his wrists that don't fit.

"It's not honorable to steal," Naila has an edge now. "They shouldn't be—"

"They think you're dead or gone," Malo interrupts. "The question is whether they'll give it back when you prove them wrong."

Naila doesn't look too sure about that.

"I don't know," Naila says. "My father, the other warriors might, but I never dealt with them."

They wait a little longer, Malo hoping these fighters, of which he counts nearly a dozen, will leave and spare him the trouble of making a decision. Naila, for her part, seems to be flipping between excitement and that fear that comes when a bluff is suddenly called—will her band actually survive a fight if she pulls them into one?

"We can't just stay here," Malo says as the sky turns an orange-purple. "Either we ask them to leave and give back your home, or we run and try to find some other place to stay."

"Leaving would mean giving up," Naila says. "Giving up what we came for."

"Then we're going," Malo says.

"Stay ready," Naila says back to the group. "We don't know what they're going to do."

Normally Malo isn't be much for head-on tactics. It's generally a blunder to show your force and march them right to the enemy. Except, he's not sure these are the enemy. And he's not leading soldiers—he's not leading people who can march in formation, or who can take battle tactics and implement them.

So he leads the mob out of the woods and startles the hunters milling about the center of the village. Some are still carrying their latest plunder as all of them turn to regard who's caught them in the act. It's a moment of truth, and Malo's hoping they'll start to retreat, or at least get cautious.

What he gets is nothing more than a couple of smiles. Not what he wants.

"Tasa, you've come at a bad time," Naila opens the conversation—Malo realizes she knows the leader, who Naila's addressing with a hard steel voice. "The Charre attacked our village. We lost many."

The leader with the feathers takes a step towards them. Up close, he's tall and the color chocolate, with layers of black tattoos spiraled around his chest and arms. His long hair is pulled tight behind his head, and he wears a long pale scar across one cheek that curls up to meet his lip, one that stretches into a sick smile as he gets a full view of Naila's force.

"This is all you have left?" Tasa almost purrs the words. "One might say you're not even a tribe anymore, Naila."

"What we have," Naila replies. "Is more than enough for a tribe. More than enough for this village. It's ours, as is what you're wearing, what your hunters are taking."

Malo has to give Naila this: she's damn brave. Foolish, even.

Tasa hardens. "You want these?" His hands pull on the bracelets. "Why? Only a tribe that means to stay alive would need these. You can't do that. There's only one man here, and he barely looks more than a boy."

Malo wants to speak, shut down this Tasa, but he stays silent when he sees Naila slide into a merciless grin of her own. This is her fight, her territory. It's up to her what happens next.

"I did not *ask* you, Tasa," Naila says. "You're going to leave what you stole. Then you will walk away from here, back to your home."

Tasa looks over her head, towards the column. "Naila is saying we need to leave." Tasa's talking to his own warriors now, and, Malo knows, to their own. "She calls us thieves, looters. The lowest of the low. I, however, believe Ignos understands the service we are providing, and is thanking us for the offer we make to you. Come with us, come back to our village. We will find space for you. Work for you."

It is, altogether, a good offer. One Malo would take if he were in charge.

"We do not need a new tribe." Naila apparently doesn't think so. "Leave, Tasa. Now."

"You spit in Ignos' face, Naila," Tasa replies. "As the price for your insolence, we will keep what we've found. You can keep your huts, your ruins."

Tulsa starts to bark orders, to tell his nine warriors to get ready to go. Naila cuts Tasa off with a series of long strides forward, right up to him. She's well shorter than Tasa, but she makes up for it by standing straight, by bearing the sheer defiance of her being towards Tasa, who can't quite manage his sardonic smile in the face of all that fierceness.

"Leave it," Naila says. "Or we'll take it back."

Malo would've cautioned her against the threat. Would have said that a fight is the last thing this group needs, the last thing they can afford. But now he's caught up in it, and he doesn't like that these worthless hunters are taking from a tribe that's already suffered. It's not honorable, and it deserves a reckoning.

One that Malo, clutching his kukri, can give.

Tasa, for his part, turns his lack of quip into a frown, into narrowed eyes and set shoulders. "You're welcome to try."

That's all he needs say. Malo, the whole group of twenty or so women and children, and Naila burst forward at Tasa's words and Naila's following battle-cry. They're brandishing their cooking knives, their rocks and stones. The one with the bow aims and looses an arrow, which flies over the heads of everyone and embeds itself in the Tier.

Malo's feet pound dry grass, his blood surges, and he feels the kukri's lethal weight in his right hand as he runs. The crowd roars around him, both Naila's villagers and Tasa's warriors calling to Ignos for glory and victory. It's exhilarating, it's madness.

Yet Malo's training kicks in and he processes the battle. Ten, counting Tasa, hunters bearing short spears and knives tucked in their belts. They array themselves in a line with the Tier to their backs, waiting for the mob to reach them. Waiting to be broken apart upon the villager's sacrificial stone.

Waiting for the villages themselves to die upon their spears.

Malo chooses a target towards the middle, a smaller warrior, more slender than Malo, who has his short spear up and ready. It's not black glass like the Charre, but bamboo with a broken rock tied to the tip. He jabs towards Malo as he closes, but the hunter telegraphs the move with a flick of his eyes and a twitch of his right arm. Malo sidesteps, flips the kukri to his left hand and, with his right, grips the spear and holds it so that the warrior can't pull his weapon back.

The kukri finds its mark, a quick dive into the warrior's chest and back out and then in again and Malo follows the last stab with a kick to knock the shocked hunter aside. Malo pulls the spear free from the weak, loose grip. Now he has the weapon he needs.

Malo turns left, catches the next warrior, busy with a pair of weathered women and their sharpened sticks, with a strike to the side. Another in and out and in jab sequence and the warrior's guard is broken. Malo leaves him to the mob.

With a moment to breathe, Malo takes stock of the fight. He's looking for a spot to stick the spear, and what he finds is disaster.

The Charre fight with the intent to take sacrifices. The Solare, from what he understands, do too: but not here, not now. Naila's group is being laid out, wounded and kicked aside, stabbed and beaten away. The hunters are doing what they been trained to do, and Naila's band doesn't have enough numbers to overcome their calm counter attacks. Their methodical stabs and switches, kicks and dodges.

Even as he stands there, Malo sees the beginnings of a retreat. Naila herself is dragging a young, wounded girl back from the line, a bloody scratch on Naila's own shoulder. Others are abandoning their knives and rocks, choosing instead to pull friends and family away from Tasa's sharp spears.

Which means Malo has to run too before Tasa realizes he's still there. So Malo skips back, out of reach as the hunters reform their line, tend to their own wounded.

Tasa, though, takes the moment and calls to Naila. "This is what you get when you bring women, children, to a warrior's game."

"Leave," Naila protests, but there's cracks in her steel now.

Tasa pulls a nasty look, and Malo readies himself to jump between an attack. But one of the hunters Malo stabbed moans from behind Tasa, and the chief turns. Tightens up his face at the sight of his own wounded, and glances back Naila.

"You can have your village, Naila. Until we come back and take it." Tasa's hunters pick up their wounded, and shuffle out of the clearing towards the north. Naila and the rest turn to their wounds, and only Malo goes to make sure Tasa keeps moving. To make sure they aren't simply doubling back for an ambush. Only when the hunters vanish deep into the trees does Malo let loose his taut muscles, take a deep breath for the first time in what feels like forever.

Tasa fought with nine other warriors. In those few moments, they wounded nearly fifteen of Naila's force. Tasa ended with four hurt that Malo saw, including the two he fought. It isn't funny, it isn't close.

"It was a slaughter," Malo tells Naila later, as the wounded receive bandages, salves, and rest in front of fires sparked to life. "If he hadn't decided to leave, we all would've died. He might have, too, but you would not have a tribe anymore."

Naila's staring at the flickering flames as though she's seeing her own grim future play out in front of her. "I know."

She turns and her tear-stained face greets Malo. He's taken aback, he wasn't sure Naila even had that emotion in her.

"We'll never catch your people now," Naila says. "Even if we did, we couldn't rescue my father. Their fathers and husbands."

Malo doesn't think any of his words will help, so he stays quiet, watches the fire. She's right. She's lucky. His eyes drift over to his black glass spear, resting on the rock besides Naila. If she lets him take it, then he could go, take the last reminder away and let her heal.

Malo's not sure how much time passes there in front of the fire, listening to its crackle and the slowly settling sounds of the wounded and exhausted around them. At some point, a saint Malo doesn't see drops a couple bowls of roasted roots and vegetables and a hunk of melon from one of the nearby trees. They eat automatically, in silence.

He's never actually lost before. Not in anything other than sparring contests or childhood games. Every engagement with the Charre, every foray against rebellious factions or jungle tribes has ended in victory. Most of them with minimal injuries. He finds losing doesn't get better as it marinates with time.

What happens instead is he turns to anger, to excuses. Naila had no reason to fight that battle, no point in risking her entirely unprepared group. She's lucky they're not all dead, a point which Malo skates to another—namely, what's he still doing here? All that's waiting by these cook fires, outside these ramshackle homes, is a cutting death whenever Tasa decides to come back.

"I think," Malo rises. "When Tasa comes back, you should go with him. Give up this place and take his offer. Keep your lives."

Naila says nothing, doesn't turn to look at him. The blankness on her face catches Malo wrong, like someone's grabbed his festering emotions and yanked them front and center.

"These people trusting you," Malo pours heat. "They will do what you say because you promise their village and their lives back, but all they're going to get is death, or a sacrifice. You're not a leader. You don't have the right to take their lives into your hands. Give them hope when you have none, because there is no hope here, Naila."

At last he gets a reaction out of her. A wince of those eyes, then a half-turned head his way.

"You mean we don't have hunters, like them. We don't have hardened warriors who know how to jab spears and knives." Naila speaks the words like a ghost, numb and dead. "Is that the only way to live in this world? Do we have to go find sacrifices like everyone else? Do I have to hold a spear?" Naila picks up Malo's weapon. "Do I have to tell the children that they have to learn to use this or they won't survive?"

"Yes." There's no time for soft words anymore.

"Then I need your help," Naila says. "I know it's not what you intended, but you're right. We won't win as we are. We're strong, yes, and we have courage." Naila runs her gaze across the sleeping forms around them. "If your way is the only way, then teach us. Make us hunters, make us warriors. Help my tribe survive."

Malo's shaking his head before Naila's finished. "I can't. I need to go. And even if I could somehow train all of you before Tasa returns, his hunters will still have experience. They'll still win."

His words rob something from Naila and she lets Malo's spear fall to the ground. This time he picks it up, stands. It's late, but the moon is bright and Malo still has a pack of supplies. If he marches hard, in a couple of days he might catch up to Jakkan and the others on the edge of the jungle. After all, one man can move so much faster than many.

He doesn't make it two steps before he hears Naila stand up behind him. Hears her sharp inhale.

"You owe us," Naila says and Malo turns to see the same defiance he witnessed on the day they took her father. "You've taken everything from us, and now you're condemning us to death too. You claim to follow Ignos, but this is against everything he stands for."

A thousand arguments sweep to Malo's lips. Protests about the impossibility of training this ragged group, about how it wasn't really him who took their husbands and fathers, about how Naila couldn't possibly hold him responsible for Tasa's actions. All those arguments die a withering death beneath the crushing guilt cascading over him.

The Charre never mean to wipe out the jungle tribes. The Solare are an endless source of sacrifices. That this one would be extinguished, would die by his people's hands... Malo's not sure he can bear that burden. He's not sure if he's capable of abandoning someone so desperate.

So he compromises with his own soul.

"If I stay," Malo says slow, feeling out his argument as he says it. "If I stay, you have to listen to me. At least regarding the fighting, the training. We'll have to be partners, Naila. Because if we aren't, we're all going to die."

The next morning sparks a string of days that flow with constant action. Naila keeps her promise, and Malo's given time with her people. After an initial run through some exercises—a sprint around the jungle, a test to see how they hold their spears, he takes the sixteen women and older children with enough strength to train and divides them into groups of four.

Each set, as the Charre call them, gets a leader, a supporting trio of a caller, supporter, and killer. Each leader gets a spear, which they manage to fashion from branches and rocks as best they can, and a series of torn, dyed cloth strips that they wind around their arms. White means run, red means attack, and yellow means they need help. When noise comes to dominate a fight, Malo's learned, having a way to communicate by sight alone can make all the difference.

Callers get the rocks and slings made from animal skins. Small knives as back-ups. Malo makes the kids the primary targets for this one, sending them up the trees to where they get their vantage points and where, with the added fall, even a lightly thrown stone can do some damage. He doesn't tell the children this, but being up high gives them a measure of safety too, a distance from the surefire carnage on ground level.

Someone has to be able to get to those that need aid, medical or otherwise. The supporters get sharpened sticks and what scrap weapons they can fashion. They also fill packs with poultices and bandages made from tightly woven moss. Malo emphasizes the stick and run technique with these four—staying out of the fight is the best way they can help those stuck in it.

And the killers. When he assigned the titles, Naila looked disappointed that she wasn't placed here, and Malo, looking at the four standing in front of him, wonders if he's made the right play. Each and every one of them is a mother, each with a child playing the role of a caller. Naila, when he told her the names, initially objects, and something in Malo twitches as he says, in reply, that the reason these women are perfect killers is because they're truly fighting for something more than themselves.

The last thing a killer can afford, after all, is a strike that falls short. Is a last effort that doesn't go all the way.

Naila hasn't looked at Malo the same way since, and her eyes hit him now with a combination of wariness and respect. Malo tries to throw out more smiles, but he feels he's revealed a dangerous part of himself, and it's not one he can hide.

So he dives into the lessons with the killers, who get the rest of the real spears in the village. Who get the crude, but sharp knives and the thicker mosswraps the village hunters used to wear. Ones made to keep claws from drawing blood, but that might turn a loose swipe of a blade.

First, the lessons are mostly simple. How to hold the

spear, how to stab and lunge or, in desperation, throw it. With knives, he emphasizes closing quickly, keeping your feet shuffling from side to side and never presenting an easy target. Work the blade in and out without lunging and giving up your options. The idea, Malo says, is to weaken, distract and disorient your enemy.

What he doesn't say is that keeping them alive allows for sacrifice. They've had too much of that.

For their part, Naila's group is eager to learn, from the oldest woman to the youngest son. Malo thinks he understands why: there's an exhilaration to being exposed to things that had been forbidden to you. Most tribes would never teach a mother how to wield the spear, would never give a young boy a pair of knives and tell them how to slice away and attack. No daughter would be taught how to string a bow or shoot an arrow with accuracy. These are molds he's breaking, and from their excitement, the breaking is long overdue.

Nights by the fire follow every hard day, spent around the crackling fire sharing progress with Naila until Malo collapses on his bedroll exhausted, wishing he was under the glowing lights of his city. Back in Damantum, away from the mosquitoes and the growing fear in his mind that no matter how much he does, this group will not be ready. That no matter how much time he has, Tasa's going to slaughter them all.

Word comes in the afternoon. One of the Callers, positioned between the village and where Naila says Tasa's tribe lives, rushes in shouting that they're coming. That it's not just ten hunters anymore, but as many as thirty.

Thirty.

Malo hears the number and goes cold. He'd been hoping Tasa would come back with his original nine, that he'd stride right into the village all haughty and confident, allowing Malo's little squads to spring a trap. Now, though, they would be so outnumbered a trap like that wouldn't matter. They'd all be dead anyway.

"How long?" he asks the Caller, a girl several years younger than Naila.

"A day's march," the Caller replies. "I saw their torches from the top of the crown."

The crown is a rise not far from the village, and one with tall trees that can give a climber a long view of the canopy. Malo's had a Caller stationed there every day and night since he formed the squads, and he can tell from the way the children fight over the shifts that contributing is doing wonders for their morale.

Even this one, with her dire report, sounds defiant. Hopeful.

"We can't wait for them," Naila says as soon as Malo dismisses the Caller.

The two of them have just sat down for yet another meal of warmed vegetables and fruit. This time, though, there's a few added scraps of meat—a hunt from the morning that managed to snag some small, furry creatures. Malo takes a bite and savors the bland, stringy food. Anything other than the taro, lettuce and beans he's been eating every meal since they returned to the village.

"Now you want to run?" Malo replies.

"No, but if we let them get here with that many, we'll die for certain."

The way Naila says that makes Malo think she has an idea, so he looks at her with the question on his face and waits. Naila looks like she's waiting for Malo to get the same idea through some magical telepathy, and when it's clear he's not going to, she takes a deep breath and plunges ahead.

"We need to hit them earlier. Surprise them."

"They're hunters, and this group is not. Run them into the trees and you'll be picked apart."

"You don't need to be a hunter to know how to move through the jungle," Naila says. "All of us have called the jungle our home for our entire lives. You couldn't follow my trail, and, according to my people, I'm not a hunter."

Naila's certainly right about one thing, and that's if Tasa's hunters get to the village with their current numbers, they're all dead. Yet the idea of fighting them in the jungle... he realizes *fight* might be the wrong word. The jungle is a big, crowded place, and a clever soul can make a lot out of its many parts.

He starts with an idea, one Naila grabs, and then they're off and talking through the night, calling over Malo's sets and assigning opportunities, laying out the path for the tribe to survive.

The first hunter picks his way through the ferns, his grip loose and his face hanging in a bored stare. No expectation of an attack a couple of hours out from the village, no thinking that the cowardly assortment waiting for them there would do anything other than die.

Which is why the child's thrown rock hits the hunter hard from the tree, scores a blow against the man's head and knocks him to the ground. Malo catches his own breath for a second, watching with bow drawn from the eves of a tall, spindly tree across the clearing. The hunter can't die here. Not till he's done what needs doing.

But the hunter still has a bit of life in him, and he stands slowly, left hand held to his temple and, when he pulls it away, showing a bit of red. Then the hunter puts his right hand to his lips and makes a chirping call while his eyes scan the trees, looking for the attacker.

When the hunter's eyes find Malo, the Charre warrior lets his arrow loose with a soft thrum.

Killing isn't something Malo undertakes lightly. It's distasteful, a waste. Yet he hopes Ignos, burning above and witnessing every second, will forgive him this one. Will understand that the hunter's body, now back-down in the dirt, is nonetheless a pleading tribute to the god from a tribe in desperate need.

Malo sets another arrow to the string. Ignores the bugs biting at his legs. His thirst after sitting in this tree for the last hour. Everything falls away as the end begins.

Answering chirps come next—the hunter's friends. Five of them weaving through the wilderness, spears in hand. These aren't like the makeshift ones wrought from bamboo and whatever sharp rock Malo could find, but actual edged stone corded onto solid shafts. Each hunter has a knife looped through a rope around their waist, along with a water skin. Mosswraps act as loose skirts, while inked tattoos cover their back and chests.

Most of the hunters wear the glowing halo of Ignos front and center, but what surrounds the god is different on every body. Malo's not close enough to identify anything other than that the symbols differ from one person to the next, but if these hunters are like Charre warriors, then every inked icon stands for something that hunter has achieved. Given the sheer number of tattoos on these, it's clear Tasa isn't bringing his tribe's youngest fighters to this battle.

The habits of experience aren't an advantage when you're facing something unpredictable.

The five stalk their way to the body of their friend and the arrow sticking out from his chest. One cups his hands in front of his mouth—about to, Malo's sure, announce a loud warning call—but before a sound escapes his lips, another missile, this one a stiff green melon, plummets from a treetop at devastating speed. It hits the hunter and shatters into a juicy pink explosion that sends its target to the ground.

As the other four turn to look at what's happened, Malo looses his second arrow. It flies straight—not that hitting a standing, still target is all that difficult for the trained Charre warrior—and the arrow embeds itself in the closest hunter's back. He collapses too, and Malo mutters a quick prayer to Ignos for forgiveness.

And runs.

The remaining three hunters give chase. Malo hears them crunching through the ferns, hooting after him. On his right, Malo sees a tree with a single slash down the bark. As soon as his foot plants even with the tree, Malo cuts hard left. There's a small, root-covered slope here leading to a muddy pit, one that's hard to see through the long ferns leaves providing cover. The warrior plants on the last root and leaps, covering most of the pit in a single bound.

But not all of it. His left foot lands in the goop and begins to sink, the cool slime sucking at his toes. Malo leans forward, grabs at the hard ground with his hands and tries to pull himself out. Behind him, he can hear them coming closer. Can hear them stop at the edge of the pit.

"Warrior! Why do you run?" one of the hunters calls to Malo. "Ignos thinks poorly of your cowardice. Of your killing."

Malo turns back, sees that the hunters are holding their spears ready, though none appear about to throw one at him. Instead, the speaker is watching him while the other two scan the treetops. They've learned.

"You claim Ignos' favor on your way to slaughter a village of women and children?" Malo replies.

"Slaughter?" the hunter shakes his head. "Tasa told us

only to take those that are willing. Those that are not go to great honor. You are the one that slaughters."

There's a moment where the hunter waits for Malo to push back on that claim, but the Charre warrior can't fight what's true, and stays silent.

"You could redeem yourself, Charre," the hunter continues a second later. "Give yourself to us. Join Ignos and atone for your crimes."

"That," Malo mutters to himself. "Is not going to happen."

With a yank and a slippery lunge, Malo gets his knees up out of the mud, pulls himself up.

"Another move, Charre, and your journey ends!" the hunter warns from behind him.

They're waiting for Malo to turn, and when he does, expectant looks paste on their faces. One who'd been watching the trees has his spear hefted, point glistening right towards Malo's heart, and the Charre warrior has no doubts the hunter could place it there before Malo made another step.

Which means it's time.

"Then I relent," Malo cries back to the hunters. "Come and take me."

He sits on the soft dirt and leaves, his legs dangling towards the mud pit. Eyes tracking to the hunters, who, themselves, appear to be unsure of what to do with their new catch. After a few moments glancing towards each other—fishing for ideas that aren't coming—the lead hunter gestures for his two fellows to make the trip. They're all wearing small coils of tan, spindly rope on their waists and Malo knows they plan on wrapping his wrists tight together.

They'll never get that chance.

The lead hunter takes up aim with the spear, keeping its

point hefted towards Malo's face as the other two begin to wade through the mud towards him. Once they're a meter along, the mud is up over their knees, making progress slow. Making them easy targets.

"Tasa should never have come back," Malo says, and at this the two coming hunters pause. "The village is not his to take."

There's no battle-cry as it happens. No cheer or call to Ignos. Just a rustle, a blur of movement, and then Naila and another woman, older, but made of iron, come around the bend and attack the lone hunter still on the back. The spears they're wielding are newer, better than the sticks the village had, and they've come directly from the bodies Malo left arrowed back in the glade.

The spears find new homes before the hunter even turns around, and the two women yank them free as the hunter collapses forward into the mud. Malo uses the moment too—he stands, slips the bow from around his shoulders and has another arrow aimed and ready. He catches Naila's face, full of triumphant fury, and shakes his head.

"Ignos demands we take them alive," Malo calls across the pit to her. "There's been too many dead today already."

The hunters, both still wielding spears, look at each other, at the angry women on the bank, and throw their weapons into the mud.

Twenty-five left, the two hunters say once they're tied and sitting in front of a fire in the village.

"Take me to Ignos if you like," one says when Naila asks why he's being so forthcoming. "Why should I hide your own death from you? Tasa is going to take this village, and no amount of your clever tricks will stop him."

"They stopped you pretty well," Naila counters.

"We were stupid. Tasa told us we were approaching a village of women and children. He was wrong, but when we fail to return, Tasa will know what's happened. He won't make our mistake."

Malo's watching the exchange, his mouth full of tart pear. This ambush was a victory, but tomorrow Tasa's main force would arrive. They managed five today, and somehow had to claim five times that tomorrow. The thought should have had the entire village spooked, but Malo didn't see a single downcast stare, hear a sharp word, or feel a hint of fear coming from any of the other villagers.

"You didn't make a mistake," Naila's still going at the

captive hunter. "We caught you. We beat you. And we'll do the same to the rest of your friends."

The hunter laughs at this and Malo's heard enough. They're not going to get anything useful from him. So Malo stands, taking a last bite of the pear, and goes behind the warrior. Naila, mouth open for another pointless retort, stops as she sees Malo draw his kukri and place the edge of the knife against the hunter's throat.

"Ignos doesn't need his sacrifices to speak," Malo whispers. "You want to keep your tongue, you'll keep quiet."

The hunter takes the hint and, with the help of a couple of wiry grandmothers who know how to tie a knot or two, Malo wraps the hunter to a tree at the edge of the village. Just to be safe, they take a scrap of cloth and gag the man too; a shout can carry a long ways in the jungle air and the last thing Malo wants to worry about now is the enemy they've already beaten.

"You didn't have to do that," Naila says later when Malo rejoins her at the fires.

"I wanted to." As he settles on the log, the tension drains away and Malo realizes how late it's getting.

Nomis, Ignos' sister, is high in a dark sky peppered with stringy clouds, casting her silvery light down through the flickering flames onto the sleeping villagers. Aside from the ones tasked with keeping watch—mostly children, high up in the trees and armed with hollowed callers—this odd collection of desperate fighters seems as content as Malo's own warriors would be the night before a battle.

And he's not the only one who's noticed. Naila's right there with him, but instead of curiosity, Malo sees compassion in the soft frown she's wearing. Worry, even.

"You've given them a chance they never had," Malo

says. "They wouldn't be here without you, fighting for their home."

"They would be alive, though."

Malo laughs lightly. "Any true warrior would tell you that the chance to die for something is far better than living long for nothing. Without you, without this, where would they be? Running in the jungle? Already taken by Tasa or another like him?"

Naila doesn't dispute this, throws Malo a slight thank-you smile. "It wasn't something I asked for. I just felt so helpless, when your people took mine. I wanted to do something. To take control."

"How does it feel?"

Naila cocks her head at him.

"To take control?" Malo asks again.

"It's scary," Naila says after a stare into the fire. "Our village always had ways to flee, points to circle to if something happened like this. I never thought I'd arrive there and, because I held your spear, find myself in charge. But, too, the position gives me something to hold onto. A purpose."

When Naila says the word, it clicks in Malo's mind. The reason he's staying. He's got his spear—he could run hard and catch up with Jakkan and the others. Instead, he's staying here, risking everything for a group of people who, in other circumstances, would love to sacrifice him atop that Tier sitting behind Malo right now.

Purpose. He has one here, one that's greater than just following orders. Taking the prescribed routine and carrying it out to fulfill Jakkan or another's objective. No, this runs deeper. It's satisfying like a warm meal, energizing like Ignos rising on a cool morning.

The feeling sticks with Malo as he and Naila talk

awhile longer, with Malo sharing stories of Damantum and its crowded streets, tall buildings, and crush of people. Until Malo notices Naila's eyes drifting shut, and makes the call to walk their dreams to morning.

And morning comes too soon.

The hooting bursts of hollowed callers knock Malo from his sleep. It takes a second to realize the grim gray fog of early morning is coating everything, with Ignos not even visible through the trees.

As he sits up, Malo reaches with his right hand to pick up his spear from the ground. With his left, he draws the kukri, stands and sees that, for the moment, none of Tasa's hunters have reached the village. But the callers are hooting, so they must be close.

The jungle goes silent again. Some of the villagers, joining Malo outside the four stone houses, are surprised. A pair of mothers turn towards their direction, but Malo makes a single click with his tongue. Gets their attention.

"They have to stop or they'll be found," Malo whispers. "They know to run."

Malo doesn't say the other reason the callers could be silent.

Instead, Malo sees the crowd around him and uses it. Malo calls his sets to their assigned areas. They don't have formations, don't have grand plans, but there's one contingency they've trained for, and it's this one. The surprise attack. It wasn't Malo's idea, but Naila's. She's seen her own tribe do it before: stream out of the jungle at the break of dawn or the dead of night and take captives before they'd wake up.

Somehow, someway, the villagers remember their training. Young and old grab their sticks and spears, their stones and knives and get where they need to be. There's no walls around the village, so they use the houses instead, position themselves along the edges, where they can't be surrounded, where they can slide back behind cover.

A pair of lanky women take the pair of bows and scramble to the top of the Tier, normally a place of honor but now a tower from which they can let loose across the entire clearing. Malo takes a second to meet their glance once they get up on the Tier and raises his kukri in a salute.

There's no cover up there, and the archers know it.

Malo joins the group at the edge of the chief's house, directly across from the Tier and nearest the jungle area from where the calls were coming.

Eight villagers, six mothers and wives and a pair of children who appear to be no more than twelve seasons old stand with him. They acknowledge his arrival with a nod, one that he returns. Naila should be somewhere to his right, the two of them holding the center-most houses on the crescent arc made by the village structures.

Now Malo sheathes the kukri, holds the spear with both hands, and embraces the taut quiet to peer into the gray shadows beyond the ferns and trees. It's an eerie stillness, marked by the tight breathing around him and the low hoots of some far off bird. A cool fog lays across the ground, only just beginning to fade away as Ignos starts to cast his light upon the jungle.

Movement. Wisps of fog dragging along behind a shadow. Ten meters away. Close enough to—

The strike comes whistles from between a pair of vine-wrapped trees. It's a rock, and it finds a target next to Malo. Strikes her in the shoulder with a bone-bruising thwack, knocking the older woman to the ground. Immediately, the set's supporter grabs the woman and pulls her back under the cover of the chief's house.

"Get back! Around the front of the houses!" Malo shouts even as the woman falls beside him.

Tasa's playing a game of range, and they can't be in the open. Can't be easy targets.

More rocks begin to whiz through the trees as the villagers retreat. No arrows though, and the hunters are aiming low. Tasa's not trying to kill. Not yet.

They fall back around the house and Malo sets up near the open stone door, facing the Tier. Through the narrow opening, he watches the pair of archers on top of the tower. Watches as they put arrows to their bowstrings, as they begin to let loose.

Those first shots change everything.

Pointed arrows aimed at the head and chest mean deadly injury. They mean you're not concerned with Ignos. And once you've sacrificed honor, your opponent has no reason to keep theirs.

So Malo and Naila had told her people to give up their honor, because if Tasa won, the village wouldn't have anything at all.

As the arrows start to fly, Tasa's hunters issue a loud and angry roar, a specific word that Malo doesn't understand and yet knows all the same. The first hunter to yell sounds right outside the house, and his cry is echoed back into the forest many times over. There won't be rocks coming back at the villagers now. It'll be arrows, throwing spears and knives. What could have been a bloodless affair, what could have ended with the prisoners tied for sacrifice, will now be a massacre one way or another.

Malo hopes they're ready.

A dozen instincts take hold of Malo at once as he sees Tasa's hunters in front of him. Hours spent during the hot Damantum days, in dirt courtyards with Charre warriors arrayed around him. Captains wearing thick lion manes stand at four corners, barking orders at them; lunge with the left, twist and sweep the leg low, draw the kukri and stab. Over and over again until the motions become a swirling dance.

In the cool mists of the early jungle morning, Malo falls into that dance again.

He lunges towards the closest hunter, whose still drawing back his short bow and only just beginning to look away from the archers on top of the Tier towards Malo. The hunter's reaction is slow, far too slow.

Malo doesn't stab deep—to do so risks catching the spear on a rib or snaring it in muscle. A quick dart into the chest and then Malo's moving towards the right side of the line, twisting his body around, pivoting on his right foot, to whip the spear around towards the next hunter, whose arrow is drawn back, about to fire.

Malo's throw is faster. His spear crosses the two meters as the hunter releases his hold on the bowstring. The spear's point—thick, sharp black-glass—slices through the arrow as it begins its forward flight. The spear embeds itself in the hunter, but Malo's too busy completing his pivot to watch, bringing up the kukri in his left hand to meet the shadow streaking towards his face.

This hunter, coming from the jungle, comes at Malo

with a Solare club. A chunk of thick wood with sharp rocks embedded all around the head, the weapons are both crude and terrible. Capable of both breaking bones and rending skin.

Malo's kukri meets the larger weapon in a crunching block that numbs Malo's wrist. The kukri, though, bites deep into the club's wood, sticking both weapons to each other and giving Malo a moment's stare into the haloed, deep blue tattoos coating the face of the hunter in front of him.

Malo's expecting to see hate there, anger, or maybe fear. The things he's seen in the eyes of tribes they've raided before. Instead, he finds determination. Steady focus. Then the moment's gone as Tasa's hunters and Naila's force of women and children clash together around them.

Malo knows he can't let the hunter get his club back, so instead of pulling the kukri out, Malo leans in as the hunter wrenches back. With his right hand, Malo punches forward, hits the hunter with a jab to the throat. He feels a snap, and the hunter drops the club, staggers backward.

Malo doesn't watch the rest.

He separates the two weapons and enters the rest of the fray, following the sounds of screams and flashes of instinct to guide him from one target to the next. The only strategy at this point is survival.

A battle has no clock, no defined duration. Malo marks its periods by moments of quiet between swinging weapons, bloody sprays and flying stones.

His line of devastation has moved beyond the chieftain's house, and while Malo's sporting a dozen cuts and bruises, while his arms are exhausted and the club is missing chunks of its body, he's still alive.

Which can't be said for many on both sides. Their

bodies, wounded or dead, litter the ground around him, and it's hard to tell if Naila's villagers are winning. Malo only knows by the continuing battle cries that all of them have not lost.

Naila, though, still lives. Malo sees her in front of him, struggling near the last house, and it's easy to see why:

Tasa's there, and he has her pushed back against the side of the building. A pair of other hunters have set up a perimeter, staking out the fight with spears of their own.

Only it's not a fight.

Naila has heart, she's determined, but Tasa's an experienced hunter and, as Malo starts to head towards them, Tasa knocks away Naila's spear with his own. Levels the point of his weapon against her chest.

Malo can't hear what Tasa's saying, and he doesn't care. Two strides into his run, as Tasa's guarding hunters orient towards him, Malo plants his left foot into the soft ground and launches the battered club.

The weapon swirls through the air, tumbling end over end in a sloppy motion that nonetheless carries it into Tasa's back. The impact makes him stumble, and one of the stone shards cuts a long red line through Tasa's skin.

Naila uses the moment. She squeezes out from under Tasa's spear, slips her left leg between Tasa's own as the hunter glares back towards Malo, and the last thing Malo sees before he has to dodge the stabbing spears of Tasa's guards is the chief falling towards the ground.

Malo, now, only has a kukri and he dances back from the probing stabs of the hunters. They're playing it safe with their short spears, feeling out Malo's flexibility, knowing they have reach. Knowing they have numbers.

Knowing they have time.

The two of them try for another dual-stab, with the left

hunter going low and the right aiming high. Again Malo hops back, but this time he lands on the front of his feet, bends his knees, and dives to the right, beneath the hunter's spear.

Malo rolls, pauses for a half-second to slash the back of the hunter's knee with his kurkri, and then keeps going. Pulls up to his feet a meter behind the two hunters, one of which is now kneeling, hands gripping his wounded, limp leg.

Much as he'd like to spare a glance back towards Naila to see how she's faring, Malo has one more hunter to deal with. This one's sporting twin arcs of red dye coming together across his chest in a circle—Ignos. He's also picked up his friend's spear, making it two long weapons against Malo's trusty kukri.

There's no waiting this time from the hunter, no caution. He jumps forward in a long lunge with his right, then tracks Malo's dodge with the spear in his left. Malo feels the burn as the second strike rakes across his shoulder, the hot wet gracing his skin.

It's desperation and blind reflex. Malo sweeps the kukri back and forth, tosses it from one hand to another as he blocks and dodges the seemingly endless stabs from the Solare hunter.

The spears score another cut, then a third along Malo's thigh and the Charre warrior knows he's not going to win this one. He can't get close. So Malo starts to backpedal, though he can't turn around to see where he's going.

Hopes that, maybe, he'll see something. Find some villager still alive, someone able to help.

The hunter, though, comes after him with a murderous gleam. There's no threats, no taunts, only the pure, focused joy of eliminating a threat.

They're both so immersed in the duel that neither one notices, for a moment, the sudden appearance of an arrow sticking out from the hunter's chest. The Solare only realizes its there when his swings suddenly fall short, when his left hand falters and the spear in it falls to the ground.

Malo meets his eyes, sees the hunter's confusion, and sees it fade a moment later as the fighter collapses.

Behind him, on to of the Tier the two fighters had wandered near, and sporting several deep injuries of her own, the one remaining archer gives Malo a quiet nod, and nocks another arrow.

Malo runs back to where Tasa and Naila were fighting —he doesn't have any idea how the rest of the battle is going. It doesn't matter anyway—if the hunters are winning, he'll be dead. If the hunters lose, but Tasa kills Naila...

But what he finds as he rounds the corner is Naila standing—dirty, sweaty, and wounded, but standing—over Tasa. Naila's holding the chieftain's spear, and its point is drawing a small stream of blood from Tasa's chest.

"You're going to leave, and you're going to tell your tribe and all the others that this village still lives. My tribe survives." Naila's more breathing the words than actually saying them, her shoulders shaking as she tries to keep her grip.

Malo comes closer, kukri in hand. His feet land on leaves and they crackle. Naila whips around, brings the spear up towards Malo, and Tasa takes advantage.

"Don't!" Malo tries to warn, but he's way too late.

Tasa sweeps his arm through Naila's left leg, picks her off her feet and dumps her down off of him. In a second, he's on her, wrestling the spear away.

In two seconds, Malo's diving into the chieftain, pushing him off Naila. Together, with Tasa managing to find Malo's left wrist and holding it, keeping the kukri away, they roll across the dirt and grass.

With his free hand, Malo goes for a swing at Tasa's face, but the chieftain slams his head forward instead, getting inside Malo's punch and slamming into Malo's chin. There's a warm splash in his mouth as Malo's teeth bite into his lip, and his skull rings as Tasa's blow drives Malo's head into the ground.

And in that moment, the chieftain rips Malo's kukri away, cutting his own hand in the process. Tasa juts his right knee into Malo's chest and the Charre feels what air he has left sputter out of his lungs.

"A cowardly attempt," Tasa whispers, turning the kukri for a stab. "Ignos would never approve."

Malo tries the same tactic, reaches for Tasa's wrist to keep the kukri away, but there's no strength. Tasa simply presses through the attempt.

"You would have made a bountiful sacrifice," Tasa whispers as he slides the knife against Malo's throat.

"You *will* make one," Naila's voice is iron, and she punctuates her words with a strong swing of Tasa's spear, sending the haft cracking into the chieftain's head.

By the time Ignos descends that night, the villagers have burned their twelve dead, along with the eight hunters that joined them. Malo stands over the flames with the remaining villagers, Naila, and the sole bright spot of the battle—a bound Tasa. Even the chieftain, though, adopts a solemn stare.

"We lost too much," Naila sighs, standing next to Malo.

With Tasa captive, the hunters called for peace, a deal the villagers, Naila and Malo included, were happy to take. In exchange for leaving with their lives, and for giving the villagers their own, the hunters left with a promise not to return except to trade. Ignos, though, demands a sacrifice from the loser of any struggle, and as Tasa began this fight, he bears the final cost of it.

"So you'll leave." Any question of staying is denied by a glance around the funeral circle.

More children than mothers and grandmothers survived. Especially the ones in the trees, whose alarms had given their families a chance to protect themselves. They are too young to carry out the essential labor—hunting, growing, building—that a true tribe needs.

"We'll find another," Naila replies. "There will be tribes looking for more members, especially children they can groom to suite their own needs."

"I thought you didn't want that?"

"What I want doesn't matter anymore. I tried that, and all we did was get these people killed. All my anger bought me was the lives of others."

Malo says nothing for a moment, but takes another look around the fire. It's quiet now, at the start of twilight. As if even the jungle senses the mourning. Sadness caresses the villager's faces, but Malo doesn't see despair. Rather, determination lurks in their set mouths, in the way even the younger ones still hold their spears. The surviving mothers have already taken charge of the orphans, too, and cook fires are lit and burning near the houses.

"They press on," Malo says. "You taught them that. You gave them honor, bravery. I don't envy any Solare or Charre tribe that tries to fight any of them. Any tribe you join will find itself blessed by Ignos beyond any expectation."

Malo can't tell if the words help Naila, but she doesn't speak anymore of losing, or of what comes next. She doesn't speak at all, and Malo, his mouth hurting and his body sore, lets the crackling night come down slow.

Morning brings early motion. Malo's up as Ignos dawns, his pack stuffed with enough provisions for the walk to Damantum, though he's hoping he'll catch up with Jakkan and the others a little beyond the jungle. Especially as he's not going alone.

"You're taking him then?" Naila says, emerging from the house to watch as Malo kicks Tasa awake.

"I think your village has seen enough death lately,"

Malo replies, then glances down at the hunter. "Besides, Tasa is a chieftain. He deserves a sacrifice worthy of his title, atop the golden altars."

"You would walk all that way, to people that abandoned you?" There's a question in Naila's eyes, one that can't be directly asked because she knows as well as he does what he would have to say.

"I have not abandoned them," Malo replies, though the words are harder to speak than he thinks. "I was asked to return with my spear." Malo holds it up. "I have it, and I mean to do as I was commanded."

The thought of staying in the jungle had flirted in Malo's mind all night, in between his dreams and the sounds of the night. These villagers, though, didn't need a fighter any longer. Any tribe they found would see Malo as a threat, and he'd likely find himself dragged to the top of a Tier. Sacrificed as an enemy of the Solare peoples.

Besides, he's longing for the sound of crashing waves instead of buzzing mosquitoes. The smells of a hundred cooking spices and the laughter of many thousands of people. A journey to the jungle is fine, but Malo knows he's a city man.

"Well then, Malo of the Charre," Naila says. "Thank you for lending me your spear."

Malo raises it slightly so that the black glass tastes Ignos' first light and scatters it across the village. Gives Naila one last nod, then pulls on the rope tied to Tasa's wrists and begins the long walk home.

THE SPEAR - PREQUEL SHORT STORY

After his band subdues an enemy village, Malo takes his eyes off a skilled captive and loses his spear when she vanishes into the jungle night. Charged by his commander to recover the weapon or never return, Malo sets off in search of the thieving girl.

A prequel to *The Skyward Saga*, *The Spear* is an action-adventure story that dives deep into the jungle to find Malo's true heart.

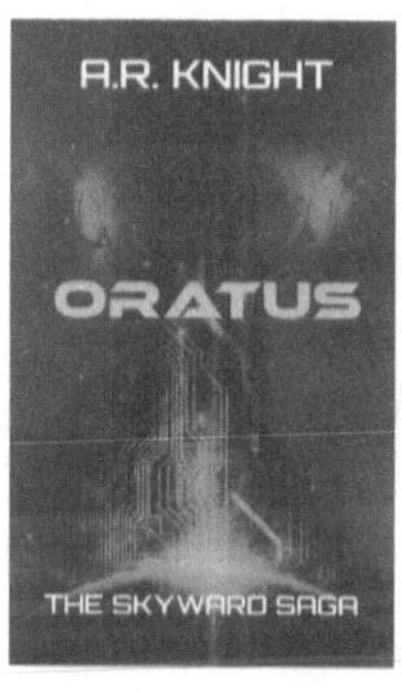

ORATUS - PREQUEL SHORT STORY

On the day she is born, Bas is expected to fight for her life.

The Oratus, a warrior species bred to bring peace and order to the galaxy, do not start quietly. From her first moments, Bas is issued a challenge: climb to the top of the Mountain. If she makes it, Bas survives. If she doesn't...

Oratus is an action-adventure prequel to *The Skyward Saga*, following the brutal first days of life for a species that knows nothing except war, survival, and the bonds forged in those moments.

STARSHOT - BOOK ONE

Caught between warring factions, Kaishi and her tribe face

extinction. When a burning meteor lights up the night, Kaishi investigates and finds a voice with answers for everything, with secrets that could let Kaishi save her people. All Kaishi has to do is promise to follow Its orders.

But this promise carries a terrible price.

Starshot is the first book *The Skyward Saga*, a completed sci-fi adventure series that features mind-bending alien encounters, far-future action, devious villains, and a heroine that won't stop fighting.

MIND'S EYE - BOOK TWO

Kaishi embraced the gifts the Sevora gave her, but becoming an empress has attracted the kind of attention that comes with claws.

Following the Sevora's guidance has brought Kaishi and her people back from ruin and into prosperity, but as miracle after miracle pours from the voice in her head to the forges in Kaishi's great city, interstellar eyes take notice.

Mind's Eye is the second book in *The Skyward Saga*, a sci-fi adventure series filled with frenetic action, weird creatures, and a universe begging to be explored.

CLARITY'S DAWN - BOOK THREE

To survive on an alien world, Kaishi must decide whether to trust the creature inside her mind, or reject it and risk everything to fight for her freedom.

Ignos lied. The alien promised to take Kaishi and her friends back

to Earth, to home. Instead, Ignos has brought them to its own world, teeming with other parasites that see the humans as hosts, and a potential gateway to their own survival.

Clarity's Dawn is the third book in *The Skyward Saga*, a sci-fi adventure series spanning alien worlds, unique technologies, and colorful characters scrambling to survive as odds mount against them.

CREATOR'S END - BOOK FOUR

Home. Kaishi can see Earth, but between her and her family stand a hostile fleet and Kaishi only has one ship that she doesn't even know how to fly.

Her sole chance at survival depends on a risky attempt to reach Earth's far side, where nobody Kaishi knows has ever been. And the Earth Kaishi finds when they reach the surface is far different than the one she knows.

Creator's End is the fourth book in *The Skyward Saga*, a sci-fi adventure series that brings peril, heart, and fascinating technology in equal measure as Kaishi and Sax look to save their species and themselves.

HUMANITY RISING - BOOK FIVE

Earth is under assault, and Kaishi has arrived to lead her people, just in time to see them destroyed.

Hiding under the mountains with continuous attacks from the skies, Kaishi marshals humanity's remnants in a final stand against overwhelming odds. Hope resides in a last ditch effort to

call out beyond the stars for help, as Kaishi climbs the cliffs to fight one final time beside her friends.

Humanity Rising is the fifth book in *The Skyward Saga*, a sci-fi adventure series that puts the galaxy at risk as species wage wars for survival, worlds are ruined in revenge, and histories are rewritten by the victors.

THE LAST CYCLE - BOOK SIX

The Sevora have been defeated, and now Kaishi and Sax come together on opposite sides, with the galaxy's most powerful force in between.

Kaishi goes from one threat to another when the same alien army that saved Earth from the Sevora invasion demands that Kaishi submit humanity to their rule. Submission comes with gifts, peace, and a promised place at the galactic table. Resistance means certain destruction.

The Last Cycle is the final book in *The Skyward Saga*, a sci-fi adventure series that brings the galaxy to the brink of cataclysmic change, where hope rests with those brave few willing to risk everything for a better future.

THE METAL MAN - PREQUEL SHORT STORY

After a disaster on the Moon, Mox's search for strength brings him to a dangerous scientist and a choice between the life Mox knows and the vengeance he desires.

The Metal Man is a sci-fi action prequel to *The Wild Nines,* running alongside Mox as he faces the most difficult choices in his life, the crucible that forges one of the most formidable mercenaries in the solar system.

WILD NINES - BOOK ONE

For Davin and his veteran mercenary crew, running security on Europa should've been easy, and was, until a deadly mistake makes the Wild Nines the number one enemy in the solar system.

Wild Nines is the first novel in *The Wild Nines* series, a fast-paced, action-driven space opera set in a corporate-controlled solar system where laws are profit-driven, and survival often depends on how fast you are on the draw.

DARK ICE - BOOK TWO

Davin tried to clear his name, and wound up owing the most dangerous man in the solar system. And it's time that debt was paid.

Dark Ice is the second novel in *The Wild Nines* series, an action-

packed space opera where humanity's expansion through the solar system is driven by blood, sweat, and greed.

ONE SHOT - BOOK THREE

Returning to the solar system's center, Davin's crew, the Wild Nines, find worlds in turmoil as uprising against corporate control consume everything they know. The battle between corporation and citizen threatens to split the Wild Nines apart, and when the rebel's ultimate plan becomes clear, Davin and his crew may be the only ones who can stop it.

One Shot is the third novel in *The Wild Nines* series, a blistering space opera that brings colorful characters to epic battles with stakes large and small, as Davin's mercenary crew must decide what their future holds.

RIVEN - BOOK ONE

The dead belong in Riven. The living on Earth. But as war fills Riven to bursting, Carver has to find a way to keep those lines clear, or there won't be much difference between the worlds for long.

Riven is the first book in *The Riven Trilogy*, a steampunk fantasy set during a twisted World War One. With action-packed adventure, humor and a little bit of love, Carver's adventure promises to keep you turning the pages, searching for answers along with the guide.

THE CYCLE - BOOK TWO

Carver thought he'd saved the world from the endless dead, but as Earth tries to find peace, a new threat targets the guides themselves, and Carver's first on its list.

The Cycle is the second book in *The Riven Trilogy*, a steampunk fantasy set during a twisted World War One. With snappy characters you'll grow to love, a unique world, and fast-paced action, Carver's attempt to save the only family he knows will have you turning the pages all the way to the end.

SPIRIT'S END - BOOK THREE

All his life, Carver wanted to save Riven, the world of the dead. Now, to save those he loves, he has to destroy it.

With the Guides in shambles and Riven overrun with furious dead, Carver embarks on a final journey to try and keep the departed where they belong. Ending Riven's growing threat, though, requires knowing how the world works, and who made it. Carver must journey through Riven's dangerous history to find an answer.

Spirit's End is the devastating conclusion to *The Riven Trilogy*, a steampunk fantasy lost between worlds. Take one last walk with Carver and his friends as they battle ancient evils, unravel Riven's final puzzle, and come together to save Earth from ruin.

PARAGON'S FALL - BOOK ONE

All his life, Aegis has defeated every villain he's come across, one punch after another. He deserves a break, but when word spreads of a plot to destroy the Paragons, Aegis must don the suit one more time.

Paragon's Fall begins a new series exploring a world run by would-be heroes, who prove to be all too human as they clash with each other, normals, and monsters from their pasts. Explore a fascinating take on the superhero genre, and how getting everything you want might be the worst thing you can imagine.

CHAMPION'S CALL - BOOK TWO

It's not easy for a legend to disappear. Mynx has been trying to fade away for years, but now Aegis is missing, and Mynx must lead the Paragons, or watch the world she built collapse into fiery disaster.

Champion's Call continues *The Hero's Code*, an action-packed superhero adventure in a near-future world where the haves and have-nots are determined not by back accounts, but by your genes.

ACKNOWLEDGMENTS

This novel is the product of my family and friends refusing to let a dream die. My wife Nicole, for letting me write in the early mornings and making sure I didn't starve. My brothers and parents for their continual comments, support, and enthusiasm.

And, of course, you, the reader, for giving me a reason to write.

A.R. Knight spins stories in a frosty house in Madison, WI, primarily owned by a pair of cats. After getting sucked into the working grind in the economic crash of the 2008, he found himself spending boring meetings soaring through space and going on grand adventures.

Eventually, spending time with podcasting, screenplays, short stories and other novels, he found a story he could fall into and a cast of characters both entertaining and full of heart.

From there, A.R. Knight plans on jumping through to other worlds and finding new stories to tell in the limitless borders of our imagination.

Thanks, as always, for reading!

For more information:
www.adamrknight.com

Dedications:

Starshot:
Nicole

Mind's Eye:
Anna and Elsa

Clarity's Dawn:
To Clyde and Emma

The Spear:
Nicole

Beyond The Sky
Ebook ISBN: 978-1-946554-49-9
Print ISBN: 978-1-946554-50-5

Published by Black Key Books
www.blackkeybooks.com